1963

stories from six authors

stories from six authors

edited by

WILLIAM E. BUCKLER, *New York University*

ARNOLD B. SKLARE, *C. W. Post College*

McGRAW-HILL *Book Company, Inc.* **1960**
New York   Toronto   London

ACKNOWLEDGMENTS

GRAHAM GREENE *"The Basement Room," "Across the Bridge," "When Greek Meets Greek," and "The Hint of an Explanation" from* Nineteen Stories *by Graham Greene. Reprinted in the United States by permission of The Viking Press, Inc.; reprinted in Canada (publisher, William Heinemann, Ltd.) by permission of Graham Greene.*

ROBERT PENN WARREN *"The Life and Work of Professor Roy Millen" (copyright 1943 by Robert Penn Warren), "The Circus in the Attic," and "Blackberry Winter" (copyright 1947 by Robert Penn Warren) from* The Circus in the Attic and Other Stories *by Robert Penn Warren. Reprinted by permission of Harcourt, Brace and Company, Inc.*

JAMES JOYCE *"Araby," "Counterparts," and "The Dead" from* Dubliners *by James Joyce (B. W. Heubsch, 1916). Reprinted by permission of The Viking Press, Inc.*

WILLIAM FAULKNER *"Barn Burning" (copyright 1939 by William Faulkner), "A Rose for Emily" (copyright 1930, 1947 by William Faulkner), and "The Bear" (copyright 1942 by Curtis Publishing Company) from* The Collected Stories of William Faulkner. *Reprinted by permission of Random House, Inc.*

HENRY JAMES *"The Figure in the Carpet," "The Lesson of the Master," and "The Madonna of the Future." Reprinted in Canada by permission of Paul R. Reynolds & Son.*

JOSEPH CONRAD *"An Outpost of Progress," "The Secret Sharer," and "Youth." Reprinted by permission of J. M. Dent & Sons, Ltd.*

08770

PREFACE

Stories from six authors is built upon a positive educational principle. Instead of offering the student a series of single stories by twenty or thirty individual authors, the editors felt that there was an advantage to be derived from reducing sharply the number of authors represented and giving the student an opportunity to look at a few authors from more than one point of view and, consequently, in more than ordinary depth.

The materials are arranged in order of complexity. Graham Greene, for all his moral subtlety, makes a conscious attempt to combine entertainment with serious purpose. Robert Penn Warren, though he is more famous as a novelist, has an enviable reputation as a short-story writer; besides the intrinsic value of his stories, it was thought that his highly developed consciousness of critical techniques might be helpful to the student beginning to wrestle with this literary form. In some respects, no British or American short-story writer is as complex as James Joyce. Often with a story surface almost parabolic in its apparent simplicity, he probes psychological subtleties which are fragile in the extreme. Even though in "Dubliners," from which these stories are taken, Joyce had not yet begun to employ those startling experimental techniques which made so great an impression on the history of modern fiction, when the student comes to Joyce, he is cutting some very permanent critical teeth. William Faulkner is, in the editors' judgment, the most challenging American short-story writer living today, and the student who has mastered Faulkner is amply prepared to follow up most other writers on his own. This brings us to James and Conrad, whose distinct styles require very careful watching in quite different ways. Joseph Conrad, through the medium of life on the sea and in exotic places, is essentially an analyst of the human conscience. We finally decided to put him last because, since we had begun with Greene, Conrad seemed to cap the whole.

The editors have no desire to overformalize the teacher's use of this volume. The foregoing is an explanation of its rationale, but the book lends itself to numerous other combinations and approaches.

The student-teacher aids included in the text are neither minimal nor, we hope, cumbersome. The introduction comments on several of the perennial problems of the student of the short story, defines essential critical terms, and suggests a point of view concerning the way literature can best be approached. At the beginning of each group of selections, there is a brief biographical-critical headnote intended to orient the student to the author he is about to read. At the end of each group of selections there are pertinent questions for discussion, a suggested interpretation for one of the stories, and questions for written composition. It is hoped that the suggested interpretations, in addition to providing some insight into both the author and the story, will arouse both teachers and students to attack or defend them.

The broad objective of this book is to help students enjoy good prose fiction through understanding and appreciation.

WILLIAM E. BUCKLER
ARNOLD B. SKLARE

CONTENTS

INTRODUCTION

The short story is an art which has adapted itself with great alacrity to the spiritual demands of the modern world. For the most part less intense and compressed than poetry, it has attracted practitioners who have labored with earnestness but without slavery to age-old forms. Less diffuse than the novel, it is more congenial to those moments of vision which, in the shifting, complex panorama of modern life, constitute one of the writer's most convenient ways of positing, for the edification or dismay of his fellow man, a unique criticism of life. Less exclusively intellectual than the essay, it enables the writer to speak to his audience through a technique that compels the reader to respond on many levels—emotional, spiritual, even physical. The short story is a concise, intense literary art form which conveys its meaning, its significance, through personal involvement in a highly selective vicarious experience.

This is not to say, of course, that it has been left to modern man to discover the fascinating charm of the brief tale well told. All literatures— profane and religious, ancient and medieval and modern—are filled with excellent examples of the storyteller's art. The episodes in the "Iliad" and the "Odyssey," the "Arabian Nights," the "Decameron," and the "Canterbury Tales" (especially the terrible "Pardoner's Tale," the comic "Nun's Priest's Tale," and the boisterous "Miller's Tale") are examples of narrative rich and compact. Both the Old Testament and the New Testament abound in brief, compelling examples of narrative art which, loosely defined, may be called short stories—the story of Herodias, Herod Antipas, and Salome; of Ruth, Naomi, and Boaz; of Judith and Susanna; of David and Goliath, David and Jonathan, David and Absalom; of Cain and Abel; of Jonah and the whale; of the temptation of Joseph by Potiphar's wife; of the Prodigal Son. And, of course, literary fables and fairy tales from Aesop to Hans Christian Andersen are major examples of the storyteller's art.

Yet it is still possible to say, with Elizabeth Bowen, that "the short story is a young art" and, with A. J. J. Ratcliff, that "the short story proper, that is, a deliberately fashioned work of art, and not just a straight forward tale of one or more events, belongs to modern times." It is now generally conceded that if one speaks in the very strictest terms of the short story as an individual form of fiction, Nikolai Gogol (1809-1852) was the first great practitioner in the short story and Edgar Allan Poe (1809-1849) was its first great theorist. The following pertinent passage from Poe was written as a review (1842, 1847) of Nathaniel Hawthorne's **Twice-told Tales:** "A skilful artist has constructed a tale. He has not fashioned his thoughts to accommodate his incidents, but having deliberately conceived a certain **single effect** to be wrought, he then combines such events, and discusses them in such tone as may best serve him in establishing this preconceived effect. If his very first sentence tend not to the outbringing of this effect, then in his very first step he has committed a blunder. In the whole composition there should be no word written of which the tendency, direct or indirect, is not to the one pre-established design. And by such means, with such care and skill, a picture is at length painted which leaves in the mind of him who contemplates it with a kindred art, a sense of the fullest satisfaction. The idea of the tale, its thesis, has been presented unblemished, because undisturbed—an end absolutely demanded, yet, in the nonce, altogether unattainable." In this one passage is contained a definition of the short story as an independent art form upon which the last hundred years have not improved. The elements which Poe stresses—(1) brevity, (2) intensity, (3) unity of effect, (4) carefully controlled tone, (5) verbal precision, and (6) the role of the reader as co-creator—are elements which any conscientious reader of serious short stories must stress in his turn today.

It will be immediately obvious that these various elements are closely interdependent. A story which is short—which, according to Poe, can be read at a single sitting—is the only kind of story which has any chance of being intense. We cannot break up the reading of a story among the routine of the day and expect to feel the cumulative emotional or intellectual force of what the author is trying to do. We may remember the plot; we may even, from one point of view, "understand" what it is the author is trying to say. But we obviously cannot thus **experience,** dramatically and emotionally, the story as a whole. We must at some point lose our sense of the story's unity, we must disremember its overtones, lose touch with its verbal texture, must become, in short, hack readers rather than responsive co-creators.

This is, admittedly, a somewhat intense view of the art of the short story. And there are those whose critical attitudes follow a different—if not diametrically opposed—course. Sir Hugh Walpole, for example: "A story should be a story: a record of things happening, full of incident and accident, swift movement, unexpected developments, leading through suspense to a climax and a satisfying denouement." Or Ellery Sedgewick: "A story is like a horse race. It is the start and finish that count most." But one needs only to be reminded of the loose, anecdotal character of the short story before Poe and Gogol and of the major achievements in the short story since Poe and Gogol——by Guy de Maupassant, Anton Chekhov, Joseph Conrad, Henry James, James Joyce, Ernest Hemingway, William Faulkner, for example——to perceive the positive contribution which this intense view generated.

But how does one talk about a given short story? Most of the people toward whom this introduction is directed will already have read a great many short stories——in school and out, among the works both of serious literary artists and of competent professional writers to whom a successful story means a check of a certain size and a better chance to sell the next story they write. It is undoubtedly true, too, that most readers will have some definite notions about which of the stories they have read are good and which are not so good. And having opinions, they will want to express them. In order to do this in such a way as to be understood by others, they will need at their command at least the rudiments of a critical vocabulary.

The fundamental terms with which one talks about the short story are few in number. For the most part, they are terms which direct one's attention to the basic questions which any good "story"——in ancient history or in yesterday's tabloid——is concerned with: who? what? when and where? how? why? The terms which these questions introduce are character, plot, setting, narrative technique, and theme.

CHARACTER

Characters are the persons in a story who do things and to whom things happen. They are to a short story what subjects and objects are to a sentence. What they **do** (or **are**) to one another constitutes the center of interest in most stories. Quantitatively, characters are either major or minor——that is, they are of central importance to the course the story follows, are the persons about whom the story revolves; or they merely support the action of the story but play a relatively insignificant part in it. Qualitatively, we may discriminate between characters, in the terminology of E. M. Forster, according to their "flatness" or their "roundness." Flat characters are "type" characters, sometimes called "stereotypes." They are delineated in outline only, and what they represent is more important than what they are as individuals. Type characters are two-dimensional—— that is, they have length and breadth but no distinctive depth. Round characters, on the other hand, are highly complex and individualized. Their responses to the stimuli provided by the plot are usually quite unpredictable. The roundness or flatness of a character in fiction can usually be determined by the ease with which he can be summed up. A flat character can be struck off in a phrase; a round character, in proportion to the care with which he is studied, resists summary description.

All this is not to say, of course, that minor characters and type characters are unimportant to the created world of the short story. They very often contribute significantly to the plot and theme. But it is safe to say that they are significant for something outside themselves—for their relation to the major characters, for example, or the part they play in the mechanism of the plot.

It used to be common to speak of the "hero" and the "villain" of a story. For these terms criticism has substituted "protagonist" (who may not be heroic) and "antagonist" (who may not be base). The protagonist is the leading character in a story (literally the "first combatant"); the antagonist is the principal character who struggles against him.

For the most part, we require of characters in a story that they (1) be drawn in sufficient detail to give us an insight into their essential natures and (2) act in harmony with their natures as we come to know them. Without the detail, we cannot understand their basic motivation; without the harmony of action, we cannot take them seriously. From an artistic point of view, at any rate, "good" and "bad" characters are characters who are well or poorly drawn.

PLOT

A distinction is usually made between characters and the actions which they perform, and there is a literal difference between the two which can easily be defined. However, since the springs of action lie within the characters, not outside them, and since the significance of action is largely dependent upon the nature and circumstances of the character who performs it, an arbitrary distinction between action and character may be more reductive than helpful. But plot is something more than action: it is a **pattern** of actions in which there is a cause-and-effect relationship between successive events. It is in his manner of combining events that the storyteller's originality is most easily seen.

The element of causality as absolutely essential to a well-made plot is succinctly set forth in the following observations by E. M. Forster: "Let us define a plot. We have defined a story as a narrative of events arranged in their time sequence. A plot is also a narrative of events, the emphasis falling on causality. 'The king died and then the queen died' is a story. 'The king died, and then the queen died of grief' is a plot. The time-sequence is preserved, but the sense of causality overshadows it. Or again: 'The queen died, no one knew why, until it was discovered that it was through grief at the death of the king.' This is a plot with mystery in it."

Aristotle has perhaps had as much to say about the nature and necessity of plots as anyone else. He spoke of plot as the "end and purpose" of tragedy, and he insisted that the actions which are the component parts of plots must be "so closely connected that the transposal or withdrawal of any one of them will disjoint and dislocate the whole." And it is Aristotle who tells us, for all time, that a unified plot is one "which has beginning, middle, and end."

A short-story writer is, by definition, committed to brevity; he has little space for expository introductions or for extended terminal mop-ups. He must get on with it, and he must have done with it. The writer of short stories must, of course, like all writers, depend for his authority on specific details, but these details—of plot, setting, character delineation, and so forth—cannot be presented in that expansive, discursive manner which is characteristic of some of the world's great novels. All narrative art depends, to some extent, upon gradualness to achieve its finest effects, but in the short story this gradualness must be of a very concentrated sort. The gradations must be there, but the steps must follow one another in very rapid succession. The short story, then, compels one to begin in **medias res**—in the very middle of the action—and it does not allow for an elaborate **denouement**—the "untying" of the major complexities of the plot. In the beginning the action will rise and at the end the action will fall, but between these two points the short story should move to its **climax**—or moment of greatest intensity—with a directness and consequential inevitability that give the short story its special shape and make of it a unique literary form.

SETTING

Events which happen to people in a certain way also happen at a certain time and in a certain place. This combination of period and locale constitutes the setting of a story. Writers vary widely in the importance they attach to setting. To one writer, the fact that a series of events takes place in Dublin in the first decade of the twentieth century or in a small town in Mississippi in the period of reconstruction after the Civil War may be of the very first importance. To another writer, "Blue Plate Diner, U.S.A." may adequately identify the "set" on which his story will work itself out. (It will be noted, of course, that short-story criticism has borrowed much of its language from the drama. Elizabeth Bowen has drawn our attention to the relationship between the short story and cinematic drama: "The short story . . . in its use of action is nearer to the drama than to the novel. The cinema, itself busy with a technique, is of the same generation: in the last thirty years the two arts have been accelerating together. They have affinities—neither is sponsored by a tradition; both, still, are self-conscious, show a self-imposed discipline and regard for form; both have, to work on, immense matter—the disorientated romanticism of the age.")

On the other hand, the reader should be careful not to confuse setting, as it is created in the words of the author, with the actual geography from which the author may have selected certain significant details. The setting of a story, like its characters and plot, requires imaginative treatment. Thomas Hardy, for example, made great use of what is known as "local color" because he felt that the series of novels and stories he was writing "seemed to require a territorial definition of some sort to lend unity to their scene." But Hardy urged his reader "to refuse steadfastly to believe" that this world did in fact exist outside the pages of his novels and stories. In other words, an author's setting is important to an understanding of his achievement as a literary artist only if the imaginary character of its geography is given appropriate attention.

NARRATIVE TECHNIQUE

A short-story writer's delineation of character, construction of plot, and creation of setting are, of course, part of his over-all narrative technique; that is, they are part of the **form** in which he presents his total conception and achieves his particular effects. And the reader would certainly want to include them in any serious consideration of how the author tells his story. In general, however, when one speaks of narrative technique, he is thinking of such matters as point of view, symbol, and tone.

By "point of view" in fiction is meant the particular angle of vision which an author uses in a story—or the point from which he views the pattern of events he chooses to relate. (The student should be careful to distinguish "point of view" in this technical sense from "attitude" or "opinion." Ultimately, of course, the two meanings of the term are related, but initially they should be sharply differentiated.) Point of view, though subject to numerous variations, has three principal forms. First, the author may use the **omniscient** point of view, that is, he may move at will from character to character and from inside and outside. Nothing is secret from him—not even a character's most subconscious. Both the first and the third persons are consistent with omniscience. The short story inherited this point of view from the novel. Second, an author may use the **first-person restrictive** point of view. He may narrate the story through one of the characters (who may be a narrator-participant or just a narrator), allowing the reader to know and understand only to the degree and in the order in which the narrator knows and understands. (Some authors are known to have constructed scale models of their setting and then placed their narrator in specific physical locations, permitting him to see only what one so located could, in fact, see.) This particular point of view has grown up with the short story and has contributed outstanding effects to the stories of such writers as James, Joyce, Conrad, and Faulkner. The student should be very careful not naively to confuse narrator with author when this point of view is used; he should, in fact, be at pains to decide to what extent the narrator is trustworthy. Third, the author may use the **third-person restrictive** point of view——that is, he may tell the story in the third person but choose one character as his "central intelligence," restricting the reader to that character's knowledge and vision.

Each of these points of view has its peculiar strength. The omniscient gives both writer and reader freer, less limited range, more direct and active participation in the springs of action from which the story flows; and it allows the author to indicate, with minimal ambiguity, the significant idea which generated the story from the beginning. The two restrictive points of view, being more indirect, have a built-in ambiguity which resists easy interpretation and challenges the reader's critical sophistication. They mask the author and invite the reader to approach the story as a work of art independent of the personality and beliefs of the person who wrote it. Such "techniques of indirection" have brought to the contemporary short story a technical subtlety (and virtuosity) which is one of its principal characteristics.

The extensive use of **symbols** has also contributed to the subtle crafts-manship of the modern short story. A symbol is something used to signify something else. More specifically, a symbol is a material object used by an artist as a mark or token of something immaterial. Thus a red rose may symbolize passion, as a lily may symbolize virginal purity. For the most part, we require of symbols that they be appropriate on both the literal and the figurative level and that they strike a nice balance between the two. If they are too obvious, they offend our critical intelligence; if they are too "private" and obscure, they defeat themselves by failing to provide even the watchful reader with a clue to their significance.

The **tone** of a story is the "quality of voice" given to it by the attitude which the author adopts toward his material. (We imply something of this when we say to someone, "Don't talk to me in that tone of voice.") Thus the tone of a story, or of a passage in a story, may be formal or solemn, or it may be intimate or bantering or ironic. Tone should always be con-sidered in connection with theme because it helps define for the reader the "program of action" (mostly mental or moral) which the author would have him follow in consequence of the new insight which the story conveys. The reader should not, of course, expect a serious theme necessarily to be enunciated in a solemn tone: theme and tone may be as effective from apparent disharmony as from close harmony.

THEME

"In outward semblance," writes Eudora Welty, "many stories have plots in common—which is of no more account than that many people have blue eyes. Plots are, indeed, what we see with. What's seen is what we're interested in." From one point of view at least, what is **seen** in a story is its theme.

The theme is the central, unifying concept, idea, or "moral" which an author intends his story to convey. It is the point, or some modification of the point, which compelled him to frame the story in the first place.

It has become a critical platitude that the theme of a story cannot beneficially be abstracted from the story itself. And this is in some sense true: a sentence which sums up the meaning of a story is not the same thing as the story itself. On the other hand, if a definition of the theme of a story is not considered as an end in itself but only as a useful means of getting at the story as a whole, it serves the cause of critical synthesis better than any other single element in the story. The story's individual parts take their shape from theme, and it is theme which their shape should ultimately render up.

A distinction should be made between "theme" and "subject matter." The subject matter of a story includes all the persons, places, and actions which a story touches upon; the theme of a story is the specific insight into life which the author posits by means of his subject matter.

We cannot end this introduction without a few brief remarks about that most essential and essentially elusive quality of all writing, **style.** All writers have a characteristic manner of expression, a certain way with words, and we cannot claim familiarity with an author until we begin to recognize in him recurrent verbal and rhythmic patterns. The words he uses, the images he evokes, the length and integrity of the sentences he composes—these and other elements are, properly scrutinized, the most faithful mirror of a writer's personality and character. Does the voice we hear in his sentences rise or fall? Is his manner grand or plain? Can he adjust his language and rhythms to the speaker and the occasion which he attempts to present? "When people talk about style," wrote F. Scott Fitzgerald, "they are always a little astonished at the newness of it, because they think that it is only **style** that they are talking about, when what they are talking about is the attempt to express a new idea with such force that it will have the originality of the thought. It is an awfully lonesome business . . . ."

Every piece of true literary art is a unique fusion of science (fact) and poetry (imagination). It is language which makes their union possible, and it is to language that we must look, finally, to judge the quality of the new creation.

GRAHAM
GREENE

GRAHAM GREENE

GRAHAM GREENE, English novelist, short-story writer, and critic, was born in Hertfordshire in 1904, educated at Oxford, and began his writing career as an editor for the London Times in 1926. Though he is without question primarily a novelist, he has intermittently written short stories, children's stories, motion-picture criticism, foreign-news reports, essays, and plays. Early in life he became a convert to Roman Catholicism, and his religion has since influenced all of his writing. However, since he has drawn painful attention to the serious moral dilemma of modern man in relation to God, his work has had dramatic impact upon all enlightened readers. He is widely read in America, and in 1952 he received the Catholic Literary Award in this country.

Readers and critics have been struck by Greene's complex two-sidedness—his capacity to produce, on the one hand, psychological thrillers, narratives peopled with sinister, violent, haunted demons of characters (what he calls "entertainments"), and on the other hand, works of serious, even somber, moral and religious reflection.

The major categories and principal titles of Greene's writings are the following: **Novels:** "The Man Within" (1929), "It's a Battlefield" (1934), "Brighton Rock" (1938), "The Power and the Glory" (1940, in the United States "The Labyrinthine Ways"), "The Heart of the Matter" (1948), "The End of the Affair" (1951), and "The Quiet American" (1955). **Short stories:** "The Basement Room" (1936, of which the title story was made into the movie "The Fallen Idol"), "Nineteen Stories" (1949), and "Twenty-one Stories" (1954). **Entertainments:** "Orient Express" (1932, in England "Stamboul Train"), "This Gun for Hire" (1936, in England "A Gun for Sale"), "The Confidential Agent" (1939), "The Ministry of Fear" (1943), "The Third Man" (1950), and "Our Man in Havana" (1958). **Travel:** "Journey without Maps" (1936) and "Another Mexico" (1939, in England "The Lawless Roads: A Mexican Journey").

Graham Greene is a student of abnormal psychology as he explores the obscure shadows which darken the soul and corrupt the spirit. But these aching human problems interest him chiefly as a reflection of the nature of the man within struggling to find his way in a world in which there appears to be no love. His thematic contention appears to be that sin and evil give rise to good and grace, with ultimate redemption, despite the way in which modern man stubbornly tries to exclude God from his consciousness.

Greene does not judge his characters with dogmatic severity, but pass judgment he most assuredly does. He belongs, ultimately, to that Arnoldian tradition of "high seriousness" which faces up to the basic moral and emotional troubles of the human heart and, in a spirit of sympathy and humility, commits itself to difficult but inevitable distinctions between good and evil.

Greene's short stories are not heavily plotted, and this is the interesting aesthetic result of one of his positive ethical tenets. "We are saved or damned by our thoughts, not by our actions," he wrote in a critique of the novels of François Mauriac, the French novelist from whom Greene claims influence. Like Mauriac, Greene fronts life directly; the subtlety of his stories lies in the delicacy of the problems which he poses.

THE BASEMENT ROOM

1

WHEN THE FRONT DOOR HAD SHUT THEM OUT AND THE BUTLER Baines had turned back into the dark heavy hall, Philip began to live. He stood in front of the nursery door, listening until he heard the engine of the taxi die out along the street. His parents were gone for a fortnight's holiday; he was "between nurses," one dismissed and the other not arrived; he was alone in the great Belgravia house with Baines and Mrs. Baines.

He could go anywhere, even through the green baize door to the pantry or down the stairs to the basement living-room. He felt a stranger in his home because he could go into any room and all the rooms were empty.

You could only guess who had once occupied them: the rack of pipes in the smoking-room beside the elephant tusks, the carved wood tobacco jar; in the bedroom the pink hangings and pale perfumes and the three-quarter finished jars of cream which Mrs. Baines had not yet cleared away; the high glaze on the never-opened piano in the drawing-room, the china clock, the silly little tables and the silver: but here Mrs. Baines was already busy, pulling down the curtains, covering the chairs in dust-sheets.

"Be off out of here, Master Philip," and she looked at him with her hateful peevish eyes, while she moved round, getting everything in order, meticulous and loveless and doing her duty.

Philip Lane went downstairs and pushed at the baize door; he looked into the pantry, but Baines was not there, then he set foot for the first time on the stairs to the basement. Again he had the sense: this is life. All his seven nursery years vibrated with the strange, the new experience. His crowded busy brain was like a city which feels the earth tremble at a distant earthquake shock. He was apprehensive, but he was happier than he had ever been. Everything was more important than before.

Baines was reading a newspaper in his shirt-sleeves. He said: "Come in, Phil, and make yourself at home. Wait a moment and I'll do the honours," and going to a white cleaned cupboard he brought out a bottle of ginger-beer and half a Dundee cake. "Half-past eleven in the morning," Baines said. "It's opening time, my boy," and he cut the cake and poured out the ginger-beer. He was more genial than Philip had ever known him, more at his ease, a man in his own home.

"Shall I call Mrs. Baines?" Philip asked, and he was glad when Baines said no. She was busy. She liked to be busy, so why interfere with her pleasure?

"A spot of drink at half-past eleven," Baines said, pouring himself out a glass of ginger-beer, "gives an appetite for chop and does no man any harm."

"A chop?" Philip asked.

"Old Coasters," Baines said, "call all food chop."

"But it's not a chop?"

"Well, it might be, you know, cooked with palm oil. And then some paw-paw to follow."

Philip looked out of the basement window at the dry stone yard, the ash-can and the legs going up and down beyond the railings.

"Was it hot there?"

"Ah, you never felt such heat. Not a nice heat, mind, like you get in the park on a day like this. Wet," Baines said, "corruption." He cut himself a slice of cake. "Smelling of rot," Baines said, rolling his eyes round the small basement room, from clean cupboard to clean cupboard, the sense of bareness, of nowhere to hide a man's secrets. With an air of regret for something lost he took a long draught of ginger-beer.

"Why did father live out there?"

"It was his job," Baines said, "same as this is mine now. And it was mine then too. It was a man's job. You wouldn't believe it now, but I've had forty niggers under me, doing what I told them to."

"Why did you leave?"

"I married Mrs. Baines."

Philip took the slice of Dundee cake in his hand and munched it round the room. He felt very old, independent and judicial; he was aware that Baines was talking to him as man to man. He never called him Master Philip as Mrs. Baines did, who was servile when she was not authoritative.

Baines had seen the world; he had seen beyond the railings, beyond the tired legs of typists, the Pimlico parade to and from Victoria. He sat there over his ginger pop with the resigned dignity of an exile; Baines didn't complain; he had chosen his fate; and if his fate was Mrs. Baines he had only himself to blame.

But today, because the house was almost empty and Mrs. Baines was upstairs and there was nothing to do, he allowed himself a little acidity.

"I'd go back tomorrow if I had the chance."

"Did you ever shoot a nigger?"

"I never had any call to shoot," Baines said. "Of course I carried a gun. But you didn't need to treat them bad. That just made them stupid. Why," Baines said, bowing his thin grey hair with embarrassment over the ginger pop, "I loved some of those damned niggers. I couldn't help loving them. There they'd be, laughing, holding hands; they liked to touch each other; it made them feel fine to know the other fellow was round.

"It didn't mean anything we could understand; two of them would go about all day without loosing hold, grown men; but it wasn't love; it didn't mean anything we could understand."

"Eating between meals," Mrs. Baines said. "What would your mother say, Master Philip?"

She came down the steep stairs to the basement, her hands full of pots of cream and salve, tubes of grease and paste. "You oughtn't to encourage him, Baines," she said, sitting down in a wicker armchair and screwing up her small ill-humoured eyes at the Coty lipstick, Pond's cream, the Leichner rouge and Cyclax powder and Elizabeth Arden astringent.

She threw them one by one into the wastepaper basket. She saved only the cold cream. "Telling the boy stories," she said. "Go along to the nursery, Master Philip, while I get lunch."

Philip climbed the stairs to the baize door. He heard Mrs. Baines's voice like the voice in a nightmare when the small Price light has guttered in the saucer and the curtains move; it was sharp and shrill and full of malice, louder than people ought to speak, exposed.

"Sick to death of your ways, Baines, spoiling the boy. Time you did some work about the house," but he couldn't hear what Baines said in reply. He pushed open the baize door, came up like a small earth animal in his grey flannel shorts into a wash of sunlight on a parquet floor, the gleam of mirrors dusted and polished and beautified by Mrs. Baines.

Something broke downstairs, and Philip sadly mounted the stairs to the nursery. He pitied Baines; it occurred to him how happily they could live together in the empty house if Mrs. Baines were called away. He didn't want to play with his Meccano sets; he wouldn't take out his train or his soldiers; he sat at the table with his chin on his hands: this is life; and suddenly he felt responsible for Baines, as if he were the master of the house and Baines an ageing servant who deserved to be cared for. There was not much one could do; he decided at least to be good.

He was not surprised when Mrs. Baines was agreeable at lunch; he was used to her changes. Now it was "another helping of meat, Master Philip," or "Master Philip, a little more of this nice pudding." It was a pudding he liked, Queen's pudding with a perfect meringue, but he wouldn't eat a second helping lest she might count that a victory. She was the kind of woman who thought that any injustice could be counterbalanced by something good to eat.

She was sour, but she liked making sweet things; one never had to complain of a lack of jam or plums; she ate well herself and added soft sugar to the meringue and the strawberry jam. The half light through the basement window set the motes moving above her pale hair like dust as she sifted the sugar, and Baines crouched over his plate saying nothing.

Again Philip felt responsibility. Baines had looked forward to this, and Baines was disappointed: everything was being spoilt. The sensation of disappointment was one which Philip could share; knowing nothing of love or jealousy or passion, he could understand better than anyone this grief, something hoped for not happening, something promised not fulfilled, something exciting turning dull. "Baines," he said, "will you take me for a walk this afternoon?"

"No," Mrs. Baines said, "no. That he won't. Not with all the silver to clean."

"There's a fortnight to do it in," Baines said.

"Work first, pleasure afterwards." Mrs. Baines helped herself to some more meringue.

Baines suddenly put down his spoon and fork and pushed his plate away. "Blast," he said.

"Temper," Mrs. Baines said softly, "temper. Don't you go breaking any more things, Baines, and I won't have you swearing in

8

front of the boy. Master Philip, if you've finished you can get down." She skinned the rest of the meringue off the pudding.

"I want to go for a walk," Philip said.

"You'll go and have a rest."

"I will go for a walk."

"Master Philip," Mrs. Baines said. She got up from the table, leaving her meringue unfinished, and came towards him, thin, menacing, dusty in the basement room. "Master Philip, you do as you're told." She took him by the arm and squeezed it gently; she watched him with a joyless passionate glitter and above her head the feet of the typists trudged back to the Victoria offices after the lunch interval.

"Why shouldn't I go for a walk?" But he weakened; he was scared and ashamed of being scared. This was life; a strange passion he couldn't understand moving in the basement room. He saw a small pile of broken glass swept into a corner by the waste-paper basket. He looked to Baines for help and only intercepted hate; the sad hopeless hate of something behind bars.

"Why shouldn't I?" he repeated.

"Master Philip," Mrs. Baines said, "you've got to do as you're told. You mustn't think just because your father's away there's nobody here to—"

"You wouldn't dare," Philip cried, and was startled by Baines's low interjection, "There's nothing she wouldn't dare."

"I hate you," Philip said to Mrs. Baines. He pulled away from her and ran to the door, but she was there before him; she was old, but she was quick.

"Master Philip," she said, "you'll say you're sorry." She stood in front of the door quivering with excitement. "What would your father do if he heard you say that?"

She put a hand out to seize him, dry and white with constant soda, the nails cut to the quick, but he backed away and put the table between them, and suddenly to his surprise she smiled; she became again as servile as she had been arrogant. "Get along with you, Master Philip," she said with glee. "I see I'm going to have my hands full till your father and mother come back."

She left the door unguarded and when he passed her she slapped him playfully. "I've got too much to do today to trouble about you. I haven't covered half the chairs," and suddenly even the upper part of the house became unbearable to him as he thought of Mrs. Baines moving round shrouding the sofas, laying out the dust sheets.

So he wouldn't go upstairs to get his cap but walked straight out across the shining hall into the street, and again, as he looked this way and looked that way, it was life he was in the middle of.

2

It was the pink sugar cakes in the window on a paper doily, the ham, the slab of mauve sausage, the wasps driving like small torpedoes across the pane that caught Philip's attention. His feet were tired by pavements; he had been afraid to cross the road, had simply walked first in one direction, then in the other. He was nearly home now; the square was at the end of the street; this was a shabby outpost of Pimlico, and he smudged the pane with his nose, looking for sweets, and saw between the cakes and ham a different Baines. He hardly recognized the bulbous eyes, the bald forehead. It was a happy, bold and buccaneering Baines, even though it was, when you looked closer, a desperate Baines.

Philip had never seen the girl. He remembered Baines had a niece and he thought that this might be her. She was thin and drawn, and she wore a white mackintosh; she meant nothing to Philip; she belonged to a world about which he knew nothing at all. He couldn't make up stories about her, as he could make them up about withered Sir Hubert Reed, the Permanent Secretary, about Mrs. Wince-Dudley, who came up once a year from Penstanley in Suffolk with a green umbrella and an enormous black handbag, as he could make them up about the upper servants in all the houses where he went to tea and games. She just didn't belong; he thought of mermaids and Undine; but she didn't belong there either, nor to the adventures of Emil, nor to the Bastables. She sat there looking at an iced pink cake in the detachment and mystery of the completely disinherited, looking at the half-used pots of powder which Baines had set out on the marble-topped table between them.

Baines was urging, hoping, entreating, commanding, and the girl looked at the tea and the china pots and cried. Baines passed his handkerchief across the table, but she wouldn't wipe her eyes; she screwed it in her palm and let the tears run down, wouldn't do anything, wouldn't speak, would only put up a silent despairing resistance to what she dreaded and wanted and refused to listen to at any price. The two brains battled over the tea-cups loving each other, and there came to Philip outside, beyond the ham and wasps and dusty Pimlico pane, a confused indication of the struggle. He was inquisitive and he didn't understand and he wanted to know. He went and stood in the doorway to see better, he was less sheltered than he had ever been; other people's lives for the first time touched and pressed and moulded. He would never escape that scene. In a week he had forgotten it, but it conditioned his career, the long austerity of his life; when he was dying he said, "Who is she?"

Baines had won; he was cocky and the girl was happy. She wiped her face, she opened a pot of powder, and their fingers touched across the table. It occurred to Philip that it would be amusing to imitate Mrs. Baines's voice and call "Baines" to him from the door.

It shrivelled them; you couldn't describe it in any other way; it made them smaller, they weren't happy any more and they weren't bold. Baines was the first to recover and trace the voice, but that didn't make things as they were. The sawdust was spilled out of the afternoon; nothing you did could mend it, and Philip was scared. "I didn't mean . . ." He wanted to say that he loved Baines, that he had only wanted to laugh at Mrs. Baines. But he had discovered that you couldn't laugh at Mrs. Baines. She wasn't Sir Hubert Reed, who used steel nibs and carried a pen-wiper in his pocket; she wasn't Mrs. Wince-Dudley; she was darkness when the night-light went out in a draught; she was the frozen blocks of earth he had seen one winter in a graveyard when someone said, "They need an electric drill"; she was the flowers gone bad and smelling in the little closet room at Penstanley. There was nothing to laugh about. You had to endure her when she was there and forget about her quickly when she was away, suppress the thought of her, ram it down deep.

Baines said, "It's only Phil," beckoned him in and gave him the pink iced cake the girl hadn't eaten, but the afternoon was broken, the cake was like dry bread in the throat. The girl left them at once; she even forgot to take the powder; like a small icicle in her white mackintosh she stood in the doorway with her back to them, then melted into the afternoon.

"Who is she?" Philip asked. "Is she your niece?"

"Oh, yes," Baines said, "that's who she is; she's my niece," and poured the last drops of water on to the coarse black leaves in the teapot.

"May as well have another cup," Baines said.

"The cup that cheers," he said hopelessly, watching the bitter black fluid drain out of the spout.

"Have a glass of ginger pop, Phil?"

"I'm sorry. I'm sorry, Baines."

"It's not your fault, Phil. Why, I could believe it wasn't you at all, but her. She creeps in everywhere." He fished two leaves out of his cup and laid them on the back of his hand, a thin soft flake and a hard stalk. He beat them with his hand: "Today," and the stalk detached itself, "tomorrow, Wednesday, Thursday, Friday, Saturday, Sunday," but the flake wouldn't come, stayed where it was, drying under his blows, with a resistance you wouldn't believe it to possess. "The tough one wins," Baines said.

He got up and paid the bill and out they went into the street. Baines said, "I don't ask you to say what isn't true. But you needn't mention to Mrs. Baines you met us here."

"Of course not," Philip said, and catching something of Sir Hubert Reed's manner, "I understand, Baines." But he didn't understand a thing; he was caught up in other people's darkness.

"It was stupid," Baines said. "So near home, but I hadn't time to think, you see. I'd got to see her."

"Of course, Baines."

"I haven't time to spare," Baines said. "I'm not young. I've got to see that she's all right."

"Of course you have, Baines."

"Mrs. Baines will get it out of you if she can."

"You can trust me, Baines," Philip said in a dry important Reed voice; and then, "Look out. She's at the window watching." And there indeed she was, looking up at them, between the lace curtains, from the basement room, speculating. "Need we go in, Baines?" Philip asked, cold lying heavy on his stomach like too much pudding; he clutched Baines's arm.

"Careful," Baines said softly, "careful."

"But need we go in, Baines? It's early. Take me for a walk in the park."

"Better not."

"But I'm frightened, Baines."

"You haven't any cause," Baines said. "Nothing's going to hurt you. You just run along upstairs to the nursery. I'll go down by the area and talk to Mrs. Baines." But even he stood hesitating at the top of the stone steps, pretending not to see her where she watched between the curtains. "In at the front door, Phil, and up the stairs."

Philip didn't linger in the hall; he ran, slithering on the parquet Mrs. Baines had polished, to the stairs. Through the drawing-room doorway on the first floor he saw the draped chairs; even the china clock on the mantel was covered like a canary's cage; as he passed it, it chimed the hour, muffled and secret under the duster.

On the nursery table he found his supper laid out: a glass of milk and a piece of bread and butter, a sweet biscuit and a little cold Queen's pudding without the meringue. He had no appetite; he strained his ears for Mrs. Baines's coming, for the sound of voices, but the basement held its secrets; the green baize door shut off that world. He drank the milk and ate the biscuit, but he didn't touch the rest, and presently he could hear the soft precise foot-falls of Mrs. Baines on the stairs: she was a good servant, she walked softly; she was a determined woman, she walked precisely.

But she wasn't angry when she came in; she was ingratiating as she opened the night nursery door—"Did you have a good walk, Master Philip?"—pulled down the blinds, laid out his pyjamas, came back to clear his supper. "I'm glad Baines found you. Your mother wouldn't have liked your being out alone." She examined the tray. "Not much appetite, have you, Master Philip? Why don't you try a little of this nice pudding? I'll bring you up some more jam for it."

"No, no, thank you, Mrs. Baines," Philip said.

"You ought to eat more," Mrs. Baines said. She sniffed round the room like a dog. "You didn't take any pots out of the waste-paper basket in the kitchen, did you, Master Philip?"

"No," Philip said.

"Of course you wouldn't. I just wanted to make sure." She patted his shoulder and her fingers flashed to his lapel; she picked off a tiny crumb of pink sugar. "Oh, Master Philip," she said, "that's why you haven't any appetite. You've been buying sweet cakes. That's not what your pocket money's for."

"But I didn't," Philip said. "I didn't."

She tasted the sugar with the tip of her tongue.

"Don't tell lies to me, Master Philip. I won't stand for it any more than your father would."

"I didn't, I didn't," Philip said. "They gave it me. I mean Baines," but she had pounced on the word "they." She had got what she wanted; there was no doubt about that, even when you didn't know what it was she wanted. Philip was angry and mis-erable and disappointed because he hadn't kept Baines's secret. Baines oughtn't to have trusted him; grown-up people should keep their own secrets, and yet here was Mrs. Baines immediately en-trusting him with another.

"Let me tickle your palm and see if you can keep a secret." But he put his hand behind him; he wouldn't be touched. "It's a secret between us, Master Philip, that I know all about them. I suppose she was having tea with him," she speculated.

"Why shouldn't she?" he said, the responsibility for Baines weighing on his spirit, the idea that he had got to keep her secret when he hadn't kept Baines's making him miserable with the unfairness of life. "She was nice."

"She was nice, was she?" Mrs. Baines said in a bitter voice he wasn't used to.

"And she's his niece."

"So that's what he said," Mrs. Baines struck softly back at him like the clock under the duster. She tried to be jocular. "The old scoundrel. Don't you tell him I know, Master Philip." She stood very still between the table and the door, thinking very hard, planning something. "Promise you won't tell. I'll give you that Meccano set, Master Philip. . . ."

He turned his back on her; he wouldn't promise, but he wouldn't tell. He would have nothing to do with their secrets, the responsibilities they were determined to lay on him. He was only anxious to forget. He had received already a larger dose of life than he had bargained for, and he was scared. "A 2A Meccano set, Master Philip." He never opened his Meccano set again, never built anything, never created anything, died, the old dilettante, sixty years later, nothing to show rather than preserve the memory of Mrs. Baines's malicious voice saying good night, her soft determined footfalls on the stairs to the basement, going down, going down.

3

The sun poured in between the curtains and Baines was beating a tattoo on the water-can. "Glory, glory," Baines said. He sat down on the end of the bed and said, "I beg to announce that Mrs. Baines has been called away. Her mother's dying. She won't be back till tomorrow."

"Why did you wake me up so early?" Philip said. He watched Baines with uneasiness; he wasn't going to be drawn in; he'd learnt his lesson. It wasn't right for a man of Baines's age to be so merry. It made a grown person human in the same way that you were human. For if a grown-up could behave so childishly, you were liable too to find yourself in their world. It was enough that it came at you in dreams: the witch at the corner, the man with a knife. So "It's very early," he complained, even though he loved Baines, even though he couldn't help being glad that Baines was happy. He was divided by the fear and the attraction of life.

"I want to make this a long day," Baines said. "This is the best time." He pulled the curtains back. "It's a bit misty. The cat's been out all night. There she is, sniffing round the area. They haven't taken in any milk at 59. Emma's shaking out the mats at 63." He said, "This was what I used to think about on the Coast: somebody shaking mats and the cat coming home. I can see it today," Baines said, "just as if I was still in Africa. Most days you don't notice what you've got. It's a good life if you don't weaken." He put a penny on the washstand. "When you've dressed, Phil, run and get a *Mail* from the barrow at the corner. I'll be cooking the sausages."

"Sausages?"

"Sausages," Baines said. "We're going to celebrate today. A fair bust." He celebrated at breakfast, reckless, cracking jokes, unaccountably merry and nervous. It was going to be a long, long day, he kept on coming back to that: for years he had waited for a long day, he had sweated in the damp Coast heat, changed shirts, gone down with fever, lain between the blankets and sweated, all in the hope of this long day, that cat sniffing round the area, a bit of mist, the mats beaten at 63. He propped the *Mail* in front of the coffee-pot and read pieces aloud. He said, "Cora Down's been married for the fourth time." He was amused, but it wasn't his idea of a long day. His long day was the Park, watching the riders in the Row, seeing Sir Arthur Stillwater pass beyond the rails ("He dined with us once in Bo; up from Freetown; he was governor there"), lunch at the Corner House for Philip's sake (he'd have preferred himself a glass of stout and some oysters at the York bar), the Zoo, the long bus ride home in the last summer light: the leaves in the Green Park were beginning to turn and the motors nuzzled out of Berkeley Street with the low sun gently glowing on their wind-screens. Baines envied no one, not Cora Down, or Sir Arthur Stillwater, or Lord Sandale, who came out on to the steps of the Army and Navy and then went back again because he hadn't got anything to do and might as well look at another paper. "I said don't let me see you touch that black again." Baines had led a man's life; everyone on top of the bus pricked their ears when he told Philip all about it.

"Would you have shot him?" Philip asked, and Baines put his head back and tilted his dark respectable man-servant's hat to a better angle as the bus swerved round the artillery memorial.

"I wouldn't have thought twice about it. I'd have shot to kill," he boasted, and the bowed figure went by, the steel helmet, the heavy cloak, the down-turned rifle and the folded hands.

"Have you got the revolver?"

"Of course I've got it," Baines said. "Don't I need it with all the burglaries there've been?" This was the Baines whom Philip loved: not Baines singing and carefree, but Baines responsible, Baines behind barriers, living his man's life.

All the buses streamed out from Victoria like a convoy of aeroplanes to bring Baines home with honour. "Forty blacks under me," and there waiting near the area steps was the proper conventional reward, love at lighting-up time.

"It's your niece," Philip said, recognizing the white mackintosh, but not the happy sleepy face. She frightened him like an unlucky number; he nearly told Baines what Mrs. Baines had said; but he didn't want to bother, he wanted to leave things alone.

"Why, so it is," Baines said. "I shouldn't wonder if she was going to have a bite of supper with us." But he said they'd play a game, pretend they didn't know her, slip down the area steps, "and here," Baines said, "we are," lay the table, put out the cold sausages, a bottle of beer, a bottle of ginger pop, a flagon of harvest burgandy. "Everyone his own drink," Baines said. "Run upstairs, Phil, and see if there's been a post."

Philip didn't like the empty house at dusk before the lights went on. He hurried. He wanted to be back with Baines. The hall lay there in quiet and shadow prepared to show him something he didn't want to see. Some letters rustled down, and someone knocked. "Open in the name of the Republic." The tumbrils rolled, the head bobbed in the bloody basket. Knock, knock, and the postman's footsteps going away. Philip gathered the letters. The slit in the door was like the grating in a jeweller's window. He remembered the policeman he had seen peer through. He had said to his nurse, "What's he doing?" and when she said, "He's seeing if everything's all right," his brain immediately filled with images of all that might be wrong. He ran to the baize door and the stairs. The girl was already there and Baines was kissing her. She leant breathless against the dresser.

"This is Emmy, Phil."

"There's a letter for you, Baines."

"Emmy," Baines said, "it's from her." But he wouldn't open it. "You bet she's coming back."

"We'll have supper, anyway," Emmy said. "She can't harm that."

"You don't know her," Baines said, "Nothing's safe. Damn it," he said, "I was a man once," and he opened the letter.

"Can I start?" Philip asked, but Baines didn't hear; he presented in his stillness and attention an example of the importance grown-up people attached to the written word: you had to write your thanks, not wait and speak them, as if letters couldn't lie. But Philip knew better than that, sprawling his thanks across a page to Aunt Alice who had given him a doll he was too old for. Letters could lie all right, but they made the lie permanent: they lay as evidence against you; they made you meaner than the spoken word.

"She's not coming back till tomorrow night," Baines said. He opened the bottles, he pulled up the chairs, he kissed Emmy again against the dresser.

"You oughtn't to," Emmy said, "with the boy here."

"He's got to learn," Baines said, "like the rest of us," and he helped Philip to three sausages. He only took one himself; he said he wasn't hungry; but when Emmy said she wasn't hungry either he stood over her and made her eat. He was timid and rough with her; he made her drink the harvest burgandy because he said she needed building up; he wouldn't take no for an answer, but when he touched her his hands were light and clumsy too, as if he were afraid to damage something delicate and didn't know how to handle anything so light.

"This is better than milk and biscuits, eh?"

"Yes," Philip said, but he was scared, scared for Baines as much as for himself. He couldn't help wondering at every bite, at every draught of the ginger pop, what Mrs. Baines would say if she ever learnt of this meal; he couldn't imagine it, there was a depth of bitterness and rage in Mrs. Baines you couldn't sound. He said, "She won't be coming back tonight?" but you could tell by the way they immediately understood him that she wasn't really away at all; she was there in the basement with them, driving them to longer drinks and louder talk, biding her time for the right cutting word. Baines wasn't really happy; he was only watching happiness from close to instead of from far away.

"No," he said, "she'll not be back till late tomorrow." He couldn't keep his eyes off happiness; he'd played around as much as other men, he kept on reverting to the Coast as if to excuse himself for his innocence; he wouldn't have been so innocent if he'd lived his life in London, so innocent when it came to tenderness. "If it was you, Emmy," he said, looking at the white dresser, the scrubbed chairs, "this'd be like a home." Already the room was not quite so harsh; there was a little dust in corners, the silver needed a final polish, the morning's paper lay untidily on a chair. "You'd better go to bed, Phil; it's been a long day."

They didn't leave him to find his own way up through the dark shrouded house; they went with him, turning on lights, touching each other's fingers on the switches; floor after floor they drove the night back; they spoke softly among the covered chairs; they watched him undress, they didn't make him wash or clean his teeth, they saw him into bed and lit his night-light and left his door ajar. He could hear their voices on the stairs, friendly, like the guests he heard at dinner-parties when they moved down to the hall, saying good night. They belonged; wherever they were they made a home. He heard a door open and a clock strike, he heard their voices for a long while, so that he felt they were not far away and he was safe. The voices didn't dwindle, they simply went out, and he could be sure that they were still somewhere not far from him, silent together in one of the many empty rooms, growing sleepy together as he grew sleepy after the long day.

He just had time to sigh faintly with satisfaction, because this too perhaps had been life, before he slept and the inevitable terrors of sleep came round him: a man with a tricolor hat beat at the door on His Majesty's service, a bleeding head lay on the kitchen table in a basket, and the Siberian wolves crept closer. He was bound hand and foot and couldn't move; they leapt round him breathing heavily; he opened his eyes and Mrs. Baines was there, her grey untidy hair in threads over his face, her black hat askew. A loose hairpin fell on the pillow and one musty thread brushed his mouth. "Where are they?" she whispered. "Where are they?"

4

Philip watched her in terror. Mrs. Baines was out of breath as if she had been searching all the empty rooms, looking under loose covers.

With her untidy grey hair and her black dress buttoned to her throat, her gloves of black cotton, she was so like the witches of his dreams that he didn't dare to speak. There was a stale smell in her breath.

"She's here," Mrs. Baines said; "you can't deny she's here." Her face was simultaneously marked with cruelty and misery; she wanted to "do things" to people, but she suffered all the time. It would have done her good to scream, but she daren't do that: it would warn them. She came ingratiatingly back to the bed where Philip lay rigid on his back and whispered, "I haven't forgotten the Meccano set. You shall have it tomorrow, Master Philip. We've got secrets together, haven't we? Just tell me where they are."

He couldn't speak. Fear held him as firmly as any nightmare. She said, "Tell Mrs. Baines, Master Philip. You love your Mrs. Baines, don't you?" That was too much; he couldn't speak, but he could move his mouth in terrified denial, wince away from her dusty image.

18

She whispered, coming closer to him, "Such deceit. I'll tell your father. I'll settle with you myself when I've found them. You'll smart; I'll see you smart." Then immediately she was still, listening. A board had creaked on the floor below, and a moment later, while she stooped listening above his bed, there came the whispers of two people who were happy and sleepy together after a long day. The night-light stood beside the mirror and Mrs. Baines could see bitterly there her own reflection, misery and cruelty wavering in the glass, age and dust and nothing to hope for. She sobbed without tears, a dry, breathless sound; but her cruelty was a kind of pride which kept her going; it was her best quality, she would have been merely pitiable without it. She went out of the door on tiptoe, feeling her way across the landing, going so softly down the stairs that no one behind a shut door could hear her. Then there was complete silence again; Philip could move; he raised his knees; he sat up in bed; he wanted to die. It wasn't fair, the walls were down again between his world and theirs; but this time it was something worse than merriment that the grown people made him share; a passion moved in the house he recognized but could not understand.

It wasn't fair, but he owed Baines everything: the Zoo, the ginger pop, the bus ride home. Even the supper called on his loyalty. But he was frightened; he was touching something he touched in dreams: the bleeding head, the wolves, the knock, knock, knock. Life fell on him with savagery; you couldn't blame him if he never faced it again in sixty years. He got out of bed, carefully from habit put on his bedroom slippers, and tiptoed to the door: it wasn't quite dark on the landing below because the curtains had been taken down for the cleaners and the light from the street came in through the tall windows. Mrs. Baines had her hand on the glass door-knob; she was very carefully turning it; he screamed, "Baines, Baines."

Mrs. Baines turned and saw him cowering in his pyjamas by the banisters; he was helpless, more helpless even than Baines, and cruelty grew at the sight of him and drove her up the stairs. The nightmare was on him again and he couldn't move; he hadn't any more courage left for ever; he'd spent it all, had been allowed no time to let it grow, no years of gradual hardening; he couldn't even scream.

But the first cry had brought Baines out of the best spare bedroom and he moved quicker than Mrs. Baines. She hadn't reached the top of the stairs before he'd caught her round the waist. She drove her black cotton gloves at his face and he bit her hand. He

"You oughtn't to do it, young fellow. Think how anxious your father and mother will be."

"They are away."

"Well, your nurse."

"I haven't got one."

"Who looks after you, then?" That question went home. Philip saw Mrs. Baines coming up the stairs at him, the heap of black cotton in the hall. He began to cry.

"Now, now, now," the sergeant said. He didn't know what to do; he wished his wife were with him; even a policewoman might have been useful.

"Don't you think it's funny," the constable said, "that there hasn't been an inquiry?"

"They think he's tucked up in bed."

"You are scared, aren't you?" the constable said. "What scared you?"

"I don't know."

"Somebody hurt you?"

"No."

"He's had bad dreams," the sergeant said. "Thought the house was on fire, I expect. I've brought up six of them. Rose is due back. She'll take him home."

"I want to go home with you," Philip said; he tried to smile at the constable, but the deceit was immature and unsuccessful.

"I'd better go," the constable said. "There may be something wrong."

"Nonsense," the sergeant said. "It's a woman's job. Tact is what you need. Here's Rose. Pull up your stockings, Rose. You're a disgrace to the Force. I've got a job of work for you." Rose shambled in: black cotton stockings drooping over her boots, a gawky Girl Guide manner, a hoarse hostile voice. "More tarts, I suppose."

"No, you've got to see this young man home." She looked at him owlishly.

"I won't go with her," Philip said. He began to cry again. "I don't like her."

"More of that womanly charm, Rose," the sergeant said. The telephone rang on his desk. He lifted the receiver. "What? What's that?" he said. "Number 48? You've got a doctor?" He put his hand over the telephone mouth. "No wonder this nipper wasn't reported," he said. "They've been too busy. An accident. Woman slipped on the stairs."

"Serious?" the constable asked. The sergeant mouthed at him;

you didn't mention the word death before a child (didn't he know? he had six of them), you made noises in the throat, you grimaced, a complicated shorthand for a word of only five letters anyway.

"You'd better go, after all," he said, "and make a report. The doctor's there."

Rose shambled from the stove; pink apply-dapply cheeks, loose stockings. She stuck her hands behind her. Her large morgue-like mouth was full of blackened teeth. "You told me to take him and now just because something interesting . . . I don't expect justice from a man . . ."

"Who's at the house?" the constable asked.

"The butler."

"You don't think," the constable said, "he saw . . ."

"Trust me," the sergeant said. "I've brought up six. I know 'em through and through. You can't teach me anything about children."

"He seemed scared about something."

"Dreams," the sergeant said.

"What name?"

"Baines."

"This Mr. Baines," the constable said to Philip, "you like him, eh? He's good to you?" They were trying to get something out of him; he was suspicious of the whole roomful of them; he said "yes" without conviction because he was afraid at any moment of more responsibilities, more secrets.

"And Mrs. Baines?"

"Yes."

They consulted together by the desk: Rose was hoarsely aggrieved; she was like a female impersonator, she bore her womanhood with an unnatural emphasis even while she scorned it in her creased stockings and her weather-exposed face. The charcoal shifted in the stove; the room was overheated in the mild late summer evening. A notice on the wall described a body found in the Thames, or rather the body's clothes: wool vest, wool pants, wool shirt with blue stripes, size ten boots, blue serge suit worn at the elbows, fifteen and a half celluloid collar. They couldn't find anything to say about the body, except its measurements, it was just an ordinary body.

"Come along," the constable said. He was interested, he was glad to be going, but he couldn't help being embarrassed by his company, a small boy in pyjamas. His nose smelt something, he didn't know what, but he smarted at the sight of the amusement they caused: the pubs had closed and the streets were full again of men making as long a day of it as they could. He hurried through the

24

less frequented streets, chose the darker pavements, wouldn't loiter, and Philip wanted more and more to loiter, pulling at his hand, dragging with his feet. He dreaded the sight of Mrs. Baines waiting in the hall: he knew now that she was dead. The sergeant's mouthings had conveyed that; but she wasn't buried, she wasn't out of sight; he was going to see a dead person in the hall when the door opened.

The light was on in the basement, and to his relief the constable made for the area steps. Perhaps he wouldn't have to see Mrs. Baines at all. The constable knocked on the door because it was too dark to see the bell, and Baines answered. He stood there in the doorway of the neat bright basement room and you could see the sad complacent plausible sentence he had prepared wither at the sight of Philip; he hadn't expected Philip to return like that in the policeman's company. He had to begin thinking all over again; he wasn't a deceptive man; if it hadn't been for Emmy he would have been quite ready to let the truth lead him where it would.

"Mr. Baines?" the constable asked.

He nodded; he hadn't found the right words; he was daunted by the shrewd knowing face, the sudden appearance of Philip there.

"This little boy from here?"

"Yes," Baines said. Philip could tell that there was a message he was trying to convey, but he shut his mind to it. He loved Baines, but Baines had involved him in secrets, in fears he didn't understand. The glowing morning thought, "This is life," had become under Baines's tuition the repugnant memory, "That was life": the musty hair across the mouth, the breathless cruel tortured inquiry, "Where are they," the heap of black cotton tipped into the hall. That was what happened when you loved: you got involved; and Philip extricated himself from life, from love, from Baines, with a merciless egotism.

There had been things between them, but he laid them low, as a retreating army cuts the wires, destroys the bridges. In the abandoned country you may leave much that is dear—a morning in the Park, an ice at a corner house, sausages for supper—but more is concerned in the retreat than temporary losses. There are old people who, as the tractors wheel away, implore to be taken, but you can't risk the rearguard for their sake: a whole prolonged retreat from life, from care, from human relationships is involved.

"The doctor's here," Baines said. He nodded at the door, moistened his mouth, kept his eyes on Philip, begging for something like a dog you can't understand. "There's nothing to be done. She slipped on these stone basement stairs. I was in here. I heard her fall." He wouldn't look at the notebook, at the constable's tiny spidery writing which got a terrible lot on one page.

"Did the boy see anything?"

"He can't have done. I thought he was in bed. Hadn't he better go up? It's a shocking thing. Oh," Baines said, losing control, "it's a shocking thing for a child."

"She's through there?" the constable asked.

"I haven't moved her an inch," Baines said.

"He'd better then—"

"Go up the area and through the hall," Baines said and again he begged dumbly like a dog: one more secret, keep this secret, do this for old Baines, he won't ask another.

"Come along," the constable said. "I'll see you up to bed. You're a gentleman; you must come in the proper way through the front door like the master should. Or will you go along with him, Mr. Baines, while I see the doctor?"

"Yes," Baines said, "I'll go." He came across the room to Philip, begging, begging, all the way with his soft old stupid expression: this is Baines, the old Coaster; what about a palm-oil chop, eh?; a man's life; forty niggers; never used a gun; I tell you I couldn't help loving them: it wasn't what we call love, nothing we could understand. The messages flickered out from the last posts at the border, imploring, beseeching, reminding: this is your old friend Baines; what about an eleven's; a glass of ginger pop won't do you any harm; sausages; a long day. But the wires were cut, the messages just faded out into the enormous vacancy of the neat scrubbed room in which there had never been a place where a man could hide his secrets.

"Come along, Phil, it's bedtime. We'll just go up the steps . . ." Tap, tap, tap, at the telegraph; you may get through, you can't tell, somebody may mend the right wire. "And in at the front door."

"No," Philip said, "no. I won't go. You can't make me go. I'll fight. I won't see her."

The constable turned on them quickly. "What's that? Why won't you go?"

"She's in the hall," Philip said. "I know she's in the hall. And she's dead. I won't see her."

"You moved her then?" the constable said to Baines. "All the way down here? You've been lying, eh? That means you had to tidy up. . . . Were you alone?"

"Emmy," Philip said, "Emmy." He wasn't going to keep any

more secrets: he was going to finish once and for all with every-thing, with Baines and Mrs. Baines and the grown-up life beyond him; it wasn't his business and never, never again, he decided, would he share their confidences and companionship. "It was all Emmy's fault," he protested with a quaver which reminded Baines that after all he was only a child; it had been hopeless to expect help there; he was a child; he didn't understand what it all meant; he couldn't read this shorthand of terror; he'd had a long day and he was tired out. You could see him dropping asleep where he stood against the dresser, dropping back into the comfortable nursery peace. You couldn't blame him. When he woke in the morning, he'd hardly remember a thing.

"Out with it," the constable said, addressing Baines with profes-sional ferocity, "who is she?" just as the old man sixty years later startled his secretary, his only watcher, asking, "Who is she? Who is she?" dropping lower and lower into death, passing on the way perhaps the image of Baines: Baines hopeless, Baines letting his head drop, Baines "coming clean."

ACROSS THE BRIDGE

"THEY SAY HE'S WORTH A MILLION," LUCIA SAID. HE SAT THERE IN the little hot damp Mexican square, a dog at his feet, with an air of immense and forlorn patience. The dog attracted your attention at once; for it was very nearly an English setter, only something had gone wrong with the tail and the feathering. Palms wilted over his head, it was all shade and stuffiness round the bandstand, radios talked loudly in Spanish from the little wooden sheds where they changed your pesos into dollars at a loss. I could tell he didn't understand a word from the way he read his newspaper—as I did myself, picking out the words which were like English ones. "He's been here a month," Lucia said. "They turned him out of Guatemala and Honduras."

You couldn't keep any secrets for five hours in this border town. Lucia had only been twenty-four hours in the place, but she knew all about Mr. Joseph Calloway. The only reason I didn't know about him (and I'd been in the place two weeks) was because I couldn't talk the language any more than Mr. Calloway could. There wasn't another soul in the place who didn't know the story —the whole story of the Halling Investment Trust and the proceedings for extradition. Any man doing dusty business in any of the wooden booths in the town is better fitted by long observation to tell Mr. Calloway's tale than I am, except that I was in—literally —at the finish. They all watched the drama proceed with immense interest, sympathy and respect. For, after all, he had a million.

Every once in a while through the long steamy day, a boy came and cleaned Mr. Calloway's shoes; he hadn't the right words to resist them—they pretended not to know his English. He must have had his shoes cleaned the day Lucia and I watched him at least half a dozen times. At midday he took a stroll across the square to the Antonio Bar and had a bottle of beer, the setter sticking to heel as if they were out for a country walk in England (he had, you may remember, one of the biggest estates in Norfolk). After his bottle of beer, he would walk down between the money-changers' huts to the Rio Grande and look across the bridge into the United States: people came and went constantly in cars. Then back to the square till lunch-time. He was staying in the best hotel, but you don't get good hotels in this border town: nobody stays in them more than a night. The good hotels were on the other side of the bridge: you could see their electric signs twenty stories high from the little square at night, like lighthouses marking the United States.

You may ask what I'd been doing in so drab a spot for a fortnight. There was no interest in the place for anyone; it was just damp and dust and poverty, a kind of shabby replica of the town across the river: both had squares in the same spots; both had the same number of cinemas. One was cleaner than the other, that was all, and more expensive, much more expensive. I'd stayed across there a couple of nights waiting for a man a tourist bureau said was driving down from Detroit to Yucatan and would sell a place in his car for some fantastically small figure—twenty dollars, I think it was. I don't know if he existed or was invented by the optimistic half-caste in the agency; anyway, he never turned up and so I waited, not much caring, on the cheap side of the river. It didn't much matter; I was living. One day I meant to give up the man from Detroit and go home or go south, but it was easier not to decide anything in a hurry. Lucia was just waiting for a car going the other way, but she didn't have to wait so long. We waited together and watched Mr. Calloway waiting—for God knows what.

I don't know how to treat this story—it was a tragedy for Mr. Calloway, it was poetic retribution, I suppose, in the eyes of the shareholders he'd ruined with his bogus transactions, and to Lucia and me, at this stage, it was pure comedy—except when he kicked the dog. I'm not a sentimentalist about dogs, I prefer people to be cruel to animals rather than to human beings, but I couldn't help being revolted at the way he'd kick that animal—with a hint of cold-blooded venom, not in anger but as if he were getting even for some trick it had played him a long while ago. That generally happened when he returned from the bridge: it was the only sign of anything resembling emotion he showed. Otherwise he looked a small, set, gentle creature with silver hair and a silver moustache, and gold-rimmed glasses, and one gold tooth like a flaw in character.

Lucia hadn't been accurate when she said he'd been turned out of Guatemala and Honduras; he'd left voluntarily when the extradition proceedings seemed likely to go through and moved north. Mexico is still not a very centralized state, and it is possible to get round governors as you can't get round cabinet ministers or judges. And so he waited there on the border for the next move. That earlier part of the story is, I suppose, dramatic, but I didn't watch it and I can't invent what I haven't seen—the long waiting in ante-rooms, the bribes taken and refused, the growing fear of arrest, and then the flight—in gold-rimmed glasses—covering his tracks as well as he could, but this wasn't finance and he was an amateur at escape. And so he'd washed up here, under my eyes and Lucia's eyes, sitting all day under the bandstand, nothing to read but a Mexican paper, nothing to do but look across the river at the United States, quite unaware, I suppose, that everyone knew everything about him, once a day kicking his dog. Perhaps in its semi-setter way it reminded him too much of the Norfolk estate—though that too, I suppose, was the reason he kept it.

And the next act again was pure comedy. I hesitate to think what this man worth a million was costing his country as they edged him out from this land and that. Perhaps somebody was getting tired of the business, and careless; anyway, they sent across two detectives, with an old photograph. He'd grown his silvery moustache since that had been taken, and he'd aged a lot, and they couldn't catch sight of him. They hadn't been across the bridge two hours when everybody knew that there were two foreign detectives in town looking for Mr. Calloway—everybody knew, that is to say, except Mr. Calloway, who couldn't talk Spanish. There were plenty of people who could have told him in English, but they didn't. It wasn't cruelty, it was a sort of awe and respect: like a bull, he was on show, sitting there mournfully in the plaza with his dog, a magnificent spectacle for which we all had ringside seats.

I ran into one of the policemen in the Bar Antonio. He was disgusted; he had had some idea that when he crossed the bridge life was going to be different, so much more colour and sun, and—I suspect—love, and all he found were wide mud streets where the nocturnal rain lay in pools, and mangy dogs, smells and cockroaches in his bedroom, and the nearest to love, the open door of the Academia Comercial, where pretty mestizo girls sat all the morning learning to typewrite. Tip-tap-tip-tap-tip—perhaps they had a dream, too—jobs on the other side of the bridge, where life was going to be so much more luxurious, refined and amusing.

We got into conversation; he seemed surprised that I knew who they both were and what they wanted. He said, "We've got information this man Calloway's in town."

"He's knocking around somewhere," I said.

"Could you point him out?"

"Oh, I don't know him by sight," I said.

He drank his beer and thought a while. "I'll go out and sit in the plaza. He's sure to pass sometime."

I finished my beer and went quickly off and found Lucia. I said, "Hurry, we're going to see an arrest." We didn't care a thing about Mr. Calloway, he was just an elderly man who kicked his dog and swindled the poor, and who deserved anything he got. So we made for the plaza; we knew Calloway would be there, but it had never occurred to either of us that the detectives wouldn't recognize him. There was quite a surge of people round the place; all the fruit-sellers and boot-blacks in town seemed to have arrived together; we had to force our way through, and there in the little green stuffy centre of the place, sitting on adjoining seats, were the two plain-clothes men and Mr. Calloway. I've never known the place so silent; everybody was on tiptoe, and the plain-clothes men were staring at the crowd looking for Mr. Calloway, and Mr. Calloway sat on his usual seat staring out over the money-changing booths at the United States.

"It can't go on. It just can't," Lucia said. But it did. It got more fantastic still. Somebody ought to write a play about it. We sat as close as we dared. We were afraid all the time we were going to laugh. The semi-setter scratched for fleas and Mr. Calloway watched the U.S.A. The two detectives watched the crowd, and the crowd watched the show with solemn satisfaction. Then one of the detectives got up and went over to Mr. Calloway. That's the end, I thought. But it wasn't, it was the beginning. For some reason they had eliminated him from their list of suspects. I shall never know why.

The man said, "You speak English?"

"I *am* English," Mr. Calloway said.

Even that didn't tear it, and the strangest thing of all was the way Mr. Calloway came alive. I don't think anybody had spoken to him like that for weeks. The Mexicans were too respectful—he was a man with a million—and it had never occurred to Lucia and me to treat him casually like a human being; even in our eyes he had been magnified by the colossal theft and the world-wide pursuit.

He said, "This is rather a dreadful place, don't you think?"

"It is," the policeman said.

"I can't think what brings anybody across the bridge."

"Duty," the policeman said gloomily. "I suppose you are passing through."

"Yes," Mr. Calloway said.

"I'd have expected over here there'd have been—you know what I mean—life. You read things about Mexico."

"Oh, life," Mr. Calloway said. He spoke firmly and precisely, as if to a committee of shareholders. "That begins on the other side."

"You don't appreciate your own country until you leave it."

"That's very true," Mr. Calloway said. "Very true."

At first it was difficult not to laugh, and then after a while there didn't seem to be much to laugh at; an old man imagining all the fine things going on beyond the international bridge. I think he thought of the town opposite as a combination of London and Norfolk—theatres and cocktail bars, a little shooting and a walk round the field at evening with the dog—that miserable imitation of a setter—poking the ditches. He'd never been across, he couldn't know that it was just the same thing over again—even the same layout; only the streets were paved and the hotels had ten more stories, and life was more expensive, and everything was a little bit cleaner. There wasn't anything Mr. Calloway would have called living—no galleries, no book-shops, just *Film Fun* and the local paper, and *Click* and *Focus* and the tabloids.

"Well," said Mr. Calloway, "I think I'll take a stroll before lunch. You need an appetite to swallow the food here. I generally go down and look at the bridge about now. Care to come too?"

The detective shook his head. "No," he said, "I'm on duty. I'm looking for a fellow." And that, of course, gave *him* away. As far as Mr. Calloway could understand, there was only one "fellow" in the world anyone was looking for—his brain had eliminated friends who were seeking their friends, husbands who might be waiting for their wives, all objectives of any search but just the one. The power of elimination was what had made him a financier—he could forget the people behind the shares.

That was the last we saw of him for a while. We didn't see him going into the Botica Paris to get his aspirin, or walking back from the bridge with his dog. He simply disappeared, and when he disappeared, people began to talk, and the detectives heard the talk. They looked silly enough, and they got busy after the very man they'd been sitting next to in the garden. Then they too disappeared. They, as well as Mr. Calloway, had gone to the state capital to see the Governor and the Chief of Police, and it must have been an amusing sight there too, as they bumped into Mr. Calloway and sat with him in the waiting-rooms. I suspect Mr. Calloway was generally shown in first, for everyone knew he was worth a million. Only in Europe is it possible for a man to be a criminal as well as a rich man.

Anyway, after about a week the whole pack of them returned by the same train. Mr. Calloway travelled Pullman, and the two policemen travelled in the day coach. It was evident that they hadn't got their extradition order.

Lucia had left by that time. The car came and went across the bridge. I stood in Mexico and watched her get out at the United States Customs. She wasn't anything in particular but she looked beautiful at a distance as she gave me a wave out of the United States and got back into the car. And I suddenly felt sympathy for Mr. Calloway, as if there were something over there which you couldn't find here, and turning round I saw him back on his old beat, with the dog at his heels.

I said "Good afternoon," as if it had been all along our habit to greet each other. He looked tired and ill and dusty, and I felt sorry for him—to think of the kind of victory he'd been winning, with so much expenditure of cash and care—the prize this dirty and dreary town, the booths of the money-changers, the awful little beauty parlours with their wicker chairs and sofas looking like the reception rooms of brothels, that hot and stuffy garden by the bandstand.

He replied gloomily, "Good morning," and the dog started to sniff at some ordure and he turned and kicked it with fury, with depression, with despair.

And at that moment a taxi with the two policemen in it passed us on its way to the bridge. They must have seen that kick; perhaps they were cleverer than I had given them credit for, perhaps they were just sentimental about animals, and thought they'd do a good deed, and the rest happened by accident. But the fact remains —those two pillars of the law set about the stealing of Mr. Calloway's dog.

He watched them go by. Then he said, "Why don't you go across?"

"It's cheaper here," I said.

"I mean just for an evening. Have a meal at that place we can see at night in the sky. Go to the theatre."

"There isn't a chance."

He said angrily, sucking his gold tooth, "Well, anyway, get away from here." He stared down the hill and up the other side. He couldn't see that that street climbing up from the bridge contained only the same money-changers' booths as this one.

I said, "Why don't *you* go?"

He said evasively, "Oh—business."

I said, "It's only a question of money. You don't *have* to pass by the bridge."

He said with faint interest, "I don't talk Spanish."

"There isn't a soul here," I said, "who doesn't talk English."

He looked at me with surprise. "Is that so?" he said. "Is that so?"

It's as I have said; he'd never tried to talk to anyone, and they respected him too much to talk to him—he was worth a million. I don't know whether I'm glad or sorry that I told him that. If I hadn't, he might be there now, sitting by the bandstand having his shoes cleaned—alive and suffering.

Three days later his dog disappeared. I found him looking for it, calling it softly and shamefacedly between the palms of the garden. He looked embarrassed. He said in a low angry voice, "I *hate* that dog. The beastly mongrel," and called "Rover, Rover" in a voice which didn't carry five yards. He said, "I bred setters once. I'd have shot a dog like that." It reminded him, I *was* right, of Norfolk, and he lived in the memory, and he hated it for its imperfection. He was a man without a family and without friends, and his only enemy was that dog. You couldn't call the law an enemy; you have to be intimate with an enemy.

Late that afternoon someone told him they'd seen the dog walking across the bridge. It wasn't true, of course, but we didn't know that then—they'd paid a Mexican five pesos to smuggle it across. So all that afternoon and the next Mr. Calloway sat in the garden having his shoes cleaned over and over again, and thinking how a dog could just walk across like that, and a human being, an immortal soul, was bound here in the awful routine of the little walk and the unspeakable meals and the aspirin at the *botica*. That dog was seeing things he couldn't see—that hateful dog. It made him mad—I think literally mad. You must remember the man had been going on for months. He had a million and he was living on two pounds a week, with nothing to spend his money on. He sat there and brooded on the hideous injustice of it. I think he'd have crossed over one day in any case, but the dog was the last straw.

Next day when he wasn't to be seen I guessed he'd gone across, and I went too. The American town is as small as the Mexican. I knew I couldn't miss him if he was there, and I was still curious. A little sorry for him, but not much.

I caught sight of him first in the only drug-store, having a Coca-Cola, and then once outside a cinema looking at the posters; he had dressed with extreme neatness, as if for a party, but there was no party. On my third time round, I came on the detectives—they were having Coca-Colas in the drug-store, and they must have missed Mr. Calloway by inches. I went in and sat down at the bar.

"Hello," I said, "you still about?" I suddenly felt anxious for Mr. Calloway, I didn't want them to meet.

One of them said, "Where's Calloway?"

"Oh," I said, "he's hanging on."

"But not his dog," he said, and laughed. The other looked a little shocked, he didn't like anyone to *talk* cynically about a dog. Then they got up—they had a car outside.

"Have another?" I said.

"No thanks. We've got to keep moving."

The man bent close and confided to me, "Calloway's on this side."

"No!" I said.

"And his dog."

"He's looking for it," the other said.

"I'm damned if he is," I said, and again one of them looked a little shocked, as if I'd insulted the dog.

I don't think Mr. Calloway was looking for his dog, but his dog certainly found him. There was a sudden hilarious yapping from the car and out plunged the semi-setter and gambolled furiously down the street. One of the detectives—the sentimental one—was into the car before we got to the door and was off after the dog. Near the bottom of the long road to the bridge was Mr. Calloway —I do believe he'd come down to look at the Mexican side when he found there was nothing but the drug-store and the cinemas and the paper shops on the American. He saw the dog coming and yelled at it to go home—"home, home, home," as if they were in Norfolk—it took no notice at all, pelting towards him. Then he saw police car coming and ran. After that, everything happened too quickly, but I think the order of events was this—the dog started across the road right in front of the car, and Mr. Calloway yelled, at the dog or the car, I don't know which. Anyway, the detective swerved—he said later, weakly, at the inquiry, that he couldn't run over a dog, and down went Mr. Calloway, in a mess of broken glass and gold rims and silver hair, and blood. The dog was on to him before any of us could reach him, licking and whimpering and licking. I saw Mr. Calloway put up his hand, and down it went across the dog's neck and the whimper rose to a stupid bark of triumph, but Mr. Calloway was dead—shock and a weak heart.

"Poor old geezer," the detective said, "I bet he really loved that dog," and it's true that the attitude in which he lay looked more like a caress than a blow. I thought it was meant to be a blow, but the detective may have been right. It all seemed to me a little too touching to be true as the old crook lay there with his arm over the dog's neck, dead with his million between the money-changers' huts, but it's as well to be humble in the face of human nature. He had come across the river for something, and it may, after all, have been the dog he was looking for. It sat there, baying its stupid and mongrel triumph across his body, like a piece of sentimental statuary. The nearest he could get to the fields, the ditches, the horizon of his home. It was comic and it was pitiable; but it wasn't less comic because the man was dead. Death doesn't change comedy to tragedy, and if that last gesture was one of affection, I suppose it was only one more indication of a human being's capacity for self-deception, our baseless optimism that is so much more appalling than our despair.

WHEN GREEK MEETS GREEK

1

WHEN THE CHEMIST HAD SHUT HIS SHOP FOR THE NIGHT HE WENT through a door at the back of the hall that served both him and the flats above, and then up two flights and a half of stairs, carrying an offering of a little box of pills. The box was stamped with his name and address: Priskett, 14, New End Street, Oxford. He was a middle-aged man with a thin moustache and scared, evasive eyes: he wore his long white coat even when he was off duty as if it had the power of protecting him like a king's uniform from his enemies. So long as he wore it he was free, as it were, from summary trial and execution.

On the top landing was a window: outside Oxford spread through the spring evening: the peevish noise of innumerable bicycles, the gas works, the prison, and the grey spires, beyond the bakers and confectioners, like paper frills. A door was marked with a visiting card, Mr. Nicholas Fennick, B.A.: the chemist rang three short times.

The man who opened the door was sixty years old at least, with snow-white hair and a pink babyish skin. He wore a mulberry velvet dinner jacket, and his glasses swung on the end of a wide black ribbon. He said with a kind of boisterousness, "Ah, Priskett, step in, Priskett. I had just sported my oak for a. moment . . ."

"I brought you some more of my pills."

"Invaluable Priskett. If only you had taken a degree—the Society of Apothecaries would have been enough—I would have appointed you resident medical officer of St. Ambrose's."

"How's the college doing?"

"Give me your company for a moment in the common-room, and you shall know all."

Mr. Fennick led the way down a little dark passage cluttered with mackintoshes: Mr. Priskett, feeling his way uneasily from mackintosh to mackintosh, kicked in front of him a pair of girl's shoes. "One day," Mr. Fennick said, "we must build . . ." and he made a broad confident gesture with his glasses that seemed to press back the walls of the common-room: a small round table covered with a landlady's cloth, three or four shiny chairs and a glass-fronted bookcase containing a copy of *Every Man His Own Lawyer*. "My niece Elisabeth," Mr. Fennick said, "my medical adviser." A very young girl with a lean pretty face nodded perfunctorily from behind a typewriter. "I am going to train Elisabeth," Mr. Fennick said, "to act as bursar. The strain of being both bursar and president of the college is upsetting my stomach. The pills . . . thank you."

Mr. Priskett said humbly, "And what do you think of the college, Miss Fennick?"

"My name's Cross," the girl said. "I think it's a good idea. I'm surprised my uncle thought of it."

"In a way it was—partly—my idea."

"I'm more surprised still," the girl said firmly.

Mr. Priskett, folding his hands in front of his white coat as though he were pleading before a tribunal, went on. "You see, I said to your uncle that with all these colleges being taken over by the military and the tutors having nothing to do they ought to start teaching by correspondence."

"A glass of audit ale, Priskett?" Mr. Fennick suggested. He took a bottle of brown ale out of a cupboard and poured out two gaseous glasses.

"Of course," Mr. Priskett pleaded, "I hadn't thought of all this —the common-room, I mean, and St. Ambrose's."

"My niece," Mr. Fennick said, "knows very little of the set-up." He began to move restlessly around the room, touching things with his hand. He was rather like an aged bird of prey inspecting the grim components of its nest.

The girl said briskly, "As I see it, Uncle is running a swindle called St. Ambrose's College, Oxford."

"Not a swindle, my dear. The advertisement was very carefully worded." He knew it by heart: every phrase had been carefully checked with his copy of *Every Man His Own Lawyer* open on the table. He repeated it now in a voice full and husky with bottled brown ale. " 'War conditions prevent you going up to Oxford. St. Ambrose's—Tom Brown's old college—has made an important break with tradition. For the period of the war only it will be possible to receive tuition by post wherever you may be, whether defending the Empire on the cold rocks of Iceland or on the burning sands of Libya, in the main street of an American town or a cottage in Devonshire . . .' "

"You've overdone it," the girl said. "You always do. That hasn't got a cultured ring. It won't catch anybody but saps."

"There are plenty of saps," Mr. Fennick said.

"Go on."

"Well, I'll skip that bit. 'Degree-diplomas will be granted at the end of three terms instead of the usual three years.' " He explained, "That gives a quick turnover. One can't wait for money these days. 'Gain a real Oxford education at Tom Brown's old college. For full particulars of tuition fees, battels, etc., write to the Bursar.' "

"And do you mean to say the University can't stop that?"

"Anybody," Mr. Fennick said with a kind of pride, "can start a college anywhere. I've never said it was part of the University."

"But battels—battels mean board and lodging."

"In this case," Mr. Fennick said, "it's quite a nominal fee, to keep your name in perpetuity on the books of the old firm—I mean the college."

"And the tuition—"

"Priskett here is the science tutor. I take history and classics. I thought that you, my dear, might tackle—economics?"

"I don't know anything about them."

"The examinations, of course, have to be rather simple—within the capacity of the tutors. (There is an excellent public library here.) And another thing—the fees are returnable if the diploma-degree is not granted."

"You mean—"

"Nobody will ever fail," Mr. Priskett brought breathlessly out with scared excitement.

"And you are really getting results?"

"I waited, my dear, until I could see the distinct possibility of at least six hundred a year for the three of us before I wired you. And today—beyond all my expectations—I have received a letter from Lord Driver. He is entering his son at St. Ambrose's."

"But how can he come here?"

"In his absence, my dear, on his country's service. The Drivers have always been a military family. I looked them up in Debrett."

"What do you think of it?" Mr. Priskett asked with anxiety and triumph.

"I think it's rich. Have you arranged a boat race?"

"There, Priskett," Mr. Fennick said proudly, raising his glass of audit ale, "I told you she was a girl of ideas."

2

Directly he heard his landlady's feet upon the stairs the elderly man with the grey shaven head began to lay his wet tea-leaves round the base of the aspidistra. When she opened the door he was dabbing the tea-leaves in tenderly with his fingers. "A lovely plant, my dear."

But she wasn't going to be softened at once: he could tell that: she waved a letter at him. "Listen," she said, "what's this Lord Driver business?"

"My name, my dear: a good Christian name like Lord George Sanger had."

"Then why don't they put Mr. Lord Driver on the letter?"

"Ignorance, just ignorance."

"I don't want any hanky-panky from my house. It's always been honest."

"Perhaps they didn't know if I was an esquire or just a plain mister, so they left it blank."

"It's sent from St. Ambrose's College, Oxford: people like that ought to know."

"It comes, my dear, of your having such a good address. W. 1. And all the gentry live in mewses." He made a half-hearted snatch at the letter, but the landlady held it out of reach.

"What are the likes of you writing to Oxford College about?"

"My dear," he said with strained dignity, "I may have been a little unfortunate: it may even be that I have spent a few years in chokey, but I have the rights of a free man."

"And a son in quod."

"Not in quod, my dear. Borstal is quite another institution. It is —a kind of college."

"Like St. Ambrose's."

"Perhaps not quite of the same rank."

He was too much for her: he was usually in the end too much for her. Before his first stay at the Scrubs he had held a number of positions as man-servant and even butler: the way he raised his eyebrows he had learned from Lord Charles Manville: he wore his clothes like an eccentric peer, and you might say that he had even learned the best way to pilfer from old Lord Bellew who had a penchant for silver spoons.

"And now, my dear, if you'd just let me have my letter?" He put his hand tentatively forward: he was as daunted by her as she was by him: they sparred endlessly and lost to each other: interminably the battle was never won—they were always afraid. This time it was his victory. She slammed the door. Suddenly, ferociously, when the door had closed, he made a little vulgar noise at the aspidistra. Then he put on his glasses and began to read.

His son had been accepted for St. Ambrose's, Oxford. The great fact stared up at him above the sprawling decorative signature of the President. Never had he been more thankful for the coincidence of his name. "It will be my great pleasure," the President wrote, "to pay personal attention to your son's career at St. Ambrose's. In these days it is an honour to welcome a member of a great military family like yours." Driver felt an odd mixture of amusement and of genuine pride. He'd put one over on them, but his breast swelled within his waistcoat at the idea that now he had a son at Oxford.

But there were two snags—minor snags when he considered how far he'd got already. It was apparently an old Oxford custom that fees should be paid in advance, and then there were the examinations. His son couldn't do them himself: Borstal would not allow it, and he wouldn't be out for another six months. Besides the whole beauty of the idea was that he should receive the gift of an Oxford degree as a kind of welcome home. Like a chess player who is always several moves ahead, he was already seeing his way around these difficulties.

The fees he felt sure in his case were only a matter of bluff: a peer could always get credit, and if there was any trouble after the degree had been awarded, he could just tell them to sue and be damned. No Oxford college would like to admit that they'd been imposed on by an old lag. But the examinations. A funny little knowing smile twitched the corners of his mouth: a memory of the Scrubs five years ago and the man they called Daddy, the Reverend Simon Milan. He was a short-time prisoner—they were all short-time prisoners at the Scrubs: no sentence of over three years was ever served there. He remembered the tall lean aristocratic parson with his iron-grey hair and his narrow face like a lawyer's which had gone somehow soft inside with too much love. A prison, when you came to think of it, contained as much knowledge as a university: there were doctors, financiers, clergy. He knew where he could find Mr. Milan: he was employed in a boarding-house near Euston Square, and for a few drinks he would do most things—he would certainly make out some fine examination papers. "I can just hear him now," Driver told himself ecstatically, "talking Latin to the warders."

3

It was autumn in Oxford: people coughed in the long queues for sweets and cakes: and the mists from the river seeped into the cinemas past the commissionaires on the look-out for people without gas-masks. A few undergraduates picked their way through the evacuated swarm: they always looked in a hurry: so much had to be got through in so little time before the army claimed them. There were lots of pickings for racketeers, Elisabeth Cross thought, but not much chance for a girl to find a husband: the oldest Oxford racket had been elbowed out by the black markets in Woodbines, toffees, tomatoes.

There had been a few days last spring when she had treated St. Ambrose's as a joke, but when she saw the money actually coming in, the whole thing seemed less amusing. Then for some weeks she was acutely unhappy—until she realized that of all the war-time rackets this was the most harmless. They were not reducing supplies like the Ministry of Food, or destroying confidence like the Ministry of Information: her uncle paid income tax, and they even to some extent educated people. The saps, when they took their diploma-degrees would know several things they hadn't known before.

But that didn't help a girl to find a husband.

She came moodily out of the matinée, carrying a bunch of papers she should have been correcting. There was only one "student" who showed any intelligence at all, and that was Lord Driver's son. The papers were forwarded from "somewhere in England" via London by his father: she had nearly found herself caught out several times on points of history, and her uncle she knew was straining his rusty Latin to the limit.

When she got home she knew that there was something in the air: Mr. Priskett was sitting in his white coat on the edge of a chair and her uncle was finishing a stale bottle of beer. When something went wrong he never opened a new bottle: he believed in happy drinking. They watched her come in in silence: Mr. Priskett's silence was gloomy, her uncle's preoccupied. Something had to be got round—it couldn't be the university authorities: they had stopped bothering him long ago—a lawyer's letter, an irascible interview, and their attempt to maintain "a monopoly of local education"—as Mr. Fennick put it—had ceased.

"Good evening," Elisabeth said. Mr. Priskett looked at Mr. Fennick and Mr. Fennick frowned.

"Has Mr. Priskett run out of pills?"

Mr. Priskett winced.

"I've been thinking," Elisabeth said, "that as we are now in the third term of the academic year, I should like a rise in salary."

Mr. Priskett drew in his breath sharply, keeping his eyes on Mr. Fennick.

"I should like another three pounds a week."

Mr. Fennick rose from the table; he glared ferociously into the top of his dark ale; his frown beetled. The chemist scraped his chair a little backward. And then Mr. Fennick spoke.

" 'We are such stuff as dreams are made on,' " he said and hiccupped slightly.

"Kidneys," Elisabeth said.

" 'Rounded by a sleep. And these our cloud-capped towers . . .' "

"You are misquoting."

" 'Vanished into air, into thin air.' "

"You've been correcting the English papers."

"Unless you allow me to think, to think rapidly and deeply, there won't be any more examination papers," Mr. Fennick said.

"Trouble?"

"I've always been a republican at heart. I don't see why we want a hereditary peerage."

"*A la lanterne,*" Elisabeth said.

"This man, Lord Driver: why should a mere accident of birth . . . ?"

"He refuses to pay?"

"It isn't that. A man like that expects credit: it's right that he should have credit. But he's written to say that he's coming down tomorrow to see his boy's college. The old fat-headed sentimental fool," Mr. Fennick said.

"I knew you'd be in trouble sooner or later."

"That's the sort of damn fool comfortless thing a girl would say."

"It just needs brain."

Mr. Fennick picked up a brass ash-tray—and then put it down again carefully.

"It's quite simple as soon as you begin to think."

"Think."

Mr. Priskett scraped a chair-leg.

"I'll meet him at the station with a taxi, and take him to, say, Balliol. Lead him straight through into the inner quad, and there you'll be, just looking as if you'd come out of the Master's lodging."

"He'll know it's Balliol."

"He won't. Anybody who knew Oxford couldn't be sap enough to send his son to St. Ambrose's."

"Of course it's true. These military families are a bit crass."

"You'll be in an enormous hurry. Consecration or something. Whip him round the Hall, the Chapel, the Library, and hand him back to me outside the Master's. I'll take him out to lunch and see him into his train. It's simple."

Mr. Fennick said broodingly, "Sometimes I think you're a terrible girl, terrible. Is there nothing you wouldn't think up?"

"I believe," Elisabeth said, "that if you're going to play your own game in a world like this, you've got to play it properly. Of course," she said, "if you are going to play a different game you go to a nunnery or to the wall and like it. But I've only got one game to play."

4

It really went off very smoothly. Driver found Elisabeth at the barrier: she didn't find him because she was expecting something different. Something about him worried her: it wasn't his clothes or the monocle he never seemed to use—it was something subtler than that. It was almost as though he were afraid of her, he was so ready to fall in with her plans. "I don't want to be any trouble, my dear, any trouble at all. I know how busy the President must be." When she explained that they would be lunching together in town, he even seemed relieved. "It's just the bricks of the dear old place," he said. "You mustn't mind my being a sentimentalist, my dear."

"Were you at Oxford?"

"No, no. The Drivers, I'm afraid, have neglected the things of the mind."

"Well, I suppose a soldier needs brains?"

He took a sharp look at her, and then answered in quite a different sort of voice, "We believed so in the Lancers." Then he strolled beside her to the taxi, twirling his monocle, and all the way up from the station he was silent, taking little quiet sideways peeks at her, appraising, approving.

"So this is St. Ambrose's," he said in a hearty voice just beside the porter's lodge and she pushed him quickly by, through the first quad towards the Master's house, where on the doorstep with a B.A. gown over his arm stood Mr. Fennick permanently posed like a piece of garden statuary. "My uncle, the President," Elisabeth said.

"A charming girl, your niece," Driver said as soon as they were alone together: he had really only meant to make conversation, but as soon as he had spoken the two old crooked minds began to move in harmony.

"She's very home-loving," Mr. Fennick said. "Our famous elms," he went on, waving his hand skywards. "St. Ambrose's rooks."

"Crooks?" Driver said with astonishment.

"Rooks. In the elms. One of our great modern poets wrote about them. 'St. Ambrose elms, oh St. Ambrose elms,' and about 'St. Ambrose rooks calling in wind and rain.' "

"Pretty. Very pretty."

"Nicely turned, I think."

"I meant your niece."

"Ah, yes. This way to the Hall. Up these steps. So often trodden, you know, by Tom Brown."

"Who was Tom Brown?"

"The great Tom Brown—one of Rugby's famous sons." He added thoughtfully, "She'll make a fine wife—and mother."

"Young men are beginning to realize that the flighty ones are not what they want for a lifetime."

They stopped by mutual consent on the top step: they nosed towards each other like two old blind sharks who each believes that what stirs the water close to him is tasty meat.

"Whoever wins her," Mr. Fennick said, "can feel proud. She'll make a fine hostess. . . ." as the future Lady Driver, he thought.

"I and my son," Driver said, "have talked seriously about marriage. He takes rather an old-fashioned view. He'll make a good husband. . . ."

They walked into the hall, and Mr. Fennick led the way round the portraits. "Our founder," he said, pointing at a full-bottomed wig. He chose it deliberately: he felt it smacked a little of himself. Before Swinburne's portrait he hesitated: then pride in St. Ambrose's conquered caution. "The great poet Swinburne," he said. "We sent him down."

"Expelled him?"

"Yes. Bad morals."

"I'm glad you are strict about those."

"Ah, your son is in safe hands at St. Ambrose's."

"It makes me very happy," Driver said. He began to scrutinize the portrait of a nineteenth-century divine. "Fine brushwork," he said. "Now religion—I believe in religion. Basis of the family." He said with a burst of confidence, "You know our young people ought to meet."

Mr. Fennick gleamed happily. "I agree."

"If he passes . . ."

"Oh, he'll certainly pass," Mr. Fennick said.

"He'll be on leave in a week or two. Why shouldn't he take his degree in person?"

"Well, there'd be difficulties."

"Isn't it the custom?"

"Not for postal graduates. The Vice-Chancellor likes to make a small distinction. But, Lord Driver, in the case of so distinguished an alumnus I suggest that I should be deputed to present the degree to your son in London."

"I'd like him to see his college."

"And so he shall in happier days. So much of the college is shut now. I would like him to visit it for the first time when its glory is restored. Allow me and my niece to call on you."

"We are living very quietly."

"Not serious financial trouble, I hope?"

"Oh, no, no."

"I'm so glad. And now let us rejoin the dear girl."

5

It always seemed to be more convenient to meet at railway stations. The coincidence didn't strike Mr. Fennick who had fortified himself for the journey with a good deal of audit ale, but it struck Elisabeth. The college lately had not been fulfilling expectations, and that was partly due to the laziness of Mr. Fennick: from his conversation lately it almost seemed as though he had begun to regard the college as only a step to something else—what, she couldn't quite make out. He was always talking about Lord Driver and his son Frederick and the responsibilities of the peerage. His republican tendencies had quite lapsed. "That dear boy," was the way he referred to Frederick, and he marked him 100% for Classics. "It's not often Latin and Greek go with military genius," he said. "A remarkable boy."

"He's not so hot on economics," Elisabeth said.

"We mustn't demand too much book-learning from a soldier."

At Paddington Lord Driver waved anxiously to them through the crowd: he wore a very new suit—one shudders to think how many coupons had been gambled away for the occasion. A little behind him was a very young man with a sullen mouth and a scar on his cheek. Mr. Fennick bustled forward: he wore a black raincoat over his shoulders like a cape and carrying his hat in his hand he disclosed his white hair venerably among the porters.

"My son—Frederick," Lord Driver said. The boy sullenly took off his hat and put it on again quickly: they wore their hair in the army very short.

"St. Ambrose's welcomes her new graduate," Mr. Fennick said. Frederick grunted.

The presentation of the degree was made in a private room at Mount Royal. Lord Driver explained that his house had been bombed—a time bomb, he added, a rather necessary explanation since there had been no raids recently. Mr. Fennick was satisfied if Lord Driver was: he had brought up a B.A. gown, a mortarboard and a Bible in his suitcase, and he made quite an imposing little ceremony between the book-table, the sofa and the radiator, reading out a Latin oration and tapping Frederick lightly on the head with the Bible. The degree-diploma had been expensively printed in two colours by an Anglo-Catholic firm. Elisabeth was the only uneasy person there. Could the world, she wondered, really contain two such saps? What was this painful feeling growing up in her that perhaps it contained four?

After a little light lunch with bottled brown beer—"almost as good, if I may say so, as our audit ale," Mr. Fennick beamed—the President and Lord Driver made elaborate moves to drive the two young people out together. "We've got to talk a little business," Mr. Fennick said, and Lord Driver hinted, "You've not been to the flickers for a year, Frederick." They were driven out together into bombed shabby Oxford Street while the old men rang cheerfully down for whisky.

"What's the idea?" Elisabeth said.

He was good-looking: she liked his scar and his sullenness; there was almost too much intelligence and purpose in his eyes. Once he took off his hat and scratched his head: Elisabeth again noticed his short hair. He certainly didn't look a military type. And his suit, like his father's, looked new and ready made. Hadn't he had any clothes to wear when he came on leave?

"I suppose," she said, "they are planning a wedding."

His eyes lit gleefully up. "I wouldn't mind," he said.

"You'd have to get leave from your C. O., wouldn't you?"

"C.O.?" he asked in astonishment, flinching a little like a boy who has been caught out, who hasn't been prepared beforehand with that question. She watched him carefully, remembering all the things that had seemed to her since the beginning odd.

"So you haven't been to the movies for a year?" she said.

"I've been on service."

"Not even an Ensa show?"

"Oh, I don't count those."

"It must be awfully like being in prison."

He grinned weakly, walking faster all the time, so that she might really have been pursuing him through the Hyde Park gates.

"Come clean," she said. "Your father's not Lord Driver."

"Oh, yes he is."

"Any more than my uncle's President of a College."

"What?" He began to laugh—it was an agreeable laugh, a laugh you couldn't trust but a laugh which made you laugh back and agree that in a crazy world like this all sorts of things didn't matter a hang. "I'm just out of Borstal," he said. "What's yours?"

"Oh, I haven't been in prison yet."

He said, "You'll never believe me, but all that ceremony—it looked phoney to me. Of course the Dad swallowed it."

"And my uncle swallowed you. I couldn't quite."

"Well, the wedding's off. In a way I'm sorry."

"I'm still free."

"Well," he said, "we might discuss it," and there in the pale autumn sunlight of the park they did discuss it—from all sorts of angles. There were bigger frauds all round them; officials of the Ministries passed carrying little portfolios: controllers of this and that purred by in motor-cars, and men with the big blank faces of advertisement hoardings strode purposefully in khaki with scarlet tabs down Park Lane from the Dorchester. Their fraud was a small one by the world's standard, and a harmless one: the boy from Borstal and the girl from nowhere at all—from the draper's counter and the semi-detached villa. "He's got a few hundred stowed away, I'm sure of that," said Fred. "He'd make a settlement if he thought he could get the President's niece."

"I wouldn't be surprised if Uncle had five hundred. He'd put it all down for Lord Driver's son."

"We'd take over this college business. With a bit of capital we could really make it go. It's just chicken feed now."

They fell in love for no reason at all, in the park, on a bench to save twopences, planning their fraud on the old frauds they knew they could outdo. Then they went back, and Elisabeth declared herself before she'd got properly inside the door. "Frederick and I want to get married." She almost felt sorry for the old fools as their faces lit suddenly simultaneously up because everything had been so easy, and then darkened with caution as they squinted at each other. "This is very surprising," Lord Driver said, and the President said, "My goodness, young people work fast."

All night the two old men planned their settlements, and the two young ones sat happily back in a corner, watching the elaborate fence, with the secret knowledge that the world is always open to the young.

THE HINT OF AN EXPLANATION

A LONG TRAIN JOURNEY ON A LATE DECEMBER EVENING, IN THIS NEW version of peace, is a dreary experience. I suppose that my fellow traveller and I could consider ourselves lucky to have a compartment to ourselves, even though the heating apparatus was not working, even though the lights went out entirely in the frequent Pennine tunnels and were too dim anyway for us to read our books without straining our eyes, and though there was no restaurant car to give at least a change of scene. It was when we were trying simultaneously to chew the same kind of dry bun bought at the same station buffet that my companion and I came together. Before that we had sat at opposite ends of the carriage, both muffled to the chin in overcoats, both bent low over type we could barely make out, but as I threw the remains of my cake under the seat our eyes met, and he laid his book down.

By the time we were half-way to Bedwell Junction we had found an enormous range of subjects for discussion; starting with buns and the weather, we had gone on to politics, the government, foreign affairs, the atom bomb, and, by an inevitable progression, God. We had not, however, become either shrill or acid. My companion, who now sat opposite me, leaning a little forward, so that our knees nearly touched, gave such an impression of serenity that it would have been impossible to quarrel with him, however much our views differed, and differ they did profoundly.

I had soon realized I was speaking to a Catholic, to someone who believed—how do they put it?—in an omnipotent and omniscient Deity, while I was what is loosely called an Agnostic. I have a certain intuition (which I do not trust, founded as it may well be on childish experiences and needs) that a God exists, and I am surprised occasionally into belief by the extraordinary coincidences that beset our path like the traps set for leopards in the jungle, but intellectually I am revolted at the whole notion of such a God who can so abandon his creatures to the enormities of Free Will. I found myself expressing this view to my companion, who listened quietly and with respect. He made no attempt to interrupt; he showed none of the impatience or the intellectual arrogance I have grown to expect from Catholics; when the lights of a wayside station flashed across his face that had escaped hitherto the rays of the one globe working in the compartment, I caught a glimpse suddenly of—what? I stopped speaking, so strong was the impression. I was carried back ten years, to the other side of the great useless conflict, to a small town, Gisors in Normandy. I was again, for a moment, walking on the ancient battlements and looking down across the grey roofs, until my eyes for some reason lit on one grey stony "back" out of the many, where the face of a middle-aged man was pressed against a windowpane (I suppose that face has ceased to exist now, just as I believe the whole town with its medieval memories has been reduced to rubble). I remembered saying to myself with astonishment, "That man is happy—completely happy." I looked across the compartment at my fellow traveller, but his face was already again in shadow. I said weakly, "When you think what God—if there is a God—allows. It's not merely the physical agonies, but think of the corruption, even of children. . . ."

He said, "Our view is so limited," and I was disappointed at the conventionality of his reply. He must have been aware of my disappointment (it was as though our thoughts were huddled as closely as ourselves for warmth), for he went on, "Of course there is no answer here. We catch hints . . ." and then the train roared into another tunnel and the lights again went out. It was the longest tunnel yet; we went rocking down it, and the cold seemed to become more intense with the darkness like an icy fog (perhaps when one sense—of sight—is robbed of sensation, the others grow more sensitive). When we emerged into the mere grey of night and the globe lit up once more, I could see that my companion was leaning back on his seat.

I repeated his last words as a question, "Hints?"

"Oh, they mean very little in cold print—or cold speech," he said, shivering in his overcoat. "And they mean nothing at all to a human being other than the man who catches them. They are not scientific evidence—or evidence at all for that matter. Events that don't, somehow, turn out as they were intended—by the human actors I mean, or by the thing behind the human actors."

"The thing?"

"The word Satan is so anthropomorphic."

I had to lean forward now: I wanted to hear what he had to say. I am—I really am, God knows—open to conviction.

He said, "One's words are so crude, but I sometimes feel pity for that thing. It is so continually finding the right weapon to use against its Enemy and the weapon breaks in its own breast. It sometimes seems to me so—powerless. You said something just now about the corruption of children. It reminded me of something in my own childhood. You are the first person—except for one—that I have thought of telling it to, perhaps because you are anonymous. It's not a very long story, and in a way it's relevant."

I said, "I'd like to hear it."

"You mustn't expect too much meaning. But to me there seems to be a hint. That's all. A hint."

He went slowly on, turning his face to the pane, though he could have seen nothing real in the whirling world outside except an occasional signal lamp, a light in a window, a small country station torn backwards by our rush, picking his words with precision. He said, "When I was a child they taught me to serve at Mass. The church was a small one, for there were very few Catholics where I lived. It was a market town in East Anglia, surrounded by flat, chalky fields and ditches—so many ditches. I don't suppose there were fifty Catholics all told, and for some reason there was a tra- dition of hostility to us. Perhaps it went back to the burning of a Protestant martyr in the sixteenth century—there was a stone marking the place near where the meat stalls stood on Wednesdays. I was only half aware of the enmity, though I knew that my school nickname of Popey Martin had something to do with my religion, and I had heard that my father was nearly excluded from the Constitutional Club when he first came to the town.

"Every Sunday I had to dress up in my surplice and serve Mass. I hated it—I have always hated dressing up in any way (which is funny when you come to think of it), and I never ceased to be afraid of losing my place in the service and doing something which would put me to ridicule. Our services were at a different hour from the Anglican, and as our small, far-from-select band trudged out of the hideous chapel the whole of the townsfolk seemed to be on the way past to the proper church—I always thought of it as the proper church. We had to pass the parade of their eyes, indifferent, supercilious, mocking; you can't imagine how seriously religion can be taken in a small town, if only for social reasons.

"There was one man in particular; he was one of the two bakers in the town, the one my family did not patronize. I don't think any of the Catholics patronized him because he was called a freethinker—an odd title, for, poor man, no one's thoughts were less free than his. He was hemmed in by his hatred—his hatred of us. He was very ugly to look at, with one wall-eye and a head the shape of a turnip, with the hair gone on the crown, and he was unmarried. He had no interests, apparently, but his baking and his hatred, though now that I am older I begin to see other sides to his nature—it did contain, perhaps, a certain furtive love. One would come across him suddenly sometimes on a country walk, especially if one were alone and it was Sunday. It was as if he rose from the ditches, and the smear of chalk on his clothes reminded one of the flour on his working overalls. He would have a stick in his hand and stab at the hedges, and if his mood were very black he would call out after one strange abrupt words like a foreign tongue—I know the meaning of those words, of course, now. Once the police went to his house because of what a boy said he'd seen, but nothing came of it except that the hate shackled him closer. His name was Blacker and he terrified me.

"I think he had a particular hatred of my father—I don't know why. My father was manager of the Midland Bank, and it's possible that at some time Blacker may have had unsatisfactory dealings with the bank; my father was a very cautious man who suffered all his life from anxiety about money—his own and other people's. If I try and picture Blacker now I see him walking along a narrow path between high windowless walls, and at the end of the path stands a small boy of ten—me. I don't know whether it's a symbolic picture or the memory of one of our encounters—our encounters somehow got more and more frequent. You talked just now about the corruption of children. That poor man was preparing to revenge himself on everything he hated—my father, the Catholics, the God whom people persisted in crediting—and that by corrupting me. He had evolved a horrible and ingenious plan.

"I remember the first time I had a friendly word from him. I was passing his shop as rapidly as I could when I heard his voice call out with a kind of sly subservience as though he were an under servant. 'Master David,' he called, 'Master David,' and I hurried on. But the next time I passed that way he was at his door (he must have seen me coming) with one of those curly cakes in his hand that we called Chelsea buns. I didn't want to take it, but he made me, and then I couldn't be other than polite when he asked me to come into his parlour behind the shop and see something very special.

"It was a small electric railway—a rare sight in those days, and he insisted on showing me how it worked. He made me turn the switches and stop and start it, and he told me that I could come in any morning and have a game with it. He used the word 'game' as though it were something secret, and it's true that I never told my family of this invitation and of how, perhaps twice a week those holidays, the desire to control that little railway became overpowering, and looking up and down the street to see if I were observed, I would dive into the shop."

Our larger, dirtier, adult train drove into a tunnel and the light went out. We sat in darkness and silence, with the noise of the train blocking our ears like wax. When we were through we didn't speak at once and I had to prick him into continuing. "An elaborate seduction," I said.

"Don't think his plans were as simple as that," my companion said, "or as crude. There was much more hate than love, poor man, in his make-up. Can you hate something you don't believe in? And yet he called himself a free-thinker. What an impossible paradox, to be free and to be so obsessed. Day by day all through those holidays his obsession must have grown, but he kept a grip; he bided his time. Perhaps that thing I spoke of gave him the strength and the wisdom. It was only a week from the end of the holidays that he spoke to me on what concerned him so deeply.

"I heard him behind me as I knelt on the floor, coupling two coaches. He said, 'You won't be able to do this, Master David, when school starts.' It wasn't a sentence that needed any comment from me any more than the one that followed. 'You ought to have it for your own, you ought,' but how skilfully and unemphatically he had sowed the longing, the idea of a possibility. . . . I was coming to his parlour every day now; you see, I had to cram every opportunity in before the hated term started again, and I suppose I was becoming accustomed to Blacker, to that wall-eye, that turnip head, that nauseating subservience. The Pope, you know, describes himself as 'the servant of the servants of God,' and Blacker—I sometimes think that Blacker was 'the servant of the servants of . . . ,' well, let it be.

"The very next day, standing in the doorway watching me play, he began to talk to me about religion. He said, with what untruth even I recognized, how much he admired the Catholics; he wished he could believe like that, but how could a baker believe? He accented 'a baker' as one might say a biologist, and the tiny train

54

spun round the gauge 0 track. He said, 'I can bake the things you eat just as well as any Catholic can,' and disappeared into his shop. I hadn't the faintest idea what he meant. Presently he emerged again, holding in his hand a little wafer. 'Here,' he said, 'eat that and tell me. . . .' When I put it in my mouth I could tell that it was made in the same way as our wafers for communion—he had got the shape a little wrong, that was all—and I felt guilty and irrationally scared. 'Tell me,' he said, 'what's the difference?'

" 'Difference?' I asked.

" 'Isn't that just the same as you eat in church?'

"I said smugly, 'It hasn't been consecrated.'

"He said, 'Do you think, if I put the two of them under a microscope, you could tell the difference?'

"But even at ten I had the answer to that question. 'No,' I said, 'the—accidents don't change,' stumbling a little on the word 'accidents' which had suddenly conveyed to me the idea of death and wounds.

"Blacker said with sudden intensity, 'How I'd like to get one of your ones in my mouth—just to see. . . .'

"It may seem odd to you, but this was the first time that the idea of transsubstantiation really lodged in my mind. I had learned it all by rote; I had grown up with the idea. The Mass was as lifeless to me as the sentences in *De Bello Gallico;* communion a routine like drill in the school-yard, but here suddenly I was in the presence of a man who took it seriously, as seriously as the priest whom naturally one didn't count—it was his job. I felt more scared than ever.

"He said, 'It's all nonsense, but I'd just like to have it in my mouth.'

" 'You could if you were a Catholic,' I said naïvely.

"He gazed at me with his one good eye, like a Cyclops. He said, 'You serve at Mass, don't you? It would be easy for you to get at one of those things. I tell you what I'd do—I'd swap this electric train for one of your wafers—consecrated, mind. It's got to be consecrated.'

" 'I could get you one out of the box,' I said. I think I still imagined that his interest was a baker's interest—to see how they were made.

" 'Oh, no,' he said, 'I want to see what your God tastes like.'

" 'I couldn't do that.'

" 'Not for a whole electric train, just for yourself? You wouldn't have any trouble at home. I'd pack it up and put a label inside that your dad could see: "For my bank manager's little boy from a grateful client." He'd be pleased as punch with that.'

"Now that we are grown men it seems a trivial temptation, doesn't it? But try to think back to your own childhood. There was a whole circuit of rails there on the floor at our feet, straight rails and curved, and a little station with porters and passengers, a tunnel, a foot-bridge, a level crossing, two signals, buffers, of course—and, above all, a turntable. The tears of longing came into my eyes when I looked at the turntable. It was my favorite piece— it looked so ugly and practical and true. I said weakly, 'I wouldn't know how.'

"How carefully he had been studying the ground! He must have slipped several times into Mass at the back of the church. It would have been no good, you understand, in a little town like that, presenting himself for communion. Everybody there knew him for what he was. He said to me, 'When you've been given communion you could just put it under your tongue a moment. He serves you and the other boy first, and I saw you once go out behind the curtain straight afterwards. You'd forgotten one of those little bottles.'

" 'The cruet,' I said.

" 'Pepper and salt.' He grinned at me jovially, and I—well, I looked at the little railway which I could no longer come and play with when term started. I said, 'You'd just swallow it, wouldn't you?'

" 'Oh, yes,' he said. 'I'd just swallow it.'

"Somehow I didn't want to play with the train any more that day. I got up and made for the door, but he detained me, gripping my lapel. He said, 'This will be a secret between you and me. Tomorrow's Sunday. You come along here in the afternoon. Put it in an envelope and post it me. Monday morning the train will be delivered bright and early.'

" 'Not tomorrow,' I implored him.

" 'I'm not interested in any other Sunday,' he said. 'It's your only chance.' He shook me gently backwards and forwards. 'It will always have to be a secret between you and me,' he said. 'Why, if anyone knew they'd take away the train and there'd be me to reckon with. I'd bleed you something awful. You know how I'm always about on Sunday walks. You can't avoid a man like me. I crop up. You wouldn't ever be safe in your own house. I know ways to get into houses when people are asleep.' He pulled me into the shop after him and opened a drawer. In the drawer was an odd looking key and a cut-throat razor. He said, 'That's a master key that opens all locks and that—that's what I bleed people with.' Then he patted my cheek with his plump floury fingers and said, 'Forget it. You and me are friends.'

"That Sunday Mass stays in my head, every detail of it, as though it had happened only a week ago. From the moment of the Confession to the moment of Consecration it had a terrible importance; only one other Mass has ever been so important to me—perhaps not even one, for this was a solitary Mass which would never happen again. It seemed as final as the last Sacrament when the priest bent down and put the wafer in my mouth where I knelt before the altar with my fellow server.

"I suppose I had made up my mind to commit this awful act—for, you know, to us it must always seem an awful act—from the moment when I saw Blacker watching from the back of the church. He had put on his best black Sunday clothes and, as though he could never quite escape the smear of his profession, he had a dab of dried talcum on his cheek, which he had presumably applied after using that cut-throat of his. He was watching me closely all the time, and I think it was fear—fear of that terrible undefined thing called bleeding—as much as covetousness that drove me to carry out my instructions.

"My fellow server got briskly up and, taking the paten, preceded Father Carey to the altar rail where the other communicants knelt. I had the Host lodged under my tongue: it felt like a blister. I got up and made for the curtain to get the cruet that I had purposely left in the sacristy. When I was there I looked quickly round for a hiding place and saw an old copy of the *Universe* lying on a chair. I took the Host from my mouth and inserted it between two sheets—a little damp mess of pulp. Then I thought: perhaps Father Carey has put out the paper for a particular purpose and he will find the Host before I have time to remove it, and the enormity of my act began to come home to me when I tried to imagine what punishment I should incur. Murder is sufficiently trivial to have its appropriate punishment, but for this act the mind boggled at the thought of any retribution at all. I tried to remove the Host, but it stuck clammily between the pages, and in desperation I tore out a piece of the newspaper and, screwing the whole thing up, stuck it in my trousers pocket. When I came back through the curtain carrying the cruet my eyes met Blacker's. He gave me a grin of encouragement and unhappiness—yes, I am sure, unhappiness. Was it perhaps that the poor man was all the time seeking something incorruptible?

"I can remember little more of that day. I think my mind was shocked and stunned, and I was caught up too in the family bustle of Sunday. Sunday in a provincial town is the day for relations. All the family are at home, and unfamiliar cousins and uncles are apt to arrive, packed in the back seats of other people's cars. I remember that some crowd of the kind descended on us and pushed Blacker temporarily out of the foreground of my mind. There was somebody called Aunt Lucy, with a loud hollow laugh that filled the house with mechanical merriment like the sound of recorded laughter from inside a hall of mirrors, and I had no opportunity to go out alone even if I had wished to. When six o'clock came and Aunt Lucy and the cousins departed and peace returned, it was too late to go to Blacker's, and at eight it was my own bed-time.

"I think I had half forgotten what I had in my pocket. As I emptied my pocket the little screw of newspaper brought quickly back the Mass, the priest bending over me, Blacker's grin. I laid the packet on the chair by my bed and tried to go to sleep, but I was haunted by the shadows on the wall where the curtains blew, the squeak of furniture, the rustle in the chimney, haunted by the presence of God there on the chair. The Host had always been to me—well, the Host. I knew theoretically, as I have said, what I had to believe, but suddenly, as someone whistled in the road outside, whistled secretively, knowingly, to me, I knew that this which I had beside my bed was something of infinite value—something a man would pay for with his whole peace of mind, something that was so hated one could love it as one loves an outcast or a bullied child. These are adult words, and it was a child of ten who lay scared in bed, listening to the whistle from the road, Blacker's whistle, but I think he felt fairly clearly what I am describing now. That is what I meant when I said this Thing, whatever it is, that seizes every possible weapon against God, is always, everywhere, disappointed at the moment of success. It must have felt as certain of me as Blacker did. It must have felt certain too of Blacker. But I wonder, if one knew what happened later to that poor man, whether one would not find again that the weapon had been turned against its own breast.

"At last I couldn't bear that whistle any more and got out of bed. I opened the curtains a little way, and there right under my window, the moonlight on his face, was Blacker. If I had stretched my hand down, his fingers reaching up could almost have touched mine. He looked up at me, flashing the one good eye, with hunger —I realize now that near-success must have developed his obsession almost to the point of madness. Desperation had driven him to the house. He whispered up at me. 'David, where is it?'

"I jerked my head back at the room. 'Give it me,' he said. 'Quick. You shall have the train in the morning.'

"I shook my head. He said, 'I've got the bleeder here, and the key. You'd better toss it down.'

" 'Go away,' I said, but I could hardly speak for fear.

" 'I'll bleed you first and then I'll have it just the same.'

" 'Oh, no, you won't,' I said. I went to the chair and picked it—Him—up. There was only one place where He was safe. I couldn't separate the Host from the paper, so I swallowed both. The newsprint stuck like a prune skin to the back of my throat, but I rinsed it down with water from the ewer. Then I went back to the window and looked down at Blacker. He began to wheedle me. 'What have you done with it, David? What's the fuss? It's only a bit of bread,' looking so longingly and pleadingly up at me that even as a child I wondered whether he could really think that, and yet desire it so much.

" 'I swallowed it,' I said.

" 'Swallowed it?'

" 'Yes,' I said. 'Go away.'

"Then something happened which seems to me now more terrible than his desire to corrupt or my thoughtless act: he began to weep —the tears ran lopsidedly out of the one good eye and his shoulders shook. I only saw his face for a moment before he bent his head and strode off, the bald turnip head shaking, into the dark. When I think of it now, it's almost as if I had seen that Thing weeping for its inevitable defeat. It had tried to use me as a weapon, and now I had broken in its hands and it wept its hopeless tears through one of Blacker's eyes."

The black furnaces of Bedwell Junction gathered around the line. The points switched and we were tossed from one set of rails to another. A spray of sparks, a signal light changing to red, tall chimneys jetting into the grey night sky, the fumes of steam from stationary engines—half the cold journey was over, and now remained the long wait for the slow cross-country train. I said, "It's an interesting story. I think I should have given Blacker what he wanted. I wonder what he would have done with it."

"I really believe," my companion said, "that he would first of all have put it under his microscope—before he did all the other things I expect he had planned."

"And the hints," I said. "I don't quite see what you mean by that."

"Oh, well," he said vaguely, "you know for me it was an odd beginning, that affair, when you come to think of it," but I never should have known what he meant had not his coat, when he rose to take the bag from the rack, come open and disclosed the collar of a priest.

I said, "I suppose you think you owe a lot to Blacker."

"Yes," he said, "you see, I am a very happy man."

QUESTIONS FOR DISCUSSION

THE BASEMENT ROOM

1. Greene is concerned with making clear the spiritual state of the seven-year-old child before his involvement in the affairs of the adults. What is his purpose in this, and how does he go about it?

2. Precisely what new awareness of the adult world does the boy, at first gradually and then suddenly, experience as a result of these encounters?

3. When Greene inserts the quotation, "In the lost childhood of Judas Christ was betrayed," he is most explicitly stating the moral of his story. Fully articulated, what is it?

4. The author makes a point of developing the character of Mr. Baines sympathetically. What fundamental knowledge of life and capacity for experience does Greene show Baines to possess?

5. Explain the irony inherent in what befalls Baines. Is there some remote parallel between the boy's denouncement of Baines and some past great historical occurrence?

6. We are, incidentally, given a view of a "poor little rich boy." What criticism of the way the boy is brought up is inherent in the story?

7. What kind of adult does the author suggest the boy will become?

ACROSS THE BRIDGE

1. The illusory quality of the American town across the bridge is emphasized. What is, after all, shown to be common to both the Mexican and the American towns? What is shown to be missing from each?

2. Explain the irony involved in Calloway's mistreatment of his dog. Show the connection between this and Calloway's fate once he crosses the bridge over which he has looked with such yearning.

3. Greene describes Calloway as "dead with his millions between the money-changers' huts." What has he wished to make clear about Calloway's life?

4. Where the author says of Calloway, "I think he'd have crossed over one day, in any case, but the dog was the last straw," what is he revealing about the financier's true dilemma about life itself?

5. The pattern of Calloway's life and the circumstances in which he finally finds himself elicit throughout a grimly humorous response on

the part of the narrator. Assuming that the financier's death gesture was one of affection for his abused dog, why would it be "only one more indication of a human being's capacity for self-deception?"

6. In connection with the assumption that Calloway was, in dying, reaching out in love to his dog, what is Greene's meaning in saying "our baseless optimism . . . is so much more appalling than our despair"?

7. What did Calloway fail to find across the bridge? How is the answer to this question important to the theme of the story?

WHEN GREEK MEETS GREEK

1. Explain how and why the title is apt.

2. What is Greene's assumption about the relationship between war and public morals, and vice versa?

3. What ironic meanings are attached to the fact that a phony educator and a phony military-aristocrat are mutually swindling one another as the world fights itself into exhaustion?

4. Explain the author's specific feeling and attitude toward all his evil characters.

5. Apart from the total story situation, patches of humor and irony occur here and there. Point these out, and tell what they contribute to the tale.

6. The two young evildoers fall very comfortably in love and into a scheme to defraud the old defrauders. What is the comment thus made about love in an immoral society?

7. Greene, in the final analysis, communicates his feeling about the human condition in our time. Explain his point of view along this line.

A SUGGESTED INTERPRETATION

THE HINT OF AN EXPLANATION

In the priest's apologia, the hint of an explanation stems from living proof that infinite good may rise out of abysmal evil. Blacker is clearly an embodiment of black evil—he deliberately chooses to trap a child barely beyond the age of reason into sinning against himself and God. But the boy, by his capacity to resist, is for the first time able to understand good. This happiness launches him on his religious life, for he has begun to sense the power of God—how God works and the nature of life. His self-realization in the priesthood——his recognition of God——is the infinite good through God which has resulted from his encounter with the diabolical man, who is thus proved to be after all subservient to God.

Much meaning should be attached to the priest's belief that Blacker, "this Thing, whatever it is, that seizes every possible weapon against God, is always, everywhere, disappointed at the moment of success." The conscious wish, the deliberate attempt to resist and to rise against God's will, Greene says, brings self-defeat, self-degradation, joylessness, despair, frustration. Yet Blacker——Satan, the Thing, whatever you call it——is covered by a mantle of dust whenever he appears in the story. Could not this be the dust of heaven? Is not this Greene's way of saying that even the Thing is one of God's fallen angels? Could not this be the reason that Blacker is granted at least a "furtive love"? Could not this be, judging from the good he ultimately causes, a further suggestion that God all-knowingly permits the choice to deny? How else may man's soul be tried?

There is every suggestion——probing, occasional lapses in speech, searching intelligence——that the second man in the train compartment, despite his affirmed agnostic views, has found only personal unhappiness in his wavering denial of God. Greene apparently believes that the perversity of Blacker and the stubbornness of the traveler in denying God are different only in degree of furtive self-delusion. Though the traveler says that he merely has "a certain intuition . . . that a God exists," he also tells the reader, "I am——I really am, God knows——open to conviction." In this uncommitted, unresolved view, Greene believes, lies the despair and dilemma of the modern intellectual who cannot accept mere hints of an explanation.

Widespread lack of belief in God is related in this story to war, to modern industrial life, to meaningless existence. "The black furnaces of Bedwell Junction gathered around the line. The points switched and we were tossed from one set of rails to another. A spray of sparks, a signal light changing to red, tall chimneys jetting into the grey night sky, the fumes of steam from the stationary engines——half the cold journey was over, and now remained the long wait for the slow cross-country train." There is very strong symbolic language here, as a counterpoint to the traveler's laconic comment that the priest's explanation "is an interesting story." The train ride itself, in the cold compartment through dark, tortuous tunnels, is suggestive of a blind, directionless life-voyage. Greene seems to be saying that even though half the cold journey of the unbelieving soul is over, there need not be merely the slow cross-country train after a long wait. One cannot, after all, see the difference between a consecrated and an unconsecrated wafer under the microscope, but for those who accept the priest's hint of an explanation of the significant difference, there is happiness, there is meaning, there is God.

SUBJECTS FOR WRITTEN COMPOSITION

1. Trace Greene's interest in the interrelationship between individual godlessness and the moral decadence of our society.

2. Show how Greene's gift for searching out and examining the evil hidden in the human heart may be the basis for his creation of characters.

3. Explain how Greene goes about providing suspense in these stories.

4. Synthesize the view of twentieth-century life we gain through Greene's stories.

5. Prepare a study of Greene's attitude as a writer toward the fallen characters in his stories.

6. Examine Greene's use of symbolism—abstract overtones of meaning through literal examples—in the appropriate stories.

7. Write a personal interpretation of "The Hint of an Explanation," "Across the Bridge," or one of the other Greene selections in this text.

8. Reconstruct Greene's religious views and show how they affect his writings.

the telescope, and for those who accept the priest's hint of an explanation of the significant difference—there is happiness, there is meaning,
there is God.

SUBJECTS FOR WRITTEN COMPOSITION

1. Trace Greene's interest in the interrelationship between individual
   goodness and the moral decadence of our society.

2. Show how Greene's gift for searching out and examining the evil
   hidden in the human heart may be the basis for his creation of characters.

3. Explain how Greene goes about providing suspense in these stories.

4. Synthesize the view of twentieth-century life we get through Greene's
   stories.

5. Prepare a study of Greene's attitude as a writer toward the fallen
   characters in his stories.

6. Examine Greene's use of symbolism—abstract overtones of meaning through literal examples—in the appropriate stories.

7. Write a personal interpretation of "The Hint of an Explanation,"
   "Across the Bridge," or one of the other Greene selections in this text.

8. Re-evaluate Greene's religious views and show how they affect his
   writings.

Robert Penn Warren

Robert Penn Warren

ROBERT PENN WARREN, poet, novelist, short-story writer, critic, textbook author, and teacher, was born in Kentucky in 1905; he acquired his formal education at Vanderbilt University, the University of California, Yale University, and at Oxford University. Well known as a teacher on many university campuses, Warren has said that, "For a person who wants to write, the advantages of teaching . . . outweigh the disadvantages; a teacher is forced to clarify—or to try to clarify—his own mind on certain questions which are necessarily involved in the business of writing."

In the 1920s Warren became associated with the so-called Agrarian Group of Southern writers, who then advocated, among other things, a return from an industrial economy to an agrarian. In the 1930s and 1940s, Warren served as one of the managing editors of the Southern Review and as an advisory editor for the Kenyon Review. From 1944 to 1945 he served as poetry consultant to the Library of Congress.

Warren is perhaps best known as a writer of prose fiction —novels and short stories. His major writings include the novels "Night Rider" (1938), "At Heaven's Gate" (1943), "All the King's Men" (1946), and "World Enough and Time" (1950), and the short stories, "The Circus in the Attic, and Other Stories" (1948). His poetical works include "XXXVI Poems" (1935), "Eleven Poems on the Same Theme" (1942), "Selected Poems, 1923–1943" (1944), and "Brother to Dragons" (1953). His college English textbooks are "Understanding Fiction" (1943), "Modern Rhetoric" (1949), and "Fundamentals of Good Writing" (1950); his collaborator on these was Cleanth Brooks.

Some of the awards and prizes bestowed upon him are the Caroline Sinkler Prize of the Poetry Society of South Carolina (1936 and 1937), the Helen Haire Levinson Prize of Poetry (1936), a Houghton Mifflin Literary Fellowship (1936), Guggenheim Awards (1940, 1947), the Shelley Memorial Prize for Poetry (cowinner, 1942), the Southern Prize (1947), and the Pulitzer Prize for Fiction (1947). To this list may be added the Meltzer Award of the Screen Writers' Guild (1950). The motion picture version of "All the King's Men" was named the best film of 1949 by the Academy of Motion Picture Arts and Sciences.

Warren's influence as a literary critic, editor, lecturer, and teacher has been impressive, but he has also earned growing popular and critical recognition as one of America's most serious and dedicated writers. The fastidiousness of his literary craftsmanship as well as his restless probing toward the center of human action—stubborn search for self-knowledge, self-recognition, self-definition —show him to be a writer of both tough intellectual substance and deep moral preoccupation. His materials largely reflect the inner conflicts of men, but there is strong emphasis given to the way in which environmental externals shape human destiny. The questions he seems to strive to answer are Who am I? Why am I what I am?

The Life and Work
of Professor Roy Millen

PROFESSOR ROY MILLEN HAD LOVED HIS WIFE DEVOTEDLY, AND NOW, in the spring of the year 1937, she was dead. He had not realized before how much she had meant to him, how his own life had described its orbit, as it were, within the steady and beneficent influence of her being. If she had dominated the course of his life, it had not been by isolated, individual acts of superior will, but rather by defining, subtly but more completely year after year, the very atmosphere he breathed. His position at the university, the long tranquil evenings at the bridge table with the light glinting subduedly on the exciting and rich designs of the royal cards, the friends at the table, the respectful greeting in the corridors and on the street, the very food he put into his mouth—all of these items had been defined by her. He had never protested against this, not even fleetingly, in the privacy of his own mind. Day after day, year after year, he had accepted it as part of the inevitable furniture of his life, just as he had accepted the sound of her voice and the expression of her face. If he felt anything, it was a kind of gratitude. Any little act he could do for her—and it comforted him now to remember that he had always tried to do the little things she wanted, especially after her health failed—had only been the proper manifestation of his gratitude, or at least of his candid admission that she had made him what he was.

The self which he now was—the man with the carefully brushed tufts of white hair on each side of the pink and hygienic-looking bald skull, the rimless pince-nez with the black cord, the well-pressed but somewhat worn suits, blue or medium gray according to the season, the cleanly cut nails, the thoughts that came into his head— that self, too, had been defined by her. And during the twenty-odd years of his life with her, he had remembered more and more rarely the other self which he had been before his marriage. He did not like to remember that other time, for those years had been painful and long, so painful that even in recollection something of the distress of the old reality could revive within him. He had bent over the long rows of cotton, with the sun bearing down on his shoulders and the humid air swimming around him. He had clerked in cross-roads stores. He had taught in the country schools of his native section, listening all day to the sullen or droning voices of the children and then tramping down some muddy road to his rented room in a tumble-down farmhouse. Later, long after those years were past, he would occasionally wonder, when the unsought recollections came to him, what had sustained him, what hope had given him strength enough to go on. Looking back, he could not say. He could not remember what strength had been in him, or remember what he had hoped for, or expected. Certainly, he had not hoped for what he had actually found. Anyway, he told himself humbly, this was better than what he had hoped for. For he had scarcely known that there could be such a life as this.

By the time he was twenty-nine he had managed to get a degree from a small denominational college. For two years then, he had better teaching jobs, and saved enough to see him through a winter at the state university. When he was thirty-seven, he received a Ph.D. in English literature. That June day he stood on the platform of the auditorium, stooped and sweating under the black robe and colored hood, as though to their weight were added the weight of all the privations and distresses which had brought him to that moment, and his outstretched hand shook. That fall, quite unexpectedly, he got a small job teaching freshmen at the university. One of the regular instructors was ill, and the head of the department thriftily surmised that Millen would take the job for little or nothing. During the year the instructor died.

"Millen is a good steady man," Dr. Saunders, the head of the department, remarked to his daughter one day toward the end of the year. "It looks as if we might just keep him on another year until we can make a permanent appointment."

"Yes," Mildred Saunders said dutifully, abstractedly. She was a tallish woman, a little past thirty, with a spindly figure and plain features. Her habitual expression was kindly, however, and she had a quiet nature. A few weeks after her father's remark, she saw Millen at a faculty reception, miserable and lonely in a corner, and talked to him, remembering what her father had said. In ministering to his embarrassment and shyness, she forgot something of her own habitual diffidence. The following year, early in the session, when Dr. Saunders had Millen to his house on some piece of academic business, Mildred Saunders saw him and asked him to come again. He came more and more frequently during the year, to sit in the shadowed and dingy parlor, his bony hands with the bitten nails moving uneasily on his knees. In May he received a permanent appointment to his job, and Mildred Saunders announced her engagement to him. She had married him, and he had been devoted to her, and now she was dead.

She had died quite suddenly and ironically, just at the time when, after years of ill health, she seemed to be getting well and strong again, and they were planning to go away on a year's leave. They were planning to go to England, where he could work in one of the great English libraries and finish his book. Six years before, he had had a leave, and they had planned to go to England to work on the book, but they had gone, in the end, to southern California. He had not protested, even to himself, at the change in plans; in fact he suggested the change. The cold, damp climate of Millersburg in winter had always been bad for his wife's asthma and neuralgia, and England might be worse. And his wife's cousins in Los Angeles would be company for her while he worked on his book. And there were some very nice libraries in California. Everybody knew that.

She had seemed better at first in California, but then, despite everything, her health had taken a turn for the worse. She had been in the hospital, and the doctors had done all they could, and the cousins had been helpful and considerate. Some days they had even gone to the hospital and he had been able to stay at home and work or go to the library. But she had been very ill, and he knew what to do for her—better, he told himself, than the cousins or even the nurses. Even after she was able to leave the hospital and go back to Millersburg she was never really well. But she was very patient and rarely lost her temper with him. Sometimes, when he sat beside her bed—for during that period she was confined to her bed almost half of the time—she would reach out to touch his hand and say: "Just leave me alone, Roy, and go work on your book. You ought to work on your book, Roy. I don't mind being alone. I've gotten used to being alone." He would say that it didn't matter, or that it was moving along nicely, that he had done quite a bit lately. Or she would say: "I'm sorry we have to spend so much money on me, Roy, when you want to go away to work on your book." Then he would try to comfort her.

She was dead now, but there was the book left for him. I have my book to do, at least I have that, he concluded as soon as the first shock of grief had worn off and he had begun to search in himself for some center of meaning for his life. Then, day after day, as he came to accept the fact of his loss and his mind dwelt more and more on his book, a kind of modest excitement grew within him —an excitement so pleasurable that once or twice, remembering in the midst of it his wife's death, he was filled with a sense of shame and remorse.

He made his plans to go abroad, to England, to work in the libraries there, as he and his wife had planned. It was what she would have him do, he told himself. And the book would be a kind of monument to her. He would dedicate the book to her. As he walked slowly back from the campus to his house in the late afternoons or early evenings of spring, he would try to compose the dedication, saying the words aloud to himself as he looked up at the paling, peach-colored sky beyond the newly leafed branches. He had decided to sail in June, as soon as he could leave after commencement.

"I hear you're going away for a year, Professor Millen," Tom Howell said, standing respectfully before Professor Millen's office desk. Then he added, in a dutiful tone, "To work on your book."

"Yes," Professor Millen said, "to work on my book." Then, as though recollecting himself, he made a little gesture toward the chair in front of the desk, and said, "Won't you have a seat, Howell?"

"Are you going to finish it in a year?" Howell asked, and sat down.

"I still have a little research to do. I have to settle a few points —points which can't be settled in libraries in this country. I have to do some work yet in one of the great English libraries." Professor Millen paused, looking over the green lawn outside his office window. "But I'll get it written within the year. Practically everything is in order. Though, of course," he paused again, looking at Tom

Howell, who listened respectfully and with what seemed to be inter-est, "I'll have to do a good deal of retouching—style and so on, you know—" he waved his hand modestly in the air, "when I get back."

"I'm hoping—" the boy hesitated, fumbling in his pocket to draw out a folded paper, "I'm hoping to be able to go abroad next year. If I can make it. That's what I wanted to see you about, Professor Millen."

"Anything I can do, I'll be glad to do."

"It's a scholarship. A French scholarship, and I was hoping you'd recommend me. I've had a lot of work with you, and all. The French Department will recommend me, but I've done my minor in English, you know. What you'd say would count a lot."

"Howell," Professor Millen said, judicially putting the tips of his fingers together and inspecting the boy, "I've never had a better student than you are. Possibly never one as good. I'll say that in my recommendation. I'll write a strong one." He felt his enthusiasm mounting as he spoke, and a warmth suffused him as though at the prospect of some piece of happiness, some success, for himself.

"I certainly appreciate it," the boy said. "This is about the only thing I've got in sight for next year, and I'm graduating. Oh, I reckon I could get a little teaching job or something for a year or two to save up some money to go on. I don't think I ought to ask my family for any more—they've been swell, putting me through college and giving me that trip to France two years back—"

"Yes, yes," Professor Millen said abstractedly, "oh, yes, you did go over one summer, didn't you?"

"Oh, that was just for fun," Howell said, "but this time it would be for work. And when I get back I ought to be able to get a pretty good job so I could save enough to get my Ph.D. quick. Up East."

"A year of study in France will be a fine opportunity," Professor Millen said. That enthusiasm and warmth which had filled him like a promise of happiness was waning now, he did not know why. He wished the boy would get up and go and leave him alone.

"Oh, it'll be an opportunity," Howell agreed, "and I'm not going to waste it. The work'll be fun, and there ought to be a little fun besides. I was in Paris for two weeks—and you know how Paris is, it sort of knocks you off your feet. You've been there?"

"Yes, yes," Professor Millen said hurriedly, impersonally, almost impatiently, averting his face from the boy and looking off across the patch of lawn, wondering why he had lied, why he had told the boy he had been to Paris. He watched some students, two boys and a girl, who moved across the sunlit, open space. They moved lingeringly. It seemed that they would never be across that bright, open space of green where the sun was. Then they were gone, hidden by the screen of foliage.

Professor Millen turned and brought his gaze to rest again on the the boy. The boy was leaning forward, his face smiling. Professor Millen saw, as for the first time, the blond, crisp hair combed back from the square forehead, the confident gaze of the blue eyes, the comfortable, confident way the coat hung from the good shoulders.

The boy stood up. "I've stayed too long. I know you've got a lot of work to do."

"No," Professor Millen said.

"And I certainly appreciate your recommendation. The address of the scholarship committee is on here," he said, and laid a printed sheet on the desk. "That's the circular, and all the information."

"I'll attend to it right away," Professor Millen said.

"Thank you," the boy said, and was gone.

For a few minutes Professor Millen sat there, his eyes on the bare wall opposite his desk. Then he read the circular. He laid it back on the desk and pressed a button. When the secretary came in, he handed her the printed sheet. "The address is on that," he said, and waited while she copied it. Then he said, "I'll give you the letter." He studied the bare wall for a moment, then began: "Gentlemen. I can truthfully say that I take the most sincere pleasure in recommending to you Mr. Thomas Howell. In my long career as a teacher I have never had a better student. He has an acute and penetrating intelligence, and, as is so often not the case with young men of his capacity, the patience and honesty of a true scholar. I am sure that if he is appointed to—" He hesitated, looking at the wall. "I am sure that—" he said at last, then stopped.

The secretary, her pencil poised above her pad, waited while Professor Millen seemed to withdraw, to sink within himself. Her foot made a slight reproachful scraping sound as she changed her position in the chair. She, too, began to look out the window, where Professor Millen's gaze now was fixed.

"That's all—for the present," Professor Millen said, suddenly. "Just hold that and I'll finish later. I've just thought—" he managed to look directly at her—"of something else I've got to do. There's something else."

After the secretary had left the office, closing the door softly behind her, he did not move for some time. Then he again looked out the window. The shadows were lengthening over the smooth lawn. The faintest premonitory flush was touching the puffs of white cloud visible toward the top of his window. Before long now he would be going home. He picked up the circular. He read it again, very carefully, dwelling on it almost painfully, as though he were an illiterate trying to extort some secret from the words. He lifted his eyes from the sheet and stared at the chair where the boy had sat leaning forward, the pleasure shining on his clear, handsome face, the good coat riding easy on his shoulders, saying "—you know how Paris is, it sort of knocks you off your feet. You've been there?"

Professor Millen let the circular slip from his lap to the floor. Then, decisively, he reached into the drawer of his desk and took out a sheet of paper. He wrote rapidly in his large, firm script:

> *Gentlemen:*
> I have been asked to recommend Mr. Thomas Howell to you for a scholarship for study in France. As you will observe from a transcript of his academic record, with which no doubt you have been provided, he has made the grade of A in all of his work in the English department of this institution, and I understand that his grades in French (his major subject) have been very high. This achievement, of course, deserves consideration, but candor compels me to say that a superficial facility and cleverness seem to characterize his mind. I do not wish to prejudice the committee against his case, and I may be wrong in my estimate; certainly, I hope that the committee will consider him very carefully. But I do feel that he lacks solidity of character, the spirit of patient inquiry, and what might be termed the philosophical bent.
>
> > *Very respectfully yours,*
> > *Roy Millen,*
> > *Professor of English.*

Without looking up, he addressed an envelope hurriedly, the pen making a dry, scratching sound. Then he blotted and stamped the envelope, inserted the sheet, put the letter into his pocket, picked up his hat, and left the office. He would, he remembered, pass a postbox on his way home.

The Circus in the Attic

LET US ASSUME THAT IT IS SUMMER. COMING FROM THE NORTH, JUST at the brow of the ridge, you catch your first view of the valley and of Bardsville. There is the wide valley of Cadman's Creek, two miles below, opening sharp upon the river. To your right, to the west, there is the silver-green shine of the river and the green-silver shine of the rank corn in the bottom lands beyond, some miles away. But the sun-glazed highway spins off ahead of you, down the valley, like a ribbon of celluloid film carelessly unspooled across green baize. And at the end is the steel bridge over the creek.

Across the creek are the long, new, raw-brick structures of the war plant set in the gashed and still red-wounded clay, one of the tin-bright stacks still releasing unwaveringly the black smoke in a single column to an improbable height in the motionless, heat-benumbed air. And there are the dilapidated piles of the old furniture factory (which made ammunition boxes for the war), the coal yards on their patch of grimed earth, which glitters like mica, and the tracks, switches, and sidings exposed among the jumble, like a tangle of dissected nerves, to glitter, too, and quiver in the incandescent light. You cannot see the stone ruin of the old mill that stands at the other end of the bridge. But you do see, beyond the creek, flung down beyond the tracks, the shanties, trailers, and pre-fabricated houses of the war workers, and beyond that the shanties of nigger town which straggle up the hill, with washing here and there hanging abjectly on crazy lines like improvised flags of surrender among ruins. But all of that is not Bardsville. Bardsville is on the river bluffs beyond.

Cadman's Creek runs west to the river to make a big "V," and on the leg of the "V" toward the river, to the west, the land is high; for the worn limestone still holds there against the erosion of frost and flood, and every spring forces the swollen red river over the cornlands to the west. As you see it from the north, there are the steeples, the water tower, and the mauve and blue slate roofs with the color and shine of a pigeon's breast, embowered in the swollen and tufted greenery, with here and there the glimpse of sober red brick, or a white wall, or a white picket fence among the trees; and, now and then, a window, miles away on Rusty-Butt Hill, flashes the sun to you like a heliograph using some code which you cannot understand. That is Bardsville. It is the county seat of Carruthers County.

As you reach the brow of the ridge, and the valley and Bardsville fill your eye, you probably do not notice the little monument by the left of the highway. It is a single shaft of granite, about ten feet high, almost concealed in a riot of purple-tufted ironweed, flame-tufted milkweed, and sassafras growth. You have noticed, of course, the big road-sign to the right, advertising Carruthers House, "Southern Hospitality at Its Most Gracious," and a dining room recommended (before the war of 1941-45) by Duncan Hines, "Country Ham our *Specialitée.*" The sign stands on the old Sykes place, and the ruinous log-house up the lane beyond the sign, sagging and windowless, under the single scrofulous cedar, weathering to earth and surrendering to the clawing hands of vine and briar, is the old Sykes house, a refuge for field mice, a lone fox, and a couple of fat blacksnakes which like to sun themselves on the stone coping of the old cistern. Not even boys go there now.

Twenty-odd years ago, a nameless old tramp crawled up there and died. His body was not found for nearly a year, long after the buzzards had lost interest. For several years thereafter, boys would go to the Sykes house to whisper with delicious shudders in the sun-dappled gloom of the half-roofless rooms and then listen to the sound of their own breathing. But the story died out of the folklore of Bardsville boyhood, even with the desperate addition of murder to spice the tale, and for another generation of boys the place was too near the highway to be romantic. Thicket and unchinked logs offered no defense, only a filter, against the whir of motors and the bleat of horns.

But Seth Sykes's name is on the monument, coupled with the name of Cassius Perkins, two heroes of Bardsville, who, as the inscription on the monument declares, gave their lives on this spot that their comrades might live and that the foot of the invader might not sully the soil of home. If you tear away the love vine from the gray granite (imported from Vermont), you can read the words. The monument was erected in 1917, as a curious backwash or eddy of the excitement and spirit of dedication evoked among the ladies of Bardsville by the coming of a new war, a war undertaken now by a united people to defend, beyond the seas, their liberty.

The new war had not yet become real in the summer of 1917. The bandages prepared at Red Cross meetings in the basement of the St. Luke's parish house or in the Sunday-school room of the Baptist Church seemed to have no more importance than the baskets prepared there for the poor before Christmas. The tears shed by mothers and sweethearts at the railroad station seemed to be no different from the tears shed when a boy went off to school or college. No armless khaki sleeve had yet appeared on the streets of Bardsville. So the tumescent, rich, meaningless emotionalism that ached sweetly in the breasts of the middle-aged ladies of the community found release and focus in the monument. The United Daughters of the Confederacy, the defenders of ancient pieties and the repositories of ignorance of history, undertook to raise the money. Bardsville had had heroes before, and it would have them again. Soon now. The monument would be an inspiration to the new heroes. So the monument appeared, and was dedicated, and while the mayor made a speech, a platoon of conscripts from a camp up in Kentucky, in untarnished khaki, with slick, scrubbed faces, stood stiffly by with the wooden embarrassment of boys trapped on the platform at high-school commencement.

Cassius Perkins and Seth Sykes had died on the old pike, on the brow of the ridge. It was the winter of 1861-62, when the Federal armies were coming down across Kentucky. The Yankees already held the towns across the Kentucky border. But Bardsville had its home guard, a few middle-aged men and a rag-tag-and-bobtail of young boys who could ride like circus performers and shoot anything that would hold powder and to whom the war was a gaudy picnic that their tyrannous mothers would not let them attend. Some of them did attend the picnic later. Some of them rode calluses on their rumps following Forrest across Mississippi and Tennessee and Alabama. Some of them huddled in the pits outside Vicksburg while the acid June sweat burned their eyes and made dewdrops on their silky boyish beards, and their shoulders ached with the interminable recoil of the rifle. But in December of 1861, Cassius Perkins was the only member of the home guard who really attended the picnic and stayed until it was over.

Cassius was one of a group of fifteen or twenty home guards who were encamped on the night of December 16, 1861, on the ridge north of Bardsville. They were on the lookout for Yankee cavalry patrols that had worked down a couple of times out of Kentucky. Their bivouac was in a grove of oaks, now gone, on top of the ridge. Their horses were tethered in a line under the trees. They had little fires and a keg of whiskey. It was like a fishing trip or a hunting party, and already the spirit of Christmas was in the air. They felt very manly. And they felt perfectly safe. For they had sent two boys up the pike to watch. "Videttes" they had proudly learned to call them. The camp, very sleepy, totally confused, and half drunk, was surprised just at dawn. The videttes had been surprised and taken without a warning shot being fired. The home guards did manage to get to their horses, did mount, mill about for a moment on the pike, and then, after a brief exchange of shots, fall back to Bardsville. Later in the day, long after the patrol had withdrawn into Kentucky, they found the body of Cassius on the pike. Seth Sykes's wife had already dragged his body to their house. Nobody knew very clearly what had happened, but it was generally understood that they had saved Bardsville.

When the monument was erected, however, an old man, Jake Velie, who had been one of the boys, remembered the time. He was an old man now, past seventy, but he seemed older, in his greasy, tattered overalls, his chin and whiskers fouled with nicotine, the stub of his right arm standing out from his shoulder like a plucked chicken's wing (he had lost the arm twenty-five years before when he was a brakeman), a derelict and a reproach to the community, squatting against a maple in the court-house yard, exuding a miasma of dried sweat and rotgut whisky. "Yeah," he said, "yeah," and spat on the sparse turf with a quick, viperish outthrust of his tendoned, dirt-crusted neck, "putten up air-y monimint to Cash Perkins. I knowed him. I wuz thar. I wuz a home guard, lak all them little pukes. Oh, we wuz sojers, I hope to tell. Layen up thar on that-air ridge in them oak trees. Them trees is gone now, gone thirty year. Layen up thar lak hit wuz a coon hunt, eaten hog meat and drinken whisky, tellen what we wuz gonna do to them Yankees. Yeah, we done hit," he said, and spat, and sank back, silent for a moment, into the miasma of rotgut and time.

Then said: "Yeah. We done hit, in a pig's eye. Layen up thar drunk, and bout day them Yankees come. Half them pukes didn't wait to pick up no guns. But they didn't aim to fergit them hosses. They wuz homeward bound, I mean to say. They tuk out home. Cept Cash. He wuz drunk. Drunk and got the wrong hoss. Mike Stafford's mean sorrel hoss couldn't nobody ride but Mike. Cash wuz drunk, but ain't no man e'er been so drunk he would ride right at him a passel of Yankees single-handed. Bet Gin'l Lee ner none of them high-toned gin'ls e'er done hit. Cash didn't do hit. That sorrel hoss was runnen away."

Then said: "Them Yankees give him his'n. They didn't stay to hem ner haw. They give hit to him. They laid him down. And none of them little pukes from town stopped to git his deathbed remarks. They wuz long-gone. And me, too."

Then, sitting under the maple, with the gray sparrow droppings staining the hot leaves above him, spat and said: "A monimint to Cash Perkins. Hit wuz an accidint. Mought as well put up air-y monimint to me fer gitten this here cut off." He waggled the stub of his arm shrouded in the hacked-off, blue shirt sleeve.

Then said: "Cash ne'er killed no Yankees. He was a likker-killer. Always wuz, time he wuz stout fer to draw a cork. Killed himself a lot of likker that night, and got on the wrong hoss. A mean sorrel hoss. Mought as well put up that monimint with a jug of cawn whisky carved on top lak hit wuz a angel on a tombstone."

But nobody was there to hear him, under the maple. All of Bardsville was out on the ridge at the dedication. All but two little colored boys, and a collie dog panting sardonically with the heat, and another old derelict like Jake Velie who lay drowsing on the grass with a straw hat over his face. Nor would Bardsville, had Bardsville been there, have believed the truth, whatever truth it was, which Jake Velie uttered out of the candor and irony of age. Not even when he leaned forward off his haunches and savagely smote the sparse turf with the flat of his hand three times and croaked: "The truth. Hit is the Gawd's truth! I wuz thar. The truth!"

They would not have believed him or his truth, for people always believe what truth they have to believe to go on being the way they are.

But Jake Velie did not know all the truth. And all who did know it had been dead a long time, those who had known the truth about how Seth Sykes died. The men of the Yankee patrol and Seth Sykes's wife had known the truth, but they were dead.

Seth Sykes had a hundred acres of ridge land, where the rains ripped off the soil every year and bore it down the furrows, and the sun all summer baked the limestone. He lived in the log house with his wife and two children, and the place was his, and was the world. What happened in the wide and inimical world outside this world was nothing to him. Men spoke to him on the street in Bardsville and told him about the war. "Secesh ain't nuthin' to me," he said, and twitched his gaunt shoulders. "Niggers," he said, "niggers ain't nuthin' to me," he said. "Take 'em outer the country ain't nuthin' to me." They told him how the Yankees would come. "Yankees," he said, "they ain't nuthin' to me. Yankees ner niggers."

He had a fight, stomp and gouge, with a man on the street in Bardsville, and lost the fight, and went home streaked with blood. He had said he hoped the Yankees would come.

Then winter fell, and Seth did not go to Bardsville any more, but holed up like a bear or a varmint in the log house on the ridge and ate the doled, haggled strips of hog meat off his razor-backs, which he had killed at the first good frost, and the squeezed and hand-weighed corn pone, and counted out the chunks of wood for the fire.

Then the Yankees came. Seth Sykes, leaning over the fireplace in the dawn to blow up the fire, heard the shots on the pike. By the time he got down to the foot of the lane, the home guards were beating it hell for leather down the ridge for town and the body of Cassius Perkins lay on the pike. Cassius Perkins was the man he had had the fight with in Bardsville.

Seth came out on the pike among the blue-clad troopers on the restless horses, nodding to them, saying good morning. He stood above the body of Cassius Perkins, flat, face-down, arms spread to clutch the pike to the bosom, and rubbed the toe of his brogan in the gravel, and said, "Secesh. What I told 'em."

He looked up at the young man with pale, silky mustaches, and said, "You the cap'n?"

"I am Lieutenant Wiggins," replied the young man, whose long-skirted blue coat seemed too big for him, and seemed to weigh too much, like a blanket thrown over a child's shoulders. The breath he uttered whitened on the still air above the yellow mustaches.

"You bossen these-here sojers?"

"I am in command," the young man said.

Seth Sykes looked down at the body on the pike. He fingered the scar along his jaw, scarcely healed, where the man on the street of Bardsville had kicked him as he lay. He took his eyes off the body and looked at the lieutenant. "You all hongry," he said, not as a question but as a statement. Then added, "I'll give you a piece of meat. You kin cook hit on a fahr." He nodded across the pike to the grove, where a little smoke yet rose from one of the campfires.

He turned up the lane, walking uneasily over the frozen, rutted ground with a rocking motion. The lieutenant followed, walking his horse at Seth's pace, the men following. They went up to the establishment. Seth Sykes went into his smoke house. One of the men dismounted and looked at the log crib by the barn. Before Seth Sykes had reappeared, he came back to the lieutenant and said, "They got corn."

"All right," the lieutenant said. "Use that wagon." He nodded to a wagon beside the barn.

When Seth Sykes came out of the smoke house, weighing a cured hog shoulder in his hands, he saw that they were spanning his mules to the wagon.

"What you doin'?" he demanded.

The lieutenant told him and added that he would be paid.

"Hit is my cawn," Seth Sykes stated without passion.

"You will be paid. I will give you an order for the money."

Seth Sykes looked at the lieutenant from head to booted and spurred heel. Then he turned deliberately, dropped the smoked shoulder, and approached the men at the wagon. He went straight up to the trooper who was holding the lead rope of the near mule. "Leave hit go," he said.

The trooper made no reply.

Seth Sykes took him by the arm and swung him round. The trooper struck him flat to the ground. Another trooper stood over him with a carbine. Seth Sykes lay there on the frozen ground, watching them put the mules in, and then load the wagon. Mrs. Sykes had run from the cabin at the noise. One of the troopers held her.

When the wagon was loaded, the lieutenant said, "Let him up." The cavalcade moved down the lane, the lieutenant in front, a trooper just behind him leading the horse which had been ridden by the trooper now driving the wagon. Two of the troopers rode behind the wagon. The wagon wheels groaned over the ruts.

They were almost at the foot of the lane when Seth Sykes rose from the ground. He ran down the lane after them. "Seth!" his wife called, "Seth!" Her voice was thin in the empty gray sky over the wide ridge.

He caught up with them just as the wagon drew onto the pike. He ran along the ditch by the pike toward the head of the column, the troopers all eyeing him incuriously. The lieutenant turned in his saddle. "Go back," he ordered sharply.

"Hit is my cawn!" Seth Sykes cried, and leaped out of the ditch to the pike and toward the lieutenant.

"Stand back!" the lieutenant cried, the authority in his voice cracking into querulousness.

Seth Sykes came on and the troopers watched him. He grabbed the lieutenant's near leg, the left leg, and shouted, "Hit is my cawn!"

The lieutenant leaned over and struck him about the head with his gauntleted fist. The horse shied and the lieutenant almost reeled from the saddle.

But the nearest trooper was on them now. He leaned from his saddle, seized Seth Sykes by the long, uncombed, matted hair, jerked his head back, and carefully put the muzzle of a pistol against the head, just above the ear, and pulled the trigger.

The body plunged, then sagged between the two horses like a dropped croker sack of nubbins.

The horses veered sharply apart, then stood. The eyes of the trooper who had fired the shot, gleaming from the crinkled, beefy face and black beard, met the eyes of the lieutenant, pale, astonished eyes above the yellow mustache.

"I didn't order you to do that," the lieutenant said uncertainly.

The bearded trooper made no reply. He looked at the body, and then sullenly replaced the weapon in its holster.

"Look!" the lieutenant cried with the tone of discovery, looking down at the blood and brains spattered on his trousers and boot.

"Look!" he cried in pain and despair and outrage, and pointed with one finger at the fouled cloth and leather. "Look, you got it all over me!"

Then he leaned over the saddlebow and, in the blank morning, under the blank eyes watching him, vomited.

After the patrol had gone on, Seth Sykes's wife came out and dragged the body back to the cabin.

That was the truth about Seth Sykes and how he became a hero.

It was corn again, as it had been in the case of Cassius Perkins, and perhaps the monument should have been erected to corn, not just a carved jug, as Jake Velie had suggested, to commemorate Cash's corn whisky, but on top of the shaft a carved jug set in the midst of a wreath of corn blades and of the spindling ears such as Seth Sykes had raised on his ridge farm. But such a monument with the jug and wreath of corn would have been no disrespect to Seth Sykes and Cassius Perkins, nor to any hero who ever died. For perhaps Seth and Cash were no different from any other heroes, men who have been drunk on whisky, or on something else as strong and heady, and have ridden runaway into the heart of the enemy, or have died defending a crib of corn, or something else, which they had sweated to make.

But the monument by the side of the dazzling concrete highway is only a simple shaft, with no jug or wreath, only the names and the inscription, which you will not stop to read. You will probably not even see the monument, for you will dip sharply over the ridge and take the long, tire-sizzling glide into the valley, over the Cadman's Creek bridge, by the Rotary Club's greeting sign, by the ruined mill, past the war plant, furniture factory, tobacco warehouses, and coal yards, and then swoop with purring motor up the rise through nigger town, where the dirt lanes fall away from each side of the concrete slab to wander among the shacks, and where a big-eyed, half-naked, chocolate pickaninny under a rose bush of red roses regards your hasty passage with the gravity of a philosopher.

You will go up the hill to the square, get gas and oil, and have lunch at the Carruthers House, overlooking the river, in the dining room where one shell from a Yankee gunboat landed in January, 1862, and made quite a mess. (The gunboats finally came up the river, were greeted with a spatter of small-arms fire from the home guard, lobbed three shells up the bluffs, and received the surrender of Bardsville.) Lunch will be served by a white girl wearing a green smock, a slash of lipstick, and an expression of indefatigable contempt; for the neat-handed, clairvoyant, grizzle-headed old colored waiters are there no more, thank you, sir. After lunch you will head out, out Chilton Avenue, up Rusty-Butt Hill and on out to hit Highway 83 and will whirl southward through the afternoon into the heart of Dixie.

Rusty-Butt Hill is the highest of the bluffs along the river, on the western leg of the "V" enclosing Bardsville. It was wooded once, great oaks and tulip trees, with a grassy glade on the western brow, above the cedars that clutched and grabbled into the limestone face, overlooking the wide river and the canebrakes beyond. One June afternoon, toward sundown, about 1778 or '79, a man named "Lem Lovehart" entered the glade and, leaning on his long rifle, looked west over the river. He wore leather breeches, the fringed doeskin smock of the frontiersman, and a coonskin cap. A powder horn and knife hung at his side, and on his back was a leather-wrapped, thong-tied bundle. He had been born thirty-five years before in a cabin in the North Carolina Piedmont, had run away from home at fifteen with a couple of hunters, had been a trader with the Cherokees, and had worked his way into the great valleys beyond the mountains, driven by a hot restlessness and a dark compulsion that he had no name for. The previous winter he had spent holed up in a hut in what is now lower Middle Tennessee, alone, and with spring had started out northwestward, in a slow, aimless, zigzag track, like a journey in a dream. He was a rather short, chunky man, with some fat streaking his brawn, given to ready sweating. His leather garments had the rank odor of the winter den, and now, tired from his climb up the bluff, he stood at the edge of the glade and sweated with the sweat of the bear fat and venison which had built the padding over his stout bones.

He found a spring down the bluff, shot two squirrels, cooked them over a handful of fire, and ate his supper as sunset drew on and the light reddened and leveled across the miles of canebrake to the west. Then he lay down on the grass, in the great stillness, broken now and then by the liquid, somnolent ripple of a robin's note or a last, lost burst of birdsong from the cedars down the bluff, and for no reason his leathery heart suddenly softened and swelled in his breast and he wept.

He did not weep because he remembered home and the brief

time of softness and affection before the years of loneliness and compulsion and hardship and violence and death began. As a matter of fact, he remembered nothing at that moment, and thought of nothing. His feeling was one of mild surprise that he should weep at all. But the tears came. Then he felt relaxed and happy, and, as night came on, slept like a child.

Three years later he led a party of settlers to the bluff. He built a cabin and married a fifteen-year-old girl, the daughter of one of the settlers. He had three children, two boys and a girl, and when the oldest was seven, was killed and scalped by a Chickasaw, seventy-five miles south, where he had gone to spy out the country.

Now his great-great-grandson, Bolton Lovehart, lives in an old brick house, halfway down the slope of Rusty-Butt Hill toward the square. The big houses of Bardsville, with the exception of a few new ones built in the flush times of the 1920's in a subdivision called Chilton Heights near the country club, are on Rusty-Butt Hill. They began to build the big houses on the hill more than a hundred years ago when the lucky sons among the sons of the pioneers were turning into land speculators and tobacco planters who shipped the leaf down the river. The first house up there was built in 1811 by Tolliver Skaggs, who had come as a big boy with the Lovehart party, who was a wild fellow known for his prowess with bottle and boot heel and knife until he got religion and became a savage Presbyterian, who prospered and lived forever, and in his old age, past ninety, said, "I come here early. I come 'mongst the first. I scalped me the first Indian. I shot the last bear. I run the first jug of whisky and I prized me the first hogshead of tobacco, and I reckin, by God, I brought civilization to Carruthers County." He told the truth, even about the Indian, and he had also built the first brick house on the hill, not a big house, but a square, solid structure among the oaks.

The other houses came during the next forty or fifty years, as the lucky grandsons of pioneers squeezed the unlucky ones off the good tobacco land or became bankers and squeezed the other lucky ones who had got good land. But none of the houses was a mansion. They were just big, solid, high-ceilinged houses, with white porticos where dogs lolled in summer and saddles and boots were flung on benches. Some time, in the thirties or forties, when the social structure of Bardsville had begun to harden, the people who lived near the square called the hill "Aristocrat Hill," with a mixture of envy and irony. And the name, in the mouths of those who lived, not near the square, but in the bottom near the creek, became "Ristycrat Hill," and then, without envy or irony, but with a great, hairy-lipped, stained-toothed, snag-toothed guffaw, "Rusty-Butt Hill." And "Rusty-Butt Hill" it has remained for all except realtors and the ladies who live in the old brick houses and see their husbands off every working morning to the insurance office, factory, office, bank, warehouse, or drug store.

Bolton Lovehart, the great-great-grandson of Lem Lovehart, lives in a house well down the hill, not one of the finest houses but safely situated on the hill. You will probably not notice the house, for it is not remarkable, except that its lawn has run to weeds and the gate is missing from the wrought-iron fence. And almost certainly you will not see Bolton Lovehart, a tall, emaciated man of sixty-seven, with no hair on his head, a gray, drooping mustache about his sweet mouth, no buttons on his wrinkled coat, and restless, clever, long-fingered hands, liver spots on the thin skin over the blue veins. You will not see him, for he, in all likelihood, will be in the attic, with the circus.

Bolton Lovehart was born in the house, the son of a man who had been a major in the Confederate Army and was, at the time of the birth, an Episcopalian minister, and of a woman whose disappointment in the marriage bed was almost forgotten in her passion for the Episcopal Church, her sickly, late-born son, and the name of "Bolton." Her passion for the first two was really an extension of her passion for the third, for only by contact with Bolton blood did the Episcopal Church (her father had been the local rector) and her son achieve their sanctity.

"Love" was not the name for her feeling for her child, which, with its very intensity of egotism, became a selfless and absorbing passion. But since there is no other name to give it and since the name, "love," has been applied to other passions equally dark and deep, it can be used for whatever it was that possessed her and possessed the child with a thousand invisible threads controlling the slightest movement of his limbs and lips and spirit like a clever puppet with beautiful chestnut curls and a lace collar on the velvet jacket.

On Sunday mornings in spring, neighbors saw the little boy, between the tall, black-garbed man and the bony, taut-faced, black-garbed woman, move down the brick walk, flanked by the rows of yellow jonquils under the oaks, moving toward the iron gate and the stone carriage block and iron hitching post surmounted by a horse's head. The little boy set his neat little booted feet (the little black boots had red buttons) on the moss-crusted bricks with the motion of prinking precision and appealing weakness, as if each step were in itself a new problem, considered and solved. The man and woman adjusted their pace to his, and it seemed forever down the thirty yards from the portico to the gate. As we look back on them, down the sixty years, they scarcely seem to move at all, to be fixed there in a photograph in an album to prove something sweet and sure about the past. But they finally reach the gate, which creaks on its hinges, and move, at the same rate, down the brick sidewalk toward St. Luke's Church.

The man, Simon Lovehart, moves with his eyes fixed down the street, as though unaware of his companions and of the street itself. He is, however, aware of them at times, in the middle of the night or on the spring street, aware of the powerful, vibrating, multitudinous web of life which binds the woman and child together, victor and victim (but which is which? he asks himself: is the present the victim of the past, or the past the victim of the present?), and when he is aware of that web and the million dark, pulsing tentacles, he feels that he stands at the end of something, on a promontory, lost, with a distant wind rushing somewhere in the night far behind him. He no longer has regrets as he stands there. He is past regrets. Should the wind blow upon him, he would draw up his coat and button it. When he brushes, by accident, against some single filmy strand of the web in his house, he stops dead still and quivers in every nerve.

He attributes his ill health to the old wound, the minnie ball that he carries in his thigh and that gives him his distinguished, scarcely disturbing limp. His left leg throbs in the night and he often lies awake for hours. When weather is brooding or the season moves into winter, the leg reminds him. The minnie ball, the size and shape of a man's thumb-tip, long since washed lovingly clean by his blood, lies precious and heavy in its warm, secret purse of his innermost flesh like a talisman or jewel, and tells him what he needs to know. It absolves him and he is lucky. He is one of the lucky ones who carries with him the explanation of everything. Not every man can prod deep in his thigh and feel his truth the size and shape of a filbert, but heavy as lead. That fact consoles Simon

Lovehart for the shock which flung him from his horse late in the afternoon of the Battle of Franklin to lie and let the hurly-burly sweep monstrously past. Man wants to know the truth and if he knows the truth he can live past all passion, and Simon Lovehart has the truth. He has the minnie ball in his thigh and the prayer book in his hand, and as he walks down the street with his wife and son he knows what he needs to know. The minnie ball and the book, they are his rod and his staff and they comfort him.

The neighbors saw little Bolton Lovehart move down the walk with his mother and father, between the jonquils. They saw him, older, let us say nine years old, walk in the wide yard on a sunny autumn afternoon, the curls on his head more discreet now, wearing tight little blue serge trousers cut off at the knee, with three buttons on the outside seam of each leg, just above the bottom. He walked slowly about the yard, peering on the ground as though he had lost something there in the brittle carpet of tawny oak leaves. He scuffed the leaves with his feet, but ever so gently.

"No," his mother had said, "you cannot go to play at the Allston house."

"Why?"

"It is not for you to question your mother. But I will tell you. The Allstons are common."

"What is 'common'?"

" 'Common' is what you must never be."

The neighbors saw him walk among the oak leaves, but they did not see him at those moments when Mrs. Lovehart would fling herself to her knees and suddenly seize him, driving her fingers into his thin back, and crush him to her bosom and crouch thus for minutes in the emptiness of one of the rooms where shadows depended like black gauze from the high ceiling. He has learned to accept this and stands patiently until she pushes him from her, rises abruptly, utters a gasp like pain, and takes her taut, yellow-tinted face from the room, into another room much like the first.

He was a good child, always obedient and studious. He read a great deal. He read the Bible and history books which his father gave him or which he took from his father's study. He had a collection of flint arrowheads gathered along the bluff back of his house. He collected stamps and knew the names of the capitals of all the countries on the big map, and the colors which they were painted on the map. He sometimes thought of himself high in the sky and looking down like God on all the world to see the countries shining with those colors in the sun. He kept his treasures in a big attic room, with the cavalry saber which his father had once unbelievably worn and wielded, and the regimental flag, from which the blue and red had unevenly faded. His mother thought that he would be a minister.

He was a good child until the summer of 1892, just before he was twelve years old. Then, quite unexpectedly, even to himself, he committed the piece of misbehavior which brought scandal into the town and caused his parents such embarrassment. One of the sects of Baptists was having a revival down in the settlement along Cadman's Creek. On still August evenings the sound of singing, though fainter than a whisper, merely a kind of rhythmic pulse in the air, came up even as far as Rusty-Butt Hill. On the last Sunday afternoon in August, the revival concluded with a big baptizing in the creek, just above the settlement, where the community waste did not pollute the waters.

That Sunday afternoon Bolton Lovehart walked out of his gate and down the hill, through town, and down to the creek. He told himself that he wanted to hunt for arrowheads down by the creek. John Sanders, a schoolmate of his, had found a flint ax-head down there. When he got as far down as Gupton's Mill, already in the nineties an abandoned mass of stonework, he heard the singing upstream. But he could see nothing, for the thickets of cane and the big shaggy willows along the stream, and the shag-bark hickories on the flat ground just back from the creek bank. He walked upstream among the weeds in the old field beside the thicket and trees. An old dog, some kind of hound bitch, the yellow hide peeled-looking over the slat ribs, had followed him down from among the shacks at the foot of the rise, and now continued after him at a respectful distance. When the dog kept after him, he turned and shouted for it to go away. It stood, fifteen feet away, and looked mournfully, searchingly at him, like guilt. He shouted again, and took a few steps on his way. The dog followed. He stooped and gathered up several stones. He hurled them, one after another, at the animal. The animal did not turn or flinch, but stood there, tail down, head down, front legs bent, waiting for the stones. The last stone struck it on the head with a flat, wooden sound. The dog did not stir or whimper. It stood there before the boy like an image of medieval hunger and scabrous, slack-dugged humility and mournful, infinite forgiveness, and shivered in the blaze of August light.

The boy was almost sick with rage and hatred, and standing there, with the eyes upon him, he felt suddenly lost, bewildered, and friendless. He felt that he had no place to go in the wide world, that nobody knew his name. When he proceeded up the creek toward the sound of singing, he resolutely did not look back. The dog followed him no farther.

At a bend in the creek, where the willows broke, he saw the singers. A gravel bar ran out here into the stream, making a riffle where the water found its way across the narrows, and damming a wide pool above. The people stood on the bank and out on the gravel bar, singing. The boy approached them, almost unnoticed. If one pair of eyes had truly fixed upon him, he would have gone away, to wander in the world, his sense of lostness and friendlessness was so great. But nobody really noticed him. He came closer and moved along the edge of the group, noiseless as a thought, to the edge of the gravel bar where he could see.

The tall preacher stood waist-deep in the green water of the pool, which softly undulated even to the farther shore, lapping the drooping boughs of willows and tossing gently the bits of twig and the yellow leaves which floated out into the open. The preacher's black coat dripped and glittered in the sunshine, and to the shining black cloth a few gold willow leaves were stuck, here and there, like spangles. As Bolton Lovehart came out on the bar, a man was leading one of the saved out into the water, a thin girl of fourteen or so, wearing a droopy white dress too big for her. The girl hung back as the water lapped up to her thighs and made the white cloth billow about her like a dancer. The man drew her forward, not too gently. She took one faltering step after him, then turned her head back and swept a wild, wide, imploring look across the sky and field and world of the uplifted singing faces. But the faces, rapt in song, offered her no help or hope. The man's hand tugged at her, drawing her into the deeper water, and suddenly her resistance faltered, her body swayed toward him, and she was drawn forward while the crowd sang, "Let the nearer waters roll. . . ."

She tried with her free hand to force down the white cloth bouffant and wreathing upon the water, but did not entirely succeed.

The preacher took her and swung her so that she faced the people. He lifted one hand to heaven and called her name and said the ritual words in the sudden silence. Then he placed a hand between her shoulder blades for support and started to lower her backward. For an instant she refused to give over, and as he was about to place his other hand upon her face to save her from strangulation, she seized it desperately in both her own and clasped it to her breast. With that, all in one motion, she let herself go, arching her back somewhat, in surrender, and letting her head fall back, with her eyes wide to the sky, as she was plunged beneath the water.

The preacher drew her quickly up. The other man took her and led her toward the gravel bar. There a fat, stubby woman dressed in a respectable black dress waited with arms outstretched, making little whimpering sounds before the song lifted again. Then the woman stepped forward one step into the water, careless of her shoes, and clasped the girl to her, soaking the black dress, then stumbled back, drawing the girl, and sank to her knees still clasping the girl, and shouted above the song, "My baby's saved! My baby's saved! Glory to Jesus and bless His holy name!" The girl stood there in the embrace, the white cloth sticking to her thin, bony body, the wet hair stringing lankly at her neck and over her cheeks, the water running down her pinched, uncertain face.

Another candidate was being led forward, a hulking boy of eighteen or twenty, who marched boldly, step for step with his conductor. Then, later, others, an old man, two women, four or five big children. And then Bolton Lovehart was there at the very edge of the water, waiting, and the man's hand took him and led him forward in the midst of song.

Immediately after his baptism, Bolton Lovehart left the crowd at the creek. But he did not go home immediately. He wandered across the field, then back to the grove near the old mill. He was not yet dry, but he hid in the thicket, under the shag-barks, and waited, for what he was not sure. He could not bring himself to think of going home nor of the night coming on. He could not bear to think of being here alone all night, in the darkness under the trees. He wished that he were dead.

But he did not die, and night did come. Just before dark, matted and damp, muddy to the knees with dust which had stuck to his wet legs, he turned in the gate of his house. He told his mother that he had fallen into the creek at the old mill. As soon as he had been bathed and dressed with clean clothes, his father was summoned to lecture him while his mother stood by with rigid face and clenched hands. By the time his father was ready to go to church for the evening service, the boy was running a high fever. Simon Lovehart had to go to church, but Mrs. Lovehart and Dr. Jordan stayed by the boy's bed.

The next day, Mrs. Lovehart learned the truth. It was all over Bardsville, over breakfast tables, at the groceries, on the humming telephone wires. But illness spared the boy his punishment, and he lay in his big bed, feeling weak and pure and sly, watching light grow on the windows in the morning and fade with evening. He did not want to die now, nor did he want to get well. He wanted to lie here forever, lapped in the long, soft rhythm of day and night, like a tide.

But he did get well, and did go back into the world, where the people were.

Just before Christmas, dressed in a new black suit with a starched white collar, he received his confirmation at St. Luke's.

"Yeah," old Ike Spackman said, leaning over his forge at the blacksmith shop, "yeah, you hear tell how they taken that boy in the 'Piscopal Church? Hear tell how his mammy bought herself the biggest lard kittle in Carruthers County and biled that-air brat a week a-forehand to git the Baptist creek water outen him 'fore them give him a bite and sup of that 'Piscopal Jesus." He slammed the glowing horseshoe in his tongs onto his anvil and gave it a couple of preliminary strokes of the hammer. "Yeah," he said, "but bet hit didn't do no good. You cain't bile a Baptist baptizen outer nobody. Once in grace, always in grace. Hit is gospel. Bet that brat right this minute is jist as Baptist as air-y mud cat."

But if Bolton Lovehart was as Baptist as any catfish in Cadman's Creek, he did not know it. His life fell back into the old pattern. He read his books and pored over his stamps and arrowheads. He now went to Professor Darter's academy for boys, where he studied hard. He was very good at his Greek and relished the praise which rewarded him.

Then, when he was sixteen, the circus came to town.

When it left, Bolton Lovehart went with it.

His flight, unlike his baptism, was carefully planned, not undertaken on impulse. He waited one afternoon until his mother was out, then brought down a suitcase from the storage room and packed it with a suit of clothes, three shirts, socks, and odds and ends of clothing, a few of his best arrowheads, and some bread and butter. He then carried the suitcase down to the river end of the Lovehart property, the pasture lot back of the unused carriage house, and hid it in a clump of elders and sumac. That night he wrote a strategic note to his mother, saying he was going to Nashville to start life for himself, and slipped downstairs after his parents were asleep (his month's allowance and a ten-dollar gold piece—a Christmas present—in his pocket), got his suitcase, and took the bluffside path to town. It was a starlight night, but he could have followed that hanging goat-track among the cedars and rotten limestone if it had been the darkest night of the year, his feet knew it so well. Not for nothing had he spent the long lonely afternoons back on the bluff, looking over the river.

If his flight, however, was carefully planned, behind that planning lay a necessity as powerful and as unanalyzed as that which had drawn him into the waters of Cadman's Creek. Or as unanalyzable; for if it had been analyzed and then its components in turn analyzed, would he not in the end have had to face, in the innermost darkness—beyond all plans, intentions, and justifications, beyond all the books ever written, the histories and sermons and prayers and the explanations of right and wrong or of heroism or cowardice—the blank-faced need swaying in the dark, coiled like the spring of his being, the unhooded, perpetual eyes gleaming imperially and giving forth the only light in that secret place, fixing deep into his own eyes with the pitiless hypnosis of destiny? But he did not try to analyze. He planned, packed the suitcase, and fled by night down the bluffside to the town, dodged the square, and found the spur track where the circus people were loading their tents, animals, and gear by the light of bonfires and flares.

He hung back, on the verge of the shadows, smelling the smell of smoke and rancid oil and stirred dust and the bold, compelling effluvium of great brutes, hearing the shouted orders and the grumbles and snarls of beasts, watching the tumult which was like a flame-streaked Dionysiac revelry or like the terror-stricken confusion of a barbarous tribe, rich in colored cloths and jangling metals and garish tinsel and savage, symbolic beasts, making ready to flee before the cosmic threat of fire or flood. When the activity had subsided somewhat, and the bonfires had burned out, he managed to hide himself in a car where he had seen men store canvas and crates. An hour later the train jerked and clanked, and undertook a grinding, jouncing motion that gradually evened out into the hum and clippety-clop of wheels on rails. When, fifteen minutes later, the locomotive whistle, far ahead and muffled, gave two blasts, he knew that it was blowing for Bedell's Crossing, ten miles from Bardsville. Shortly after that he fell asleep on the canvas and only awoke with broad day.

The train was motionless now. He sneaked from his hiding. There was nobody about the open space by the track except an old man wearing overalls, lop-sided high-heeled boots, and a sombrero, sitting on a box and eating a sandwich. The old man did not see him get off the car. Bolton could see that the train was on the edge of a city, for roofs and tall buildings were in the distance beyond the sheds on the other side of the cinder-packed loading area. He did not know the name of the city.

He went over to the sheds, walked in their cover on the other side of them from the man, up to a point which would make him seem, when he emerged, to come from the city. Then he approached the old man, said his name was "Joe Randall," and said he wanted a job. He was an orphan, he said.

"You're a God-blasted tom-fool," the old man said, eyeing him with bleared, squint eyes from under the sombrero.

"I want a job," the boy said, feeling strong and certain, and not afraid of the old man. He had never felt this way before. "Anything," he said. "I'll do anything."

"You don't look stout," the old man said, eyeing the stringy, tallish boy with the perspicacity and contempt of a horse trader inspecting an inferior animal.

"I'm stronger than I look," the boy said.

"You're a God-blasted fool," the old man said, "but you kin tote water fer the critters. You kin feed 'em."

The old man was one of the menagerie hands, nameless in the circus but for the name "Tim," old, chivvied about, broken. He saw a week, maybe two weeks ahead, a time in which he could boss the boy about, loaf a little on his job, before whatever happened that would happen about the tom-fool kid who wasn't any more an orphan than he was the Angel Gabriel. Whatever happened, it would not be his fault. He didn't know anything. He hadn't said he would pay anything. There was always some grub, scraps from the mess car.

So Bolton Lovehart toted water and lugged baskets and buckets of food for the animals, bloody messes of meat or damp mixtures of stuff, and tossed hay, under the direction of the old man. The first day somebody stole his suitcase. He didn't care. He didn't care about anything, not even his sore back and aching arms or the nausea of fatigue. He ate scrap food which Tim provided and slept on straw in a boxcar.

On the afternoon of the second day, just before the show opened, a burly man in a gray tweed suit, with a cigar and diamond ring, came up to him. "What's your name?" he demanded.

"Joe Randall," the boy replied.

"You're a lying little snot," the man said. Then, "Look here, I want to know your name. I'm manager of this show and, by God, I'm not going to have any trouble with the cops on account of some lying little snot. What's your name?"

"Joe Randall," the boy said, and still felt the sweet, unaccustomed strength and certainty under his fear.

The manager was about to say something, but just then another man came hurrying up and spoke to him.

"I'll fix you later," the manager promised the boy, and turned away.

That afternoon after the show, the detective and Simon Lovehart came. The note about going to Nashville and Mrs. Lovehart's fear of scandal had delayed their arrival. But here they were, standing in the middle of the circus lot, among the tents and cages and bedlam, with Bolton Lovehart, no longer strong and certain, before them.

That evening they took the train out of Memphis to Bardsville.

Once back home, everything was as it had been before. The boys at the academy that fall, it is true, tried to make him tell them about the circus. He was, for the moment, a kind of hero among them. But he could not even enjoy that. The memory was like an old sore healing slowly, or a broken bone retarding his motions, making him careful of gesture or speech. But there were his books. He could read the books, get the praise of teacher or parent, spend hours in the attic with the stamps and flag and saber and arrowheads (the best ones gone now, missing with the stolen suitcase), sit on the bluffside in the smoky autumn afternoons, walk wordlessly about the house, putting his feet down carefully on the betraying floor, or, when his parents spoke to him, answering dutifully, "Yes, Mother." Or, "Yes, Father." Or, "Yes, Mother, yes. I'm sorry I made you nervous. Yes, I'll sit still." He learned to sit very still, spying on her yellow-tinted face at the edge of the circle of lamplight.

He graduated from the academy, first in his class. His prize was a Greek Testament, delivered to him by Professor Darter up on the platform. His mother and father talked of sending him to college that fall, to the University of the South, the Episcopal university, up at Sewanee, Tennessee, in the mountains. He thought of the mountains. He had never seen mountains, only pictures—the Himalayas, the Matterhorn, Pike's Peak, Mt. Shasta, the Andes, pictures in books—great crags reared like masonry, the black pines, and beyond, the glittering, white Saturnian purity of the peak under the stars. He knew Sewanee would not be like that, but the picture was in his head, in his dreams. He knew that the mountains in East Tennessee were not like that, just big hills with trees on them, just bigger hills than the hills in Carruthers County. Sewanee was just more of Tennessee. But the picture was there and would not go away.

Then his father died. Simon Lovehart had a stroke as he walked one morning in early September up the brick walk to his house. He fell across the mossed bricks, among the few premonitory, tawny, little oak leaves and the now faded green spears of the jonquil plants bordering the walk. Mrs. Lovehart saw him fall. She ran from the house and crouched by his side, under the oaks, lifting her head to utter wild cries of anguish that might have been wild cries of triumph. And in the sequel they were wild cries of triumph; for no one knows the meaning of the cry of passion he utters until the flesh of the passion is long since withered away to show the austere, logical articulation of fact with fact in the skeleton of Time.

The neighbors heard the cries, came to carry the man into his house, and laid him in his bed. Simon Lovehart revived and lay with his long limbs outstretched and his eyes closed. He had known it all before, long before on the field of Franklin, the shock that unhorsed him and flung him to earth under the thunder and tattered swirl of smoke and failing plunge of the banners. And he knew again, in the foreshortening and fusion of time, the pure, essential astonishment at the clap of peace out of fury. *Everything is so easy,* he thought, marveling, *everything in the world.* But he had known this a long time now. So he lay there for two more days and nights, dying with a decorous and cunning celerity like spilled quicksilver finding its way down a dark rat-hole.

Before he died, after strength enough for speech had come back to him, Bolton Lovehart came in to see him. The boy stood by the bed, waiting, hearing the grind and wheeze of breathing in the gloom. Then he said: "Father." Then: "Father."

"It—is—all right—son," the voice from the bed said, like a voice from a long way off and a long time back.

He knelt by the bed, holding one of his father's hands, cold and waxy to his touch. He thought his heart would burst, and mixed with his grief was a sense of discovery, the discovery of the man on the bed. A thousand questions leaped into his mind. He felt that he had to ask his father those questions, now, now before it was too late: *Father, what was the name of that old coon dog you had when you were a boy—I forgot his name, Father—Father, what was the name of the Wilcox boy, the boy you played with when you were little—Father, did it hurt when you were shot, Father— Father, what book did you like best when you were growing up— Father, did you ever talk to General Forrest—Father, did you hunt arrowheads when you were a boy—Father—* But he knew that it was too late, he would never know those things, for they were slipping through his fingers, like a handful of water dropping onto dry sand, and he heard the distant voice again, saying: "Be good—to your mother—son. She is a—good woman—she means—everything —for your good—son—"

He listened to the voice, which was like a weary explanation, an apology, promised to be good, and left the room. An hour later Simon Lovehart was dead.

The boy did not go to Sewanee that fall. He lived the life he had lived before, except for the fact that he did not go to the academy now. He read a great deal, the books he thought the freshmen would be studying up at Sewanee. He walked along the bluffs. He sat in the evenings with his mother, the lamp between them on the living room table.

In June, Sam Jackson, a friend from the academy who had gone to Sewanee the fall before, came back to Bardsville. On the summer afternoons, Sam would sit for hours on the porch with Bolton, telling him about Sewanee, answering his questions. Then they would go up to the attic or out to the bluffs. Mrs. Lovehart, sitting in the shadows of the living room, just inside the open window, would listen to every word they spoke, and as she listened, her heart was like stone in her breast. But it was worse when they went off to the attic or wandered down by the bluffs where she could not follow them and hear.

One day at dinner she said to her son, "Son, don't you think you ought to begin to get ready to go?"

"Go where?"

"Why, to Sewanee. This fall."

She watched the flash of animation on the boy's face, saw the hand tremble with which he laid the fork on the plate. "Mother—" he managed to begin. "Mother, I didn't know—why, I—"

She briskly cut him off. "You must get ready to go," she said. "You must write for admission again. I must get your clothes ready. There are so many things. You must go." And added, with a quick glance at his face: "You must not think of me."

"Mother—" he began.

"You are young," she said. "You must not think of me."

They finished the meal in silence.

He went to Sewanee. At Christmas he came home. His mother gave him a party with Sam Jackson and some of the boys from the academy class and their girls. Sara Darter, daughter of Professor Darter, came as Bolton's girl. They drank grape-juice punch, and ate sandwiches and cakes, and sang Christmas songs. Bolton went to parties at the houses of the other boys and girls on the hill. And back home, late at night, his mother would wait up for him, to ask him questions about the party or about Sewanee and to tell him how happy and proud she was that he had done good work. He went back to Sewanee in January.

But he was back home again by the first of March. His mother had had a heart attack. She was never to be well again. Her bed was moved down to the little back sitting room on the first floor, with a table of medicine bottles, a Bible and a prayer book beside it. On good days she sat propped on pillows in a big basket chair, staring through the windows, if it was summer, or into the fire, if it was winter. Bolton spent much of his time with her. Almost always he prepared her medicine. "I don't mind it—I really don't," she would say, "when you give it to me." And she would smile up at him from the pillows. She had grown almost pretty after the heart attack, young-looking, fresh, and clear-eyed, the yellow hue gone from her complexion, with a shy virginal quality which she must have had as a very young girl when Major Simon Lovehart, the veteran with the distinguished limp, had come to court her.

Bolton went on with his studies, reading his father's books, borrowing books from Professor Darter, ordering books from Nashville or Louisville. In the next summer, when Sam Jackson was home from Sewanee, he slyly interrogated him, and thought: *I've learned more than Sam. I know more than Sam.* He went to parties that summer, but he always came home early—to give his mother her medicine. And sometimes after he had given her the draught, he would go up to his room to read, or if the weather was not too hot, to the big attic, and he might hear music from beyond the trees or catch the flicker of Japanese lanterns strung across a lawn up the hill.

Late in the summer, his mother suggested that he go back to Sewanee. Not then, but the second term. "I want you to go," she said. "I want you to be happy. I went down into the Valley of the Shadow for you, son, and I want you to be happy."

"I know more than Sam Jackson," he said, and got up and left the room.

So the next four years passed, the parties fewer and fewer for him each summer and Christmas vacation, as the faces changed, as the boys and girls he had known married and settled down, or moved away. He could not talk to the younger boys, and the young girls were like strangers. And he was strange to them, a lanky young man with thinning black hair and very clean, unfashionable clothes that always looked awry on his nervous bones. He saw more of Professor Darter than of anyone else. And of Sara Darter.

He thought he was in love with Sara Darter. She was a thin, nervous girl, with big black eyes straining out of the dead white of her face. She might, in appearance, have been his sister. She was two years older than he. She knew how to make him feel at ease. He wrote poems and mailed them to her. And when they were alone together in Professor Darter's living room in the evening, before he had to go home to give his mother her medicine, they would clutch and cling, kissing with a desperate and sad excitement, waiting for the Professor's shuffling step in the hall.

He was writing a book. Or rather, he was getting ready to write a book. It was to be the history of Carruthers County. "Bolton is writing a book," Mrs. Lovehart would confide to the Episcopalian ladies who dutifully came to call. And when the husbands of those ladies would say to their wives, "That Lovehart boy, he ought to be getting a job. The old lady is living off her capital, I bet. Simon was well fixed, but it won't last forever," the wives would say that Bolton was writing a book. That explained everything. He began to make talks to the Bardsville Ladies' Study Club and to the St. Luke's Men's Bible Class. The Bardsville *Gazette* recorded each event: "Mr. Bolton Lovehart, one of our most promising young authors . . ."

But Bolton did get a job. He got a job teaching in Professor Darter's academy. He taught there two winters. It was understood between him and Sara that they were to be married. When things got straightened out. Then Professor Darter died.

He left no money. Just the house and a mortgage on it and enough to put him decently underground. Bolton ran the academy for the rest of the year. Sara Darter wept often now, and Bolton tried to comfort her. But once when he put his arms around her and tried to kiss her, she struck him savagely on the chest, with clenched fists, and screamed at him with furious words which he could not interpret.

For a month after that she was very calm, submitting to his caresses when he came to see her, breathing shallowly and staring across the room. Then one night she said, "You've got to get a specialist to see your mother."

"But Dr. Jordan, he—"

But she cut him off. "If you don't do it," she declared, "I won't marry you."

He saw Dr. Jordan. "Son," the doctor said, "I don't mind you getting in anybody. I'm just an old country doctor, and it won't hurt my feelings. A heart's a funny thing, now. It's not like appendicitis or lockjaw or a gunshot. A heart is right in the middle of a man, or a woman for that matter, and in a manner of speaking it is them themselves. In a manner of speaking."

"What do you mean?" Bolton demanded.

The doctor studied the young man's face. Then he shrugged. "Nothing," he said. "It is just a manner of speaking. Of saying a doctor don't know much. Leastways, not an old country doctor like me, in a town like Bardsville."

"Will you get a specialist?"

"Son," Dr. Jordan said, "it won't hurt my feelings. That time I tried—I tried two or three times, now I recollect—your mother wouldn't hear of it. Nigh bit my head off. She said—"

"You tried?"

"Sure, son. Didn't you know?"

Bolton Lovehart stood there in the middle of the cluttered office, breathing the dusty odor of the worn horsehair furniture and the metallic tang of disinfectant, and his own heart took a leap and turn in his bosom like a bass when it strikes the barb. "You tried?" he demanded in a whisper.

"Sure, son."

"Do it!" Bolton Lovehart said with sudden authority, feeling the surge of strength and certainty that he had felt twelve years before, that morning when he had stood before the old circus roustabout and demanded a job.

"Son," Dr. Jordan said, studying him, "you get your mother's consent, and it suits me."

"I'll get it," Bolton declared.

It all seemed easy as he walked home down the familiar street in broad day. It was easy, and everything was going to be different. And it seemed easy that night, when, after he had given his mother her medicine, he stood by the bed and looked down at her. She seemed so frail and innocent, with that clear girlish quality, so willless and trusting. It would be easy. So he told her, in detail, how he was worried that she got no better, that he had seen Dr. Jordan, that Dr. Jordan had agreed to having a specialist in, a big man from Nashville, from the university there.

It had been easy. She lay there perfectly silent while his reasonable voice went on, her clear eyes on him, and he almost thought that he detected a smile on her lips. So he smiled back and leaned as though to pat her hand.

He had almost touched her before he caught the words she was saying. She was speaking in a vibrant whisper through the lips that still seemed to smile, saying: "You—you, my son—to sneak behind my back. Oh, it is heinous! To sneak behind my back, like a thief. When I am ill. When I am the mother that bore you. That went down into the Valley of the Shadow. Oh, it is heinous. And you sneak and conspire—" The words came out, the vibrant, sibilant whisper, from the lips that still seemed to smile.

"Mother!" he exclaimed. "Mother!" And tried to take her hand.

But she heaved herself back in the bed, half rising. "Don't touch me!" she cried. "Oh, you are all against me. Everybody! Everybody! Don't touch me," she cried as he tried to take her hand. "It is the kiss of Judas! Oh, you want me dead, you want me to die!"

She swept her arm wide, knocking two bottles from the table, lunging back against the headboard as though to elude an attacker.

"Mother!" he exclaimed.

"Oh, you want me to die—flesh of my flesh, and you want me to die!" And she uttered again the wild, undecipherable, ambiguous, untranslatable cries which she had uttered by the fallen body of Simon Lovehart among the tawny oak leaves of autumn and the spears of jonquil plants.

Then she fell back, gasping and panting, pale as a sheet, clutching her bosom, seemingly unconscious, with the smile returned to her lips.

Dr. Jordan arrived. He worked over her a long time before she came to. Then her eyes fixed on her son. "Go," she said, in the same whisper as before, "go from my sight!"

He went and stood in the hall, waiting.

Dr. Jordan finally came out, closed the door softly behind him, and said, "She's in a bad way."

"Will she—" Bolton Lovehart began, "will she—" But he could not speak the word, "die."

"Will she die?" Dr. Jordan framed the question for him. He shook his head. "I don't know, son. I'm an old country doctor, and I don't know. But I do know this: we better get that specialist."

Bolton Lovehart could not speak. He could not say why he could not get the specialist. His lips worked, but he could not speak.

Dr. Jordan inspected his face under the hanging electric bulb of the back hall. (The house had been wired a few years before.) Then Dr. Jordan shrugged slightly. "Maybe," he said, "maybe it'll all come out all right." He turned and went into the front hall and picked up his flappy old panama from the table.

Bolton Lovehart still stood in the back hall, under the hanging bulb, long after the front door had closed.

Mrs. Lovehart was very sick for a long time, about a month. Then she sat again in her basket chair in the living room, looking across the lawn. Everything was as though nothing had happened, as though that night had been nothing but a bad dream now lost in the honest daylight. Neither ever said a word about it to the other.

Bolton Lovehart, however, had to say something to Sara Darter. After his mother was better, he told her exactly what had happened, or at least those parts which he could bear to tell, and apologized for withholding the truth earlier. "So you see, Sara," he wound up. "Yes," she said, "I see." And patted his hand.

The next night when he came to see her, she seduced him with a cold, pertinacious, clumsy methodicalness based on dark hints and whispered lore and inept experiment, there on the red plush sofa in Professor Darter's parlor, under the portrait of Professor Darter and the serried eyes of dead grandfathers and grandmothers peering through the gloom, while from the room above came the faint rhythmic creak of the rocking chair of the old aunt who now lived in the house.

The next day Sara Darter left Bardsville. She had borrowed five hundred dollars from Mr. Dorrity, vice president of the bank, an old friend of her father. She went to Nashville, enrolled in a secretarial school, and later got a job in the city. The house was sold a few months after her departure, and every stick of furniture, every plate and cup, the pictures on the walls, the carefully mended linen in the drawers, the knickknacks and souvenirs from the mahogany whatnot. "Everything," the ladies of Bardsville whispered, "literally everything. Sold. Even her mother's wedding dress. I saw it at the auction. Thrown down like an old dust rag. That girl, she has no heart." And again: "Throwing her poor old aunt out in the world. After she had come to take care of her. That poor old woman. Not a place to lay her head, and that girl her nearest of blood."

Sara Darter did not hear the whispers or catch the sidewise glances, sharp as pins. She took her school course, got her job, and after a while married an insurance salesman, a widower, in the office where she worked. She had left Bardsville, and she never came back. The plan for her leaving, however, had come to her suddenly, like a revelation, the day before that last evening with Bolton Lovehart. That last encounter with him had not been part of the plan. Or if it was a part, it was a part that had not showed itself above the surface of the stream, where the trivial debris and drift moiled and spun in the light, but wallowed in the dark central depth of the current, like an old log, black and waterlogged, sucked up from the mud, and borne in secret to the rock-tossed, rapid narrows where the waters boiled over with a last fury into the placid reaches below, and where in that final, funneled rush the unwieldy inner burden heaved and lunged upward, black, blunt, big, and dripping, like a blind fish from a cave, hurled into light.

She had not planned the act, and once it was accomplished, she did not speculate about its meaning and motive. Once done, it seemed like something which had always had its existence, waiting not for her doing but for her recognition. It was done, but it had always existed, even before her doing, an expiation *or* a vengeance, or an expiation *and* a vengeance, inextricably interfused, the violent act caught like the very face of life between two mirrors, to be reflected, mirror within answering mirror, expiation and vengeance, vengeance and expiation, forever in opposite directions, forever toward the inwardness of self and forever toward the outwardness of the world, into twin infinities. But expiation for what? Vengeance on whom? Sara Darter did not have to answer those questions. Instead, she had to live, and she took the already packed suitcase out from under her bed the next morning, in the room grown suddenly strange, like the room where one stops overnight after a disaster, and caught the ten-forty train.

She was gone, and behind her were the voices, which say everything if we hear them, and which say nothing if we do not hear them. And Bolton Lovehart did not hear them. What he heard was nothing, and what he knew was a victory and a betrayal. One of those things is enough to live by, and if you have both, you can live, and he lived. He lived in the way people live, by finding life where he could find it. Which is always easy, for every act justifies itself like a flower, and every day, like the step of a child, is its own problem and its own solution. And years are nothing but so many days laid end to end. If you can live one day you can live forever.

In 1913 the first moving picture house in Bardsville opened. There had been moving pictures before, in tents, with the drone of the projecting machine and the tinkle of the piano like the moment in a revival meeting when the piano strikes a few notes, waiting in the eddy of silence for the singers to catch breath and drown the music, and now waiting for the locomotive to plunge forward, thunderless but for the frantic bass of the piano, or waiting for the horse and rider to come plunging across the screen with soundless hoofs. But now the moving pictures were to be in a real theater. It was the old opera house, where traveling companies had come to play *Thorns and Orange Blossoms* and *The Widowed Bride,* with preposterous stances and an excess of emotion. Now signs painted on canvas were hung out front, and there was a booth with a glass front where tickets were to be sold. Miss Lucile MacIntyre, who had taught music in Bardsville for thirty years, was to be at the piano. Bolton Lovehart got the job of collecting tickets at the inside door.

He collected tickets for two weeks, every evening except Sunday, and on Saturday afternoons. He stood in the cramped lobby, with his trousers too short on his bony shanks and his sleeves too short on the wrists, stooping forward to take the ticket with a kind of creaky ceremoniousness, like an old man being gallant to a young girl. (But he was not an old man, only thirty-three.) And when the face above the proffered ticket was one he had known on the hill from boyhood, he would say gravely, "Good evening, Miss Liza," or, "Good evening, Mr. Lawrence, I hope you enjoy the performance," with the air of an impresario. Then, when everybody was inside, and the show was on, he would slip to the door of the theater and stand in the shadow, and peer through a crack in the heavy red curtain at the screen, where Ben Hur whirled across in his victorious chariot or some dark-haired, full-busted beauty in a black dress, gorgeous with jewels and fringes, jerkily paced a rich room and wept or flung herself passionately into the arms of an obviously panting lover wearing a dress shirt, while Miss Lucile MacIntyre's piano defined, like a machine, the motion of the soul.

This lasted for two weeks.

One evening he came home after the show and went to his mother's room to give her the medicine. As he entered, he saw that she was propped up against the bare headboard of the bed, ignoring the pillows, staring at him. "Mother—" he said in alarm. "Mother, are you worse?"

"Yes," she replied, "I am worse. To know what I know."

"I'll call Dr. Jordan. Why didn't you ring for Marybelle to get him? I'll—"

But she stopped him with an abrupt gesture. "Come here," she commanded. And when he stopped at the foot of the bed, she gestured again. "Closer," she said. And he came around to the side where the medicine table was.

"Where have you been?" she asked.

"At the show," he said.

"Yes," she said, and echoed, "at the show."

He waited, stifling a crazy impulse to run from the room, from the house.

"At the show," she whispered. And whispered again, "No shame. To lie to me. To go behind my back. Your own mother, who gave you life. Who gave you suck. Have you no shame?"

"Mother—" he began.

"To bring shame on me. You, my son—a common ticket-taker. Oh, your father would turn in his grave. A ticket-taker."

"I've got to do something," he burst out. "I'm thirty-three. I've got to do something."

"You don't have to do that. And lie and sneak to do it. You have your work. You have your book. You can finish your book. And then I'll be proud of you."

"Yes," he said, "I can finish my book."

"Promise me," she said, keeping her eyes on him, "that you will not go back there. That you will not shame me. That you will let me live out my life and not spit on me as I bear my cross. That you will not place thorns on my brow."

He did not speak for a moment.

"Promise me," she said, her voice again in a whisper.

"I promise," he said, whispering, too.

"Come closer," she said. "Give me your hand," she said.

He did so, and she drew him down. He sank to his knees by the bed. "My son," she said, and placed her hand on his head. It was light as a feather, but enough to make his head sink against the covers, while she patted his head and toyed with his hair and he felt the coldness of the fingers where she touched the bald spot in the back.

Then she said, "Son, you are right. You must do something. I'll take my affairs out of Mr. Dorrity's hands. You can manage my affairs. Then you will be ready when I pass on to the Other Shore. I shall pay you. I shall pay you well. You can manage my affairs. And write your book. Then I can die happy. And be proud that you are my son."

The voice went on and on, and the fingers toyed with his hair.

The next day he went back to his book, the piles of notes and the pages of manuscript written in a large, irregular, boyish hand, the history of Carruthers County—Carruthers County, where Bardsville was and where Lem Lovehart, so many years before, had lain down on the bluff amid the last birdsong of a June evening and wept. But Bolton Lovehart knew nothing of that, and in the chapter already written about the founding of the town—called "The Coming of the Fathers"—there was, of course, no mention of the episode.

He could not work in his room. Nothing would come right. And so he moved his table to the attic.

That winter, just after Christmas, he began to make the circus. One day in middle December he had gone to the square on an errand, to talk with Mr. Dorrity at the bank, in fact, and had seen the toy exhibit in the windows of Sellars' Hardware Store. He had stood there a long time before the window. In the middle of the window, dominating the exhibit, was a circus. There were wooden animals, painted, with jointed legs. The lions and tigers sat on little platforms. An elephant reared on a tub. There was a ring master dressed in black cloth, a girl acrobat with a stiff little skirt and a painted smirk on her face and eyes far too large and blue, a clown swathed in spotted cloth, balancing on top of a ladder, held there by a slot in his wooden foot. After a while Bolton Lovehart tore himself from the window and went on to the Planter's Fidelity Bank to see Mr. Dorrity, whose friendly burden of the Lovehart affairs had been doubled since Bolton Lovehart had undertaken to handle them. Mr. Dorrity now had to spend hours with him every month.

That same day Bolton Lovehart got some soft pine from the lumber yard, and bought a strong jackknife and a set of water colors. He laid those things on a shelf in his attic and did not touch them for ten days. He worked at the book. But the wood and paints and knife were there. The day after Christmas, late in the evening, long after he had given his mother the medicine and kissed her good night, in the timeless silence of the night, he began.

It took him a week to make the tiger. It was a silly-looking, stiff-legged thing, blunt-headed, not much like a tiger. When he tried to paint it, he found that the wood absorbed the water colors like a blotter and blurred all outlines. So he had to get oil paints. He had to order them from Nashville. He waited impatiently all the days before the package arrived. Then the colored girl, Marybelle, delivered it to the hand of his mother. He had to lie to her.

He told her that he was going to make a map of Carruthers County. He felt no guilt about the lie and was surprised at himself.

The tiger was a poor thing, but when the color was on and it stood before him on his table, he felt, for a moment, the tremulous echo of the old excitement he had felt that night, years back, when he stood in the shadows and watched the flame-streaked, hoarse tumult as the circus was loaded.

The next animal, a lion, was better. And the elephant was better still. He had managed, after two weeks of experiment and effort, to make legs that would bend. By summer he had made a human figure, the ring master, and had dressed it, pricking his fingers at the unaccustomed sewing. He even gave the ring master a ferocious black mustache of a snippet of black yarn glued on. Then he made the girl acrobat, with blue eyes and a skirt of silk. That was his masterpiece.

But beside the masterpiece, the other things looked so sad and inept. He had to begin again. So night after night that summer, in the hot, dead attic air, he would lean over his table, with the sweat dripping from his face down on the wood or metal or cloth. The electric fan which he bought did little good. But he could not work downstairs. For nobody knew what went on up there, behind the always bolted door, in the big room where shadows and cobwebs massed in the corners and hung from the slanting, damp-ringed ceiling, where the arrowheads, long since washed clean of whatever hot blood had stained them, lay in orderly rows on sagging shelves with the albums of stamps, where the notes and books were stacked on a table, where the saber and the faded regimental colors of Simon Lovehart's regiment hung on the wall at the end of a gable. People going home late at night would see the light in the Lovehart attic, a faint gleam beyond the dense oak boughs, and would say, "That Lovehart boy's working on his book. He's a hard worker. Maybe he will amount to something."

Bolton Lovehart did still work at the book. Or at least he would read over the stacks of notes, or take new notes, or perhaps write a page now and then in his boyish script. This was before the time of the monument to Cassius Perkins and Seth Sykes, but he found out what he could about them from old men who gave him fragments of the official story. And he wrote a chapter called "The Battle of Bardsville." But all the writing went slowly. It was easier to gather material. Sometimes he spent whole days at the court house, fumbling through the dusty, sour-smelling papers in the vault of the clerk of the circuit court or of the county court clerk. Or he would hire a boy to drive him in a rig from the livery stable out into the country to talk with some old resident. But all of this was only in the daytime. The nights were his own.

So the months stretched into the year, and the year became another year, and his fingers grew cleverer and cleverer. And with the growth of skill, the passion for perfection grew to torment him. When he finished some new creature to add to the little throng which cluttered the shelves and floor, or devised some new apparatus for the circus, he felt for one moment, up there above the world, the peace and purity of spirit that comes when vision and cunning are commensurate. But next day, after he had risen early to go up to the attic to verify the happiness of the night before, he would spy, in the critical sunlight, some flaw, some ineptitude, and he would almost hate the thing he had made and his fingers would itch for the steady feel of the knife or awl and the softness of the wood. He could scarcely wait for night to come.

As the years grew and the painted eyes of animals and girl acrobats and riders and ring masters and clowns circled about him, so his world constricted to that orbit. He still made talks, but more and more infrequently, to the study club, and the Bardsville *Gazette* still recorded each event with the old phrases: "Mr. Bolton Lovehart, one of our most promising young authors . . ." He still worked at his book, but the words he wrote, like the words he spoke to the club, seemed more and more strange to him, more and more a penance he had to pay for an old crime or a price he had to pay for a new happiness. He went to church every Sunday. He still attended to his mother's affairs, wrote receipts for rent checks, arranged for painters and plumbers to repair, more and more infrequently, the little houses she rented, paid her taxes, and kept her accounts.

The war of 1917-18 came and passed. But it was not for him. He did not even read the papers. The bugles and uniforms were nothing to him, or the tears and kisses and speeches. When the news of the armistice came, when the whistles blew, and the bells rang and people ran out into the street, even there on the hill, and shouted, the noises scarcely reached him in the attic. He did not even bother to come down to find out what the tumult meant.

That night, however, he did go down to the square to see the bonfire and hear the music and the speeches (made from a hastily erected platform at the foot of the Confederate monument in front of the court house) and the shouting and singing. The crowd sang:

> *Smile a while, I've kissed you sad adieu,*
> *When the clouds roll by I'll come to you. . . .*

There in the crowd he did experience a kind of happiness. He was happy in their happiness, with the happiness of a ghost who blesses out of his own steady peace the flickering joy of the living and wishes them well. He could afford to wish them well. He had his own victory.

Then he went back home to his victory, kissed his mother good night, and went up to the attic. The excitement of the night passed. The debris was cleaned from the square, and the platform in front of the monument knocked down. The wounded and the whole came home to listen to greetings on the streets of Bardsville, and then forgot, almost as quickly as others forgot, the event over which the skin grew back, leaving scarcely a scar.

As the years passed, he grew more and more attentive and tender with his mother. She seemed impervious to time, still fresh-cheeked, even though the flesh sagged a little and even though the color seemed to hint sometimes of the mortician's rouge applied with unusual subtlety, still bright-eyed, even though the eyes themselves sank a little more, year by year, into the delicately arched sockets. She lived as though sustained in the heart of a timeless peace, lying among embroidered counterpanes (grown slightly yellow), propped among lace pillows (artfully mended), smiling in benediction. The long lie he lived, the secret locked in the attic and never suspected by a breathing soul, gave him the right to love her perfectly at last. For he hugged a dear truth to him: you can only love perfectly in terms of a great betrayal.

Then she died. She woke up in the middle of the night with a stab of pain and a sudden suffocation, and with astonishment knew that it was her heart. With that first astonishment came the black fear, brute fear like a tremendous maw opening before her. And with the fear were the words in her mind, like the words of another self: *Oh, I won't do it. I won't go, they can't make me go, not now when I've got everything fixed like I want it, when I'm happy,*

oh, so happy, oh, I won't go. I won't go, they can't make me go!
But she knew she was going. The fangs of that great black maw
were closing on her, dripping with cold saliva. Then, suddenly,
fear and refusal were lost in the simple sense of outrage, a stupendous outrage, at the deceitful, sneaking little heart. Oh, it was
heinous! It had lain there inside her all those years, doing her will,
pretending to love her, giving her instant obedience, and planning
this, this, this. Like the kitten she had had as a child, that had
lain on her knee, purring, and then had scratched her, and she had
felt this same outrage and had flung the nasty thing from her, out
of the second-story window, to thud on the bricks of the drive.
Now she clawed at her breast to tear out the treacherous, sneaking
little beast of a heart and fling it away. Oh, she would fix it! She
would never again have a sneaking little heart like this. Oh, this
was worse than the kitten that scratched her. This was worse than
the son, flesh of her flesh, who had sneaked behind her back and
tried to betray her. This was worse than anything, for this was
her own dear heart, herself, herself, doing this to herself, doing
this to Louise Bolton, to pretty little, nice little Louise Bolton. Oh,
she would tell her father!

Then it did it.

That was in 1934, when Mrs. Lovehart was eighty-seven years
old. But next morning when her son found her, she did not, even
then, look her age. In the last instant her face had relaxed, and
except for the paleness, she looked herself, the pretty little old
lady who might smile any moment.

The doctor came, not Dr. Jordan (dead now for years), but a
young man, sun-tanned from the links, full of confidence. "She
probably died very quickly," he said, by way of comfort, snapping
his case shut.

"She died," Bolton Lovehart echoed, musingly, wonderingly, almost in a whisper as to himself. Then to the doctor, out loud, "She
died—look, she died in here, all alone, at night, by herself at
night—"

"It was probably very sudden," the doctor said, with a faint
hint of irritation. "Very little pain, probably. And at her age—"

"She died," Bolton Lovehart whispered, "at night—all by herself."

And he saw himself alone. Forever alone, in the house. And he
would die alone in one of the dark rooms, at night, or in the attic,

falling to the floor among the hateful, painted eyes of the creatures he had made.

He was alone in the house now. The Negro woman came and cooked his meals, and passed a dust cloth wearily over furniture in a kind of ritualistic incompetence, and slammed the back door and went away at first dusk. Bolton Lovehart tried at first to keep on with the old routine, but he found himself sitting there in the attic at his table, doing nothing, brooding into emptiness. The reason for his occupation was gone. The old pleasure was gone, the compulsion. There was no need to lie any more. He wandered the house at night, from room to room, in a blaze of electric light, all the lights turned on. Or he sat in the living room, in the dark, staring out of the window. On some nights he fell asleep in the basket chair and was there all night.

Now and then, the necessity for attending to his affairs would draw him out into the world. He would wander down to the bottoms where the rental houses were, little better than shacks now, falling paintlessly to pieces, and knock at the doors to meet the sullen face of a man or the bitter face of a woman, children peering like animals from about her skirts, and ask for the rent. Sometimes they gave him a little like grudging alms. Sometimes they began to talk in whining or bullying voices, but he could never attend properly to the words they said. Sometimes they said nothing, just looked at him and shut the door, or looked at him, wordlessly, until he wandered off like a man who has been caught in a shameful act. Mr. Dorrity was dead now, and there was nobody to tell him what to say, what to do. But there was a little bank stock left, and that, even in the bad times of the thirties, kept him going.

The bank stock and the church kept him going. The bank stock gave him something to eat. The church gave him a reason for eating. He was no more religious than before, but he went there, to every service. He had not gone much in the last years of his mother's life, but at the funeral people had been kind, even people whose names he had forgotten. The church was a place to go, away from the house, away from the attic, away from himself and all the years.

If it had not been for the church he would never have met Mrs. Parton.

Mrs. Parton was the daughter of a poor, scratch-living farmer in the county just south of Carruthers County, a lean country full of bare limestone and blackjack oak and sassafras, with moonshine stills, even in the days before Prohibition, back in the cedar thickets. She had married Mr. Parton when she was just a girl and he was a drummer for a wholesale hardware company, working that district. But back about 1920, Mr. Parton had got the agency for a cheap automobile in Bardsville and had prospered, begotten a son, and had died, leaving Mrs. Parton with a fair bank account to make her way as best she could in the life of Bardsville.

Mr. Parton had been no asset to Mrs. Parton's ambitions. He had been definitely common, with his chewed cigar, his back slapping, his country drummer's manner. But pretty little blonde Mrs. Parton had caught on fast. Out of the corner of her innocent, china-blue eyes she watched what people were like, and her tight little mind snapped up and ticketed away every bit of old gossip or new scandal, every tone of contempt or admiration. In the end she knew Bardsville better than Bardsville knew itself. And knowledge is power.

Knowledge is power and patience can move mountains. Mrs. Parton was nothing if not patient. She could wait. She never obtruded herself. She never took a step before she was sure of her footing. She was willing and unresentful and agreeable, and she carried her head modestly. She had seen every rung of the ladder, every stage of the ascent, but nobody suspected her knowledge. She joined the PTA when her child was in school, and was active in the Presbyterian Church. Then she learned to play "five hundred" and joined a card club. She watched her grammar. She subscribed to a national organization which sent her a good book every month, and she sometimes read the book. She had gone in for color on her clothes when she first came to Bardsville, but the right magazines and the sight of certain ladies on the streets had modified her ideas. By 1930 she was a member of the Episcopal Church, but the transition from Presbyterianism had been so gradual that people scarcely noticed it. By 1934 she had learned to drink cocktails. "Just one," she would say, "just one. Oh, no, thank you, I only take one." And she never took but one, or at most two, in public, though now and then, safe at home, in the evening, she would pull the shades and make herself a shakerful and drink it and go to bed and lie hot and dizzy and shaking in the dark, and feel her body flow tinglingly away from her. But she knew what she wanted. There was still a long way to go from her pleasant little brick house, tastefully decorated according to the magazines, at the foot of Rusty-Butt Hill.

She married Bolton Lovehart, and moved into the house. In one sense, though neither she nor Bolton Lovehart knew it, she had as much right to be in the house as he did. For Lovehart blood was in her veins, too. She, too, was descended from old Lem Lovehart, by the daughter he had left when the Chickasaw scalped him. That daughter had married a settler of Bardsville who then pioneered into the scrub country to the south, where the recollection of Lovehart was lost and only the secret blood in the veins remained.

Mrs. Parton was then in her late thirties, still prettyish, a little full in the body, but with the innocent china-blue eyes and good ankles. Bolton Lovehart was fifty-nine. That was in 1939.

She made few changes in the Lovehart house except to bring order and cleanliness. The old furniture and knick-knacks, shabby and battered as they were, kept their places. She was too smart to be caught in that trap. Changes could come later, if there were changes to be made. She knew that the attic room was always locked with a good padlock, but after the first questions she held her peace. Her husband had said that that was where he kept his books and papers, his "work," his "book," and that he didn't want anything disturbed. A few times when he was out of the house, she did try to open the lock with a batch of old keys she had found, but without success. It was a good lock. And she had no reason to disbelieve her husband. He did go up there sometimes and stay for a while. And she knew he was cranky and set in his ways. Everybody had always said he was cranky. So she could wait. She had waited to satisfy more important longings than curiosity.

Her son, Jasper Parton, came to live in the house, too. He was about nineteen then, a well-built, brawny lad, with the undefinable promise, however, of fat and slackness. He had curly brown hair, a wide, heavy mouth, full of good teeth which he showed often in an expectant smile when he looked around after he had made some remark. He laughed readily, and most readily at his own words. He would say something and roll his large brown eyes like a comic stallion, and then laugh. He had the habit of rubbing his hands together, or pulling at his fingers to crack the knuckles. He called his mother "Old Girl," or "My Little Chickadee," and was accustomed to slap her on the rump in playful good spirits. He soon got the habit of slapping Bolton Lovehart on the shoulder, and calling him "Pop," or "Pop, Old Boy." His mother was disturbed by this at first, but she soon saw that her husband didn't mind, that he really seemed to like it.

Bolton Lovehart did like it. He liked everything about the new life. He liked the friends his wife brought home (though she brought few people, for she was gradually preparing to drop some of them), and even tried to learn to play bridge. And he especially liked Jasper's girl, Janie Murphy, a good-looking, well-mannered girl, with few words but a nice, direct look at you out of her gray eyes. Bolton Lovehart sank into the new happiness with a sense of perpetual surprise. He had not even suspected that things might be this way.

Mrs. Lovehart did not like Janie Murphy. Or rather, she did not like or dislike Janie Murphy: she disliked the idea of Janie Murphy. Janie Murphy would not do. Not with old Tom Murphy for a father. And a Catholic to boot. But she could wait, and wait in perfect confidence.

So when in the fall of 1940 her son was drafted for military service, she was almost glad. He would forget Janie. She was sure of that. And the war was far away. It was far away across the ocean where it belonged.

Bolton Lovehart was almost happy, too, when the draft came. He liked Jasper, but the event gave him a sense of excitement, of having his finger somehow on the pulse of the world. He went to the station with the boy when he left. "Good-bye, Pop," the boy said with good-humored contempt, and rolled his eyes. "Take care of yourself," he said, and slapped the old man on the shoulder. Bolton Lovehart wanted to say something, he didn't know what, but something which was swelling in his heart. "My boy—" he began, "my son—" Then he fumbled for words.

"Tootle-oo, Pop," the boy said, and swung up to the platform of the coach, grinned over all of Bardsville, and disappeared from sight.

Bolton Lovehart got the habit of going downtown early for the morning paper. He began to read magazines and books about Europe and the war. He got the habit of stopping on street corners or in the post office to talk with men about the situation. "In so far as I have been able to inform myself," he would begin, and clear his throat, then proceed. About any other subject in the world, the men would not have listened. But the war was coming and they listened. And after Bolton Lovehart had left, one of them would say, "You know, Old Lovehart has got a head on him. He's read all those books."

Another might say, "Yeah, he might as well have read 'em. He never did a damned thing else all his life. Me, I had to get out and chase the almighty dollar. Give me nothing else to do and I'd sit on my tail and read me some books."

But they listened. And one day Bolton Lovehart was asked to speak to the Kiwanis Club on the European situation. He became the town authority on the subject. He made speeches to all the clubs in town, and at the high school. Whatever he had been waiting for all his life now seemed to be his. He was happy.

When the war came, what had been happiness was transformed almost overnight into a kind of bliss, of excitement, which even on the dullest day glowed unwinkingly in his bosom. Sometimes it surprised him, the sense of lightness and meaning inside him, and he would stop about his occupation or stand in the street and demand of himself, *Is this me, is it me?* He was busy all the time now. He had to read all the books and magazines and newspapers and take notes. Somebody had to find out things and tell people, explain to them. Somebody had to work for paper collection and rubber collection. Somebody had to work for bond drives and Red Cross drives.

He lived for the morning paper and the radio broadcasts. The long story of the early defeats, detail by detail, wrenched him to the core, but in the pain was the stab of life, a clean quickening and a dedication. He was walking up the street from town, where he had gone for the morning mail, hoping for a letter from Jasper, when he heard the news of Bataan. Mr. Sullivan, who lived down the hill, stopped him and said, "They just surrendered. Bataan has surrendered. I just heard it on the radio."

"Thank you," Bolton Lovehart murmured, and after Mr. Sullivan had gone on, stood there in the street steadily breathing the sweet spring air, letting the tears run down his cheeks, feeling the exquisite sensation in his bosom. He reached out, timidly, to touch the bark of the old maple which grew between the pavement and the street. The coarseness of the bark was a vibrant delight to his fingers. He touched it humbly. He looked up at the tree, at the tinted, waxy beginnings of buds, then swung his gaze over the street, the houses, the trees, the springing lawns, and up at the great, rain-washed, glowing sky. It was all real. It was real.

In the scrub county just south of Carruthers County a big army post had been established, and a new concrete road, straight as a knife edge, had been driven through the red clay and limestone hills, a white slab over which the red clay bled streakingly down in wet weather from the cuts where clay and limestone looked like a gigantic side of beef brutally slashed open. In the evenings the lost boys, bulging or scrawny in khaki, wearing big clumsy shoes like plow boys, wandered the streets of Bardsville, or hung around the restaurants and drug stores and pool rooms. They got drunk and shouted in the streets or went down to the bottom to the whores or stood in wordless groups on street corners, staring with a wistful and penal humility out of their strange world into a strange world.

The town had to take care of them, and every one was a hero and precious in the early months before they became a curse and a burden. The town turned an old hall into a recreation center. Church people had a soldier to dinner every Sunday. People gave parties for them on Saturday night. Bolton Lovehart worked indefatigably on the recreation committee of St. Luke's. And the Loveharts gave parties. They filled the big old living room with boys and a scattering of regular army non-coms, leather-faced, mature men, who gorged on sandwiches and cake and coffee and beer, and made the house rock with laughter, and the blare of the radio turned up full. Sometimes in the racket two or three of the regular army non-coms would go into the back parlor and talk to Mrs. Lovehart and drink beer with her. Occasionally, with a show of giggling and theatrical furtiveness, she would give them a drop of something stronger than beer.

Bolton Lovehart could afford to buy sandwiches and beer for the boys. The pinch of the 1930's was over. He had sold, for a handsome figure, a strip of his property down in the bottom. The war plant stood on it. And the parties were his delight.

The best parties occurred when Jasper came home on his infrequent leaves, brawny and laughing, a lieutenant now. They then had the girls in and they danced to the radio, shaking the house, making the room dizzy with smoke. That was the best. Bolton Lovehart sat by the wall, watching everything, his whole being absorbed into everything, and the bliss in his bosom glowed white and hot like a live ember when the blast from the bellows hits it.

Among the girls who came to these parties was Janie Murphy. There was nothing Mrs. Lovehart could do about that if Jasper wanted it. But she was still confident. When word came that Jasper was to be sent overseas, there was a hard kernel of satisfaction in the middle of her grief. Everything would be all right now. He would forget that Janie.

Jasper came home on his last leave. And he married Janie Murphy. They eloped up into Kentucky, in the middle of the night. It had happened on the spur of the moment. Jasper had had no intention of marrying Janie Murphy, or anybody else. But she adored him. Every glance, every gesture, her hands clinging to him, flattered his vanity. And the excitement of going overseas roused an unexpected sentimentality in his nature. He thought about having a dear little wife back home. And having Janie Murphy as his wife was the only way to get Janie Murphy. He had found that out. Even the excitement of the last leave hadn't changed that fact. She wept and clung to him, but she was a good little Catholic girl. She was a good little Catholic girl, but when, on impulse late one evening, he proposed that they elope, she let her scruples be overruled. She loved him so. They were married by a bleary justice of the peace, sleepy and half-dressed, whom they had roused from bed. Jasper promised that they would get married by a priest later.

They went on up into Kentucky and had a three-day honeymoon and saw a horse race, and up in the hotel room she even drank whisky with him, she loved him so much. They would get married by the priest when they got home to Bardsville, he said. When they got back, there was no time—or at least not enough time—for Jasper had new orders to report immediately.

"Oh, you might take time, it won't take much time," she begged him.

But he said, "Kiddo, look here. Orders is orders. This is the army, kiddo. And, chicken, you and me, we are married good as anybody. Don't let 'em tell you different."

"But, Jasper—you—"

"Sure, kiddo. When I get back. Sure, and don't you love me?"

On the train he leaned back and propped his feet up. For the moment he was almost glad to get away. Just for a sort of a breath of fresh air, you might say. Sure, she was the stuff. Sure, he loved the kid. She was his little wife and she sure had what it took, no matter what those priests had told her. He'd knock that nonsense out of her.

He leaned back and drowsed. He thought how he would have something to tell the fellows, how he had got married. He'd laugh and say with mock woe how she had thrown the hooks into him. *But, boy*, he would say, *boy, I tell you, it is easy punishment. What she has got. Listen here, let me tell you, she* . . . He could scarcely wait to get to camp and tell the fellows.

Mrs. Lovehart made the best of the situation. She did not lose hope. The event was passing almost unnoticed in Bardsville. So many strange things happened every day now, with the war on, and new people, and people acting funny and doing things they had never done before, behaving the way they had never expected to behave. So she put the best face possible on the marriage, and referred to it as little as possible. But her husband could talk of little else. He wanted to stop people on the street and tell them about it. She could have strangled him. Sitting alone, thinking of him down the street telling somebody, she could have coldly strangled him with her bare hands. Her hands clenched, her breath came quick, and she thought of doing it. She suddenly loathed him, everything about him, everything, everything. She had always loathed him. It rose up inside her. She suddenly knew it. The thought filled the room, like light.

Bolton Lovehart's excitement about the marriage, however, did not last long. There was the war itself, the committees and drives, and the letters from Jasper. When one of the rare letters came, he would read parts of it to anybody in town whom he could stop on the street. "You know my boy Jasper," he would say, "you know Jasper. He's a lieutenant. In Sicily now. I know you'd like to hear what he has written. I find it very informative." Then he would read the letter.

He wrote often and sent Jasper money, more money than he could afford.

Jasper Parton was killed in Italy. It was a great blow for Mrs. Lovehart. It shook her confidence in the world, and in all she had learned, and in herself. It was, at first, an even greater shock for Bolton Lovehart, but even the grief was absorbed into life, into his occupations, the conversations on the street: "My son—you remember my boy Jasper, who was killed in Italy—" And there were the other boys. Nothing would be too good for them now. And then he got his great idea.

One of the ladies' organizations of St. Luke's was having a bazaar to raise money for the Red Cross. The bazaar was to fall on December 5th, when Christmas was already on the way. It was Christmas that made him think of it, for it had been the Christmas-toy display in the hardware store long ago which had started the whole thing. He would give his circus to the bazaar to be sold for toys. He said nothing to his wife about the matter, but began to spend all his days and evenings in the attic. He was retouching such of the poor creatures as needed retouching, replacing costumes that had faded, packing them in neat boxes. Then they were all carried to the church, where, the night before the bazaar, he worked for hours in the recreation room, arranging them in a great circus, setting up tight ropes and bars and trapezes, sprinkling finely ground sawdust in the rings, adjusting the animals on their stands. He did not finish until after two o'clock.

The circus was a great success. It was the hit of the bazaar. Children were crazy about it. Broken up and sold piece by piece it brought nearly two hundred dollars for the Red Cross. And for Jasper. The Bardsville *Gazette* ran a photograph of Mr. Lovehart standing beside the circus: "Prominent Citizen Has Secret Hobby. Gives proceeds to Red Cross." The death of Jasper had brought the secret circus out into the world to live, to be enjoyed, to be used and broken in the end. There was some kind of atonement in this, Bolton Lovehart felt, for the long lie, for all the past, and he felt resigned now even to the death of Jasper.

Jasper Parton was killed on the banks of a swift river—what would pass for nothing better than a creek back home in Tennessee—under the shadow of snow-stung rocks in the Apennines. He had crossed the stream, with two companies, on an unsteady pontoon bridge, by the ruins of a stone bridge, under machine-gun fire from Germans above the little road, up in the rocks. A couple of planes got through the murk and knocked out the position. Just in time, too, for the clouds were thickening, lower and lower. The men strung out up the little road, in the mountain quiet, and spread up the ridge, feeling it out. It was very quiet, except for gunfire, far to the west. Then the Germans hit. Two other machine guns, which had remained silent during the crossing, opened on the men who had remained near the bridge. Then the troops appeared, out of the earth, among the rocks, ready to rush the bridge. It was an effective surprise.

The Americans up the road began piling back, but it was a good distance. They were cut off. It was Jasper and two of the other men near the bridge who blocked the rush and held it. They managed to get a machine gun placed in the lee of an outcropping of rock. One of the men was killed. Jasper was hit, but not badly. It was Jasper who, at the last minute, sent the survivor back, and stayed until the grenades got him. He had stayed long enough.

Jasper Parton was awarded the Congressional Medal.

His wife, Janie Murphy Parton, was to go to Washington to receive the medal.

"To think," Mrs. Lovehart said in her bitterness, "to think that he named her his next of kin. To think—that girl—and he was only married to her four days. Four days before he went away." It was cruel. It was too cruel, she decided.

"You go to Washington, too," Bolton Lovehart comforted her. "You'll go, my dear."

"I'll not go! Not with that girl. I'll not go. She can have it. She got Jasper and now she can have that medal."

"You must go," her husband urged. "I'll take you. You must go for Jasper's sake."

She swore that she would not go. But she went to Washington, and saw that girl receive the medal. She had, however, her own satisfactions. Great men shook her own hand and murmured their congratulations and sympathy. Only when, back in the hotel room, she saw the picture in the paper, the picture of that girl with the medal, and herself in the background, did the bitterness surge up so powerfully that nothing else mattered. She tore the paper across and flung herself on the bed. She had been robbed of everything.

It was better back in Bardsville. People back in Bardsville at least knew the difference between Mrs. Bolton Lovehart and that Murphy girl. So when the celebration occurred in Bardsville, that girl did not crowd her out. She sat on the platform next to the mayor, with her husband, who was to speak a few words, the rector of St. Luke's and Colonel Malcolm, from the army post down in the forgotten county of her birth. That girl was up there, too, but far over to one side, looking frightened and lost. Mrs. Lovehart could see her out of the corner of her eye. She was pleased with what she saw. *She has no composure*, she thought. *She can't keep her hands still, she is picking one of her nails*, she thought. She surreptitiously spread her own small, well-shaped, well-manicured fingers in her lap and studied them, her head slightly bowed in her characteristic modest way.

Bolton Lovehart's speech was the most successful of his life. His words were slow and halting at the beginning, his gestures cranky and unsure. For the first few minutes his voice droned along, saying what people expected him to say, but what they strained forward to hear above the muffled coughs and the cautious scraping of feet. Then, still uncertain, in that dry, pedantic voice of a school teacher or Sunday-school superintendent, he said, "We do not come here tonight to honor Jasper Parton. We cannot honor him. That medal—the highest recognition this country can give a citizen—does not honor him. Or any man who died, far away in a foreign land. He does not need any honor. We come here tonight because we are to be honored. By him. Because one morning in a foreign land, he did us honor. He did honor to Bardsville, and to all of us. We grieve for him. I grieve for him. He was not my son. You all know that. I have no son. But I want to think of him as my son. I want to think of him and of all who went away as my sons. For they are all our sons—every one of them is the son of each of us—I want to think of him—as my—son—for they all— they all—"

He could not continue. He did not break down. He showed no emotion. He simply stopped and the words would not come any more. For a moment he looked out to the people, and then turned and sat down stiffly in his chair.

There was music after that. They stood and sang the national anthem.

At the reception afterwards, he stood quietly, almost somnam- bulistically, beside Mrs. Lovehart, and the people came to shake their hands.

But Janie Murphy had slipped away. She had walked across the square and down the dark streets beyond, not able to hold the tears any longer, down to one of the side streets, to the house of old Tom Murphy.

The newspapers, the radio reports, the conversations were full of victories now. The final victory was certain. Housewives, waiting their turn in the butcher shop, grumbled a little now. Sometimes soldiers from the camp to the south would wait on the edge of the highway just out of town with lifted arms, late at night, and watch the cars whizz past. Not many got invited to Sunday dinner any more. People knew that these boys would never get overseas, would never fight in jungles or in icy mountains or ruined towns. They would never die in foreign lands. They would stay here in the camp a while and then be sent home. They were a nuisance, a burden, and little more. Even the merchants and café owners were tired of them. But Bolton Lovehart was not tired. He would do what he could for them. There were still the parties up at the Lovehart house, the free beer, sandwiches, and cigarettes, and the loud radio.

He still went to committee meetings, still tried to arrange entertainments for the soldiers, still worked at bond selling and in Red Cross drives. He still stopped people on the street to tell them something he had read about, to refer to Jasper Parton: "You know Jasper—my boy that was killed in Italy—well, he used to say, he used to predict—" But people did not listen closely to him any more. Their eyes wandered from his face and they moved restlessly.

One night he went to a bond meeting in a village some ten miles from Bardsville. He got home late, long after midnight. Mr. Simmons, the rector, let him out of the car at the gate and drove away. Bolton Lovehart saw that the light was on in the living room. He assumed that his wife was waiting up for him, though that would have been unusual. As he opened the front door, he saw two men's hats lying on the table. Then, once in the hall, he saw the men waiting for him, standing in the middle of the living room. One of the men he recognized as Milt Suggs, the sheriff. The other man he did not know, but he looked like the kind of man a sheriff would have with him.

The sheriff apologized: "We just come in." Then: "Didn't nobody answer, and the door was open, so we just come in. Hope you didn't mind."

"Of course not," Bolton Lovehart said, his face, however, showing his question.

The sheriff was uneasy, shifting from foot to foot. "Mr. Lovehart," he finally managed, "it's—it's about Mrs. Lovehart."

"What?"

"It's Mrs. Lovehart," the sheriff said, and stopped again.

"Tell me," Bolton Lovehart ordered. "Tell me!"

"Well," the sheriff said. "Well—" Then he got himself together. "She's dead," he said. "Done killed."

Mrs. Lovehart was killed that night in an accident on the highway. She and a certain Captain Cartwright, who had been at the wheel, had driven at high speed into the back of a heavy truck parked on the shoulder of the highway ten miles south of town. They had both been drinking. Bolton Lovehart knew Captain Cartwright, a big, red-faced, burly man, fiftyish, who had been a sergeant in the regular army for years before the war and had received a commission for distinguished service in action and had been sent back to the training camps. He had come to the Lovehart house now and then. He and Mrs. Lovehart were killed instantly in the collision. Both bodies were severely mangled.

The last victories came. The last blood was shed in the ruined streets of Berlin. Half the world away, American fleets lifted some dream island in the morning light and the bombardment began, while landing craft skeetered crazily shoreward like water insects and the planes poured steadily overhead. People in Bardsville knew how it was. They could see it in the newsreel after the feature. Then the bomb fell on Hiroshima.

It meant nothing, however, to Bolton Lovehart. For some time now, all day long and far into the night, he had sat in the attic, leaning over his table, where lay the block of soft pine, the glue pot, the wire, the awl, the knife, the paint tubes and brushes, the bits of cloth and needles and scissors. Finally, he had found his way back.

Some of the forward-looking business men of Bardsville have formed a corporation and have bought the war plant, where small arms ammunition was made. Plastics will now be manufactured there. The old furniture factory is operating day and night since the strike has been settled. New houses are going up in the bottoms to replace some of the more decrepit shacks occupied by the war workers. Many of those workers will stay, the Chamber of Commerce confidently predicts, people drawn from the red clay hills to the south, the banks of sluggish, stippled, moccasin-drowsing creeks over toward the Mississippi, the cross-roads settlements, and the slums of Memphis. Bardsville now has nearly twenty thousand people.

Janie Murphy Parton has just married again. She went through a period of great anguish. It was anguish not only for the loss of Jasper Parton, whom she had loved so much, but an anguish of guilt. She felt that she was the cause of his death. She had sinned in marrying him outside the church, and her punishment had been to lose him. For a long time she could scarcely keep from killing herself, especially after the trip to Washington and the medal, which was the public mark of her guilt. She resisted that impulse, and then it seemed that she would die. Nobody could feel such anguish, day and night, and live. Nothing she could do and nothing Father Donnelly could say seemed to help her.

But she lived. And she has married Murray James, a foreman at the furniture factory, a man ten years older than she, a big, quiet man, very strong and very kind. He satisfies her in every way much better than Jasper Parton ever did, and she loves him better, even, than she ever loved Jasper Parton. She knows this, and she knows that now, at last, in this way she has truly killed poor, vain, cheap, laughing, eye-rolling, heroic Jasper. Knowing this, she sometimes wakes up in the night and out of this new guilt in her happiness, she weeps silently and sweetly a while and then reaches over to take the big, coarse hand of Murray James and hold it between both her own and listen to his breathing.

This occurs less frequently in recent weeks, and soon now she will let Jasper go. He will go away where he belongs, to join the circus in the attic. He will join Seth Sykes and drunken Cash Perkins and all the heroes who ever died for all their good reasons, and old Lem Lovehart, who laid himself down amid birdsong at dusk and was scalped by a Chickasaw, and Simon Lovehart with the wound and the prayer book as his truth, and Louise Bolton Lovehart with her dear, treacherous heart in her bosom, and the kitten little Louise Bolton flung from her window to thud on the paving bricks, and the bloodless arrowheads and the fading flag of Simon Lovehart's regiment, and the song, "Let the nearer waters roll," which they sang at the baptizing and the song they sang in the square the night of the armistice in 1918, and the painted animals carved from wood and the sinister ring master and the girl acrobat with the frivolous skirt and round blue painted eyes, and all the things by which Bardsville had lived, and found life worth living, and died. And Jasper will be at home there.

Blackberry Winter

To Joseph Warren and Dagmar Beach

IT WAS GETTING INTO JUNE AND PAST EIGHT O'CLOCK IN THE morning, but there was a fire—even if it wasn't a big fire, just a fire of chunks—on the hearth of the big stone fireplace in the living room. I was standing on the hearth, almost into the chimney, hunched over the fire, working my bare toes slowly on the warm stone. I relished the heat which made the skin of my bare legs warp and creep and tingle, even as I called to my mother, who was somewhere back in the dining room or kitchen, and said: "But it's June, I don't have to put them on!"

"You put them on if you are going out," she called.

I tried to assess the degree of authority and conviction in the tone, but at that distance it was hard to decide. I tried to analyze the tone, and then I thought what a fool I had been to start out the back door and let her see that I was barefoot. If I had gone out the front door or the side door she would never have known, not till dinner time anyway, and by then the day would have been half gone and I would have been all over the farm to see what the storm had done and down to the creek to see the flood. But it had never crossed my mind that they would try to stop you from going barefoot in June, no matter if there had been a gully-washer and a cold spell.

Nobody had ever tried to stop me in June as long as I could

remember, and when you are nine years old, what you remember seems forever; for you remember everything and everything is important and stands big and full and fills up Time and is so solid that you can walk around and around it like a tree and look at it. You are aware that time passes, that there is a movement in time, but that is not what Time is. Time is not a movement, a flowing, a wind then, but is, rather, a kind of climate in which things are, and when a thing happens it begins to live and keeps on living and stands solid in Time like the tree that you can walk around. And if there is a movement, the movement is not Time itself, any more than a breeze is climate, and all the breeze does is to shake a little the leaves on the tree which is alive and solid. When you are nine, you know that there are things that you don't know, but you know that when you know something you know it. You know how a thing has been and you know that you can go barefoot in June. You do not understand that voice from back in the kitchen which says that you cannot go barefoot outdoors and run to see what has happened and rub your feet over the wet shivery grass and make the perfect mark of your foot in the smooth, creamy, red mud and then muse upon it as though you had suddenly come upon that single mark on the glistening auroral beach of the world. You have never seen a beach, but you have read the book and how the footprint was there.

The voice had said what it had said, and I looked savagely at the black stockings and the strong, scuffed brown shoes which I had brought from my closet as far as the hearth rug. I called once more, "But it's June," and waited.

"It's June," the voice replied from far away, "but it's blackberry winter."

I had lifted my head to reply to that, to make one more test of what was in that tone, when I happened to see the man.

The fireplace in the living room was at the end; for the stone chimney was built, as in so many of the farmhouses in Tennessee, at the end of a gable, and there was a window on each side of the chimney. Out of the window on the north side of the fireplace I could see the man. When I saw the man I did not call out what I had intended, but, engrossed by the strangeness of the sight, watched him, still far off, come along the path by the edge of the woods.

What was strange was that there should be a man there at all.

That path went along the yard fence, between the fence and the woods which came right down to the yard, and then on back past the chicken runs and on by the woods until it was lost to sight where the woods bulged out and cut off the back field. There the path disappeared into the woods. It led on back, I knew, through the woods and to the swamps, skirted the swamp where the big trees gave way to sycamores and water oaks and willows and tangled cane, and then led on to the river. Nobody ever went back there except people who wanted to gig frogs in the swamp or to fish in the river or to hunt in the woods, and those people, if they didn't have a standing permission from my father, always stopped to ask permission to cross the farm. But the man whom I now saw wasn't, I could tell even at that distance, a sportsman. And what would a sportsman have been doing down there after a storm? Besides, he was coming from the river, and nobody had gone down there that morning. I knew that for a fact, because if anybody had passed, certainly if a stranger had passed, the dogs would have made a racket and would have been out on him. But this man was coming up from the river and had come up through the woods. I suddenly had a vision of him moving up the grassy path in the woods, in the green twilight under the big trees, not making any sound on the path, while now and then, like drops off the eaves, a big drop of water would fall from a leaf or bough and strike a stiff oak leaf lower down with a small, hollow sound like a drop of water hitting tin. That sound, in the silence of the woods, would be very significant.

When you are a boy and stand in the stillness of woods, which can be so still that your heart almost stops beating and makes you want to stand there in the green twilight until you feel your very feet sinking into and clutching the earth like roots and your body breathing slow through its pores like the leaves—when you stand there and wait for the next drop to drop with its small, flat sound to a lower leaf, that sound seems to measure out something, to put an end to something, to begin something, and you cannot wait for it to happen and are afraid it will not happen, and then when it has happened, you are waiting again, almost afraid.

But the man whom I saw coming through the woods in my mind's eye did not pause and wait, growing into the ground and breathing with the enormous, soundless breathing of the leaves. Instead, I saw him moving in the green twilight inside my head as he was moving at that very moment along the path by the edge of the woods, coming toward the house. He was moving steadily, but not fast, with his shoulders hunched a little and his head thrust forward, like a man who has come a long way and has a long way to go. I shut my eyes for a couple of seconds, thinking that when I opened them he would not be there at all. There was no place for him to have come from, and there was no reason for him to come where he was coming, toward our house. But I opened my eyes, and there he was, and he was coming steadily along the side of the woods. He was not yet even with the back chicken yard.

"Mama," I called.

"You put them on," the voice said.

"There's a man coming," I called, "out back."

She did not reply to that, and I guessed that she had gone to the kitchen window to look. She would be looking at the man and wondering who he was and what he wanted, the way you always do in the country, and if I went back there now she would not notice right off whether or not I was barefoot. So I went back to the kitchen.

She was standing by the window. "I don't recognize him," she said, not looking around at me.

"Where could he be coming from?" I asked.

"I don't know," she said.

"What would he be doing down at the river? At night? In the storm?"

She studied the figure out the window, then said, "Oh, I reckon maybe he cut across from the Dunbar place."

That was, I realized, a perfectly rational explanation. He had not been down at the river in the storm, at night. He had come over this morning. You could cut across from the Dunbar place if you didn't mind breaking through a lot of elder and sassafras and blackberry bushes which had about taken over the old cross path, which nobody ever used any more. That satisfied me for a moment, but only for a moment. "Mama," I asked, "what would he be doing over at the Dunbar place last night?"

Then she looked at me, and I knew I had made a mistake, for she was looking at my bare feet. "You haven't got your shoes on," she said.

But I was saved by the dogs. That instant there was a bark which I recognized as Sam, the collie, and then a heavier, churning kind of bark which was Bully, and I saw a streak of white as Bully tore round the corner of the back porch and headed out for the man. Bully was a big, bone-white bull dog, the kind of dog that they used to call a farm bull dog but that you don't see any more, heavy chested and heavy headed, but with pretty long legs. He could take a fence as light as a hound. He had just cleared the white paling fence toward the woods when my mother ran out to the back porch and began calling, "Here you, Bully! Here you!"

Bully stopped in the path, waiting for the man, but he gave a few more of those deep, gargling savage barks that reminded you of something down a stone-lined well. The red clay mud, I saw, was splashed up over his white chest and looked exciting, like blood.

The man, however, had not stopped walking even when Bully took the fence and started at him. He had kept right on coming. All he had done was to switch a little paper parcel which he carried from the right hand to the left, and then reach into his pants pocket to get something. Then I saw the glitter and knew that he had a knife in his hand, probably the kind of mean knife just made for devilment and nothing else, with a blade as long as the blade of a frog-sticker, which will snap out ready when you press a button in the handle. That knife must have had a button in the handle, or else how could he have had the blade out glittering so quick and with just one hand?

Pulling his knife against the dogs was a funny thing to do, for Bully was a big, powerful brute and fast, and Sam was all right. If those dogs had meant business, they might have knocked him down and ripped him before he got a stroke in. He ought to have picked up a heavy stick, something to take a swipe at them with and something which they could see and respect when they came at him. But he apparently did not know much about dogs. He just held the knife blade close against the right leg, low down, and kept on moving down the path.

Then my mother had called, and Bully had stopped. So the man let the blade of the knife snap back into the handle, and dropped it into his pocket, and kept on coming. Many women would have been afraid with the strange man who they knew had that knife in his pocket. That is, if they were alone in the house with nobody but a nine-year-old boy. And my mother was alone, for my father had gone off, and Dellie, the cook, was down at her cabin because she wasn't feeling well. But my mother wasn't afraid. She wasn't a big woman, but she was clear and brisk about everything she did and looked everybody and everything right in the eye from her own blue eyes in her tanned face. She had been the first woman in the county to ride a horse astride (that was back when she was a girl and long before I was born), and I have seen her snatch up a pump gun and go out and knock a chicken hawk out of the air like a busted skeet when he came over her chicken yard. She was a steady and self-reliant woman, and when I think of her now after all the years she has been dead, I think of her brown hands, not big, but somewhat square for a woman's hands, with square-cut nails. They looked, as a matter of fact, more like a young boy's hands than a grown woman's. But back then it never crossed my mind that she would ever be dead.

She stood on the back porch and watched the man enter the back gate, where the dogs (Bully had leaped back into the yard) were dancing and muttering and giving sidelong glances back to my mother to see if she meant what she had said. The man walked right by the dogs, almost brushing them, and didn't pay them any attention. I could see now that he wore old khaki pants, and a dark wool coat with stripes in it, and a gray felt hat. He had on a gray shirt with blue stripes in it, and no tie. But I could see a tie, blue and reddish, sticking in his side coat-pocket. Everything was wrong about what he wore. He ought to have been wearing blue jeans or overalls, and a straw hat or an old black felt hat, and the coat, granting that he might have been wearing a wool coat and not a jumper, ought not to have had those stripes. Those clothes, despite the fact that they were old enough and dirty enough for any tramp, didn't belong there in our back yard, coming down the path, in Middle Tennessee, miles away from any big town, and even a mile off the pike.

When he got almost to the steps, without having said anything, my mother, very matter-of-factly, said, "Good morning."

"Good morning," he said, and stopped and looked her over. He did not take off his hat, and under the brim you could see the perfectly unmemorable face, which wasn't old and wasn't young, or thick or thin. It was grayish and covered with about three days of stubble. The eyes were a kind of nondescript, muddy hazel, or something like that, rather bloodshot. His teeth, when he opened his mouth, showed yellow and uneven. A couple of them had been knocked out. You knew that they had been knocked out, because there was a scar, not very old, there on the lower lip just beneath the gap.

"Are you hunting work?" my mother asked him.

"Yes," he said—not "yes, mam"—and still did not take off his hat.

"I don't know about my husband, for he isn't here," she said, and didn't mind a bit telling the tramp, or whoever he was, with the mean knife in his pocket, that no man was around, "but I can give you a few things to do. The storm has drowned a lot of my chicks. Three coops of them. You can gather them up and bury them. Bury them deep so the dogs won't get at them. In the woods. And fix the coops the wind blew over. And down yonder beyond that pen by the edge of the woods are some drowned poults. They got out and I couldn't get them in. Even after it started to rain hard. Poults haven't got any sense."

"What are them things—poults?" he demanded, and spat on the brick walk. He rubbed his foot over the spot, and I saw that he wore a black, pointed-toe low shoe, all cracked and broken. It was a crazy kind of shoe to be wearing in the country.

"Oh, they're young turkeys," my mother was saying. "And they haven't got any sense. I oughtn't to try to raise them around here with so many chickens, anyway. They don't thrive near chickens, even in separate pens. And I won't give up my chickens." Then she stopped herself and resumed briskly on the note of business. "When you finish that, you can fix my flower beds. A lot of trash and mud and gravel has washed down. Maybe you can save some of my flowers if you are careful."

"Flowers," the man said, in a low, impersonal voice which seemed to have a wealth of meaning, but a meaning which I could not fathom. As I think back on it, it probably was not pure contempt. Rather, it was a kind of impersonal and distant marveling that he should be on the verge of grubbing in a flower bed. He said the word, and then looked off across the yard.

"Yes, flowers," my mother replied with some asperity, as though she would have nothing said or implied against flowers. "And they were very fine this year." Then she stopped and looked at the man. "Are you hungry?" she demanded.

"Yeah," he said.

"I'll fix you something," she said, "before you get started." She turned to me. "Show him where he can wash up," she commanded, and went into the house.

I took the man to the end of the porch where a pump was and where a couple of wash pans sat on a low shelf for people to use before they went into the house. I stood there while he laid down his little parcel wrapped in newspaper and took off his hat and looked around for a nail to hang it on. He poured the water and plunged his hands into it. They were big hands, and strong looking, but they did not have the creases and the earth-color of the hands of men who work outdoors. But they were dirty, with black dirt ground into the skin and under the nails. After he had washed his hands, he poured another basin of water and washed his face. He dried his face, and with the towel still dangling in his grasp, stepped over to the mirror on the house wall. He rubbed one hand over the stubble on his face. Then he carefully inspected his face, turning first one side and then the other, and stepped back and settled his striped coat down on his shoulders. He had the movements of a man who has just dressed up to go to church or a party —the way he settled his coat and smoothed it and scanned himself in the mirror.

Then he caught my glance on him. He glared at me for an instant out of the bloodshot eyes, then demanded in a low, harsh voice, "What you looking at?"

"Nothing," I managed to say, and stepped back a step from him.

He flung the towel down, crumpled, on the shelf, and went toward the kitchen door and entered without knocking.

My mother said something to him which I could not catch. I started to go in again, then thought about my bare feet, and decided to go back of the chicken yard, where the man would have to come to pick up the dead chicks. I hung around behind the chicken house until he came out.

He moved across the chicken yard with a fastidious, not quite finicking motion, looking down at the curdled mud flecked with bits of chicken-droppings. The mud curled up over the soles of his black shoes. I stood back from him some six feet and watched him pick up the first of the drowned chicks. He held it up by one foot and inspected it.

There is nothing deader looking than a drowned chick. The feet

134

curl in that feeble, empty way which back when I was a boy, even if I was a country boy who did not mind hog-killing or frog-gigging, made me feel hollow in the stomach. Instead of looking plump and fluffy, the body is stringy and limp with the fluff plastered to it, and the neck is long and loose like a little string of rag. And the eyes have that bluish membrane over them which makes you think of a very old man who is sick about to die.

The man stood there and inspected the chick. Then he looked all around as though he didn't know what to do with it.

"There's a great big old basket in the shed," I said, and pointed to the shed attached to the chicken house.

He inspected me as though he had just discovered my presence, and moved toward the shed.

"There's a spade there, too," I added.

He got the basket and began to pick up the other chicks, picking each one up slowly by a foot and then flinging it into the basket with a nasty, snapping motion. Now and then he would look at me out of the blood-shot eyes. Every time he seemed on the verge of saying something, but he did not. Perhaps he was building up to say something to me, but I did not wait that long. His way of looking at me made me so uncomfortable that I left the chicken yard.

Besides, I had just remembered that the creek was in flood, over the bridge, and that people were down there watching it. So I cut across the farm toward the creek. When I got to the big tobacco field I saw that it had not suffered much. The land lay right and not many tobacco plants had washed out of the ground. But I knew that a lot of tobacco round the country had been washed right out. My father had said so at breakfast.

My father was down at the bridge. When I came out of the gap in the osage hedge into the road, I saw him sitting on his mare over the heads of the other men who were standing around, admiring the flood. The creek was big here, even in low water; for only a couple of miles away it ran into the river, and when a real flood came, the red water got over the pike where it dipped down to the bridge, which was an iron bridge, and high over the floor and even the side railings of the bridge. Only the upper iron work would show, with the water boiling and frothing red and white around it. That creek rose so fast and so heavy because a few miles back it came down out of the hills, where the gorges filled up with water in no time when a rain came. The creek ran in a deep bed with limestone bluffs along both sides until it got within three quarters of a mile of the bridge, and when it came out from between those bluffs in flood it was boiling and hissing and steaming like water from a fire hose.

Whenever there was a flood, people from half the county would come down to see the sight. After a gully-washer there would not be any work to do anyway. If it didn't ruin your crop, you couldn't plow and you felt like taking a holiday to celebrate. If it did ruin your crop, there wasn't anything to do except to try to take your mind off the mortgage, if you were rich enough to have a mortgage, and if you couldn't afford a mortgage you needed something to take your mind off how hungry you would be by Christmas. So people would come down to the bridge and look at the flood. It made something different from the run of days.

There would not be much talking after the first few minutes of trying to guess how high the water was this time. The men and kids just stood around, or sat their horses or mules, as the case might be, or stood up in the wagon beds. They looked at the strangeness of the flood for an hour or two, and then somebody would say that he had better be getting on home to dinner and would start walking down the gray, puddled limestone pike, or would touch heel to his mount and start off. Everybody always knew what it would be like when he got down to the bridge, but people always came. It was like church or a funeral. They always came, that is, if it was summer and the flood unexpected. Nobody ever came down in winter to see high water.

When I came out of the gap in the bodock hedge, I saw the crowd, perhaps fifteen or twenty men and a lot of kids, and saw my father sitting his mare, Nellie Gray. He was a tall, limber man and carried himself well. I was always proud to see him sit a horse, he was so quiet and straight, and when I stepped through the gap of the hedge that morning, the first thing that happened was, I remember, the warm feeling I always had when I saw him up on a horse, just sitting. I did not go toward him, but skirted the crowd on the far side, to get a look at the creek. For one thing, I was not sure what he would say about the fact that I was barefoot. But the first thing I knew, I heard his voice calling, "Seth!"

I went toward him, moving apologetically past the men, who bent their large, red or thin, sallow faces above me. I knew some of the men, and knew their names, but because those I knew were there in a crowd, mixed with the strange faces, they seemed foreign to me, and not friendly. I did not look up at my father until I was almost within touching distance of his heel. Then I looked up and tried to read his face, to see if he was angry about my being barefoot. Before I could decide anything from that impassive, high-boned face, he had leaned over and reached a hand to me. "Grab on," he commanded.

I grabbed on and gave a little jump, and he said, "Up-see-daisy!" and whisked me, light as a feather, up to the pommel of his McClellan saddle.

"You can see better up here," he said, slid back on the cantle a little to make me more comfortable, and then, looking over my head at the swollen, tumbling water, seemed to forget all about me. But his right hand was laid on my side, just above my thigh, to steady me.

I was sitting there as quiet as I could, feeling the faint stir of my father's chest against my shoulders as it rose and fell with his breath, when I saw the cow. At first, looking up the creek, I thought it was just another big piece of driftwood steaming down the creek in the ruck of water, but all at once a pretty good-size boy who had climbed part way up a telephone pole by the pike so that he could see better yelled out, "Golly-damn, look at that-air cow!"

Everybody looked. It was a cow all right, but it might just as well have been driftwood; for it was dead as a chunk, rolling and roiling down the creek, appearing and disappearing, feet up or head up, it didn't matter which.

The cow started up the talk again. Somebody wondered whether it would hit one of the clear places under the top girder of the bridge and get through or whether it would get tangled in the drift and trash that had piled against the upright girders and braces. Somebody remembered how about ten years before so much drift-wood had piled up on the bridge that it was knocked off its founda-tions. Then the cow hit. It hit the edge of the drift against one of the girders, and hung there. For a few seconds it seemed as though it might tear loose, but then we saw that it was really caught. It bobbed and heaved on its side there in a slow, grinding, uneasy fashion. It had a yoke around its neck, the kind made out of a forked limb to keep a jumper behind fence.

"She shore jumped one fence," one of the men said.

And another: "Well, she done jumped her last one, fer a fack."

Then they began to wonder about whose cow it might be. They decided it must belong to Milt Alley. They said that he had a cow that was a jumper, and kept her in a fenced-in piece of ground up the creek. I had never seen Milt Alley, but I knew who he was. He was a squatter and lived up the hills a way, on a shirt-tail patch of set-on-edge land, in a cabin. He was pore white trash. He had lots of children. I had seen the children at school, when they came. They were thin-faced, with straight, sticky-looking, dough-colored hair, and they smelled something like old sour buttermilk, not because they drank so much buttermilk but because that is the sort of smell which children out of those cabins tend to have. The big Alley boy drew dirty pictures and showed them to the little boys at school.

That was Milt Alley's cow. It looked like the kind of cow he would have, a scrawny, old, sway-backed cow, with a yoke around her neck. I wondered if Milt Alley had another cow.

"Poppa," I said, "do you think Milt Alley has got another cow?"

"You say 'Mr. Alley,' " my father said quietly.

"Do you think he has?"

"No telling," my father said.

Then a big gangly boy, about fifteen, who was sitting on a scraggly little old mule with a piece of croker sack thrown across the saw-tooth spine, and who had been staring at the cow, suddenly said to nobody in particular, "Reckin anybody ever et drownt cow?"

He was the kind of boy who might just as well as not have been the son of Milt Alley, with his faded and patched overalls ragged at the bottom of the pants and the mud-stiff brogans hanging off his skinny, bare ankles at the level of the mule's belly. He had said what he did, and then looked embarrassed and sullen when all the eyes swung at him. He hadn't meant to say it, I am pretty sure now. He would have been too proud to say it, just as Milt Alley would have been too proud. He had just been thinking out loud, and the words had popped out.

There was an old man standing there on the pike, an old man with a white beard. "Son," he said to the embarrassed and sullen boy on the mule, "you live long enough and you'll find a man will eat anything when the time comes."

"Time gonna come fer some folks this year," another man said.

"Son," the old man said, "in my time I et things a man don't like to think on. I was a sojer and I rode with Gin'l Forrest, and them things we et when the time come. I tell you. I et meat what got up and run when you taken out yore knife to cut a slice to put on the fire. You had to knock it down with a carbeen butt, it was so active. That-air meat would jump like a bullfrog, it was so full of skippers."

But nobody was listening to the old man. The boy on the mule turned his sullen sharp face from him, dug a heel into the side of the mule and went off up the pike with a motion which made you think that any second you would hear mule bones clashing inside that lank and scrofulous hide.

"Cy Dundee's boy," a man said, and nodded toward the figure going up the pike on the mule.

"Reckin Cy Dundee's young-uns seen times they'd settle fer drownt cow," another man said.

The old man with the beard peered at them both from his weak, slow eyes, first at one and then at the other. "Live long enough," he said, "and a man will settle fer what he kin git."

Then there was silence again, with the people looking at the red, foam-flecked water.

My father lifted the bridle rein in his left hand, and the mare turned and walked around the group and up the pike. We rode on up to our big gate, where my father dismounted to open it and let me myself ride Nellie Gray through. When he got to the lane that led off from the drive about two hundred yards from our house, my father said, "Grab on." I grabbed on, and he let me down to the ground. "I'm going to ride down and look at my corn," he said. "You go on." He took the lane, and I stood there on the drive and watched him ride off. He was wearing cowhide boots and an old hunting coat, and I thought that that made him look very military, like a picture. That and the way he rode.

I did not go to the house. Instead, I went by the vegetable garden and crossed behind the stables, and headed down for Dellie's cabin. I wanted to go down and play with Jebb, who was Dellie's little boy about two years older than I was. Besides, I was cold. I shivered as I walked, and I had gooseflesh. The mud which crawled up between my toes with every step I took was like ice. Dellie would have a fire, but she wouldn't make me put on shoes and stockings.

Dellie's cabin was of logs, with one side, because it was on a slope, set on limestone chunks, with a little porch attached to it, and had a little whitewashed fence around it and a gate with plow-points on a wire to clink when somebody came in, and had two big white oaks in the yard and some flowers and a nice privy in the back with some honeysuckle growing over it. Dellie and Old Jebb, who was Jebb's father and who lived with Dellie and had lived with her for twenty-five years even if they never had got married, were careful to keep everything nice around their cabin. They had the name all over the community for being clean and clever Negroes. Dellie and Jebb were what they used to call "white-folks' niggers." There was a big difference between their cabin and the other two cabins farther down where the other tenants lived. My father kept the other cabins weatherproof, but he couldn't undertake to go down and pick up after the litter they strewed. They didn't take the trouble to have a vegetable patch like Dellie and Jebb or to make preserves from wild plum, and jelly from crab apple the way Dellie did. They were shiftless, and my father was always threatening to get shed of them. But he never did. When they finally left, they just up and left on their own, for no reason, to go and be shiftless somewhere else. Then some more came. But meanwhile they lived down there, Matt Rawson and his family, and Sid Turner and his, and I played with their children all over the farm when they weren't working. But when I wasn't around they were mean sometimes to Little Jebb. That was because the other tenants down there were jealous of Dellie and Jebb.

I was so cold that I ran the last fifty yards to Dellie's gate. As soon as I had entered the yard, I saw that the storm had been hard on Dellie's flowers. The yard was, as I have said, on a slight slope, and the water running across had gutted the flower beds and washed out all the good black woods-earth which Dellie had brought in. What little grass there was in the yard was plastered sparsely down on the ground, the way the drainage water had left it. It reminded me of the way the fluff was plastered down on the skin of the drowned chicks that the strange man had been picking up, up in my mother's chicken yard.

I took a few steps up the path to the cabin, and then I saw that the drainage water had washed a lot of trash and filth out from under Dellie's house. Up toward the porch, the ground was not clean any more. Old pieces of rag, two or three rusted cans, pieces of rotten rope, some hunks of old dog dung, broken glass, old paper, and all sorts of things like that had washed out from under Dellie's house to foul her clean yard. It looked just as bad as the yards of the other cabins, or worse. It was worse, as a matter of fact, because it was a surprise. I had never thought of all that filth being under Dellie's house. It was not anything against Dellie that the stuff had been under the cabin. Trash will get under any house. But I did not think of that when I saw the foulness which had washed out on the ground which Dellie sometimes used to sweep with a twig broom to make nice and clean.

I picked my way past the filth, being careful not to get my bare feet on it, and mounted to Dellie's door. When I knocked, I heard her voice telling me to come in.

It was dark inside the cabin, after the daylight, but I could make out Dellie piled up in bed under a quilt, and Little Jebb crouched by the hearth, where a low fire simmered. "Howdy," I said to Dellie, "how you feeling?"

Her big eyes, the whites surprising and glaring in the black face, fixed on me as I stood there, but she did not reply. It did not look like Dellie, or act like Dellie, who would grumble and bustle around our kitchen, talking to herself, scolding me or Little Jebb, clanking pans, making all sorts of unnecessary noises and mutterings like an old-fashioned black steam thrasher engine when it has got up an extra head of steam and keeps popping the governor and rumbling and shaking on its wheels. But now Dellie just lay up there on the bed, under the patch-work quilt, and turned the black face, which I scarcely recognized, and the glaring white eyes to me.

"How you feeling?" I repeated.

"I'se sick," the voice said croakingly out of the strange black face which was not attached to Dellie's big, squat body, but stuck out from under a pile of tangled bedclothes. Then the voice added: "Mighty sick."

"I'm sorry," I managed to say.

The eyes remained fixed on me for a moment, then they left me and the head rolled back on the pillow. "Sorry," the voice said, in a flat way which wasn't question or statement of anything. It was just the empty word put into the air with no meaning or expression, to float off like a feather or a puff of smoke, while the big eyes, with the whites like the peeled white of hard-boiled eggs, stared at the ceiling.

"Dellie," I said after a minute, "there's a tramp up at the house. He's got a knife."

She was not listening. She closed her eyes.

I tiptoed over to the hearth where Jebb was and crouched beside him. We began to talk in low voices. I was asking him to get out his train and play train. Old Jebb had put spool wheels on three cigar boxes and put wire links between the boxes to make a train for Jebb. The box that was the locomotive had the top closed and a length of broom stick for a smoke stack. Jebb didn't want to get the train out, but I told him I would go home if he didn't. So he got out the train, and the colored rocks, and fossils of crinoid stems, and other junk he used for the load, and we began to push it around, talking the way we thought trainmen talked, making a chuck-chucking sound under the breath for the noise of the locomotive and now and then uttering low, cautious toots for the whistle. We got so interested in playing train that the toots got louder. Then, before he thought, Jebb gave a good, loud *toot-toot*, blowing for a crossing.

"Come here," the voice said from the bed.

Jebb got up slow from his hands and knees, giving me a sudden, naked, inimical look.

"Come here!" the voice said.

Jebb went to the bed. Dellie propped herself weakly up on one arm, muttering, "Come closer."

Jebb stood closer.

"Last thing I do, I'm gonna do it," Dellie said. "Done tole you to be quiet."

Then she slapped him. It was an awful slap, more awful for the kind of weakness which it came from and brought to focus. I had seen her slap Jebb before, but the slapping had always been the kind of easy slap you would expect from a good-natured, grumbling Negro woman like Dellie. But this was different. It was awful. It was so awful that Jebb didn't make a sound. The tears just popped out and ran down his face, and his breath came sharp, like gasps.

Dellie fell back. "Cain't even be sick," she said to the ceiling.

"Git sick and they won't even let you lay. They tromp all over you. Cain't even be sick." Then she closed her eyes.

I went out of the room. I almost ran getting to the door, and I did run across the porch and down the steps and across the yard, not caring whether or not I stepped on the filth which had washed out from under the cabin. I ran almost all the way home. Then I thought about my mother catching me with the bare feet. So I went down to the stables.

I heard a noise in the crib, and opened the door. There was Big Jebb, sitting on an old nail keg, shelling corn into a bushel basket. I went in, pulling the door shut behind me, and crouched on the floor near him. I crouched there for a couple of minutes before either of us spoke, and watched him shelling the corn.

He had very big hands, knotted and grayish at the joints, with calloused palms which seemed to be streaked with rust with the rust coming up between the fingers to show from the back. His hands were so strong and tough that he could take a big ear of corn and rip the grains right off the cob with the palm of his hand, all in one motion, like a machine. "Work long as me," he would say, "and the good Lawd'll give you a hand lak cass-ion won't nuthin' hurt." And his hands did look like cast iron, old cast iron streaked with rust.

He was an old man, up in his seventies, thirty years or more older than Dellie, but he was strong as a bull. He was a squat sort of man, heavy in the shoulders, with remarkably long arms, the kind of build they say the river natives have on the Congo from paddling so much in their boats. He had a round bullet-head, set on powerful shoulders. His skin was very black, and the thin hair on his head was now grizzled like tufts of old cotton batting. He had small eyes and a flat nose, not big, and the kindest and wisest old face in the world, the blunt, sad, wise face of an old animal peering tolerantly out on the goings-on of the merely human creatures before him. He was a good man, and I loved him next to my mother and father. I crouched there on the floor of the crib and watched him shell corn with the rusty cast-iron hands, while he looked down at me out of the little eyes set in the blunt face.

"Dellie says she's might sick," I said.

"Yeah," he said.

"What's she sick from?"

"Woman-mizry," he said.

"What's woman-mizry?"

"Hit comes on 'em," he said. "Hit just comes on 'em when the time comes."

"What is it?"

"Hit is the change," he said. "Hit is the change of life and time."

"What changes?"

"You too young to know."

"Tell me."

"Time come and you find out everthing."

I knew that there was no use in asking him any more. When I asked him things and he said that, I always knew that he would not tell me. So I continued to crouch there and watch him. Now that I had sat there a little while, I was cold again.

"What you shiver fer?" he asked me.

"I'm cold. I'm cold because it's blackberry winter," I said.

"Maybe 'tis and maybe 'tain't," he said.

"My mother says it is."

"Ain't sayen Miss Sallie doan know and ain't sayen she do. But folks doan know everthing."

"Why isn't it blackberry winter?"

"Too late fer blackberry winter. Blackberries done bloomed."

"She said it was."

"Blackberry winter just a leetle cold spell. Hit come and then hit go away, and hit is growed summer of a sudden lak a gunshot. Ain't no tellen hit will go way this time."

"It's June," I said.

"June," he replied with great contempt. "That what folks say. What June mean? Maybe hit is come cold to stay."

"Why?"

"Cause this-here old yearth is tahrd. Hit is tahrd and ain't gonna perduce. Lawd let hit come rain one time forty days and forty nights, 'cause He wus tahrd of sinful folks. Maybe this-here old yearth say to the Lawd, Lawd, I done plum tahrd, Lawd, lemme rest. And Lawd say, Yearth, you done yore best, you give 'em cawn and you give 'em taters, and all they think on is they gut, and, Yearth, you kin take a rest."

"What will happen?"

"Folks will eat up everthing. The yearth won't perduce no more. Folks cut down all the trees and burn 'em cause they cold, and the yearth won't grow no more. I been tellen 'em. I been tellen folks. Sayen, maybe this year, hit is the time. But they doan listen to me, how the yearth is tahrd. Maybe this year they find out."

"Will everything die?"

"Everthing and everbody, hit will be so."

"This year?"

"Ain't no tellen. Maybe this year."

"My mother said it is blackberry winter," I said confidently, and got up.

"Ain't sayen nuthin' agin Miss Sallie," he said.

I went to the door of the crib. I was really cold now. Running, I had got up a sweat and now I was worse.

I hung on the door, looking at Jebb, who was shelling corn again.

"There's a tramp came to the house," I said. I had almost forgotten the tramp.

"Yeah."

"He came by the back way. What was he doing down there in the storm?"

"They comes and they goes," he said, "and ain't no tellen."

"He had a mean knife."

"The good ones and the bad ones, they comes and they goes. Storm or sun, light or dark. They is folks and they comes and they goes lak folks."

I hung on the door, shivering.

He studied me a moment, then said, "You git on to the house. You ketch yore death. Then what yore mammy say?"

I hesitated.

"You git," he said.

When I came to the back yard, I saw that my father was standing by the back porch and the tramp was walking toward him. They began talking before I reached them, but I got there just as my father was saying, "I'm sorry, but I haven't got any work. I got all the hands on the place I need now. I won't need any extra until wheat thrashing."

The stranger made no reply, just looked at my father.

My father took out his leather coin purse, and got out a half-dollar. He held it toward the man. "This is for half a day," he said.

The man looked at the coin, and then at my father, making no motion to take the money. But that was the right amount. A dollar a day was what you paid them back in 1910. And the man hadn't even worked half a day.

Then the man reached out and took the coin. He dropped it into the right side pocket of his coat. Then he said, very slowly and without feeling: "I didn't want to work on your — farm."

He used the word which they would have frailed me to death for using.

I looked at my father's face and it was streaked white under the sunburn. Then he said, "Get off this place. Get off this place or I won't be responsible."

The man dropped his right hand into his pants pocket. It was the pocket where he kept the knife. I was just about to yell to my father about the knife when the hand came back out with nothing in it. The man gave a kind of twisted grin, showing where the teeth had been knocked out above the new scar. I thought that instant how maybe he had tried before to pull a knife on somebody else and had got his teeth knocked out.

So now he just gave that twisted, sickish grin out of the un-memorable, grayish face, and then spat on the brick path. The glob landed just about six inches from the toe of my father's right boot. My father looked down at it, and so did I. I thought that if the glob had hit my father's boot something would have happened. I looked down and saw the bright glob, and on one side of it my father's strong cowhide boots, with the brass eyelets and the leather thongs, heavy boots splashed with good red mud and set solid on the bricks, and on the other side the pointed-toe, broken, black shoes, on which the mud looked so sad and out of place. Then I saw one of the black shoes move a little, just a twitch first, then a real step backward.

The man moved in a quarter circle to the end of the porch, with my father's steady gaze upon him all the while. At the end of the porch, the man reached up to the shelf where the wash pans were to get his little newspaper-wrapped parcel. Then he disappeared around the corner of the house and my father mounted the porch and went into the kitchen without a word.

I followed around the house to see what the man would do. I wasn't afraid of him now, no matter if he did have the knife. When I got around in front, I saw him going out the yard gate and starting up the drive toward the pike. So I ran to catch up with him. He was sixty yards or so up the drive before I caught up.

I did not walk right up even with him at first, but trailed him, the way a kid will, about seven or eight feet behind, now and then running two or three steps in order to hold my place against his longer stride. When I first came up behind him, he turned to give me a look, just a meaningless look, and then fixed his eyes up the drive and kept on walking.

When we had got around the bend in the drive which cut the house from sight, and were going along by the edge of the woods, I decided to come up even with him. I ran a few steps, and was by his side, or almost, but some feet off to the right. I walked along in this position for a while, and he never noticed me. I walked along until we got within sight of the big gate that let on the pike.

Then I said: "Where did you come from?"

He looked at me then with a look which seemed almost surprised that I was there. Then he said, "It ain't none of yore business."

We went on another fifty feet.

Then I said, "Where are you going?"

He stopped, studied me dispassionately for a moment, then suddenly took a step toward me and leaned his face down at me. The lips jerked back, but not in any grin, to show where the teeth were knocked out and to make the scar on the lower lip come white with the tension.

He said: "Stop following me. You don't stop following me and I cut yore throat, you little son-of-a-bitch."

Then he went on to the gate, and up the pike.

That was thirty-five years ago. Since that time my father and mother have died. I was still a boy, but a big boy, when my father got cut on the blade of a mowing machine and died of lockjaw. My mother sold the place and went to town to live with her sister. But she never took hold after my father's death, and she died within three years, right in middle life. My aunt always said, "Sallie just died of a broken heart, she was so devoted." Dellie is dead, too, but she died, I heard, quite a long time after we sold the farm.

As for Little Jebb, he grew up to be a mean and ficey Negro. He killed another Negro in a fight and got sent to the penitentiary, where he is yet, the last I heard tell. He probably grew up to be mean and ficey from just being picked on so much by the children of the other tenants, who were jealous of Jebb and Dellie for being thrifty and clever and being white-folks' niggers.

Old Jebb lived forever. I saw him ten years ago and he was

about a hundred then, and not looking much different. He was living in town then, on relief—that was back in the Depression—when I went to see him. He said to me: "Too strong to die. When I was a young feller just comen on and seen how things wuz, I prayed the Lawd. I said, Oh, Lawd, gimme strength and meke me strong fer to do and to in-dure. The Lawd hearkened to my prayer. He give me strength. I was in-duren proud fer being strong and me much man. The Lawd give me my prayer and my strength. But now He done gone off and fergot me and left me alone with my strength. A man doan know what to pray fer, and him mortal."

Jebb is probably living yet, as far as I know.

That is what has happened since the morning when the tramp leaned his face down at me and showed his teeth and said: "Stop following me. You don't stop following me and I cut yore throat, you little son-of-a-bitch." That was what he said, for me not to follow him. But I did follow him, all the years.

QUESTIONS FOR DISCUSSION

THE LIFE AND WORK OF PROFESSOR ROY MILLEN

1. Professor Millen, doctor of philosophy and teacher of long experience, has looked forward patiently to an opportunity to finish his book. Are there causes other than his wife's illness which have prevented him from so doing?

2. Professor Millen's struggles to get his degree and the way in which he came to his university job are detailed. What questions are raised about his "solidity of character," "spirit of patient inquiry," and "philosophical bent"?

3. The student obviously represents something that rouses the teacher's deep animosity. In the light of what we know of the teacher, what would you say that something is?

4. We are told that the student has earned A grades but lacks real intellectual substance and scholarly patience. Does Professor Millen merely invent this last part as an excuse, or could it be the truth?

5. Problems inherent in the relationship between persons separated by age are posed. How would you define these problems?

6. We may safely assume that the chief purpose of this story is not to discourage students from asking teachers for letters of recommendation. What, then, does the story have as an objective?

THE CIRCUS IN THE ATTIC

1. What does Warren achieve by devoting so many pages to background before he introduces Bolton Lovehart?

2. The author permits a particular attitude of his to obtrude upon the early part of the story, an attitude about the Civil War. What does he show his feelings to be?

3. The story encompasses three wars—the Civil War and World Wars I and II—which establish the limits of the time span covered. How does Bolton Lovehart's connection with and reaction to each of these wars serve to underscore the story motif of a changing South?

4. ". . . for people always believe what truth they have to believe to go on being the way they are." What application do these words, appearing early, have to the overtones of meaning suggested by the story?

5. Explain how false pride, against a backdrop of disintegrating social patterns and structures, is an element in the author's development of character.

6. Bolton Lovehart's leisurely manner of life without economic stress conforms to the traditional pattern associated with gentility and aristocracy in the Old South. What are the distinguishing characteristics and attributes of this life of "quality"; what apparent effects does it have upon those who live it; and why does it appear anomalous to the twentieth century?

7. Bolton's circus in the attic obviously represents escape from reality. From what is he withdrawing? Are the answers to this question suggestive of symbolical meanings related to development in the South?

8. The discrepancy between illusion and reality is a theme central to the story. Explain.

A SUGGESTED INTERPRETATION

BLACKBERRY WINTER

This is the story of a boy and a man. As a portion of the boy's day at a particular time and place is brilliantly illuminated, we are given an intimation of what the man thinks life was and is. That day long ago, surely, is only a representative spot of time utilized to pin-point a turning, a spiritual metamorphosis unsuited to bold tracing or direct articulation.

That which may be talked about directly throughout the story is the force of the spring flood, which is not unlike the latent power stirring in the boy. The turbulent and torrential waters, which signal the frightening thrust of life itself, help communicate the sense of displacement and far-reaching natural mutation. In living through the pervasive, final wet chill of spring, the boy is exposed primarily not to a glimpse of evil but rather to one of uncontained, dynamic energy. He is both disturbed and excited to discover that the carefully circumscribed, neatly arranged world he knows is not simply what it appears to be——that life has in its main stream hard times, struggles, and hidden obstacles. At the moment of the story, however, this young creature, alive with strange forces not unlike despair, is fortified by the bulwark of a reassuring parental relationship.

The tramp appears quite mysteriously, almost out of the flood. Insolent, disorderly, unruly, he is an embodiment of that challenging, 'rightening, and unknown life force that must be understood, tamed, even subdued. But clearly, this is a savage, wild force that wants not to be questioned, not to be fathomed. That the boy, out of the security and well-being of his own back yard, almost dumbly chooses to pursue the inscrutable tramp is indicative of the restless curiosity which will characterize his development in life.

In the process of saying these things, the story frames certain other, deeper questions. What are the sources of human action, the obscure beginnings which gradually come to motivate and dominate a human life? Why is man impelled by stubborn defiance arduously to pursue the imaginative life of the spirit, to seek answers to marvelously unanswerable questions? Why does the writer chase after the struggles, hard times, and hidden obstacles in the intellectually adventurous main stream of life? Why does one attempt to expose a part of life through the painful disciplines of writing?

Apart from these meanings which are implicit, the story is an open exposition of a young boy's reverie, showing his capacity to transform experience imaginatively. Literal understandings are effectively communicated through meticulously chosen details put together in meaningful patterns. Metaphor, especially, is notably utilized; the figures of speech contain startling surprises which, by their vividness, bring the reader eye to eye with what is happening. The mode of casting thoughts into words and sentences is characterized by honesty and directness. We learn that homespun plainness has its own luster. Earthiness and authenticity are achieved with appropriate local vocabulary and conversation. The boy's searching perceptiveness and his healthy state of well-being in relation to his parents are elicited with clarity but without sentimentality. Quite without considering any overtones of meaning, the outward story justifies itself and stands alone.

Blackberry winter is a time of maturation and ripening. By throwing a floodlight of luminous memory backward upon a boy in Tennessee, Robert Penn Warren has explored the soil of planting, the climate of growth, the time of harvest.

SUBJECTS FOR WRITTEN COMPOSITION

1. Explore Warren's use of symbolism—his technique for revealing or suggesting general truths and abstract, intangible ideas through concrete actualities. Work out a personal critical-interpretive study of "Blackberry Winter" or "Circus in the Attic."

2. Study Warren's use of metaphor. After searching out his more noteworthy figures of speech and listing them, prepare a composition analyzing their substance and qualities.

3. Write a theme on Warren's use of local color. Show the various components of this aspect of his writing and demonstrate your understanding of how it relates to and is an integral part of any one of his plots.

4. Analyze the author's capacity to reveal psychological insight and motivation of character. Tell how this talent works to provide a fuller view of what is happening in the stories.

5. Warren seems not to be afraid to deal honestly with such "sacred cows" as academic life and Southern tradition. Show what "myths" or basic assumptions he undertakes to upset in either or both of these areas.

6. Compare and contrast Warren's boy in "Blackberry Winter" with Joyce's boy in "Araby." Show the essential likenesses and differences between their characters and problems.

James
Joyce

James Joyce

JAMES JOYCE, the most famous of all Irish novelists, was born near Dublin, the heart of Ireland's intellectual and artistic life, in 1882. He was trained by the Jesuits, who at one time hoped that he would join their order; but Joyce early became estranged from the Jesuits and defected from the Catholic Church. In fact, he made a titanic effort to free himself of all aspects of the past— family, religion, country—that were local and provincial. In 1902 he left Ireland and spent most of his adult life in Trieste, Zurich, and Paris. The next twenty years brought Joyce his share of struggles—with poverty, which he fought off by teaching languages and working as a bank clerk; with extremely weak eyesight; with publishers, who were shy of the extraordinary originality of his literary productions; and principally with the necessities of his own creative spirit. After the publication of "Ulysses" in 1922, Joyce was relieved, through the gift of an Eng-lishwoman, from the necessity of earning his living, and gave himself over entirely to literary work, seventeen years of which was devoted to the writing of "Finnegans Wake" (1939). Joyce died in 1941.

Joyce's total literary output was not large, but he did work in most of the traditional genres: lyric poems, "Chamber Music" (1907); short stories, "Dubliners" (1914); a play, "Exiles" (1915); a short novel, "A Portrait of the Artist as a Young Man" (1916); a novel of epic proportions, "Ulysses" (1922). "Finnegans Wake" (1939) is hard to categorize: it is not so much a novel as an experimental creation **sui generis,** in a style so private as to be almost incomprehensible.

This relationship of Joyce to the idea of genre is important because it points up his concern with art as technique. A literary genre has, like myth, the weight of history behind it, and is, so to speak, the product of hundreds of years of "literary wisdom." From the beginning, therefore, the student will do well to take careful note of Joyce's way with words and structural patterns. His sentences, for example, are as much aural as visual and, being aural, they appeal to the voice as well as to the mind. This is not to say that Joyce lacked an interest in life in its painful length and breadth. On the contrary, his remarkable creative energy was spent on technique not for its own sake but as a method of both discovering truth and revealing it. He was a keen observer of reality, which he loved with genuine frankness, and he attempted always to get at the truth behind the appearance. Further, Joyce was never a mere theorist: like the Sophocles of Arnold's description, he saw life steadily and he saw it whole. For example, although Joyce voluntarily exiled himself from Ireland, Ireland as subject matter was never very far from his imagination; he had a microscopic knowledge of Dublin life which he used to full advantage. But, like Robert Browning, he was determined that his art should "no wise speak to men,/ Only to mankind. . . ." Hence his aloofness from Irish nationalism and the universal quality even of his treatment of the squalid aspects of life in his native city.

Joyce was one of the most completely dedicated literary artists. "Welcome, O life!" he declared in the words of Stephen Dedalus, "I go to encounter for the millionth time the reality of experience and to forge in the smithy of my soul the uncreated conscience of my race."

Araby

NORTH RICHMOND STREET, BEING BLIND, WAS A QUIET STREET EXCEPT at the hour when the Christian Brothers' School set the boys free. An uninhabited house of two storeys stood at the blind end, detached from its neighbours in a square ground. The other houses of the street, conscious of decent lives within them, gazed at one another with brown imperturbable faces.

The former tenant of our house, a priest, had died in the back drawing-room. Air, musty from having been long enclosed, hung in all the rooms, and the waste room behind the kitchen was littered with old useless papers. Among these I found a few paper-covered books, the pages of which were curled and damp: *The Abbot,* by Walter Scott, *The Devout Communicant* and *The Memoirs of Vidocq.* I liked the last best because its leaves were yellow. The wild garden behind the house contained a central apple-tree and a few straggling bushes under one of which I found the late tenant's rusty bicycle-pump. He had been a very charitable priest; in his will he had left all his money to institutions and the furniture of his house to his sister.

When the short days of winter came dusk fell before we had well eaten our dinners. When we met in the street the houses had grown sombre. The space of sky above us was the colour of everchanging violet and towards it the lamps of the street lifted their feeble lanterns. The cold air stung us and we played till our bodies glowed. Our shouts echoed in the silent street. The career of our play brought us through the dark muddy lanes behind the houses where we ran the gauntlet of the rough tribes from the cottages, to the back doors of the dark dripping gardens where odours arose from the ashpits, to the dark odorous stables where a coachman smoothed and combed the horse or shook music from the buckled harness. When we returned to the street light from the kitchen windows had filled the areas. If my uncle was seen turning the corner we hid in the shadow until we had seen him safely housed. Or if Mangan's sister came out on the doorstep to call her brother in to his tea we watched her from our shadow peer up and down the street. We waited to see whether she would remain or go in and, if she remained, we left our shadow and walked up to Mangan's steps resignedly. She was waiting for us, her figure defined by the light from the half-opened door. Her brother always teased her before he obeyed and I stood by the railings looking at her. Her dress swung as she moved her body and the soft rope of her hair tossed from side to side.

Every morning I lay on the floor in the front parlour watching her door. The blind was pulled down to within an inch of the sash so that I could not be seen. When she came out on the doorstep my heart leaped. I ran to the hall, seized my books and followed her. I kept her brown figure always in my eye and, when we came near the point at which our ways diverged, I quickened my pace and passed her. This happened morning after morning. I had never spoken to her, except for a few casual words, and yet her name was like a summons to all my foolish blood.

Her image accompanied me even in places the most hostile to romance. On Saturday evenings when my aunt went marketing I had to go to carry some of the parcels. We walked through the flaring streets, jostled by drunken men and bargaining women, amid the curses of labourers, the shrill litanies of shop-boys who stood on guard by the barrels of pigs' cheeks, the nasal chanting of street-singers, who sang a *come-all-you* about O'Donovan Rossa, or a ballad about the troubles in our native land. These noises converged in a single sensation of life for me: I imagined that I bore my chalice safely through a throng of foes. Her name sprang to my lips at moments in strange prayers and praises which I myself did not understand. My eyes were often full of tears (I could not tell why) and at times a flood from my heart seemed to pour itself out into my bosom. I thought little of the future. I did not know whether I would ever speak to her or not or, if I spoke to her, how I could tell her of my confused adoration.

But my body was like a harp and her words and gestures were like fingers running upon the wires.

One evening I went into the back drawing-room in which the priest had died. It was a dark rainy evening and there was no sound in the house. Through one of the broken panes I heard the rain impinge upon the earth, the fine incessant needles of water playing in the sodden beds. Some distant lamp or lighted window gleamed below me. I was thankful that I could see so little. All my senses seemed to desire to veil themselves and, feeling that I was about to slip from them, I pressed the palms of my hands together until they trembled, murmuring: *"O love! O love!"* many times.

At last she spoke to me. When she addressed the first words to me I was so confused that I did not know what to answer. She asked me was I going to *Araby.* I forgot whether I answered yes or no. It would be a splendid bazaar, she said she would love to go.

"And why can't you?" I asked.

While she spoke she turned a silver bracelet round and round her wrist. She could not go, she said, because there would be a retreat that week in her convent. Her brother and two other boys were fighting for their caps and I was alone at the railings. She held one of the spikes, bowing her head towards me. The light from the lamp opposite our door caught the white curve of her neck, lit up her hair that rested there and, falling, lit up the hand upon the railing. It fell over one side of her dress and caught the white border of a petticoat, just visible as she stood at ease.

"It's well for you," she said.

"If I go," I said, "I will bring you something."

What innumerable follies laid waste my waking and sleeping thoughts after that evening! I wished to annihilate the tedious intervening days. I chafed against the work of school. At night in my bedroom and by day in the classroom her image came between me and the page I strove to read. The syllables of the word *Araby* were called to me through the silence in which my soul luxuriated and cast an Eastern enchantment over me. I asked for leave to go to the bazaar on Saturday night. My aunt was surprised and hoped it was not some Freemason affair. I answered few questions in class. I watched my master's face pass from amiability to sternness; he hoped I was not beginning to idle. I could not call my wandering thoughts together. I had hardly any patience with the serious work of life which, now that it stood between me and my desire, seemed to me child's play, ugly monotonous child's play.

On Saturday morning I reminded my uncle that I wished to go to the bazaar in the evening. He was fussing at the hallstand, looking for the hat-brush, and answered me curtly:

"Yes, boy, I know."

As he was in the hall I could not go into the front parlour and lie at the window. I felt the house in bad humour and walked slowly towards the school. The air was pitilessly raw and already my heart misgave me.

When I came home to dinner my uncle had not yet been home. Still it was early. I sat staring at the clock for some time and, when its ticking began to irritate me, I left the room. I mounted the staircase and gained the upper part of the house. The high cold empty gloomy rooms liberated me and I went from room to room singing. From the front window I saw my companions playing below in the street. Their cries reached me weakened and indistinct and, leaning my forehead against the cool glass, I looked over at the dark house where she lived. I may have stood there for an hour, seeing nothing but the brown-clad figure cast by my imagination, touched discreetly by the lamplight at the curved neck, at the hand upon the railings and at the border below the dress.

When I came downstairs again I found Mrs. Mercer sitting at the fire. She was an old garrulous woman, a pawnbroker's widow, who collected used stamps for some pious purpose. I had to endure the gossip of the tea-table. The meal was prolonged beyond an hour and still my uncle did not come. Mrs. Mercer stood up to go: she was sorry she couldn't wait any longer, but it was after eight o'clock and she did not like to be out late, as the night air was bad for her. When she had gone I began to walk up and down the room, clenching my fists. My aunt said:

"I'm afraid you may put off your bazaar for this night of Our Lord."

At nine o'clock I heard my uncle's latchkey in the halldoor. I heard him talking to himself and heard the hallstand rocking when it had received the weight of his overcoat. I could interpret these signs. When he was midway through his dinner I asked him to give me the money to go to the bazaar. He had forgotten.

"The people are in bed and after their first sleep now," he said.

I did not smile. My aunt said to him energetically:

"Can't you give him the money and let him go? You've kept him late enough as it is."

My uncle said he was very sorry he had forgotten. He said he believed in the old saying: "All work and no play makes Jack a dull boy." He asked me where I was going and, when I had told him a second time he asked me did I know *The Arab's Farewell to His Steed*. When I left the kitchen he was about to recite the opening lines of the piece to my aunt.

I held a florin tightly in my hand as I strode down Buckingham Street towards the station. The sight of the streets thronged with buyers and glaring with gas recalled to me the purpose of my journey. I took my seat in a third-class carriage of a deserted train. After an intolerable delay the train moved out of the station slowly. It crept onward among ruinous houses and over the twinkling river. At Westland Row Station a crowd of people pressed to the carriage doors; but the porters moved them back, saying that it was a special train for the bazaar. I remained alone in the bare carriage. In a few minutes the train drew up beside an improvised wooden platform. I passed out on to the road and saw by the lighted dial of a clock that it was ten minutes to ten. In front of me was a large building which displayed the magical name.

I could not find any sixpenny entrance and, fearing that the bazaar would be closed, I passed in quickly through a turnstile, handing a shilling to a weary-looking man. I found myself in a big hall girdled at half its height by a gallery. Nearly all the stalls were closed and the greater part of the hall was in darkness. I recognised a silence like that which pervades a church after a service. I walked into the centre of the bazaar timidly. A few people were gathered about the stalls which were still open. Before a curtain, over which the words *Café Chantant* were written in coloured lamps, two men were counting money on a salver. I listened to the fall of the coins.

Remembering with difficulty why I had come I went over to one of the stalls and examined porcelain vases and flowered tea-sets. At the door of the stall a young lady was talking and laughing with two young gentlemen. I remarked their English accents and listened vaguely to their conversation.

"O, I never said such a thing!"

"O, but you did!"

"O, but I didn't!"

"Didn't she say that?"

"Yes. I heard her."

"O, there's a . . . fib!"

Observing me the young lady came over and asked me did I wish to buy anything. The tone of her voice was not encouraging; she seemed to have spoken to me out of a sense of duty. I looked humbly at the great jars that stood like eastern guards at either side of the dark entrance to the stall and murmured:

"No, thank you."

The young lady changed the position of one of the vases and went back to the two young men. They began to talk of the same subject. Once or twice the young lady glanced at me over her shoulder.

I lingered before her stall, though I knew my stay was useless, to make my interest in her wares seem the more real. Then I turned away slowly and walked down the middle of the bazaar. I allowed the two pennies to fall against the sixpence in my pocket. I heard a voice call from one end of the gallery that the light was out. The upper part of the hall was now completely dark.

Gazing up into the darkness I saw myself as a creature driven and derided by vanity; and my eyes burned with anguish and anger.

Counterparts

THE BELL RANG FURIOUSLY AND, WHEN MISS PARKER WENT TO THE tube, a furious voice called out in a piercing North of Ireland accent:

"Send Farrington here!"

Miss Parker returned to her machine, saying to a man who was writing at a desk:

"Mr. Alleyne wants you upstairs."

The man muttered *"Blast* him!" under his breath and pushed back his chair to stand up. When he stood up he was tall and of great bulk. He had a hanging face, dark wine-coloured, with fair eyebrows and moustache: his eyes bulged forward slightly and the whites of them were dirty. He lifted up the counter and, passing by the clients, went out of the office with a heavy step.

He went heavily upstairs until he came to the second landing, where a door bore a brass plate with the inscription *Mr. Alleyne.* Here he halted, puffing with labour and vexation, and knocked. The shrill voice cried:

"Come in!"

The man entered Mr. Alleyne's room. Simultaneously Mr. Alleyne, a little man wearing gold-rimmed glasses on a clean-shaven face, shot his head up over a pile of documents. The head itself was so pink and hairless it seemed like a large egg reposing on the papers. Mr. Alleyne did not lose a moment:

"Farrington? What is the meaning of this? Why have I always to complain of you? May I ask you why you haven't made a copy of that contract between Bodley and Kirwan? I told you it must be ready by four o'clock."

"But Mr. Shelley said, sir——"

"*Mr. Shelley said, sir.* . . . Kindly attend to what I say and not to what *Mr. Shelley says, sir.* You have always some excuse or another for shirking work. Let me tell you that if the contract is not copied before this evening I'll lay the matter before Mr. Crosbie. . . . Do you hear me now?"

"Yes, sir."

"Do you hear me now? . . . Ay and another little matter! I might as well be talking to the wall as talking to you. Understand once for all that you get a half an hour for your lunch and not an hour and a half. How many courses do you want, I'd like to know. . . . Do you mind me now?"

"Yes, sir."

Mr. Alleyne bent his head again upon his pile of papers. The man stared fixedly at the polished skull which directed the affairs of Crosbie & Alleyne, gauging its fragility. A spasm of rage gripped his throat for a few moments and then passed, leaving after it a sharp sensation of thirst. The man recognised the sensation and felt that he must have a good night's drinking. The middle of the month was passed and, if he could get the copy done in time, Mr. Alleyne might give him an order on the cashier. He stood still, gazing fixedly at the head upon the pile of papers. Suddenly Mr. Alleyne began to upset all the papers, searching for something. Then, as if he had been unaware of the man's presence till that moment, he shot up his head again, saying:

"Eh? Are you going to stand there all day? Upon my word, Farrington, you take things easy!"

"I was waiting to see . . ."

"Very good, you needn't wait to see. Go downstairs and do your work."

The man walked heavily towards the door and, as he went out of the room, he heard Mr. Alleyne cry after him that if the contract was not copied by evening Mr. Crosbie would hear of the matter.

He returned to his desk in the lower office and counted the sheets which remained to be copied. He took up his pen and dipped it in the ink but he continued to stare stupidly at the last words he had written: *In no case shall the said Bernard Bodley be* . . . The evening was falling and in a few minutes they would be lighting the gas: then he could write. He felt that he must slake the thirst in his throat. He stood up from his desk and, lifting the counter as before, passed out of the office. As he was passing out the chief clerk looked at him inquiringly.

"It's all right, Mr. Shelley," said the man, pointing with his finger to indicate the objective of his journey.

The chief clerk glanced at the hat-rack, but, seeing the row complete, offered no remark. As soon as he was on the landing the man pulled a shepherd's plaid cap out of his pocket, put it on his head and ran quickly down the rickety stairs. From the street door he walked on furtively on the inner side of the path towards the corner and all at once dived into a doorway. He was now safe in the dark snug of O'Neill's shop, and, filling up the little window that looked into the bar with his inflamed face, the colour of dark wine or dark meat, he called out:

"Here, Pat, give us a g.p., like a good fellow."

The curate brought him a glass of plain porter. The man drank it at a gulp and asked for a caraway seed. He put his penny on the counter and, leaving the curate to grope for it in the gloom, retreated out of the snug as furtively as he had entered it.

Darkness, accompanied by a thick fog, was gaining upon the dusk of February and the lamps in Eustace Street had been lit. The man went up by the houses until he reached the door of the office, wondering whether he could finish his copy in time. On the stairs a moist pungent odour of perfumes saluted his nose: evidently Miss Delacour had come while he was out in O'Neill's. He crammed his cap back again into his pocket and re-entered the office, assuming an air of absent mindedness.

"Mr. Alleyne has been calling for you," said the chief clerk severely. "Where were you?"

The man glanced at the two clients who were standing at the counter as if to intimate that their presence prevented him from answering. As the clients were both male the chief clerk allowed himself a laugh.

"I know that game," he said. "Five times in one day is a little bit. . . . Well, you better look sharp and get a copy of our correspondence in the Delacour case for Mr. Alleyne."

This address in the presence of the public, his run upstairs and the porter he had gulped down so hastily confused the man and, as he sat down at his desk to get what was required, he realised how hopeless was the task of finishing his copy of the contract before half past five. The dark damp night was coming and he longed to spend it in the bars, drinking with his friends amid the glare of gas and the clatter of glasses. He got out the Delacour correspondence and passed out of the office. He hoped Mr. Alleyne would not discover that the last two letters were missing.

The moist pungent perfume lay all the way up to Mr. Alleyne's room. Miss Delacour was a middle-aged woman of Jewish appearance. Mr. Alleyne was said to be sweet on her or on her money. She came to the office often and stayed a long time when she came. She was sitting beside his desk now in an aroma of perfumes, smoothing the handle of her umbrella and nodding the great black feather in her hat. Mr. Alleyne had swivelled his chair round to face her and thrown his right foot jauntily upon his left knee. The man put the correspondence on the desk and bowed respectfully but neither Mr. Alleyne nor Miss Delacour took any notice of his bow. Mr. Alleyne tapped a finger on the correspondence and then flicked it towards him as if to say: *"That's all right: you can go."*

The man returned to the lower office and sat down again at his desk. He stared intently at the incomplete phrase: *In no case shall the said Bernard Bodley be* . . . and thought how strange it was that the last three words began with the same letter. The chief clerk began to hurry Miss Parker, saying she would never have the letters typed in time for post. The man listened to the clicking of the machine for a few minutes and then set to work to finish his copy. But his head was not clear and his mind wandered away to the glare and rattle of the public-house. It was a night for hot punches. He struggled on with his copy, but when the clock struck five he had still fourteen pages to write. Blast it! He couldn't finish it in time. He longed to execrate aloud, to bring his fist down on something violently. He was so enraged that he wrote *Bernard Bernard* instead of *Bernard Bodley* and had to begin again on a clean sheet.

He felt strong enough to clear out the whole office single-handed. His body ached to do something, to rush out and revel in violence. All the indignities of his life enraged him. . . . Could he ask the cashier privately for an advance? No, the cashier was no good, no damn good: he wouldn't give an advance. . . . He knew where he would meet the boys: Leonard and O'Halloran and Nosey Flynn. The barometer of his emotional nature was set for a spell of riot.

His imagination had so abstracted him that his name was called twice before he answered. Mr. Alleyne and Miss Delacour were stand-

ing outside the counter and all the clerks had turned round in antic-
ipation of something. The man got up from his desk. Mr. Alleyne
began a tirade of abuse, saying that two letters were missing. The man
answered that he knew nothing about them, that he had made a faithful copy. The tirade continued: it was so bitter and violent that the
man could hardly restrain his fist from descending upon the head of
the manikin before him:

"I know nothing about any other two letters," he said stupidly.

"*You—know—nothing*. Of course you know nothing," said Mr. Alleyne. "Tell me," he added, glancing first for approval to the lady
beside him, "do you take me for a fool? Do you think me an utter
fool?"

The man glanced from the lady's face to the little egg-shaped head
and back again; and, almost before he was aware of it, his tongue had
found a felicitous moment:

"I don't think, sir," he said, "that that's a fair question to put to me."

There was a pause in the very breathing of the clerks. Everyone
was astounded (the author of the witticism no less than his neighbours) and Miss Delacour, who was a stout amiable person, began to
smile broadly. Mr. Alleyne flushed to the hue of a wild rose and his
mouth twitched with a dwarf's passion. He shook his fist in the man's
face till it seemed to vibrate like the knob of some electric machine:

"You impertinent ruffian! You impertinent ruffian! I'll make short
work of you! Wait till you see! You'll apologise to me for your impertinence or you'll quit the office instanter! You'll quit this, I'm telling you, or you'll apologise to me!"

He stood in a doorway opposite the office watching to see if the
cashier would come out alone. All the clerks passed out and finally
the cashier came out with the chief clerk. It was no use trying to say
a word to him when he was with the chief clerk. The man felt that
his position was bad enough. He had been obliged to offer an abject
apology to Mr. Alleyne for his impertinence but he knew what a
hornet's nest the office would be for him. He could remember the way
in which Mr. Alleyne had hounded little Peake out of the office in
order to make room for his own nephew. He felt savage and thirsty
and revengeful, annoyed with himself and with everyone else. Mr.
Alleyne would never give him an hour's rest; his life would be a hell
to him. He had made a proper fool of himself this time. Could he
not keep his tongue in his cheek? But they had never pulled together

from the first, he and Mr. Alleyne, ever since the day Mr. Alleyne had overheard him mimicking his North of Ireland accent to amuse Higgins and Miss Parker: that had been the beginning of it. He might have tried Higgins for the money, but sure Higgins never had anything for himself. A man with two establishments to keep up, of course he couldn't. . . .

He felt his great body again aching for the comfort of the public-house. The fog had begun to chill him and he wondered could he touch Pat in O'Neill's. He could not touch him for more than a bob—and a bob was no use. Yet he must get money somewhere or other: he had spent his last penny for the g.p. and soon it would be too late for getting money anywhere. Suddenly, as he was fingering his watch-chain, he thought of Terry Kelly's pawn-office in Fleet Street. That was the dart! Why didn't he think of it sooner?

He went through the narrow alley of Temple Bar quickly, muttering to himself that they could all go to hell because he was going to have a good night of it. The clerk in Terry Kelly's said *A crown!* but the consignor held out for six shillings; and in the end the six shillings was allowed him literally. He came out of the pawn-office joyfully, making a little cylinder of the coins between his thumb and fingers. In Westmoreland Street the footpaths were crowded with young men and women returning from business and ragged urchins ran here and there yelling out the names of the evening editions. The man passed through the crowd, looking on the spectacle generally with proud satisfaction and staring masterfully at the office-girls. His head was full of the noises of tram-gongs and swishing trolleys and his nose already sniffed the curling fumes of punch. As he walked on he preconsidered the terms in which he would narrate the incident to the boys:

"So, I just looked at him—coolly, you know, and looked at her. Then I looked back at him again—taking my time, you know. 'I don't think that that's a fair question to put to me,' says I."

Nosey Flynn was sitting up in his usual corner of Davy Byrne's and, when he heard the story, he stood Farrington a half-one, saying it was as smart a thing as ever he heard. Farrington stood a drink in his turn. After a while O'Halloran and Paddy Leonard came in and the story was repeated to them. O'Halloran stood tailors of malt, hot, all round and told the story of the retort he had made to the chief clerk when he was in Callan's of Fownes's Street; but, as the retort was after the manner of the liberal shepherds in the eclogues, he had to admit that it was not as clever as Farrington's retort. At this Farrington told the boys to polish off that and have another.

Just as they were naming their poisons who should come in but Higgins! Of course he had to join in with the others. The men asked him to give his version of it, and he did so with great vivacity for the sight of five small hot whiskies was very exhilarating. Everyone roared laughing when he showed the way in which Mr. Alleyne shook his fist in Farrington's face. Then he imitated Farrington, saying, *"And here was my nabs, as cool as you please,"* while Farrington looked at the company out of his heavy dirty eyes, smiling and at times drawing forth stray drops of liquor from his moustache with the aid of his lower lip.

When that round was over there was a pause. O'Halloran had money but neither of the other two seemed to have any; so the whole party left the shop somewhat regretfully. At the corner of Duke Street Higgins and Nosey Flynn bevelled off to the left while the other three turned back towards the city. Rain was drizzling down on the cold streets and, when they reached the Ballast Office, Farrington suggested the Scotch House. The bar was full of men and loud with the noise of tongues and glasses. The three men pushed past the whining match-sellers at the door and formed a little party at the corner of the counter. They began to exchange stories. Leonard introduced them to a young fellow named Weathers who was performing at the Tivoli as an acrobat and knockabout *artiste*. Farrington stood a drink all round. Weathers said he would take a small Irish and Apollinaris. Farrington, who had definite notions of what was what, asked the boys would they have an Apollinaris too; but the boys told Tim to make theirs hot. The talk became theatrical. O'Halloran stood a round and then Farrington stood another round, Weathers protesting that the hospitality was too Irish. He promised to get them in behind the scenes and introduce them to some nice girls. O'Halloran said that he and Leonard would go, but that Farrington wouldn't go because he was a married man; and Farrington's heavy dirty eyes leered at the company in token that he understood he was being chaffed. Weathers made them all have just one little tincture at his expense and promised to meet them later on at Mulligan's in Poolbeg Street.

When the Scotch House closed they went round to Mulligan's. They went into the parlour at the back and O'Halloran ordered small hot specials all round. They were all beginning to feel mellow. Farrington was just standing another round when Weathers came back. Much to Farrington's relief he drank a glass of bitter this time. Funds were getting low but they had enough to keep them going. Presently two young women with big hats and a young man in a check suit came in and sat at a table close by. Weathers saluted them and told the company that they were out of the Tivoli. Farrington's eyes wandered at every moment in the direction of one of the young women. There was something striking in her appearance. An immense scarf of peacock-blue muslin was wound round her hat and knotted in a great bow under her chin; and she wore bright yellow gloves, reaching to the elbow. Farrington gazed admiringly at the plump arm which she moved very often and with much grace; and when, after a little time, she answered his gaze he admired still more her large dark brown eyes. The oblique staring expression in them fascinated him. She glanced at him once or twice and, when the party was leaving the room, she brushed against his chair and said "O, pardon!" in a London accent. He watched her leave the room in the hope that she would look back at him, but he was disappointed. He cursed his want of money and cursed all the rounds he had stood, particularly all the whiskies and Apollinaris which he had stood to Weathers. If there was one thing that he hated it was a sponge. He was so angry that he lost count of the conversation of his friends.

When Paddy Leonard called him he found that they were talking about feats of strength. Weathers was showing his biceps muscle to the company and boasting so much that the other two had called on Farrington to uphold the national honour. Farrington pulled up his sleeve accordingly and showed his biceps muscle to the company. The two arms were examined and compared and finally it was agreed to have a trial of strength. The table was cleared and the two men rested their elbows on it, clasping hands. When Paddy Leonard said "Go!" each was to try to bring down the other's hand on to the table. Farrington looked very serious and determined.

The trial began. After about thirty seconds Weathers brought his opponent's hand slowly down on to the table. Farrington's dark wine coloured face flushed darker still with anger and humiliation at having been defeated by such a stripling.

"You're not to put the weight of your body behind it. Play fair," he said.

"Who's not playing fair?" said the other.

"Come on again. The two best out of three."

The trial began again. The veins stood out on Farrington's forehead, and the pallor of Weathers' complexion changed to peony. Their hands and arms trembled under the stress. After a long struggle Weathers again brought his opponent's hand slowly on to the table. There was a murmur of applause from the spectators. The curate, who was standing beside the table, nodded his red head towards the victor and said with stupid familiarity:

"Ah! that's the knack!"

"What the hell do you know about it?" said Farrington fiercely, turning on the man. "What do you put in your gab for?"

"Sh, sh!" said O'Halloran, observing the violent expression of Farrington's face. "Pony up, boys. We'll have just one little smahan more and then we'll be off."

A very sullen-faced man stood at the corner of O'Connell Bridge waiting for the little Sandy-mount tram to take him home. He was full of smouldering anger and revengefulness. He felt humiliated and discontented; he did not even feel drunk; and he had only twopence in his pocket. He cursed everything. He had done for himself in the office, pawned his watch, spent all his money; and he had not even got drunk. He began to feel thirsty again and he longed to be back again in the hot reeking public-house. He had lost his reputation as a strong man, having been defeated twice by a mere boy. His heart swelled with fury and, when he thought of the woman in the big hat who had brushed against him and said *Pardon!* his fury nearly choked him.

His tram let him down at Shelbourne Road and he steered his great body along in the shadow of the wall of the barracks. He loathed returning to his home. When he went in by the side-door he found the kitchen empty and the kitchen fire nearly out. He bawled upstairs:

"Ada! Ada!"

His wife was a little sharp-faced woman who bullied her husband when he was sober and was bullied by him when he was drunk. They had five children. A little boy came running down the stairs.

"Who is that?" said the man, peering through the darkness.

"Me, pa."

"Who are you? Charlie?"

"No, pa. Tom."

"Where's your mother?"

"She's out at the chapel."

"That's right. . . . Did she think of leaving any dinner for me?"

"Yes, pa. I——"

"Light the lamp. What do you mean by having the place in darkness? Are the other children in bed?"

The man sat down heavily on one of the chairs while the little boy lit the lamp. He began to mimic his son's flat accent, saying half to himself: *"At the chapel. At the chapel, if you please!"* When the lamp was lit he banged his fist on the table and shouted:

"What's for my dinner?"

"I'm going . . . to cook it, pa," said the little boy.

The man jumped up furiously and pointed to the fire.

"On that fire! You let the fire out! By God, I'll teach you to do that again!"

He took a step to the door and seized the walking-stick which was standing behind it.

"I'll teach you to let the fire out!" he said, rolling up his sleeve in order to give his arm free play.

The little boy cried *"O, pa!"* and ran whimpering round the table, but the man followed him and caught him by the coat. The little boy looked about him wildly but, seeing no way of escape, fell upon his knees.

"Now, you'll let the fire out the next time!" said the man, striking at him vigorously with the stick. "Take that, you little whelp!"

The boy uttered a squeal of pain as the stick cut his thigh. He clasped his hands together in the air and his voice shook with fright.

"O, pa!" he cried. "Don't beat me, pa! And I'll . . . I'll say a *Hail Mary* for you. . . . I'll say a *Hail Mary* for you, pa, if you don't beat me. . . . I'll say a *Hail Mary*. . . ."

The Dead

LILY, THE CARETAKER'S DAUGHTER, WAS LITERALLY RUN OFF HER FEET.
Hardly had she brought one gentleman into the little pantry behind
the office on the ground floor and helped him off with his overcoat
than the wheezy hall-door bell clanged again and she had to scamper
along the bare hallway to let in another guest. It was well for her
she had not to attend to the ladies also. But Miss Kate and Miss Julia
had thought of that and had converted the bathroom upstairs into a
ladies' dressing-room. Miss Kate and Miss Julia were there, gossiping
and laughing and fussing, walking after each other to the head of
the stairs, peering down over the banisters and calling down to Lily
to ask her who had come.

It was always a great affair, the Misses Morkan's annual dance.
Everybody who knew them came to it, members of the family, old
friends of the family, the members of Julia's choir, any of Kate's pupils
that were grown up enough, and even some of Mary Jane's pupils too.
Never once had it fallen flat. For years and years it had gone off in
splendid style, as long as anyone could remember; ever since Kate and
Julia, after the death of their brother Pat, had left the house in
Stoney Batter and taken Mary Jane, their only niece, to live with
them in the dark, gaunt house on Usher's Island, the upper part of
which they had rented from Mr. Fulham, the corn-factor on the
ground floor. That was a good thirty years ago if it was a day. Mary
Jane, who was then a little girl in short clothes, was now the main

prop of the household, for she had the organ in Haddington Road. She had been through the Academy and gave a pupils' concert every year in the upper room of the Antient Concert Rooms. Many of her pupils belonged to the better-class families on the Kingstown and Dalkey line. Old as they were, her aunts also did their share. Julia, though she was quite grey, was still the leading soprano in Adam and Eve's, and Kate, being too feeble to go about much, gave music lessons to beginners on the old square piano in the back room. Lily, the caretaker's daughter, did housemaid's work for them. Though their life was modest, they believed in eating well; the best of everything: diamond-bone sirloins, three-shilling tea and the best bottled stout. But Lily seldom made a mistake in the orders, so that she got on well with her three mistresses. They were fussy, that was all. But the only thing they would not stand was back answers.

Of course, they had good reason to be fussy on such a night. And then it was long after ten o'clock and yet there was no sign of Gabriel and his wife. Besides they were dreadfully afraid that Freddy Malins might turn up screwed. They would not wish for worlds that any of Mary Jane's pupils should see him under the influence; and when he was like that it was sometimes very hard to manage him. Freddy Malins always came late, but they wondered what could be keeping Gabriel: and that was what brought them every two minutes to the banisters to ask Lily had Gabriel or Freddy come.

"O, Mr. Conroy," said Lily to Gabriel when she opened the door for him, "Miss Kate and Miss Julia thought you were never coming. Good-night, Mrs. Conroy."

"I'll engage they did," said Gabriel, "but they forget that my wife here takes three mortal hours to dress herself."

He stood on the mat, scraping the snow from his goloshes, while Lily led his wife to the foot of the stairs and called out:

"Miss Kate, here's Mrs. Conroy."

Kate and Julia came toddling down the dark stairs at once. Both of them kissed Gabriel's wife, said she must be perished alive, and asked was Gabriel with her.

"Here I am as right as the mail, Aunt Kate! Go on up. I'll follow," called out Gabriel from the dark.

He continued scraping his feet vigorously while the three women went upstairs, laughing, to the ladies' dressing-room. A light fringe of snow lay like a cape on the shoulders of his overcoat and like toecaps on the toes of his goloshes; and, as the buttons of his overcoat slipped with a squeaking noise through the snow-stiffened frieze, a cold, fragrant air from out-of-doors escaped from crevices and folds.

"Is it snowing again, Mr. Conroy?" asked Lily.

She had preceded him into the pantry to help him off with his overcoat. Gabriel smiled at the three syllables she had given his surname and glanced at her. She was a slim, growing girl, pale in complexion and with hay-coloured hair. The gas in the pantry made her look still paler. Gabriel had known her when she was a child and used to sit on the lowest step nursing a rag doll.

"Yes, Lily," he answered, "and I think we're in for a night of it."

He looked up at the pantry ceiling, which was shaking with the stamping and shuffling of feet on the floor above, listened for a moment to the piano and then glanced at the girl, who was folding his overcoat carefully at the end of a shelf.

"Tell me, Lily," he said in a friendly tone, "do you still go to school?"

"O no, sir," she answered. "I'm done schooling this year and more."

"O, then," said Gabriel gaily, "I suppose we'll be going to your wedding one of these fine days with your young man, eh?"

The girl glanced back at him over her shoulder and said with great bitterness:

"The men that is now is only all palaver and what they can get out of you."

Gabriel coloured, as if he felt he had made a mistake and, without looking at her, kicked off his goloshes and flicked actively with his muffler at his patent-leather shoes.

He was a stout, tallish young man. The high colour of his cheeks pushed upwards even to his forehead, where it scattered itself in a few formless patches of pale red; and on his hairless face there scintillated restlessly the polished lenses and the bright gilt rims of the glasses which screened his delicate and restless eyes. His glossy black hair was parted in the middle and brushed in a long curve behind his ears where it curled slightly beneath the groove left by his hat.

When he had flicked lustre into his shoes he stood up and pulled his waistcoat down more tightly on his plump body. Then he took a coin rapidly from his pocket.

"O Lily," he said, thrusting it into her hands, "it's Christmas-time, isn't it? Just . . . here's a little. . . ."

He walked rapidly towards the door.

"O no, sir!" cried the girl, following him. "Really, sir, I wouldn't take it."

"Christmas-time! Christmas-time!" said Gabriel, almost trotting to the stairs and waving his hand to her in deprecation.

The girl, seeing that he had gained the stairs, called out after him: "Well, thank you, sir."

He waited outside the drawing-room door until the waltz should finish, listening to the skirts that swept against it and to the shuffling of feet. He was still discomposed by the girl's bitter and sudden retort. It had cast a gloom over him which he tried to dispel by arranging his cuffs and the bows of his tie. He then took from his waistcoat pocket a little paper and glanced at the headings he had made for his speech. He was undecided about the lines from Robert Browning, for he feared they would be above the heads of his hearers. Some quotation that they would recognise from Shakespeare or from the Melodies would be better. The indelicate clacking of the men's heels and the shuffling of their soles reminded him that their grade of culture differed from his. He would only make himself ridiculous by quoting poetry to them which they could not understand. They would think that he was airing his superior education. He would fail with them just as he had failed with the girl in the pantry. He had taken up a wrong tone. His whole speech was a mistake from first to last, an utter failure.

Just then his aunts and his wife came out of the ladies' dressing-room. His aunts were two small, plainly dressed old women. Aunt Julia was an inch or so the taller. Her hair, drawn low over the tops of her ears, was grey; and grey also, with darker shadows, was her large flaccid face. Though she was stout in build and stood erect, her slow eyes and parted lips gave her the appearance of a woman who did not know where she was or where she was going. Aunt Kate was more vivacious. Her face, healthier than her sister's, was all puckers and creases, like a shrivelled red apple, and her hair, braided in the same old-fashioned way, had not lost its ripe nut colour.

They both kissed Gabriel frankly. He was their favourite nephew, the son of their dead elder sister, Ellen, who had married T. J. Conroy of the Port and Docks.

"Gretta tells me you're not going to take a cab back to Monkstown to-night, Gabriel," said Aunt Kate.

"No," said Gabriel, turning to his wife, "we had quite enough of that last year, hadn't we? Don't you remember, Aunt Kate, what a cold Gretta got out of it? Cab windows rattling all the way, and the east wind blowing in after we passed Merrion. Very jolly it was. Gretta caught a dreadful cold."

Aunt Kate frowned severely and nodded her head at every word.

"Quite right, Gabriel, quite right," she said. "You can't be too careful."

"But as for Gretta there," said Gabriel, "she'd walk home in the snow if she were let."

Mrs. Conroy laughed.

"Don't mind him, Aunt Kate," she said. "He's really an awful bother, what with green shades for Tom's eyes at night and making him do the dumb-bells, and forcing Eva to eat the stirabout. The poor child! And she simply hates the sight of it! . . . O, but you'll never guess what he makes me wear now!"

She broke out into a peal of laughter and glanced at her husband, whose admiring and happy eyes had been wandering from her dress to her face and hair. The two aunts laughed heartily, too, for Gabriel's solicitude was a standing joke with them.

"Goloshes!" said Mrs. Conroy. "That's the latest. Whenever it's wet underfoot I must put on my goloshes. To-night even, he wanted me to put them on, but I wouldn't. The next thing he'll buy me will be a diving suit."

Gabriel laughed nervously and patted his tie reassuringly, while Aunt Kate nearly doubled herself, so heartily did she enjoy the joke. The smile soon faded from Aunt Julia's face and her mirthless eyes were directed towards her nephew's face. After a pause she asked:

"And what are goloshes, Gabriel?"

"Goloshes, Julia!" exclaimed her sister. "Goodness me, don't you know what goloshes are? You wear them over your . . . over your boots, Gretta, isn't it?"

"Yes," said Mrs. Conroy. "Guttapercha things. We both have a pair now. Gabriel says everyone wears them on the continent."

"O, on the continent," murmured Aunt Julia, nodding her head slowly.

Gabriel knitted his brows and said, as if he were slightly angered:

"It's nothing very wonderful, but Gretta thinks it very funny because she says the word reminds her of Christy Minstrels."

"But tell me, Gabriel," said Aunt Kate, with brisk tact. "Of course, you've seen about the room. Gretta was saying . . ."

"O, the room is all right," replied Gabriel. "I've taken one in the Gresham."

"To be sure," said Aunt Kate, "by far the best thing to do. And the children, Gretta, you're not anxious about them?"

"O, for one night," said Mrs. Conroy. "Besides, Bessie will look after them."

"To be sure," said Aunt Kate again. "What a comfort it is to have a girl like that, one you can depend on! There's that Lily, I'm sure I don't know what has come over her lately. She's not the girl she was at all."

Gabriel was about to ask his aunt some questions on this point, but she broke off suddenly to gaze after her sister, who had wandered down the stairs and was craning her neck over the banisters.

"Now, I ask you," she said almost testily, "where is Julia going? Julia! Julia! Where are you going?"

Julia, who had gone half way down one flight, came back and announced blandly:

"Here's Freddy."

At the same moment a clapping of hands and a final flourish of the pianist told that the waltz had ended. The drawing-room door was opened from within and some couples came out. Aunt Kate drew Gabriel aside hurriedly and whispered into his ear:

"Slip down, Gabriel, like a good fellow and see if he's all right, and don't let him up if he's screwed. I'm sure he's screwed. I'm sure he is."

Gabriel went to the stairs and listened over the banisters. He could hear two persons talking in the pantry. Then he recognised Freddy Malins' laugh. He went down the stairs noisily.

"It's such a relief," said Aunt Kate to Mrs. Conroy, "that Gabriel is here. I always feel easier in my mind when he's here. . . . Julia, there's Miss Daly and Miss Power will take some refreshment. Thanks for your beautiful waltz, Miss Daly. It made lovely time."

A tall wizen-faced man, with a stiff grizzled moustache and swarthy skin, who was passing out with his partner, said:

"And may we have some refreshment, too, Miss Morkan?"

"Julia," said Aunt Kate summarily, "and here's Mr. Browne and Miss Furlong. Take them in, Julia, with Miss Daly and Miss Power."

"I'm the man for the ladies," said Mr. Browne, pursing his lips until his moustache bristled and smiling in all his wrinkles. "You know, Miss Morkan, the reason they are so fond of me is——"

He did not finish his sentence, but, seeing that Aunt Kate was out of earshot, at once led the three young ladies into the back room. The middle of the room was occupied by two square tables placed end to end, and on these Aunt Julia and the caretaker were straightening and smoothing a large cloth. On the sideboard were arrayed dishes and plates, and glasses and bundles of knives and forks and spoons. The top of the closed square piano served also as a sideboard for viands and sweets. At a smaller sideboard in one corner two young men were standing, drinking hop-bitters.

Mr. Browne led his charges thither and invited them all, in jest, to some ladies' punch, hot, strong and sweet. As they said they never took anything strong, he opened three bottles of lemonade for them. Then he asked one of the young men to move aside, and, taking hold of the decanter, filled out for himself a goodly measure of whisky. The young men eyed him respectfully while he took a trial sip.

"God help me," he said, smiling, "it's the doctor's orders."

His wizened face broke into a broader smile, and the three young ladies laughed in musical echo to his pleasantry, swaying their bodies to and fro, with nervous jerks of their shoulders. The boldest said:

"O, now, Mr. Browne, I'm sure the doctor never ordered anything of the kind."

Mr. Browne took another sip of his whisky and said, with sidling mimicry:

"Well, you see, I'm like the famous Mrs. Cassidy, who is reported to have said: 'Now, Mary Grimes, if I don't take it, make me take it, for I feel I want it.'"

His hot face had leaned forward a little too confidentially and he had assumed a very low Dublin accent so that the young ladies, with one instinct, received his speech in silence. Miss Furlong, who was one of Mary Jane's pupils, asked Miss Daly what was the name of the pretty waltz she had played; and Mr. Browne, seeing that he was ignored, turned promptly to the two young men who were more appreciative.

A red-faced young woman, dressed in pansy, came into the room, excitedly clapping her hands and crying:

"Quadrilles! Quadrilles!"

Close on her heels came Aunt Kate, crying:

"Two gentlemen and three ladies, Mary Jane!"

"O, here's Mr. Bergin and Mr. Kerrigan," said Mary Jane. "Mr. Kerrigan, will you take Miss Power? Miss Furlong, may I get you a partner, Mr. Bergin. O, that'll just do now."

"Three ladies, Mary Jane," said Aunt Kate.

The two young gentlemen asked the ladies if they might have the pleasure, and Mary Jane turned to Miss Daly.

"O, Miss Daly, you're really awfully good, after playing for the last two dances, but really we're so short of ladies to-night."

"I don't mind in the least, Miss Morkan."

"But I've a nice partner for you, Mr. Bartell D'Arcy, the tenor. I'll get him to sing later on. All Dublin is raving about him."

"Lovely voice, lovely voice!" said Aunt Kate.

As the piano had twice begun the prelude to the first figure Mary Jane led her recruits quickly from the room. They had hardly gone when Aunt Julia wandered slowly into the room, looking behind her at something.

"What is the matter, Julia?" asked Aunt Kate anxiously. "Who is it?"

Julia, who was carrying in a column of table-napkins, turned to her sister and said, simply, as if the question had surprised her:

"It's only Freddy, Kate, and Gabriel with him."

In fact right behind her Gabriel could be seen piloting Freddy Malins across the landing. The latter, a young man of about forty, was of Gabriel's size and build, with very round shoulders. His face was fleshy and pallid, touched with colour only at the thick hanging lobes of his ears and at the wide wings of his nose. He had coarse features, a blunt nose, a convex and receding brow, tumid and protruded lips. His heavy-lidded eyes and the disorder of his scanty hair made him look sleepy. He was laughing heartily in a high key at a story which he had been telling Gabriel on the stairs and at the same time rubbing the knuckles of his left fist backwards and forwards into his left eye.

"Good-evening, Freddy," said Aunt Julia.

Freddy Malins bade the Misses Morkan good-evening in what seemed an offhand fashion by reason of the habitual catch in his voice and then, seeing that Mr. Browne was grinning at him from the sideboard, crossed the room on rather shaky legs and began to repeat in an undertone the story he had just told to Gabriel.

"He's not so bad, is he?" said Aunt Kate to Gabriel.

Gabriel's brows were dark but he raised them quickly and answered: "O, no, hardly noticeable."

"Now, isn't he a terrible fellow!" she said. "And his poor mother made him take the pledge on New Year's Eve. But come on, Gabriel, into the drawing-room."

Before leaving the room with Gabriel she signalled to Mr. Browne by frowning and shaking her forefinger in warning to and fro. Mr. Browne nodded in answer and, when she had gone, said to Freddy Malins:

"Now, then, Teddy, I'm going to fill you out a good glass of lemonade just to buck you up."

Freddy Malins, who was nearing the climax of his story, waved the offer aside impatiently but Mr. Browne, having first called Freddy Malins' attention to a disarray in his dress, filled out and handed him a full glass of lemonade. Freddy Malins' left hand accepted the glass mechanically, his right hand being engaged in the mechanical readjustment of his dress. Mr. Browne, whose face was once more wrinkling with mirth, poured out for himself a glass of whisky while Freddy Malins exploded, before he had well reached the climax of his story, in a kink of high-pitched bronchitic laughter and, setting down his untasted and overflowing glass, began to rub the knuckles of his left fist backwards and forwards into his left eye, repeating words of his last phrase as well as his fit of laughter would allow him.

Gabriel could not listen while Mary Jane was playing her Academy piece, full of runs and difficult passages, to the hushed drawing-room. He liked music but the piece she was playing had no melody for him and he doubted whether it had any melody for the other listeners, though they had begged Mary Jane to play something. Four young men, who had come from the refreshment-room to stand in the doorway at the sound of the piano, had gone away quietly in couples after a few minutes. The only persons who seemed to follow the music were Mary Jane herself, her hands racing along the key-board or lifted from it at the pauses like those of a priestess in momentary imprecation, and Aunt Kate standing at her elbow to turn the page.

Gabriel's eyes, irritated by the floor, which glittered with beeswax under the heavy chandelier, wandered to the wall above the piano. A picture of the balcony scene in *Romeo and Juliet* hung there and beside it was a picture of the two murdered princes in the Tower which Aunt Julia had worked in red, blue and brown wools when she was a girl. Probably in the school they had gone to as girls that kind of work had been taught for one year. His mother had worked for him as a birthday present a waistcoat of purple tabinet, with little foxes' heads upon it, lined with brown satin and having round mulberry buttons. It was strange that his mother had had no musical talent though Aunt Kate used to call her the brains carrier of the Morkan family. Both she and Julia had always seemed a little proud of their serious and matronly sister. Her photograph stood before the pierglass. She held an open book on her knees and was pointing out something in it to Constantine who, dressed in a man-o'-war suit, lay at her feet. It was she who had chosen the names of her sons for she was very sensible of the dignity of family life. Thanks to her, Constantine was now senior curate in Balbriggan and, thanks to her, Gabriel himself had taken his degree in the Royal University. A shadow passed over his face as he remembered her sullen opposition to his marriage. Some slighting phrases she had used still rankled in his memory; she had once spoken of Gretta as being country cute and that was not true of Gretta at all. It was Gretta who had nursed her during all her last long illness in their house at Monkstown.

He knew that Mary Jane must be near the end of her piece for she was playing again the opening melody with runs of scales after every bar and while he waited for the end the resentment died down in his heart. The piece ended with a trill of octaves in the treble and a final deep octave in the bass. Great applause greeted Mary Jane as, blushing and rolling up her music nervously, she escaped from the room. The most vigorous clapping came from the four young men in the doorway who had gone away to the refreshment-room at the beginning of the piece but had come back when the piano had stopped.

Lancers were arranged. Gabriel found himself partnered with Miss Ivors. She was a frank-mannered talkative young lady, with a freckled face and prominent brown eyes. She did not wear a low-cut bodice and the large brooch which was fixed in the front of her collar bore on it an Irish device and motto.

When they had taken their places she said abruptly:

"I have a crow to pluck with you."

"With me?" said Gabriel.

She nodded her head gravely.

"What is it?" asked Gabriel, smiling at her solemn manner.

"Who is G. C.?" answered Miss Ivors, turning her eyes upon him.

Gabriel coloured and was about to knit his brows, as if he did not understand, when she said bluntly:

"O, innocent Amy! I have found out that you write for *The Daily Express.* Now, aren't you ashamed of yourself?"

"Why should I be ashamed of myself?" asked Gabriel, blinking his eyes and trying to smile.

"Well, I'm ashamed of you," said Miss Ivors frankly. "To say you'd write for a paper like that. I didn't think you were a West Briton."

A look of perplexity appeared on Gabriel's face. It was true that he wrote a literary column every Wednesday in *The Daily Express,* for which he was paid fifteen shillings. But that did not make him a West Briton surely. The books he received for review were almost more welcome than the paltry cheque. He loved to feel the covers and turn over the pages of newly printed books. Nearly every day when his teaching in the college was ended he used to wander down the quays to the second-hand booksellers, to Hickey's on Bachelor's Walk, to Webb's or Massey's on Aston's Quay, or to O'Clohissey's in the by-street. He did not know how to meet her charge. He wanted to say that literature was above politics. But they were friends of many years' standing and their careers had been parallel, first at the University and then as teachers: he could not risk a grandiose phrase with her. He continued blinking his eyes and trying to smile and murmured lamely that he saw nothing political in writing reviews of books.

When their turn to cross had come he was still perplexed and inattentive. Miss Ivors promptly took his hand in a warm grasp and said in a soft friendly tone:

"Of course, I was only joking. Come, we cross now."

When they were together again she spoke of the University question and Gabriel felt more at ease. A friend of hers had shown her his review of Browning's poems. That was how she had found out the secret: but she liked the review immensely. Then she said suddenly:

"O, Mr. Conroy, will you come for an excursion to the Aran Isles this summer? We're going to stay there a whole month. It will be splendid out in the Atlantic. You ought to come. Mr. Clancy is coming, and Mr. Kilkelly and Kathleen Kearney. It would be splendid for Gretta too if she'd come. She's from Connacht, isn't she?"

"Her people are," said Gabriel shortly.

"But you will come, won't you?" said Miss Ivors, laying her warm hand eagerly on his arm.

"The fact is," said Gabriel, "I have just arranged to go——"

"Go where?" asked Miss Ivors.

"Well, you know, every year I go for a cycling tour with some fellows and so——"

"But where?" asked Miss Ivors.

"Well, we usually go to France or Belgium or perhaps Germany," said Gabriel awkwardly.

"And why do you go to France and Belgium," said Miss Ivors, "instead of visiting your own land?"

"Well," said Gabriel, "it's partly to keep in touch with the languages and partly for a change."

"And haven't you your own language to keep in touch with—Irish?" asked Miss Ivors.

"Well," said Gabriel, "if it comes to that, you know, Irish is not my language."

Their neighbours had turned to listen to the cross-examination. Gabriel glanced right and left nervously and tried to keep his good humour under the ordeal which was making a blush invade his forehead.

"And haven't you your own land to visit," continued Miss Ivors, "that you know nothing of, your own people, and your own country?"

"O, to tell you the truth," retorted Gabriel suddenly, "I'm sick of my own country, sick of it!"

"Why?" asked Miss Ivors.

Gabriel did not answer for his retort had heated him.

"Why?" repeated Miss Ivors.

They had to go visiting together and, as he had not answered her, Miss Ivors said warmly:

"Of course, you've no answer."

Gabriel tried to cover his agitation by taking part in the dance with great energy. He avoided her eyes for he had seen a sour expression on her face. But when they met in the long chain he was surprised to feel his hand firmly pressed. She looked at him from under her brows for a moment quizzically until he smiled. Then, just as the chain was about to start again, she stood on tiptoe and whispered into his ear:

"West Briton!"

When the lancers were over Gabriel went away to a remote corner of the room where Freddy Malins' mother was sitting. She was a stout feeble old woman with white hair. Her voice had a catch in it like her son's and she stuttered slightly. She had been told that Freddy had come and that he was nearly all right. Gabriel asked her whether she had had a good crossing. She lived with her married daughter in Glasgow and came to Dublin on a visit once a year. She answered placidly that she had had a beautiful crossing and that the captain had been most attentive to her. She spoke also of the beautiful house her daughter kept in Glasgow, and of all the friends they had there. While her tongue rambled on Gabriel tried to banish from his mind all memory of the unpleasant incident with Miss Ivors. Of course the girl or woman, or whatever she was, was an enthusiast but there was a time for all things. Perhaps he ought not to have answered her like that. But she had no right to call him a West Briton before people, even in joke. She had tried to make him ridiculous before people, heckling him and staring at him with her rabbit's eyes.

He saw his wife making her way towards him through the waltzing couples. When she reached him she said into his ear:

"Gabriel, Aunt Kate wants to know won't you carve the goose as usual. Miss Daly will carve the ham and I'll do the pudding."

"All right," said Gabriel.

"She's sending in the younger ones first as soon as this waltz is over so that we'll have the table to ourselves."

"Were you dancing?" asked Gabriel.

"Of course I was. Didn't you see me? What row had you with Molly Ivors?"

"No row. Why? Did she say so?"

"Something like that. I'm trying to get that Mr. D'Arcy to sing. He's full of conceit, I think."

"There was no row," said Gabriel moodily, "only she wanted me to go for a trip to the west of Ireland and I said I wouldn't."

His wife clasped her hands excitedly and gave a little jump.

"O, do go, Gabriel," she cried. "I'd love to see Galway again."

"You can go if you like," said Gabriel coldly.

She looked at him for a moment, then turned to Mrs. Malins and said:

"There's a nice husband for you, Mrs. Malins."

While she was threading her way back across the room Mrs. Malins, without adverting to the interruption, went on to tell Gabriel what beautiful places there were in Scotland and beautiful scenery. Her son-in-law brought them every year to the lakes and they used to go fishing. Her son-in-law was a splendid fisher. One day he caught a beautiful big fish and the man in the hotel cooked it for their dinner.

Gabriel hardly heard what she said. Now that supper was coming near he began to think again about his speech and about the quotation. When he saw Freddy Malins coming across the room to visit his mother Gabriel left the chair free for him and retired into the embrasure of the window. The room had already cleared and from the back room came the clatter of plates and knives. Those who still remained in the drawing-room seemed tired of dancing and were conversing quietly in little groups. Gabriel's warm trembling fingers tapped the cold pane of the window. How cool it must be outside! How pleasant it would be to walk out alone, first along by the river and then through the park! The snow would be lying on the branches of the trees and forming a bright cap on the top of the Wellington Monument. How much more pleasant it would be there than at the supper-table!

He ran over the headings of his speech: Irish hospitality, sad memories, the Three Graces, Paris, the quotation from Browning. He repeated to himself a phrase he had written in his review: "One feels that one is listening to a thought-tormented music." Miss Ivors had praised the review. Was she sincere? Had she really any life of her own behind all her propagandism? There had never been any ill-feeling between them until that night. It unnerved him to think that she would be at the supper-table, looking up at him while he spoke with her critical quizzing eyes. Perhaps she would not be sorry to see him fail in his speech. An idea came into his mind and gave him courage. He would say, alluding to Aunt Kate and Aunt Julia: "Ladies and Gentlemen, the generation which is now on the wane among us may have had its faults but for my part I think it had certain qualities of hospitality, of humour, of humanity, which the new and very serious and hypereducated generation that is growing up around us seems to me to lack." Very good: that was one for Miss Ivors. What did he care that his aunts were only two ignorant old women?

A murmur in the room attracted his attention. Mr. Browne was advancing from the door, gallantly escorting Aunt Julia, who leaned upon his arm, smiling and hanging her head. An irregular musketry of applause escorted her also as far as the piano and then, as Mary Jane seated herself on the stool, and Aunt Julia, no longer smiling, half turned so as to pitch her voice fairly into the room, gradually ceased. Gabriel recognised the prelude. It was that of an old song of Aunt Julia's—*Arrayed for the Bridal*. Her voice, strong and clear in tone, attacked with great spirit the runs which embellish the air and though she sang very rapidly she did not miss even the smallest of the grace notes. To follow the voice, without looking at the singer's face, was to feel and share the excitement of swift and secure flight. Gabriel applauded loudly with all the others at the close of the song and loud applause was borne in from the invisible supper-table. It sounded so genuine that a little colour struggled into Aunt Julia's face as she bent to replace in the music-stand the old leather-bound song-book that had her initials on the cover. Freddy Malins, who had listened with his head perched sideways to hear her better, was still applauding when everyone else had ceased and talking animatedly to his mother who nodded her head gravely and slowly in acquiescence. At last, when he could clap no more, he stood up suddenly and hurried across the room to Aunt Julia whose hand he seized and held in both his hands, shaking it when words failed him or the catch in his voice proved too much for him.

"I was just telling my mother," he said, "I never heard you sing so well, never. No, I never heard your voice so good as it is to-night. Now! Would you believe that now? That's the truth. Upon my word and honour that's the truth. I never heard your voice sound so fresh and so . . . so clear and fresh, never."

Aunt Julia smiled broadly and murmured something about compliments as she released her hand from his grasp. Mr. Browne extended his open hand towards her and said to those who were near him in the manner of a showman introducing a prodigy to an audience:

"Miss Julia Morkan, my latest discovery!"

He was laughing very heartily at this himself when Freddy Malins turned to him and said:

"Well, Browne, if you're serious you might make a worse discovery. All I can say is I never heard her sing half so well as long as I am coming here. And that's the honest truth."

"Neither did I," said Mr. Browne. "I think her voice has greatly improved."

Aunt Julia shrugged her shoulders and said with meek pride:

"Thirty years ago I hadn't a bad voice as voices go."

"I often told Julia," said Aunt Kate emphatically, "that she was simply thrown away in that choir. But she never would be said by me."

She turned as if to appeal to the good sense of the others against a refractory child while Aunt Julia gazed in front of her, a vague smile of reminiscence playing on her face.

"No," continued Aunt Kate, "she wouldn't be said or led by anyone, slaving there in that choir night and day, night and day. Six o'clock on Christmas morning! And all for what?"

"Well, isn't it for the honour of God, Aunt Kate?" asked Mary Jane, twisting round on the piano-stool and smiling.

Aunt Kate turned fiercely on her niece and said:

"I know all about the honour of God, Mary Jane, but I think it's not at all honourable for the pope to turn out the women out of the choirs that have slaved there all their lives and put little whipper-snappers of boys over their heads. I suppose it is for the good of the Church if the pope does it. But it's not just, Mary Jane, and it's not right."

She had worked herself into a passion and would have continued in defence of her sister for it was a sore subject with her but Mary Jane, seeing that all the dancers had come back, intervened pacifically:

"Now, Aunt Kate, you're giving scandal to Mr. Browne who is of the other persuasion."

Aunt Kate turned to Mr. Browne, who was grinning at this allusion to his religion, and said hastily:

"O, I don't question the pope's being right. I'm only a stupid old woman and I wouldn't presume to do such a thing. But there's such a thing as common everyday politeness and gratitude. And if I were in Julia's place I'd tell that Father Healey straight up to his face . . ."

"And besides, Aunt Kate," said Mary Jane, "we really are all hungry and when we are hungry we are all very quarrelsome."

"And when we are thirsty we are also quarrelsome," added Mr. Browne.

"So that we had better go to supper," said Mary Jane, "and finish the discussion afterwards."

On the landing outside the drawing-room Gabriel found his wife and Mary Jane trying to persuade Miss Ivors to stay for supper. But Miss Ivors, who had put on her hat and was buttoning her cloak, would not stay. She did not feel in the least hungry and she had already overstayed her time.

"But only for ten minutes, Molly," said Mrs. Conroy. "That won't delay you."

"To take a pick itself," said Mary Jane, "after all your dancing."

"I really couldn't," said Miss Ivors.

"I am afraid you didn't enjoy yourself at all," said Mary Jane hopelessly.

"Ever so much, I assure you," said Miss Ivors, "but you really must let me run off now."

"But how can you get home?" asked Mrs. Conroy.

"O, it's only two steps up the quay."

Gabriel hesitated a moment and said:

"If you will allow me, Miss Ivors, I'll see you home if you are really obliged to go."

But Miss Ivors broke away from them.

"I won't hear of it," she cried. "For goodness' sake go in to your suppers and don't mind me. I'm quite well able to take care of myself."

"Well, you're the comical girl, Molly," said Mrs. Conroy frankly.

"*Beannacht libh*," cried Miss Ivors, with a laugh, as she ran down the staircase.

Mary Jane gazed after her, a moody puzzled expression on her face, while Mrs. Conroy leaned over the banisters to listen for the hall-door. Gabriel asked himself was he the cause of her abrupt departure. But she did not seem to be in ill humour: she had gone away laughing. He stared blankly down the staircase.

At the moment Aunt Kate came toddling out of the supper-room, almost wringing her hands in despair.

"Where is Gabriel?" she cried. "Where on earth is Gabriel? There's everyone waiting in there, stage to let, and nobody to carve the goose!"

"Here I am, Aunt Kate!" cried Gabriel, with sudden animation, "ready to carve a flock of geese, if necessary."

A fat brown goose lay at one end of the table and at the other end, on a bed of creased paper strewn with sprigs of parsley, lay a great ham, stripped of its outer skin and peppered over with crust crumbs, a neat paper frill round its shin and beside this was a round of spiced beef. Between these rival ends ran parallel lines of side-dishes: two little minsters of jelly, red and yellow; a shallow dish full of blocks of blancmange and red jam, a large green leaf-shaped dish with a stalk-shaped handle, on which lay bunches of purple raisins and peeled almonds, a companion dish on which lay a solid rectangle of Smyrna figs, a dish of custard topped with grated nutmeg, a small bowl full of chocolates and sweets wrapped in gold and silver papers and a glass vase in which stood some tall celery stalks. In the centre of the table there stood, as sentries to a fruit-stand which upheld a pyramid of oranges and American apples, two squat old-fashioned decanters of cut glass, one containing port and the other dark sherry. On the closed square piano a pudding in a huge yellow dish lay in waiting and behind it were three squads of bottles of stout and ale and minerals, drawn up according to the colours of their uniforms, the first two black, with brown and red labels, the third and smallest squad white, with transverse green sashes.

Gabriel took his seat boldly at the head of the table and, having looked to the edge of the carver, plunged his fork firmly into the goose. He felt quite at ease now for he was an expert carver and liked nothing better than to find himself at the head of a well-laden table.

"Miss Furlong, what shall I send you?" he asked. "A wing or a slice of the breast?"

"Just a small slice of the breast."

"Miss Higgins, what for you?"

"O, anything at all, Mr. Conroy."

While Gabriel and Miss Daly exchanged plates of goose and plates of ham and spiced beef Lily went from guest to guest with a dish of hot floury potatoes wrapped in a white napkin. This was Mary Jane's idea and she had also suggested apple sauce for the goose but Aunt Kate had said that plain roast goose without any apple sauce had always been good enough for her and she hoped she might never eat worse. Mary Jane waited on her pupils and saw that they got the best slices and Aunt Kate and Aunt Julia opened and carried across from the piano bottles of stout and ale for the gentlemen and bottles of minerals for the ladies. There was a great deal of confusion and laughter and noise, the noise of orders and counter-orders, of knives and forks, of corks and glass-stoppers. Gabriel began to carve second helpings as soon as he had finished the first round without serving himself. Everyone protested loudly so that he compromised by taking a long draught of stout for he had found the carving hot work. Mary Jane settled down quietly to her supper but Aunt Kate and Aunt Julia were still toddling round the table, walking on each other's heels, getting in each other's way and giving each other unheeded orders. Mr. Browne begged of them to sit down and eat their suppers and so did Gabriel but they said there was time enough, so that, at last, Freddy Malins stood up and, capturing Aunt Kate, plumped her down on her chair amid general laughter.

When everyone had been well served Gabriel said, smiling:

"Now, if anyone wants a little more of what vulgar people call stuffing let him or her speak."

A chorus of voices invited him to begin his own supper and Lily came forward with three potatoes which she had reserved for him.

"Very well," said Gabriel amiably, as he took another preparatory draught, "kindly forget my existence, ladies and gentlemen, for a few minutes."

He set to his supper and took no part in the conversation with which the table covered Lily's removal of the plates. The subject of talk was the opera company which was then at the Theatre Royal. Mr. Bartell D'Arcy, the tenor, a dark-complexioned young man with a smart moustache, praised very highly the leading contralto of the company but Miss Furlong thought she had a rather vulgar style of production. Freddy Malins said there was a negro chieftain singing in the second part of the Gaiety pantomime who had one of the finest tenor voices he had ever heard.

"Have you heard him?" he asked Mr. Bartell D'Arcy across the table.

"No," answered Mr. Bartell D'Arcy carelessly.

"Because," Freddy Malins explained, "now I'd be curious to hear your opinion of him. I think he has a grand voice."

"It takes Teddy to find out the really good things," said Mr. Browne familiarly to the table.

"And why couldn't he have a voice too?" asked Freddy Malins sharply. "Is it because he's only a black?"

Nobody answered this question and Mary Jane led the table back to the legitimate opera. One of her pupils had given her a pass for *Mignon.* Of course it was very fine, she said, but it made her think of poor Georgina Burns. Mr. Browne could go back farther still, to the old Italian companies that used to come to Dublin—Tietjens, Ilma de Murzka, Campanini, the great Trebelli Giuglini, Ravelli, Aramburo. Those were the days, he said, when there was something like singing to be heard in Dublin. He told too of how the top gallery of the old Royal used to be packed night after night, of how one night an Italian tenor had sung five encores to *Let me like a Soldier fall,* introducing a high C every time and of how the gallery boys would sometimes in their enthusiasm unyoke the horses from the carriage of some great *prima donna* and pull her themselves through the streets to her hotel. Why did they never play the grand old operas now, he asked, *Dinorah, Lucrezia Borgia?* Because they could not get the voices to sing them: that was why.

"O, well," said Mr. Bartell D'Arcy, "I presume there are as good singers to-day as there were then."

"Where are they?" asked Mr. Browne defiantly.

"In London, Paris, Milan," said Mr. Bartell D'Arcy warmly. "I suppose Caruso, for example, is quite as good, if not better than any of the men you have mentioned."

"Maybe so," said Mr. Browne. "But I may tell you I doubt it strongly."

"O, I'd give anything to hear Caruso sing," said Mary Jane.

"For me," said Aunt Kate, who had been picking a bone, "there was only one tenor. To please me, I mean. But I suppose none of you ever heard of him."

"Who was he, Miss Morkan?" asked Mr. Bartell D'Arcy politely.

"His name," said Aunt Kate, "was Parkinson. I heard him when he was in his prime and I think he had then the purest tenor voice that was ever put into a man's throat."

"Strange," said Mr. Bartell D'Arcy. "I never even heard of him."

"Yes, yes, Miss Morkan is right," said Mr. Browne. "I remember hearing of old Parkinson but he's too far back for me."

"A beautiful, pure, sweet, mellow English tenor," said Aunt Kate with enthusiasm.

Gabriel having finished, the huge pudding was transferred to the table. The clatter of forks and spoons began again. Gabriel's wife served out spoonfuls of the pudding and passed the plates down the table. Midway down they were held up by Mary Jane, who replenished them with raspberry or orange jelly or with blancmange and jam. The pudding was of Aunt Julia's making and she received praises for it from all quarters. She herself said that it was not quite brown enough.

"Well, I hope, Miss Morkan," said Mr. Browne, "that I'm brown enough for you because, you know, I'm all brown."

All the gentlemen, except Gabriel, ate some of the pudding out of compliment to Aunt Julia. As Gabriel never ate sweets the celery had been left for him. Freddy Malins also took a stalk of celery and ate it with his pudding. He had been told that celery was a capital thing for the blood and he was just then under doctor's care. Mrs. Malins, who had been silent all through the supper, said that her son was going down to Mount Melleray in a week or so. The table then spoke of Mount Melleray, how bracing the air was down there, how hospitable the monks were and how they never asked for a penny-piece from their guests.

"And do you mean to say," asked Mr. Browne incredulously, "that a chap can go down there and put up there as if it were a hotel and live on the fat of the land and then come away without paying anything?"

"O, most people give some donation to the monastery when they leave," said Mary Jane.

"I wish we had an institution like that in our Church," said Mr. Browne candidly.

He was astonished to hear that the monks never spoke, got up at two in the morning and slept in their coffins. He asked what they did it for.

"That's the rule of the order," said Aunt Kate firmly.

"Yes, but why?" asked Mr. Browne.

Aunt Kate repeated that it was the rule, that was all. Mr. Browne still seemed not to understand. Freddy Malins explained to him, as best he could, that the monks were trying to make up for the sins committed by all the sinners in the outside world. The explanation was not very clear for Mr. Browne grinned and said:

"I like that idea very much but wouldn't a comfortable spring bed do them as well as a coffin?"

"The coffin," said Mary Jane, "is to remind them of their last end."

As the subject had grown lugubrious it was buried in a silence of the table during which Mrs. Malins could be heard saying to her neighbour in an indistinct undertone:

"They are very good men, the monks, very pious men."

The raisins and almonds and figs and apples and oranges and chocolates and sweets were now passed about the table and Aunt Julia invited all the guests to have either port or sherry. At first Mr. Bartell D'Arcy refused to take either but one of his neighbours nudged him and whispered something to him upon which he allowed his glass to be filled. Gradually as the last glasses were being filled the conversation ceased. A pause followed, broken only by the noise of the wine and by unsettlings of chairs. The Misses Morkan, all three, looked down at the tablecloth. Someone coughed once or twice and then a few gentlemen patted the table gently as a signal for silence. The silence came and Gabriel pushed back his chair and stood up.

The patting at once grew louder in encouragement and then ceased altogether. Gabriel leaned his ten trembling fingers on the tablecloth and smiled nervously at the company. Meeting a row of upturned faces he raised his eyes to the chandelier. The piano was playing a waltz tune and he could hear the skirts sweeping against the drawing-room door. People, perhaps, were standing in the snow on the quay outside, gazing up at the lighted windows and listening to the waltz music. The air was pure there. In the distance lay the park where the trees were weighted with snow. The Wellington Monument wore a gleaming cap of snow that flashed westward over the white field of Fifteen Acres.

He began:

"Ladies and Gentlemen,

"It has fallen to my lot this evening, as in years past, to perform a very pleasing task but a task for which I am afraid my poor powers as a speaker are all too inadequate."

"No, no!" said Mr. Browne.

"But, however that may be, I can only ask you to-night to take the will for the deed and to lend me your attention for a few moments while I endeavour to express to you in words what my feelings are on this occasion.

"Ladies and Gentlemen, it is not the first time that we have gathered together under this hospitable roof, around this hospitable board. It is not the first time that we have been the recipients—or perhaps, I had better say, the victims—of the hospitality of certain good ladies."

He made a circle in the air with his arm and paused. Everyone laughed or smiled at Aunt Kate and Aunt Julia and Mary Jane who all turned crimson with pleasure. Gabriel went on more boldly:

"I feel more strongly with every recurring year that our country has no tradition which does it so much honour and which it should guard so jealously as that of its hospitality. It is a tradition that is unique as far as my experience goes (and I have visited not a few places abroad) among the modern nations. Some would say, perhaps, that with us it is rather a failing than anything to be boasted of. But granted even that, it is, to my mind, a princely failing, and one that I trust will long be cultivated among us. Of one thing, at least, I am sure. As long as this one roof shelters the good ladies aforesaid—and I wish from my heart it may do so for many and many a long year to come—the tradition of genuine warm-hearted courteous Irish hospitality, which our forefathers have handed down to us and which we in turn must hand down to our descendants, is still alive among us."

A hearty murmur of assent ran round the table. It shot through Gabriel's mind that Miss Ivors was not there and that she had gone away discourteously: and he said with confidence in himself:

"Ladies and Gentlemen,

"A new generation is growing up in our midst, a generation actuated by new ideas and new principles. It is serious and enthusiastic for these new ideas and its enthusism, even when it is misdirected, is, I believe, in the main sincere. But we are living in a sceptical and, if I may use the phrase, a thought-tormented age: and sometimes I fear that this new generation, educated or hypereducated as it is, will lack those qualities of humanity, of hospitality, of kindly humour which belonged to an older day. Listening to-night to the names of all those great singers of the past it seemed to me, I must confess, that we were living in a less spacious age. Those days might, without exaggeration, be called spacious days: and if they are gone beyond recall let us hope, at least, that in gatherings such as this we shall still speak of them with pride and affection, still cherish in our hearts the memory of those dead and gone great ones whose fame the world will not willingly let die."

"Hear, hear!" said Mr. Browne loudly.

"But yet," continued Gabriel, his voice falling into a softer inflection, "there are always in gatherings such as this sadder thoughts that will recur to our minds: thoughts of the past, of youth, of changes, of absent faces that we miss here to-night. Our path through life is strewn with many such sad memories: and were we to brood upon them always we could not find the heart to go on bravely with our work among the living. We have all of us living duties and living affections which claim, and rightly claim, our strenuous endeavours.

"Therefore, I will not linger on the past. I will not let any gloomy moralising intrude upon us here to-night. Here we are gathered to-gether for a brief moment from the bustle and rush of our everyday routine. We are met here as friends, in the spirit of good-fellowship, as colleagues, also to a certain extent, in the true spirit of *camaraderie,* and as the guests of—what shall I call them?—the Three Graces of the Dublin musical world."

The table burst into applause and laughter at this allusion. Aunt Julia vainly asked each of her neighbours in turn to tell her what Gabriel had said.

"He says we are the Three Graces, Aunt Julia," said Mary Jane.

Aunt Julia did not understand but she looked up, smiling, at Gabriel, who continued in the same vein:

"Ladies and Gentlemen,

"I will not attempt to play to-night the part that Paris played on another occasion. I will not attempt to choose between them. The task would be an invidious one and one beyond my poor powers. For when I view them in turn, whether it be our chief hostess herself, whose good heart, whose too good heart, has become a byword with all who knew her, or her sister, who seems to be gifted with perennial youth and whose singing must have been a surprise and a revelation to us all to-night, or, last but not least, when I consider our youngest hostess, talented, cheerful, hard-working and the best of nieces, I confess, Ladies and Gentlemen, that I do not know to which of them I should award the prize."

Gabriel glanced down at his aunts and, seeing the large smile on Aunt Julia's face and the tears which had risen to Aunt Kate's eyes, hastened to his close. He raised his glass of port gallantly, while every member of the company fingered a glass expectantly, and said loudly:

"Let us toast them all three together. Let us drink to their health, wealth, long life, happiness and prosperity and may they long continue to hold the proud and self-won position which they hold in their profession and the position of honour and affection which they hold in our hearts."

All the guests stood up, glass in hand, and turning towards the three seated ladies, sang in unison, with Mr. Browne as leader:

> For they are jolly gay fellows,
> For they are jolly gay fellows,
> For they are jolly gay fellows,
> Which nobody can deny.

Aunt Kate was making frank use of her handkerchief and even Aunt Julia seemed moved. Freddy Malins beat time with his pudding-fork and the singers turned towards one another, as if in melodious conference, while they sang with emphasis:

> Unless he tells a lie,
> Unless he tells a lie,

Then, turning once more towards their hostesses, they sang:

> For they are jolly gay fellows,
> For they are jolly gay fellows,
> For they are jolly gay fellows,
> Which nobody can deny.

The acclamation which followed was taken up beyond the door of the supper-room by many of the other guests and renewed time after time, Freddy Malins acting as officer with his fork on high.

The piercing morning air came into the hall where they were standing so that Aunt Kate said:

"Close the door, somebody. Mrs. Malins will get her death of cold."

"Browne is out there, Aunt Kate," said Mary Jane.

"Browne is everywhere," said Aunt Kate, lowering her voice.

Mary Jane laughed at her tone.

"Really," she said archly, "he is very attentive."

"He has been laid on here like the gas," said Aunt Kate in the same tone, "all during the Christmas."

She laughed herself this time good-humouredly and then added quickly:

"But tell him to come in, Mary Jane, and close the door. I hope to goodness he didn't hear me."

At that moment the hall-door was opened and Mr. Browne came in from the door-step, laughing as if his heart would break. He was dressed in a long green overcoat with mock astrakhan cuffs and collar and wore on his head an oval fur cap. He pointed down the snow-covered quay from where the sound of shrill prolonged whistling was borne in.

"Teddy will have all the cabs in Dublin out," he said.

Gabriel advanced from the little pantry behind the office, struggling into his overcoat, and, looking round the hall, said:

"Gretta not down yet?"

"She's getting on her things, Gabriel," said Aunt Kate.

"Who's playing up there?" asked Gabriel.

"Nobody. They're all gone."

"O no, Aunt Kate," said Mary Jane. "Bartell D'Arcy and Miss O'Callaghan aren't gone yet."

"Someone is fooling at the piano anyhow," said Gabriel.

Mary Jane glanced at Gabriel and Mr. Browne and said with a shiver:

"It makes me feel cold to look at you two gentlemen muffled up like that. I wouldn't like to face your journey home at this hour."

"I'd like nothing better this minute," said Mr. Browne stoutly, "than a rattling fine walk in the country or a fast drive with a good spanking goer between the shafts."

"We used to have a very good horse and trap at home," said Aunt Julia sadly.

"The never-to-be-forgotten Johnny," said Mary Jane, laughing.

Aunt Kate and Gabriel laughed too.

"Why, what was wonderful about Johnny?" asked Mr. Browne.

"The late lamented Patrick Morkan, our grandfather, that is," explained Gabriel, "commonly known in his later years as the old gentleman, was a glue-boiler."

"O, now, Gabriel," said Aunt Kate, laughing, "he had a starch mill."

"Well, glue or starch," said Gabriel, "the old gentleman had a horse by the name of Johnny. And Johnny used to work in the old gentleman's mill, walking round and round in order to drive the mill. That was all very well; but now comes the tragic part about Johnny. One fine day the old gentleman thought he'd like to drive out with the quality to a military review in the park."

"The Lord have mercy on his soul," said Aunt Kate compassionately.

"Amen," said Gabriel. "So the old gentleman, as I said, harnessed Johnny and put on his very best tall hat and his very best stock collar and drove out in grand style from his ancestral mansion somewhere near Back Lane, I think."

Everyone laughed, even Mrs. Malins, at Gabriel's manner and Aunt Kate said:

"O, now, Gabriel, he didn't live in Back Lane, really. Only the mill was there."

"Out from the mansion of his forefathers," continued Gabriel, "he drove with Johnny. And everything went on beautifully until Johnny came in sight of King Billy's statue: and whether he fell in love with the horse King Billy sits on or whether he thought he was back again in the mill, anyhow he began to walk round the statue."

Gabriel paced in a circle round the hall in his goloshes amid the laughter of the others.

"Round and round he went," said Gabriel, "and the old gentleman, who was a very pompous old gentleman, was highly indignant. 'Go on, sir! What do you mean, sir? Johnny! Johnny! Most extraordinary conduct! Can't understand the horse!'"

The peals of laughter which followed Gabriel's imitation of the incident was interrupted by a resounding knock at the hall door. Mary Jane ran to open it and let in Freddy Malins. Freddy Malins, with his hat well back on his head and his shoulders humped with cold, was puffing and steaming after his exertions.

"I could only get one cab," he said.

"O, we'll find another along the quay," said Gabriel.

"Yes," said Aunt Kate. "Better not keep Mrs. Malins standing in the draught."

Mrs. Malins was helped down the front steps by her son and Mr. Browne and, after many manœuvres, hoisted into the cab. Freddy Malins clambered in after her and spent a long time settling her on the seat, Mr. Browne helping him with advice. At last she was settled comfortably and Freddy Malins invited Mr. Browne into the cab. There was a good deal of confused talk, and then Mr. Browne got into the cab. The cabman settled his rug over his knees, and bent down for the address. The confusion grew greater and the cabman was directed differently by Freddy Malins and Mr. Browne, each of whom had his head out through a window of the cab. The difficulty was to know where to drop Mr. Browne along the route, and Aunt Kate, Aunt Julia and Mary Jane helped the discussion from the door-step with cross-directions and contradictions and abundance of laughter. As for Freddy Malins he was speechless with laughter. He popped his head in and out of the window every moment to the great danger of his hat, and told his mother how the discussion was progressing, till at last Mr. Browne shouted to the bewildered cabman above the din of everybody's laughter:

"Do you know Trinity College?"

"Yes, sir," said the cabman.

"Well, drive bang up against Trinity College gates," said Mr. Browne, "and then we'll tell you where to go. You understand now?"

"Yes, sir," said the cabman.

"Make like a bird for Trinity College."

"Right, sir," said the cabman.

The horse was whipped up and the cab rattled off along the quay amid a chorus of laughter and adieus.

Gabriel had not gone to the door with the others. He was in a dark part of the hall gazing up the staircase. A woman was standing near the top of the first flight, in the shadow also. He could not see her face but he could see the terra-cotta and salmon-pink panels of her skirt which the shadow made appear black and white. It was his wife. She was leaning on the banisters, listening to something. Gabriel was surprised at her stillness and strained his ear to listen also. But he could hear little save the noise of laughter and dispute on the front steps, a few chords struck on the piano and a few notes of a man's voice singing.

He stood still in the gloom of the hall, trying to catch the air that the voice was singing and gazing up at his wife. There was grace and mystery in her attitude as if she were a symbol of something. He asked himself what is a woman standing on the stairs in the shadow, listening to distant music, a symbol of. If he were a painter he would paint her in that attitude. Her blue felt hat would show off the bronze of her hair against the darkness and the dark panels of her skirt would show off the light ones. *Distant Music* he would call the picture if he were a painter.

The hall-door was closed; and Aunt Kate, Aunt Julia and Mary Jane came down the hall, still laughing.

"Well, isn't Freddy terrible?" said Mary Jane. "He's really terrible."

Gabriel said nothing but pointed up the stairs towards where his wife was standing. Now that the hall-door was closed the voice and the piano could be heard more clearly. Gabriel held up his hand for them to be silent. The song seemed to be in the old Irish tonality and the singer seemed uncertain both of his words and of his voice. The voice, made plaintive by distance and by the singer's hoarseness, faintly illuminated the cadence of the air with words expressing grief:

> *O, the rain falls on my heavy locks*
> *And the dew wets my skin,*
> *My babe lies cold . . .*

"O," exclaimed Mary Jane. "It's Bartell D'Arcy singing and he wouldn't sing all the night. O' I'll get him to sing a song before he goes."

"O, do, Mary Jane," said Aunt Kate.

Mary Jane brushed past the others and ran to the staircase, but before she reached it the singing stopped and the piano was closed abruptly.

"O, what a pity!" she cried. "Is he coming down, Gretta?"

Gabriel heard his wife answer yes and saw her come down towards them. A few steps behind her were Mr. Bartell D'Arcy and Miss O'Callaghan.

"O, Mr. D'Arcy," cried Mary Jane, "it's downright mean of you to break off like that when we were all in raptures listening to you."

"I have been at him all the evening," said Miss O'Callaghan, "and Mrs. Conroy, too, and he told us he had a dreadful cold and couldn't sing."

"O, Mr. D'Arcy," said Aunt Kate, "now that was a great fib to tell."

"Can't you see that I'm as hoarse as a crow?" said Mr. D'Arcy roughly.

He went into the pantry hastily and put on his overcoat. The others, taken aback by his rude speech, could find nothing to say. Aunt Kate wrinkled her brows and made signs to the others to drop the subject. Mr. D'Arcy stood swathing his neck carefully and frowning.

"It's the weather," said Aunt Julia, after a pause.

"Yes, everybody has colds," said Aunt Kate readily, "everybody."

"They say," said Mary Jane, "we haven't had snow like it for thirty years; and I read this morning in the newspapers that the snow is general all over Ireland."

"I love the look of snow," said Aunt Julia sadly.

"So do I," said Miss O'Callaghan. "I think Christmas is never really Christmas unless we have the snow on the ground."

"But poor Mr. D'Arcy doesn't like the snow," said Aunt Kate, smiling.

Mr. D'Arcy came from the pantry, fully swathed and buttoned, and in a repentant tone told them the history of his cold. Everyone gave him advice and said it was a great pity and urged him to be very careful of his throat in the night air. Gabriel watched his wife, who did not join in the conversation. She was standing right under the dusty fanlight and the flame of the gas lit up the rich bronze of her hair, which he had seen her drying at the fire a few days before. She was in the same attitude and seemed unaware of the talk about her. At last she turned towards them and Gabriel saw that there was colour on her cheeks and that her eyes were shining. A sudden tide of joy went leaping out of his heart.

"Mr. D'Arcy," she said, "what is the name of that song you were singing?"

"It's called *The Lass of Aughrim,*" said Mr. D'Arcy, "but I couldn't remember it properly. Why? Do you know it?"

"*The Lass of Aughrim,*" she repeated. "I couldn't think of the name."

"It's a very nice air," said Mary Jane. "I'm sorry you were not in voice to-night."

"Now, Mary Jane," said Aunt Kate, "don't annoy Mr. D'Arcy. I won't have him annoyed."

Seeing that all were ready to start she shepherded them to the door, where good-night was said:

"Well, good-night, Aunt Kate, and thanks for the pleasant evening."

"Good-night, Gabriel. Good-night, Gretta!"

"Good-night, Aunt Kate, and thanks ever so much. Good-night, Aunt Julia."

"O, good-night, Gretta, I didn't see you."

"Good-night, Mr. D'Arcy. Good-night, Miss O'Callaghan."

"Good-night, Miss Morkan."

"Good-night, again."

"Good-night, all. Safe home."

"Good-night. Good-night."

The morning was still dark. A dull, yellow light brooded over the houses and the river; and the sky seemed to be descending. It was slushy underfoot; and only streaks and patches of snow lay on the roofs, on the parapets of the quay and on the area railings. The lamps were still burning redly in the murky air and, across the river, the palace of the Four Courts stood out menacingly against the heavy sky.

She was walking on before him with Mr. Bartell D'Arcy, her shoes in a brown parcel tucked under one arm and her hands holding her skirt up from the slush. She had no longer any grace of attitude, but Gabriel's eyes were still bright with happiness. The blood went bounding along his veins; and the thoughts went rioting through his brain, proud, joyful, tender, valorous.

She was walking on before him so lightly and so erect that he longed to run after her noiselessly, catch her by the shoulders and say something foolish and affectionate into her ear. She seemed to him so frail that he longed to defend her against something and then to be alone with her. Moments of their secret life together burst like stars upon his memory. A heliotrope envelope was lying beside his breakfast-cup and he was caressing it with his hand. Birds were twittering in the ivy and the sunny web of the curtain was shimmering along the floor: he could not eat for happiness. They were standing on the crowded platform and he was placing a ticket inside the warm palm of her glove. He was standing with her in the cold, looking in through a grated window at a man making bottles in a roaring furnace. It was very cold. Her face, fragrant in the cold air, was quite close to his; and suddenly he called out to the man at the furnace:

"Is the fire hot, sir?"

But the man could not hear with the noise of the furnace. It was just as well. He might have answered rudely.

A wave of yet more tender joy escaped from his heart and went coursing in warm flood along his arteries. Like the tender fire of stars moments of their life together, that no one knew of or would ever know of, broke upon and illumined his memory. He longed to recall to her those moments, to make her forget the years of their dull existence together and remember only their moments of ecstasy. For the years, he felt, had not quenched his soul or hers. Their children, his writing, her household cares had not quenched all their souls' tender fire. In one letter that he had written to her then he had said: "Why is it that words like these seem to me so dull and cold? Is it because there is no word tender enough to be your name?"

Like distant music these words that he had written years before were borne towards him from the past. He longed to be alone with her. When the others had gone away, when he and she were in the room in the hotel, then they would be alone together. He would call her softly:

"Gretta!"

Perhaps she would not hear at once: she would be undressing. Then something in his voice would strike her. She would turn and look at him. . . .

At the corner of Winetavern Street they met a cab. He was glad of its rattling noise as it saved him from conversation. She was looking out of the window and seemed tired. The others spoke only a few words, pointing out some building or street. The horse galloped along wearily under the murky morning sky, dragging his old rattling box after his heels, and Gabriel was again in a cab with her, galloping to catch the boat, galloping to their honeymoon.

As the cab drove across O'Connell Bridge Miss O'Callaghan said:

"They say you never cross O'Connell Bridge without seeing a white horse."

"I see a white man this time," said Gabriel.

"Where?" asked Mr. Bartell D'Arcy.

Gabriel pointed to the statue, on which lay patches of snow. Then he nodded familiarly to it and waved his hand.

"Good-night, Dan," he said gaily.

When the cab drew up before the hotel, Gabriel jumped out and, in spite of Mr. Bartell D'Arcy's protest, paid the driver. He gave the man a shilling over his fare. The man saluted and said:

"A prosperous New Year to you, sir."

"The same to you," said Gabriel cordially.

She leaned for a moment on his arm in getting out of the cab and while standing at the curbstone, bidding the others good-night. She leaned lightly on his arm, as lightly as when she had danced with him a few hours before. He had felt proud and happy then, happy that she was his, proud of her grace and wifely carriage. But now, after the kindling again of so many memories, the first touch of her body, musical and strange and perfumed, sent through him a keen pang of lust. Under cover of her silence he pressed her arm closely to his side; and, as they stood at the hotel door, he felt that they had escaped from their lives and duties, escaped from home and friends and run away together with wild and radiant hearts to a new adventure.

An old man was dozing in a great hooded chair in the hall. He lit a candle in the office and went before them to the stairs. They followed him in silence, their feet falling in soft thuds on the thickly carpeted stairs. She mounted the stairs behind the porter, her head bowed in the ascent, her frail shoulders curved as with a burden, her skirt girt tightly about her. He could have flung his arms about her hips and held her still, for his arms were trembling with desire to seize her and only the stress of his nails against the palms of his hands held the wild impulse of his body in check. The porter halted on the stairs to settle his guttering candle. They halted, too, on the steps below him. In the silence Gabriel could hear the falling of the molten wax into the tray and the thumping of his own heart against his ribs.

The porter led them along a corridor and opened a door. Then he set his unstable candle down on a toilet-table and asked at what hour they were to be called in the morning.

"Eight," said Gabriel.

The porter pointed to the tap of the electric-light and began a muttered apology, but Gabriel cut him short.

"We don't want any light. We have light enough from the street. And I say," he added, pointing to the candle, "you might remove that handsome article, like a good man."

The porter took up his candle again, but slowly, for he was surprised by such a novel idea. Then he mumbled good-night and went out. Gabriel shot the lock to.

A ghastly light from the street lamp lay in a long shaft from one window to the door. Gabriel threw his overcoat and hat on a couch and crossed the room towards the window. He looked down into the street in order that his emotion might calm a little. Then he turned and leaned against a chest of drawers with his back to the light. She had taken off her hat and cloak and was standing before a large swinging mirror, unhooking her waist. Gabriel paused for a few moments, watching her, and then said:

"Gretta!"

She turned away from the mirror slowly and walked along the shaft of light towards him. Her face looked so serious and weary that the words would not pass Gabriel's lips. No, it was not the moment yet.

"You looked tired," he said.

"I am a little," she answered.

"You don't feel ill or weak?"

"No, tired: that's all."

She went on to the window and stood there, looking out. Gabriel waited again and then fearing that diffidence was about to conquer him, he said abruptly:

"By the way, Gretta!"

"What is it?"

"You know that poor fellow Malins?" he said quickly.

"Yes. What about him?"

"Well, poor fellow, he's a decent sort of chap, after all," continued Gabriel in a false voice. "He gave me back that sovereign I lent him, and I didn't expect it, really. It's a pity he wouldn't keep away from that Browne, because he's not a bad fellow, really."

He was trembling now with annoyance. Why did she seem so abstracted? He did not know how he could begin. Was she annoyed, too, about something? If she would only turn to him or come to him of her own accord! To take her as she was would be brutal. No, he must see some ardour in her eyes first. He longed to be master of her strange mood.

"When did you lend him the pound?" she asked, after a pause.

Gabriel strove to restrain himself from breaking out into brutal language about the sottish Malins and his pound. He longed to cry to her from his soul, to crush her body against his, to overmaster her. But he said:

"O, at Christmas, when he opened that little Christmas-card shop in Henry Street."

He was in such a fever of rage and desire that he did not hear her come from the window. She stood before him for an instant, looking at him strangely. Then, suddenly raising herself on tip-toe and resting her hands lightly on his shoulders, she kissed him.

"You are a very generous person, Gabriel," she said.

Gabriel, trembling with delight at her sudden kiss and at the quaintness of her phrase, put his hands on her hair and began smoothing it back, scarcely touching it with his fingers. The washing had made it fine and brilliant. His heart was brimming over with happiness. Just when he was wishing for it she had come to him of her own accord.

Perhaps her thoughts had been running with his. Perhaps she had felt the impetuous desire that was in him, and then the yielding mood had come upon her. Now that she had fallen to him so easily, he wondered why he had been so diffident.

He stood, holding her head between his hands. Then, slipping one arm swiftly about her body and drawing her towards him, he said softly:

"Gretta, dear, what are you thinking about?"

She did not answer nor yield wholly to his arm. He said again, softly:

"Tell me what it is, Gretta. I think I know what is the matter. Do I know?"

She did not answer at once. Then she said in an outburst of tears:

"O, I am thinking about that song, *The Lass of Aughrim*."

She broke loose from him and ran to the bed and, throwing her arms across the bed-rail, hid her face. Gabriel stood stock-still for a moment in astonishment and then followed her. As he passed in the way of the cheval-glass he caught sight of himself in full length, his broad, well-filled shirt-front, the face whose expression always puzzled him when he saw it in a mirror, and his glimmering gilt-rimmed eyeglasses. He halted a few paces from her and said:

"What about the song? Why does that make you cry?"

She raised her head from her arms and dried her eyes with the back of her hand like a child. A kinder note than he had intended went into his voice.

"Why, Gretta?" he asked.

"I am thinking about a person long ago who used to sing that song."

"And who was the person long ago?" asked Gabriel, smiling.

"It was a person I used to know in Galway when I was living with my grandmother," she said.

The smile passed away from Gabriel's face. A dull anger began to gather again at the back of his mind and the dull fires of his lust began to glow angrily in his veins.

"Someone you were in love with?" he asked ironically.

"It was a young boy I used to know," she answered, "named Michael Furey. He used to sing that song, *The Lass of Aughrim*. He was very delicate."

Gabriel was silent. He did not wish her to think that he was interested in this delicate boy.

"I can see him so plainly," she said, after a moment. "Such eyes as he had: big, dark eyes! And such an expression in them—an expression!"

"O, then, you are in love with him?" said Gabriel.

"I used to go out walking with him," she said, "when I was in Galway."

A thought flew across Gabriel's mind.

"Perhaps that was why you wanted to go to Galway with that Ivors girl?" he said coldly.

She looked at him and asked in surprise:

"What for?"

Her eyes made Gabriel feel awkward. He shrugged his shoulders and said:

"How do I know? To see him, perhaps."

She looked away from him along the shaft of light towards the window in silence.

"He is dead," she said at length. "He died when he was only seventeen. Isn't it a terrible thing to die so young as that?"

"What was he?" asked Gabriel, still ironically.

"He was in the gasworks," she said.

Gabriel felt humiliated by the failure of his irony and by the evocation of this figure from the dead, a boy in the gasworks. While he had been full of memories of their secret life together, full of tenderness and joy and desire, she had been comparing him in her mind with another. A shameful consciousness of his own person assailed him. He saw himself as a ludicrous figure, acting as a pennyboy for his aunts, a nervous, well-meaning sentimentalist, orating to vulgarians and idealising his own clownish lusts, the pitiable fatuous fellow he had caught a glimpse of in the mirror. Instinctively he turned his back more to the light lest she might see the shame that burned upon his forehead.

He tried to keep up his tone of cold interrogation, but his voice when he spoke was humble and indifferent.

"I suppose you were in love with this Michael Furey, Gretta," he said.

"I was great with him at that time," she said.

Her voice was veiled and sad. Gabriel, feeling now how vain it would be to try to lead her whither he had purposed, caressed one of her hands and said, also sadly:

"And what did he die of so young, Gretta? Consumption, was it?"

"I think he died for me," she answered.

A vague terror seized Gabriel at this answer, as if, at that hour when he had hoped to triumph, some impalpable and vindictive being was coming against him, gathering forces against him in its vague world. But he shook himself free of it with an effort of reason and continued to caress her hand. He did not question her again, for he felt that she would tell him of herself. Her hand was warm and moist: it did not respond to his touch, but he continued to caress it just as he had caressed her first letter to him that spring morning.

"It was in the winter," she said, "about the beginning of the winter when I was going to leave my grandmother's and come up here to the convent. And he was ill at the time in his lodgings in Galway and wouldn't be let out, and his people in Oughterard were written to. He was in decline, they said, or something like that. I never knew rightly."

She paused for a moment and sighed.

"Poor fellow," she said. "He was very fond of me and he was such a gentle boy. We used to go out together, walking, you know, Gabriel, like the way they do in the country. He was going to study singing only for his health. He had a very good voice, poor Michael Furey."

"Well; and then?" asked Gabriel.

"And then when it came to the time for me to leave Galway and come up to the convent he was much worse and I wouldn't be let see him so I wrote him a letter saying I was going up to Dublin and would be back in the summer, and hoping he would be better then."

She paused for a moment to get her voice under control, and then went on:

"Then the night before I left, I was in my grandmother's house in Nuns' Island, packing up, and I heard gravel thrown up against the window. The window was so wet I couldn't see, so I ran downstairs as I was and slipped out the back into the garden and there was the poor fellow at the end of the garden, shivering."

"And did you not tell him to go back?" asked Gabriel.

"I implored of him to go home at once and told him he would get his death in the rain. But he said he did not want to live. I can see his eyes as well as well! He was standing at the end of the wall where there was a tree."

"And did he go home?" asked Gabriel.

"Yes, he went home. And when I was only a week in the convent he died and he was buried in Oughterard, where his people came from. O, the day I heard that, that he was dead!"

She stopped, choking with sobs, and, overcome by emotion, flung herself face downward on the bed, sobbing in the quilt. Gabriel held her hand for a moment longer, irresolutely, and then, shy of intruding on her grief, let it fall gently and walked quietly to the window.

She was fast asleep.

Gabriel, leaning on his elbow, looked for a few moments unresentfully on her tangled hair and half-open mouth, listening to her deep-drawn breath. So she had had that romance in her life: a man had died for her sake. It hardly pained him now to think how poor a part he, her husband, had played in her life. He watched her while she slept, as though he and she had never lived together as man and wife. His curious eyes rested long upon her face and on her hair: and, as he thought of what she must have been then, in that time of her first girlish beauty, a strange, friendly pity for her entered his soul. He did not like to say even to himself that her face was no longer beautiful, but he knew that it was no longer the face for which Michael Furey had braved death.

Perhaps she had not told him all the story. His eyes moved to the chair over which she had thrown some of her clothes. A petticoat string dangled to the floor. One boot stood upright, its limp upper fallen down: the fellow of it lay upon its side. He wondered at his riot of emotions of an hour before. From what had it proceeded? From his aunt's supper, from his own foolish speech, from the wine and dancing, the merry-making when saying good-night in the hall, the pleasure of the walk along the river in the snow. Poor Aunt Julia! She, too, would soon be a shade with the shade of Patrick Morkan and his horse. He had caught that haggard look upon her face for a moment when she was singing *Arrayed for the Bridal*. Soon, perhaps, he would be sitting in that same drawing-room, dressed in black, his silk hat on his knees. The blinds would be drawn down and Aunt Kate would be sitting beside him, crying and blowing her nose and telling him how Julia had died. He would cast about in his mind for some words that might console her, and would find only lame and useless ones. Yes, yes: that would happen very soon.

The air of the room chilled his shoulders. He stretched himself cautiously along under the sheets and lay down beside his wife. One by one, they were all becoming shades. Better pass boldly into that other world, in the full glory of some passion, than fade and wither dismally with age. He thought of how she who lay beside him had locked in her heart for so many years that image of her lover's eyes when he had told her that he did not wish to live.

Generous tears filled Gabriel's eyes. He had never felt like that himself towards any woman, but he knew that such a feeling must be love. The tears gathered more thickly in his eyes and in the partial darkness he imagined he saw the form of a young man standing under a dripping tree. Other forms were near. His soul had approached that region where dwell the vast hosts of the dead. He was conscious of, but could not apprehend, their wayward and flickering existence. His own identity was fading out into a grey impalpable world: the solid world itself, which these dead had one time reared and lived in, was dissolving and dwindling.

A few light taps upon the pane made him turn to the window. It had begun to snow again. He watched sleepily the flakes, silver and dark, falling obliquely against the lamplight. The time had come for him to set out on his journey westward. Yes, the newspapers were right, snow was general all over Ireland. It was falling on every part of the dark central plain, on the treeless hills, falling softly upon the Bog of Allen and, farther westward, softly falling into the dark mutinous Shannon waves. It was falling, too, upon every part of the lonely churchyard on the hill where Michael Furey lay buried. It lay thickly drifted on the crooked crosses and headstones, on the spears of the little gate, on the barren thorns. His soul swooned slowly as he heard the snow falling faintly through the universe and faintly falling, like the descent of their last end, upon all the living and the dead.

QUESTIONS FOR DISCUSSION

ARABY

1. The boy in the story is experiencing a serious but nonetheless familiar kind of personal crisis. What is the nature of that crisis?

2. Joyce has the boy recall: ". . . I imagined that I bore my chalice safely through a throng of foes. . . ." How does this make clearer a conflict which appears in the story? What is the "chalice"? Who are the "foes"?

3. The writer presents us with a boy of fertile imagination and marked tenderness and sensitivity. Can you put your finger on the points in the story where these qualities are revealed?

4. This story is set in a big city. How does the author communicate this fact to us?

5. Touches both of humor and satire are worked into the narrative. Show where they appear and explain what they contribute to the total effect.

6. Explain the possible relationships between the title and the plot situation.

COUNTERPARTS

1. Episodes in this story occur against a background of workaday environment. In the light of the story line, what basic social facts or assumptions does Joyce appear to accept?

2. Joyce employs a cyclic series of related incidents in developing the story line—that is, each action precipitates a compensating counteraction. How would you relate this technique to Joyce's conception of life?

3. This story probes some of the ordinary stresses and strains which shape and modify human reactions to experience. In Joyce's view as revealed in the story, to what extent can man master these forces which shape day-to-day patterns of living?

4. How would you characterize the mood of the story? By what techniques does Joyce create this mood?

5. Whisky, bars, and drinking are woven into the fabric of the narrative. Define the role these elements play in the development of the story and relate them to the larger view of life that results.

6. What, or who, are the "counterparts"?

7. Analyze the degree of self-awareness that Farrington shows toward his behavior. Does Joyce's awareness of Farrington coincide with that the character has of himself? Explain how differences which exist in these points of view are exploited by the writer to give greater force of meaning.

A SUGGESTED INTERPRETATION

THE DEAD

"The Dead" serves to crystallize the disturbing realization that past human experience is constantly impinging upon and modifying the present moment of life. This is another way of saying that individuals are subtly made aware of the past through a continuous stream of half-articulated personal memories and remembrances.

Gabriel's burden of memory, however, as the story suggests, is much heavier and more keenly felt than that of the other characters, for two reasons. First, he apparently is much more perceptive, sensitive, and intelligent than they, and therefore sees, feels, and understands life around him much more fully. Second, his memories are more than of merely personal experience: he "remembers" the entire history of his land and is weighted down with this. Awareness of the past saddens him and creates for him a personal conflict because, in his everyday real life, he has intellectually liberated himself from these old dark clouds.

By the same unsolicited gift of remembrance that joins him spiritually to the past, he is awkwardly isolated from the unperceptive people around him. The other persons in the story—the humble and the vain—mechanically act out their roles in life according to established patterns. Only Gabriel, the disengaged observer with a retrospective awareness, seems able to see beyond these rigid patterns to a freer, more flexible mode of life, despite his feelings for "the dead." But he is, clearly, isolated from everybody else, and he knows that he is isolated.

Nonetheless, to go on bravely with one's work among the living, as he sententiously remarks in his after-dinner speech, should be one's aim in life. To succumb to the overwhelming sad tide of time gone by, to permit the engulfing memory of human struggles against darkness to paralyze one from affirmative action, would be to deny life and yield to the dead. To live successfully in a land where the unhappy past is always felt, where the presence of shades and spirits is compelling and obtrusive, one must vigorously affirm the life of fact and enlightened action. Perhaps pushed by fear of being overtaken and vanquished by the past, Gabriel cries, in a desperate moment, "I'm sick of my country, sick of it."

And so the first half circle of the plot line has for its backdrop the soiree at the maiden aunts', seen through Gabriel's bifocal lenses on a dual level of perception. The evening is magnificently illuminated by snatches of carefully authentic conversation, second-rate music, questionable wit, minor personality clashes, and large portions of sentimentality. Each movement and grouping is painted as a brilliant little mosaic, much like an imaginary painting such as the one in which Gabriel himself sees his wife as she stands quietly in the dark at the top of the stairs.

Gabriel's wife emerges dramatically from the crowd to complete the circle of the plot, in a line painlessly joined to its beginning by Gabriel's controlling point of view.

The complex interplay between man and wife is bewildering in the force with which it underscores the inadequacy of verbal communication between people who know each other well. Indeed, the words exchanged become only vague, simplified symbols for the undertow of deep, complex feelings which is really at the heart of the matter.

In the final analysis, then, Gabriel, who has openly and valorously proclaimed his determination (indeed, his urgent necessity) not to be vanquished by the dead, is so vanquished. The hauntingly memorable final paragraph—poetic in its overtones—in which Gabriel fully faces the dead, tells us that he may have great difficulty tomorrow carrying on his work among the living.

SUBJECTS FOR WRITTEN COMPOSITION

1. Explain how Joyce employs trenchant wit and satire—intellectually humorous criticism of certain aspects of human folly and failing—in these stories.

2. Analyze Joyce's use of conventional story structure. Show to what extent he utilizes such standard literary techniques as inevitable plot lines; arithmetically balanced numbers and kinds of characters; neatly arranged outcomes, and so forth.

3. Prepare a paper on Joyce as a realist. Show how and to what degree he maintains a fidelity to real life in presenting his story material.

4. "Araby" takes the form of the recall by a mature adult of his thoughts and experiences as a young adolescent. Examine this problem in "point of view." Explain how Joyce handles it and try to determine how successful he is.

5. Discuss the major sociologic and economic components of Joyce's world as revealed in the stories in this text. Outline the picture we obtain of Dublin life.

6. Through a close analysis and interpretation of the character of the boy in "Araby," explain how and to what extent he is in harmony or disagreement with the world around him.

7. Prepare an analytical-interpretive paper on "The Dead." Present your critical views on the overtones of meaning in the story.

8. Compose a paper dealing with Joyce's attitudes toward Ireland and the Irish as shown in these tales. Explain his relationship as a writer to the people, situations, and scenes he deals with.

William Faulkner

William Faulkner

WILLIAM FAULKNER, American novelist and Nobel Laureate, was born in Oxford, Mississippi, in 1897, and except for short intervals, he has lived his entire life in his native county. Though he attended the university sporadically as a young man, he never took a degree; Faulkner's formal grammar and high school training was equally incomplete.

After several unhappy months trying to make his way in New York and a full year tramping about Europe, Faulkner returned to Mississippi and began to write steadily—chiefly novels, some short stories, and a bit of poetry. Principal works from the list of novels are "Soldier's Pay" (1926), "Mosquitoes" (1927), "Sartoris" (1929), "The Sound and the Fury" (1929), "As I Lay Dying" (1930), "Sanctuary" (1931), "Light in August" (1932), "Pylon" (1933), "Absalom! Absalom!" (1936), "The Unvanquished" (1938), "The Wild Palms" (1939), "The Hamlet" (1940), "Intruder in the Dust" (1948), "Requiem for a Nun" (1951), and "A Fable" (1954). The short stories are "These Thirteen" (1931), "Go Down Moses, and Other Stories" (1942), and "Collected Stories" (1950); the poems are "The Marble Faun" (1924) and

"A Green Bough" (1933). "The Faulkner Reader," various selections collected from his writings, appeared in 1954.

In the short interval since the mid-forties—at which period he was read and admired only by a relatively few faithful—Faulkner has emerged dramatically into national and international fame and stature. Now all his work is exhaustively studied in the graduate schools, in the scholarly and critical journals, and in the consciousness of an ever-widening circle of devoted supporters. It was Robert Penn Warren who, in 1946, said, "The study of Faulkner is the most challenging single task in contemporary American literature for criticism to undertake. Here is a novelist who, in mass of work, in scope of material, in range of effect, in reportorial accuracy and symbolic subtlety, in philosophical weight, can be put beside the masters of our own past literature." For the sum total of his achievement Faulkner was awarded in 1950 the Nobel Prize for Literature; in 1955 he won the National Book Award for Fiction and the Pulitzer Prize for Literature.

The eloquent expression of his artistic credo, uttered when accepting his Nobel Award at Stockholm in 1950, is now widely known. In part, he said, "I feel that this award was not made to me as a man but to my work— a life's work in the agony and sweat of the human spirit, not for glory and least of all for profit, but to create out of the materials of the human spirit something which did not exist before. . . . I believe that man will not merely endure: he will prevail. He is immortal, not because he alone among creatures has an inexhaustible voice, but because he has a soul, a spirit capable of compassion and sacrifice and endurance. . . . The poet's voice need not merely be the record of man, it can be one of the props, the pillars to help him endure and prevail."

Faulkner's achievement is, of course, still being weighed, but there is small doubt that for sheer imaginative range (he has invented a whole Southern county and peopled it), searching moral concern (his work embodies striking parables for all men), and penetrating psychological truth (he succeeds in unmasking all corners of the human heart), he will rightfully be confirmed as one of America's mid-century literary giants.

Barn Burning

THE STORE IN WHICH THE JUSTICE OF THE PEACE'S COURT
was sitting smelled of cheese. The boy, crouched on his nail
keg at the back of the crowded room, knew he smelled cheese,
and more: from where he sat he could see the ranked shelves
close-packed with the solid, squat, dynamic shapes of tin cans
whose labels his stomach read, not from the lettering which
meant nothing to his mind but from the scarlet devils and the
silver curve of fish—this, the cheese which he knew he smelled
and the hermetic meat which his intestines believed he smelled
coming intermittent gusts momentary and brief between the
other constant one, the smell and sense just a little of fear because mostly of despair and grief, the old fierce pull of blood.
He could not see the table where the Justice sat and before
which his father and his father's enemy (*our enemy* he thought
in that despair; *ourn! mine and hisn both! He's my father!*)
stood, but he could hear them, the two of them that is, because his father had said no word yet:

"But what proof have you, Mr. Harris?"

"I told you. The hog got into my corn. I caught it up and
sent it back to him. He had no fence that would hold it. I
told him so, warned him. The next time I put the hog in my
pen. When he came to get it I gave him enough wire to patch

up his pen. The next time I put the hog up and kept it. I rode down to his house and saw the wire I gave him still rolled on to the spool in his yard. I told him he could have the hog when he paid me a dollar pound fee. That evening a nigger came with the dollar and got the hog. He was a strange nigger. He said, 'He say to tell you wood and hay kin burn.' I said, 'What?' 'That whut he say to tell you,' the nigger said. 'Wood and hay kin burn.' That night my barn burned. I got the stock out but I lost the barn."

"Where is the nigger? Have you got him?"

"He was a strange nigger, I tell you. I don't know what became of him."

"But that's not proof. Don't you see that's not proof?"

"Get that boy up here. He knows." For a moment the boy thought too that the man meant his older brother until Harris said, "Not him. The little one. The boy," and, crouching, small for his age, small and wiry like his father, in patched and faded jeans even too small for him, with straight, uncombed, brown hair and eyes gray and wild as storm scud, he saw the men between himself and the table part and become a lane of grim faces, at the end of which he saw the Justice, a shabby, collarless, graying man in spectacles, beckoning him. He felt no floor under his bare feet; he seemed to walk beneath the palpable weight of the grim turning faces. His father, stiff in his black Sunday coat donned not for the trial but for the moving, did not even look at him. *He aims for me to lie,* he thought, again with that frantic grief and despair. *And I will have to do hit.*

"What's your name, boy?" the Justice said.

"Colonel Sartoris Snopes," the boy whispered.

"Hey?" the Justice said. "Talk louder. Colonel Sartoris? I reckon anybody named for Colonel Sartoris in this country can't help but tell the truth, can they?" The boy said nothing. *Enemy! Enemy!* he thought; for a moment he could not even see, could not see that the Justice's face was kindly nor discern that his voice was troubled when he spoke to the man named Harris: "Do you want me to question this boy?" But he could hear, and during those subsequent long seconds while there was absolutely no sound in the crowded little room save that of quiet and intent breathing it was as if he had swung outward at the end of a grape vine, over a ravine, and at the top of the swing had been caught in a prolonged instant of mesmerized gravity, weightless in time.

"No!" Harris said violently, explosively. "Damnation! Send him out of here!" Now time, the fluid world, rushed beneath him again, the voices coming to him again through the smell of cheese and sealed meat, the fear and despair and the old grief of blood:

"This case is closed. I can't find against you, Snopes, but I can give you advice. Leave this country and don't come back to it."

His father spoke for the first time, his voice cold and harsh, level, without emphasis: "I aim to. I don't figure to stay in a country among people who . . ." he said something unprintable and vile, addressed to no one.

"That'll do," the Justice said. "Take your wagon and get out of this country before dark. Case dismissed."

His father turned, and he followed the stiff black coat, the wiry figure walking a little stiffly from where a Confederate provost's man's musket ball had taken him in the heel on a stolen horse thirty years ago, followed the two backs now, since his older brother had appeared from somewhere in the crowd, no taller than the father but thicker, chewing tobacco steadily, between the two lines of grim-faced men and out of the store and across the worn gallery and down the sagging steps and among the dogs and half-grown boys in the mild May dust, where as he passed a voice hissed:

"Barn burner!"

Again he could not see, whirling; there was a face in a red haze, moonlike, bigger than the full moon, the owner of it half again his size, he leaping in the red haze toward the face, feeling no blow, feeling no shock when his head struck the earth, scrabbling up and leaping again, feeling no blow this time either and tasting no blood, scrabbling up to see the other boy in full flight and himself already leaping into pursuit as his father's hand jerked him back, the harsh, cold voice speaking above him: "Go get in the wagon."

It stood in a grove of locusts and mulberries across the road. His two hulking sisters in their Sunday dresses and his mother and her sister in calico and sunbonnets were already in it, sitting on and among the sorry residue of the dozen and more movings which even the boy could remember—the battered stove, the broken beds and chairs, the clock inlaid with mother-of-pearl, which would not run, stopped at some fourteen minutes past two o'clock of a dead and forgotten day and time, which had been his mother's dowry. She was crying, though when she saw him she drew her sleeve across her face and began to descend from the wagon. "Get back," the father said.

"He's hurt. I got to get some water and wash his . . ."

"Get back in the wagon," his father said. He got in too, over the tail-gate. His father mounted to the seat where the older brother already sat and struck the gaunt mules two savage blows with the peeled willow, but without heat. It was not even sadistic; it was exactly that same quality which in later years would cause his descendants to over-run the engine before putting a motor car into motion, striking and reining back in the same movement. The wagon went on, the store with its quiet crowd of grimly watching men dropped behind; a curve in the road hid it. *Forever* he thought. *Maybe he's done satisfied now, now that he has* . . . stopping himself, not to say it aloud even to himself. His mother's hand touched his shoulder.

"Does hit hurt?" she said.

"Naw," he said. "Hit don't hurt. Lemme be."

"Can't you wipe some of the blood off before hit dries?"

"I'll wash to-night," he said. "Lemme be, I tell you."

The wagon went on. He did not know where they were going. None of them ever did or ever asked, because it was always somewhere, always a house of sorts waiting for them a day or two days or even three days away. Likely his father had already arranged to make a crop on another farm before he . . . Again he had to stop himself. He (the father) always did. There was something about his wolflike independence and even courage when the advantage was at least neutral which impressed strangers, as if they got from his latent ravening ferocity not so much a sense of dependability as a feeling that his ferocious conviction in the rightness of his own actions would be of advantage to all whose interest lay with his.

That night they camped in a grove of oaks and beeches where a spring ran. The nights were still cool and they had a fire against it, of a rail lifted from a nearby fence and cut into lengths—a small fire, neat, niggard almost, a shrewd fire; such fires were his father's habit and custom always, even in freezing weather. Older, the boy might have remarked this and wondered why not a big one; why should not a man who had not only seen the waste and extravagance of war, but who had in his blood an inherent voracious prodigality with material not his own, have burned everything in sight? Then he might have gone a step farther and thought that that was the reason: that niggard blaze was the living fruit of nights passed during those four years in the woods hiding from all men, blue or gray, with his strings of horses (captured horses, he called them). And older still, he might have divined the true reason: that the element of fire spoke to some deep mainspring of his father's being, as the element of steel or of powder spoke to other men, as the one weapon for the preservation of integrity, else breath were not worth the breathing, and hence to be regarded with respect and used with discretion.

But he did not think this now and he had seen those same niggard blazes all his life. He merely ate his supper beside it and was already half asleep over his iron plate when his father called him, and once more he followed the stiff back, the stiff and ruthless limp, up the slope and on to the starlit road where, turning, he could see his father against the stars but without face or depth—a shape black, flat, and bloodless as though cut from tin in the iron folds of the frockcoat which had not been made for him, the voice harsh like tin and without heat like tin:

"You were fixing to tell them. You would have told him." He didn't answer. His father struck him with the flat of his hand on the side of the head, hard but without heat, exactly as he had struck the two mules at the store, exactly as he would strike either of them with any stick in order to kill a horse fly, his voice still without heat or anger: "You're getting to be a man. You got to learn. You got to learn to stick to your own blood or you ain't going to have any blood to stick to you. Do you think either of them, any man there this morning, would? Don't you know all they wanted was a chance to get at me because they knew I had them beat? Eh?" Later, twenty years later, he was to tell himself, "If I had said they wanted only truth, justice, he would have hit me again." But now he said nothing. He was not crying. He just stood there. "Answer me," his father said.

"Yes," he whispered. His father turned.

"Get on to bed. We'll be there tomorrow."

To-morrow they were there. In the early afternoon the wagon stopped before a paintless two-room house identical almost with the dozen others it had stopped before even in the boy's ten years, and again, as on the other dozen occasions, his mother and aunt got down and began to unload the wagon, although his two sisters and his father and brother had not moved.

"Likely hit ain't fitten for hawgs," one of the sisters said.

"Nevertheless, fit it will and you'll hog it and like it," his father said. "Get out of them chairs and help your Ma unload."

The two sisters got down, big, bovine, in a flutter of cheap ribbons; one of them drew from the jumbled wagon bed a battered lantern, the other a worn broom. His father handed the reins to the older son and began to climb stiffly over the wheel. "When they get unloaded, take the team to the barn and feed them." Then he said, and at first the boy thought he was still speaking to his brother: "Come with me."

"Me?" he said.

"Yes," his father said. "You."

"Abner," his mother said. His father paused and looked back—the harsh level stare beneath the shaggy, graying, irascible brows.

"I reckon I'll have a word with the man that aims to begin to-morrow owning me body and soul for the next eight months."

They went back up the road. A week ago—or before last night, that is—he would have asked where they were going, but not now. His father had struck him before last night but never before had he paused afterward to explain why; it was as if the blow and the following calm, outrageous voice still rang, repercussed, divulging nothing to him save the terrible handicap of being young, the light weight of his few years, just heavy enough to prevent his soaring free of the world as it seemed to be ordered but not heavy enough to keep him footed solid in it, to resist it and try to change the course of its events.

Presently he could see the grove of oaks and cedars and the other flowering trees and shrubs where the house would be, though not the house yet. They walked beside a fence massed with honeysuckle and Cherokee roses and came to a gate swinging open between two brick pillars, and now, beyond a sweep of drive, he saw the house for the first time and at that instant he forgot his father and the terror and despair both, and even when he remembered his father again (who had not stopped) the terror and despair did not return. Because, for all the twelve movings, they had sojourned until now in a poor country, a land of small farms and fields and houses, and he had never seen a house like this before. *Hit's big as a courthouse* he thought quietly, with a surge of peace and joy whose reason he could not have thought into words, being too young for that: *They are safe from him. People whose lives are a part of this peace and dignity are beyond his touch, be no more to them than a buzzing wasp: capable of stinging for a little moment but that's all; the spell of this peace and dignity rendering even the barns and stable and cribs which belong to it impervious to the puny flames he might contrive* . . . this, the peace and joy, ebbing for an instant as he looked again at the stiff black back, the stiff and implacable limp of the figure which was not dwarfed by the house, for the reason that it had never looked big anywhere and which now, against the serene columned backdrop, had more than ever that impervious quality of something cut ruthlessly from tin, depthless, as though, sidewise to the sun, it would cast no shadow. Watching him, the boy remarked the absolutely undeviating course which his father held and saw the stiff foot come squarely down in a pile of fresh droppings where a horse had stood in the drive and which his father could have avoided by a simple change of stride. But it ebbed only for a moment, though he could not have thought this into words either, walking on in the spell of the house, which he could even want but without envy, without sorrow, certainly never with that ravening and jealous rage which unknown to him walked in the ironlike black coat before him. *Maybe he will feel it too. Maybe it will even change him now from what maybe he couldn't help but be.*

They crossed the portico. Now he could hear his father's stiff foot as it came down on the boards with clocklike finality, a sound out of all proportion to the displacement of the body it bore and which was not dwarfed either by the white door before it, as though it had attained to a sort of vicious and ravening minimum not to be dwarfed by anything—the flat, wide, black hat, the formal coat of broadcloth which had once been black but which had now the friction-glazed greenish cast of the bodies of old house flies, the lifted sleeve which was too large, the lifted hand like a curled claw. The door opened so promptly that the boy knew the Negro must have been watching them all the time, an old man with neat grizzled hair, in a linen jacket, who stood barring the door with his body, saying, "Wipe yo foots, white man, fo you come in here. Major ain't home nohow."

"Get out of my way, nigger," his father said, without heat too, flinging the door back and the Negro also and entering, his hat still on his head. And now the boy saw the prints of the stiff foot on the doorjamb and saw them appear on the pale rug behind the machinelike deliberation of the foot which seemed to bear (or transmit) twice the weight which the body compassed. The Negro was shouting "Miss Lula! Miss Lula!" somewhere behind them, then the boy, deluged as though by a warm wave by a suave turn of carpeted stair and a pendant glitter of chandeliers and a mute gleam of gold frames, heard the swift feet and saw her too, a lady—perhaps he had never seen her like before either—in a gray, smooth gown with lace at the throat and an apron tied at the waist and the sleeves turned back, wiping cake or biscuit dough from her hands with a towel as she came up the hall, looking not at his father at all but at the tracks on the blond rug with an expression of incredulous amazement.

"I tried," the Negro cried. "I tole him to . . ."

"Will you please go away?" she said in a shaking voice. "Major de Spain is not at home. Will you please go away?"

His father had not spoken again. He did not speak again. He did not even look at her. He just stood stiff in the center of the rug, in his hat, the shaggy iron-gray brows twitching slightly above the pebble-colored eyes as he appeared to examine the house with brief deliberation. Then with the same deliberation he turned; the boy watched him pivot on the good leg and saw the stiff foot drag round the arc of the turning, leaving a final long and fading smear. His father never looked at it, he never once looked down at the rug. The Negro held the door. It closed behind them, upon the hysteric and indistinguishable woman-wail. His father stopped at the top of the steps and scraped his boot clean on the edge of it. At the gate he stopped again. He stood for a moment, planted stiffly on the stiff foot, looking back at the house. "Pretty and white, ain't it?" he said. "That's sweat. Nigger sweat. Maybe it ain't white enough yet to suit him. Maybe he wants to mix some white sweat with it."

Two hours later the boy was chopping wood behind the house within which his mother and aunt and the two sisters (the mother and aunt, not the two girls, he knew that; even at this distance and muffled by walls the flat loud voices of the two girls emanated an incorrigible idle inertia) were setting up the stove to prepare a meal, when he heard the hooves and saw the linen-clad man on a fine sorrel mare, whom he recognized even before he saw the rolled rug in front of the Negro youth following on a fat bay carriage horse—a suffused, angry face vanishing, still at full gallop, beyond the corner of the house where his father and brother were sitting in the two tilted chairs; and a moment later, almost before he could have put the axe down, he heard the hooves again and watched the sorrel mare go back out of the yard, already galloping again. Then his father began to shout one of the sisters' names, who presently emerged backward from the kitchen door dragging the rolled rug along the ground by one end while the other sister walked behind it.

"If you ain't going to tote, go on and set up the wash pot," the first said.

"You, Sarty!" the second shouted, "Set up the wash pot!" His father appeared at the door, framed against that shabbiness, as he had been against that other bland perfection, impervious to either, the mother's anxious face at his shoulder.

"Go on," the father said. "Pick it up." The two sisters stooped, broad, lethargic; stooping, they presented an incredible expanse of pale cloth and a flutter of tawdry ribbons.

"If I thought enough of a rug to have to git hit all the way from France I wouldn't keep hit where folks coming in would have to tromp on hit," the first said. They raised the rug.

"Abner," the mother said. "Let me do it."

"You go back and git dinner," his father said. "I'll tend to this."

From the woodpile through the rest of the afternoon the boy watched them, the rug spread flat in the dust beside the bubbling wash-pot, the two sisters stooping over it with that profound and lethargic reluctance, while the father stood over them in turn, implacable and grim, driving them though never raising his voice again. He could smell the harsh homemade lye they were using; he saw his mother come to the door once and look toward them with an expression not anxious now but very like despair; he saw his father turn, and he fell to with the axe and saw from the corner of his eye his father raise from the ground a flattish fragment of field stone and examine it and return to the pot, and this time his mother actually spoke: "Abner. Abner. Please don't. Please, Abner."

Then he was done too. It was dusk; the whippoorwills had already begun. He could smell coffee from the room where they would presently eat the cold food remaining from the mid-afternoon meal, though when he entered the house he realized they were having coffee again probably because there was a fire on the hearth, before which the rug now lay spread over the backs of the two chairs. The tracks of his father's foot were gone. Where they had been were now long, water-cloudy scoria-tions resembling the sporadic course of a lilliputian mowing machine.

It still hung there while they ate the cold food and then went to bed, scattered without order or claim up and down the two rooms, his mother in one bed, where his father would later lie, the older brother in the other, himself, the aunt, and the two sisters on pallets on the floor. But his father was not in bed yet. The last thing the boy remembered was the depthless, harsh silhouette of the hat and coat bending over the rug and it seemed to him that he had not even closed his eyes when the silhouette was standing over him, the fire almost dead behind it, the stiff foot prodding him awake. "Catch up the mule," his father said.

When he returned with the mule his father was standing in the black door, the rolled rug over his shoulder. "Ain't you going to ride?" he said.

"No. Give me your foot."

He bent his knee into his father's hand, the wiry, surprising power flowed smoothly, rising, he rising with it, on to the mule's bare back (they had owned a saddle once; the boy could remember it though not when or where) and with the same effortlessness his father swung the rug up in front of him. Now in the starlight they retraced the afternoon's path, up the dusty road rife with honeysuckle, through the gate and up the black tunnel of the drive to the lightless house, where he sat on the mule and felt the rough warp of the rug drag across his thighs and vanish.

"Don't you want me to help?" he whispered. His father did not answer and now he heard again that stiff foot striking the hollow portico with that wooden and clocklike deliberation, that outrageous overstatement of the weight it carried. The rug, hunched, not flung (the boy could tell that even in the darkness) from his father's shoulder struck the angle of wall and floor with a sound unbelievably loud, thunderous, then the foot again, unhurried and enormous; a light came on in the house and the boy sat, tense, breathing steadily and quietly and just a little fast, though the foot itself did not increase its beat at all, descending the steps now; now the boy could see him.

"Don't you want to ride now?" he whispered. "We kin both ride now," the light within the house altering now, flaring up and sinking. *He's coming down the stairs now,* he thought. He had already ridden the mule up beside the horse block; presently his father was up behind him and he doubled the reins over and slashed the mule across the neck, but before the animal could begin to trot the hard, thin arm came round him, the hard, knotted hand jerking the mule back to a walk.

In the first red rays of the sun they were in the lot, putting plow gear on the mules. This time the sorrel mare was in the lot before he heard it at all, the rider collarless and even bareheaded, trembling, speaking in a shaking voice as the woman in the house had done, his father merely looking up once before stooping again to the hame he was buckling, so that the man on the mare spoke to his stooping back:

"You must realize you have ruined that rug. Wasn't there anybody here, any of your women . . ." he ceased, shaking, the boy watching him, the older brother leaning now in the stable door, chewing, blinking slowly and steadily at nothing apparently. "It cost a hundred dollars. But you never had a hundred dollars. You never will. So I'm going to charge you twenty bushels of corn against your crop. I'll add it in your contract and when you come to the commissary you can sign it.

That won't keep Mrs. de Spain quiet but maybe it will teach you to wipe your feet off before you enter her house again."

Then he was gone. The boy looked at his father, who still had not spoken or even looked up again, who was now adjusting the logger-head in the hame.

"Pap," he said. His father looked at him—the inscrutable face, the shaggy brows beneath which the gray eyes glinted coldly. Suddenly the boy went toward him, fast, stopping as suddenly. "You done the best you could!" he cried. "If he wanted hit done different why didn't he wait and tell you how? He won't git no twenty bushels! He won't git none! We'll gether hit and hide hit! I kin watch . . ."

"Did you put the cutter back in the straight stock like I told you?"

"No, sir," he said.

"Then go do it."

That was Wednesday. During the rest of that week he worked steadily, at what was within his scope and some which was beyond it, with an industry that did not need to be driven nor even commanded twice; he had this from his mother, with the difference that some at least of what he did he liked to do, such as splitting wood with the half-size axe which his mother and aunt had earned, or saved money somehow, to present him with at Christmas. In company with the two older women (and on one afternoon, even one of the sisters), he built pens for the shoat and the cow which were a part of his father's contract with the landlord, and one afternoon, his father being absent, gone somewhere on one of the mules, he went to the field.

They were running a middle buster now, his brother holding the plow straight while he handled the reins, and walking beside the straining mule, the rich black soil shearing cool and damp against his bare ankles, he thought *Maybe this is the end of it. Maybe even that twenty bushels that seems hard to have to pay for just a rug will be a cheap price for him to stop forever and always from being what he used to be;* thinking, dreaming now, so that his brother had to speak sharply to him to mind the mule: *Maybe he even won't collect the twenty bushels. Maybe it will all add up and balance and vanish—corn, rug, fire; the terror and grief, the being pulled two ways like between two teams of horses—gone, done with for ever and ever.*

Then it was Saturday; he looked up from beneath the mule he was harnessing and saw his father in the black coat and hat. "Not that," his father said. "The wagon gear." And then, two hours later, sitting in the wagon bed behind his father and brother on the seat, the wagon accomplished a final curve, and he saw the weathered paintless store with its tattered tobacco and patent-medicine posters and the tethered wagons and saddle animals below the gallery. He mounted the gnawed steps behind his father and brother, and there again was the lane of quiet, watching faces for the three of them to walk through. He saw the man in spectacles sitting at the plank table and he did not need to be told this was a Justice of the Peace; he sent one glare of fierce, exultant, partisan defiance at the man in collar and cravat now, whom he had seen but twice before in his life, and that on a galloping horse, who now wore on his face an expression not of rage but of amazed unbelief which the boy could not have known was at the incredible circumstance of being sued by one of his own tenants, and came and stood against his father and cried at the Justice: "He ain't done it! He ain't burnt . . ."

"Go back to the wagon," his father said.

"Burnt?" the Justice said. "Do I understand this rug was burned too?"

"Does anybody here claim it was?" his father said. "Go back to the wagon." But he did not, he merely retreated to the rear of the room, crowded as that other had been, but not to sit down this time, instead, to stand pressing among the motionless bodies, listening to the voices:

"And you claim twenty bushels of corn is too high for the damage you did to the rug?"

"He brought the rug to me and said he wanted the tracks washed out of it. I washed the tracks out and took the rug back to him."

"But you didn't carry the rug back to him in the same condition it was in before you made the tracks on it."

His father did not answer, and now for perhaps half a minute there was no sound at all save that of breathing, the faint, steady suspiration of complete and intent listening.

"You decline to answer that, Mr. Snopes?" Again his father did not answer. "I'm going to find against you, Mr. Snopes. I'm going to find that you were responsible for the injury to Major de Spain's rug and hold you liable for it. But twenty bushels of corn seems a little high for a man in your circumstances to have to pay. Major de Spain claims it cost a hundred dollars. October corn will be worth about fifty cents. I figure that if Major de Spain can stand a ninety-five dollar loss on something he paid cash for, you can stand a five-dollar loss you haven't earned yet. I hold you in damages to Major de Spain to the amount of ten bushels of corn over and above your contract with him, to be paid to him out of your crop at gathering time. Court adjourned."

It had taken no time hardly, the morning was but half begun. He thought they would return home and perhaps back to the field, since they were late, far behind all other farmers. But instead his father passed on behind the wagon, merely indicating with his hand for the older brother to follow with it, and crossed the road toward the blacksmith shop opposite, pressing on after his father, overtaking him, speaking, whispering up at the harsh, calm face beneath the weathered hat: "He won't git no ten bushels neither. He won't git one. We'll . . ." until his father glanced for an instant down at him, the face absolutely calm, the grizzled eyebrows tangled above the cold eyes, the voice almost pleasant, almost gentle: "You think so? Well, we'll wait till October anyway."

The matter of the wagon—the setting of a spoke or two and the tightening of the tires—did not take long either, the business of the tires accomplished by driving the wagon into the spring branch behind the shop and letting it stand there, the mules nuzzling into the water from time to time, and the boy on the seat with the idle reins, looking up the slope and through the sooty tunnel of the shed where the slow hammer rang and where his father sat on an upended cypress bolt, easily, either talking or listening, still sitting there when the boy brought the dripping wagon up out of the branch and halted it before the door.

"Take them on to the shade and hitch," his father said. He did so and returned. His father and the smith and a third man squatting on his heels inside the door were talking, about crops and animals; the boy, squatting too in the ammoniac dust and hoof-parings and scales of rust, heard his father tell a long and unhurried story out of the time before the birth of the older brother even when he had been a professional horsetrader. And then his father came up beside him where he stood before a tattered last year's circus poster on the other side of the store, gazing rapt and quiet at the scarlet horses, the incredible poisings and convolutions of tulle and tights and the painted leers of comedians, and said, "It's time to eat."

But not at home. Squatting beside his brother against the front wall, he watched his father emerge from the store and produce from a paper sack a segment of cheese and divide it carefully and deliberately into three with his pocket knife and produce crackers from the same sack. They all three squatted on the gallery and ate, slowly, without talking; then in the store again, they drank from a tin dipper tepid water smelling of the cedar bucket and of living beech trees. And still they did not go home. It was a horse lot this time, a tall rail fence upon and along which men stood and sat and out of which one by one horses were led, to be walked and trotted and then cantered back and forth along the road while the slow swapping and buying went on and the sun began to slant westward, they—the three of them—watching and listening, the older brother with his muddy eyes and his steady, inevitable tobacco, the father commenting now and then on certain of the animals, to no one in particular.

It was after sundown when they reached home. They ate supper by lamplight, then, sitting on the doorstep, the boy watched the night fully accomplished, listening to the whip-poorwills and the frogs, when he heard his mother's voice: "Abner! No! No! Oh, God. Oh, God. Abner!" and he rose, whirled, and saw the altered light through the door where a candle stub now burned in a bottle neck on the table and his father, still in the hat and coat, at once formal and burlesque as though dressed carefully for some shabby and ceremonial violence, emptying the reservoir of the lamp back into the five-gallon kerosene can from which it had been filled, while the mother tugged at his arm until he shifted the lamp to the other hand and flung her back, not savagely or viciously, just hard, into the wall, her hands flung out against the wall for balance, her mouth open and in her face the same quality of hopeless despair as had been in her voice. Then his father saw him standing in the door.

"Go to the barn and get that can of oil we were oiling the wagon with," he said. The boy did not move. Then he could speak.

"What . . ." he cried. "What are you . . ."

"Go get that oil," his father said. "Go."

Then he was moving, running, outside the house, toward the stable: this the old habit, the old blood which he had not been permitted to choose for himself, which had been bequeathed him willy nilly and which had run for so long (and who knew where, battening on what of outrage and savagery and lust) before it came to him. *I could keep on,* he thought. *I could run on and on and never look back, never need to see his face again. Only I can't. I can't,* the rusted can in his hand now, the liquid sploshing in it as he ran back to the house and into it, into the sound of his mother's weeping in the next room, and handed the can to his father.

"Ain't you going to even send a nigger?" he cried. "At least you sent a nigger before!"

This time his father didn't strike him. The hand came even faster than the blow had, the same hand which had set the can on the table with almost excruciating care flashing from the can toward him too quick for him to follow it, gripping him by the back of his shirt and on to tiptoe before he had seen it quit the can, the face stooping at him in breathless and frozen ferocity, the cold, dead voice speaking over him to the older brother who leaned against the table, chewing with that steady, curious, sidewise motion of cows:

"Empty the can into the big one and go on. I'll ketch up with you."

"Better tie him up to the bedpost," the brother said.

"Do like I told you," the father said. Then the boy was moving, his bunched shirt and the hard, bony hand between his shoulder-blades, his toes just touching the floor, across the room and into the other one, past the sisters sitting with spread heavy thighs in the two chairs over the cold hearth, and to where his mother and aunt sat side by side on the bed, the aunt's arms about his mother's shoulders.

"Hold him," the father said. The aunt made a startled movement. "Not you," the father said. "Lennie. Take hold of him. I want to see you do it." His mother took him by the wrist. "You'll hold him better than that. If he gets loose don't you know what he is going to do? He will go up yonder." He jerked his head toward the road. "Maybe I'd better tie him."

"I'll hold him," his mother whispered.

"See you do then." Then his father was gone, the stiff foot heavy and measured upon the boards, ceasing at last.

Then he began to struggle. His mother caught him in both arms, he jerking and wrenching at them. He would be stronger in the end, he knew that. But he had no time to wait for it. "Lemme go!" he cried. "I don't want to have to hit you!"

"Let him go!" the aunt said. "If he don't go, before God, I am going up there myself!"

"Don't you see I can't?" his mother cried. "Sarty! Sarty! No! No! Help me, Lizzie!"

Then he was free. His aunt grasped at him but it was too late. He whirled, running, his mother stumbled forward on to her knees behind him, crying to the nearer sister: "Catch him, Net! Catch him!" But that was too late too, the sister (the sisters were twins, born at the same time, yet either of them now gave the impression of being, encompassing as much living meat and volume and weight as any other two of the family) not yet having begun to rise from the chair, her head, face, alone merely turned, presenting to him in the flying instant an astonishing expanse of young female features untroubled by any surprise even, wearing only an expression of bovine interest. Then he was out of the room, out of the house, in the mild dust of the starlit road and the heavy rifeness of honeysuckle, the pale ribbon unspooling with terrific slowness under his running feet, reaching the gate at last and turning in, running, his heart and lungs drumming, on up the drive toward the lighted house, the lighted door. He did not knock, he burst in, sobbing for breath, incapable for the moment of speech; he saw the astonished face of the Negro in the linen jacket without knowing when the Negro had appeared.

"De Spain!" he cried, panted. "Where's . . ." then he saw the white man too emerging from a white door down the hall. "Barn!" he cried. "Barn!"

"What?" the white man said. "Barn?"

"Yes!" the boy cried. "Barn!"

"Catch him!" the white man shouted.

But it was too late this time too. The Negro grasped his shirt, but the entire sleeve, rotten with washing, carried away, and he was out that door too and in the drive again, and had actually never ceased to run even while he was screaming into the white man's face.

Behind him the white man was shouting, "My horse! Fetch my horse!" and he thought for an instant of cutting across the park and climbing the fence into the road, but he did not know the park nor how high the vine-massed fence might be and he dared not risk it. So he ran on down the drive, blood and breath roaring; presently he was in the road again though he could not see it. He could not hear either: the galloping mare was almost upon him before he heard her, and even then he held his course, as if the very urgency of his wild grief and need must in a moment more find him wings, waiting until the ultimate instant to hurl himself aside and into the weed-choked roadside ditch as the horse thundered past and on, for an instant in furious silhouette against the stars, the tranquil early summer night sky which, even before the shape of the horse and rider vanished, stained abruptly and violently upward: a long, swirling roar incredible and soundless, blotting the stars, and he springing up and into the road again, running again, knowing it was too late yet still running even after he heard the shot and, an instant later, two shots, pausing now without knowing he had ceased to run, crying "Pap! Pap!", running again before he knew he had begun to run, stumbling, tripping over something and scrabbling up again without ceasing to run, looking backward over his shoulder at the glare as he got up, running on among the invisible trees, panting, sobbing, "Father! Father!"

At midnight he was sitting on the crest of a hill. He did not know it was midnight and he did not know how far he had come. But there was no glare behind him now and he sat now, his back toward what he had called home for four days anyhow, his face toward the dark woods which he would enter when breath was strong again, small, shaking steadily in the chill darkness, hugging himself into the remainder of his thin, rotten shirt, the grief and despair now no longer terror and fear but just grief and despair. *Father. My father,* he thought. "He was brave!" he cried suddenly, aloud but not loud, no more than a whisper: "He was! He was in the war! He was in Colonel Sartoris' cav'ry!" not knowing that his father had gone to that war a private in the fine old European sense, wearing no uniform, admitting the authority of and giving fidelity to no man or army or flag, going to war as Malbrouck himself did: for booty—it meant nothing and less than nothing to him if it were enemy booty or his own.

The slow constellations wheeled on. It would be dawn and then sun-up after a while and he would be hungry. But that would be to-morrow and now he was only cold, and walking would cure that. His breathing was easier now and he decided to get up and go on, and then he found that he had been asleep because he knew it was almost dawn, the night almost over.

He could tell that from the whippoorwills. They were everywhere now among the dark trees below him, constant and inflectioned and ceaseless, so that, as the instant for giving over to the day birds drew nearer and nearer, there was no interval at all between them. He got up. He was a little stiff, but walking would cure that too as it would the cold, and soon there would be the sun. He went on down the hill, toward the dark woods within which the liquid silver voices of the birds called unceasing—the rapid and urgent beating of the urgent and quiring heart of the late spring night. He did not look back.

A Rose for Emily

WHEN MISS EMILY GRIERSON DIED, OUR WHOLE TOWN WENT TO her funeral: the men through a sort of respectful affection for a fallen monument, the women mostly out of curiosity to see the inside of her house, which no one save an old man-servant —a combined gardener and cook—had seen in at least ten years.

It was a big, squarish frame house that had once been white, decorated with cupolas and spires and scrolled balconies in the heavily lightsome style of the seventies, set on what had once been our most select street. But garages and cotton gins had encroached and obliterated even the august names of that neighborhood; only Miss Emily's house was left, lifting its stubborn and coquettish decay above the cotton wagons and the gasoline pumps—an eyesore among eyesores. And now Miss Emily had gone to join the representatives of those august names where they lay in the cedar-bemused cemetery among the ranked and anonymous graves of Union and Confederate soldiers who fell at the battle of Jefferson.

Alive, Miss Emily had been a tradition, a duty, and a care; a sort of hereditary obligation upon the town, dating from that day in 1894 when Colonel Sartoris, the mayor—he who fathered the edict that no Negro woman should appear on the streets without an apron—remitted her taxes, the dispensation dating from the death of her father on into perpetuity. Not that Miss Emily would have accepted charity. Colonel Sartoris invented an involved tale to the effect that Miss Emily's father had loaned money to the town, which the town, as a matter of business, preferred this way of repaying. Only a man of Colonel Sartoris' generation and thought could have invented it, and only a woman could have believed it.

When the next generation, with its more modern ideas, became mayors and aldermen, this arrangement created some little dissatisfaction. On the first of the year they mailed her a tax notice. February came, and there was no reply. They wrote her a formal letter, asking her to call at the sheriff's office at her convenience. A week later the mayor wrote her himself, offering to call or to send his car for her, and received in reply a note on paper of an archaic shape, in a thin, flowing calligraphy in faded ink, to the effect that she no longer went out at all. The tax notice was also enclosed, without comment.

They called a special meeting of the Board of Aldermen. A deputation waited upon her, knocked at the door through which no visitor had passed since she ceased giving china-painting lessons eight or ten years earlier. They were admitted by the old Negro into a dim hall from which a stairway mounted into still more shadow. It smelled of dust and disuse—a close, dank smell. The Negro led them into the parlor. It was furnished in heavy, leather-covered furniture. When the Negro opened the blinds of one window, they could see that the leather was cracked; and when they sat down, a faint dust rose sluggishly about their thighs, spinning with slow motes in the single sun-ray. On a tarnished gilt easel before the fireplace stood a crayon portrait of Miss Emily's father.

They rose when she entered—a small, fat woman in black, with a thin gold chain descending to her waist and vanishing into her belt, leaning on an ebony cane with a tarnished gold head. Her skeleton was small and spare; perhaps that was why what would have been merely plumpness in another was obesity in her. She looked bloated, like a body long submerged in motionless water, and of that pallid hue. Her eyes, lost in the fatty ridges of her face, looked like two small pieces of coal pressed into a lump of dough as they moved from one face to another while the visitors stated their errand.

She did not ask them to sit. She just stood in the door and listened quietly until the spokesman came to a stumbling halt. Then they could hear the invisible watch ticking at the end of the gold chain.

Her voice was dry and cold. "I have no taxes in Jefferson. Colonel Sartoris explained it to me. Perhaps one of you can gain access to the city records and satisfy yourselves."

"But we have. We are the city authorities, Miss Emily. Didn't you get a notice from the sheriff, signed by him?"

"I received a paper, yes," Miss Emily said. "Perhaps he considers himself the sheriff . . . I have no taxes in Jefferson."

"But there is nothing on the books to show that, you see. We must go by the—"

"See Colonel Sartoris. I have no taxes in Jefferson."

"But, Miss Emily—"

"See Colonel Sartoris." (Colonel Sartoris had been dead almost ten years.) "I have no taxes in Jefferson. Tobe!" The Negro appeared. "Show these gentlemen out."

2

So she vanquished them, horse and foot, just as she had vanquished their fathers thirty years before about the smell. That was two years after her father's death and a short time after her sweetheart—the one we believed would marry her—had deserted her. After her father's death she went out very little; after her sweetheart went away, people hardly saw her at all. A few of the ladies had the temerity to call, but were not received, and the only sign of life about the place was the Negro man—a young man then—going in and out with a market basket.

"Just as if a man—any man—could keep a kitchen properly," the ladies said; so they were not surprised when the smell developed. It was another link between the gross, teeming world and the high and mighty Griersons.

A neighbor, a woman, complained to the mayor, Judge Stevens, eighty years old.

"But what will you have me do about it, madam?" he said.

"Why, send her word to stop it," the woman said. "Isn't there a law?"

"I'm sure that won't be necessary," Judge Stevens said. "It's probably just a snake or a rat that nigger of hers killed in the yard. I'll speak to him about it."

The next day he received two more complaints, one from a man who came in diffident deprecation. "We really must do something about it, Judge. I'd be the last one in the world to bother Miss Emily, but we've got to do something." That night the Board of Aldermen met—three graybeards and one younger man, a member of the rising generation.

"It's simple enough," he said. "Send her word to have her place cleaned up. Give her a certain time to do it in, and if she don't . . ."

"Dammit, sir," Judge Stevens said, "will you accuse a lady to her face of smelling bad?"

So the next night, after midnight, four men crossed Miss Emily's lawn and slunk about the house like burglars, sniffing along the base of the brickwork and at the cellar openings while one of them performed a regular sowing motion with his hand out of a sack slung from his shoulder. They broke open the cellar door and sprinkled lime there, and in all the outbuildings. As they recrossed the lawn, a window that had been dark was lighted and Miss Emily sat in it, the light behind her, and her upright torso motionless as that of an idol. They crept quietly across the lawn and into the shadow of the locusts that lined the street. After a week or two the smell went away.

That was when people had begun to feel really sorry for her. People in our town, remembering how old lady Wyatt, her great-aunt, had gone completely crazy at last, believed that the Griersons held themselves a little too high for what they really were. None of the young men were quite good enough for Miss Emily and such. We had long thought of them as a tableau, Miss Emily a slender figure in white in the background, her father a spraddled silhouette in the foreground, his back to her and clutching a horsewhip, the two of them framed by the back-flung front door. So when she got to be thirty and was still single, we were not pleased exactly, but vindicated; even with insanity in the family she wouldn't have turned down all of her chances if they had really materialized.

When her father died, it got about that the house was all that was left to her; and in a way, people were glad. At last they could pity Miss Emily. Being left alone, and a pauper, she had become humanized. Now she too would know the old thrill and the old despair of a penny more or less.

The day after his death all the ladies prepared to call at the house and offer condolence and aid, as is our custom. Miss Emily met them at the door, dressed as usual and with no trace of grief on her face. She told them that her father was not dead. She did that for three days, with the ministers calling on her, and the doctors, trying to persuade her to let them dispose of the body. Just as they were about to resort to law and force, she broke down, and they buried her father quickly.

We did not say she was crazy then. We believed she had to do that. We remembered all the young men her father had driven away, and we knew that with nothing left, she would have to cling to that which had robbed her, as people will.

3

She was sick for a long time. When we saw her again, her hair was cut short, making her look like a girl, with a vague resemblance to those angels in colored church windows—sort of tragic and serene.

The town had just let the contracts for paving the sidewalks, and in the summer after her father's death they began the work. The construction company came with niggers and mules and machinery, and a foreman named Homer Barron, a Yankee—a big, dark, ready man, with a big voice and eyes lighter than his face. The little boys would follow in groups to hear him cuss the niggers, and the niggers singing in time to the rise and fall of picks. Pretty soon he knew everybody in town. Whenever you heard a lot of laughing anywhere about the square, Homer Barron would be in the center of the group. Presently we began to see him and Miss Emily on Sunday afternoons driving in the yellow-wheeled buggy and the matched team of bays from the livery stable.

At first we were glad that Miss Emily would have an interest, because the ladies all said, "Of course a Grierson would not think seriously of a Northerner, a day laborer." But there were still others, older people, who said that even grief could not cause a real lady to forget *noblesse oblige*—without calling it *noblesse oblige*. They just said, "Poor Emily. Her kinsfolk should come to her." She had some kin in Alabama; but years ago her father had fallen out with them over the estate of old lady Wyatt, the crazy woman, and there was no communication between the two families. They had not even been represented at the funeral.

And as soon as the old people said, "Poor Emily," the whispering began. "Do you suppose it's really so?" they said to one another. "Of course it is. What else could . . ." This behind their hands; rustling of craned silk and satin behind jalousies closed upon the sun of Sunday afternoon as the thin, swift clop-clop-clop of the matched team passed: "Poor Emily."

She carried her head high enough—even when we believed that she was fallen. It was as if she demanded more than ever the recognition of her dignity as the last Grierson; as if it had wanted that touch of earthiness to reaffirm her imperviousness. Like when she bought the rat poison, the arsenic. That was over a year after they had begun to say "Poor Emily," and while the two female cousins were visiting her.

"I want some poison," she said to the druggist. She was over thirty then, still a slight woman, though thinner than usual, with cold, haughty black eyes in a face the flesh of which was strained across the temples and about the eyesockets as you imagine a lighthouse-keeper's face ought to look. "I want some poison," she said.

"Yes, Miss Emily. What kind? For rats and such? I'd recom—"

"I want the best you have. I don't care what kind."

The druggist named several. "They'll kill anything up to an elephant. But what you want is—"

"Arsenic," Miss Emily said. "Is that a good one?"

"Is . . . arsenic? Yes, ma'am. But what you want—"

"I want arsenic."

The druggist looked down at her. She looked back at him, erect, her face like a strained flag. "Why, of course," the druggist said. "If that's what you want. But the law requires you to tell what you are going to use it for."

Miss Emily just stared at him, her head tilted back in order to look him eye for eye, until he looked away and went and got the arsenic and wrapped it up. The Negro delivery boy brought her the package; the druggist didn't come back. When she opened the package at home there was written on the box, under the skull and bones: "For rats."

4

So the next day we all said, "She will kill herself"; and we said it would be the best thing. When she had first begun to be seen with Homer Barron, we had said, "She will marry him." Then we said, "She will persuade him yet," because Homer himself had remarked—he liked men, and it was known that he drank with the younger men in the Elks' Club—that he was not a marrying man. Later we said, "Poor Emily" behind the jalousies as they passed on Sunday afternoon in the glittering buggy, Miss Emily with her head high and Homer Barron with his hat cocked and a cigar in his teeth, reins and whip in a yellow glove.

Then some of the ladies began to say that it was a disgrace to the town and a bad example to the young people. The men did not want to interfere, but at last the ladies forced the Baptist minister—Miss Emily's people were Episcopal—to call upon her. He would never divulge what happened during that interview, but he refused to go back again. The next Sunday they again drove about the streets, and the following day the minister's wife wrote to Miss Emily's relations in Alabama.

So she had blood-kin under her roof again and we sat back to watch developments. At first nothing happened. Then we were sure that they were to be married. We learned that Miss Emily had been to the jeweler's and ordered a man's toilet set in silver, with the letters H. B. on each piece. Two days later we learned that she had bought a complete outfit of men's clothing, including a nightshirt, and we said, "They are married." We were really glad. We were glad because the two female cousins were even more Grierson than Miss Emily had ever been.

So we were not surprised when Homer Barron—the streets had been finished some time since—was gone. We were a little disappointed that there was not a public blowing-off, but we believed that he had gone on to prepare for Miss Emily's coming, or to give her a chance to get rid of the cousins. (By that time it was a cabal, and we were all Miss Emily's allies to help circumvent the cousins.) Sure enough, after another week they departed. And, as we had expected all along, within three days Homer Barron was back in town. A neighbor saw the Negro man admit him at the kitchen door at dusk one evening.

And that was the last we saw of Homer Barron. And of Miss Emily for some time. The Negro man went in and out with the market basket, but the front door remained closed. Now and then we would see her at a window for a moment, as the men did that night when they sprinkled the lime, but for almost six months she did not appear on the streets. Then we knew that this was to be expected too; as if that quality of her father which had thwarted her woman's life so many times had been too virulent and too furious to die.

When we next saw Miss Emily, she had grown fat and her

hair was turning gray. During the next few years it grew grayer and grayer until it attained an even pepper-and-salt iron-gray, when it ceased turning. Up to the day of her death at seventy-four it was still that vigorous iron-gray, like the hair of an active man.

From that time on her front door remained closed, save during a period of six or seven years, when she was about forty, during which she gave lessons in china-painting. She fitted up a studio in one of the downstairs rooms, where the daughters and granddaughters of Colonel Sartoris' contemporaries were sent to her with the same regularity and in the same spirit that they were sent to church on Sundays with a twenty-five-cent piece for the collection plate. Meanwhile her taxes had been remitted.

Then the newer generation became the backbone and the spirit of the town, and the painting pupils grew up and fell away and did not send their children to her with boxes of color and tedious brushes and pictures cut from the ladies' magazines. The front door closed upon the last one and remained closed for good. When the town got free postal delivery, Miss Emily alone refused to let them fasten the metal numbers above her door and attach a mailbox to it. She would not listen to them.

Daily, monthly, yearly we watched the Negro grow grayer and more stooped, going in and out with the market basket. Each December we sent her a tax notice, which would be returned by the post office a week later, unclaimed. Now and then we would see her in one of the downstairs windows—she had evidently shut up the top floor of the house—like the carven torso of an idol in a niche, looking or not looking at us, we could never tell which. Thus she passed from generation to generation—dear, inescapable, impervious, tranquil, and perverse.

And so she died. Fell ill in the house filled with dust and shadows, with only a doddering Negro man to wait on her. We did not even know she was sick; we had long since given up trying to get any information from the Negro. He talked to no one, probably not even to her, for his voice had grown harsh and rusty, as if from disuse.

She died in one of the downstairs rooms, in a heavy walnut bed with a curtain, her gray head propped on a pillow yellow and moldy with age and lack of sunlight.

5

The Negro met the first of the ladies at the front door and let them in, with their hushed, sibilant voices and their quick, curious glances, and then he disappeared. He walked right through the house and out the back and was not seen again.

The two female cousins came at once. They held the funeral on the second day, with the town coming to look at Miss Emily beneath a mass of bought flowers, with the crayon face of her father musing profoundly above the bier and the ladies sibilant and macabre; and the very old men—some in their brushed Confederate uniforms—on the porch and the lawn, talking of Miss Emily as if she had been a contemporary of theirs, believing that they had danced with her and courted her perhaps, confusing time with its mathematical progression, as the old do, to whom all the past is not a diminishing road but, instead, a huge meadow which no winter ever quite touches, divided from them now by the narrow bottle-neck of the most recent decade of years.

Already we knew that there was one room in that region above stairs which no one had seen in forty years, and which would have to be forced. They waited until Miss Emily was decently in the ground before they opened it.

The violence of breaking down the door seemed to fill this room with pervading dust. A thin, acrid pall as of the tomb seemed to lie everywhere upon this room decked and furnished as for a bridal: upon the valance curtains of faded rose color, upon the rose-shaded lights, upon the dressing table, upon the delicate array of crystal and the man's toilet things backed with tarnished silver, silver so tarnished that the monogram was obscured. Among them lay a collar and tie, as if they had just been removed, which, lifted, left upon the surface a pale crescent in the dust. Upon a chair hung the suit, carefully folded; beneath it the two mute shoes and the discarded socks.

The man himself lay in the bed.

For a long while we just stood there, looking down at the profound and fleshless grin. The body had apparently once lain in the attitude of an embrace, but now the long sleep that outlasts love, that conquers even the grimace of love, had cuckolded him. What was left of him, rotted beneath what was left of the nightshirt, had become inextricable from the bed in which he lay; and upon him and upon the pillow beside him lay that even coating of the patient and biding dust.

Then we noticed that in the second pillow was the indentation of a head. One of us lifted something from it, and leaning forward, that faint and invisible dust dry and acrid in the nostrils, we saw a long strand of iron-gray hair.

The Bear

HE WAS TEN. BUT IT HAD ALREADY BEGUN, LONG BEFORE
that day when at last he wrote his age in two figures and he
saw for the first time the camp where his father and Major
de Spain and old General Compson and the others spent two
weeks each November and two weeks again each June. He had
already inherited then, without ever having seen it, the tremendous bear with one trap-ruined foot which, in an area almost a hundred miles deep, had earned itself a name, a definite
designation like a living man.

He had listened to it for years: the long legend of corn-
cribs rifled, of shotes and grown pigs and even calves carried
bodily into the woods and devoured, of traps and deadfalls
overthrown and dogs mangled and slain, and shotgun and even
rifle charges delivered at point-blank range and with no more
effect than so many peas blown through a tube by a boy—a
corridor of wreckage and destruction beginning back before
he was born, through which sped, not fast but rather with the
ruthless and irresistible deliberation of a locomotive, the shaggy
tremendous shape.

It ran in his knowledge before he ever saw it. It looked
and towered in his dreams before he even saw the unaxed
woods where it left its crooked print, shaggy, huge, red-eyed,

251

not malevolent but just big—too big for the dogs which tried to bay it, for the horses which tried to ride it down, for the men and the bullets they fired into it, too big for the very country which was its constricting scope. He seemed to see it entire with a child's complete divination before he ever laid eyes on either—the doomed wilderness whose edges were being constantly and punily gnawed at by men with axes and plows who feared it because it was wilderness, men myriad and nameless even to one another in the land where the old bear had earned a name, through which ran not even a mortal animal but an anachronism, indomitable and invincible, out of an old dead time, a phantom, epitome and apotheosis of the old wild life at which the puny humans swarmed and hacked in a fury of abhorrence and fear, like pygmies about the ankles of a drowsing elephant: the old bear solitary, indomitable and alone, widowered, childless, and absolved of mortality—old Priam reft of his old wife and having outlived all his sons.

Until he was ten, each November he would watch the wagon containing the dogs and the bedding and food and guns and his father and Tennie's Jim, the Negro, and Sam Fathers, the Indian, son of a slave woman and a Chickasaw chief, depart on the road to town, to Jefferson, where Major de Spain and the others would join them. To the boy, at seven, eight, and nine, they were not going into the Big Bottom to hunt bear and deer, but to keep yearly rendezvous with the bear which they did not even intend to kill. Two weeks later they would return, with no trophy, no head and skin. He had not expected it. He had not even been afraid it would be in the wagon. He believed that even after he was ten and his father would let him go too, for those two weeks in November, he would merely make another one, along with his father and Major de Spain and General Compson and the others, the dogs which feared to bay at it and the rifles and shotguns which failed even to bleed it, in the yearly pageant of the old bear's furious immortality.

Then he heard the dogs. It was in the second week of his first time in the camp. He stood with Sam Fathers against a big oak beside the faint crossing where they had stood each dawn for nine days now, hearing the dogs. He had heard them once before, one morning last week—a murmur, sourceless, echoing through the wet woods, swelling presently into separate voices which he could recognize and call by name. He had raised and cocked the gun as Sam told him and stood motionless again while the uproar, the invisible course, swept up and past and faded; it seemed to him that he could actually see the deer, the buck, blond, smoke-colored, elongated with speed, fleeing, vanishing, the woods, the gray solitude, still ringing even when the cries of the dogs had died away.

"Now let the hammers down," Sam said.

"You knew they were not coming here too," he said.

"Yes," Sam said. "I want you to learn how to do when you didn't shoot. It's after the chance for the bear or the deer has done already come and gone that men and dogs get killed."

"Anyway," he said, "it was just a deer."

Then on the tenth morning he heard the dogs again. And he readied the too-long, too-heavy gun as Sam had taught him, before Sam even spoke. But this time it was no deer, no ringing chorus of dogs running strong on a free scent, but a moiling yapping an octave too high, with something more than indecision and even abjectness in it, not even moving very fast, taking a long time to pass completely out of hearing, leaving then somewhere in the air that echo, thin, slightly hysterical, abject, almost grieving, with no sense of a fleeting, unseen, smoke-colored, grass-eating shape ahead of it, and Sam, who had taught him first of all to cock the gun and take position where he could see everywhere and then never move again, had himself moved up beside him; he could hear Sam breathing at his shoulder, and he could see the arched curve of the old man's inhaling nostrils.

"Hah," Sam said. "Not even running. Walking."

"Old Ben!" the boy said. "But up here!" he cried. "Way up here!"

"He do it every year," Sam said. "Once. Maybe to see who in camp this time, if he can shoot or not. Whether we got the dog yet that can bay and hold him. He'll take them to the river, then he'll send them back home. We may as well go back too; see how they look when they come back to camp."

When they reached the camp the hounds were already there, ten of them crouching back under the kitchen, the boy and Sam squatting to peer back into the obscurity where they had huddled, quiet, the eyes luminous, glowing at them and vanishing, and no sound, only that effluvium of something more than dog, stronger than dog and not just animal, just beast because still there had been nothing in front of that abject and almost painful yapping save the solitude, the wilderness, so that when the eleventh hound came in at noon and with all the others watching even old Uncle Ash, who called himself first a cook— Sam daubed the tattered ear and the raked shoulder with turpentine and axle grease, to the boy it was still no living creature, but the wilderness which, leaning for the moment down, had patted lightly once the hound's temerity.

"Just like a man," Sam said. "Just like folks. Put off as long as she could having to be brave, knowing all the time that sooner or later she would have to be brave to keep on living with herself, and knowing all the time beforehand what was going to happen to her when she done it."

That afternoon, himself on the one-eyed wagon mule which did not mind the smell of blood or, as they told him, of bear, and with Sam on the other one, they rode for more than three hours through the rapid, shortening winter day. They followed no path, no trail even that he could see; almost at once they were in a country which he had never seen before. Then he knew why Sam had made him ride the mule which would not spook. The sound one stopped short and tried to whirl and bolt even as Sam got down, blowing its breath, jerking and wrenching at the rein, while Sam held it, coaxing it forward with his voice, since he could not risk tying it, drawing it forward while the boy got down from the marred one.

Then, standing beside Sam in the gloom of the dying afternoon, he looked down at the rotted over-turned log, gutted and scored with claw marks and, in the wet earth beside it, the print of the enormous warped two-toed foot. He knew now what he had smelled when he peered under the kitchen where the dogs huddled. He realized for the first time that the bear which had run in his listening and loomed in his dreams since before he could remember to the contrary, and which, therefore, must have existed in the listening and dreams of his father and Major de Spain and even old General Compson, too, before they began to remember in their turn, was a mortal animal, and that if they had departed for the camp each November without any actual hope of bringing its trophy back, it was not because it could not be slain, but because so far they had had no actual hope to.

"Tomorrow," he said.

"We'll try tomorrow," Sam said. "We ain't got the dog yet."

"We've got eleven. They ran him this morning."

"It won't need but one," Sam said. "He ain't here. Maybe he ain't nowhere. The only other way will be for him to run by accident over somebody that has a gun."

"That wouldn't be me," the boy said. "It will be Walter or Major or—"

"It might," Sam said. "You watch close in the morning. Because he's smart. That's how come he has lived this long. If he gets hemmed up and has to pick out somebody to run over, he will pick out you."

"How?" the boy said. "How will he know—" He ceased. "You mean he already knows me, that I ain't never been here before, ain't had time to find out yet whether I—" He ceased again, looking at Sam, the old man whose face revealed nothing until it smiled. He said humbly, not even amazed, "It was me he was watching. I don't reckon he did need to come but once."

The next morning they left the camp three hours before daylight. They rode this time because it was too far to walk, even the dogs in the wagon; again the first gray light found him in a place which he had never seen before, where Sam had placed him and told him to stay and then departed. With the gun which was too big for him, which did not even belong to him, but to Major de Spain, and which he had fired only once—at a stump on the first day, to learn the recoil and how to reload it —he stood against a gum tree beside a little bayou whose black still water crept without movement out of a canebrake and crossed a small clearing and into cane again, where, invisible, a bird—the big woodpecker called Lord-to-God by Negroes— clattered at a dead limb.

It was a stand like any other, dissimilar only in incidentals to the one where he had stood each morning for ten days; a territory new to him, yet no less familiar than that other one which, after almost two weeks, he had come to believe he knew a little—the same solitude, the same loneliness through which human beings had merely passed without altering it, leaving no mark, no scar, which looked exactly as it must have looked when the first ancestor of Sam Fathers' Chickasaw predecessors crept into it and looked about, club or stone ax or bone arrow drawn and poised; different only because, squatting at the edge of the kitchen, he smelled the hounds huddled and cringing beneath it and saw the raked ear and shoulder of the one who, Sam said, had had to be brave once in order to live with herself, and saw yesterday in the earth beside the gutted log the print of the living foot.

He heard no dogs at all. He never did hear them. He only heard the drumming of the woodpecker stop short off and knew that the bear was looking at him. He never saw it. He did not know whether it was in front of him or behind him. He did not move, holding the useless gun, which he had not even had warning to cock and which even now he did not cock, tasting in his saliva that taint as of brass which he knew now because he had smelled it when he peered under the kitchen at the huddled dogs.

Then it was gone. As abruptly as it had ceased, the woodpecker's dry, monotonous clatter set up again, and after a while he even believed he could hear the dogs—a murmur, scarce a sound even, which he had probably been hearing for some time before he even remarked it, drifting into hearing and then out again, dying away. They came nowhere near him.

If it was a bear they ran, it was another bear. It was Sam himself who came out of the cane and crossed the bayou, followed by the injured bitch of yesterday. She was almost at heel, like a bird dog, making no sound. She came and crouched against his leg, trembling, staring off into the cane.

"I didn't see him," he said. "I didn't, Sam!"

"I know it," Sam said. "He done the looking. You didn't hear him neither, did you?"

"No," the boy said. "I—"

"He's smart," Sam said. "Too smart." He looked down at the hound, trembling faintly and steadily against the boy's knee. From the raked shoulder a few drops of fresh blood oozed and clung. "Too big. We ain't got the dog yet. But maybe someday. Maybe not next time. But someday."

So I must see him, he thought. *I must look at him.* Otherwise, it seemed to him that it would go on like this forever, as it had gone on with his father and Major de Spain, who was older than his father, and even with old General Compson, who had been old enough to be a brigade commander in 1865. Otherwise, it would go on so forever, next time and next time, after and after and after. It seemed to him that he could never see the two of them, himself and the bear, shadowy in the limbo from which time emerged, becoming time; the old bear absolved of mortality and himself partaking, sharing a little of it, enough of it. And he knew now what he had smelled in the huddled dogs and tasted in his saliva. He recognized fear. *So I will have to see him,* he thought, without dread or even hope. *I will have to look at him.*

It was in June of the next year. He was eleven. They were in camp again, celebrating Major de Spain's and General Compson's birthdays. Although the one had been born in September and the other in the depth of winter and in another decade, they had met for two weeks to fish and shoot squirrels and turkey and run coons and wildcats with the dogs at night. That is, he and Boon Hoggenbeck and the Negroes fished and shot squirrels and ran the coons and cats, because the proved hunters, not only Major de Spain and old General Compson, who spent those two weeks sitting in a rocking chair before a tremendous iron pot of Brunswick stew, stirring and tasting, with old Ash to quarrel with about how he was making it and Tennie's Jim to pour whiskey from the demijohn into the tin dipper from which he drank it, but even the boy's father and Walter Ewell, who were still young enough, scorned such, other than shooting the wild gobblers with pistols for wagers on their marksmanship.

Or, that is, his father and the others believed he was hunting squirrels. Until the third day, he thought that Sam Fathers believed that too. Each morning he would leave the camp right after breakfast. He had his own gun now, a Christmas present. He went back to the tree beside the bayou where he had stood that morning. Using the compass which old General Compson had given him, he ranged from that point; he was teaching himself to be a better-than-fair woodsman without knowing he was doing it. On the second day he even found the gutted log where he had first seen the crooked print. It was almost completely crumbled now, healing with unbelievable speed, a passionate and almost visible relinquishment, back into the earth from which the tree had grown.

He ranged the summer woods now, green with gloom; if anything, actually dimmer than in November's gray dissolution, where, even at noon, the sun fell only in intermittent dappling upon the earth, which never completely dried out and which crawled with snakes—moccasins and water snakes and rattlers, themselves the color of the dappling gloom, so that he would not always see them until they moved, returning later and later, first day, second day, passing in the twilight of the third evening the little log pen enclosing the log stable where Sam was putting up the horses for the night.

"You ain't looked right yet," Sam said.

He stopped. For a moment he didn't answer. Then he said peacefully, in a peaceful rushing burst as when a boy's miniature dam in a little brook gives way, "All right. But how? I went to the bayou. I even found that log again. I—"

"I reckon that was all right. Likely he's been watching you. You never saw his foot?"

"I," the boy said—"I didn't—I never thought—"

"It's the gun," Sam said. He stood beside the fence motion-less—the old man, the Indian, in the battered faded overalls and the five-cent straw hat which in the Negro's race had been the badge of his enslavement and was now the regalia of his freedom. The camp—the clearing, the house, the barn and its tiny lot with which Major de Spain in his turn had scratched punily and evanescently at the wilderness—faded in the dusk, back into the immemorial darkness of the woods. *The gun,* the boy thought. *The gun.*

"Be scared," Sam said. "You can't help that. But don't be afraid. Ain't nothing in the woods going to hurt you unless you corner it, or it smells that you are afraid. A bear or a deer, too, has got to be scared of a coward the same as a brave man has got to be."

The gun, the boy thought.

"You will have to choose," Sam said.

He left the camp before daylight, long before Uncle Ash would wake in his quilts on the kitchen floor and start the fire for breakfast. He had only the compass and a stick for snakes. He could go almost a mile before he would begin to need the compass. He sat on a log, the invisible compass in his invisible hand, while the secret night sounds, fallen still at his move-ments, scurried again and then ceased for good, and the owls ceased and gave over to the waking of day birds, and he could see the compass. Then he went fast yet still quietly; he was becoming better and better as a woodsman, still without having yet realized it.

He jumped a doe and a fawn at sunrise, walked them out of the bed, close enough to see them—the crash of undergrowth, the white scut, the fawn scudding behind her faster than he had believed it could run. He was hunting right, upwind, as Sam had taught him; not that it mattered now. He had left the gun; of his own will and relinquishment he had accepted not a gambit, not a choice, but a condition in which not only the bear's heretofore inviolable anonymity but all the old rules and balances of hunter and hunted had been abrogated. He would not even be afraid, not even in the moment when the fear would take him completely—blood, skin, bowels, bones, memory from the long time before it became his memory—all save that thin, clear, immortal lucidity which alone differed him from this bear and from all the other bear and deer he would ever kill in the humility and pride of his skill and endurance, to which Sam had spoken when he leaned in the twilight on the lot fence yesterday.

By noon he was far beyond the little bayou, farther into the new and alien country than he had ever been. He was traveling now not only by the old, heavy, biscuit-thick silver watch which had belonged to his grandfather. When he stopped at last, it was for the first time since he had risen from the log at dawn when he could see the compass. It was far enough. He had left the camp nine hours ago; nine hours from now, dark would have already been an hour old. But he didn't think that. He thought, *All right. Yes. But what?* and stood for a moment, alien and small in the green and topless solitude, answering his own question before it had formed and ceased. It was the watch, the compass, the stick—the three lifeless mechanicals with which for nine hours he had fended the wilderness off: he hung the watch and compass carefully on a bush and leaned the stick beside them and relinquished completely to it.

He had not been going very fast for the last two or three hours. He went no faster now, since distance would not matter even if he could have gone fast. And he was trying to keep a bearing on the tree where he had left the compass, trying to complete a circle which would bring him back to it or at least intersect itself, since direction would not matter now either. But the tree was not there, and he did as Sam had schooled him—made the next circle in the opposite direction, so that the two patterns would bisect somewhere, but crossing no print of his own feet, finding the tree at last, but in the wrong place— no bush, no compass, no watch—and the tree not even the tree, because there was a down log beside it and he did what Sam Fathers had told him was the next thing and the last.

As he sat down on the log he saw the crooked print—the warped, tremendous, two-toed indentation which, even as he watched it, filled with water. As he looked up, the wilderness coalesced, solidified—the glade, the tree he sought, the bush, the watch and the compass glinting where a ray of sunshine touched them. Then he saw the bear. It did not emerge, appear; it was just there, immobile, solid, fixed in the hot dappling of the green and windless noon, not as big as he had dreamed it, but as big as he had expected it, bigger, dimensionless, against the dappled obscurity, looking at him where he sat quietly on the log and looked back at it.

Then it moved. It made no sound. It did not hurry. It crossed the glade, walking for an instant into the full glare of the sun; when it reached the other side it stopped again and looked back at him across one shoulder while his quiet breathing inhaled and exhaled three times.

Then it was gone. It didn't walk into the woods, the undergrowth. It faded, sank back into the wilderness as he had watched a fish, a huge old bass, sink and vanish into the dark depths of its pool without even any movement of its fins.

He thought, *It will be next fall.* But it was not next fall, nor the next nor the next. He was fourteen then. He had killed his buck, and Sam Fathers had marked his face with the hot blood, and in the next year he killed a bear. But even before that accolade he had become as competent in the woods as many grown men with the same experience; by his fourteenth year he was a better woodsman than most grown men with more. There was no territory within thirty miles of the camp that he did not know—bayou, ridge, brake, landmark, tree and path. He could have led anyone to any point in it without deviation, and brought them out again. He knew the game trails that even Sam Fathers did not know; in his thirteenth year he found a buck's bedding place, and unbeknown to his father he borrowed Walter Ewell's rifle and lay in wait at dawn and killed the buck when it walked back to the bed, as Sam had told him how the old Chickasaw fathers did.

But not the old bear, although by now he knew its footprints better than he did his own, and not only the crooked one. He could see any one of three sound ones and distinguish it from any other, and not only by its size. There were other bears within these thirty miles which left tracks almost as large, but this was more than that. If Sam Fathers had been his mentor and the back-yard rabbits and squirrels at home his kindergarten, then the wilderness the old bear ran was his college, the old male bear itself, so long unwifed and childless as to have become its own ungendered progenitor, was his alma mater. But he never saw it.

He could find the crooked print now almost whenever he liked, fifteen or ten or five miles, or sometimes nearer the camp than that. Twice while on stand during the three years he heard the dogs strike its trail by accident; on the second time they jumped it seemingly, the voices high, abject, almost human in hysteria, as on that first morning two years ago. But not the bear itself. He would remember that noon three years ago, the glade, himself and the bear fixed during that moment in the windless and dappled blaze, and it would seem to him that it had never happened, that he had dreamed that too. But it had happened. They had looked at each other, they had emerged from the wilderness old as earth, synchronized to the instant by something more than the blood that moved the flesh and bones which bore them, and touched, pledged something, affirmed, something more lasting than the frail web of bones and flesh which any accident could obliterate.

Then he saw it again. Because of the very fact that he thought of nothing else, he had forgotten to look for it. He was still hunting with Walter Ewell's rifle. He saw it cross the end of a long blow-down, a corridor where a tornado had swept, rushing through rather than over the tangle of trunks and branches as a locomotive would have, faster than he had ever believed it could move, almost as fast as a deer even, because a deer would have spent most of that time in the air, faster than he could bring the rifle sights up with it. And now he knew what had been wrong during all the three years. He sat on a log, shaking and trembling as if he had never seen the woods before nor anything that ran them, wondering with incredulous amazement how he could have forgotten the very thing which Sam Fathers had told him and which the bear itself had proved the next day and had now returned after three years to reaffirm.

And now he knew what Sam Fathers had meant about the right dog, a dog in which size would mean less than nothing. So when he returned alone in April—school was out then, so that the sons of farmers could help with the land's planting, and at last his father had granted him permission, on his promise to be back in four days—he had the dog. It was his own, a mongrel of the sort called by Negroes a fyce, a ratter, itself not much bigger than a rat and possessing that bravery which had long since stopped being courage and had become foolhardiness.

It did not take four days. Alone again, he found the trail on the first morning. It was not a stalk; it was an ambush. He timed the meeting almost as if it were an appointment with a human being. Himself holding the fyce muffled in a feed sack and Sam Fathers with two of the hounds on a piece of a plow-line rope, they lay down wind of the trail at dawn of the second morning. They were so close that the bear turned without even running, as if in surprised amazement at the shrill and frantic uproar of the released fyce, turning at bay against the trunk of a tree, on its hind feet; it seemed to the boy that it would never stop rising, taller and taller, and even the two hounds seemed to take a desperate and despairing courage from the fyce, following it as it went in.

Then he realized that the fyce was actually not going to stop. He flung, threw the gun away, and ran; when he overtook and grasped the frantically pin-wheeling little dog, it seemed to him that he was directly under the bear.

He could smell it, strong and hot and rank. Sprawling, he looked up to where it loomed and towered over him like a cloudburst and colored like a thunderclap, quite familiar, peacefully and even lucidly familiar, until he remembered: This was the way he had used to dream about it. Then it was gone. He didn't see it go. He knelt, holding the frantic fyce with both hands, hearing the abashed wailing of the hounds drawing farther and farther away, until Sam came up. He carried the gun. He laid it down quietly beside the boy and stood looking down at him.

"You've done seed him twice now with a gun in your hands," he said. "This time you couldn't have missed him."

The boy rose. He still held the fyce. Even in his arms and clear of the ground, it yapped frantically, straining and surging after the fading uproar of the two hounds like a tangle of wire springs. He was panting a little, but he was neither shaking nor trembling now.

"Neither could you!" he said. "You had the gun! Neither did you!"

"And you didn't shoot," his father said. "How close were you?"

"I don't know, sir," he said. "There was a big wood tick inside his right hind leg. I saw that. But I didn't have the gun then."

"But you didn't shoot when you had the gun," his father said. "Why?"

But he didn't answer, and his father didn't wait for him to, rising and crossing the room, across the pelt of the bear which the boy had killed two years ago and the larger one which his father had killed before he was born, to the bookcase beneath the mounted head of the boy's first buck. It was the room which his father called the office, from which all the plantation business was transacted; in it for the fourteen years of his life he had heard the best of all talking. Major de Spain would be there and sometimes old General Compson, and Walter Ewell and Boon Hoggenback and Sam Fathers and Tennie's Jim, too, were hunters, knew the woods and what ran them.

He would hear it, not talking himself but listening—the wilderness, the big woods, bigger and older than any recorded document of white man fatuous enough to believe he had bought any fragment of it or Indian ruthless enough to pretend that any fragment of it had been his to convey. It was of the men, not white nor black nor red, but men, hunters with the will and hardihood to endure and the humility and skill to survive, and the dogs and the bear and deer juxtaposed and reliefed against it, ordered and compelled by and within the wilderness in the ancient and unremitting contest by the ancient and immitigable rules which voided all regrets and brooked no quarter, the voices quiet and weighty and deliberate for retrospection and recollection and exact remembering, while he squatted in the blazing firelight as Tennie's Jim squatted, who stirred only to put more wood on the fire and to pass the bottle from one glass to another. Because the bottle was always present, so that after a while it seemed to him that those fierce instants of heart and brain and courage and wiliness and speed were concentrated and distilled into the brown liquor which not women, not boys and children, but only hunters drank, drinking not of the blood they had spilled but some condensation of the wild immortal spirit, drinking it moderately, humbly even, not with the pagan's base hope of acquiring the virtues of cunning and strength and speed, but in salute to them.

His father returned with the book and sat down again and opened it. "Listen," he said. He read the five stanzas aloud, his voice quiet and deliberate in the room where there was no fire now because it was already spring. Then he looked up. The boy watched him. "All right," his father said. "Listen." He read again, but only the second stanza this time, to the end of it, the last two lines, and closed the book and put it on the table beside him. "She cannot fade, though thou hast not thy bliss, forever wilt thou love, and she be fair," he said.

"He's talking about a girl," the boy said.

"He had to talk about something," his father said. Then he said, "He was talking about truth. Truth doesn't change. Truth is one thing. It covers all things which touch the heart—honor and pride and pity and justice and courage and love. Do you see now?"

He didn't know. Somehow it was simpler than that. There was an old bear, fierce and ruthless, not merely just to stay alive, but with the fierce pride of liberty and freedom, proud enough of the liberty and freedom to see it threatened without fear or even alarm; nay, who at times even seemed deliberately to put that freedom and liberty in jeopardy in order to savor them, to remind his old strong bones and flesh to keep supple and quick to defend and preserve them. There was an old man, son of a Negro slave and an Indian king, inheritor on the one side of the long chronicle of a people who had learned humility through suffering, and pride through the endurance which survived the suffering and injustice, and on the other side, the chronicle of a people even longer in the land than the first, yet who no longer existed in the land at all save in the solitary brotherhood of an old Negro's alien blood and the wild and invincible spirit of an old bear. There was a boy who wished to learn humility and pride in order to become skillful and worthy in the woods, who suddenly found himself becoming so skillful so rapidly that he feared he would never become worthy because he had not learned humility and pride, although he had tried to, until one day and as suddenly he discovered that an old man who could not have defined either had led him, as though by the hand, to that point where an old bear and a little mongrel of a dog showed him that, by possessing one thing other, he would possess them both.

And a little dog, nameless and mongrel and many-fathered, grown, yet weighing less than six pounds, saying as if to itself, "I can't be dangerous, because there's nothing much smaller than I am; I can't be fierce, because they would call it just a noise; I can't be humble, because I'm already too close to the ground to genuflect; I can't be proud, because I wouldn't be near enough to it for anyone to know who was casting the shadow, and I don't even know that I'm not going to heaven, because they have already decided that I don't possess an immortal soul. So all I can be is brave. But it's all right. I can be that, even if they still call it just noise."

That was all. It was simple, much simpler than somebody talking in a book about youth and a girl he would never need to grieve over, because he could never approach any nearer her and would never have to get any farther away. He had heard about a bear, and finally got big enough to trail it, and he trailed it four years and at last met it with a gun in his hands and he didn't shoot. Because a little dog— But he could have shot long before the little dog covered the twenty yards to where the bear waited, and Sam Fathers could have shot at any time during that interminable minute while Old Ben stood on his hind feet over them. He stopped. His father was watching him gravely across the spring-rife twilight of the room; when he spoke, his words were as quiet as the twilight, too, not loud, because they did not need to be because they would last. "Courage, and honor, and pride," his father said, "and pity, and love of justice and of liberty. They all touch the heart, and what the heart holds to becomes truth, as far as we know the truth. Do you see now?"

Sam, and Old Ben, and Nip, he thought. And himself too. He had been all right too. His father had said so. "Yes, sir," he said.

QUESTIONS FOR DISCUSSION

BARN BURNING

1. Point to the specific scenes and passages which underscore the special way in which point of view is treated in the story. Explain fully how and where different points of view are merged and separated.

2. How is the point of view exploited to create tautness and suspense?

3. Enumerate the particular details and circumstances selected by the writer to place the story in a certain place at a certain time.

4. Select typical sentences which illustrate how Faulkner puts ideas into words. What are the characteristics and attributes of these sentences?

5. Explain the natures of the conflict or conflicts in the story.

6. How do we learn what we know of the secondary characters— mother, aunt, sisters, older brother, Major? What is the author's technique for sketching them in?

7. What does the character of the father show? What appears to motivate his actions?

8. To what effect does Faulkner create ambiguities in the father's character before fully unmasking it?

9. What is the nature of the choice the boy finally and instinctively makes?

10. Explain how delusion and deception are fundamental to the story.

11. What accepted ideas does Faulkner expose?

A ROSE FOR EMILY

1. From what point of view is the story narrated? What is the attitude of the narrator toward his subject matter?

2. Explain the probable circumstances of Homer Barron's death.

3. What motives are offered for Miss Emily's behavior toward Barron, both before and after his death?

4. Comment upon the view given of life in a small town.

5. Explain the nature of the changing social scene against which the story is enacted.

6. What does Faulkner achieve by withholding his final shocker—the point of fact toward which the entire story is directed—until the last sentence?

7. Does the use of such unconventional material seem artistically justified within the context of the story?

8. Explain the theme of the story in terms of false pride, decadent social forms and values, romantic delusions, and psychoses.

A SUGGESTED INTERPRETATION

THE BEAR
The initiation by ordeal of a youth into the tribal fold is traced. Ennobled by his questing, the boy establishes his own identity as well as his relationship to others; he begins to understand the code by which he must live; and he achieves an intimation of the soaring spirit which leads men on. His ultimate encounter with the bear provides the moment of truth for which his own spirit has been searching. We experience a strong hope that a principled man, schooled in "the old verities and truths of the heart," is now emergent. We know that man will "endure and prevail."

Early in the story, when the .injured hound returns to camp from encounter with the bear, Sam says of her, "Just like folks. Put off as long as she could having to be brave, knowing all the time that sooner or later she would have to be brave to keep on living with herself, and knowing all the time beforehand what was going to happen to her when she done it." This is a statement of the nature of the ordeal facing the lad.

Through successive stages of growth during those trying, juvenescent years, the young man starts to understand (in his own terms) the lasting truths that extend far back into racial consciousness and are the basic part of man's accumulated wisdom. He comes to know he is brave—without bravado—and that bravery leads on to immortality. The woods are life and are enduring; the land has wisdom and strength. It takes greater courage to **live** in a country—to settle it, to people it, to inhabit it—than it does merely to explore and chart it. A brave youth with "love and honor and pity and pride and compassion and sacrifice" is the salt of the earth. The boy quickly becomes skillful and adroit at mechanically finding his way through the woods of life, but the land and the people close to the land—and the bear—help him discover what life is and how it must be lived.

The bear is symbolic of the savage, undefeated, undying, proud spirit of life. None of the men can shoot the animal down; none wishes to. It is the bear with its fierce, brave spirit that gives meaning to the woods, and it is from the primeval forest that the bear itself has gained force and spirit to survive, to endure, to prevail. And so the boy does not shoot the bear. Sam Fathers, "the Indian, son of a slave woman and a Chickasaw chief," knows the land and bear better than anyone else, and so he guides the boy and fathers him; but Sam, too, does not shoot the bear. Into a fraternity of such brave, humble men the boy is initiated.

The boy's real father apprehends life on a somewhat more sophisticated plane than the primitive boy and his guide. But this only serves to show that profound truth is not altered, even though interpreted differently. And it serves further to show that one part of truth, once recognized, leads to recognition of all that is truth. In reading out from Keats, the father poetically suggests that the lad's experience touches upon that unattainable something great toward which men ceaselessly struggle, thereby giving dignity to their lives. It was the ecstasy of seeing the bear—without destroying the beast—that, the father felt, gave enduring moment and fulfillment to the boy. However approached, the story concludes with a reassuring, affirmative, " 'Yes, sir,' " about brave people with "a soul, a spirit capable of compassion and sacrifice and endurance."

SUBJECTS FOR WRITTEN COMPOSITION

1. Present an interpretation of any of the Faulkner stories, based on a close reading of the text.

2. To project his serious moral preoccupation with facets of contemporary life, Faulkner utilizes the South as a source of symbols. Show what phases of modern life Faulkner is morally concerned with and how these problems are of a universal rather than a merely Southern nature.

3. Faulkner is more interested in why his people do what they do than in what they do. Demonstrate Faulkner's capacity to explore and reveal the motivation of his characters.

4. Faulkner and Warren both talk about the South. Explain how and if the attitudes of both or of each of these writers toward that region could be applied equally to the East, Midwest, West, and so forth.

5. Compare and contrast the boys in Faulkner's "Barn Burning" and "The Bear"; Faulkner's "The Bear" and Warren's "Blackberry Winter"; or Faulkner's "The Bear" and Joyce's "Araby." Show where and how their problems are essentially alike or different.

Henry James

Henry James

HENRY JAMES, like T. S. Eliot in our own time, was an ambiguous national. He was born in New York City and remained a citizen of the United States until the year before his death, when he became a naturalized British subject. James spent five years of his youth in travel and schooling abroad. In 1869–1870 he returned to Europe, and after a stay in Italy, he settled permanently in England. James did not take to formal schooling, but he compensated for the lack of a stable, supervised education by intensive independent reading; and however one may appraise the emotional security of his formative years, there can be no question of the intellectual stimulation which he received from a father who was a close student of Swedenborgianism and an elder brother, William, who became America's most distinguished pragmatic philosopher.

Compared with some of his contemporary writers, Henry James remained remarkably uninvolved in the public affairs of his day. He never married, and he led no social or political crusades. Coupled with the fact that he was never dogged by poverty, this general serenity enabled him to produce a body of literary work which is distinguished by quality, variety, and mass. He wrote books of travel ("A Little Tour in France," "Italian Hours," "English Hours," "The American Scene"); books of literary criticism ("French Poets and Novelists," "Partial Portraits," "Essays in London," "Notes on Novelists"—in addition to essays and prefaces posthumously collected as "Notes and Reviews," "The Art of the Novel: Critical Prefaces," "The Scenic Art," and so forth); autobiographical sketches ("A Small Boy and Others," "Notes of a Son and Brother," the fragmentary "Terminations"); a life of Nathaniel Hawthorne; several forgotten plays; nearly a hundred short stories: and more than a dozen distinguished novels, of which the following are the most famous: "Roderick Hudson" (1875), "The American" (1877), "Portrait of a Lady" (1881), "The Princess Casamassima" (1886), "The Tragic Muse" (1890), "The Wings of the Dove" (1902), "The Ambassadors" (1903), "The Golden Bowl" (1904). James left two unfinished novels, "The Ivory Tower" and "The Sense of the Past."

Henry James is among the most subtle writers of prose fiction in English. Possessed of an abiding self-consciousness which was the outgrowth of his essentially shy nature and his failure to attract a popular following for his work, James wrote again and again on the theme of art and the artist. Determined that his novels and short stories should be finished, self-sufficient works of art rather than merely vehicles of communication from author to reader, he strove to withdraw from the surface of his work and let the work itself become all in all. In the process, he created some of the most influential techniques of modern fiction, and can almost be said to have established the vocabulary with which twentieth-century criticism talks of the novel and short story.

James, like Joyce, made little effort to simplify the task of his readers. He was fascinated by most resistant materials—mental and emotional experience and moral motivation—and like Flaubert, he was sensitive to linguistic subtlety and nuance. Further, there are few storytellers whose "point of view" requires more careful watching. The critical challenge which the writings of Henry James present to the student is indeed a real one.

The Figure in the Carpet

1

I HAD DONE A FEW THINGS AND EARNED A FEW PENCE—I HAD perhaps even had time to begin to think I was finer than was perceived by the patronising; but when I take the little measure of my course (a fidgety habit, for it's none of the longest yet) I count my real start from the evening George Corvick, breathless and worried, came in to ask me a service. He had done more things than I, and earned more pence, though there were chances for cleverness I thought he sometimes missed. I could only, however, that evening declare to him that he never missed one for kindness. There was almost rapture in hearing it proposed to me to prepare for *The Middle*, the organ of our lucubrations, so called from the position in the week of its day of appearance, an article for which he had made himself responsible and of which, tied up with a stout string, he laid on my table the subject. I pounced upon my opportunity—that is on the first volume of it—and paid scant attention to my friend's explanation of his appeal. What explanation could be more to the point than my obvious fitness for the task? I had written on Hugh Vereker, but never a word in *The Middle*, where my dealings were mainly with the ladies and the minor poets. This was his new novel, an advance copy, and whatever much or little it should do for his reputation I was clear on the spot as to what it should do for mine. Moreover

275

if I always read him as soon as I could get hold of him I had a particular reason for wishing to read him now: I had accepted an invitation to Bridges for the following Sunday, and it had been mentioned in Lady Jane's note that Mr. Vereker was to be there. I was young enough for a flutter at meeting a man of his renown, and innocent enough to believe the occasion would demand the display of an acquaintance with his "last."

Corvick, who had promised a review of it, had not even had time to read it; he had gone to pieces in consequence of news requiring—as on precipitate reflexion he judged—that he should catch the night-mail to Paris. He had had a telegram from Gwendolen Erme in answer to his letter offering to fly to her aid. I knew already about Gwendolen Erme; I had never seen her, but I had my ideas, which were mainly to the effect that Corvick would marry her if her mother would only die. That lady seemed now in a fair way to oblige him; after some dreadful mistake about a climate or a "cure" she had suddenly collapsed on the return from abroad. Her daughter, unsupported and alarmed, desiring to make a rush for home but hesitating at the risk, had accepted our friend's assistance, and it was my secret belief that at sight of him Mrs. Erme would pull round. His own belief was scarcely to be called secret; it discernibly at any rate differed from mine. He had showed me Gwendolen's photograph with the remark that she wasn't pretty but was awfully interesting; she had published at the age of nineteen a novel in three volumes, "Deep Down," about which, in *The Middle*, he had been really splendid. He appreciated my present eagerness and undertook that the periodical in question should do no less; then at the last, with his hand on the door, he said to me: "Of course you'll be all right, you know." Seeing I was a trifle vague he added: "I mean you won't be silly."

"Silly—about Vereker! Why what do I ever find him but awfully clever?"

"Well, what's that but silly? What on earth does 'awfully clever' mean? For God's sake try to get *at* him. Don't let him suffer by our arrangement. Speak of him, you know, if you can, as *I* should have spoken of him."

I wondered an instant. "You mean as far and away the biggest of the lot—that sort of thing?"

Corvick almost groaned. "Oh you know, I don't put them back to back that way; it's the infancy of art! But he gives me a pleasure so rare; the sense of"—he mused a little— "something or other."

I wondered again. "The sense, pray, of what?"

"My dear man, that's just what I want *you* to say!"

Even before he had banged the door I had begun, book in hand, to prepare myself to say it. I sat up with Vereker half the night; Corvick couldn't have done more than that. He was awfully clever—I stuck to that, but he wasn't a bit the biggest of the lot. I didn't allude to the lot, however; I flattered myself that I emerged on this occasion from the infancy of art. "It's all right," they declared vividly at the office; and when the number appeared I felt there was a basis on which I could meet the great man. It gave me confidence for a day or two—then that confidence dropped. I had fancied him reading it with relish, but if Corvick wasn't satisfied how could Vereker himself be? I reflected indeed that the heat of the admirer was sometimes grosser even than the appetite of the scribe. Corvick at all events wrote me from Paris a little ill-humouredly. Mrs. Erme was pulling round, and I hadn't at all said what Vereker gave him the sense of.

2

The effect of my visit to Bridges was to turn me out for more profundity. Hugh Vereker, as I saw him there, was of a contact so void of angles that I blushed for the poverty of imagination involved in my small precautions. If he was in spirits it wasn't because he had read my review; in fact on the Sunday morning I felt sure he hadn't read it, though *The Middle* had been out three days and bloomed, I assured myself, in the stiff garden of periodicals which gave one of the ormolu tables the air of a stand at a station. The impression he made on me personally was such that I wished him to read it, and I corrected to this end with a surreptitious hand what might be wanting in the careless conspicuity of the sheet. I'm afraid

I even watched the result of my manœuvre, but up to luncheon I watched in vain.

When afterwards, in the course of our gregarious walk, I found myself for half an hour, not perhaps without another manœuvre, at the great man's side, the result of his affability was a still livelier desire that he shouldn't remain in ignorance of the peculiar justice I had done him. It wasn't that he seemed to thirst for justice; on the contrary I hadn't yet caught in his talk the faintest grunt of a grudge—a note for which my young experience had already given me an ear. Of late he had had more recognition, and it was pleasant, as we used to say in *The Middle*, to see how it drew him out. He wasn't of course popular, but I judged one of the sources of his good humour to be precisely that his success was independent of that. He had none the less become in a manner the fashion; the critics at least had put on a spurt and caught up with him. We had found out at last how clever he was, and he had had to make the best of the loss of his mystery. I was strongly tempted, as I walked beside him, to let him know how much of that unveiling was my act; and there was a moment when I probably should have done so had not one of the ladies of our party, snatching a place at his other elbow, just then appealed to him in a spirit comparatively selfish. It was very discouraging: I almost felt the liberty had been taken with myself.

I had had on my tongue's end, for my own part, a phrase or two about the right word at the right time; but later on I was glad not to have spoken, for when on our return we clustered at tea I perceived Lady Jane, who had not been out with us, brandishing *The Middle* with her longest arm. She had taken it up at her leisure; she was delighted with what she had found, and I saw that, as a mistake in a man may often be a felicity in a woman, she would practically do for me what I hadn't been able to do for myself. "Some sweet little truths that needed to be spoken," I heard her declare, thrusting the paper at rather a bewildered couple by the fireplace. She grabbed it away from them again on the reappearance of Hugh Vereker, who after our walk had been upstairs to change something. "I know you don't in general look at this kind of thing, but it's an occasion really for doing so. You *haven't* seen it? Then you must. The man has actually got *at* you, at what *I* always feel, you know." Lady Jane threw into her eyes a look evidently intended to give an idea of what she always felt; but she added that she couldn't have expressed it. The man in the paper expressed it in a striking manner. "Just see there, and there, where I've dashed it, how he brings it out." She had literally marked for him the brightest patches of my prose, and if I was a little amused Vereker himself may well have been. He showed how much he was when before us all Lady Jane wanted to read something aloud. I liked at any rate the way he defeated her purpose by jerking the paper affectionately out of her clutch. He'd take it upstairs with him and look at it on going to dress. He did this half an hour later—I saw it in his hand when he repaired to his room. That was the moment at which, thinking to give her pleasure, I mentioned to Lady Jane that I was the author of the review. I did give her pleasure, I judged, but perhaps not quite so much as I had expected. If the author was "only me" the thing didn't seem quite so remarkable. Hadn't I had the effect rather of diminishing the lustre of the article than of adding to my own? Her ladyship was subject to the most extraordinary drops. It didn't matter; the only effect I cared about was the one it would have on Vereker up there by his bedroom fire.

At dinner I watched for the signs of this impression, tried to fancy some happier light in his eyes; but to my disappointment Lady Jane gave me no chance to make sure. I had hoped she'd call triumphantly down the table, publicly demand if she hadn't been right. The party was large—there were people from outside as well, but I had never seen a table long enough to deprive Lady Jane of a triumph. I was just reflecting in truth that this interminable board would deprive *me* of one when the guest next to me, dear woman—she was Miss Poyle, the vicar's sister, a robust unmodulated person—had the happy inspiration and the unusual courage to address herself across it to Vereker, who was opposite, but not directly, so that when he replied they were both leaning forward. She inquired, artless body, what he thought of Lady Jane's "panegyric," which she had read—not connecting it however with her right-hand neighbour; and while I strained my ear for his reply I heard him, to my stupefaction, call back gaily, his mouth full of bread: "Oh it's all right—the usual twaddle!"

I had caught Vereker's glance as he spoke, but Miss Poyle's surprise was a fortunate cover for my own. "You mean he doesn't do you justice?" said the excellent woman.

Vereker laughed out, and I was happy to be able to do the same. "It's a charming article," he tossed us.

Miss Poyle thrust her chin half across the cloth. "Oh you're so deep!" she drove home.

"As deep as the ocean! All I pretend is that the author doesn't see—" But a dish was at this point passed over his shoulder, and we had to wait while he helped himself.

"Doesn't see what?" my neighbour continued.

"Doesn't see anything."

"Dear me—how very stupid!"

"Not a bit," Vereker laughed again. "Nobody does."

The lady on his further side appealed to him and Miss Poyle sank back to myself. "Nobody sees anything!" she cheerfully announced; to which I replied that I had often thought so too, but had somehow taken the thought for a proof on my own part of a tremendous eye. I didn't tell her the article was mine; and I observed that Lady Jane, occupied at the end of the table, had not caught Vereker's words.

I rather avoided him after dinner, for I confess he struck me as cruelly conceited, and the revelation was a pain. "The usual twaddle"—my acute little study! That one's admiration should have had a reserve or two could gall him to that point? I had thought him placid, and he was placid enough; such a surface was the hard polished glass that encased the bauble of his vanity. I was really ruffled, and the only comfort was that if nobody saw anything George Corvick was quite as much out of it as I. This comfort however was not sufficient, after the ladies had dispersed, to carry me in the proper manner—I mean in a spotted jacket and humming an air—into the smoking-room. I took my way in some dejection to bed; but in the passage I encountered Mr. Vereker, who had been up once more to change, coming out of his room. *He* was humming an air and had on a spotted jacket, and as soon as he saw me his gaiety gave a start.

"My dear young man," he exclaimed, "I'm so glad to lay

hands on you! I'm afraid I most unwittingly wounded you by those words of mine at dinner to Miss Poyle. I learned but half an hour ago from Lady Jane that you're the author of the little notice in *The Middle*."

I protested that no bones were broken; but he moved with me to my own door, his hand, on my shoulder, kindly feeling for a fracture; and on hearing that I had come up to bed he asked leave to cross my threshold and just tell me in three words what his qualification of my remarks had represented. It was plain he really feared I was hurt, and the sense of his solicitude suddenly made all the difference to me. My cheap review fluttered off into space, and the best things I had said in it became flat enough beside the brilliancy of his being there. I can see him there still, on my rug, in the firelight and his spotted jacket, his fine clear face all bright with the desire to be tender to my youth. I don't know what he had at first meant to say, but I think the sight of my relief touched him, excited him, brought up words to his lips from far within. It was so these words presently conveyed to me something that, as I afterwards knew, he had never uttered to any one. I've always done justice to the generous impulse that made him speak; it was simply compunction for a snub unconsciously administered to a man of letters in a position inferior to his own, a man of letters moreover in the very act of praising him. To make the thing right he talked to me exactly as an equal and on the ground of what we both loved best. The hour, the place, the unexpectedness deepened the impression: he couldn't have done anything more intensely effective.

3

"I don't quite know how to explain it to you," he said, "but it was the very fact that your notice of my book had a spice of intelligence, it was just your exceptional sharpness, that produced the feeling—a very old story with me, I beg you to believe—under the momentary influence of which I used in speaking to that good lady the words you so naturally resent. I don't read the things in the newspapers unless they're thrust upon me as that one was—it's always one's best friend who does it! But I used to read them sometimes—ten years ago. I dare say they were in general rather stupider then; at any rate it always struck me they missed my little point with a perfection exactly as admirable when they patted me on the back as when they kicked me in the shins. Whenever since I've happened to have a glimpse of them they were still blazing away—still missing it, I mean, deliciously. *You* miss it, my dear fellow, with inimitable assurance; the fact of your being awfully clever and your article's being awfully nice doesn't make a hair's breadth of difference. It's quite with you rising young men," Vereker laughed, "that I feel most what a failure I am!"

I listened with keen interest; it grew keener as he talked. "*You* a failure—heavens! What then may your 'little point' happen to be?"

"Have I got to *tell* you, after all these years and labours?" There was something in the friendly reproach of this—jocosely exaggerated—that made me, as an ardent young seeker for truth, blush to the roots of my hair. I'm as much in the dark as ever, though I've grown used in a sense to my obtuseness; at that moment, however, Vereker's happy accent made me appear to myself, and probably to him, a rare dunce. I was on the point of exclaiming "Ah yes, don't tell me: for my honour, for that of the craft, don't!" when he went on in a manner that showed he had read my thought and had his own idea of the probability of our some day redeeming ourselves. "By my little point I mean—what shall I call it?—the particular thing I've written my books most *for*. Isn't there for every writer a particular thing of that sort, the thing that most makes him apply himself, the thing without the effort to achieve which he wouldn't write at all, the very passion of his passion, the part of the business in which, for him, the flame of art burns most intensely? Well, it's *that!*"

I considered a moment—that is I followed at a respectful distance, rather gasping. I was fascinated—easily, you'll say; but I wasn't going after all to be put off my guard. "Your description's certainly beautiful, but it doesn't make what you describe very distinct."

"I promise you it would be distinct if it should dawn on you at all." I saw that the charm of our topic overflowed for my companion into an emotion as lively as my own. "At any rate," he went on, "I can speak for myself: there's an idea in my work without which I wouldn't have given a straw for the whole job. It's the finest fullest intention of the lot, and the application of it has been, I think, a triumph of patience, of ingenuity. I ought to leave that to somebody else to say; but that nobody does say it is precisely what we're talking about. It stretches, this little trick of mine, from book to book, and everything else, comparatively, plays over the surface of it. The order, the form, the texture of my books will perhaps someday constitute for the initiated a complete representation of it. So it's naturally the thing for the critic to look for. It strikes me," my visitor added, smiling, "even as the thing for the critic to find."

This seemed a responsibility indeed. "You call it a little trick?"

"That's only my little modesty. It's really an exquisite scheme."

"And you hold that you've carried the scheme out?"

"The way I've carried it out is the thing in life I think a bit well of myself for."

I had a pause. "Don't you think you ought—just a trifle—to assist the critic?"

"Assist him? What else have I done with every stroke of my pen? I've shouted my intention in his great blank face!" At this, laughing out again, Vereker laid his hand on my shoulder to show the allusion wasn't to my personal appearance.

"But you talk about the initiated. There must therefore, you see, *be* initiation."

"What else in heaven's name is criticism supposed to be?" I'm afraid I coloured at this too; but I took refuge in repeating that his account of his silver lining was poor in something or other that a plain man knows things by. "That's only because you've never had a glimpse of it," he returned. "If you had had one the element in question would soon have become practically all you'd see. To me it's exactly as palpable as the marble of this chimney. Besides, the critic just *isn't* a plain man: if he were, pray, what would he be doing in his neighbour's garden? You're anything but a plain man yourself, and the very *raison d'être* of you all is that you're little demons of subtlety. If my great affair's a secret, that's only because it's a secret in spite of itself—the amazing event has made it one. I not only never took the smallest precaution to keep it so, but never dreamed of any such accident. If I had I shouldn't in advance have had the heart to go on. As it was, I only became aware little by little, and meanwhile I had done my work."

"And now you quite like it?" I risked.

"My work?"

"Your secret. It's the same thing."

"Your guessing that," Vereker replied, "is a proof that you're as clever as I say!" I was encouraged by this to remark that he would clearly be pained to part with it, and he confessed that it was indeed with him now the great amusement of life. "I live almost to see if it will ever be detected." He looked at me for a jesting challenge; something far within his eyes seemed to peep out. "But I needn't worry—it won't!"

"You fire me as I've never been fired," I declared; "you make me determined to do or die." Then I asked: "Is it a kind of esoteric message?"

His countenance fell at this—he put out his hand as if to bid me good-night. "Ah my dear fellow, it can't be described in cheap journalese!"

I knew of course he'd be awfully fastidious, but our talk had made me feel how much his nerves were exposed. I was unsatisfied—I kept hold of his hand. "I won't make use of the expression then," I said, "in the article in which I shall eventually announce my discovery, though I dare say I shall have hard work to do without it. But meanwhile, just to hasten that difficult birth, can't you give a fellow a clue?" I felt much more at my ease.

"My whole lucid effort gives him the clue—every page and line and letter. The thing's as concrete there as a bird in a cage, a bait on a hook, a piece of cheese in a mouse-trap. It's stuck into every volume as your foot is stuck into your shoe. It governs every line, it chooses every word, it dots every i, it places every comma."

I scratched my head. "Is it something in the style or something in the thought? An element of form or an element of feeling?"

He indulgently shook my hand again, and I felt my questions to be crude and my distinctions pitiful. "Good-night, my dear boy—don't bother about it. After all, you do like a fellow."

"And a little intelligence might spoil it?" I still detained him.

He hesitated. "Well, you've got a heart in your body. Is that an element of form or an element of feeling? What I contend that nobody has ever mentioned in my work is the organ of life."

"I see—it's some idea *about* life, some sort of philosophy. Unless it be," I added with the eagerness of a thought perhaps still happier, "some kind of game you're up to with your style, something you're after in the language. Perhaps it's a preference for the letter P!" I ventured profanely to break out. "Papa, potatoes, prunes—that sort of thing?" He was suitably indulgent: he only said I hadn't got the right letter. But his amusement was over; I could see he was bored. There was nevertheless something else I had absolutely to learn. "Should you be able, pen in hand, to state it clearly yourself— to name it, phrase it, formulate it?"

"Oh," he almost passionately sighed, "if I were only, pen in hand, one of *you* chaps!"

"That would be a great chance for you of course. But why should you despise us chaps for not doing what you can't do yourself?"

"Can't do?" He opened his eyes. "Haven't I done it in twenty volumes? I do it in my way," he continued. "Go *you* and do it in yours."

"Ours is so devilish difficult," I weakly observed.

"So's mine! We each choose our own. There's no compulsion. You won't come down and smoke?"

"No. I want to think this thing out."

"You'll tell me then in the morning that you've laid me bare?"

"I'll see what I can do; I'll sleep on it. But just one word more," I added. We had left the room—I walked again with him a few steps along the passage. "This extraordinary 'general intention,' as you call it—for that's the most vivid description I can induce you to make of it—is then, generally, a sort of buried treasure?"

His face lighted. "Yes, call it that, though it's perhaps not for me to do so."

"Nonsense!" I laughed. "You know you're hugely proud of it."

"Well, I didn't propose to tell you so; but it *is* the joy of my soul!"

"You mean it's a beauty so rare, so great?"

He waited a little again. "The loveliest thing in the world!" We had stopped, and on these words he left me; but at the end of the corridor, while I looked after him rather yearningly, he turned and caught sight of my puzzled face. It made him earnestly, indeed I thought quite anxiously, shake his head and wave his finger. "Give it up—give it up!"

This wasn't a challenge—it was fatherly advice. If I had had one of his books at hand I'd have repeated my recent act of faith—I'd have spent half the night with him. At three o'clock in the morning, not sleeping, remembering moreover how indispensable he was to Lady Jane, I stole down to the library with a candle. There wasn't, so far as I could discover, a line of his writing in the house.

4

Returning to town I feverishly collected them all; I picked out each in its order and held it up to the light. This gave me a maddening month, in the course of which several things took place. One of these, the last, I may as well immediately mention, was that I acted on Vereker's advice: I renounced my ridiculous attempt. I could really make nothing of the business; it proved a dead loss. After all I had always, as he had himself noted, liked him; and what now occurred was simply that my new intelligence and vain preoccupation damaged my liking. I not only failed to run a general intention to earth, I found myself missing the subordinate intentions I had formerly enjoyed. His books didn't even remain the charming things they had been for me; the exasperation of my search put me out of conceit of them. Instead of being a pleasure the more they became a resource the less; for from the moment I was unable to follow up the author's hint I of course felt it a point of honour not to make use professionally of my knowledge of them. I *had* no knowledge—nobody had any. It was humiliating, but I could bear it—they only annoyed me now. At last they even bored me, and I accounted for my confusion—perversely, I allow—by the idea that Vereker had made a fool of me. The buried treasure was a bad joke, the general intention a monstrous *pose*.

The great point of it all is, however, that I told George Corvick what had befallen me and that my information had an immense effect on him. He had at last come back, but so, unfortunately, had Mrs. Erme, and there was as yet, I could see, no question of his nuptials. He was immensely stirred up by the anecdote I had brought from Bridges; it fell in so completely with the sense he had had from the first that there was more in Vereker than met the eye. When I remarked that the eye seemed what the printed page had been expressly invented to meet he immediately accused me of being spiteful because I had been foiled. Our commerce had always that pleasant latitude. The thing Vereker had mentioned to me was exactly the thing he, Corvick, had wanted me to speak of in my review. On my suggesting at last that with the assistance I had now given him he would doubtless be prepared to speak of it himself he admitted freely that before doing this there was more he must understand. What he would have said, had he reviewed the new book, was that there was evidently in the writer's inmost art something to *be* understood. I hadn't so much as hinted at that: no wonder the writer hadn't been flattered! I asked Corvick what he really considered he meant by his own supersubtlety, and, unmistakably kindled, he replied: "It isn't for the vulgar—it isn't for the vulgar!" He had hold of the tail of something: he would pull hard, pull it right out. He pumped me dry on Vereker's strange confidence and, pronouncing me the luckiest of mortals, mentioned half-a-dozen questions he wished to goodness I had had the gumption to put. Yet on the other hand he didn't want to be told too much—it would spoil the fun of seeing what would come. The failure of *my* fun was at the moment of our meeting not complete, but I saw it ahead, and Corvick saw that I saw it. I, on my side, saw likewise that one of the first things he would do would be to rush off with my story to Gwendolen.

On the very day after my talk with him I was surprised by the receipt of a note from Hugh Vereker, to whom our encounter at Bridges had been recalled, as he mentioned, by his falling, in a magazine, on some article to which my signature was attached. "I read it with great pleasure," he wrote, "and remembered under its influence our lively conversation by your bedroom fire. The consequence of this has been that I begin to measure the temerity of my having saddled you with a knowledge that you may find something of a burden. Now that the fit's over I can't imagine how I came to be moved so much beyond my wont. I had never before mentioned, no matter in what state of expansion, the fact of my little secret, and I shall never speak of that mystery again. I was accidentally so much more explicit with you than it had ever entered into my game to be, that I find this game—I mean the pleasure of playing it—suffers considerably. In short, if you can understand it, I've rather spoiled my sport. I really don't want to give anybody what I believe you clever young men call the tip. That's of course a selfish solicitude, and I name it to you for what it may be worth to you. If you're disposed to humour me don't repeat my revelation. Think me demented—it's your right; but don't tell anybody why."

The sequel to this communication was that as early on the morrow as I dared I drove straight to Mr. Vereker's door. He occupied in those years one of the honest old houses in Kensington Square. He received me immediately, and as soon as I came in I saw I hadn't lost my power to minister to his mirth. He laughed out at sight of my face, which doubtless expressed my perturbation. I had been indiscreet—my compunction was great. "I *have* told somebody," I panted, "and I'm sure that person will by this time have told somebody else! It's a woman, into the bargain."

"The person you've told?"

"No, the other person. I'm quite sure he must have told her."

"For all the good it will do her—or do *me!* A woman will never find out."

"No, but she'll talk all over the place: she'll do just what you don't want."

Vereker thought a moment, but wasn't so disconcerted as I had feared: he felt that if the harm was done it only served him right. "It doesn't matter—don't worry."

"I'll do my best, I promise you, that your talk with me shall go no further."

"Very good; do what you can."

"In the meantime," I pursued, "George Corvick's possession of the tip may, on his part, really lead to something."

"That will be a brave day."

I told him about Corvick's cleverness, his admiration, the intensity of his interest in my anecdote; and without making too much of the divergence of our respective estimates mentioned that my friend was already of opinion that he saw much further into a certain affair than most people. He was quite as fired as I had been at Bridges. He was moreover in love with the young lady: perhaps the two together would puzzle something out.

Vereker seemed struck with this. "Do you mean they're to be married?"

"I dare say that's what it will come to."

"That may help them," he conceded, "but we must give them time!"

I spoke of my own renewed assault and confessed my difficulties; whereupon he repeated his former advice: "Give it up, give it up!" He evidently didn't think me intellectually equipped for the adventure. I stayed half an hour, and he was most good-natured, but I couldn't help pronouncing him a man of unstable moods. He had been free with me in a mood, he had repented in a mood, and now in a mood he had turned indifferent. This general levity helped me to believe that, so far as the subject of the tip went, there wasn't much in it. I contrived however to make him answer a few more questions about it, though he did so with visible impatience. For himself, beyond doubt, the thing we were all so blank about was vividly there. It was something, I guessed, in the primal plan; something like a complex figure in a Persian carpet. He highly approved of this image when I used it, and he used another himself. "It's the very string," he said, "that my pearls are strung on!" The reason of his note to me had been that he really didn't want to give us a grain of succour —our density was a thing too perfect in its way to touch. He had formed the habit of depending on it, and if the spell was to break it must break by some force of its own. He comes back to me from that last occasion—for I was never to speak to him again—as a man with some safe preserve for sport. I wondered as I walked away where he had got *his* tip.

5

When I spoke to George Corvick of the caution I had received he made me feel that any doubt of his delicacy would be almost an insult. He had instantly told Gwendolen, but Gwendolen's ardent response was in itself a pledge of discretion. The question would now absorb them and would offer them a pastime too precious to be shared with the crowd. They appeared to have caught instinctively at Vereker's high idea of enjoyment. Their intellectual pride, however, was not such as to make them indifferent to any further light I might throw on the affair they had in hand. They were indeed of the "artistic temperament," and I was freshly struck with my colleague's power to excite himself over a question of art. He'd call it letters, he'd call it life, but it was all one thing. In what he said I now seemed to understand that he spoke equally for Gwendolen, to whom, as soon as Mrs. Erme was sufficiently better to allow her a little leisure, he made a point of introducing me. I remember our going together one Sunday in August to a huddled house in Chelsea, and my renewed envy of Corvick's possession of a friend who had some light to mingle with his own. He could say things to her that I could never say to him. She had indeed no sense of humour and, with her pretty way of holding her head on one side, was one of those persons whom you want, as the phrase is, to shake, but who have learnt Hungarian by themselves. She conversed perhaps in Hungarian with Corvick; she had remarkably little English for his friend. Corvick afterwards told me that I had chilled her by my apparent indisposition to oblige them with the detail of what Vereker had said to me. I allowed that I felt I had given thought enough to that indication: hadn't I even made up my mind that it was vain and would lead nowhere? The importance they attached to it was irritating and quite envenomed my doubts.

That statement looks unamiable, and what probably happened was that I felt humiliated at seeing other persons deeply beguiled by an experiment that had brought me only chagrin. I was out in the cold while, by the evening fire, under the lamp, they followed the chase for which I myself had sounded the horn. They did as I had done, only more deliberately and sociably—they went over their author from the beginning. There was no hurry, Corvick said—the future was before them and the fascination could only grow; they would take him page by page, as they would take one of the classics, inhale him in slow draughts and let him sink all the way in. They would scarce have got so wound up, I think, if they hadn't been in love: poor Vereker's inner meaning gave them endless occasion to put and to keep their young heads together. None the less it represented the kind of problem for which Corvick had a special aptitude, drew out the particular pointed patience of which, had he lived, he would have given more striking and, it is to be hoped, more fruitful examples. He at least was, in Vereker's words, a little demon of subtlety. We had begun by disputing, but I soon saw that without my stirring a finger his infatuation would have its bad hours. He would bound off on false scents as I had done—he would clap his hands over new lights and see them blown out by the wind of the turned page. He was like nothing, I told him, but the maniacs who embrace some bedlamitical theory of the cryptic character of Shakespeare. To this he replied that if we had had Shakespeare's own word for his being cryptic he would at once have accepted it. The case there was altogether different—we had nothing but the word of Mr. Snooks. I returned that I was stupefied to see him attach such importance even to the word of Mr. Vereker. He wanted thereupon to know if I treated Mr. Vereker's word as a lie. I wasn't perhaps prepared, in my unhappy rebound, to go so far as that, but I insisted that till the contrary was proved I should view it as too fond an imagination. I didn't, I confess, say—I didn't at that time quite know—all I felt. Deep down, as Miss Erme would have said, I was uneasy, I was expectant. At the core of my disconcerted state—for my wonted curiosity lived in its ashes—was the sharpness of a sense that Corvick would at least probably come out somewhere. He made, in defence of his credulity, a great point of the fact that from of old, in his study of this genius, he had caught whiffs and hints of he didn't know what, faint wandering notes of a hidden music. That was just the rarity, that was the charm: it fitted so perfectly into what I reported.

If I returned on several occasions to the little house in Chelsea I dare say it was as much for news of Vereker as for news of Miss Erme's ailing parent. The hours spent there by Corvick were present to my fancy as those of a chessplayer bent with a silent scowl, all the lamplit winter, over his board and his moves. As my imagination filled it out the picture held me fast. On the other side of the table was a ghostlier form, the faint figure of an antagonist good-humouredly but a little wearily secure—an antagonist who leaned back in his chair with his hands in his pockets and a smile on his fine clear face. Close to Corvick, behind him, was a girl who had begun to strike me as pale and wasted and even, on more familiar view, as rather handsome, and who rested on his shoulder and hung on his moves. He would take up a chessman and hold it poised a while over one of the little squares, and then would put it back in its place with a long sigh of disappointment. The young lady, at this, would slightly but uneasily shift her position and look across, very hard, very long, very strangely, at their dim participant. I had asked them at an early stage of the business if it mightn't contribute to their success to have some closer communication with him. The special circumstances would surely be held to have given me a right to introduce them. Corvick immediately replied that he had no wish to approach the altar before he had prepared the sacrifice. He quite agreed with our friend both as to the delight and as to the honour of the chase—he would bring down the animal with his own rifle. When I asked him if Miss Erme were as keen a shot he said after thinking: "No, I'm ashamed to say she wants to set a trap. She'd give anything to see him; she says she requires another tip. She's really quite morbid about it. But she must play fair—she *shan't* see him!" he emphatically added. I wondered if they hadn't even quarrelled a little on the subject—a suspicion not corrected by the way he more than once exclaimed to me: "She's quite incredibly literary, you know—quite fantastically!" I remember his saying of her that she felt in italics and thought in capitals. "Oh when I've run him to earth," he also said, "then, you know, I shall knock at his door. Rather—I beg you to believe. I'll have it from his own lips: 'Right you are, my boy; you've done it this time!' He shall crown me victor—with the critical laurel."

Meanwhile he really avoided the chances London life might have given him of meeting the distinguished novelist; a danger, however, that disappeared with Vereker's leaving England for an indefinite absence, as the newspapers announced—going to the south for motives connected with the health of his wife, which had long kept her in retirement. A year—more than a year—had elapsed since the incident at Bridges, but I had had no further sight of him. I think I was at bottom rather ashamed —I hated to remind him that, though I had irremediably missed his point, a reputation for acuteness was rapidly overtaking me. This scruple led me a dance; kept me out of Lady Jane's house, made me even decline, when in spite of my bad manners she was a second time so good as to make me a sign, an invitation to her beautiful seat. I once became aware of her under Vereker's escort at a concert, and was sure I was seen by them, but I slipped out without being caught. I felt, as on that occasion I splashed along in the rain, that I couldn't have done anything else; and yet I remember saying to myself that it was hard, was even cruel. Not only had I lost the books, but I had lost the man himself: they and their author had been alike spoiled for me. I knew too which was the loss I most regretted. I had taken to the man still more than I had ever taken to the books.

6

Six months after our friend had left England George Corvick, who made his living by his pen, contracted for a piece of work which imposed on him an absence of some length and a journey of some difficulty, and his undertaking of which was much of a surprise to me. His brother-in-law had become editor of a great provincial paper, and the great provincial paper, in a fine flight of fancy, had conceived the idea of sending a "special commissioner" to India. Special commissioners had begun, in the "metropolitan press," to be the fashion, and the journal in question must have felt it had passed too long for a mere country cousin. Corvick had no hand, I knew, for the big brush of the correspondent, but that was his brother-in-law's affair, and the fact that a particular task was not in his line was apt to be with himself exactly a reason for accepting it. He was prepared to out-Herod the metropolitan press; he took solemn precautions against priggishness, he exquisitely outraged taste. Nobody ever knew it—that offended principle was all his own. In addition to his expenses he was to be conveniently paid, and I found myself able to help him, for the usual fat book, to a plausible arrangement with the usual fat publisher. I naturally inferred that his obvious desire to make a little money was not unconnected with the prospect of a union with Gwendolen Erme. I was aware that her mother's opposition was largely addressed to his want of means and of lucrative abilities, but it so happened that, on my saying the last time I saw him something that bore on the question of his separation from our young lady, he brought out with an emphasis that startled me: "Ah I'm not a bit engaged to her, you know!"

"Not overtly," I answered, "because her mother doesn't like you. But I've always taken for granted a private understanding."

"Well, there *was* one. But there isn't now." That was all he said save something about Mrs. Erme's having got on her feet again in the most extraordinary way—a remark pointing, as I supposed, the moral that private understandings were of little use when the doctor didn't share them. What I took the liberty of more closely inferring was that the girl might in some way have estranged him. Well, if he had taken the turn of jealousy, for instance, it could scarcely be jealousy of me. In that case—over and above the absurdity of it—he wouldn't have gone away just to leave us together. For some time before his going we had indulged in no allusion to the buried treasure, and from his silence, which my reserve simply emulated, I had drawn a sharp conclusion. His courage had dropped, his ardour had gone the way of mine—this appearance at least he left me to scan. More than that he couldn't do; he couldn't face the triumph with which I might have greeted an explicit admission. He needn't have been afraid, poor dear, for I had by this time lost all need to triumph. In fact I considered I showed magnanimity in not reproaching him with his collapse, for the sense of his having thrown up the game made me feel more than ever how much I at last depended on him. If Corvick had broken down I should never know; no one would be of any use if *he* wasn't. It wasn't a bit true I had ceased to care for knowledge; little by little my curiosity not only had begun to ache again, but had become the familiar torment of my days and my nights. There are doubtless people to whom torments of such an order appear hardly more natural than the contortions of disease; but I don't after all know why I should in this connexion so much as mention them. For the few persons, at any rate, abnormal or not, with whom my anecdote is concerned, literature was a game of skill, and skill meant courage, and courage meant honour, and honour meant passion, meant life. The stake on the table was a special substance and our roulette the revolving mind, but we sat round the green board as intently as the grim gamblers at Monte Carlo. Gwendolen Erme, for that matter, with her white face and her fixed eyes, was of the very type of the lean ladies one had met in the temples of chance. I recognized in Corvick's absence that she made this analogy vivid. It was extravagant, I admit, the way she lived for the art of the pen. Her passion visibly preyed on her, and in her presence I felt almost tepid. I got hold of "Deep Down" again: it was a desert in which she had lost herself, but in which too she had dug a wonderful hole in the sand—a cavity out of which Corvick had still more remarkably pulled her.

Early in March I had a telegram from her, in consequence of which I repaired immediately to Chelsea, where the first thing she said to me was: "He has got it, he has got it!"

She was moved, as I could see, to such depths that she must mean the great thing. "Vereker's idea?"

"His general intention. George has cabled from Bombay."

She had the missive open there; it was emphatic though concise. "Eureka. Immense." That was all—he had saved the cost of the signature. I shared her emotion, but I was disappointed. "He doesn't say what it is."

"How could he—in a telegram? He'll write it."

"But how does he know?"

"Know it's the real thing? Oh I'm sure that when you see it you do know. *Vera incessu patuit dea!*"

"It's you, Miss Erme, who are a 'dear' for bringing me such news!"—I went all lengths in my high spirits. "But fancy finding our goddess in the temple of Vishnu! How strange of George to have been able to go into the thing again in the midst of such different and such powerful solicitations!"

"He hasn't gone into it, I know; it's the thing itself, let severely alone for six months, that has simply sprung out at him like a tigress out of the jungle. He didn't take a book with him—on purpose; indeed he wouldn't have needed to—he knows every page, as I do, by heart. They all worked in him together, and some day somewhere, when he wasn't thinking, they fell, in all their superb intricacy, into the one right combination. The figure in the carpet came out. That's the way he knew it would come and the real reason—you didn't in the least understand, but I suppose I may tell you now—why he went and why I consented to his going. We knew the change would do it—that the difference of thought, of scene, would give the needed touch, the magic shake. We had perfectly, we had admirably calculated. The elements were all in his mind, and in the *secousse* of a new intense experience they just struck light." She positively struck light herself—she was literally, facially luminous. I stammered something about unconscious cerebration, and she continued: "He'll come right home—this will bring him."

"To see Vereker, you mean?"

"To see Vereker—and to see *me*. Think what he'll have to tell me!"

I hesitated. "About India?"

"About fiddlesticks! About Vereker—about the figure in the carpet."

"But, as you say, we shall surely have that in a letter."

She thought like one inspired, and I remembered how Corvick had told me long before that her face was interesting. "Perhaps it can't be got into a letter if it's 'immense.'"

"Perhaps not if it's immense bosh. If he has hold of something that can't be got into a letter he hasn't hold of *the* thing. Vereker's own statement to me was exactly that the 'figure' *would* fit into a letter."

"Well, I cabled to George an hour ago—two words," said Gwendolen.

"Is it indiscreet of me to ask what they were?"

She hung fire, but at last brought them out. "'Angel, write.'"

"Good!" I cried. "I'll make it sure—I'll send him the same."

7

My words however were not absolutely the same—I put something instead of "angel"; and in the sequel my epithet seemed the more apt, for when eventually we heard from our traveller it was merely, it was thoroughly to be tantalised. He was magnificent in his triumph, he described his discovery as stupendous; but his ecstasy only obscured it—there were to be no particulars till he should have submitted his conception to the supreme authority. He had thrown up his commission, he had thrown up his book, he had thrown up everything but the instant need to hurry to Rapallo, on the Genoese shore, where Vereker was making a stay. I wrote him a letter which was to await him at Aden—I besought him to relieve my suspense. That he had found my letter was indicated by a telegram which, reaching me after weary days and in the absence of any answer to my laconic dispatch to him at Bombay, was evidently intended as a reply to both communications. Those few words were in familiar French, the French of the day, which Corvick often made use of to show he wasn't a prig. It had for some persons the opposite effect, but his message may fairly be paraphrased. "Have patience; I want to see, as it breaks on you, the face you'll make!" "*Tellement envie de voir ta tête!*"—that was what I had to sit down with. I can certainly not be said to have sat down, for I seem to remember myself at this time as rattling constantly between the little house in Chelsea and my own.

Our impatience, Gwendolen's and mine, was equal, but I kept hoping her light would be greater. We all spent during this episode, for people of our means, a great deal of money in telegrams and cabs, and I counted on the receipt of news from Rapallo immediately after the junction of the discoverer with the discovered. The interval seemed an age, but late one day I heard a hansom precipitated to my door with the crash engendered by a hint of liberality. I lived with my heart in my mouth and accordingly bounded to the window—a movement which gave me a view of a young lady erect on the footboard of the vehicle and eagerly looking up at my house. At sight of me she flourished a paper with a movement that brought me straight down, the movement with which, in melodramas, handkerchiefs and reprieves are flourished at the foot of the scaffold.

"Just seen Vereker—not a note wrong. Pressed me to bosom —keeps me a month." So much I read on her paper while the cabby dropped a grin from his perch. In my excitement I paid him profusely and in hers she suffered it; then as he drove away we started to walk about and talk. We had talked, heaven knows, enough before, but this was a wondrous lift. We pictured the whole scene at Rapallo, where he would have written, mentioning my name, for permission to call; that is *I* pictured it, having more material than my companion, whom I felt hang on my lips as we stopped on purpose before shop-windows we didn't look into. About one thing we were clear; if he was staying on for fuller communication we should at least have a letter from him that would help us through the dregs of delay. We understood his staying on, and yet each of us saw, I think, that the other hated it. The letter we were clear about arrived; it was for Gwendolen, and I called on her in time to save her the trouble of bringing it to me. She didn't read it out, as was natural enough; but she repeated to me what it chiefly embodied. This consisted of the remarkable statement that he'd tell her after they were married exactly what she wanted to know.

"Only *then*, when I'm his wife—not before," she explained. "It's tantamount to saying—isn't it?—that I must marry him straight off!" She smiled at me while I flushed with disappointment, a vision of fresh delay that made me at first unconscious of my surprise. It seemed more than a hint that on me as well he would impose some tiresome condition. Suddenly, while she reported several more things from his letter, I remembered what he had told me before going away. He had found Mr. Vereker deliriously interesting and his own possession of the secret a real intoxication. The buried treasure was all gold and gems. Now that it was there it seemed to grow and grow before him; it would have been, through all time and taking all tongues, one of the most wonderful flowers of literary art. Nothing, in especial, once you were face to face with it, could show for more consummately *done*. When once it came out it came out, was there with a splendour that made you ashamed; and there hadn't been, save in the bottomless vulgarity of the age, with every one tasteless and tainted, every sense stopped, the smallest reason why it should have been overlooked. It was great, yet so simple, was simple, yet so great, and the final knowledge of it was an experience quite apart. He intimated that the charm of such an experience, the desire to drain it, in its freshness, to the last drop, was what kept him there close to the source. Gwendolen, frankly radiant as she tossed me these fragments, showed the elation of a prospect more assured than my own. That brought me back to the question of her marriage, prompted me to ask if what she meant by what she had just surprised me with was that she was under an engagement.

"Of course I am!" she answered. "Didn't you know it?" She seemed astonished, but I was still more so, for Corvick had told me the exact contrary. I didn't mention this however; I only reminded her how little I had been on that score in her confidence, or even in Corvick's, and that moreover I wasn't in ignorance of her mother's interdict. At bottom I was troubled by the disparity of the two accounts; but after a little I felt Corvick's to be the one I least doubted. This simply reduced me to asking myself if the girl had on the spot improvised an engagement—vamped up an old one or dashed off a new—in order to arrive at the satisfaction she desired. She must have had resources of which I was destitute, but she made her case slightly more intelligible by returning presently: "What the state of things has been is that we felt of course bound to do nothing in mamma's lifetime."

"But now you think you'll just dispense with mamma's consent?"

"Ah it mayn't come to that!" I wondered what it might come to, and she went on: "Poor dear, she may swallow the dose. In fact, you know," she added with a laugh, "she really *must!*"—a proposition of which, on behalf of every one concerned, I fully acknowledged the force.

8

Nothing more vexatious had ever happened to me than to become aware before Corvick's arrival in England that I shouldn't be there to put him through. I found myself abruptly called to Germany by the alarming illness of my younger brother, who, against my advice, had gone to Munich to study, at the feet indeed of a great master, the art of portraiture in oils. The near relative who made him an allowance had threatened to withdraw it if he should, under specious pretexts, turn for superior truth to Paris—Paris being somehow, for a Cheltenham aunt, the school of evil, the abyss. I deplored this prejudice at the time, and the deep injury of it was now visible—first in the fact that it hadn't saved the poor boy, who was clever frail and foolish, from congestion of the lungs, and second in the greater break with London to which the event condemned me. I'm afraid that what was uppermost in my mind during several anxious weeks was the sense that if we had only been in Paris I might have run over to see Corvick. This was actually out of the question from every point of view: my brother, whose recovery gave us both plenty to do, was ill for three months, during which I never left him and at the end of which we had to face the absolute prohibition of a return to England. The consideration of climate imposed itself, and he was in no state to meet it alone. I took him to Meran and there spent the summer with him, trying to show him by example how to get back to work and nursing a rage of another sort that I tried *not* to show him.

The whole business proved the first of a series of phenomena so strangely interlaced that, taken all together—which was how I had to take them—they form as good an illustration as I can recall of the manner in which, for the good of his soul doubtless, fate sometimes deals with a man's avidity. These incidents certainly had larger bearings than the comparatively meagre consequence we are here concerned with—though I feel that consequence also a thing to speak of with some respect. It's mainly in such a light, I confess, at any rate, that the ugly fruit of my exile is at this hour present to me. Even at first indeed the spirit in which my avidity, as I have called it, made me regard that term owed no element of ease to the fact that before coming back from Rapallo George Corvick addressed me in a way I objected to. His letter had none of the sedative action I must to-day profess myself sure he had wished to give it, and the march of occurrences was not so ordered as to make up for what it lacked. He had begun on the spot, for one of the quarterlies, a great last word on Vereker's writings, and this exhaustive study, the only one that would have counted, have existed, was to turn on the new light, to utter—oh so quietly!—the unimagined truth. It was in other words to trace the figure in the carpet through every convolution, to reproduce it in every tint. The result, according to my friend, would be the greatest literary portrait ever painted, and what he asked of me was just to be so good as not to trouble him with questions till he should hang up his masterpiece before me. He did me the honour to declare that, putting aside the great sitter himself, all aloft in his indifference, I was individually the connoisseur he was most working for. I was therefore to be a good boy and not try to peep under the curtain before the show was ready: I should enjoy it all the more if I sat very still.

I did my best to sit very still, but I couldn't help giving a jump on seeing in *The Times*, after I had been a week or two in Munich and before, as I knew, Corvick had reached London, the announcement of the sudden death of poor Mrs. Erme. I instantly, by letter, appealed to Gwendolen for particulars, and she wrote me that her mother had yielded to long-threatened failure of the heart. She didn't say, but I took the liberty of reading into her words, that from the point of view of her marriage and also of her eagerness, which was quite a match for mine, this was a solution more prompt than could have been expected and more radical than waiting for the old lady to swallow the dose. I candidly admit indeed that at the time

—for I heard from her repeatedly—I read some singular things into Gwendolen's words and some still more extraordinary ones into her silences. Pen in hand, this way, I live the time over, and it brings back the oddest sense of my having been, both for months and in spite of myself, a kind of coerced spectator. All my life had taken refuge in my eyes, which the procession of events appeared to have committed itself to keep astare. There were days when I thought of writing to Hugh Vereker and simply throwing myself on his charity. But I felt more deeply that I hadn't fallen quite so low—besides which, quite properly, he would send me about my business. Mrs. Erme's death brought Corvick straight home, and within the month he was united "very quietly"— as quietly, I seemed to make out, as he meant in his article to bring out his *trouvaille*—to the young lady he had loved and quitted. I use this last term, I may parenthetically say, because I subsequently grew sure that at the time he went to India, at the time of his great news from Bombay, there had been no positive pledge between them whatever. There had been none at the moment she was affirming to me the very opposite. On the other hand he had certainly become engaged the day he returned. The happy pair went down to Torquay for their honeymoon, and there, in a reckless hour, it occurred to poor Corvick to take his young bride a drive. He had no command of that business: this had been brought home to me of old in a little tour we had once made together in a dogcart. In a dogcart he perched his companion for a rattle over Devonshire hills, on one of the likeliest of which he brought his horse, who, it was true, had bolted, down with such violence that the occupants of the cart were hurled forward and that he fell horribly on his head. He was killed on the spot; Gwendolen escaped unhurt.

I pass rapidly over the question of this unmitigated tragedy, of what the loss of my best friend meant for me, and I complete my little history of my patience and my pain by the frank statement of my having, in a postscript to my very first letter to her after the receipt of the hideous news, asked Mrs. Corvick whether her husband mightn't at least have finished the great article on Vereker. Her answer was as prompt as my question: the article, which had been barely begun, was a mere heartbreaking scrap. She explained that our friend, abroad, had just settled down to it when interrupted by her mother's death, and that then, on his return, he had been kept from work by the engrossments into which that calamity was to plunge them. The opening pages were all that existed; they were striking, they were promising, but they didn't unveil the idol. That great intellectual feat was obviously to have formed his climax. She said nothing more, nothing to enlighten me as to the state of her own knowledge —the knowledge for the acquisition of which I had fancied her prodigiously acting. This was above all what I wanted to know: had *she* seen the idol unveiled? Had there been a private ceremony for a palpitating audience of one? For what else but that ceremony had the nuptials taken place? I didn't like as yet to press her, though when I thought of what had passed between us on the subject in Corvick's absence her reticence surprised me. It was therefore not till much later, from Meran, that I risked another appeal, risked it in some trepidation, for she continued to tell me nothing. "Did you hear in those few days of your blighted bliss," I wrote, "what we desired so to hear?" I said "we" as a little hint; and she showed me she could take a little hint. "I heard everything," she replied, "and I mean to keep it to myself!"

9

It was impossible not to be moved with the strongest sympathy for her, and on my return to England I showed her every kindness in my power. Her mother's death had made her means sufficient, and she had gone to live in a more convenient quarter. But her loss had been great and her visitation cruel; it never would have occurred to me, moreover, to suppose she could come to feel the possession of a technical tip, of a piece of literary experience, a counterpoise to her grief. Strange to say, none the less, I couldn't help believing after I had seen her a few times that I caught a glimpse of some such oddity. I hasten to add that there had been other things I couldn't help believing, or at least imagining; and as I never felt I was really clear about these, so, as to the point I here touch on, I give her memory the benefit of the doubt. Stricken and solitary, highly accomplished and now, in her deep mourning, her maturer grace and her uncomplaining sorrow, incontestably handsome, she presented herself as leading a life of singular dignity and beauty. I had at first found a way to persuade myself that I should soon get the better of the reserve formulated, the week after the catastrophe, in her reply to an appeal as to which I was not unconscious that it might strike her as mistimed. Certainly that reserve was something of a shock to me—certainly it puzzled me the more I thought of it and even though I tried to explain it (with moments of success) by an imputation of exalted sentiments, of superstitious scruples, of a refinement of loyalty. Certainly it added at the same time hugely to the price of Vereker's secret, precious as this mystery already appeared. I may as well confess abjectly that Mrs. Corvick's unexpected attitude was the final tap on the nail that was to fix fast my luckless idea, convert it into the obsession of which I'm for ever conscious.

But this only helped me the more to be artful, to be adroit, to allow time to elapse before renewing my suit. There were plenty of speculations for the interval, and one of them was deeply absorbing. Corvick had kept his information from his young friend till after the removal of the last barrier to their intimacy—then only had he let the cat out of the bag. Was it Gwendolen's idea, taking a hint from him, to liberate this animal only on the basis of the renewal of such a relation? Was the figure in the carpet traceable or describable only for husbands and wives—for lovers supremely united? It came back to me in a mystifying manner that in Kensington Square, when I mentioned that Corvick would have told the girl he loved, some word had dropped from Vereker that gave colour to this possibility. There might be little in it, but there was enough to make me wonder if I should have to marry Mrs. Corvick to get what I wanted. Was I prepared to offer her this price for the blessing of her knowledge? Ah that way madness lay!—so I at least said to myself in bewildered hours. I could see meanwhile the torch she refused to pass on flame away in her chamber of memory—pour through her eyes a light that shone in her lonely house. At the end of six months I was fully sure of what this warm presence made up to her for. We had talked again and again of the man who had brought us together—of his talent, his character, his personal charm, his certain career, his dreadful doom, and even of his clear purpose in that great study which was to have been a supreme literary portrait, a kind of critical Vandyke or Velasquez. She had conveyed to me in abundance that she was tongue-tied by her perversity, by her piety, that she would never break the silence it had not been given to the "right person," as she said, to break. The hour, however, finally arrived. One evening when I had been sitting with her longer than usual I laid my hand firmly on her arm. "Now at last what *is* it?"

She had been expecting me and was ready. She gave a long slow soundless headshake, merciful only in being inarticulate. This mercy didn't prevent its hurling at me the largest finest coldest "Never!" I had yet, in the course of a life that had known denials, had to take full in the face. I took it and was aware that with the hard blow the tears had come into my eyes. So for a while we sat and looked at each other; after which I slowly rose. I was wondering if some day she would accept me; but this was not what I brought out. I said as I smoothed down my hat: "I know what to think then. It's nothing!"

A remote disdainful pity for me gathered in her dim smile; then she spoke in a voice that I hear at this hour. "It's my *life!*" As I stood at the door she added: "You've insulted him!"

"Do you mean Vereker?"

"I mean the Dead!"

I recognized when I reached the street the justice of her charge. Yes, it was her life—I recognised that too; but her life none the less made room with the lapse of time for another interest. A year and a half after Corvick's death she published in a single volume her second novel, "Overmastered," which I pounced on in the hope of finding in it some tell-tale echo or some peeping face. All I found was a much better book than her younger performance, showing I thought the better company she had kept. As a tissue tolerably intricate it was a carpet with a figure of its own; but the figure was not the figure I was looking for. On sending a review of it to *The Middle* I was surprised to learn from the office that a notice was already in type. When the paper came out I had no hesitation in attributing this article, which I thought rather vulgarly overdone, to Drayton Deane, who in the old days had been something of a friend of Corvick's, yet had only within a few weeks made the acquaintance of his widow. I had had an early copy of the book, but Deane had evidently had an earlier. He lacked all the same the light hand with which Corvick had gilded the gingerbread—he laid on the tinsel in splotches.

10

Six months later appeared "The Right of Way," the last chance, though we didn't know it, that we were to have to redeem ourselves. Written wholly during Vereker's sojourn abroad, the book had been heralded, in a hundred paragraphs, by the usual ineptitudes. I carried it, as early a copy as any, I this time flattered myself, straightaway to Mrs. Corvick. This was the only use I had for it; I left the inevitable tribute of *The Middle* to some more ingenious mind and some less irritated temper. "But I already have it," Gwendolen said. "Drayton Deane was so good as to bring it to me yesterday, and I've just finished it."

"Yesterday? How did he get it so soon?"

"He gets everything so soon! He's to review it in *The Middle*."

"He—Drayton Deane—review Vereker?" I couldn't believe my ears.

"Why not? One fine ignorance is as good as another."

I winced but I presently said: "You ought to review him yourself!"

"I don't 'review,'" she laughed. "I'm reviewed!"

Just then the door was thrown open. "Ah yes, here's your reviewer!" Drayton Deane was there with his long legs and his tall forehead: he had come to see what she thought of "The Right of Way," and to bring news that was singularly relevant. The evening papers were just out with a telegram on the author of that work, who, in Rome, had been ill for some days with an attack of malarial fever. It had at first not been thought grave, but had taken, in consequence of complications, a turn that might give rise to anxiety. Anxiety had indeed at the latest hour begun to be felt.

I was struck in the presence of these tidings with the fundamental detachment that Mrs. Corvick's overt concern quite failed to hide: it gave me the measure of her consummate independence. That independence rested on her knowledge, the knowledge which nothing now could destroy and which nothing could make different. The figure in the carpet might take on another twist or two, but the sentence had virtually been written. The writer might go down to his grave: she was the person in the world to whom—as if she had been his favoured heir—his continued existence was least of a need. This reminded me how I had observed at a particular moment —after Corvick's death—the drop of her desire to see him face to face. She had got what she wanted without that. I had been sure that if she hadn't got it she wouldn't have been restrained from the endeavour to sound him personally by those superior reflexions, more conceivable on a man's part than on a woman's, which in my case had served as a deterrent. It wasn't however, I hasten to add, that my case, in spite of this invidious comparison, wasn't ambiguous enough. At the thought that Vereker was perhaps at that moment dying there rolled over me a wave of anguish—a poignant sense of how inconsistently I still depended on him. A delicacy that it was my one compensation to suffer to rule me had left the Alps and the Apennines between us, but the sense of the waning occasion suggested that I might in my despair at last have gone to him. Of course I should really have done nothing of the sort. I remained five minutes, while my companions talked of the new book, and when Drayton Deane appealed to me for my opinion of it I made answer, getting up, that I detested Hugh Vereker and simply couldn't read him. I departed with the moral certainty that as the door closed behind me Deane would brand me for awfully superficial. His hostess wouldn't contradict *that* at least.

I continue to trace with a briefer touch our intensely odd successions. Three weeks after this came Vereker's death, and before the year was out the death of his wife. That poor lady I had never seen, but I had had a futile theory that, should she survive him long enough to be decorously accessible, I might approach her with the feeble flicker of my plea. Did she know and if she knew would she speak? It was much to be presumed that for more reasons than one she would have nothing to say; but when she passed out of all reach I felt renouncement indeed my appointed lot. I was shut up in my obsession for ever—my gaolers had gone off with the key. I find myself quite as vague as a captive in a dungeon about the time that further elapsed before Mrs. Corvick became the wife of Drayton Deane. I had foreseen, through my bars, this end of the business, though there was no indecent haste and our friendship had rather fallen off. They were both so "awfully intellectual" that it struck people as a suitable match, but I had measured better than any one the wealth of understanding the bride would contribute to the union. Never, for a marriage in literary circles—so the newspapers described the alliance—had a lady been so bravely dowered. I began with due promptness to look for the fruit of the affair—that fruit, I mean, of which the premonitory symptoms would be peculiarly visible in the husband. Taking for granted the splendour of the other party's nuptial gift, I expected to see him make a show commensurate with his increase of means. I knew what his means had been—his article on "The Right of Way" had distinctly given one the figure. As he was now exactly in the position in which still more exactly I was not I watched from month to month, in the likely periodicals, for the heavy message poor Corvick had been unable to deliver and the responsibility of which would have fallen on his successor. The widow and wife would have broken by the rekindled hearth the silence that only a widow and wife might break, and Deane would be as aflame with the knowledge as Corvick in his own hour, as Gwendolen in hers, had been. Well, he was aflame doubtless, but the fire was apparently not to become a public blaze. I scanned the periodicals in vain: Drayton Deane filled them with exuberant pages, but he withheld the page I most feverishly sought. He wrote on a thousand subjects, but never on the subject of Vereker. His special line was to tell truths that other people either "funked," as he said, or overlooked, but he never told the only truth that seemed to me in these days to signify. I met the couple in those literary circles referred to in the papers: I have sufficiently intimated that it was only in such circles we were all constructed to revolve. Gwendolen was more than ever committed to them by the publication of her third novel, and I myself definitely classed by holding the opinion that this work was inferior to its immediate predecessor. Was it worse because she had been keeping worse company? If her secret was, as she had told me, her life—a fact discernible in her increasing bloom, an air of conscious privilege that, cleverly corrected by pretty charities, gave distinction to her appearance—it had yet not a direct influence on her work. That only made one—everything only made one—yearn the more for it; only rounded it off with a mystery finer and subtler.

11

It was therefore from her husband I could never remove my eyes: I beset him in a manner that might have made him uneasy. I went even so far as to engage him in conversation. *Didn't* he know, hadn't he come into it as a matter of course? —that question hummed in my brain. Of course he knew; otherwise he wouldn't return my stare so queerly. His wife had told him what I wanted and he was amiably amused at my impotence. He didn't laugh—he wasn't a laugher: his system was to present to my irritation, so that I should crudely expose myself, a conversational blank as vast as his big bare brow. It always happened that I turned away with a settled conviction from these unpeopled expanses, which seemed to complete each other geographically and to symbolise together Drayton Deane's want of voice, want of form. He simply hadn't the art to use what he knew; he literally was incompetent to take up the duty where Corvick had left it. I went still further—it was the only glimpse of happiness I had. I made up my mind that the duty didn't appeal to him. He wasn't interested, he didn't care. Yes, it quite comforted me to believe him too stupid to have joy of the thing I lacked. He was as stupid after as he had been before, and that deepened for me the golden glory in which the mystery was wrapped. I had of course none the less to recollect that his wife might have imposed her conditions and exactions. I had above all to remind myself that with Vereker's death the major incentive dropped. He was still there to be honoured by what might be done—he was no longer there to give it his sanction. Who alas but he had the authority?

Two children were born to the pair, but the second cost the mother her life. After this stroke I seemed to see another ghost of a chance. I jumped at it in thought, but I waited a certain time for manners, and at last my opportunity arrived in a remunerative way. His wife had been dead a year when I met Drayton Deane in the smoking-room of a small club of which we were both members, but where for months—perhaps because I rarely entered it—I hadn't seen him. The room was empty and the occasion propitious. I deliberately offered him, to have done with the matter for ever, that advantage for which I felt he had long been looking.

"As an older acquaintance of your late wife's than even you were," I began, "you must let me say to you something I have on my mind. I shall be glad to make any terms with you that you see fit to name for the information she must have had from George Corvick—the information, you know, that had come to *him*, poor chap, in one of the happiest hours of his life, straight from Hugh Vereker."

He looked at me like a dim phrenological bust. "The information—?"

"Vereker's secret, my dear man—the general intention of his books: the string the pearls were strung on, the buried treasure, the figure in the carpet."

He began to flush—the numbers on his bumps to come out. "Vereker's books had a general intention?"

I stared in my turn. "You don't mean to say you don't know it?" I thought for a moment he was playing with me. "Mrs. Deane knew it; she had it, as I say, straight from Corvick, who had, after infinite search and to Vereker's own delight, found the very mouth of the cave. Where *is* the mouth? He told after their marriage—and told alone—the person who, when the circumstances were reproduced, must have told *you*. Have I been wrong in taking for granted that she admitted you, as one of the highest privileges of the relation in which you stood to her, to the knowledge of which she was after

Corvick's death the sole depository? All *I* know is that that knowledge is infinitely precious, and what I want you to understand is that if you'll in your turn admit me to it you'll do me a kindness for which I shall be lastingly grateful."

He had turned at last very red; I dare say he had begun by thinking I had lost my wits. Little by little he followed me: on my own side I stared with a livelier surprise. Then he spoke. "I don't know what you're talking about."

He wasn't acting—it was the absurd truth. "She *didn't* tell you—?"

"Nothing about Hugh Vereker."

I was stupefied; the room went round. It had been too good even for that! "Upon your honour?"

"Upon my honour. What the devil's the matter with you?" he growled.

"I'm astounded—I'm disappointed. I wanted to get it out of you."

"It isn't *in* me!" he awkwardly laughed. "And even if it were—"

"If it were you'd let me have it—oh yes, in common humanity. But I believe you. I see—I see!" I went on, conscious, with the full turn of the wheel, of my great delusion, my false view of the poor man's attitude. What I saw, though I couldn't say it, was that his wife hadn't thought him worth enlightening. This struck me as strange for a woman who had thought him worth marrying. At last I explained it by the reflexion that she couldn't possibly have married him for his understanding. She had married him for something else.

He was to some extent enlightened now, but he was even more astonished, more disconcerted: he took a moment to compare my story with his quickened memories. The result of his meditation was his presently saying with a good deal of rather feeble form: "This is the first I hear of what you allude to. I think you must be mistaken as to Mrs. Drayton Deane's having had any unmentioned, and still less any unmentionable, knowledge of Hugh Vereker. She'd certainly have wished it— should it have borne on his literary character—to be used."

"It *was* used. She used it herself. She told me with her own lips that she 'lived' on it."

I had no sooner spoken than I repented of my words; he grew so pale that I felt as if I had struck him. "Ah 'lived'—!" he murmured, turning short away from me.

My compunction was real; I laid my hand on his shoulder. "I beg you to forgive me—I've made a mistake. You *don't* know what I thought you knew. You could, if I had been right, have rendered me a service; and I had my reasons for assuming that you'd be in a position to meet me."

"Your reasons?" he echoed. "What were your reasons?"

I looked at him well; I hesitated; I considered. "Come and sit down with me here and I'll tell you." I drew him to a sofa, I lighted another cigar and, beginning with the anecdote of Vereker's one descent from the clouds, I recited to him the extraordinary chain of accidents that had, in spite of the original gleam, kept me till that hour in the dark. I told him in a word just what I've written out here. He listened with deepening attention, and I became aware, to my surprise, by his ejaculations, by his questions, that he would have been after all not unworthy to be trusted by his wife. So abrupt an experience of her want of trust had now a disturbing effect on him; but I saw the immediate shock throb away little by little and then gather again into waves of wonder and curiosity—waves that promised, I could perfectly judge, to break in the end with the fury of my own highest tides. I may say that to-day as victims of unappeased desire there isn't a pin to choose between us. The poor man's state is almost my consolation; there are really moments when I feel it to be quite my revenge.

The Lesson of the Master

1

HE HAD BEEN TOLD THE LADIES WERE AT CHURCH, BUT THIS
was corrected by what he saw from the top of the steps—
they descended from a great height in two arms, with a circular sweep of the most charming effect—at the threshold of
the door which, from the long bright gallery, overlooked the
immense lawn. Three gentlemen, on the grass, at a distance,
sat under the great trees, while the fourth figure showed a
crimson dress that told as a "bit of colour" amid the fresh
rich green. The servant had so far accompanied Paul Overt
as to introduce him to this view, after asking him if he wished
first to go to his room. The young man declined that privilege,
conscious of no disrepair from so short and easy a journey
and always liking to take at once a general perceptive possession of a new scene. He stood there a little with his eyes on
the group and on the admirable picture, the wide grounds of
an old country house near London—that only made it better—
on a splendid Sunday in June. "But that lady, who's *she?*"
he said to the servant before the man left him.

"I think she's Mrs. St. George, sir."

"Mrs. St. George, the wife of the distinguished—" Then Paul
Overt checked himself, doubting if a footman would know.

"Yes, sir—probably, sir," said his guide, who appeared to

wish to intimate that a person staying at Summersoft would naturally be, if only by alliance, distinguished. His tone, however, made poor Overt himself feel for the moment scantly so.

"And the gentlemen?" Overt went on.

"Well, sir, one of them's General Fancourt."

"Ah, yes, I know; thank you." General Fancourt was distinguished, there was no doubt of that, for something he had done, or perhaps even hadn't done—the young man couldn't remember which—some years before in India. The servant went away, leaving the glass doors open into the gallery, and Paul Overt remained at the head of the wide double staircase, saying to himself that the place was sweet and promised a pleasant visit, while he leaned on the balustrade of fine old ironwork which, like all the other details, was of the same period as the house. It all went together and spoke in one voice—a rich English voice of the early part of the eighteenth century. It might have been church-time on a summer's day in the reign of Queen Anne: the stillness was too perfect to be modern, the nearness counted so as distance, and there was something so fresh and sound in the originality of the large smooth house, the expanse of beautiful brickwork that showed for pink rather than red and that had been kept clear of messy creepers by the law under which a woman with a rare complexion disdains a veil. When Paul Overt became aware that the people under the trees had noticed him he turned back through the open doors into the great gallery which was the pride of the place. It marched across from end to end and seemed—with its bright colours, its high panelled windows, its faded flowered chintzes, its quickly-recognised portraits and pictures, the blue-and-white china of its cabinets and the attenuated festoons and rosettes of its ceiling—a cheerful, upholstered avenue into the other century.

Our friend was slightly nervous; that went with his character as a student of fine prose, went with the artist's general disposition to vibrate; and there was a particular thrill in the idea that Henry St. George might be a member of the party. For the young aspirant he had remained a high literary figure, in spite of the lower range of production to which he had fallen after his three first great successes, the comparative absence of quality in his later work. There had been moments when Paul Overt almost shed tears for this; but now that he was near him—he had never met him—he was conscious only of the fine original source and of his own immense debt. After he had taken a turn or two up and down the gallery he came out again and descended the steps. He was but slenderly supplied with a certain social boldness—it was really a weakness in him—so that, conscious of a want of acquaintance with the four persons in the distance, he gave way to motions recommended by their not committing him to a positive approach. There was a fine English awkwardness in this—he felt that too as he sauntered vaguely and obliquely across the lawn, taking an independent line. Fortunately there was an equally fine English directness in the way one of the gentlemen presently rose and made as if to "stalk" him, though with an air of conciliation and reassurance. To this demonstration Paul Overt instantly responded, even if the gentleman were not his host. He was tall, straight and elderly and had, like the great house itself, a pink smiling face, and into the bargain a white moustache. Our young man met him halfway while he laughed and said: "Er—Lady Watermouth told us you were coming; she asked me just to look after you." Paul Overt thanked him, liking him on the spot, and turned round with him to walk toward the others. "They've all gone to church—all except us," the stranger continued as they went; "we're just sitting here—it's so jolly." Overt pronounced it jolly indeed: it was such a lovely place. He mentioned that he was having the charming impression for the first time.

"Ah, you've not been here before?" said his companion. "It's a nice little place—not much to *do*, you know." Overt wondered what he wanted to "do"—he felt that he himself was doing so much. By the time they came to where the others sat he had recognised his initiator for a military man and—such was the turn of Overt's imagination—he had found him thus still more sympathetic. He would naturally have a need for action, for deeds at variance with the pacific pastoral scene. He was evidently so good-natured, however, that he accepted the inglorious hour for what it was worth. Paul Overt shared it with him and with his companions for the next twenty minutes; the latter looked at him and he looked at them without knowing much who they were, while the talk went on without much telling him even what it meant. It seemed indeed to mean nothing in particular; it wandered, with casual pointless pauses and short terrestrial flights, amid names of persons and places—names which, for our friend, had no great power of evocation. It was all sociable and slow, as was right and natural of a warm Sunday morning.

His first attention was given to the question, privately considered, of whether one of the two younger men would be Henry St. George. He knew many of his distinguished contemporaries by their photographs, but had never, as happened, seen a portrait of the great misguided novelist. One of the gentlemen was unimaginable—he was too young; and the other scarcely looked clever enough, with such mild, undiscriminating eyes. If those eyes were St. George's the problem presented by the ill-matched parts of his genius would be still more difficult of solution. Besides, the deportment of their proprietor was not, as regards the lady in the red dress, such as could be natural, toward the wife of his bosom, even to a writer accused by several critics of sacrificing too much to manner. Lastly, Paul Overt had a vague sense that if the gentleman with the expressionless eyes bore the name that had set his heart beating faster (he also had contradictory, conventional whiskers—the young admirer of the celebrity had never in a mental vision seen *his* face in so vulgar a frame) he would have given him a sign of recognition or of friendliness, would have heard of him a little, would know something about "Ginistrella," would have an impression of how that fresh fiction had caught the eye of real criticism. Paul Overt had a dread of being grossly proud, but even morbid modesty might view the authorship of "Ginistrella" as constituting a degree of identity. His soldierly friend became clear enough: he was "Fancourt," but was also "the General"; and he mentioned to the new visitor in the course of a few moments that he had but lately returned from twenty years' service abroad.

"And now you remain in England?" the young man asked.

"Oh, yes; I've bought a small house in London."

"And I hope you like it," said Overt, looking at Mrs. St. George.

"Well, a little house in Manchester Square—there's a limit to the enthusiasm *that* inspires."

"Oh, I meant being home again—being back in Piccadilly."

"My daughter likes Piccadilly—that's the main thing. She's very fond of art and music and literature and all that kind of thing. She missed it in India and she finds it in London, or she hopes she'll find it. Mr. St. George has promised to help her—he has been awfully kind to her. She has gone to church—she's fond of that too—but they'll all be back in a quarter of an hour. You must let me introduce you to her—she'll be so glad to know you. I daresay she has read every blest word you've written."

"I shall be delighted—I haven't written so very many," Overt pleaded, feeling, and without resentment, that the General at least was vagueness itself about that. But he wondered a little why, expressing this friendly disposition, it didn't occur to the doubtless eminent soldier to pronounce the word that would put him in relation with Mrs. St. George. If it was a question of introductions Miss Fancourt—apparently as yet unmarried—was far away, while the wife of his illustrious confrère was almost between them. This lady struck Paul Overt as altogether pretty, with a surprising juvenility and a high smartness of aspect, something that—he could scarcely have said why—served for mystification. St. George certainly had every right to a charming wife, but he himself would never have imagined the important little woman in the aggressively Parisian dress the partner for life, the *alter ego*, of a man of letters. That partner in general, he knew, that second self, was far from presenting herself in a single type: observation had taught him that she was not inveterately, not necessarily plain. But he had never before seen her look so much as if her prosperity had deeper foundations than an ink-spotted study-table littered with proof-sheets. Mrs. St. George might have been the wife of a gentleman who "kept" books rather than wrote them, who carried on great affairs in the City and made better bargains than those that poets mostly make with publishers. With this she hinted at a success more personal—a success peculiarly stamping the age in which society, the world of conversation, is a great drawing-room with the City for its antechamber. Overt numbered her years at first as some thirty, and then ended by believing that she might approach her fiftieth. But she somehow in this case juggled away the excess and the difference—you only saw them in a rare glimpse, like the rabbit in the conjurer's sleeve. She was extraordinarily white, and her every element and item was pretty; her eyes, her ears, her hair, her voice, her hands, her feet—to which her relaxed attitude in her wicker chair gave a great publicity—and the numerous ribbons and trinkets with which she was bedecked. She looked as if she had put on her best clothes to go to church and then had decided they were too good for that and had stayed at home. She told a story of some length about the shabby way Lady Jane had treated the Duchess, as well as an anecdote in relation to a purchase she had made in Paris—on her way back from Cannes; made for Lady Egbert, who had never refunded the money. Paul Overt suspected her of a tendency to figure great people as larger than life, until he noticed the manner in which she handled Lady Egbert, which was so sharply mutinous that it reassured him. He felt he should have understood her better if he might have met her eye; but she scarcely so much as glanced at him. "Ah, here they come—all the good ones!" she said at last; and Paul Overt admired at his distance the return of the churchgoers—several persons, in couples and threes, advancing in a flicker of sun and shade at the end of a large green vista formed by the level grass and the overarching boughs.

"If you mean to imply that *we're* bad, I protest," said one of the gentlemen—"after making one's self agreeable all the morning!"

"Ah, if they've found you agreeable—!" Mrs. St. George gaily cried. "But if we're good the others are better."

"They must be angels then," said the amused General.

"Your husband was an angel, the way he went off at your bidding," the gentleman who had first spoken declared to Mrs. St. George.

"At my bidding?"

"Didn't you make him go to church?"

"I never made him do anything in my life but once—when I made him burn up a bad book. That's all!" At her "That's all!" our young friend broke into an irrepressible laugh; it lasted only a second, but it drew her eyes to him. His own met them, though not long enough to help him to understand her; unless it were a step towards this that he saw on the instant how the burnt book—the way she alluded to it!— would have been one of her husband's finest things.

"A bad book?" her interlocutor repeated.

"I didn't like it. He went to church because your daughter went," she continued to General Fancourt. "I think it my duty to call your attention to his extraordinary demonstrations to your daughter."

"Well, if you don't mind them I don't!" the General laughed.

"*Il s'attache à ses pas.* But I don't wonder—she's so charming."

"I hope she won't make him burn any books!" Paul Overt ventured to exclaim.

"If she'd make him write a few it would be more to the purpose," said Mrs. St. George. "He has been of a laziness of late—!"

Our young man stared—he was so struck with the lady's phraseology. Her "Write a few" seemed to him almost as good as her "That's all." Didn't she, as the wife of a rare artist, know what it was to produce *one* perfect work of art? How in the world did she think they were turned off? His private conviction was that, admirably as Henry St. George wrote, he had written for the last ten years, and especially for the last five, only too much, and there was an instant during which he felt inwardly solicited to make this public. But before he had spoken a diversion was affected by the return of the absentees. They strolled up dispersedly—there were eight or ten of them—and the circle under the trees rearranged itself as they took their place in it. They made it much larger, so that Paul Overt could feel—he was always feeling that sort of thing, as he said to himself—that if the company had already been interesting to watch the interest would now become intense. He shook hands with his hostess, who welcomed him without many words, in the manner of a woman able to trust him to understand and conscious that so pleasant an occasion would in every way speak for itself. She offered him no particular facility for sitting by her, and when they had all subsided again he found himself still next General Fancourt, with an unknown lady on his other flank.

"That's my daughter—that one opposite," the General said to him without loss of time. Overt saw a tall girl, with magnificent red hair, in a dress of pretty grey-green tint and of a limp silken texture, a garment that clearly shirked every modern effect. It had therefore somehow the stamp of the latest thing, so that our beholder quickly took her for nothing if not contemporaneous.

"She's very handsome—very handsome," he repeated while he considered her. There was something noble in her head, and she appeared fresh and strong.

Her good father surveyed her with complacency, remarking soon: "She looks too hot—that's her walk. But she'll be all right presently. Then I'll make her come over and speak to you."

"I should be sorry to give you that trouble. If you were to take me over *there*—!" the young man murmured.

"My dear sir, do you suppose I put myself out that way? I don't mean for you, but for Marian," the General added.

"*I* would put myself out for her soon enough," Overt replied; after which he went on: "Will you be so good as to tell me which of those gentlemen is Henry St. George?"

"The fellow talking to my girl. By Jove, he *is* making up to her—they're going off for another walk."

"Ah, is that he—really?" Our friend felt a certain surprise, for the personage before him seemed to trouble a vision which had been vague only while not confronted with the reality. As soon as the reality dawned, the mental image, retiring with a sigh, became substantial enough to suffer a slight wrong. Overt, who had spent a considerable part of his short life in foreign lands, made now, but not for the first time, the reflexion that whereas in those countries he had almost always recognised the artist and the man of letters by his personal "type," the mould of his face, the character of his head, the expression of his figure, and even the indications of his dress, so in England this identification was as little as possible a matter of course, thanks to the greater conformity, the habit of sinking the profession instead of advertising it, the general diffusion of the air of the gentleman—the gentleman committed to no particular set of ideas. More than once, on returning to his own country, he had said to himself about people met in society: "One sees them in this place and that, and one even talks with them; but to find out what they *do* one would really have to be a detective." In respect to several individuals whose work he was the opposite of "drawn to"—perhaps he was wrong—he found himself adding, "No wonder they conceal it—when it's so bad!" He noted that oftener than in France and in Germany his artist looked like a gentleman—that is, like an English one—while, certainly outside a few exceptions, his gentleman didn't look like an artist. St. George was not one of the exceptions; that circumstance he definitely apprehended before the great man had turned his back to walk off with Miss Fancourt. He certainly looked better behind than any foreign man of letters—showed for beautifully correct in his tall black hat and his superior frock coat. Somehow, all the same, these very garments—he wouldn't have minded them so much on a weekday—were disconcerting to Paul Overt, who forgot for the moment that the head of the profession was not a bit better dressed than himself. He had caught a glimpse of a regular face, a fresh colour, a brown moustache, and a pair of eyes surely never visited by a fine frenzy, and he promised himself to study these denotements on the first occasion. His superficial sense was that their owner might have passed for a lucky stockbroker—a gentleman driving eastward every morning from a sanitary suburb in a smart dogcart. That carried out the impression already derived from his wife. Paul's glance, after a moment, travelled back to this lady, and he saw how her own had followed her husband as he moved off with Miss Fancourt. Overt permitted himself to wonder a little if she were jealous when another woman took him away. Then he made out that Mrs. St. George wasn't glaring at the indifferent maiden. Her eyes rested but on her husband, and with unmistakable serenity. That was the way she wanted him to be—she liked his conventional uniform. Overt longed to hear more about the book she had induced him to destroy.

As they all came out from luncheon General Fancourt took
hold of him with an "I say, I want you to know my girl!"
as if the idea had just occurred to him and he hadn't spoken
of it before. With the other hand he possessed himself all
paternally of the young lady. "You know all about him. I've
seen you with his books. She reads everything—everything!"
he went on to Paul. The girl smiled at him and then laughed
at her father. The General turned away and his daughter
spoke—"Isn't papa delightful?"

"He is indeed, Miss Fancourt."

"As if I read you because I read 'everything'!"

"Oh, I don't mean for saying that," said Paul Overt. "I
liked him from the moment he began to be kind to me. Then
he promised me this privilege."

"It isn't for you he means it—it's for me. If you flatter
yourself that he thinks of anything in life but me you'll find
you're mistaken. He introduces everyone. He thinks me in-
satiable."

"You speak just like him," laughed our youth.

"Ah, but sometimes I want to"—and the girl coloured. "I
don't read everything—I read very little. But I *have* read
you."

"Suppose we go into the gallery," said Paul Overt. She
pleased him greatly, not so much because of this last remark—
though that of course was not too disconcerting—as because,
seated opposite to him at luncheon, she had given him for
half an hour the impression of her beautiful face. Something
else had come with it—a sense of generosity, of an enthusiasm
which, unlike many enthusiasms, was not all manner. That
was not spoiled for him by his seeing that the repast had
placed her again in familiar contact with Henry St. George. Sitting next her this celebrity was also opposite our young man,
who had been able to note that he multiplied the attentions
lately brought by his wife to the General's notice. Paul Overt
had gathered as well that this lady was not in the least discomposed by these fond excesses and that she gave every sign
of an unclouded spirit. She had Lord Masham on one side of
her and on the other the accomplished Mr. Mulliner, editor of

the new high-class lively evening paper which was expected to meet a want felt in circles increasingly conscious that Conservatism must be made amusing, and unconvinced when assured by those of another political colour that it was already amusing enough. At the end of an hour spent in her company Paul Overt thought her still prettier than at the first radiation, and if her profane allusions to her husband's work had not still rung in his ears he should have liked her—so far as it could be a question of that in connexion with a woman to whom he had not yet spoken and to whom probably he should never speak if it were left to her. Pretty women were a clear need to his genius, and for the hour it was Miss Fancourt who supplied the want. If Overt had promised himself a closer view the occasion was now of the best, and it brought consequences felt by the young man as important. He saw more in St. George's face, which he liked the better for its not having told its whole story in the first three minutes. That story came out as one read, in short instalments—it was excusable that one's analogies should be somewhat professional—and the text was a style considerably involved, a language not easy to translate at sight. There were shades of meaning in it and a vague perspective of history which receded as you advanced. Two facts Paul had particularly heeded. The first of these was that he liked the measured mask much better at inscrutable rest than in social agitation; its almost convulsive smile above all displeased him (as much as any impression from that source could), whereas the quiet face had a charm that grew in proportion as stillness settled again. The change to the expression of gaiety excited, he made out, very much the private protest of a person sitting gratefully in the twilight when the lamp is brought in too soon. His second reflexion was that, though generally adverse to the flagrant use of ingratiating arts by a man of age "making up" to a pretty girl, he was not in this case too painfully affected: which seemed to prove either that St. George had a light hand or the air of being younger than he was, or else that Miss Fancourt's own manner somehow made everything right.

Overt walked with her into the gallery, and they strolled to the end of it, looking at the pictures, the cabinets, the charming vista, which harmonised with the prospect of the summer afternoon, resembling it by a long brightness, with great divans and old chairs that figured hours of rest. Such a place as that had the added merit of giving those who came into it plenty to talk about. Miss Fancourt sat down with her new acquaintance on a flowered sofa, the cushions of which, very numerous, were tight ancient cubes of many sizes, and presently said: "I'm so glad to have a chance to thank you."

"To thank me—?" He had to wonder.

"I liked your book so much. I think it splendid."

She sat there smiling at him, and he never asked himself which book she meant; for after all he had written three or four. That seemed a vulgar detail, and he wasn't even gratified by the idea of the pleasure she told him—her handsome bright face told him—he had given her. The feeling she appealed to, or at any rate the feeling she excited, was something larger, something that had little to do with any quickened pulsation of his own vanity. It was responsive admiration of the life she embodied, the young purity and richness of which appeared to imply that real success was to resemble *that,* to live, to bloom, to present the perfection of a fine type, not to have hammered out headachy fancies with a bent back at an ink-stained table. While her grey eyes rested on him—there was a widish space between these, and the division of her rich-coloured hair, so thick that it ventured to be smooth, made a free arch above them—he was almost ashamed of that exercise of the pen which it was her present inclination to commend. He was conscious he should have liked better to please her in some other way. The lines of her face were those of a woman grown, but the child lingered on in her complexion and in the sweetness of her mouth. Above all she was natural—that was indubitable now; more natural than he had supposed at first, perhaps on account of her esthetic toggery, which was conventionally unconventional, suggesting what he might have called a tortuous spontaneity. He had feared that sort of thing in other cases, and his fears had been justified; for, though he was an artist to the essence, the modern reactionary nymph, with the brambles of the woodland caught in her folds and a look as if the satyrs had toyed with her hair, made him shrink, not as a man of starch and patent leather, but as a man potentially himself a poet or even a faun. The girl was really more candid than her costume, and the best proof of it was her supposing her liberal character suited by any uniform. This was a fallacy, since if she was draped as a pessimist he was sure she liked the taste of life. He thanked her for her appreciation—aware at the same time that he didn't appear to thank her enough and that she might think him ungracious. He was afraid she would ask him to explain something he had written, and he always winced at that—perhaps too timidly—for to his own ear the explanation of a work of art sounded fatuous. But he liked her so much as to feel a confidence that in the long run he should be able to show her he wasn't rudely evasive. Moreover, she surely wasn't quick to take offence, wasn't irritable; she could be trusted to wait. So when he said to her, "Ah, don't talk of anything I've done, don't talk of it *here;* there's another man in the house who's the actuality!"—when he uttered this short sincere protest it was with the sense that she would see in the words neither mock humility nor the impatience of a successful man bored with praise.

"You mean Mr. St. George—isn't he delightful?"

Paul Overt met her eyes, which had a cool morning light that would have half-broken his heart if he hadn't been so young. "Alas, I don't know him. I only admire him at a distance."

"Oh, you *must* know him—he wants so to talk to you," returned Miss Fancourt, who evidently had the habit of saying the things that, by her quick calculation, would give people pleasure. Paul saw how she would always calculate on everything's being simple between others.

"I shouldn't have supposed he knew anything about me," he professed.

"He does then—everything. And if he didn't I should be able to tell him."

"To tell him everything?" our friend smiled.

"You talk just like the people in your book," she answered.

"Then they must all talk alike."

She thought a moment, not a bit disconcerted. "Well, it must be so difficult. Mr. St. George tells me it *is*—terribly. I've tried too—and I find it so. I've tried to write a novel."

"Mr. St. George oughtn't to discourage you," Paul went so far as to say.

"You do much more—when you wear that expression."

"Well, after all, why try to be an artist?" the young man pursued. "It's so poor—so poor!"

"I don't know what you mean," said Miss Fancourt, who looked grave.

"I mean as compared with being a person of action—as living your works."

"But what's art but an intense life—if it be real?" she asked. "I think it's the only one—everything else is so clumsy!" Her companion laughed, and she brought out with her charming serenity what next struck her. "It's so interesting to meet so many celebrated people."

"So I should think—but surely it isn't new to you."

"Why, I've never seen anyone—anyone: living always in Asia."

The way she talked of Asia somehow enchanted him. "But doesn't that continent swarm with great figures? Haven't you administered provinces in India and had captive rajahs and tributary princes chained to your car?"

It was as if she didn't care even *should* he amuse himself at her cost. "I was with my father, after I left school to go out there. It was delightful being with him—we're alone together in the world, he and I—but there was none of the society I like best. One never heard of a picture—never of a book, except bad ones."

"Never of a picture? Why, wasn't all life a picture?"

She looked over the delightful place where they sat. "Nothing to compare to this. I adore England!" she cried.

It fairly stirred in him the sacred chord. "Ah, of course I don't deny that we must do something with her, poor old dear, yet!"

"She hasn't been touched, really," said the girl.

"Did Mr. St. George say that?"

There was a small and, as he felt, harmless spark of irony in his question; which, however, she answered very simply, not noticing the insinuation. "Yes, he says England hasn't been touched—not considering all there is," she went on eagerly. "He's so interesting about our country. To listen to him makes one want so to do something."

"It would make *me* want to," said Paul Overt, feeling

strongly, on the instant, the suggestion of what she said and that of the emotion with which she said it, and well aware of what an incentive, on St. George's lips, such a speech might be.

"Oh, you—as if you hadn't! I should like so to hear you talk together," she added ardently.

"That's very genial of you; but he'd have it all his own way. I'm prostrate before him."

She had an air of earnestness. "Do you think, then, he's so perfect?"

"Far from it. Some of his later books seem to me of a queerness—!"

"Yes, yes—he knows that."

Paul Overt stared. "That they seem to me of a queerness—?"

"Well, yes, or at any rate that they're not what they should be. He told me he didn't esteem them. He has told me such wonderful things—he's so interesting."

There was a certain shock for Paul Overt in the knowledge that the fine genius they were talking of had been reduced to so explicit a confession and had made it, in his misery, to the first comer; for though Miss Fancourt was charming what was she after all but an immature girl encountered at a country-house? Yet precisely this was part of the sentiment he himself had just expressed: he would make way completely for the poor peccable great man, not because he didn't read him clear, but altogether because he did. His consideration was half composed of tenderness for superficialities which he was sure their perpetrator judged privately, judged more ferociously than anyone, and which represented some tragic intellectual secret. He would have his reasons for his psychology *à fleur de peau,* and these reasons could only be cruel ones, such as would make him dearer to those who already were fond of him. "You excite my envy. I have my reserves, I discriminate—but I love him," Paul said in a moment. "And seeing him for the first time this way is a great event for me."

"How momentous—how magnificent!" cried the girl. "How delicious to bring you together!'

"*Your* doing it—that makes it perfect," our friend returned.

"He's as eager as you," she went on. "But it's so odd you shouldn't have met."

"It's not really so odd as it strikes you. I've been out of England so much—made repeated absences all these last years."

She took this in with interest. "And yet you write of it as well as if you were always here."

"It's just the being away perhaps. At any rate the best bits, I suspect, are those that were done in dreary places abroad."

"And why were they dreary?"

"Because they were health-resorts—where my poor mother was dying."

"Your poor mother?"—she was all sweet wonder.

"We went from place to place to help her to get better. But she never did. To the deadly Riviera (I hate it!), to the high Alps, to Algiers, and far away—a hideous journey—to Colorado."

"And she isn't better?" Miss Fancourt went on.

"She died a year ago."

"Really?—like mine! Only that's years since. Some day you must tell me about your mother," she added.

He could at first, on this, only gaze at her. "What right things you say! If you say them to St. George I don't wonder he's in bondage."

It pulled her up for a moment. "I don't know what you mean. He doesn't make speeches and professions at all—he isn't ridiculous."

"I'm afraid you consider, then, that I am."

"No, I don't"—she spoke it rather shortly. And then she added: "He understands—understands everything."

The young man was on the point of saying jocosely: "And I don't—is that it?" But these words, in time, changed themselves to others slightly less trivial. "Do you suppose he understands his wife?"

Miss Fancourt made no direct answer, but after a moment's hesitation put in: "Isn't she charming?"

"Not in the least!"

"Here he comes. Now you must know him," she went on. A small group of visitors had gathered at the other end of the gallery and had been there overtaken by Henry St. George, who strolled in from a neighbouring room. He stood near them a moment, not falling into the talk but taking up an old miniature from a table and vaguely regarding it. At the end of a minute he became aware of Miss Fancourt and her companion in the distance; whereupon, laying down his miniature, he approached them with the same procrastinating air, his hands in his pockets and his eyes turned, right and left, to the pictures. The gallery was so long that this transit took some little time, especially as there was a moment when he stopped to admire the fine Gainsborough. "He says Mrs. St. George has been the making of him," the girl continued in a voice slightly lowered.

"Ah, he's often obscure!" Paul laughed.

"Obscure?" she repeated as if she heard it for the first time. Her eyes rested on her other friend, and it wasn't lost upon Paul that they appeared to send out great shafts of softness. "He's going to speak to us!" she fondly breathed. There was a sort of rapture in her voice, and our friend was startled. "Bless my soul, does she care for him like *that?*—is she in love with him?" he mentally inquired. "Didn't I tell you he was eager?" she had meanwhile asked of him.

"It's eagerness dissimulated," the young man returned as the subject of their observation lingered before his Gainsborough. "He edges toward us shyly. Does he mean that she saved him by burning that book?"

"That book? what book did she burn?" The girl quickly turned her face to him.

"Hasn't he told you, then?"

"Not a word."

"Then he doesn't tell you everything!" Paul had guessed that she pretty much supposed he did. The great man had now resumed his course and come nearer; in spite of which his more qualified admirer risked a profane observation. "St. George and the Dragon is what the anecdote suggests!"

His companion, however, didn't hear it; she smiled at the dragon's adversary. "He *is* eager—he is!" she insisted.

"Eager for you—yes."

But meanwhile she had called out: "I'm sure you want to know Mr. Overt. You'll be great friends, and it will always be delightful to me to remember I was here when you first met and that I had something to do with it."

There was a freshness of intention in the words that carried them off; nevertheless our young man was sorry for Henry St. George, as he was sorry at any time for any person publicly invited to be responsive and delightful. He would have been so touched to believe that a man he deeply admired should care a straw for him that he wouldn't play with such a presumption if it were possibly vain. In a single glance of the eye of the pardonable master he read—having the sort of divination that belonged to his talent—that this personage had ever a store of friendly patience, which was part of his rich outfit, but was versed in no printed page of a rising scribbler. There was even a relief, a simplification, in that: liking him so much already for what he had done, how could one have liked him any more for a perception which must at the best have been vague? Paul Overt got up, trying to show his compassion, but at the same instant he found himself encompassed by St. George's happy personal art—a manner of which it was the essence to conjure away false positions. It all took place in a moment. Paul was conscious that he knew him now, conscious of his handshake and of the very quality of his hand; of his face, seen nearer and consequently seen better, of a general fraternising assurance, and in particular of the circumstance that St. George didn't dislike him (as yet at least) for being imposed by a charming but too gushing girl, attractive enough without such danglers. No irritation at any rate was reflected in the voice with which he questioned Miss Fancourt as to some project of a walk—a general walk of the company round the park. He had soon said something to Paul about a talk— "We must have a tremendous lot of talk; there are so many things, aren't there?"—but our friend could see this idea wouldn't in the present case take very immediate effect. All the same he was extremely happy, even after the matter of the walk had been settled—the three presently passed back to the other part of the gallery, where it was discussed with several members of the party; even when, after they had all gone out together, he found himself for half an hour conjoined with Mrs. St. George. Her husband had taken the advance with Miss Fancourt, and this pair were quite out of sight. It was the prettiest of rambles for a summer afternoon—a grassy circuit, of immense extent, skirting the limit of the park within. The park was completely surrounded by its old mottled but perfect red wall, which, all the way on their left, constituted in itself an object of interest. Mrs. St. George mentioned to him the surprising number of acres thus enclosed, together with numerous other facts relating to the property and the family, and the family's other properties: she couldn't too strongly urge on him the importance of seeing their other houses. She ran over the names of these and rang the changes on them with the facility of practice, making them appear an almost endless list. She had received Paul Overt very amiably on his breaking ground with her by the mention of his joy in having just made her husband's acquaintance, and struck him as so alert and so accommodating a little woman that he was rather ashamed of his *mot* about her to Miss Fancourt; though he reflected that a hundred other people, on a hundred occasions, would have been sure to make it. He got on with Mrs. St. George, in short, better than he expected; but this didn't prevent her suddenly becoming aware that she was faint with fatigue and must take her way back to the house by the shortest cut. She professed that she hadn't the strength of a kitten and was a miserable wreck; a character he had been too preoccupied to discern in her while he wondered in what sense she could be held to have been the making of her husband. He had arrived at a glimmering of the answer when she announced that she must leave him, though this perception was of course provisional. While he was in the very act of placing himself at her disposal for the return, the situation underwent a change; Lord Masham had suddenly turned up, coming back to them, overtaking them, emerging from the shrubbery—Overt could scarcely have said how he appeared —and Mrs. St. George had protested that she wanted to be left alone and not to break up the party. A moment later she was walking off with Lord Masham. Our friend fell back and joined Lady Watermouth, to whom he presently mentioned that Mrs. St. George had been obliged to renounce the attempt to go further.

"She oughtn't to have come out at all," her ladyship rather grumpily remarked.

"Is she so very much of an invalid?"

"Very bad indeed." And his hostess added with still greater austerity: "She oughtn't really to come to one!" He wondered what was implied by this, and presently gathered that it was not a reflexion on the lady's conduct or her moral nature: it only represented that her strength was not equal to her aspirations.

3

The smoking-room at Summersoft was on the scale of the rest of the place—high light commodious and decorated with such refined old carvings and mouldings that it seemed rather a bower for ladies who should sit at work at fading crewels than a parliament of gentlemen smoking strong cigars. The gentlemen mustered there in considerable force on the Sunday evening, collecting mainly at one end, in front of one of the cool fair fireplaces of white marble, the entablature of which was adorned with a delicate little Italian "subject." There was another in the wall that faced it, and, thanks to the mild summer night, a fire in neither; but a nucleus for aggregation was furnished on one side by a table in the chimney-corner laden with bottles, decanters and tall tumblers. Paul Overt was a faithless smoker; he would puff a cigarette for reasons with which tobacco had nothing to do. This was particularly the case on the occasion of which I speak; his motive was the vision of a little direct talk with Henry St. George. The "tremendous" communion of which the great man had held out hopes to him earlier in the day had not yet come off, and this saddened him considerably, for the party was to go its several ways immediately after breakfast on the morrow. He had, however, the disappointment of finding that apparently the author of "Shadowmere" was not disposed to prolong his vigil. He wasn't among the gentlemen assembled when Paul entered, nor was he one of those who turned up, in bright habiliments, during the next ten minutes. The young man waited a little, wondering if he had only gone to put on something extraordinary; this would account for his delay as well as contribute further to Overt's impression of his tendency to do the approved superficial thing. But he didn't arrive—he must have been putting on something more extraordinary than was probable. Our hero gave him up, feeling a little injured, a little wounded, at this loss of twenty coveted words. He wasn't angry, but he puffed his cigarette sighingly, with the sense of something rare possibly missed. He wandered away with his regret and moved slowly round the room, looking at the old prints on the walls. In this attitude he presently felt a hand on his shoulder and a friendly voice in his ear: "This is good. I hoped I should find you. I came down on purpose." St. George was there without a change of dress and with a fine face—his graver one—to which our young man all in a flutter responded. He explained that it was only for the Master—the idea of a little talk—that he had sat up, and that, not finding him, he had been on the point of going to bed.

"Well, you know, I don't smoke—my wife doesn't let me," said St. George, looking for a place to sit down. "It's very good for me—very good for me. Let us take that sofa."

"Do you mean smoking's good for you?"

"No, no—her not letting me. It's a great thing to have a wife who's so sure of all the things one can do without. One might never find them out one's self. She doesn't allow me to touch a cigarette." They took possession of a sofa at a distance from the group of smokers, and St. George went on: "Have you got one yourself?"

"Do you mean a cigarette?"

"Dear no—a wife!"

"No; and yet I'd give up my cigarette for one."

"You'd give up a good deal more than that," St. George returned. "However, you'd get a great deal in return. There's a something to be said for wives," he added, folding his arms and crossing his outstretched legs. He declined tobacco altogether and sat there without returning fire. His companion stopped smoking, touched by his courtesy; and after all they were out of the fumes, their sofa was in a faraway corner. It would have been a mistake, St. George went on, a great mistake for them to have separated without a little chat; "for I know all about you," he said, "I know you're very remarkable. You've written a very distinguished book."

"And how do you know it?" Paul asked.

"Why, my dear fellow, it's in the air, it's in the papers, it's everywhere." St. George spoke with the immediate familiarity of a confrère—a tone that seemed to his neighbour the very rustle of the laurel. "You're on all men's lips and, what's better, on all women's. And I've just been reading your book."

"Just? You hadn't read it this afternoon," said Overt.

"How do you know that?"

"I think you should know how I know it," the young man laughed.

"I suppose Miss Fancourt told you."

"No indeed—she led me rather to suppose you had."

"Yes—that's much more what she'd do. Doesn't she shed a rosy glow over life? But you didn't believe her?" asked St. George.

"No, not when you came to us there."

"Did I pretend? did I pretend badly?" But without waiting for an answer to this St. George went on: "You ought always to believe such a girl as that—always, always. Some women are meant to be taken with allowances and reserves; but you must take *her* just as she is."

"I like her very much," said Paul Overt.

Something in his tone appeared to excite on his companion's part a momentary sense of the absurd; perhaps it was the air of deliberation attending this judgment. St. George broke into a laugh to reply. "It's the best thing you can do with her. She's a rare young lady! In point of fact, however, I confess I hadn't read you this afternoon."

"Then you see how right I was in this particular case not to believe Miss Fancourt."

"How right? how can I agree to that when I lost credit by it?"

"Do you wish to pass exactly for what she represents you? Certainly you needn't be afraid," Paul said.

"Ah, my dear young man, don't talk about passing—for the likes of me! I'm passing away—nothing else than that. She has a better use for her young imagination (isn't it fine?) than in 'representing' in any way such a weary wasted used-up animal!" The Master spoke with a sudden sadness that produced a protest on Paul's part; but before the protest could be uttered he went on, reverting to the latter's striking novel: "I had no idea you were so good—one hears of so many things. But you're surprisingly good."

"I'm going to be surprisingly better," Overt made bold to reply.

"I see that, and it's what fetches me. I don't see so much else—as one looks about—that's going to be surprisingly better. They're going to be consistently worse—most of the things. It's so much easier to be worse—heaven knows I've found it so. I'm not in a great glow, you know, about what's breaking out all over the place. But you *must* be better, you really must keep it up. I haven't, of course. It's very difficult— that's the devil of the whole thing, keeping it up. But I see you'll be able to. It will be a great disgrace if you don't."

"It's very interesting to hear you speak of yourself; but I don't know what you mean by your allusions to your having fallen off," Paul Overt observed with pardonable hypocrisy. He liked his companion so much now that the fact of any decline of talent or of care had ceased for the moment to be vivid to him.

"Don't say that—don't say that," St. George returned gravely, his head resting on the top of the sofa-back and his eyes on the ceiling. "You know perfectly what I mean. I haven't read twenty pages of your book without seeing that you can't help it."

"You make me very miserable," Paul ecstatically breathed.

"I'm glad of that, for it may serve as a kind of warning. Shocking enough it must be, especially to a young fresh mind, full of faith—the spectacle of a man meant for better things sunk at my age in such dishonour." St. George, in the same contemplative attitude, spoke softly but deliberately, and without perceptible emotion. His tone indeed suggested an impersonal lucidity that was practically cruel—cruel to himself— and made his young friend lay an argumentative hand on his arm. But he went on while his eyes seemed to follow the graces of the eighteenth-century ceiling: "Look at me well, take my lesson to heart—for it *is* a lesson. Let that good come of it at least that you shudder with your pitiful impression, and that this may help to keep you straight in the future. Don't become in your old age what I have in mine—the depressing, the deplorable illustration of the worship of false gods!"

"What do you mean by your old age?" the young man asked.

"It has made me old. But I like your youth."

Paul answered nothing—they sat for a minute in silence. They heard the others going on about the governmental majority. Then "What do you mean by false gods?" he inquired.

His companion had no difficulty whatever in saying, "The idols of the market; money and luxury and 'the world'; placing one's children and dressing one's wife; everything that drives one to the short and easy way. Ah, the vile things they make one do!"

"But surely one's right to want to place one's children."

"One has no business to have any children," St. George placidly declared. "I mean, of course, if one wants to do anything good."

"But aren't they an inspiration—an incentive?"

"An incentive to damnation, artistically speaking."

"You touch on very deep things—things I should like to discuss with you," Paul said. "I should like you to tell me volumes about yourself. This is a great feast for *me!*"

"Of course it is, cruel youth. But to show you I'm still not incapable, degraded as I am, of an act of faith, I'll tie my vanity to the stake for you and burn it to ashes. You must come and see me—you must come and see us," the Master quickly substituted. "Mrs. St. George is charming; I don't know whether you've had any opportunity to talk with her. She'll be delighted to see you; she likes great celebrities, whether incipient or predominant. You must come and dine—my wife will write to you. Where are you to be found?"

"This is my little address"—and Overt drew out his pocketbook and extracted a visiting-card. On second thoughts, however, he kept it back, remarking that he wouldn't trouble his friend to take charge of it but would come and see him straightway in London and leave it at his door if he should fail to obtain entrance.

"Ah, you'll probably fail; my wife's always out—or when she isn't out is knocked up from having *been* out. You must come and dine—though that won't do much good either, for my wife insists on big dinners." St. George turned it over further, but then went on: "You must come down and see us in the country, that's the best way; we've plenty of room and it isn't bad."

"You've a house in the country?" Paul asked enviously.

"Ah, not like this! But we have a sort of place we go to—an hour from Euston. That's one of the reasons."

"One of the reasons?"

"Why my books are so bad."

"You must tell me all the others!" Paul longingly laughed.

His friend made no direct rejoinder to this, but spoke again abruptly. "Why have I never seen you before?"

The tone of the question was singularly flattering to our hero, who felt it to imply the great man's now perceiving he had for years missed something. "Partly, I suppose, because there has been no particular reason why you should see me. I haven't lived in the world—in your world. I've spent many years out of England, in different places abroad."

"Well, please don't do it any more. You must do England—there's such a lot of it."

"Do you mean I must write about it?"—and Paul struck the note of the listening candour of a child.

"Of course you must. And tremendously well, do you mind? That takes off a little of my esteem for this thing of yours—that it goes on abroad. Hang 'abroad'! Stay at home and do things here—do subjects we can measure."

"I'll do whatever you tell me," Overt said, deeply attentive. "But pardon me if I say I don't understand how you've been reading my book," he added. "I've had you before me all the afternoon, first in that long walk, then at tea on the lawn, till we went to dress for dinner, and all the evening at dinner and in this place."

St. George turned his face about with a smile. "I gave it but a quarter of an hour."

"A quarter of an hour's immense, but I don't understand where you put it in. In the drawing-room after dinner you weren't reading—you were talking to Miss Fancourt."

"It comes to the same thing, because we talked about 'Ginistrella.' She described it to me—she lent me her copy."

"Lent it to you?"

"She travels with it."

"It's incredible," Paul blushed.

"It's glorious for you, but it also turned out very well for me. When the ladies went off to bed she kindly offered to send the book down to me. Her maid brought it to me in the hall, and I went to my room with it. I hadn't thought of coming here, I do that so little. But I don't sleep early, I always have to read an hour or two. I sat down to your novel on the spot, without undressing, without taking off anything but my coat. I think that's a sign my curiosity had been strongly aroused about it. I read a quarter of an hour, as I tell you, and even in a quarter of an hour I was greatly struck."

"Ah, the beginning isn't very good—it's the whole thing!" said Overt, who had listened to this recital with extreme interest. "And you laid down the book and came after me?" he asked.

"That's the way it moved me. I said to myself, 'I see it's off his own bat, and he's there, by the way, and the day's over, and I haven't said twenty words to him.' It occurred to me that you'd probably be in the smoking-room and that it wouldn't be too late to repair my omission. I wanted to do something civil to you, so I put on my coat and came down. I shall read your book again when I go up."

Our friend faced round in his place—he was touched as he had scarce ever been by the picture of such a demonstration in his favour. "You're really the kindest of men. *Cela s'est passé comme ça?*—and I've been sitting here with you all this time and never apprehended it and never thanked you!"

"Thank Miss Fancourt—it was she who wound me up. She has made me feel as if I had read your novel."

"She's an angel from heaven!" Paul declared.

"She is indeed. I've never seen anyone like her. Her interest in literature's touching—something quite peculiar to herself; she takes it all so seriously. She feels the arts and she wants to feel them more. To those who practise them it's almost humiliating—her curiosity, her sympathy, her good faith. How can anything be as fine as she supposes it?"

"She's a rare organisation," the younger man sighed.

"The richest I've ever seen—an artistic intelligence really of the first order. And lodged in such a form!" St. George exclaimed.

"One would like to represent such a girl as that," Paul continued.

"Ah, there it is—there's nothing like life!" said his companion. "When you're finished, squeezed dry and used up and you think the sack's empty, you're still appealed to, you still get touches and thrills, the idea springs up—out of the lap of the actual—and shows you there's always something to be done. But I shan't do it—she's not for me!"

"How do you mean, not for you?"

"Oh, it's all over—she's for you, if you like."

"Ah, much less!" said Paul. "She's not for a dingy little man of letters; she's for the world, the bright rich world of bribes and rewards. And the world will take hold of her—it will carry her away."

"It will try—but it's just a case in which there may be a fight. It would be worth fighting, for a man who had it in him, with youth and talent on his side."

These words rang not a little in Paul Overt's consciousness—they held him briefly silent. "It's a wonder she has remained as she is; giving herself away so—with so much to give away."

"Remaining, you mean, so ingenuous—so natural? Oh, she doesn't care a straw—she gives away because she overflows. She has her own feelings, her own standards; she doesn't keep remembering that she must be proud. And then she hasn't been here long enough to be spoiled; she has picked up a fashion or two, but only the amusing ones. She's a provincial—a provincial genius," St. George went on; "her very blunders are charming, her mistakes are interesting. She has come back from Asia with all sorts of excited curiosities and unappeased appetites. She's first-rate herself and she expends herself on the second-rate. She's life herself and she takes a rare interest in imitations. She mixes all things up, but there are none in regard to which she hasn't perceptions. She sees things in a perspective—as if from the top of the Himalayas—and she enlarges everything she touches. Above all she exaggerates—to herself, I mean. She exaggerates you and me!"

There was nothing in that description to allay the agitation caused in our younger friend by such a sketch of a fine subject. It seemed to him to show the art of St. George's admired hand, and he lost himself in gazing at the vision—this hovered there before him—of a woman's figure which should be part of the glory of a novel. But at the end of a moment the thing had turned into smoke, and out of the smoke—the last puff of a big cigar—proceeded the voice of General Fancourt, who had left the others and come and planted himself before the gentlemen on the sofa. "I suppose that when you fellows get talking you sit up half the night."

"Half the night?—*jamais de la vie!* I follow a hygiene"—and St. George rose to his feet.

"I see—you're hothouse plants," laughed the General. "That's the way you produce your flowers."

"I produce mine between ten and one every morning—I bloom with a regularity!" St. George went on.

"And with a splendour!" added the polite General, while Paul noted how little the author of "Shadowmere" minded, as he phrased it to himself, when addressed as a celebrated story-teller. The young man had an idea *he* should never get used to that; it would always make him uncomfortable—from the suspicion that people would think they had to—and he would want to prevent it. Evidently his great colleague had toughened and hardened—had made himself a surface. The group of men had finished their cigars and taken up their bedroom candle-sticks; but before they all passed out Lord Watermouth invited the pair of guests who had been so absorbed together to "have" something. It happened that they both declined; upon which General Fancourt said: "Is that the hygiene? You don't water the flowers?"

"Oh, I should drown them!" St. George replied; but, leaving the room still at his young friend's side, he added whimsically, for the latter's benefit, in a lower tone: "My wife doesn't let me."

"Well, I'm glad I'm not one of you fellows!" the General richly concluded.

The nearness of Summersoft to London had this consequence, chilling to a person who had had a vision of sociability in a railway carriage, that most of the company, after break-fast, drove back to town, entering their own vehicles, which had come out to fetch them, while their servants returned by train with their luggage. Three or four young men, among whom was Paul Overt, also availed themselves of the common convenience; but they stood in the portico of the house and saw the others roll away. Miss Fancourt got into a victoria with her father after she had shaken hands with our hero and said, smiling in the frankest way in the world, "I *must* see you more. Mrs. St. George is so nice; she has promised to ask us both to dinner together." This lady and her husband took their places in a perfectly appointed brougham—she required a closed carriage—and as our young man waved his hat to them in response to their nods and flourishes he reflected that, taken together, they were an honourable image of success, of the material rewards and the social credit of literature. Such things were not the full measure, but he nevertheless felt a little proud for literature.

4

Before a week had elapsed he met Miss Fancourt in Bond Street, at a private view of the works of a young artist in "black-and-white" who had been so good as to invite him to the stuffy scene. The drawings were admirable, but the crowd in the one little room was so dense that he felt himself up to his neck in a sack of wool. A fringe of people at the outer edge endeavoured by curving forward their backs and presenting, below them, a still more convex surface of resistance to the pressure of the mass, to preserve an interval between their noses and the glazed mounts of the pictures; while the central body, in the comparative gloom projected by a wide horizontal screen hung under the skylight and allowing only a margin for the day, remained upright, dense, and vague, lost in the contemplation of its own ingredients. This contemplation sat especially in the sad eyes of certain female heads, surmounted with hats of strange convolution and plumage, which rose on long necks above the others. One of the heads, Paul perceived, was much the most beautiful of the collection, and his next discovery was that it belonged to Miss Fancourt. Its beauty was enhanced by the glad smile she sent him across surrounding obstructions, a smile that drew him to her as fast as he could make his way. He had seen for himself at Summersoft that the last thing her nature contained was an affectation of indifference; yet even with this circumspection he took a fresh satisfaction in her not having pretended to await his arrival with composure. She smiled as radiantly as if she wished to make him hurry, and as soon as he came within earshot she broke out in her voice of joy: "He's here—he's here; he's coming back in a moment!"

"Ah, your father?" Paul returned as she offered him her hand.

"Oh, dear no, this isn't in my poor father's line. I mean Mr. St. George. He has just left me to speak to someone—he's coming back. It's he who brought me—wasn't it charming?"

"Ah that gives him a pull over me—I couldn't have 'brought' you, could I?"

"If you had been so kind as to propose it—why not you as well as he?" the girl returned with a face that, expressing no cheap coquetry, simply affirmed a happy fact.

"Why he's a *père de famille*. They've privileges," Paul explained. And then quickly: "Will you go to see places with *me?*" he asked.

"Anything you like," she smiled. "I know what you mean, that girls have to have a lot of people—!" Then she broke off: "I don't know; I'm free. I've always been like that—I can go about with anyone. I'm so glad to meet you," she added with a sweet distinctness that made those near her turn around.

"Let me at least repay that speech by taking you out of this squash," her friend said. "Surely people aren't happy here!"

"No, they're awfully *mornes,* aren't they? But I'm very happy indeed and I promised Mr. St. George to remain on this spot till he comes back. He's going to take me away. They send him invitations for things of this sort—more than he wants. It was so kind of him to think of me."

"They also send me invitations of this kind—more than *I* want. And if thinking of *you* will do it—!" Paul went on.

"Oh, I delight in them—everything that's life, everything that's London!"

"They don't have private views in Asia, I suppose," he laughed. "But what a pity that for this year, even in this gorged city, they're pretty well over."

"Well, next year will do, for I hope you believe we're going to be friends always. Here he comes!" Miss Fancourt continued before Paul had time to respond.

He made out St. George in the gaps of the crowd, and this perhaps led to his hurrying a little to say: "I hope that doesn't mean I'm to wait till next year to see you."

"No, no—aren't we to meet at dinner on the twenty-fifth?" she panted with an eagerness as happy as his own.

"That's almost next year. Is there no means of seeing you before?"

She stared with all her brightness. "Do you mean you'd *come?*"

"Like a shot, if you'll be so good as to ask me!"

"On Sunday then—this next Sunday?"

"What have I done that you should doubt it?" the young man asked with delight.

Miss Fancourt turned instantly to St. George, who had now joined them, and announced triumphantly: "He's coming on Sunday—this next Sunday!"

"Ah, my day—my day too!" said the famous novelist, laughing, to their companion.

"Yes, but not yours only. You shall meet in Manchester Square; you shall talk—you shall be wonderful!"

"We don't meet often enough," St. George allowed, shaking hands with his disciple. "Too many things—ah, too many things! But we must make it up in the country in September. You won't forget you've promised me that?"

"Why, he's coming on the twenty-fifth—you'll see him then," said the girl.

"On the twenty-fifth?" St. George asked vaguely.

"We dine with you; I hope you haven't forgotten. He's dining out that day," she added gaily to Paul.

"Oh, bless me, yes—that's charming! And you're coming? My wife didn't tell me," St. George said to him. "Too many things—too many things!" he repeated.

"Too many people—too many people!" Paul exclaimed, giving ground before the penetration of an elbow.

"You oughtn't to say that. They all read you."

"Me? I should like to see them! Only two or three at most," the young man returned.

"Did you ever hear anything like that? He knows, haughtily, how good he is!" St. George declared, laughing, to Miss Fancourt. "They read *me*, but that doesn't make me like them any better. Come away from them, come away!" And he led the way out of the exhibition.

"He's going to take me to the Park," Miss Fancourt observed to Overt with elation as they passed along the corridor that led to the street.

"Ah, does he go there?" Paul asked, taking the fact for a somewhat unexpected illustration of St. George's *moeurs*.

"It's a beautiful day—there'll be a great crowd. We're going to look at the people, to look at types," the girl went on. "We shall sit under the trees; we shall walk by the Row."

"I go once a year—on business," said St. George, who had overheard Paul's question.

"Or with a country cousin, didn't you tell me? I'm the country cousin!" she continued over her shoulder to Paul as their friend drew her toward a hansom to which he had signalled. The young man watched them get in; he returned, as he stood there, the friendly wave of the hand with which, ensconced in the vehicle beside her, St. George took leave of him. He even lingered to see the vehicle start away and lose itself in the confusion of Bond Street. He followed it with his eyes; it put to him embarrassing things. "She's not for *me*!" the great novelist had said emphatically at Summersoft; but his manner of conducting himself toward her appeared not quite in harmony with such a conviction. How could he have behaved differently if she *had* been for him? An indefinite envy rose in Paul Overt's heart as he took his way on foot alone; a feeling addressed alike, strangely enough, to each of the occupants of the hansom. How much he should like to rattle about London with such a girl! How much he should like to go and look at "types" with St. George!

The next Sunday at four o'clock he called in Manchester Square, where his secret wish was gratified by his finding Miss Fancourt alone. She was in a large bright friendly occupied room, which was painted red all over, draped with the quaint cheap florid stuffs that are represented as coming from southern and eastern countries, where they are fabled to serve as the counterpanes of the peasantry, and bedecked with pottery of vivid hues, ranged on casual shelves, and with many water-colour drawings from the hand (as the visitor

344

learned) of the young lady herself, commemorating with a brave breadth the sunsets, the mountains, the temples and palaces of India. He sat an hour—more than an hour, two hours—and all the while no one came in. His hostess was so good as to remark, with her liberal humanity, that it was delightful they weren't interrupted: it was so rare in London, especially at that season, that people got a good talk. But luckily now, of a fine Sunday, half the world went out of town, and that made it better for those who didn't go, when these others were in sympathy. It was the defect of London —one of two or three, the very short list of those she recognised in the teeming world city she adored—that there were too few good chances for talk: you never had time to carry anything far.

"Too many things, too many things!" Paul said, quoting St. George's exclamation of a few days before.

"Ah, yes, for him there are too many—his life's too complicated."

"Have you seen it *near?* That's what I should like to do; it might explain some mysteries," the visitor went on. She asked him what mysteries he meant, and he said: "Oh, peculiarities of his work, inequalities, superficialities. For one who looks at it from the artistic point of view it contains a bottomless ambiguity."

She became at this, on the spot, all intensity. "Ah, do describe that more—it's so interesting. There are no such suggestive questions. I'm so fond of them. He thinks he's a failure —fancy!" she beautifully wailed.

"That depends on what his ideal may have been. With his gifts it ought to have been high. But till one knows what he really proposed to himself—! Do *you* know by chance?" the young man broke off.

"Oh, he doesn't talk to me about himself. I can't make him. It's too provoking."

Paul was on the point of asking what, then, he did talk about, but discretion checked it and he said instead: "Do you think he's unhappy at home?"

She seemed to wonder. "At home?"

"I mean in his relations with his wife. He has a mystifying little way of alluding to her."

"Not to me," said Marian Fancourt with her clear eyes. "That wouldn't be right, would it?" she asked gravely.

"Not particularly so; I'm glad he doesn't mention her to you. To praise her might bore you, and he has no business to do anything else. Yet he knows you better than me."

"Ah, but he respects *you!*" the girl cried as with envy.

Her visitor stared a moment, then broke into a laugh. "Doesn't he respect you?"

"Of course, but not in the same way. He respects what you've done—he told me so the other day."

Paul drank it in, but retained his faculties. "When you went to look at types?"

"Yes—we found so many: he has such an observation of them! He talked a great deal about your book. He says it's really important."

"Important! Ah the grand creature!"—and the author of the work in question groaned for joy.

"He was wonderfully amusing, he was inexpressibly droll, while we walked about. He sees everything; he has so many comparisons and images, and they're always exactly right. *C'est d'un trouvé,* as they say!"

"Yes, with his gifts, such things as he ought to have done!" Paul sighed.

"And don't you think he *has* done them?"

Ah, it was just the point. "A part of them, and of course even that part's immense. But he might have been one of the greatest. However, let us not make this an hour of qualifications. Even as they stand," our friend earnestly concluded, "his writings are a mine of gold."

To this proposition she ardently responded, and for half an hour the pair talked over the Master's principal productions. She knew them well—she knew them even better than her visitor, who was struck with her critical intelligence and with something large and bold in the movement in her mind. She said things that startled him and that evidently had come to her directly; they weren't picked-up phrases—she placed them too well. St. George had been right about her being first-rate, about her not being afraid to gush, not remembering that she must be proud. Suddenly something came back to her, and she said: "I recollect that he did speak of

Mrs. St. George to me once. He said, apropos of something or other, that she didn't care for perfection."

"That's a great crime in an artist's wife," Paul returned.

"Yes, poor thing!" and the girl sighed with a suggestion of many reflexions, some of them mitigating. But she presently added: "Ah perfection, perfection—how one ought to go in for it! I wish *I* could."

"Every one can in his way," her companion opined.

"In *his* way, yes—but not in hers. Women are so hampered —so condemned! Yet it's a kind of dishonour if you don't, when you want to *do* something, isn't it?" Miss Fancourt pursued, dropping one train in her quickness to take up another, an accident that was common with her. So these two young persons sat discussing high themes in their eclectic drawing-room, in their London "season"—discussing, with extreme seriousness, the high theme of perfection. It must be said in extenuation of this eccentricity that they were interested in the business. Their tone had truth and their emotion beauty; they weren't posturing for each other or for someone else.

The subject was so wide that they found themselves reducing it; the perfection to which for the moment they agreed to confine their speculations was that of the valid, the exemplary work of art. Our young woman's imagination, it appeared, had wandered far in that direction, and her guest had the rare delight of feeling in their conversation a full interchange. This episode will have lived for years in his memory and even in his wonder; it had the quality that fortune distils in a single drop at a time—the quality that lubricates many ensuing frictions. He still, whenever he likes, has a vision of the room, the bright red sociable talkative room with the curtains that, by a stroke of successful audacity, had the note of vivid blue. He remembers where certain things stood, the particular book open on the table and the almost intense odour of the flowers placed, at the left, somewhere behind him. These facts were the fringe, as it were, of a fine special agitation which had its birth in those two hours and of which perhaps the main sign was in its leading him inwardly and repeatedly to breathe, "I had no idea there was any one like this—I had no idea there was any one like this!" Her freedom amazed him and charmed him—it seemed so to simplify the practical question. She was on the footing of an independent personage—a motherless girl who had passed out of her teens and had a position and responsibilities, who wasn't held down to the limitations of a little miss. She came and went with no dragged duenna, she received people alone, and, though she was totally without hardness, the question of protection or patronage had no relevancy in regard to her. She gave such an impression of the clear and the noble combined with the easy and the natural that in spite of her eminent modern situation she suggested no sort of sisterhood with the "fast" girl. Modern she was indeed, and made Paul Overt, who loved old colour, the golden glaze of time, think with some alarm of the muddled palette of the future. He couldn't get used to her interest in the arts he cared for; it seemed too good to be real—it was so unlikely an adventure to tumble into such a well of sympathy. One might stray into the desert easily—that was on the cards and that was the law of life; but it was too rare an accident to stumble on a crystal well. Yet if her aspirations seemed at one moment too extravagant to be real they struck him at the next as too intelligent to be false. They were both high and lame, and, whims for whims, he preferred them to any he had met in a like relation. It was probable enough she would leave them behind—exchange them for politics or "smartness" or mere prolific maternity, as was the custom of scribbling daubing educated flattered girls in an age of luxury and a society of leisure. He noted that the watercolours on the walls of the room she sat in had mainly the quality of being naïves, and reflected that naïveté in art is like a zero in a number: its importance depends on the figure it is united with. Meanwhile, however, he had fallen in love with her. Before he went away, at any rate, he said to her: "I thought St. George was coming to see you today, but he doesn't turn up."

For a moment he supposed she was going to cry *"Comment donc?* Did you come here only to meet him?" But the next he became aware of how little such a speech would have fallen in with any note of flirtation he had as yet perceived in her. She only replied: "Ah, yes, but I don't think he'll come. He recommended me not to expect him." Then she gaily but all gently added: "He said it wasn't fair to you. But I think I could manage two."

"So could I," Paul Overt returned, stretching the point a little to meet her. In reality his appreciation of the occasion was so completely an appreciation of the woman before him that another figure in the scene, even so esteemed a one as St. George, might for the hour have appealed to him vainly. He left the house wondering what the great man had meant by its not being fair to him; and, still more than that, whether he had actually stayed away from the force of that idea. As he took his course through the Sunday solitude of Manchester Square, swinging his stick and with a good deal of emotion fermenting in his soul, it appeared to him he was living in a world strangely magnanimous. Miss Fancourt had told him it was possible she should be away, and that her father should be, on the following Sunday, but that she had the hope of a visit from him in the other event. She promised to let him know should their absence fail, and then he might act accordingly. After he had passed into one of the streets that open from the Square he stopped, without definite intentions, looking sceptically for a cab. In a moment he saw a hansom roll through the place from the other side and come a part of the way toward him. He was on the point of hailing the driver when he noticed a "fare" within; then he waited, seeing the man prepare to deposit his passenger by pulling up at one of the houses. The house was apparently the one he himself had just quitted; at least he drew that inference as he recognised Henry St. George in the person who stepped out of the hansom. Paul turned off as quickly as if he had been caught in the act of spying. He gave up his cab—he preferred to walk; he would go nowhere else. He was glad St. George hadn't renounced his visit altogether—that would have been too absurd. Yes, the world was magnanimous, and even he himself felt so as, on looking at his watch, he noted but six o'clock, so that he could mentally congratulate his successor on having an hour still to sit in Miss Fancourt's drawing-room. He himself might use that hour for another visit, but by the time he reached the Marble Arch the idea of such a course had become incongruous to him. He passed beneath that architectural effort and walked into the Park till he had got upon the spreading grass. Here he continued to walk; he took his way across the elastic turf and came out by the Serpentine. He watched with a friendly eye the diversions of the London people, he bent a glance almost encouraging on the young ladies paddling their sweethearts about the lake and the guardsmen tickling tenderly with their bearskins the artificial flowers in the Sunday hats of their partners. He prolonged his meditative walk; he went into Kensington Gardens, he sat upon the penny chairs, he looked at the little sail-boats launched upon the round pond and was glad he had no engagement to dine. He repaired for this purpose, very late, to his club, where he found himself unable to order a repast and told the waiter to bring whatever there was. He didn't even observe what he was served with, and he spent the evening in the library of the establishment, pretending to read an article in an American magazine. He failed to discover what it was about; it appeared in a dim way to be about Marian Fancourt.

Quite late in the week she wrote to him that she was not to go into the country—it had only just been settled. Her father, she added, would never settle anything, but put it all on her. She felt her responsibility—she had to—and since she was forced this was the way she had decided. She mentioned no reasons, which gave our friend all the clearer field for bold conjecture about them. In Manchester Square on this second Sunday he esteemed his fortune less good, for she had three or four other visitors. But there were three or four compensations; perhaps the greatest of which was that, learning how her father had after all, at the last hour, gone out of town alone, the bold conjecture I just now spoke of found itself becoming a shade more bold. And then her presence was her presence, and the personal red room was there and was full of it, whatever phantoms passed and vanished, emitting incomprehensible sounds. Lastly, he had the resource of staying till every one had come and gone and of believing this grateful to her, though she gave no particular sign. When they were alone together he came to his point. "But St. George did come—last Sunday. I saw him as I looked back."

"Yes, but it was the last time."

"The last time?"

"He said he would never come again."

Paul Overt stared. "Does he mean he wishes to cease to see you?"

"I don't know what he means," the girl bravely smiled. "He won't at any rate see me here."

"And pray why not?"

"I haven't the least idea," said Marian Fancourt, whose visitor found her more perversely sublime than ever yet as she professed this clear helplessness.

5

"Oh, I say, I want you to stop a little," Henry St. George said to him at eleven o'clock the night he dined with the head of the profession. The company—none of it indeed *of* the profession—had been numerous and was taking its leave; our young man, after bidding good-night to his hostess, had put out his hand in farewell to the master of the house. Besides drawing from the latter the protest I have cited, this movement provoked a further priceless word about their chance now to have a talk, their going into his room, his having still everything to say. Paul Overt was all delight at this kindness; nevertheless he mentioned in weak jocose qualification the bare fact that he had promised to go to another place which was at a considerable distance.

"Well, then, you'll break your promise, that's all. You quite awful humbug!" St. George added in a tone that confirmed our young man's ease.

"Certainly I'll break it—but it was a real promise."

"Do you mean to Miss Fancourt? You're following her?" his friend asked.

He answered by a question. "Oh, is *she* going?"

"Base impostor!" his ironic host went on. "I've treated you handsomely on the article of that young lady: I won't make another concession. Wait three minutes—I'll be with you." He gave himself to his departing guests, accompanied the long-trained ladies to the door. It was a hot night, the windows were open, the sound of the quick carriages and of the linkmen's call came into the house. The affair had rather glittered; a sense of festal things was in the heavy air: not only the influence of that particular entertainment, but the suggestion of the wide hurry of pleasure which in London on summer nights fills so many of the happier quarters of the complicated town. Gradually Mrs. St. George's drawing-room emptied itself; Paul was left alone with his hostess, to whom he explained the motive of his waiting. "Ah, yes, some intellectual, some *professional*, talk," she leered; "at this season doesn't one miss it? Poor dear Henry, I'm so glad!" The young man looked out of the window a moment, at the called hansoms that lurched up, at the smooth broughams that rolled away. When he turned round Mrs. St. George had disappeared; her husband's voice rose to him from below—he was laughing and talking, in the portico, with some lady who awaited her carriage. Paul had solitary possession, for some minutes, of the warm deserted rooms where the covered tinted lamplight was soft, the seats had been pushed about, and the odour of flowers lingered. They were large, they were pretty, they contained objects of value; everything in the picture told of a "good house." At the end of five minutes a servant came in with a request from the Master that he would join him downstairs; upon which, descending, he followed his conductor through a long passage to an apartment thrown out, in the rear of the habitation, for the special requirements, as he guessed, of a busy man of letters.

St. George was in his shirt-sleeves in the middle of a large high room—a room without windows, but with a wide skylight at the top, that of a place of exhibition. It was furnished as a library, and the serried bookshelves rose to the ceiling, a surface of incomparable tone produced by dimly gilt "backs" interrupted here and there by the suspension of old prints and drawings. At the end furthest from the door of admission was a tall desk, of great extent, at which the person using it could write only in the erect posture of a clerk in a counting-house; and stretched from the entrance to this structure was a wide plain band of crimson cloth, as straight as a garden path and almost as long, where, in his mind's eye, Paul at once beheld the Master pace to and fro during vexed hours—hours, that is, of admirable composition. The servant gave him a coat, an old jacket with a hang of experience, from a cupboard in the wall, retiring afterwards with the garment he had taken off. Paul Overt welcomed the coat; it was a coat for talk, it promised confidences—having visibly received so many—and had tragic literary elbows. "Ah, we're practical—we're practical!" St. George said as he saw his visitor look the place over. "Isn't it a good big cage for going round and round? My wife invented it and she locks me up here every morning."

Our young man breathed—by way of tribute—with a certain oppression. "You don't miss a window—a place to look out?"

"I did at first awfully; but her calculation was just. It saves time, it has saved me many months in these ten years. Here I stand, under the eye of day—in London of course, very often, it's rather a bleared old eye—walled in to my trade. I can't get away—so the room's a fine lesson in concentration. I've learnt the lesson, I think; look at that big bundle of proof and acknowledge it." He pointed to a fat roll of papers, on one of the tables, which had not been undone.

"Are you bringing out another—?" Paul asked in a tone the fond deficiencies of which he didn't recognise till his companion burst out laughing, and indeed scarce even then.

"You humbug, you humbug!"—St. George appeared to enjoy caressing him, as it were, with that opprobrium. "Don't I know what you think of them?" he asked, standing there with his hands in his pockets and with a new kind of smile. It was as if he were going to let his young votary see him all now.

"Upon my word in that case you know more than I do!" the latter ventured to respond, revealing a part of the torment of being able neither clearly to esteem nor distinctly to renounce him.

"My dear fellow," said the more and more interesting Master, "don't imagine I talk about my books specifically; they're not a decent subject—*il ne manquerait plus que ça!* I'm not so bad as you may apprehend. About myself, yes, a little, if you like; though it wasn't for that I brought you down here. I want to ask you something—very much indeed; I value this chance. Therefore sit down. We're practical, but there *is* a sofa, you see—for she does humour my poor bones so far. Like all really great administrators and disciplinarians she knows when wisely to relax." Paul sank into the corner of a deep leathern couch, but his friend remained standing and explanatory. "If you don't mind, in this room, this is my habit. From the door to the desk and from the desk to the door. That shakes up my imagination gently; and don't you see what a good thing it is that there's no window for her to fly out of? The eternal standing as I write (I stop at that bureau and put it down, when anything comes, and so we go on) was rather wearisome at first, but we adopted it with an eye to the long run: you're in better order—if your legs don't break down!—and you can keep it up for more years. Oh, we're practical—we're practical!" St. George repeated, going to the table and taking up all mechanically the bundle of proofs. But, pulling off the wrapper, he had a change of attention that appealed afresh to our hero. He lost himself a moment, examining the sheets of his new book, while the younger man's eyes wandered over the room again.

"Lord, what good things I should do if I had such a charming place as this to do them in!" Paul reflected. The outer world, the world of accident and ugliness, was so successfully excluded, and within the rich protecting square, beneath the patronising sky, the dream-figures, the summoned company, could hold their particular revel. It was a fond prevision of Overt's rather than an observation on actual data, for which occasions had been too few, that the Master thus more closely viewed would have the quality, the charming gift, of flashing out, all surprisingly, in personal intercourse and at moments of suspended or perhaps even of diminished expectation. A happy relation with him would be a thing proceeding by jumps, not by traceable stages.

"Do you read them—really?" he asked, laying down the proofs on Paul's inquiring of him how soon the work would be published. And when the young man answered, "Oh, yes, always," he was moved to mirth again by something he caught in his manner of saying that. "You go to see your grandmother on her birthday—and very proper it is, especially as she won't last for ever. She has lost every faculty and every sense; she neither sees, nor hears, nor speaks; but all customary pieties and kindly habits are respectable. Only you're strong if you *do* read 'em! *I* couldn't, my dear fellow.

You *are* strong, I know; and that's just a part of what I wanted to say to you. You're very strong indeed. I've been going into your other things—they've interested me immensely. Some one ought to have told me about them before—some one I could believe. But whom can one believe? You're wonderfully on the right road—it's awfully decent work. Now do you mean to keep it up?—that's what I want to ask you."

"Do I mean to do others?" Paul asked, looking up from his sofa at his erect inquisitor and feeling partly like a happy little boy when the schoolmaster is gay, and partly like some pilgrim of old who might have consulted a world-famous oracle. St. George's own performance had been infirm, but as an adviser he would be infallible.

"Others—others? Ah, the number won't matter; one other would do, if it were really a further step—a throb of the same effort. What I mean is, have you it in your heart to go in for some sort of decent perfection?"

"Ah, decency, ah, perfection—!" the young man sincerely sighed. "I talked of them the other Sunday with Miss Fancourt."

It produced on the Master's part a laugh of odd acrimony. "Yes, they'll 'talk' of them as much as you like! But they'll do little to help one to them. There's no obligation of course; only you strike me as capable," he went on. "You must have thought it all over. I can't believe you're without a plan. That's the sensation you give me, and it's so rare that it really stirs one up—it makes you remarkable. If you haven't a plan, if you *don't* mean to keep it up, surely you're within your rights; it's nobody's business, no one can force you, and not more than two or three people will notice you don't go straight. The others—*all* the rest, every blest soul in England, will think you do—will think you *are* keeping it up: upon my honour they will! I shall be one of the two or three who know better. Now the question is whether you can do it for two or three. Is that the stuff you're made of?"

It locked his guest a minute as in closed throbbing arms. "I could do it for one, if you were the one."

"Don't say that; I don't deserve it; it scorches me," he protested with eyes suddenly grave and glowing. "The 'one' is of course one's self, one's conscience, one's idea, the singleness of one's aim. I think of that pure spirit as a man thinks of a woman he has in some detested hour of his youth loved and forsaken. She haunts him with reproachful eyes, she lives for ever before him. As an artist, you know, I've married for money." Paul stared and even blushed a little, confounded by this avowal; whereupon his host, observing the expression of his face, dropped a quick laugh and pursued: "You don't follow my figure. I'm not speaking of my dear wife, who had a small fortune—which, however, was not my bribe. I fell in love with her, as many other people have done. I refer to the mercenary muse whom I led to the altar of literature. Don't, my boy, put your nose into *that* yoke. The awful jade will lead you a life!"

Our hero watched him, wondering and deeply touched. "Haven't you been happy!"

"Happy? It's a kind of hell."

"There are things I should like to ask you," Paul said after a pause.

"Ask me anything in all the world. I'd turn myself inside out to save you."

"To 'save' me?" he quavered.

"To make you stick to it—to make you see it through. As I said to you the other night at Summersoft, let my example be vivid to you."

"Why, your books are not so bad as that," said Paul, fairly laughing and feeling that if ever a fellow had breathed the air of art—!

"So bad as what?"

"Your talent's so great that it's in everything you do, in what's less good as well as in what's best. You've some forty volumes to show for it—forty volumes of wonderful life, of rare observation, of magnificent ability."

"I'm very clever, of course I know that"—but it was a thing, in fine, this author made nothing of. "Lord, what rot they'd all be if I hadn't been! I'm a successful charlatan," he went on—"I've been able to pass off my system. But do you know what it is? It's *carton-pierre*."

"*Carton-pierre?*" Paul was struck, and gaped.

"Lincrusta-Walton!"

"Ah, don't say such things—you make me bleed!" the

younger man protested. "I see you in a beautiful fortunate home, living in comfort and honour."

"Do you call it honour?"—his host took him up with an intonation that often comes back to him. "That's what I want *you* to go in for. I mean the real thing. This is brummagem."

"Brummagem?" Paul ejaculated while his eyes wandered, by a movement natural at the moment, over the luxurious room.

"Ah, they make it so well today—it's wonderfully deceptive!"

Our friend thrilled with the interest and perhaps even more with the pity of it. Yet he wasn't afraid to seem to patronise when he could still so far envy. "Is it deceptive that I find you living with every appearance of domestic felicity—blest with a devoted, accomplished wife, with children whose acquaintance I haven't yet had the pleasure of making, but who *must* be delightful young people, from what I know of their parents?"

St. George smiled as for the candour of his question. "It's all excellent, my dear fellow—heaven forbid I should deny it. I've made a great deal of money; my wife has known how to take care of it, to use it without wasting it, to put a good bit of it by, to make it fructify. I've got a loaf on the shelf; I've got everything in fact but the great thing."

"The great thing?" Paul kept echoing.

"The sense of having done the best—the sense which is the real life of the artist and the absence of which is his death, of having drawn from his intellectual instrument the finest music that nature had hidden in it, of having played it as it should be played. He either does that or he doesn't—and if he doesn't he isn't worth speaking of. Therefore, precisely, those who really know *don't* speak of him. He may still hear a great chatter, but what he hears most is the incorruptible silence of Fame. I've squared her, you may say, for my little hour—but what's my little hour? Don't imagine for a moment," the Master pursued, "that I'm such a cad as to have brought you down here to abuse or to complain of my wife to you. She's a woman of distinguished qualities, to whom my obligations are immense; so that, if you please, we'll say nothing about her. My boys—my children are all boys—are straight and strong, thank God, and have no poverty of growth about them, no penury of needs. I receive periodically the most satisfactory attestation from Harrow, from Oxford, from Sandhurst—oh, we've done the best for them!—of their eminence as living thriving consuming organisms."

"It must be delightful to feel that the son of one's loins is at Sandhurst," Paul remarked enthusiastically.

"It is—it's charming. Oh, I'm a patriot!"

The young man then could but have the greater tribute of questions to pay. "Then what did you mean—the other night at Summersoft—by saying that children are a curse?"

"My dear youth, on what basis are we talking?" and St. George dropped upon the sofa at a short distance from him. Sitting a little sideways he leaned back against the opposite arm with his hands raised and interlocked behind his head. "On the supposition that a certain perfection's possible and even desirable—isn't it so? Well, all I say is that one's children interfere with perfection. One's wife interferes. Marriage interferes."

"You think, then, the artist shouldn't marry?"

"He does so at his peril—he does so at his cost."

"Not even when his wife's in sympathy with his work?"

"She never is—she can't be! Women haven't a conception of such things."

"Surely they on occasion work themselves," Paul objected.

"Yes, very badly indeed. Oh, of course, often, they think they understand, they think they sympathise. Then it is they're most dangerous. Their idea is that you shall do a great lot and get a great lot of money. Their great nobleness and virtue, their exemplary conscientiousness as British females, is in keeping you up to that. My wife makes all my bargains with my publishers for me, and has done so for twenty years. She does it consummately well—that's why I'm really pretty well off. Aren't you the father of their innocent babes, and will you withhold from them their natural sustenance? You asked me the other night if they're not an immense incentive. Of course they are—there's no doubt of that!"

Paul turned it over: it took, from eyes he had never felt

open so wide, so much looking at. "For myself I've an idea I need incentives."

"Ah, well, then, *n'en parlons plus!*" his companion handsomely smiled.

"*You* are an incentive, I maintain," the young man went on. "You don't affect me in the way you'd apparently like to. Your great success is what I see—the pomp of Ennismore Gardens!"

"Success?"—St. George's eyes had a cold fine light. "Do you call it success to be spoken of as you'd speak of me if you were sitting here with another artist—a young man intelligent and sincere like yourself? Do you call it success to make you blush—as you *would* blush!—if some foreign critic (some fellow, of course I mean, who should know what he was talking about and should have shown you he did, as foreign critics like to show it) were to say to you: 'He's the one, in this country, whom they consider the most perfect, isn't he?' Is it success to be the occasion of a young Englishman's having to stammer as you would have to stammer at such a moment for old England? No, no; success is to have made people wriggle to another tune. Do try it!"

Paul continued all gravely to glow. "Try what?"

"Try to do some really good work."

"Oh, I want to, heaven knows!"

"Well, you can't do it without sacrifices—don't believe that for a moment," the Master said. "I've made none. I've had everything. In other words, I've missed everything."

"You've had the full rich masculine human general life, with all the responsibilities and duties and burdens and sorrows and joys—all the domestic and social initiations and complications. They must be immensely suggestive, immensely amusing," Paul anxiously submitted.

"Amusing?"

"For a strong man—yes."

"They've given me subjects without number, if that's what you mean; but they've taken away at the same time the power to use them. I've touched a thousand things, but which one of them have I turned into gold? The artist has to do only with that—he knows nothing of any baser metal. I've led the life of the world, with my wife and my progeny; the clumsy conventional expensive materialised vulgarised brutalised life of London. We've got everything handsome, even a carriage—we're perfect Philistines and prosperous hospitable eminent people. But, my dear fellow, don't try to stultify yourself and pretend you don't know what we *haven't* got. It's bigger than all the rest. Between artists—come!" the Master wound up. "You know as well as you sit there that you'd put a pistol ball into your brain if you had written my books!"

It struck his listener that the tremendous talk promised by him at Summersoft had indeed come off, and with a promptitude, a fulness, with which the latter's young imagination had scarcely reckoned. His impression fairly shook him and he throbbed with the excitement of such deep soundings and such strange confidences. He throbbed indeed with the conflict of his feelings—bewilderment and recognition and alarm, enjoyment and protest and assent, all commingled with tenderness (and a kind of shame in the participation) for the sores and bruises exhibited by so fine a creature, and with a sense of the tragic secret nursed under his trappings. The idea of *his*, Paul Overt's, becoming the occasion of such an act of humility made him flush and pant, at the same time that his consciousness was in certain directions too much alive not to swallow—and not intensely to taste—every offered spoonful of the revelation. It had been his odd fortune to blow upon the deep waters, to make them surge and break in waves of strange eloquence. But how couldn't he give out a passionate contradiction of his host's last extravagance, how couldn't he enumerate to him the parts of his work he loved, the splendid things he had found in it, beyond the compass of any other writer of the day? St. George listened a while, courteously; then he said, laying his hand on his visitor's: "That's all very well; and if your idea's to do nothing better, there's no reason you shouldn't have as many good things as I—as many human and material appendages, as many sons or daughters, a wife with as many gowns, a house with as many servants, a stable with as many horses, a heart with as many aches." The Master got up when he had spoken thus—he stood a moment—near the sofa, looking down on his agitated pupil. "Are you possessed of any property?" it occurred to him to ask.

"None to speak of."

"Oh, well then there's no reason why you shouldn't make a goodish income—if you set about it the right way. Study *me* for that—study me well. You may really have horses."

Paul sat there some minutes without speaking. He looked straight before him—he turned over many things. His friend had wandered away, taking up a parcel of letters from the table where the roll of proofs had lain. "What was the book Mrs. St. George made you burn—the one she didn't like?" our young man brought out.

"The book she made me burn—how did you know that?" The Master looked up from his letters quite without the facial convulsion the pupil had feared.

"I heard her speak of it at Summersoft."

"Ah, yes—she's proud of it. I don't know—it was rather good."

"What was it about?"

"Let me see." And he seemed to make an effort to remember. "Oh, yes—it was about myself." Paul gave an irrepressible groan for the disappearance of such a production, and the elder man went on: "Oh, but *you* should write it—*you* should do me." And he pulled up—from the restless motion that had come upon him; his fine smile a generous glare. "There's a subject, my boy: no end of stuff in it!"

Again Paul was silent, but it was all tormenting. "Are there no women who really understand—who can take part in a sacrifice?"

"How can they take part? They themselves are the sacrifice. They're the idol and the altar and the flame."

"Isn't there even *one* who sees further?" Paul continued.

For a moment St. George made no answer; after which, having torn up his letters, he came back to the point all ironic. "Of course I know the one you mean. But not even Miss Fancourt."

"I thought you admired her so much."

"It's impossible to admire her more. Are you in love with her?" St. George asked.

"Yes," Paul Overt presently said.

"Well, then, give it up."

Paul stared. "Give up my 'love'?"

"Bless me, no. Your idea." And then as our hero but still gazed: "The one you talked with her about. The idea of a decent perfection."

"She'd help it—she'd help it!" the young man cried.

"For about a year—the first year, yes. After that she'd be as a millstone round its neck."

Paul frankly wondered. "Why, she has a passion for the real thing, for good work—for everything you and I care for most."

" 'You and I' is charming, my dear fellow!" his friend laughed. "She has it indeed, but she'd have a still greater passion for her children—and very proper too. She'd insist on everything's being made comfortable, advantageous, propitious for them. That isn't the artist's business."

"The artist—the artist! Isn't he a man all the same?"

St. George had a grand grimace. "I mostly think not. You know as well as I what he has to do: the concentration, the finish, the independence he must strive for from the moment he begins to wish his work really decent. Ah, my young friend, his relation to women, and especially to the one he's most intimately concerned with, is at the mercy of the damning fact that whereas he can in the nature of things have but one standard, they have about fifty. That's what makes them so superior," St. George amusingly added. "Fancy an artist with a change of standards as you'd have a change of shirts or of dinner plates. To *do* it—to do it and make it divine— is the only thing he has to think about. 'Is it done or not?' is his only question. Not 'Is it done as well as a proper solicitude for my dear little family will allow?' He has nothing to do with the relative—he has only to do with the absolute; and a dear little family may represent a dozen relatives."

"Then you don't allow him the common passions and affections of men?" Paul asked.

"Hasn't he a passion, an affection, which includes all the rest? Besides, let him have all the passions he likes—if he only keeps his independence. He must be able to be poor."

Paul slowly got up. "Why, then, did you advise me to make up to her?"

St. George laid a hand on his shoulder. "Because she'd make a splendid wife! And I hadn't read you then."

The young man had a strained smile. "I wish you had left me alone!"

"I didn't know that that wasn't good enough for you," his host returned.

"What a false position, what a condemnation of the artist, that he's a mere disfranchised monk and can produce his effect only by giving up personal happiness. What an arraignment of art!" Paul went on with a trembling voice.

"Ah, you don't imagine by chance that I'm defending art? 'Arraignment'—I should think so! Happy the societies in which it hasn't made its appearance, for from the moment it comes they have a consuming ache, they have an incurable corruption, in their breast. Most assuredly is the artist in a false position! But I thought we were taking him for granted. Pardon me," St. George continued: " 'Ginistrella' made me!"

Paul stood looking at the floor—one o'clock struck, in the stillness, from a neighbouring church-tower. "Do you think she'd ever look at me?" he put to his friend at last.

"Miss Fancourt—as a suitor? Why shouldn't I think it? That's why I've tried to favour you—I've had a little chance or two of bettering your opportunity."

"Forgive my asking you, but do you mean by keeping away yourself?" Paul said with a blush.

"I'm an old idiot—my place isn't there," St. George stated gravely.

"I'm nothing yet, I've no fortune; and there must be so many others," his companion pursued.

The Master took this considerably in, but made little of it. "You're a gentleman and a man of genius. I think you might do something."

"But if I must give that up—the genius?"

"Lots of people, you know, think I've kept mine," St. George wonderfully grinned.

"You've a genius for mystification!" Paul declared, but grasping his hand gratefully in attenuation of this judgment.

"Poor, dear boy, I do worry you! But try, try, all the same. I think your chances are good and you'll win a great prize."

Paul held fast the other's hand a minute; he looked into the strange deep face. "No, I *am* an artist—I can't help it!"

"Ah, show it then!" St. George pleadingly broke out. "Let me see before I die the thing I most want, the thing I yearn for: a life in which the passion—ours—is really intense. If you can be rare don't fail of it! Think what it is—how it counts—how it lives!"

They had moved to the door and he had closed both his hands over his companion's. Here they paused again and our hero breathed deep. "I want to live!"

"In what sense?"

"In the greatest."

"Well, then, stick to it—see it through."

"With your sympathy—your help?"

"Count on that—you'll be a great figure to me. Count on my highest appreciation, my devotion. You'll give me satisfaction—if that has any weight with you!" After which, as Paul appeared still to waver, his host added: "Do you remember what you said to me at Summersoft?"

"Something infatuated, no doubt!"

" 'I'll do anything in the world you tell me.' You said that."

"And you hold me to it?"

"Ah, what am I?" the Master expressively sighed.

"Lord, what things I shall have to do!" Paul almost moaned as he departed.

6

"It goes on too much abroad—hang abroad!" These or something like them had been the Master's remarkable words in relation to the action of "Ginistrella"; and yet, though they had made a sharp impression on the author of that work, like almost all spoken words from the same source, he a week after the conversation I have noted left England for a long absence and full of brave intentions. It is not a perversion of the truth to pronounce that encounter the direct cause of his departure. If the oral utterance of the eminent writer had the privilege of moving him deeply it was especially on his turning it over at leisure, hours and days later, that it appeared to yield him its full meaning and exhibit its extreme importance. He spent the summer in Switzerland and, having in September begun a new task, determined not to cross the Alps till he should have made a good start. To this end he returned to a quiet corner he knew well, on the edge of the Lake of Geneva and within sight of the towers of Chillon: a region and a view for which he had an affection that sprang from old associations and was capable of mysterious revivals and refreshments. Here he lingered late, till the snow was on the nearer hills, almost down to the limit to which he could climb when his stint, on the shortening afternoons, was performed. The autumn was fine, the lake was blue, and his book took form and direction. These felicities, for the time, embroidered his life, which he suffered to cover him with its mantle. At the end of six weeks he felt he had learnt St. George's lesson by heart, had tested and proved its doctrine. Nevertheless he did a very inconsistent thing: before crossing the Alps he wrote to Marian Fancourt. He was aware of the perversity of this act, and it was only as a luxury, an amusement, the reward of a strenuous autumn, that he justified it. She had asked of him no such favour when, shortly before he left London, three days after their dinner in Ennismore Gardens, he went to take leave of her. It was true she had had no ground—he hadn't named his intention of absence. He had kept his counsel for want of due assurance: it was that particular visit that was, the next thing, to settle the matter. He had paid the visit to see how much he really cared for her, and quick departure, without so much as an explicit farewell, was the sequel to this inquiry, the answer to which had created within him a deep yearning. When he wrote her from Clarens he noted that he owed her an explanation (more than three months after!) for not having told her what he was doing.

She replied now briefly but promptly, and gave him a striking piece of news: that of the death, a week before, of Mrs. St. George. This exemplary woman had succumbed, in the country, to a violent attack of inflammation of the lungs—he would remember that for a long time she had been delicate. Miss Fancourt added that she believed her husband was overwhelmed by the blow; he would miss her too terribly—she had been everything in life to him. Paul Overt, on this, immediately wrote to St. George. He would from the day of their parting have been glad to remain in communication with him, but had hitherto lacked the right excuse for troubling so busy a man. Their long nocturnal talk came back to him in every detail, but this was no bar to an expression of proper sympathy with the head of the profession, for hadn't that very talk made it clear that the late accomplished lady was the influence that ruled his life? What catastrophe could be more cruel than the extinction of such an influence? This was to be exactly the tone taken by St. George in answering his young friend upwards of a month later. He made no allusion of course to their important discussion. He spoke of his wife as frankly and generously as if he had quite forgotten that occasion, and the feeling of deep bereavement was visible in his words. "She took everything off my hands—off my mind. She carried on our life with the greatest art, the rarest devotion, and I was free, as few men can have been, to drive my pen, to shut myself up with my trade. This was a rare service—the highest she could have rendered me. Would I could have acknowledged it more fitly!"

A certain bewilderment, for our hero, disengaged itself from these remarks: they struck him as a contradiction, a retraction, strange on the part of a man who hadn't the excuse of witlessness. He had certainly not expected his correspondent to rejoice in the death of his wife, and it was perfectly in order that the rupture of a tie of more than twenty years should have left him sore. But if she had been so clear a blessing what in the name of consistency had the dear man meant by turning *him* upside down that night—by dosing him to that degree, at the most sensitive hour of his life, with the doctrine of renunciation? If Mrs. St. George was an irreparable loss, then her husband's inspired advice had been a bad joke and renunciation was a mistake. Overt was on the point of rushing back to London to show that, for his part, he was perfectly willing to consider it so, and he went so far as to take the manuscript of the first chapters of his new book out of his table-drawer and insert it into a pocket of his portmanteau. This led to his catching a glimpse of certain pages he hadn't looked at for months, and that accident, in turn, to his being struck with the high promise they revealed—a rare result of such retrospections, which it was his habit to avoid as much as possible: they usually brought home to him that the glow of composition might be a purely subjective and misleading emotion. On this occasion a certain belief in himself disengaged itself whimsically from the serried erasures of his first draft, making him think it best after all to pursue his present trial to the end. If he could write so well under the rigour of privation it might be a mistake to change the conditions before that spell had spent itself. He would go back to London of course, but he would go back only when he should have finished his book. This was the vow he privately made, restoring his manuscript to the table-drawer. It may be added that it took him a long time to finish his book, for the subject was as difficult as it was fine, and he was literally embarrassed by the fulness of his notes. Something within him warned him he must make it supremely good—otherwise he should lack, as regards his private behaviour, a handsome excuse. He had a horror of this deficiency and found himself as firm as need be on the question of the lamp and the file. He crossed the Alps at last and spent the winter, the spring, the ensuing summer, in Italy, where still, at the end of a twelvemonth, his task was unachieved. "Stick to it—see it through": this general injunction of St. George's was good also for the particular case. He applied it to the utmost, with the result that when in its slow order the summer had come round again he felt he had given all that was in him. This time he put his papers into his portmanteau, with the address of his publisher attached, and took his way northward.

He had been absent from London for two years; two years which, seeming to count as more, had made such a difference in his own life—through the production of a novel far stronger, he believed, than "Ginistrella"—that he turned out into Piccadilly, the morning after his arrival, with a vague expectation of changes, of finding great things had happened. But there were few transformations in Piccadilly—only three or four big red houses where there had been low black ones— and the brightness of the end of June peeped through the rusty railings of the Green Park and glittered in the varnish of the rolling carriages as he had seen it in other, more cursory Junes. It was a greeting he appreciated; it seemed friendly and pointed, added to the exhilaration of his finished book, of his having his own country and the huge oppressive amusing city that suggested everything, that contained everything, under his hand again. "Stay at home and do things here—do subjects we can measure," St. George had said; and now it struck him he should ask nothing better than to stay at home for ever. Late in the afternoon he took his way to Manchester Square, looking out for a number he hadn't forgotten. Miss Fancourt, however, was not at home, so that he turned rather dejectedly from the door. His movement brought him face to face with a gentleman just approaching it and recognised on another glance as Miss Fancourt's father. Paul saluted this personage, and the General returned the greeting with his customary good manner—a manner so good, however, that you could never tell whether it meant he placed you. The disappointed caller felt the impulse to address him; then, hesitating, became both aware of having no particular remark to make, and convinced that though the old soldier remembered him he remembered him wrong. He therefore went his way without computing the irresistible effect his own evident recognition would have on the General, who never neglected a chance to gossip. Our young man's face was expressive, and observation seldom let it pass. He hadn't taken ten steps before he heard himself called after with a friendly semi-articulate "Er—I beg your pardon!" He turned round and the General, smiling at him from the porch, said: "Won't you come in? I won't leave you the advantage of me!" Paul declined to come in, and then felt regret, for Miss Fancourt, so late in the afternoon, might return at any moment. But her father gave him no second chance; he appeared mainly to wish not to have struck him as ungracious. A further look at the visitor had recalled something, enough at least to enable him to say: "You've come back, you've come back?" Paul was on the point of replying that he had come back the night before, but he suppressed, the next instant, this strong light on the immediacy of his visit and, giving merely a general assent, alluded to the young lady he deplored not having found. He had come late in the hope she would be in. "I'll tell her—I'll tell her," said the old man; and then he added quickly, gallantly: "You'll be giving us something new? It's a long time, isn't it?" Now he remembered him right.

"Rather long. I'm very slow," Paul explained. "I met you at Summersoft a long time ago."

"Oh, yes—with Henry St. George. I remember very well. Before his poor wife—" General Fancourt paused a moment, smiling a little less. "I daresay you know."

"About Mrs. St. George's death? Certainly—I heard at the time."

"Oh, no, I mean—I mean he's to be married."

"Ah, I've not heard that!" But just as Paul was about to add "To whom?" the General crossed his intention.

"When did you come back? I know you've been away—by my daughter. She was very sorry. You ought to give her something new."

"I came back last night," said our young man, to whom something had occurred which made his speech for the moment a little thick.

"Ah, most kind of you to come so soon. Couldn't you turn up at dinner?"

"At dinner?" Paul just mechanically repeated, not liking to ask whom St. George was going to marry, but thinking only of that.

"There are several people, I believe. Certainly St. George. Or afterwards if you like better. I believe my daughter expects—" He appeared to notice something in the visitor's raised face (on his steps he stood higher) which led him to interrupt himself, and the interruption gave him a momentary sense of awkwardness, from which he sought a quick issue. "Perhaps, then, you haven't heard she's to be married."

Paul gaped again. "To be married?"

"To Mr. St. George—it has just been settled. Odd marriage, isn't it?" Our listener uttered no opinion on this point: he only continued to stare. "But I daresay it will do—she's so awfully literary!" said the General.

Paul had turned very red. "Oh, it's a surprise—very interesting, very charming! I'm afraid I can't dine—so many thanks!"

"Well, you must come to the wedding!" cried the General. "Oh, I remember that day at Summersoft. He's a great man, you know."

"Charming—charming!" Paul stammered for retreat. He shook hands with the General and got off. His face was red and he had the sense of its growing more and more crimson. All the evening at home—he went straight to his rooms and remained there dinnerless—his cheek burned at intervals as if it had been smitten. He didn't understand what had happened to him, what trick had been played him, what treachery practised. "None, none," he said to himself. "I've nothing to do with it. I'm out of it—it's none of my business." But that bewildered murmur was followed again and again by the incongruous ejaculation: "Was it a plan—was it a plan?" Sometimes he cried to himself, breathless, "Have I been duped, sold, swindled?" If at all, he was an absurd, an abject victim. It was as if he hadn't lost her till now. He had renounced her, yes; but that was another affair—that was a closed but not a locked door. Now he seemed to see the door quite slammed in his face. Did he expect her to wait—was she to give him his time like that: two years at a stretch? He didn't know what he had expected—he only knew what he hadn't. It wasn't this—it wasn't this. Mystification bitterness and wrath rose and boiled in him when he thought of the deference, the devotion, the credulity with which he had listened to St. George. The evening wore on and the light was long; but even when it had darkened he remained without a lamp. He had flung himself on the sofa, where he lay through the hours with his eyes either closed or gazing at the gloom, in the attitude of a man teaching himself to bear something, to bear having been made a fool of. He had made it too easy —that idea passed over him like a hot wave. Suddenly, as he heard eleven o'clock strike, he jumped up, remembering what General Fancourt had said about his coming after dinner. He'd go—he'd see her at least; perhaps he should see what it meant. He felt as if some of the elements of a hard sum had been given him and the others were wanting: he couldn't do his sum till he had got all his figures.

He dressed and drove quickly, so that by half-past eleven he was at Manchester Square. There were a good many carriages at the door—a party was going on; a circumstance which at the last gave him a slight relief, for now he would rather see her in a crowd. People passed him on the staircase; they were going away, going "on" with the hunted herdlike movement of London society at night. But sundry groups remained in the drawing-room, and it was some minutes, as she didn't hear him announced, before he discovered and spoke to her. In this short interval he had seen St. George talking to a lady before the fireplace; but he at once looked away, feeling unready for an encounter, and therefore couldn't be sure the author of "Shadowmere" noticed him. At all events he didn't come over; though Miss Fancourt did as soon as she saw him—she almost rushed at him, smiling rustling radiant beautiful. He had forgotten what her head, what her face offered to the sight; she was in white, there were gold figures on her dress and her hair was a casque of gold. He saw in a single moment that she was happy, happy with an aggressive splendour. But she wouldn't speak to him of that, she would speak only of himself.

"I'm so delighted; my father told me. How kind of you to come!" She struck him as so fresh and brave, while his eyes moved over her, that he said to himself irresistibly: "Why to *him*, why not to youth, to strength, to ambition, to a future? Why, in her rich young force, to failure, to abdication, to superannuation?" In his thought at that sharp moment he blasphemed even against all that had been left of his faith in the peccable master. "I'm so sorry I missed you," she went on. "My father told me. How charming of you to have come so soon!"

"Does that surprise you?" Paul Overt asked.

"The first day? No, from you—nothing that's nice." She was interrupted by a lady who bade her good-night, and he seemed to read that it cost her nothing to speak to him in that tone; it was her old liberal lavish way, with a certain added amplitude that time had brought; and if this manner began to operate on the spot, at such a juncture in her history, perhaps in the other days too it had meant just as little or as much—a mere mechanical charity, with the difference now that she was satisfied, ready to give but in want of nothing. Oh, she was satisfied—and why shouldn't she be? Why shouldn't she have been surprised at his coming the first day—for all the good she had ever got from him? As the lady continued to hold her attention Paul turned from her with a strange irritation in his complicated artistic soul and a sort of disinterested disappointment. She was so happy that it was almost stupid—a disproof of the extraordinary intelligence he had formerly found in her. Didn't she know how bad St. George could be, hadn't she recognised the awful thinness—? If she didn't she was nothing, and if she did why such an insolence of serenity? This question expired as our young man's eyes settled at last on the genius who had advised him in a great crisis. St. George was still before the chimney-piece, but now he was alone—fixed, waiting, as if he meant to stop after every one—and he met the clouded gaze of the young friend so troubled as to the degree of his right (the right his resentment would have enjoyed) to regard himself as a victim. Somehow the ravage of the question was checked by the Master's radiance. It was as fine in its way as Marian Fancourt's, it denoted the happy human being; but also it represented to Paul Overt that the author of "Shadowmere" had now definitely ceased to count—ceased to count as a writer. As he smiled a welcome across the place he was almost *banal*, was almost smug. Paul fancied that for a moment he hesitated to make a movement, as if, for all the world, he *had* his bad conscience; then they had already met in the middle of the room and had shaken hands—expressively, cordially on St. George's part. With which they had passed back together to where the elder man had been standing, while St. George said: "I hope you're never going away again. I've been dining here; the General told me." He was handsome, he was young, he looked as if he had still a great fund of life. He bent the friendliest, most unconfessing eyes on his disciple of a couple of years before; asked him about everything, his health, his plans, his late occupations, the new book. "When will it be out—soon, soon, I hope? Splendid, eh? That's right; you're a comfort, you're a luxury! I've read you all over again these last six months." Paul waited to see if he'd tell him what the General had told him in the afternoon and what Miss Fancourt, verbally, at least, of course hadn't. But as it didn't come out he at last put the question, "Is it true, the great news I hear—that you're to be married?"

"Ah, you *have* heard it, then?"

"Didn't the General tell you?" Paul asked.

The Master's face was wonderful. "Tell me what?"

"That he mentioned it to me this afternoon?"

"My dear fellow, I don't remember. We've been in the midst of people. I'm sorry, in the case, that I lose the pleasure, myself, of announcing to you a fact that touches me so nearly. It *is* a fact, strange as it may appear. It has only just become one. Isn't it ridiculous?" St. George made this speech without confusion, but on the other hand, so far as our friend could judge, without latent impudence. It struck his interlocutor that, to talk so comfortably and coolly, he must simply have forgotten what had passed between them. His next words, however, showed he hadn't, and they produced, as an appeal to Paul's own memory, an effect which would have been ludicrous if it hadn't been cruel. "Do you recall the talk we had at my house that night, into which Miss Fancourt's name entered? I've often thought of it since."

"Yes; no wonder you said what you did"—Paul was careful to meet his eyes.

"In the light of the present occasion? Ah, but there was no light then. How could I have foreseen this hour?"

"Didn't you think it probable?"

"Upon my honour, no," said Henry St. George. "Certainly I owe you that assurance. Think how my situation has changed."

"I see—I see," our young man murmured.

His companion went on as if, now that the subject had been broached, he was, as a person of imagination and tact, quite ready to give every satisfaction—being both by his genius and his method so able to enter into everything another might feel. "But it's not only that; for honestly, at my age, I never dreamed—a widower with big boys and with so little else! It has turned out differently from anything one could have dreamed, and I'm fortunate beyond all measure. She has been so free, and yet she consents. Better than any one else perhaps

—for I remember how you liked her before you went away, and how she liked you—you can intelligently congratulate me."

"She has been so free!" Those words made a great impression on Paul Overt, and he almost writhed under that irony in them as to which it so little mattered whether it was designed or casual. Of course she had been free, and appreciably perhaps by his own act; for wasn't the Master's allusion to her having liked him a part of the irony too? "I thought that by your theory you disapproved of a writer's marrying."

"Surely—surely. But you don't call me a writer?"

"You ought to be ashamed," said Paul.

"Ashamed of marrying again?"

"I won't say that—but ashamed of your reasons."

The elder man beautifully smiled. "You must let me judge of them, my good friend."

"Yes; why not? For you judged wonderfully of mine."

The tone of these words appeared suddenly, for St. George, to suggest the unsuspected. He stared as if divining a bitterness. "Don't you think I've been straight?"

"You might have told me at the time perhaps."

"My dear fellow, when I say I couldn't pierce futurity—!"

"I mean afterwards."

The Master wondered. "After my wife's death?"

"When this idea came to you."

"Ah, never, never! I wanted to save you, rare and precious as you are."

Poor Overt looked hard at him. "Are you marrying Miss Fancourt to save me?"

"Not absolutely, but it adds to the pleasure. I shall be the making of you," St. George smiled. "I was greatly struck, after our talk, with the brave, devoted way you quitted the country, and still more perhaps with your force of character in remaining abroad. You're very strong—you're wonderfully strong."

Paul tried to sound his shining eyes; the strange thing was that he seemed sincere—not a mocking fiend. He turned away, and as he did so heard the Master say something about his giving them all the proof, being the joy of his old age. He faced him again, taking another look. "Do you mean to say you've stopped writing?"

"My dear fellow, of course I have. It's too late. Didn't I tell you?"

"I can't believe it!"

"Of course you can't—with your own talent! No, no; for the rest of my life I shall only read *you*."

"Does she know that—Miss Fancourt?"

"She will—she will." Did he mean this, our young man wondered, as a covert intimation that the assistance he should derive from that young lady's fortune, moderate as it was, would make the difference of putting it in his power to cease to work ungratefully an exhausted vein? Somehow, standing there in the ripeness of his successful manhood, he didn't suggest that any of his veins were exhausted. "Don't you remember the moral I offered myself to you that night as pointing?" St. George continued. "Consider at any rate the warning I am at present."

This was too much—he *was* the mocking fiend. Paul turned from him with a mere nod for good-night and the sense in a sore heart that he might come back to him and his easy grace, his fine way of arranging things, some time in the far future, but he couldn't fraternise with him now. It was necessary to his soreness to believe for the hour in the intensity of his grievance—all the more cruel for its not being a legal one. It was doubtless in the attitude of hugging this wrong that he descended the stairs without taking leave of Miss Fancourt, who hadn't been in view at the moment he quitted the room. He was glad to get out into the honest dusky unsophisticating night, to move fast, to take his way home on foot. He walked a long time, going astray, paying no attention. He was thinking of too many other things. His steps recovered their direction, however, and at the end of an hour he found himself before his door in the small inexpensive empty street. He lingered, questioning himself still before going in, with nothing around and above him but moonless blackness, a bad lamp or two, and a few far-away dim stars. To these last faint features he raised his eyes; he had been saying to himself that he should have been "sold" indeed, diabolically sold, if now, on his new foundation, at the end of a year, St. George were to put forth something of his prime quality—something of the type of "Shadowmere" and finer than his finest. Greatly as he admired his talent Paul literally hoped such an incident wouldn't occur; it seemed to him just then that he shouldn't be able to bear it. His late adviser's words were still in his ears—"You're very strong, wonderfully strong." Was he really? Certainly he would have to be, and it might a little serve for revenge. *Is* he? the reader may ask in turn, if his interest has followed the perplexed young man so far. The best answer to that perhaps is that he's doing his best, but that it's too soon to say. When the new book came out in the autumn Mr. and Mrs. St. George found it really magnificent. The former still has published nothing, but Paul doesn't even yet feel safe. I may say for him, however, that if this event were to occur he would really be the very first to appreciate it: which is perhaps a proof that the Master was essentially right and that nature had dedicated him to intellectual, not to personal passion.

The Madonna of the Future

1

WE HAD BEEN TALKING ABOUT THE MASTERS WHO HAD ACHIEVED but a single masterpiece—the artists and poets who but once in their lives had known the divine afflatus and touched the high level of perfection. Our host had shown us a charming little cabinet picture by a painter whose name we had never heard, and who, after this single spasmodic bid for fame, had appeared to relapse into obscurity and mediocrity. There was some discussion as to the frequency of this inconsequence; during which I noted H—— sit silent, finishing his cigar with a meditative air and looking at the picture, which was being handed round the table. "I don't know how common a case it is," he said at last, "but I've seen it. I've known a poor fellow who painted his one masterpiece, and who"—he added with a smile—"didn't even paint that. He made his bid for fame and missed it." We all knew H—— for a clever man who had seen much of men and manners and had a great stock of reminiscences. Some one immediately questioned him further, and while I was engrossed with the raptures of my neighbour over the precious object in circulation he was induced to tell his tale. If I were to doubt whether it would bear repeating, I should only have to remember how that charming woman our hostess, who had left the table, ventured back, in rustling rose-colour, to pronounce our lingering a want of gallantry, and, then finding us under the spell, sank into her chair in spite of our cigars and heard the story out so graciously that when the catastrophe was reached she glanced across and showed me a tear in each of her beautiful eyes.

It relates to my youth and to Italy: two very fine things! (H—— began.) I had arrived late in the evening at Florence and, while I finished my bottle of wine at supper, had fancied that, tired traveller though I was, I might pay such a place a finer compliment than by going vulgarly to bed. A narrow passage wandered darkly away out of the little square before my hotel and looked as if it bored into the heart of Florence. I followed it and at the end of ten minutes emerged upon a great piazza filled only with the mild autumn moonlight. Opposite rose the Palazzo Vecchio, like some huge civic fortress, with the great bell-tower springing from its embattled verge even as a mountain-pine from the edge of a cliff. At the base, in the great projected shadow, gleamed certain dim sculptures which I wonderingly approached. One of the images, on the left of the palace door, was a magnificent colossus who shone through the dusky air like a sentinel roused by some alarm and in whom I at once recognised Michael Angelo's famous David. I turned with a certain relief from his heroic sinister strength to a slender figure in bronze poised beneath the high light loggia which opposes the free and elegant span of its arches to the dead masonry of the palace; a figure supremely shapely and graceful, markedly gentle almost, in spite of his holding out with his light nervous arm the snaky head of the slaughtered Gorgon. His name—as, unlike the great David, he still stands there—is Perseus, and you may read his story not in the Greek mythology but in the memoirs of Benvenuto Cellini. Glancing from one of these fine fellows to the other, I probably uttered some irrepressible commonplace of praise, for, as if provoked by my voice, a man rose from the steps of the loggia, where he had been sitting in the shadow, and addressed me in proper English—a small slim personage clad in some fashion of black velvet tunic (as it seemed) and with a mass of auburn hair, which shimmered in the moonlight, escaping from a little beretto of the *cinquecento*. In a tone of the most insinuating deference he proceeded to appeal to me for my "impressions." He was romantic, fantastic, slightly unreal. Hovering in that consecrated neighbourhood he might have passed for the genius of esthetic hospitality—if the genius of esthetic hospitality wasn't commonly some shabby little custode who flourishes a calico pocket-handkerchief and openly resents the divided franc. This analogy was made none the less complete by his breaking into discourse as I threw myself diffidently back upon silence.

"I've known Florence long, sir, but I've never known her so lovely as to-night. It's as if the ghosts of her past were abroad in the empty streets. The present is sleeping; the past hovers about us like a dream made visible. Fancy the old Florentines strolling up in couples to pass judgment on the last performance of Michael, of Benvenuto! We should come in for a precious lesson if we might overhear what they say. The plainest burgher of them, in his cap and gown, had a taste in the matter. That was the prime of art, sir. The sun stood high in heaven, and his broad and equal blaze made the darkest places bright and the dullest eyes clear. We live in the evening of time. We grope in the grey dusk, carrying each our poor little taper of selfish and painful wisdom, holding it up to the great models and to the dim idea, and seeing nothing but overwhelming greatness and dimness. The days of illumination are gone. But do you take my refreshing idea"—and he grew suddenly almost familiar in this visionary fervour—"my idea that the light of that time rests upon us here for an hour? I've never seen the David so grand, the Perseus so fair! Even the inferior productions of John of Bologna and of Baccio Bandinelli seem to realise the artist's dream. I feel as if the moonlit air were charged with the secrets of the masters, and as if, standing here in religious attention, we might—well, witness a revelation!" Perceiving at this moment, I suppose, my halting comprehension reflected in my puzzled face, this interesting rhapsodist paused and blushed. Then with a melancholy smile: "You think me a moonstruck charlatan, I suppose. It's not my habit to hang about the piazza and pounce upon innocent tourists. But to-night, I confess, I'm under the charm. And then, somehow, I seemed to take you too for an artist!"

"I'm not an artist, I'm sorry to say, as you must understand the term. But pray make no apologies. I *am* also under the charm, and your eloquent remarks," I declared, "have only deepened it."

"If you're not an artist, you're worthy to be one!" he returned with flattering frankness. "A young man who arrives at Florence late in the evening and, instead of going prosaically to bed or hanging over the travellers' book at his hotel, walks forth without loss of time to render homage to these blest objects is a young man after my own heart!"

The mystery was suddenly solved; my friend was the most characteristic of compatriots. He would *have* to be one of "us," of the famished race—for we were at least a pair—to take the situation so to heart. "None the less so, I trust," I answered, "if the young man is a sordid New Yorker."

"New Yorkers have often been munificent patrons of art!" he answered urbanely.

For a moment I was alarmed. Was his irrepressible passion mere Yankee enterprise?—was he simply a desperate brother of the brush who had posted himself here to extort an "order" from a sauntering tourist? But I wasn't called to defend myself. A great brazen note broke suddenly from the far-off summit of the bell-tower above us and sounded the first stroke of midnight. My companion started, apologised for detaining me and prepared to retire. But he seemed to offer so lively a promise of further entertainment that I was loth to part with him and suggested we should proceed homeward together. He cordially assented; so we turned out of the Piazza, passed down before the statued arcade of the Uffizi and came out upon the Arno. What course we took I hardly remember, but we roamed far and wide for an hour, my companion delivering by snatches a positively moon-touched esthetic lecture. I listened in puzzled fascination, wondering who the deuce he might be. He confessed with a melancholy but all-respectful headshake to an origin identical with my own. "We're the disinherited of Art! We're condemned to be superficial! We're excluded from the magic circle! The soil of American perception is a poor little barren artificial deposit! Yes, we're wedded to imperfection! An American, to excel, has just ten times as much to learn as a European! We lack the deeper sense! We have neither taste nor tact nor force! How *should* we have them? Our crude and garish climate, our silent past, our deafening present, the constant pressure about us of unlovely conditions, are as void of all that nourishes and prompts and inspires the artist as my sad heart is void of bitterness in saying so! We poor aspirants must live in perpetual exile."

"You seem fairly at home in exile," I made answer, "and Florence seems to me a very easy Siberia. But do you know my own thought? Nothing is so idle as to talk about our want of a nursing air, of a kindly soil, of opportunity, of inspiration, of the things that help. The only thing that helps is to do something fine. There's no law in our glorious Constitution against that. Invent, create, achieve. No matter if you've to study fifty times as much as one of these. What else are you an artist for? Be you our Moses," I added, laughing and laying my hand on his shoulder, "and lead us out of the house of bondage!"

"Golden words, golden words, young man!"—my friend rose to it beautifully. " 'Invent, create, achieve'! Yes, that's our business; I know it well. Don't take me, in heaven's name, for one of your barren complainers, of the falsely fastidious, who have neither talent nor faith! I'm at work!"—and he glanced about him and lowered his voice as if this were quite a peculiar secret—"I'm at work night and day. I've undertaken, believe me, a creation. I'm no Moses; I'm only a poor patient artist; but it would be a fine thing if I were to cause some slender stream of beauty to flow in our thirsty land! Don't think me a monster of conceit," he went on as he saw me smile at the avidity with which he adopted my illustration; "I confess that I *am* in one of those moods when great things seem possible! This is one of my—shall I say inspired?—nights: I dream waking! When the south wind blows over Florence at midnight it seems to coax the soul from all the fair things locked away in her churches and galleries; it comes into my own little studio with the moonlight; it sets my heart beating too deeply for rest. You see I'm always adding a thought to my conception. This evening I felt I couldn't sleep unless I had communed with the genius of Buonarotti!"

He seemed really to know his Florence through and through and had no need to tell me he loved her. I saw he was an old devotee and had taken her even from the first to his heart. "I owe her everything," he put it—"it's only since I came here that I've really lived, intellectually and esthetically speaking. One by one all profane desires, all mere worldly aims, have dropped away from me and left me nothing but my pencil, my little note-book"—he tapped his breast pocket—"and the worship of the pure masters, those who were pure because they were innocent and those who were pure because they were strong!"

"And have you been very productive all this time?" I found myself too interested to keep from asking.

He was silent a while before replying. "Not in the vulgar sense! I've chosen never to manifest myself by imperfection. The good in every performance I've reabsorbed into the generative force of new creations; the bad—there's always plenty of that—I've religiously destroyed. I may say with some satisfaction that I've not added a grain to the rubbish of the world. As a proof of my conscientiousness"—and he stopped short, eyeing me with extraordinary candour, as if the proof were to be overwhelming—"I've never sold a picture! 'At least no merchant traffics in my heart!' Do you remember that divine line in Browning? My little studio has never been profaned by superficial feverish mercenary work. It's a temple of labour but of leisure! Art is long. If we work for ourselves of course we must hurry. If we work for *her* we must often pause. She can wait!"

This had brought us to my hotel door, somewhat to my relief, I confess, for I had begun to feel unequal to the society of a genius of this heroic strain. I left him, however, not without expressing a friendly hope that we should meet again. The next morning my curiosity had not abated; I was anxious to see him by common daylight. I counted on meeting him in one of the many art-haunts of the so rich little city, and I was gratified without delay. I found him in the course of the morning in the Tribune of the Uffizi—that little treasure-chamber of world-famous things. He had turned his back on the Venus de' Medici and, with his arms resting on the rail that protects the pictures and his head buried in his hands, was lost in the contemplation of that superb neighbouring triptych of Andrea Mantegna—a work which has neither the material splendour nor the commanding force of some of its neighbours, but which, glowing there with the loveliness of patient labour, suits possibly a more constant need of the soul. I looked at the picture for some time over his shoulder; at last, with a heavy sigh, he turned away and our eyes met. As he recognised me he coloured for the consciousness of what I brought back: he recalled perhaps that he had made a fool of himself overnight. But I offered him my hand with a frankness that assured him I was no scoffer. I knew him by his great nimbus of red hair; otherwise he was much altered. His midnight mood was over, and he looked as haggard as an actor by daylight. He was much older than I had supposed, and had less bravery of costume and attitude. He seemed quite the poor patient artist he had proclaimed himself, and the fact that he had never sold a picture was more conceivable doubtless than commendable. His velvet coat was threadbare and his short slouched hat, of an antique pattern, revealed a rustiness that marked it an "original" and not one of the picturesque reproductions that members of his craft sometimes affect. His eye was mild and heavy, and his expression singularly gentle and acquiescent; the more so for a certain pale facial spareness which I hardly knew whether to refer to the consuming fire of genius or to a meagre diet. A very little talk, however, cleared his brow and brought back his flow.

"And this is your first visit to these enchanted halls?" he cried. "Happy, thrice happy youth!"—with which, taking me by the arm, he prepared to lead me to each of the pre-eminent works in turn and show me the flower of the array. Before we left the Mantegna, however, I felt him squeeze me and give it a loving look. "*He* was not in a hurry," he murmured. "*He* knew nothing of 'raw Haste, half-sister to Delay'!" How sound a critic he might have been didn't seem to me even then to concern me—it so served that he was an amusing one; overflowing with opinions and theories, sympathies and aversions, with disquisition and gossip and anecdote. He inclined more than I approved to the sentimental proposition, was too fond, I thought, of superfine shades and of discovering subtle intentions and extracting quintessences. At moments too he plunged into the sea of metaphysics and floundered a while in waters that were not for my breasting. But his abounding knowledge and frequent felicities told a touching story of long attentive hours in all such worshipful companies; there was a reproach to my wasteful saunterings in his systematic and exhaustive attack. "There are two moods," I remember his saying, "in which we may walk through galleries—the critical and the ideal. They seize us at their pleasure, and we can never tell which is to take its turn. The critical, oddly, is the genial one, the friendly, the condescending. It relishes the pretty trivialities of art, its vulgar cleverness, its conscious graces. It has a kindly greeting for anything which looks as if, according to his light, the painter had enjoyed doing it—for the little Dutch cabbages and kettles, for the taper fingers and breezy mantles of late-coming Madonnas, for the little blue-hilled, broken-bridged, pastoral, classical landscapes. Then there are the days of fierce, fastidious longing—solemn churchfeasts of the taste or the faith—when all vulgar effort and all petty success is a weariness and everything but the best, the best of the best, disgusts. In these hours we're relentless aristocrats of attitude. We'll not take Michael for granted, we'll not swallow Raphael whole!"

The gallery of the Uffizi is not only rich in its possessions, but peculiarly fortunate in that fine architectural accident or privilege which unites it—with the breadth of river and city between them—to the princely extent of the Pitti. The Louvre and the Vatican hardly give you such a sense of sustained enclosure as those long passages projected over street and stream to establish an inviolate transition between the two palaces of art. We paced the clear tunnel in which those precious drawings by eminent hands hang chaste and grey above the swirl and murmur of the yellow Arno, and reached the grand-ducal, the palatial saloons. Grand-ducal as they are, they must be pronounced imperfect show-rooms, since, thanks to their deep-set windows and their massive mouldings, it is rather a broken light that reaches the pictured walls. But here the masterpieces hang thick, so that you see them in a deep diffused lustre of their own. And the great chambers, with their superb dim ceilings, their outer wall in splendid shadow and the sombre opposite glow of toned canvas and gleaming gold, make themselves almost as fine a picture as the Titians and Raphaels they imperfectly reveal. We lingered briefly before many a Raphael and Titian; but I saw my friend was impatient and I suffered him at last to lead me directly to the goal of our journey—the most tenderly fair of Raphael's virgins, the Madonna of the Chair. Of all the fine pictures of the world, it was to strike me at once as the work with which criticism has least to do. None betrays less effort, less of the mechanism of success and of the irrepressible discord between conception and result that sometimes faintly invalidates noble efforts. Graceful, human, near to our sympathies as it is, it has nothing of manner, of method, nothing almost of style; it blooms there in a softness as rounded and as instinct with harmony as if it were an immediate exhalation of genius. The figure imposes on the spectator a spell of submission which he scarce knows whether he has given to heavenly purity or to earthly charm. He is intoxicated with the fragrance of the tenderest blossom of maternity that ever bloomed among men.

"That's what I call a fine picture," said my companion after we had gazed a while in silence. "I've a right to say so, for I've copied it so often and so carefully that I could repeat it now with my eyes shut. Other works are Raphael: this is Raphael himself. Others you can praise, you can qualify, you can measure, explain, account for: this you can only love and admire. I don't know in what seeming he walked here below while this divine mood was upon him; but after it surely he could do nothing but die—this world had nothing more to teach him. Think of it a while, my friend, and you'll admit that I'm not raving. Think of his seeing that spotless image not for a moment, for a day, in a happy dream or a restless fever-fit, not as a poet in a five minutes' frenzy—time to snatch his phrase and scribble his immortal stanza; but for days together, while the slow labour of the brush went on, while the foul vapours of life interposed and the fancy ached with tension, fixed, radiant, distinct, as we see it now! What a master, certainly! But ah what a seer!"

"Don't you imagine," I fear I profanely asked, "that he had a model, and that some pretty young woman—"

"As pretty a young woman as you please! It doesn't diminish the miracle. He took his hint of course, and the young woman possibly sat smiling before his canvas. But meanwhile the painter's idea had taken wings. No lovely human outline could charm it to vulgar fact. He saw the fair form made perfect; he rose to the vision without tremor, without effort of wing; he communed with it face to face and resolved into finer and lovelier truth the purity which completes it as the fragrance completes the rose. That's what they call idealism; the word's vastly abused, but the thing's good. It's my own creed at any rate. Lovely Madonna, model at once and muse, I call you to witness that I too am an idealist!"

"An idealist then"—and I really but wanted to draw him further out—"an idealist is a gentleman who says to Nature in the person of a beautiful girl: 'Go to, you're all wrong! Your fine's coarse, your bright's dim, your grace is *gaucherie*. This is the way you should have done it! Isn't the chance against him?"

He turned on me at first almost angrily—then saw that I was but sowing the false to reap the true. "Look at that picture," he said, "and cease your irreverent mockery! Idealism is *that!* There's no explaining it; one must feel the flame. It says nothing to Nature, or to any beautiful girl, that they won't both forgive. It says to the fair woman: 'Accept me as your artist-friend, lend me your beautiful face, trust me, help me, and your eyes shall be half my masterpiece.' No one so loves and respects the rich realities of nature as the artist whose imagination intensifies them. He knows what a fact may hold—whether Raphael knew, you may judge by his inimitable portrait, behind us there, of Tommaso Inghirami—but his fancy hovers above it as Ariel in the play hovers above the sleeping prince. There's only one Raphael, but an artist may still be an artist. As I said last night, the days of illumination are gone; visions are rare; we've to look long to have them. But in meditation we may still cultivate the ideal; round it, smooth it, perfect it. The result, the result"—here his voice faltered suddenly and he fixed his eyes for a moment on the picture; when they met my own again they were full of tears—"the result may be less than this, but still it may be good, it may be *great!*" he cried with vehemence. "It may hang somewhere, through all the years, in goodly company, and keep the artist's memory warm. Think of being known to mankind after some such fashion as this; of keeping pace with the restless centuries and the changing world; of living on and on in the cunning of an eye and a hand that belong to the dust of ages, a delight and a law to remote generations; of making beauty more and more a force and purity more and more an example!"

"Heaven forbid," I smiled, "that I should take the wind out
of your sails! But doesn't it occur to you that besides being
strong in his genius Raphael was happy in a certain good faith
of which we've lost the trick? There are people, I know, who
deny that his spotless Madonnas are anything more than pretty
blondes of that period, enhanced by the Raphaelesque touch,
which they declare to be then as calculating and commercial
as any other. Be that as it may, people's religious and esthetic
needs went arm in arm, and there was, as I may say, a demand
for the Blessed Virgin, visible and adorable, which must have
given firmness to the artist's hand. I'm afraid there's no demand now."

My friend momentarily stared—he shivered and shook his
ears under this bucketful of cold water. But he bravely kept
up his high tone. "There's always a demand—that ineffable
type is one of the eternal needs of man's heart; only pious souls
long for it in silence, almost in shame. Let it appear and their
faith grows brave. How *should* it appear in this corrupt generation? It can't be made to order. It could indeed when the
order came trumpet-toned from the lips of the Church herself
and was addressed to genius panting with inspiration. But it
can spring now only from the soil of passionate labour and
culture. Do you really fancy that while from time to time a
man of complete artistic vision is born into the world such an
image can perish? The man who paints it has painted everything. The subject admits of every perfection—form, colour,
expression, composition. It can be as simple as you please and
yet as rich; as broad and free and yet as full of delicate detail.
Think of the chance for flesh in the little naked nestling child,
irradiating divinity; of the chance for drapery in the chaste
and ample garment of the mother. Think of the great story
you compress into that simple theme. Think above all of the
mother's face and its ineffable suggestiveness, of the mingled
burden of joy and trouble, the tenderness turned to worship
and the worship turned to far-seeing pity. Then look at it all
in perfect line and lovely colour, breathing truth and beauty
and mastery."

"*Anch' io son pittore!*" I laughed. "Unless I'm mistaken *you*
have a masterpiece on the stocks. If you put all that in, you'll
do more than Raphael himself did. Let me know when your

picture's finished, and wherever in the wide world I may be I'll post back to Florence and pay my respects to—the *Madonna of the future*!"

His face, at this, had a flush of consciousness, and he seemed to sigh half in protest, half in resignation. "I don't often mention my picture by name. I detest this modern custom of premature publicity. A great work needs silence, privacy, mystery. And then, do you know, people are so cruel, so frivolous, so unable to imagine a man's wishing to paint a Madonna at this time of day, that I've been laughed at, positively laughed at, sir!"—and his poor, guilty blush deepened. "I don't know what has prompted me to be so frank and trustful with you. You look as if you wouldn't laugh at me. My dear young man"—and he laid his hand on my arm—"I'm worthy of respect. Whatever my limitations may be, I'm honest. There's nothing grotesque in a pure ambition or in a life devoted to it."

2

There was something so admirably candid in his look and tone that further questions seemed to savour just then of indiscretion. I had repeated opportunity to put as many as I would, however, for after this we spent much time together. Daily, for a fortnight, we met under agreement that he should help me to intimacy with the little treasure-city. He knew it so well and had studied it with so pious a patience, he was so deeply versed both in its greater and its minor memories, he had become in short so fond and familiar a Florentine, that he was an ideal *valet de place* and I was glad enough to leave dryer documents at home and learn what I wanted from his lips and his example. He talked of Florence as a devoted old lover might still speak of an old incomparable mistress who remained proof against time; he liked to describe how he had lost his heart to her at first sight. "It's the fashion to make all cities of the feminine gender, but as a rule it's a monstrous mistake. Is Florence of the same sex as New York, as Chicago, as London, as Liverpool? She's the sole perfect lady of them all; one feels toward her as some sensitive aspiring youth feels to some beautiful older woman with a 'history.' She fills you with a presumptuous gallantry." This disinterested passion seemed to stand my friend instead of the common social ties; he led a lonely life and cared for nothing but his work. I was duly flattered by his having taken my uninstructed years into his favour and by his generous sacrifice of precious hours to my society. We spent them in historic streets and consecrated nooks, in churches and convents and galleries, spent them above all in study of those early paintings in which Florence is so rich, returning ever and anon, with restless sympathies, to find in these tender blossoms of art a fragrance and savour more precious than the full-fruited knowledge of the later works. We lingered often in the mortuary chapel of San Lorenzo, where we watched Michael Angelo's dim-visaged warrior sit like some awful Genius of Doubt and brood behind his eternal mask upon the mysteries of life. We stood more than once in the little convent chambers where Fra Angelico wrought as if an angel indeed had held his hand, and gathered that sense of scattered dews and early bird-notes which makes an hour among his relics resemble a morning stroll in some monkish garden. We did all this and much more—wandered into obscure shrines, damp courts, and dusty palace-rooms, in quest of lingering hints of fresco and lurking treasures of sculpture.

I was more and more impressed with my companion's remarkable singleness of purpose. Everything became a pretext for one of his high-flown excursions. Nothing could be seen or said that didn't lead him sooner or later to a glowing discourse on the true, the beautiful and the good. If my friend was not a genius, he was certainly a natural rhapsodist, or even a harmless madman; and I found the play of his temper, his humour, and his candid and unworldly character as quaint as if he had been a creature from another planet. He seemed indeed to know very little of this one, and lived and moved altogether in his boundless province of art. A creature more unsullied by the accidents of life it's impossible to conceive, and I sometimes questioned the reality of an artistic virtue, an esthetic purity, on which some profane experience hadn't rubbed off a little more. It was hard to have to accept him as of our own hard-headed stock; but after all there could be no better sign of his

American star than the completeness of his reaction in favour of vague profits. The very heat of his worship was a mark of conversion; those born within sight of the temple take their opportunities more for granted. He had, moreover, all our native mistrust for intellectual discretion and our native relish for sonorous superlatives. As a critic he rather ignored proportion and degree; his recognitions had a generous publicity, his discriminations were all discoveries. The small change of appreciation seemed to him in fine no coin for a gentleman to handle; and yet with all this overflow of opinion and gesture he remained in himself a mystery. His professions were practically, somehow, all masks and screens, and his personal allusions, as to his ambiguous background, mere wavings of the dim lantern. He was modest and proud, in other words, and never spoke of his domestic matters. He was evidently poor, and yet must have had some slender independence, since he could afford to make so merry over the fact that his culture of ideal beauty had never brought him a penny. His poverty, I supposed, was his motive for neither inviting me to his lodging nor mentioning its whereabouts. We met either in some public place or at my hotel, where I entertained him as freely as I might without appearing to be prompted by charity. He appeared for the most part hungry, and this was his nearest approach to human grossness. I made a point of never seeming to cross a certain line with him, but, each time we met, I ventured to make some respectful allusion to the *magnum opus,* to inquire, if I might, as to its health and progress. "We're getting on, with the Lord's help," he would say with a bravery that never languished; "I think we can't be said not to be doing well. You see I've the grand advantage that I lose no time. These hours I spend with you are pure profit. They bring me in a harvest of incentives. Just as the truly religious soul is always at worship, the genuine artist is always in labour. He takes his property wherever he finds it—he learns some precious secret from every object that stands up in the light. If you but knew—in connexion with something to be done—of the rapture of observing and remembering, of applying one's notes. I take in at every glance some hint for light, for colour, for style. When I get home I pour out my treasures into the lap of my Madonna. Oh, I'm not idle! *Nulla dies sine linea.*"

I had been introduced meanwhile to an American lady whose drawing-room had long formed an attractive place of reunion for strangers of supposed distinction. She lived on a fourth floor and was not rich; but she offered her visitors very good tea, little cakes at option, and conversation not quite to match. Her conversation had mainly a high esthetic pitch, for Mrs. Coventry was famously "artistic." Her apartment was a sort of miniature Pitti Palace. She possessed "early masters" by the dozen—a cluster of Peruginos in her dining room, a Giotto in her boudoir, an Andrea del Sarto over her drawing-room chimney-piece. Surrounded by these treasures and by innumerable bronzes, mosaics, majolica dishes, and little worm-eaten diptychs covered with angular saints on gilded backgrounds, she enjoyed the dignity of a social high-priestess of the arts. She always wore on her bosom a huge, if reduced, copy of the Madonna della Seggiola. Gaining her ear quietly one evening I asked her whether she knew among our compatriots in the place of a certain eccentric but charming Mr. Theobald.

"Know him, know poor Theobald?"—her answer was as public as if I had owed it to the bell-crier. "All Florence knows him, his flamed-coloured locks, his black velvet coat, his interminable harangues on the Beautiful and his wondrous Madonna that mortal eye has never seen and that mortal patience has quite given up expecting."

"Really," I asked, "you don't believe in his wondrous Madonna?"

"My dear ingenuous youth," rejoined my shrewd friend, "has he made a convert of you? Well, we all believed in him once; he came down upon Florence—that is on our little colony here—and took the town by storm. Another Raphael, at the very least, had been born among men, and our poor dear barbarous country was to have the credit of him. Hadn't he the very hair of Raphael flowing down on his shoulders? The hair, alas—it's his difficulty—appears to have to do duty for the head! We swallowed him whole, however; we hung on his lips and proclaimed his genius from the house-tops. The women were dying to sit to him for their portraits and be made immortal like Leonardo's Gioconda. We decided that his manner was a good deal like Leonardo's—'esoteric' and indescribable and fascinating. Well, it has all remained esoteric, and nobody can describe what nobody has ever seen. The months, the years have passed and the miracle has hung fire; our master has never produced his masterpiece. He has passed hours in the galleries and churches, posturing, musing, and gazing; he has talked more about his subject—about every subject—than any human being before has ever talked about anything, but has never put brush to canvas. We had all subscribed, as it were, to the great performance; but as it never came off people began to ask for their money again. I was one of the last of the faithful; I carried devotion so far as to sit to him for my head. If you could have seen the horrible creature he made of me, you'd recognise that even a woman with no more vanity than will tie her bonnet straight must have cooled off then. The man didn't know the very alphabet of drawing. His strong point, he intimated, was his sentiment; but is it a consolation, when one has been painted a fright, to know that the man has particularly enjoyed doing it? One by one, I confess, we fell away from the faith, and Mr. Theobald didn't lift his little finger to preserve us. At the first hint that we were tired of waiting and that we should like the show to begin he was off in a huff. 'Great work requires time, contemplation, privacy, mystery! O ye of little faith!' We answered that we didn't insist on a great work; that the five-act tragedy might come at his convenience; that we merely asked for something to keep us from yawning, some light little *lever de rideau.* On that the poor dear man took his stand as a genius misconceived and persecuted, a martyr to his opinions, and washed his hands of us from that hour! No, I believe he does me the honour to consider me the head and front of the conspiracy formed to nip his glory in the bud—a bud that has taken twenty years to blossom. Ask him if he knows me, and he'll tell you I'm a horribly ugly old woman who has vowed his destruction because he doesn't see his way to paint her in the style of Titian's Flora. I'm afraid that since then he has had none but chance followers, innocent strangers like yourself, who have taken him at his word. The mountain's still in labour; I haven't heard that the mouse has been born. I pass him once in a while in the galleries, and he fixes his great dark eyes on me with a sublimity of indifference, as if I were a bad copy of a Sassoferrato! It's ever so long now since I heard that he was making studies for a Madonna who was to be a *résumé* of all the other Madonnas of the Italian school—like that antique Venus who borrowed a nose from one great image and an ankle from another. It's certainly a grand idea. The parts may be fine, but when I think of my unhappy portrait I tremble for the whole. He has communicated this *trouvaille,* under pledge of solemn secrecy, to fifty chosen spirits, to every one he has ever been able to buttonhole for five minutes. I suppose he wants to get an order for it, and he's not to blame; for goodness knows how he lives. I see by your blush" —my friend freely proceeded—"that you've been honoured with his confidence. You needn't be ashamed, my dear young man; a man of your age is none the worse for a certain generous credulity. Only allow me this word of advice: keep your credulity out of your pockets! Don't pay for the picture till it's delivered. You haven't been treated to a peep at it, I imagine? No more have your fifty predecessors in the faith. There are people who doubt there's any picture to be seen. I shouldn't myself be surprised if, when one runs him to earth, one finds scarce more than in that terrible little tale of Balzac's—a mere mass of incoherent scratches and daubs, a jumble of dead paint!"

I listened to this bold sketch in silent wonder. It had a painfully plausible sound, it set the seal on shy suspicions of my own. My hostess was satirical, but was neither unveracious nor vindictive. I determined to let my judgment wait upon events. Possibly she was right, but if she was wrong she was cruelly wrong. Her version of my friend's eccentricities made me impatient to see him again and examine him in the light of public opinion. On our next meeting I at once asked him if he knew Mrs. Coventry. He laid his hand on my arm with a sadder, though perhaps sharper, look than had ever yet come into his face. "Has she got *you* into training? She's a most vain woman. She's empty and scheming, and she pretends to be serious and kind. She prattles about Giotto's second manner and Vittoria Colonna's liaison with 'Michael'—one would suppose Michael lived across the way and was expected in to take a hand at whist—but she knows as little about art, and about the conditions of production, as I know about the stock-market.

She profanes sacred things," he more vehemently went on. "She cares for you only as someone to hand teacups in that horrible humbugging little parlor with its trumpery Peruginos! If you can't dash off a new picture every three days and let her hand it round among her guests, she tells them you're a low fraud and that they must have nothing to do with you."

This attempt of mine to test Mrs. Coventry's understanding of our poor friend was made in the course of a late afternoon walk to the quiet old church of San Miniato, on one of the hill-tops which directly overlook the city, from whose gates you are guided to it by a stony and cypress-bordered walk, the most fitting of avenues to a shrine. No spot is more propitious to rest and thought than the broad terrace in front of the church, where, lounging against the parapet, you may glance in slow alternation from the black and yellow marbles of the church-façade, seamed and cracked with time and wind-sown with a tender flora of their own, down to the full domes and slender towers of Florence and over to the blue sweep of the wide-mouthed cup of mountains in whose hollow this choicest handful of the spoils of time has been stored away for keeping. I had proposed, as a diversion from the painful memories evoked by Mrs. Coventry's name, that Theobald should go with me the next evening to the opera, where some work rarely played was to be given. He declined, as I half-expected, for I had noted that he regularly kept his evenings in reserve and never alluded to his manner of passing them. "You've reminded me before," I put to him, "of that charming speech of the Florentine painter in Alfred de Musset's *Lorenzaccio:'I do no harm to any one. I pass my days in my studio. On Sunday I go to the Annunziata or to Santa Maria; the monks think I have a voice; they dress me in a white gown and a red cap, and I take a share in the choruses; sometimes I do a little solo: these are the only times I go into public. In the evening, I visit my sweetheart; when the night is fine, we pass it on her balcony.'* I don't know whether you've a sweetheart or whether she has a balcony. But if you *are* so happy it's certainly better than trying to hold out against a third-rate prima donna."

He made no immediate answer, but at last he turned to me solemnly. "Can you look upon a beautiful woman with reverent eyes?"

"Really," I said, "I don't pretend to be sheepish, but I should be sorry to think myself impudent." And I asked him what in the world he meant. When at last I had assured him that if the question was of his giving me such an exhibition I would accept it on the terms he should impose, he made known to me—with an air of religious mystery—that it was in his power to introduce me to the most beautiful woman in Italy: "A beauty with a beautiful soul."

"Upon my word," I said, "you're extremely fortunate. I'm not less so, but you do keep cards up your sleeve."

"This woman's beauty," he returned, "is a revelation, a lesson, a morality, a poem! It's my daily study." Of course after this I lost no time in reminding him of what, before we parted, had taken the shape of a promise. "I feel somehow," he had said, "as if it were a violation of that privacy in which I've always studied and admired her. Therefore what I'm doing for you—well, my friend, is friendship. No hint of her existence has ever fallen from my lips. But with too great a familiarity we're apt to lose a sense of the real value of things, and you'll perhaps throw some new light on what I show you and offer a fresher appreciation."

We went accordingly by appointment to a certain ancient house in the heart of Florence—the precinct of the Mercato Vecchio—and climbed a dark, steep staircase to its highest flight. Theobald's worshipped human type seemed hung as far above the line of common vision as his artistic ideal was lifted over the usual practice of men. He passed without knocking into the dark vestibule of a small apartment where, opening an inner door, he ushered me into a small saloon. The room affected me as mean and sombre, though I caught a glimpse of white curtains swaying gently at an open window. At a table, near a lamp, sat a woman dressed in black, working at a piece of embroidery. As my guide entered she looked up with a serene smile; then, seeing me, she made a movement of surprise and rose with stately grace. He stepped nearer, taking her hand and kissing it with an indescribable air of immemorial usage. As he bent his head she looked at me askance and had, I thought, a perfectly human change of colour.

"This is the sublime Serafina!"—Theobald frankly waved me forward. "And this is a friend and a lover of the arts," he added, introducing me. I received a smile, a curtsey, and a request to be seated.

The most beautiful woman in Italy was a person of a generous Italian type and of a great simplicity of demeanour. Seated again at her lamp with her embroidery, she seemed to have nothing whatever to say. Theobald, bending to her in a sort of Platonic ecstasy, asked her a dozen paternally tender questions about her health, her state of mind, her occupations and the progress of her needlework, which he examined minutely and summoned me to admire. It was one of the pieces of some ecclesiastical vestment—ivory satin wrought with an elaborate design of silver and gold. She made answer in a full rich voice, but with a brevity I couldn't know whether to attribute to native reserve or to the profane constraint of my presence. She had been that morning to confession; she had also been to market and had bought a chicken for dinner. She felt very happy; she had nothing to complain of except that the people for whom she was making her vestment and who furnished her materials should be willing to put such rotten silver thread into the garment, as one might say, of the Lord. From time to time, as she took her slow stitches, she raised her eyes and covered me with a glance which seemed at first to express but a placid curiosity, but in which, as I saw it repeated, I thought I perceived the dim glimmer of an attempt to establish an understanding with me at the expense of our companion. Meanwhile, as mindful as possible of Theobald's injunction of reverence, I considered the lady's personal claims to the fine compliment he had paid her.

That she was indeed a beautiful woman I recognised as soon as I had recovered from the surprise of finding her without the freshness of youth. Her appearance was of the sort which, in losing youth, loses little of its greater merit, expressed for the most part as it was in form and structure and, as Theobald would have said, in "composition." She was broad and ample, low-browed and large-eyed, dark and pale. Her thick brown hair hung low beside her cheek and ear and seemed to drape her head with a covering as chaste and formal as the veil of a nun. The poise and carriage of this head were admirably free and noble, and all the more effective that their freedom was at moments discreetly corrected by a little sanctimonious droop which harmonised admirably with the level gaze of her dark and quiet eye. A strong serene physical nature, with the placid temper which comes of no nerves and no troubles, seemed this lady's comfortable portion. She was dressed in plain dull black, save for a dark blue kerchief which was folded across her bosom and exposed a glimpse of her massive throat. Over this kerchief was suspended a little silver cross. I admired her greatly, yet with a considerable reserve. A certain mild intellectual apathy was the very mark of her complexion and form, and always seemed to round and enrich them; but this bourgeoise Egeria, if I viewed her right, betrayed rather a vulgar stagnation of mind. There might have once been a dim spiritual light in her face, but it had long since begun to wane. And furthermore, in plain prose, she was growing stout. My disappointment amounted very nearly to complete disenchantment when Theobald, as if to facilitate my covert inspection, declaring that the lamp was very dim and that she would ruin her eyes without more light, rose and addressed himself to a couple of candles on the mantelpiece, which he lighted and transferred to the table. In this improved clearness I made our hostess out a very mature person. She was neither haggard nor worn nor grey, but she was thick and coarse. The beautiful soul my friend had promised me seemed scarce worth making such a point of; it dwelt in no deeper principle than some accident of quietude, some matronly mildness of lip and brow. I should have been ready even to pronounce her sanctified bend of the head nothing more inward than the trick of a person always working at embroidery. It might have been even a slightly more sinister symptom, for in spite of her apparently admirable dullness this object of our all-candid homage practically dropped a hint that she took the situation rather less seriously than her friend. When he rose to light the candles she looked across at me with a quick intelligent smile and tapped her forehead with her forefinger; then, as from a sudden feeling of compassionate loyalty to poor Theobald I preserved a blank face, she gave a little shrug and resumed her work.

What was the relation of this singular couple? Was he the most ardent of friends or the most discreet of lovers? Did she regard him as an eccentric swain whose benevolent admiration of her beauty she was not ill-pleased to humour at the small cost of having him climb into her little parlour and gossip of summer nights? With her decent and sombre dress, her simple gravity and that fine piece of priestly stitching, she looked like some pious lay-member of a sisterhood living by special permission outside her convent walls. Or was she maintained here aloft by her admirer in comfortable leisure, so that he might have before him the perfect eternal type, uncorrupted and untarnished by the struggle for existence? Her shapely hands, I observed, were very fair and white; they lacked the traces of what is called honest toil.

"And the pictures, how do they come on?" she asked of Theobald after a long pause.

"Oh, in their own fine, quiet way! I've here a friend whose sympathy and encouragement give me new faith and ardour."

Our hostess turned to me, gazed at me a moment rather inscrutably, and then, repeating the vivid reference to the contents of our poor friend's head she had used a minute before, "He has a magnificent genius!" she said with perfect gravity.

"I'm inclined to think so"—I was amused in spite of myself.

"Eh, why do you smile?" she cried. "If you doubt what I say, you must see the *santo bambino!*" And she took the lamp and conducted me to the other side of the room, where, on the wall, in a plain black frame, hung a large drawing in red chalk. Beneath it was attached a little bowl for holy-water. The drawing represented a very young child, entirely naked, half-nestling back against his mother's gown, but with his two little arms outstretched as in the act of benediction. It had been thrown off with singular freedom and directness, but was none the less vivid with the sacred bloom of infancy. A dimpled elegance and grace, which yet didn't weaken its expression, recalled the touch of Correggio. "That's what he can do!" said my hostess. "It's the blessed little boy I lost. It's his very image, and the Signor Teobaldo, a generous person if there ever was one, gave it me as a gift. He has given me many things besides!"

I looked at the picture for some time—certainly it had a charm. Turning back to our friend I assured him that if it were hung amid the drawings in the Uffizi and labelled with a glorious name it would bravely hold its own. My praise seemed to give him joy; he pressed my hands—his eyes filled with tears. I had apparently quickened his desire to expatiate on the history of the drawing, for he rose and took leave of our companion, kissing her hand with the same mild ardour as before. It occurred to me that the offer of a similar piece of gallantry on my own part might help me to know what manner of woman she was. When she felt my intention she withdrew her hand, dropped her eyes solemnly, and made a severe curtsey. Theobald took my arm and led me rapidly into the street.

"And what do you think of the sublime Serafina?" he cried with anxiety.

"She's certainly a fine figure of a woman," I answered without ceremony.

He eyed me an instant askance and then seemed hurried along by the current of remembrance. "You should have seen the mother and the child together, seen them as I first saw them—the mother with her head draped in a shawl, a divine trouble in her face and the bambino pressed to her bosom. You'd have said, I'm sure, that Raphael had found his match in common chance. I was coming back one summer night from a long walk in the country when I met this apparition at the city gate. The woman held out her hand and I hardly knew whether to say 'What do you want?' or to fall down and worship. She asked for a little money and received what I gave her with the holy sweetness with which the Santissima Vergine receives the offerings of the faithful. I saw she was beautiful and pale—she might have stepped out of the stable of Bethlehem! I gave her money and helped her on her way into the town. I had guessed her story. She too was a maiden mother, but she had been turned out into the world in her shame. I felt in all my pulses that here was my subject marvellously realised. It was as if I had had like one of the monkish artists of old a miraculous vision. I rescued the poor creatures, cherished them, watched them as I would have done some precious work of art, some lovely fragment of fresco discovered in a mouldering cloister. In a month—as if to deepen and sanctify the sadness and sweetness of it all—the poor little child died. When she felt he was going she lifted him up to me for ten minutes—so as not to lose him *all*—and

I made that sketch. You saw a feverish haste in it, I suppose; I wanted to spare the poor little mortal the pain of his position. After that I doubly valued the mother. She's the simplest, sweetest, most natural creature that ever bloomed in this brave old land of Italy. She lives in the memory of her child, in her gratitude for the scanty kindness I've been able to show her, and in her simple instinctive imperturbable piety. She's not even conscious of her beauty; my admiration has never made her vain. Heaven yet knows that I've made no secret what I think of it. You must have taken in the extraordinary clearness and modesty of her look. Was there ever such a truly virginal brow, such a natural classic elegance in the wave of the hair and the arch of the forehead? I've studied her; I may say I know her. I've absorbed her little by little, I've made her my own, my mind's stamped and imbued, and I've determined how to clinch the impression. I shall at last invite her to sit for me!"

" 'At last—at last'?" I repeated in amazement. "Do you mean she has never done so yet?"

"I've not really—since that first time—made her *pose*," he said with a shade of awkwardness. "I've taken notes, you know; I've got my grand fundamental impression. That's the great thing! But I've not actually put her to the inconvenience —so to call it—to which I'd have put a common model."

What had become for the moment of my perception and my tact I'm at a loss to say; in their absence I was unable to repress a headlong exclamation. I was destined to regret it. We had stopped at a turning and beneath a lamp. "My poor friend," I exclaimed, laying my hand on his shoulder, "you've *dawdled!* She's an old, old woman—for a maiden mother."

It was as if I had brutally struck him; I shall never forget the long slow almost ghastly look of pain with which he answered me. "Dawdled?—old, old?" he stammered. "Are you joking?"

"Why, my dear fellow, I suppose you don't take her for anything *but* mature?"

He drew a long breath and leaned against a house, looked at me with questioning, protesting, reproachful eyes. At last starting forward and grasping my arm: "Answer me solemnly: does she seem to you really and truly old? Is she wrinkled, is she faded—am I blind?" he demanded.

Then at last I understood the immensity of his illusion; how, one by one, the noiseless years had ebbed away and left him brooding in charmed inaction, for ever preparing for a work for ever deferred. It struck me almost as a kindness now to tell him the plain truth. "I should be sorry to say you're blind," I returned, "but I think you're rather unfortunately deceived. You've lost time in effortless contemplation. Your friend was once young and fresh and virginal; but you see that must have been some years ago. Still, she has fine things left. By all means make her sit for you." But I broke down; his face was too horribly reproachful.

He took off his hat and stood passing his handkerchief mechanically over his forehead. " 'Fine things left'?" he stared. "Do you speak as if other people had helped themselves—?"

"Why, my dear man," I smiled, "the years have helped themselves! But she has what the French call—don't they?—*de beaux restes?*"

Oh, how he gaped and how something seemed to roll over him! "I must make my Madonna out of *de beaux restes!* What a masterpiece she'll be! Old—old! Old—old!" he re-echoed.

"Never mind her age," I cried, revolted by what I had done; "never mind my impression of her! You have your memory, your notes, your genius. Finish your picture in a month. I pronounce it beforehand a masterpiece and hereby offer you for it any sum you may choose to ask."

He kept staring, but seemed scarce to understand me. "Old —old!" he kept stupidly repeating. "If she's old what am I? If her beauty has faded where, where is my strength? Has life been a dream? Have I worshipped too long? Have I loved too well?" The charm in truth was broken. That the chord of illusion should have snapped at my light accidental touch showed how it had been weakened by excessive tension. The poor fellow's sense of wasted time, of vanished opportunity, surged in upon his soul in waves of darkness. He suddenly dropped his head and burst into tears.

I led him homeward with all possible tenderness, but I attempted neither to check his grief, to restore his equanimity nor to unsay the hard truth. When we reached my hotel I tried to induce him to come in. "We'll drink a glass of wine," I smiled, "to the completion of the Madonna."

With a violent effort he held up his head, mused for a moment with a formidably sombre frown and then, giving me his hand, "I'll finish it," he vowed, "in a month! No, no, in a fortnight! After all I have it *here!*" And he smote his forehead. "Of course she's old! She can afford to have it said of her—a woman who has made twenty years pass like a twelvemonth! Old—old! Why, sir, she shall be eternal!"

I wished to see him safely to his own door, but he waved me back and walked away with an air of resolution, whistling and swinging his cane. I waited a moment—then followed him at a distance and saw him proceed to cross the Santa Trinità Bridge. When he reached the middle he suddenly paused, as if his strength had deserted him, and leaned upon the parapet gazing over into the Arno. I was careful to keep him in sight; I confess I passed ten very nervous minutes. He recovered himself at last and went his way slowly and with hanging head.

That I had really startled him into a bolder use of his long-garnered stores of knowledge and taste, into the vulgar effort and hazard of production, seemed at first reason enough for his continued silence and absence; but as day followed day without his either calling or sending me a line and without my meeting him in his customary haunts, in the galleries, in the chapel at San Lorenzo, or even strolling between the Arno-side and the great hedge-screen of verdure which, along the drive of the Cascine, throws the fair occupants of the open carriages into such becoming relief—as for more than a week I got neither tidings nor sight of him, I began to fear I might have fatally offended him and that instead of giving a wholesome push to his talent, or at least to his faith, I had done it a real harm. I had a wretched suspicion I might have made him ill. My stay at Florence was drawing to a close, and it was important that before resuming my journey I should assure myself of the truth. Theobald had to the last kept his lodging a secret, and I was at a loss how to follow him up. The simplest course was to make inquiry of the object of his homage who neighboured with the Mercato Vecchio, and I confess that unsatisfied curiosity as to the lady herself counselled it as well. Perhaps I had done her injustice, perhaps she was as immortally fresh and fair as he conceived her. I was at any rate anxious to set eyes once more on the ripe enchantress who had made twenty years, as he had said, pass like a twelve-month. I repaired accordingly one morning to her abode, climbed the interminable staircase, and reached her door. It stood ajar, and, while I hesitated to enter, a little serving-maid came clattering out with an empty cooking-pot, as if she had just performed some savoury errand. The inner door too was open; so I crossed the little vestibule and reached the room in which I had formerly been received. It hadn't its evening aspect. The table, or one end of it, was spread for a late breakfast, before which sat a gentleman—an individual at least of the male sex—doing execution upon a beefsteak and onions and a bottle of wine. At his elbow, in intimate nearness, was placed the lady of the house. Her attitude, as I arrived, was not that of an enchantress. With one hand she held in her lap a plate of smoking maccaroni; with the other she had lifted high in air one of the pendulous filaments of this succulent compound and was in the act of slipping it gently down her throat. On the uncovered end of the table, facing her companion, were ranged half-a-dozen small statuettes, of some snuff-coloured substance resembling terra-cotta. He, brandishing his knife with ardour, was apparently descanting on their merits.

Evidently I darkened the door. My hostess dropped her maccaroni—into her mouth, and rose hastily with a harsh exclamation and a flushed face. I forthwith felt sure that the sublime Serafina's secret was still better worth knowing than I had supposed, and that the way to learn it was to take it for granted. I summoned my best Italian, I smiled and bowed and apologised for my intrusion; and in a moment, whether or no I had dispelled the lady's irritation, I had at least made her prudent. I must put myself at my ease; I must take a seat. This was another friend of hers—also an artist, she declared with a smile that had turned to the gracious. Her companion wiped his moustache and bowed with great civility. I saw at a glance that he was equal to the situation. He was presumably the author of the statuettes on the table and knew a money-spending *forestiere* when he saw one. He was a small active man, with a clever, impudent tossed-up nose, a sharp little black eye, conscious of many things at once, and the cocked-up moustache of a trooper. On the side of his head he wore jauntily one of the loose velvet caps affected by sculptors in damp studios, and I observed that his feet were encased in bright "worked" slippers. On Serafina's remarking with dignity that I was the friend of Mr. Theobald he broke out into the fantastic French of which Italians are sometimes so insistently lavish, declaring without reserve that Mr. Theobald was a magnificent genius.

"I'm sure I don't know," I answered with a shrug. "If you're in a position to affirm it you've the advantage of me. I've seen nothing from his hand but the bambino yonder, which certainly is fine."

He had it that the bambino was a masterpiece—in the maniera Correggiesca. It was only a pity, he added with a knowing laugh, that the sketch hadn't been made on some good bit of honeycombed old panel. The sublime Serafina hereupon protested that Mr. Theobald was the soul of honour and didn't lend himself to that style of manufacture. "I'm not a judge of genius," she said, "and I know nothing of pictures. I'm a poor, simple widow; but I'm sure *nostro signore* has the heart of an angel and the virtue of a saint. He's my great benefactor," she made no secret of it. The after-glow of the somewhat sinister flush with which she had greeted me still lingered in her cheek and perhaps didn't favour her beauty; I couldn't but judge it a wise custom of Theobald's to visit her only by candle-light. She was coarse and her poor adorer a poet.

"I've the greatest esteem for him," I stated; "it's for that reason I've been so uneasy at not seeing him for ten days. Have you seen him? Is he perhaps ill?"

"Ill? Heaven forbid!" cried Serafina with genuine vehemence.

Her companion uttered a rapid expletive and reproached her with not having been to see him. She hesitated a moment, then simpered the least bit and bridled. "He comes to see me—without reproach! But it wouldn't be the same for me to go to him, though indeed you may almost call him a man of holy life."

"He has the greatest admiration for you," I said. "He'd have been honoured by your visit."

She looked at me a moment sharply. "More admiration than you. Admit that!" Of course I protested with all the eloquence at my command, and my ambiguous hostess then confessed that she had taken no fancy to me on my former visit and that, our friend not having returned, she believed I had poisoned his mind against her. "It would be no kindness to the poor gentleman, I can tell you that," she said. "He has come to see me every evening for years. It's a long friendship! No one knows him as I do."

"I don't pretend to know him or to understand him. I can only esteem and—I think I may say—love him. Nevertheless he seems to me a little—!" And I touched my forehead and waved my hand in the air.

Serafina glanced at her companion as for inspiration. He contented himself with shrugging his shoulders while he filled his glass again. The padrona hereupon treated me to a look of more meaning than quite consorted with her noble blankness. "Ah, but it's for that that *I* love him! The world has so little kindness for such persons. It laughs at them and despises them and cheats them. He's too good for this wicked life. It's his blest imagination that he finds a little Paradise up here in my poor apartment. If he thinks so, how can I help it? He has a strange belief—really I ought to be ashamed to tell you—that I resemble the Madonna Santissima, heaven forgive me! I let him think what he pleases so long as it makes him happy. He was very kind to me once and I'm not one who forgets a favour. So I receive him every evening civilly, and ask after his health, and let him look at me on this side and that. For that matter, I may say it without vanity, I was worth looking at once. And he's not always amusing, *poveretto*! He sits sometimes for an hour without speaking a word, or else he talks away, without stopping, about art and nature and beauty and duty, about fifty fine things that are all so much Latin to me. I beg you to under-

stand that he has never said a word to me I mightn't honour-
ably listen to. He may be a little cracked, but he's one of the
blessed saints."

"Eh, eh," cried the man, "the blessed saints were all a little
cracked!"

Serafina, I surmised, left part of her story untold; what
she said sufficed to make poor Theobald's own statement still
more affecting than I had already found its strained simplicity. "It's a strange fortune, certainly," she went on, "to
have such a friend as this dear man—a friend who's less than
a lover, yet more than a brother." I glanced at her comrade,
who continued to smirk in a mystifying manner while he
twisted the ends of his moustache between his copious mouth-
fuls. Was *he* less than a lover? "But what will you have?"
Serafina pursued. "In this hard world one mustn't ask too
many questions; one must take what comes and keep what
one gets. I've kept my *amoroso* for twenty years, and I do
hope that, at this time of day, signore, you've not come to
turn him against me!"

I assured her I had no such intention, and that I should
vastly regret disturbing Mr. Theobald's habits or convictions.
On the contrary I was alarmed about him and would at once
go in search of him. She gave me his address and a florid
account of her sufferings at his non-appearance. She had
not been to him for various reasons; chiefly because she was
afraid of displeasing him, as he had always made such a
mystery of his home. "You might have sent this gentleman!"
I however ventured to suggest.

"Ah," cried the gentleman, "he admires Madonna Serafina,
but he wouldn't admire me whom he doesn't take for Saint
Joseph!" And then confidentially, his finger on his nose: "His
taste's terribly severe!"

I was about to withdraw after having promised that I
would inform our hostess of my friend's condition, when her
companion, who had risen from table and girded his loins
apparently for the onset, grasped me gently by the arm and
led me before the row of statuettes. "I perceive by your conversation, signore, that you're a patron of the arts. Allow
me to request your honourable attention for these modest
products of my own ingenuity. They are brand-new, fresh

from my atelier, and have never been exhibited in public. I have brought them here to receive the verdict of this dear lady, who's a good critic, for all she may pretend to the contrary. I'm the inventor of this peculiar style of statuette—of subject, manner, material, everything. Touch them, I pray you; handle them freely—you needn't fear. Delicate as they look, it's impossible they should break! My various creations have met with great success. They're especially admired by the American *conoscenti*. I've sent them all over Europe—to London, Paris, Vienna! You may have noticed some little specimens in Paris, on the *grand boulevard*"—he aimed at the French sound of the words—"in a shop of which they constitute the specialty. There's always a crowd about the window. They form a very pleasing ornament for the mantel-shelf of a gay young bachelor, for the boudoir of a pretty woman. You couldn't make a prettier present to a person with whom you should wish to exchange a harmless joke. It's not classic art, signore, of course; but, between ourselves, isn't classic art sometimes rather a bore? Caricature, burlesque, *la charge*, has hitherto been confined to paper, to the pen and pencil. Now it has been my inspiration to introduce it into statuary. For this purpose I've invented a peculiar plastic compound which you will permit me not to divulge. That's my secret, signore! It's as light, you perceive, as cork, and yet firm as alabaster! I frankly confess that I really pride myself as much on this little stroke of chemical ingenuity as upon the other element of novelty in my creations—my types. What do you say to my types, signore? The idea's bold; does it strike you as happy? Cats and monkeys—monkeys and cats— all human life is there! Human life, of course I mean, viewed with the eye of the satirist! To combine sculpture and satire, signore, has been my unprecedented ambition. I flatter myself I've not egregiously failed."

As this jaunty Juvenal of the chimney-piece thus persuasively proceeded he took up his little groups successively from the table, held them aloft, turned them about, rapped them with his knuckles and gazed at them lovingly, his head on one side. They consisted each, with a vengeance, of a cat and a monkey, occasionally draped, in some preposterously sentimental conjunction. They exhibited a certain sameness of motive and illustrated chiefly the different phases of what, in fine terms, might have been called the amorous advance and the amorous alarm; but they were strikingly clever and expressive, and were at once very dreadful little beasts and very natural men and women. I confess, however, that they failed to amuse me. I was doubtless not in a mood to enjoy them, for they seemed to me peculiarly cynical and vulgar. Their imitative felicity was revolting. As I looked askance at the complacent little artist, brandishing them between finger and thumb and caressing them with the fondest eye, he struck me as himself little more than an exceptionally intelligent ape. I mustered an admiring grin, however, and he blew another blast. "My figures are studied from life! I've a little menagerie of monkeys whose frolics I follow by the hour. As for the cats, one has only to look out of one's back window! Since I've begun to examine these expressive little brutes I've made many profound observations. Speaking, signore, to a man of imagination, I may say that my little designs are not without a philosophy of their own. Truly, I don't know whether the cats and monkeys imitate us, or whether it's we who imitate them." I congratulated him on his philosophy, and he resumed: "You'll do me the honour to admit that I've handled my subjects with delicacy. Eh, it was needed, *signore mio*. I've been just a bit free, but not too free—eh, *dica*? Just a scrap of a hint, you know! You may see as much or as little as you please. These little groups, however, are no measure of my invention. If you'll favour me with a call at my studio I think you'll admit that my combinations are really infinite. I likewise execute figures to command. You've perhaps some little motive—the fruit of your philosophy of life, signore— which you'd like to have interpreted. I can promise to work it up to your satisfaction; it shall have as many high lights and sharp accents as you please! Allow me to present you with my card and to remind you that my prices are moderate. Only sixty francs for a little group like that. My statuettes are as durable as bronze—*aere perennius*, signore—and, between ourselves, I think they're more amusing!"

As I pocketed his card I turned an eye on Madonna Serafina, wondering whether she had a sense for contrasts. She had picked up one of the little couples and was tenderly dusting it with a feather broom.

What I had just seen and heard had so deepened my compassionate interest in my deluded friend that I took a summary leave, making my way directly to the house designated by this remarkable woman. It was in an obscure corner of the opposite side of the town and presented a sombre and squalid appearance. A withered crone, in the doorway, on my inquiring for Theobald, welcomed me with a mumbled blessing and an expression of relief at the poor gentleman's having at last a caller. His lodging appeared to consist of a single room at the top of the house. On getting no answer to my knock I opened the door, supposing him absent; so that it gave me a certain shock to find him but seated helpless and dumb. His chair was near the single window, facing an easel which supported a large canvas. On my entering he looked up at me blankly, without changing his position, which was that of absolute lassitude and dejection, his arms loosely folded, his legs stretched before him, his head hanging on his breast. Advancing into the room I saw how vividly his face answered to his attitude. He was pale, haggard, and unshaven, and his dull and sunken eye gazed at me without a spark of recognition. My fear had been that he would greet me with fierce reproaches, as the cruelly officious patron who had turned his contentment to bitterness, and I was relieved to find my appearance excite no visible resentment. "Don't you know me?"—I put out my hand. "Have you already forgotten me?"

He made no response, but kept his position stupidly and left me staring about the room. It spoke, the poor place, all plaintively for itself. Shabby, sordid, naked, it contained, beyond the wretched bed, but the scantiest provision for personal comfort. It was bedroom at once and studio—a grim ghost of a studio. A few dusty casts and prints on the walls, three or four old canvases turned face inward and a rusty-looking colour-box formed, with the easel at the window, the sum of its appurtenances. The whole scene savoured horribly of indigence. Its only wealth was the picture on the easel, presumably the famous Madonna. Averted as this was from the door I was unable to see its face; but at last, sickened by my impression of vacant misery, I passed behind Theobald eagerly and tenderly. I can scarcely say I was surprised at what I found—a canvas that was a mere dead blank cracked and discoloured by time. This was his immortal work! Though not surprised, I confess I was powerfully moved, and I think that for five minutes I couldn't have trusted myself to speak. At last my silent nearness affected him; he stirred and turned and then rose, looking at me with a slow return of intelligence. I murmured some kind ineffective nothings about his being ill and needing advice and care, but he seemed absorbed in the effort to recall distinctly what had last passed between us. "You were right," he said with a pitiful smile, "I'm a dawdler! I'm a failure! I shall do nothing more in this world. You opened my eyes, and though the truth is bitter I bear you no grudge. Amen! I've been sitting here for a week face to face with it, the terrible truth, face to face with the past, with my weakness and poverty and nullity. I shall never touch a brush! I believe I've neither eaten nor slept. Look at that canvas!" he went on as I relieved my emotion by an urgent request that he would come home with me and dine. "That was to have contained my masterpiece! Isn't it a promising foundation? The elements of it are all *here*." And he tapped his forehead with that mystic confidence which had so often marked the gesture for me before. "If I could only transpose them into some brain that has the hand, the will! Since I've been sitting here taking stock of my intellects, I've come to believe that I've the material for a hundred masterpieces. But my hand's paralysed now and they'll never be painted. I never began! I waited and waited to be worthier to begin— I wasted my life in preparation. While I fancied my creation was growing it was only dying. I've taken the whole business too hard. Michael Angelo didn't when he went at the Lorenzo. He did his best at a venture, and his venture's immortal. *That's* mine!" And he pointed with a gesture I shall never forget at the empty canvas. "I suppose we're a genus by ourselves in the providential scheme—we talents that can't act, that can't do nor dare! We take it out in talk, in study, in plans and promises, in visions! But our visions, let me tell you," he cried with a toss of his head, "have a way of

410

being brilliant, and a man has not lived in vain who has seen the things *I've* seen! Of course you won't believe in them when that bit of worm-eaten cloth is all I have to show for them; but to convince you, to enchant and astound the world, I need only the hand of Raphael. His brain I already have. A pity, you'll say, that I haven't his modesty! Ah, let me boast and babble now—it's all I have left! I'm the half of a genius! Where in the wide world is my other half? Lodged perhaps in the vulgar soul, the cunning ready fingers of some dull copyist or some trivial artisan who turns out by the dozen his easy prodigies of touch! But it's not for me to sneer at him; he at least does something. He's not a dawdler. Well for me if I had been vulgar and clever and reckless, if I could have shut my eyes and taken my leap."

What to say to the poor fellow, what to do for him, seemed hard to determine; I chiefly felt I must break the spell of his present inaction and draw him out of the haunted air of the little room it was such cruel irony to call a studio. I can't say I persuaded him to come forth with me; he simply suffered himself to be led, and when we began to walk in the warm light of day I was able to appreciate his great weakness. Nevertheless he seemed in a manner to revive; he even murmured to me at last that he should like to go to the Pitti Gallery. I shall never forget our melancholy stroll through those gorgeous halls, every picture on whose walls glowed, to my stricken sight, with an insolent renewal of strength and lustre. The eyes and lips of the great portraits reflected for me a pitying scorn of the dejected pretender who had dreamed of competing with their triumphant authors. The celestial candour even of the Madonna of the Chair, as we paused in perfect silence before her, broke into the strange smile of the women of Leonardo. Perfect silence indeed marked our whole progress—the silence of a deep farewell; for I felt in all my pulses, as Theobald, leaning on my arm, dragged one heavy foot after the other, that he was looking his last. When we came out he was so exhausted that instead of taking him to my hotel to dine I called a cab and drove him straight to his own poor lodging. He had sunk into the deepest lethargy; he lay back in the vehicle with his eyes closed, as pale as death, his faint breathing interrupted at intervals by a gasp like a smothered sob or a vain attempt to speak. With the help of the old woman who had admitted me before and who emerged from a dark back court I contrived to lead him up the long, steep staircase and lay him on his wretched bed. To her I gave him in charge while I prepared in all haste to call a doctor. But she followed me out of the room with a pitiful clasping of her hands.

"Poor dear blessed gentleman," she wailed—"is he dying?"

"Possibly. How long has he been so bad?"

"Since a certain night he passed ten days ago. I came up in the morning to make his poor bed, and found him sitting up in his clothes before that great dirty canvas he keeps there. Poor dear strange man, he says his prayers to it! He hadn't been to bed—nor even since then, as you may say. What has happened to him? Has he found out about *quella cattiva donna?*" she panted with a glittering eye and a toothless grin.

"Prove at least that one old woman can be faithful," I said, "and watch him well till I come back." My return was delayed through the absence of the English physician, who was away on a round of visits and whom I vainly pursued from house to house before I overtook him. I brought him to Theobald's bedside none too soon. A violent fever had seized our patient, whose case was evidently grave. A couple of hours later on I knew he had brain-fever. From this moment I was with him constantly, but I am far from wishing fully to report his illness. Excessively painful to witness, it was happily brief. Life burned out in delirium. One night in particular that I passed at his pillow, listening to his wild snatches of regret, of aspiration, of rapture and awe at the phantasmal pictures with which his brain seemed to swarm, comes back to my memory now like some stray page from a lost masterpiece of tragedy. Before a week was over we had buried him in the little Protestant cemetery on the way to Fiesole. Madonna Serafina, whom I had caused to be informed of his state, had come in person, I was told, to inquire about its progress; but she was absent from his funeral, which was attended but by a scanty concourse of mourners. Half-a-dozen old Florentine sojourners, in spite of the prolonged estrangement that had preceded his death, had felt the kindly impulse

412

to honour his grave. Among them was my friend Mrs. Coventry, whom I found, on my departure, waiting in her carriage at the gate of the cemetery.

"Well," she said, relieving at last with a significant smile the solemnity of our immediate greeting, "and the greatest of all Madonnas? Have you seen her after all?"

"I've seen her," I said; "she's mine—by bequest. But I shall never show her to you."

"And why not, pray?"

"Because you wouldn't understand her!"

She rather glared at me. "Upon my word you're polite!"

"Pardon me—I'm sad and vexed and bitter." And with reprehensible rudeness I marched away. I was impatient to leave Florence; my friend's blighted spirit met my eyes in all aspects. I had packed my trunk to start for Rome that night, and meanwhile, to beguile my unrest, I aimlessly paced the streets. Chance led me at last to the church of San Lorenzo. Remembering poor Theobald's phrase about Michael Angelo—"He did his best at a venture"—I went in and turned my steps to the chapel of the tombs. Viewing in sadness the sadness of its immortal treasures, I could say to myself while I stood there that they needed no ampler commentary than those simple words. As I passed through the church again to leave it, a woman, turning away from one of the side-altars, met me face to face. The black shawl depending from her head draped becomingly the handsome face of Madonna Serafina. She stopped as she recognised me, and I saw she wished to speak. Her brow was lighted and her ample bosom heaved in a way that seemed to portend a certain sharpness of reproach. But some expression of my own then drew the sting from her resentment, and she addressed me in a tone in which bitterness was tempered by an acceptance of anticlimax that had been after all so long and so wondrously postponed. "I know it was you, now, who separated us," she said. "It was a pity he ever brought you to see me! Of course, you couldn't think of me as he did. Well, the Lord gave him, the Lord has taken him. I've just paid for a nine days' mass for his soul. And I can tell you this, signore—I never deceived him. Who put it into his head that I was made to live on holy thoughts and fine phrases? It was his own imagination, and it pleased him to think so. Did he suffer much?" she added more softly and after a pause.

"His sufferings were great, but they were short."

"And did he speak of me?" She had hesitated and dropped her eyes; she raised them with her question, and revealed in their sombre stillness a gleam of feminine confidence which for the moment revived and enhanced her beauty. Poor Theobald! Whatever name he had given his passion it was still her fine eyes that had charmed him.

"Be contented, madam," I answered gravely.

She lowered her lids again and was silent. Then exhaling a full rich sigh as she gathered her shawl together: "He was a magnificent genius!"

I bowed assent and we separated.

Passing through a narrow side street on my way back to my hotel, I noted above a doorway a sign that it seemed to me I had read before. I suddenly remembered it for identical with the superscription of a card that I had carried for an hour in my waistcoat-pocket. On the threshold stood the ingenius artist whose claims to public favour were thus distinctly signalised, smoking a pipe in the evening air and giving the finishing polish with a bit of rag to one of his inimitable "combinations." I caught the expressive curl of a couple of tails. He recognized me, removed his little red cap with an obsequious bow, and motioned me to enter his studio. I returned his salute and passed on, vexed with the apparition. For a week afterwards, whenever I was seized among the ruins of triumphant Rome with some peculiarly poignant memory of Theobald's transcendent illusions and deplorable failure, I seemed to catch the other so impertinent and so cynical echo: "Cats and monkeys, monkeys and cats—all human life is there!"

QUESTIONS FOR DISCUSSION

THE FIGURE IN THE CARPET

1. The figure in the carpet, or Vereker's "general intention," is, of course, the focal point of interest. Applied here, what does James make the words "general intention" mean?

2. The author chooses not to give answer to the "mystery" question raised in the story. It is safe to assume, therefore, that he is chiefly interested in the main question raised **by** the story. What is that question? How does James answer it?

3. Elements of frustration, perversity, and intellectual tenacity are measured into the story. Point out where and to what degree each appears, and tell how all these forces relate to the central question posed by the story.

4. Unexpected accidents and delays prevent the narrator from gaining his objective. Aside from their obvious use as extensions of the plot, what specific story components do they add?

5. "For the few persons, at any rate, abnormal or not, with whom my anecdote is concerned, literature was a game of skill, and skill meant courage, and courage meant honour, and honour meant passion, meant life. The stake on the table was a special substance and our roulette the revolving mind, but we sat round the green board as intently as the grim gamblers at Monte Carlo." With this quotation as a basis, explain: (a) the kind of people this story is about; (b) the kind of people for whom this story is written; and (c) the sort of problem James takes as story material.

THE LESSON OF THE MASTER

1. James deftly analyzes the personal relationship between the younger and older writer. Explore the binding substance of this friendship.

2. We find James speaking through both of these different imaginary writers. Does he present equally fair and sympathetic treatment for the problems of each? Explain.

3. The author offers a distinct possibility that Paul Overt was duped by St. George. Explain this, and tell why or why not you think he was.

4. Two brief but notable descriptive passages occur in the first pages of the story. These passages are strongly suggestive of techniques and scenes from the French Impressionist school of painting. Whether you

wish to make this comparison or not, explain the components of Jamesian description.

5. Basic assumptions are found in the story regarding the relationship of the writer to society. What are they?

6. This story occupies itself chiefly with the question of how a writer may achieve a lasting quality of artistic perfection. What answer does James give to this question?

A SUGGESTED INTERPRETATION

THE MADONNA OF THE FUTURE

Three ideas of enduring interest are at the core of this story about art: (1) Of what does the act of artistic creation consist? (2) Is a completed second-rate art object more desirable than the vision for one that is first rate? (3) What is required for a renaissance?

The ideas, then, draw the author out. Whether as an afterthought or as an incompletely executed forethought, he gives his story the limited first-person point of view through an anonymous American narrator. But we are not brought back to the drawing-room frame attached at the beginning. Our spokesman remains not only unnamed but undeveloped as a character, except for what we learn of him as a result of his reactions to the events which take place. Theobald, the "mute, inglorious Milton," although the central character, likewise remains only an idea, while Mrs. Coventry and Serafina and her paramour are merely conventional foils. On James's own terms, therefore, the reader is inevitably urged to fasten his greatest attention upon the ideas with which the story starts and stops.

For those few writers and aestheticians passionately concerned with the philosophy of beauty, the question of what the act of artistic creation consists in has continuously been a spur to speculation. Through Theobald, Henry James suggests (and endorses) the notion that art of consummate, sublime perfection is the product of a deep intuitive perception. In effect, James says that before a great painting can be put to canvas the artist must be able to see it—with every perfectly conceived detail—in the refining fires of his own luminous creative imagination. A fully apprehended painting exists in the artist's brain first of all; transposition to canvas is, with learnable technical virtuosity, a mechanical act. Theobald has experienced the truly important first step, but, intoxicated (and long-sustained) by his inner vision, he has lost necessary contact with reality and has succumbed before the enormity of the act of getting the painting outside of himself.

That James respects this condition is suggested by the sympathetic way he has the narrator behave toward our rather ludicrous and somewhat mad virtuoso. Mrs. Coventry, the unbelieving Philistine, is incapable of understanding that Theobald's sincere devotion to the artistic ideal of perfection is alone sufficient cause for courteous approbation. Serafina, the fallen angel who through a cloudy religious feeling reacts patiently toward the genius, exploits him.

Serafina's shabby gentleman caller then serves to raise the issue of whether an unobjectified first-rate inner vision such as Theobald's is preferable to a completed second-rate artistic production. James says "yes." In the story, imperfect art is patently commercial, frankly erotic, and vulgarly promoted by its creator, debasing by its fraudulent existence the sublimity of Theobald's ideal.

That the city most dramatically embodying the feeling of the Renaissance—Florence, with its unique museums chockablock with art treasures—should be Theobald's spiritual home is altogether appropriate. That he and the narrator be American, however, is not an absolute requirement.

James, an expatriated American, often wrote about the impact of highly developed, complex European civilization upon ingenuous, unsophisticated Americans. Since this story was originally published in an American magazine, it seems likely that James's thesis was intended to have particular meaning for readers in this country. Theobald says, "We're the disinherited of Art! We're condemned to be superficial! We're excluded from the magic circle! The soil of American perception is a poor little barren artificial deposit! Yes, we're wedded to imperfection! An American, to excel, has just ten times as much to learn as a European! We lack the deeper sense! We have neither taste nor tact nor force! How **should** we have them? Our crude and garish climate, our silent past, our deafening present, the constant pressure about us of unlovely conditions, are as void of all that nourishes and prompts and inspires the artist as my sad heart is void of bitterness in saying so! We poor aspirants must live in perpetual exile."

In reply to this outburst, the spokesman for James makes a special exhortation to Americans, urging them to hasten the arrival of the Madonna of the future. " 'Nothing is so idle as to talk about our want of a nursing air, of a kindly soil, of opportunity, of inspiration, of the things that help. The only thing that helps is to do something fine. There's no law in our glorious Constitution against that. Invent, create, achieve.' "

The idea with which James was chiefly taken now becomes clearer: What is required for a renaissance in art? It is here that the spiritual fervor and belief of Theobald come into play, for James thinks that a widespread devotion to a vision of artistic perfection would be requisite to a second Renaissance. Theobald's mildly psychotic dedication to art is an evangelical protest against the indifferent-to-art world in which he finds himself. The Madonna of the future——the spiritual motherhood needed for sublime artistic rebirth——is still to appear, but not until there are fewer Mrs. Coventrys and Serafinas and more Theobalds and believers in Theobalds.

SUBJECTS FOR WRITTEN COMPOSITION

1. Using as a basis these stories about writers and artists, write a paper on James's aesthetic, his philosophy of art. Synthesize the main ideas in each story to provide the core of the composition.

2. Prepare a theme on James as a creator of suspense. Analyze the specific ingredients which contribute to the state of being undecided or undetermined, the state of suspense.

3. To develop an understanding of James's handling of character, write a composition on the typical Jamesian hero. Through a synthesis of material in these stories, explain the following elements about James's protagonist: (a) his basic beliefs; (b) his social standing and background; (c) his purpose in life; (d) his chief pursuits and accomplishments; and (e) his mode of conversation and conduct.

4. Analyze the social milieu or environment in these James stories. Present a fully developed picture of the view we get of society through James.

5. Write a paper on the nature of the conflict——the clash of ideas or persons——in these stories. Reveal the special qualities of this conflict as it relates to character and subject matter.

6. Compose a theme on James's style——his specific mode of putting thoughts into words. Analyze the variety and kinds of his sentences; the construction and execution of his paragraphs; the design and plan of his over-all structure; the quality and character of his vocabulary; the distinction and frequency of his punctuation; and the syntax and rhythm of his prose.

Joseph Conrad

Joseph Conrad

JOSEPH CONRAD was born Teodor Jósef Konrad Korzen-
iowski in 1857, the child of Polish parents living in the
Russian Ukraine. When he died in 1924, he was a British
subject, a veteran of twenty years' service on French and
English ships, and a master novelist in English. Conrad's
remarkable command of written English (he always spoke
it with an accent) had deep origins. His father was an
avid reader of English literature in translation, and it was
thus that as a boy Conrad read his Shakespeare and his
Dickens. When, after more than fifteen years in the British
merchant navy, Conrad took up his labors as a novelist,
he wrote in English not simply because it was his adopted
tongue, but because English was a language which had
mastered him.

During the thirty years which he devoted to writing novels and short stories (1894–1924), Conrad produced the equivalent of two full-length novels every three years. The best and most famous of his novel-length stories are, "The Nigger of the 'Narcissus'" (1897), "Lord Jim" (1900), "Nostromo" (1904), and "Victory" (1915); but many of Conrad's other novels—"An Outcast of the Islands" (1896), "Under Western Eyes" (1911), "Chance" (1913), "The Arrow of Gold" (1919)—are excellent by most standards, even though they fall below the high mark of Conrad's best. Among his short stories, the following must be considered masterpieces: "Youth," "Heart of Darkness," "An Outpost of Progress," "The Secret Sharer," "Typhoon," and "The Mirror of the Sea."

That Conrad wrote so much in English is remarkable; that he wrote so well is phenomenal. He could describe a scene, pose a problem, and evoke an atmosphere in a manner unsurpassed; he did not use words sparingly (except in passages of dialogue), but few discerning readers would want to dispense with any that appear on a Conrad page.

Joseph Conrad does not fall easily into the traditional patterns of Anglo-American prose fiction. Like James before him and like Steinbeck and Hemingway after, he frequently employed in his novels and stories the point of view of a character (in Conrad's case it was Marlow) who, as a kind of spectator-participant, filters the story through to the reader and provides clues as to its right interpretation. As for his subject matter, however, Conrad usually chose seafaring life, and except for Tobias Smollett in the eighteenth century and Captain Frederick Marryat in the nineteenth, there was no living English tradition to guide him. Conrad constantly probed the most fundamental questions of good and evil; life at sea was thus a vital vehicle—first, because it was what Conrad knew best, and second, because it provided him with a kind of formal microcosm in which to formulate his moral definitions. And however much the student may be fascinated by Conrad's life and language, he will miss his author unless he comes firmly to grips with the moral problems posed.

An outpost of progress

1

THERE WERE TWO WHITE MEN IN CHARGE OF THE TRADING STATION. Kayerts, the chief, was short and fat; Carlier, the assistant, was tall, with a large head and a very broad trunk perched upon a long pair of thin legs. The third man on the staff was a Sierra Leone nigger, who maintained that his name was Henry Price. However, for some reason or other, the natives down the river had given him the name of Makola, and it stuck to him through all his wanderings about the country. He spoke English and French with a warbling accent, wrote a beautiful hand, understood bookkeeping, and cherished in his innermost heart the worship of evil spirits. His wife was a negress from Loanda, very large and very noisy. Three children rolled about in sunshine before the door of his low, shed-like dwelling. Makola, taciturn and impenetrable, despised the two white men. He had charge of a small clay store house with a dried-grass roof, and pretended to keep a correct account of beads, cotton cloth, red kerchiefs, brass wire, and other trade goods it contained. Besides the storehouse and Makola's hut, there was only one large building in the cleared ground of the station. It was built neatly of reeds, with a veranda on all the four sides. There were three rooms in it. The one in the middle was the living room, and had two rough tables and a few stools in it. The other two were the bedrooms for the white men. Each had a bedstead and a mosquito net for all furniture. The plank floor was littered with the belongings of the white men; open half-empty boxes, torn wearing apparel, old boots; all the things dirty, and all the things broken, that accumulate mysteriously round untidy men. There was also another dwelling place some distance away from the buildings. In it, under a tall cross much out of the perpendicular, slept the man who had seen the beginning of all this; who had planned and had watched the construction of this outpost of progress. He had been, at home, an unsuccessful painter who, weary of pursuing fame on an empty stomach, had gone out there through high protections. He had been the first chief of that station. Makola had watched the energetic artist die of fever in the just finished house with his usual kind of "I told you so" indifference. Then, for a time, he dwelt alone with his family, his account books, and the Evil Spirit that rules the lands under the equator. He got on very well with his god. Perhaps he had propitiated him by a promise of more white men to play with, by and by. At any rate the director of the Great Trading Company, coming up in a steamer that resembled an enormous sardine box with a flat-roofed shed erected on it, found the station in good order, and Makola as usual quietly diligent. The director had the cross put up over the first agent's grave, and appointed Kayerts to the post. Carlier was told off as second in charge. The director was a man ruthless and efficient, who at times, but very imperceptibly, indulged in grim humor. He made a speech to Kayerts and Carlier, pointing out to them the promising aspect of their station. The nearest trading post was about three hundred miles away. It was an exceptional opportunity for them to distinguish themselves and to earn percentages on the trade. This appointment was a favor done to beginners. Kayerts was moved almost to tears by his director's kindness. He would, he said, by doing his best, try to justify the flattering confidence, etc., etc. Kayerts had been in the Administration of the Telegraphs, and knew how to express himself correctly. Carlier, an ex-noncommissioned officer of cavalry in an army guaranteed from harm by several European powers, was less impressed. If there were commissions to get, so much the better; and, trailing a sulky glance over the river, the forests, the impenetrable bush that seemed to cut off the station from the rest of the world, he muttered between his teeth, "We shall see, very soon."

Next day, some bales of cotton goods and a few cases of provisions having been thrown on shore, the sardine-box steamer went off, not to return for another six months. On the deck the director touched his cap to the two agents, who stood on the bank waving their hats, and turning to an old servant of the Company on his passage to headquarters, said, "Look at those two imbeciles. They must be mad at home to send me such specimens. I told those fellows to plant a vegetable garden, build new storehouses and fences, and construct a landing stage. I bet nothing will be done! They won't know how to begin. I always thought the station on this river useless, and they just fit the station!"

"They will form themselves there," said the old stager with a quiet smile.

"At any rate, I am rid of them for six months," retorted the director.

The two men watched the steamer round the bend, then, ascending arm in arm the slope of the bank, returned to the station. They had been in this vast and dark country only a very short time, and as yet always in the midst of other white men, under the eye and guidance of their superiors. And now, dull as they were to the subtle influences of surroundings, they felt themselves very much alone, when suddenly left unassisted to face the wilderness; a wilderness rendered more strange, more incomprehensible by the mysterious glimpses of the vigorous life it contained. They were two perfectly insignificant and incapable individuals, whose existence is only rendered possible through the high organization of civilized crowds. Few men realize that their life, the very essence of their character, their capabilities and their audacities, are only the expression of their belief in the safety of their surroundings. The courage, the composure, the confidence; the emotions and principles; every great and every insignificant thought belongs not to the individual but to the crowd: to the crowd that believes blindly in the irresistible force of its institutions and of its morals, in the power of its police and of its opinion. But the contact with pure unmitigated savagery, with primitive nature and primitive man, brings sudden and profound trouble into the heart. To the sentiment of being alone of one's kind, to the clear perception of the loneliness of one's thoughts, of one's sensations—to the negation of the habitual, which is safe, there is added the affirmation of the unusual, which is dangerous; a suggestion of things vague, uncontrollable, and repulsive, whose discomposing intrusion excites the imagination and tries the civilized nerves of the foolish and the wise alike.

Kayerts and Carlier walked arm in arm, drawing close to one another as children do in the dark; and they had the same, not altogether unpleasant, sense of danger which one half suspects to be imaginary. They chatted persistently in familiar tones. "Our station is prettily situated," said one. The other assented with enthusiasm, enlarging volubly on the beauties of the situation. Then they passed near the grave. "Poor devil!" said Kayerts. "He died of fever, didn't he?" muttered Carlier, stopping short. "Why," retorted

Kayerts, with indignation, "I've been told that the fellow exposed himself recklessly to the sun. The climate here, everybody says, is not at all worse than at home, as long as you keep out of the sun. Do you hear that, Carlier? I am chief here, and my orders are that you should not expose yourself to the sun!" He assumed his superiority jocularly, but his meaning was serious. The idea that he would, perhaps, have to bury Carlier and remain alone, gave him an inward shiver. He felt suddenly that this Carlier was more precious to him here, in the center of Africa, than a brother could be anywhere else. Carlier, entering into the spirit of the thing, made a military salute and answered in a brisk tone, "Your orders shall be attended to, chief!" Then he burst out laughing, slapped Kayerts on the back and shouted, "We shall let life run easily here! Just sit still and gather in the ivory those savages will bring. This country has its good points, after all!" They both laughed loudly while Carlier thought: "That poor Kayerts; he is so fat and unhealthy. It would be awful if I had to bury him here. He is a man I respect." . . . Before they reached the veranda of their house they called one another "my dear fellow."

The first day they were very active, pottering about with hammers and nails and red calico, to put up curtains, make their house habitable and pretty; resolved to settle down comfortably to their new life. For them an impossible task. To grapple effectually with even purely material problems requires more serenity of mind and more lofty courage than people generally imagine. No two beings could have been more unfitted for such a struggle. Society, not from any tenderness, but because of its strange needs, had taken care of those two men, forbidding them all independent thought, all initiative, all departure from routine; and forbidding it under pain of death. They could only live on condition of being machines. And now, released from the fostering care of men with pens behind the ears, or of men with gold lace on the sleeves, they were like those lifelong prisoners who, liberated after many years, do not know what use to make of their freedom. They did not know what use to make of their faculties, being both, through want of practice, incapable of independent thought.

At the end of two months Kayerts often would say, "If it was not for my Melie, you wouldn't catch me here." Melie was his daughter. He had thrown up his post in the Administration of the Telegraphs, though he had been for seventeen years perfectly happy there, to earn a dowry for his girl. His wife was dead, and the child was being brought up by his sisters. He regretted the streets, the pavements, the cafés, his friends of many years; all the things he used to see, day after day; all the thoughts suggested by familiar things—the thoughts effortless, monotonous, and soothing of a Government clerk; he regretted all the gossip, the small enmities, the mild venom, and the little jokes of Government offices. "If I had had a decent brother-in-law," Carlier would remark, "a fellow with a heart, I would not be here." He had left the army and had made himself so obnoxious to his family by his laziness and impudence, that an exasperated brother-in-law had made superhuman efforts to procure him an appointment in the Company as a second-class agent. Having not a penny in the world he was compelled to accept this means of livelihood as soon as it became quite clear to him that there was nothing more to squeeze out of his relations. He, like Kayerts, regretted his old life. He regretted the clink of saber and spurs on a fine afternoon, the barrack-room witticisms, the girls of garrison towns; but, besides, he had also a sense of grievance. He was evidently a much ill-used man. This made him moody, at times. But the two men got on well together in the fellowship of their stupidity and laziness. Together they did nothing, absolutely nothing, and enjoyed the sense of the idleness for which they were paid. And in time they came to feel something resembling affection for one another.

They lived like blind men in a large room, aware only of what came in contact with them (and of that only imperfectly), but unable to see the general aspect of things. The river, the forest, all the great land throbbing with life, were like a great emptiness. Even the brilliant sunshine disclosed nothing intelligible. Things appeared and disappeared before their eyes in an unconnected and aimless kind of way. The river seemed to come from nowhere and flow nowhither. It flowed through a void. Out of that void, at times, came canoes, and men with spears in their hands would suddenly crowd the yard of the station. They were naked, glossy black, ornamented with snowy shells and glistening brass wire, perfect of limb. They made an uncouth babbling noise when they spoke, moved in a stately manner, and sent quick, wild glances out of their startled, never-resting eyes. Those warriors would squat in long rows, four or more deep, before the veranda, while their chiefs bargained for hours with Makola over an elephant tusk. Kayerts sat on his chair and looked down on the proceedings, understanding nothing. He stared at them with his round blue eyes, called out to Carlier, "Here, look! look at that fellow there—and that other one, to the left. Did you ever see such a face? Oh, the funny brute!"

Carlier, smoking native tobacco in a short wooden pipe, would swagger up twirling his mustaches, and surveying the warriors with haughty indulgence, would say:

"Fine animals. Brought any bone? Yes? It's not any too soon. Look at the muscles of that fellow—third from the end. I wouldn't care to get a punch on the nose from him. Fine arms, but legs no good below the knee. Couldn't make cavalry men of them." And after glancing down complacently at his own shanks, he always concluded. "Pah! Don't they stink! You, Makola! Take that herd over to the fetish" (the storehouse was in every station called the fetish, perhaps because of the spirit of civilization it contained) "and give them up some of the rubbish you keep there. I'd rather see it full of bone than full of rags.

Kayerts approved.

"Yes, yes! Go and finish that palaver over there, Mr. Makola. I will come round when you are ready, to weigh the tusk. We must be careful." Then turning to his companion: "This is the tribe that lives down the river; they are rather aromatic. I remember, they had been once before here. D'ya hear that row? What a fellow has got to put up with in this dog of a country! My head is split."

Such profitable visits were rare. For days the two pioneers of trade and progress would look on their empty courtyard in the vibrating brilliance of vertical sunshine. Below the high bank, the silent river flowed on glittering and steady. On the sands in the middle of the stream, hippos and alligators sunned themselves side by side. And stretching away in all directions, surrounding the insignificant cleared spot of the trading post, immense forests, hiding fateful complications of fantastic life, lay in the eloquent silence of mute greatness. The two men understood nothing, cared for nothing but for the passage of days that separated them from the steamer's return. Their predecessor had left some torn books. They took up these wrecks of novels, and, as they had never read anything of the kind before, they were surprised and amused. Then during long days there were interminable and silly discussions about plots and personages. In the center of Africa they made acquaintance of Richelieu and of d'Artagnan, of Hawk's Eye and of Father Goriot, and of many other people. All these imaginary personages became subjects for gossip as if they had been living friends. They discounted their virtues, suspected their motives, decried their successes; were scandalized at their duplicity or were doubtful about their courage. The accounts of crimes filled them with indignation, while tender or pathetic passages moved them deeply. Carlier cleared his throat and said in a soldierly voice, "What nonsense!" Kayerts, his round eyes suffused with tears, his fat cheeks quivering, rubbed his bald head, and declared, "This is a splendid book. I had no idea there were such clever fellows in the world." They also found some old copies of a home paper. That print discussed what it was pleased to call "Our Colonial Expansion" in high-flown language. It spoke much of the rights and duties of civilization, of the sacredness of the civilizing work, and extolled the merits of those who went about bringing light, and faith and commerce to the dark places of the earth. Carlier and Kayerts read, wondered, and began to think better of themselves. Carlier said one evening, waving his hand about, "In a hundred years, there will be perhaps a town here. Quays, and warehouses, and barracks, and—and—billiard rooms. Civilization, my boy, and virtue—and all. And then, chaps will read that two good fellows, Kayerts and Carlier, were the first civilized men to live in this very spot!" Kayerts nodded, "Yes, it is a consolation to think of that." They seemed to forget their dead predecessor; but, early one day, Carlier went out and replanted the cross firmly. "It used to make me squint whenever I walked that way," he explained to Kayerts over the morning coffee. "It made me squint, leaning over so much. So I just planted it upright. And solid, I promise you! I suspended myself with both hands to the crosspiece. Not a move. Oh, I did that properly."

At times Gobila came to see them. Gobila was the chief of the neighboring villages. He was a gray-headed savage, thin and black, with a white cloth round his loins and a mangy panther skin hanging over his back. He came up with long strides of his skeleton legs, swinging a staff as tall as himself, and, entering the common room of the station, would squat on his heels to the left of the door. There he sat, watching Kayerts, and now and then making a speech which the other did not understand. Kayerts, without interrupting his occupation, would from time to time say in a friendly manner: "How goes it, you old image?" and they would smile at one another. The two whites had a liking for that old and incomprehensible creature, and called him Father Gobila. Gobila's manner was paternal, and he seemed really to love all white men. They all appeared to him very young, indistinguishably alike (except for stature), and he knew that they were all brothers, and also immortal. The death of the artist, who was the first white man whom he knew intimately, did not disturb this belief, because he was firmly convinced that the white stranger had pretended to die and got himself buried for some mysterious purpose of his own, into which it was useless to inquire. Perhaps it was his way of going home to his own country? At any rate, these were his brothers, and he transferred his absurd affection to them. They returned it in a way. Carlier slapped him on the back, and recklessly struck off matches for his amusement. Kayerts was always ready to let him have a sniff at the ammonia bottle. In short, they behaved just like that other white creature that had hidden itself in a hole in the ground. Gobila considered them attentively. Perhaps they were the same being with the other—or one of them was. He couldn't decide—clear up that mystery; but he remained always very friendly. In consequence of that friendship the women of Gobila's village walked in single file through the reedy grass, bringing every morning to the station, fowls, and sweet potatoes, and palm wine, and sometimes a goat. The Company never provisions the stations fully, and the agents required those local supplies to live. They had them through the good will of Gobila, and lived well. Now and then one of them had a bout of fever, and the other nursed him with gentle devotion. They did not think much of it. It left them weaker, and their appearance changed for the worse. Carlier was hollow-eyed and irritable. Kayerts showed a drawn, flabby face above the rotundity of his stomach, which gave him a weird aspect. But being constantly together, they did not notice the change that took place gradually in their appearance, and also in their dispositions.

Five months passed in that way.

Then, one morning, as Kayerts and Carlier, lounging in their chairs under the veranda, talked about the approaching visit of the steamer, a knot of armed men came out of the forest and advanced towards the station. They were strangers to that part of the country. They were tall, slight, draped classically from neck to heel in blue fringed cloths, and carried percussion muskets over their bare right shoulders. Makola showed signs of excitement, and ran out of the storehouse (where he spent all his days) to meet these visitors. They came into the courtyard and looked about them with steady, scornful glances. Their leader, a powerful and determined-looking Negro with bloodshot eyes, stood in front of the veranda and made a long speech. He gesticulated much and ceased very suddenly.

There was something in his intonation, in the sounds of the long sentences he used, that startled the two whites. It was like a reminiscence of something not exactly familiar, and yet resembling the speech of civilized men. It sounded like one of those impossible languages which sometimes we hear in our dreams.

"What lingo is that?" said the amazed Carlier. "In the first moment I fancied the fellow was going to speak French. Anyway, it is a different kind of gibberish to what we ever heard."

"Yes," replied Kayerts. "Hey, Makola, what does he say? Where do they come from? Who are they?"

But Makola, who seemed to be standing on hot bricks, answered hurriedly, "I don't know. They come from very far. Perhaps Mrs. Price will understand. They are perhaps bad men."

The leader, after waiting for a while, said something sharply to Makola, who shook his head. Then the man, after looking round, noticed Makola's hut and walked over there. The next moment Mrs. Makola was heard speaking with great volubility. The other strangers—they were six in all—strolled about with an air of ease, put their heads through the door of the storeroom, congregated round the grave, pointed understandingly at the cross, and generally made themselves at home.

"I don't like those chaps—and, I say, Kayerts, they must be from the coast; they've got firearms," observed the sagacious Carlier.

Kayerts also did not like those chaps. They both, for the first time, became aware that they lived in conditions where the unusual may be dangerous, and that there was no power on earth outside of themselves to stand between them and the unusual. They became uneasy, went in and loaded their revolvers. Kayerts said, "We must order Makola to tell them to go away before dark."

The strangers left in the afternoon, after eating a meal prepared for them by Mrs. Makola. The immense woman was excited, and talked much with the visitors. She rattled away shrilly, pointing here and there at the forests and at the river. Makola sat apart and watched. At times he got up and whispered to his wife. He accompanied the strangers across the ravine at the back of the station-ground, and returned slowly looking very thoughtful. When questioned by the white men he was very strange, seemed not to understand, seemed to have forgotten French—seemed to have forgotten how to speak altogether. Kayerts and Carlier agreed that the nigger had had too much palm wine.

There was some talk about keeping a watch in turn, but in the evening everything seemed so quiet and peaceful that they retired as usual. All night they were disturbed by a lot of drumming in the villages. A deep, rapid roll near by would be followed by another far off—then all ceased. Soon short appeals would rattle out here and there, then all mingle together, increase, become vigorous and sustained, would spread out over the forest, roll through the night, unbroken and ceaseless, near and far, as if the whole land had been one immense drum booming out steadily an appeal to heaven. And through the deep and tremendous noise sudden yells that resembled snatches of songs from a madhouse darted shrill and high in discordant jets of sound which seemed to rush far above the earth and drive all peace from under the stars.

Carlier and Kayerts slept badly. They both thought they had heard shots fired during the night—but they could not agree as to the direction. In the morning Makola was gone somewhere. He returned about noon with one of yesterday's strangers, and eluded all Kayerts' attempts to close with him: had become deaf apparently. Kayerts wondered. Carlier, who had been fishing off the bank, came back and remarked while he showed his catch, "The niggers seem to be in a deuce of a stir; I wonder what's up. I saw about fifteen canoes cross the river during the two hours I was there fishing." Kayerts, worried, said, "Isn't this Makola very queer today?" Carlier advised, "Keep all our men together in case of some trouble."

2

There were ten station men who had been left by the Director. Those fellows, having engaged themselves to the Company for six months (without having any idea of a month in particular and only a very faint notion of time in general), had been serving the cause of progress for upwards of two years. Belonging to a tribe from a very distant part of the land of darkness and sorrow, they did not run away, naturally supposing that as wandering strangers they would be killed by the inhabitants of the country; in which they were right. They lived in straw huts on the slope of a ravine overgrown with reedy grass, just behind the station buildings. They were not happy, regretting the festive incantations, the sorceries, the human sacrifices of their own land; where they also had parents, brothers, sisters, admired chiefs, respected magicians, loved friends, and other ties supposed generally to be human. Besides, the rice rations served out by the Company did not agree with them, being a food unknown to their land, and to which they could not get used. Consequently they were unhealthy and miserable. Had they been of any other tribe they would have made up their minds to die—for nothing is easier to certain savages than suicide—and so have escaped from the puzzling difficulties of existence. But belonging, as they did, to a warlike tribe with filed teeth, they had more grit, and went on stupidly living through disease and sorrow. They did very little work, and had lost their splendid physique. Carlier and Kayerts doctored them assiduously without being able to bring them back into condition again. They were mustered every morning and told off to different tasks—grass-cutting, fence-building, tree-felling, etc., etc., which no power on earth could induce them to execute efficiently. The two whites had practically very little control over them.

In the afternoon Makola came over to the big house and found Kayerts watching three heavy columns of smoke rising above the forests. "What is that?" asked Kayerts. "Some villages burn," answered Makola, who seemed to have regained his wits. Then he said abruptly: "We have got very little ivory; bad six months' trading. Do you like get a little more ivory?"

"Yes," said Kayerts, eagerly. He thought of percentages which were low.

"Those men who came yesterday are traders from Loanda who have got more ivory than they can carry home. Shall I buy? I know their camp."

"Certainly," said Kayerts. "What are those traders?"

"Bad fellows," said Makola, indifferently. "They fight with people, and catch women and children. They are bad men, and got guns. There is a great disturbance in the country. Do you want ivory?"

"Yes," said Kayerts. Makola said nothing for a while. Then: "Those workmen of ours are no good at all," he muttered, looking round. "Station in very bad order, sir. Director will growl. Better get a fine lot of ivory, then he say nothing."

"I can't help it; the men won't work," said Kayerts. "When will you get that ivory?"

"Very soon," said Makola. "Perhaps tonight. You leave it to me, and keep indoors, sir. I think you had better give some palm wine to our men to make a dance this evening. Enjoy themselves. Work better tomorrow. There's plenty palm wine—gone a little sour."

Kayerts said "yes," and Makola, with his own hands carried big calabashes to the door of his hut. They stood there till the evening, and Mrs. Makola looked into every one. The men got them at sunset. When Kayerts and Carlier retired, a big bonfire was flaring before the men's huts. They could hear their shouts and drumming. Some men from Gobila's village had joined the station hands, and the entertainment was a great success.

In the middle of the night, Carlier waking suddenly, heard a man shout loudly; then a shot was fired. Only one. Carlier ran out and met Kayerts on the veranda. They were both startled. As they went across the yard to call Makola, they saw shadows moving in the night. One of them cried, "Don't shoot! It's me, Price." Then Makola appeared close to them. "Go back, go back, please," he urged, "you spoil all." "There are strange men about," said Carlier.

"Never mind; I know," said Makola. Then he whispered, "All right. Bring ivory. Say nothing! I know my business." The two white men reluctantly went back to the house, but did not sleep. They heard footsteps, whispers, some groans. It seemed as if a lot of men came in, dumped heavy things on the ground, squabbled a long time, then went away. They lay on their hard beds and thought: "This Makola is invaluable." In the morning Carlier came out, very sleepy, and pulled at the cord of the big bell. The station hands mustered every morning to the sound of the bell. That morning nobody came. Kayerts turned out also, yawning. Across the yard they saw Makola come out of his hut, a tin basin of soapy water in his hand. Makola, a civilized nigger, was very neat in his person. He threw the soapsuds skillfully over a wretched little yellow cur he had, then turning his face to the agent's house, he shouted from the distance, "All the men gone last night!"

They heard him plainly, but in their surprise they both yelled out together: "What!" Then they stared at one another. "We are in a proper fix now," growled Carlier. "It's incredible!" muttered Kayerts. "I will go to the huts and see," said Carlier, striding off. Makola coming up found Kayerts standing alone.

"I can hardly believe it," said Kayerts, tearfully. "We took care of them as if they had been our children."

"They went with the coast people," said Makola after a moment of hesitation.

"What do I care with whom they went—the ungrateful brutes!" exclaimed the other. Then with sudden suspicion, and looking hard at Makola, he added: "What do you know about it?"

Makola moved his shoulders, looking down on the ground. "What do I know? I think only. Will you come and look at the ivory I've got there? It is a fine lot. You never saw such."

He moved towards the store. Kayerts followed him mechanically, thinking about the incredible desertion of the men. On the ground before the door of the fetish lay six splendid tusks.

"What did you give for it?" asked Kayerts, after surveying the lot with satisfaction.

"No regular trade," said Makola. "They brought the ivory and gave it to me. I told them to take what they most wanted in the station. It is a beautiful lot. No station can show such tusks. Those traders wanted carriers badly, and our men were no good here. No trade, no entry in books; all correct."

Kayerts nearly burst with indignation. "Why!" he shouted, "I believe you have sold our men for these tusks!" Makola stood impassive and silent, "I—I—will—I," stuttered Kayerts. "You fiend!" he yelled out.

"I did the best for you and the Company," said Makola, imperturbably. "Why you shout so much? Look at this tusk."

"I dismiss you! I will report you—I won't look at the tusk. I forbid you to touch them. I order you to throw them into the river. You—you!"

"You very red, Mr. Kayerts. If you are so irritable in the sun, you will get fever and die—like the first chief!" pronounced Makola impressively.

They stood still, contemplating one another with intense eyes, as if they had been looking with effort across immense distances. Kayerts shivered. Makola had meant no more than he said, but his words seemed to Kayerts full of ominous menace! He turned sharply and went away to the house. Makola retired into the bosom of his family; and the tusks, left lying before the store, looked very large and valuable in the sunshine.

Carlier came back on the veranda. "They're all gone, hey?" asked Kayerts from the far end of the common room in a muffled voice. "You did not find anybody?"

"Oh, yes," said Carlier, "I found one of Gobila's people lying dead before the huts—shot through the body. We heard that shot last night."

Kayerts came out quickly. He found his companion staring grimly over the yard at the tusks, away by the store. They both sat in silence for a while. Then Kayerts related his conversation with Makola. Carlier said nothing. At the midday meal they ate very little. They hardly exchanged a word that day. A great silence seemed to lie heavily over the station and press on their lips. Makola did not open the store; he spent the day playing with his children. He lay full-length on a mat outside his door, and the youngsters sat on his chest and clambered all over him. It was a touching picture. Mrs. Makola was busy cooking all day as usual. The white men made a somewhat better meal in the evening. Afterwards, Carlier smoking his pipe strolled over to the store; he stood for a long time over the tusks, touched one or two with his foot, even tried to lift the largest one by its small end. He came back to his chief, who had not stirred from the veranda, threw himself in the chair and said:

"I can see it! They were pounced upon while they slept heavily after drinking all that palm wine you've allowed Makola to give them. A put-up job! See? The worst is, some of Gobila's people were there, and got carried off too, no doubt. The least drunk woke up, and got shot for his sobriety. This is a funny country. What will you do now?"

"We can't touch it, of course," said Kayerts.

"Of course not," assented Carlier.

"Slavery is an awful thing," stammered out Kayerts in an unsteady voice.

"Frightful—the sufferings," grunted Carlier with conviction.

They believed their words. Everybody shows a respectful deference to certain sounds that he and his fellows can make. But about feelings people really know nothing. We talk with indignation or enthusiasm; we talk about oppression, cruelty, crime, devotion, self-sacrifice, virtue, and we know nothing real beyond the words. Nobody knows what suffering or sacrifice mean—except, perhaps the victims of the mysterious purpose of these illusions.

Next morning they saw Makola very busy setting up in the yard the big scales used for weighing ivory. By and by Carlier said: "What's that filthy scoundrel up to?" and lounged out into the yard. Kayerts followed. They stood watching. Makola took no notice. When the balance was swung true, he tried to lift a tusk into the scale. It was too heavy. He looked up helplessly without a word, and for a minute they stood round that balance as mute and still as three statues. Suddenly Carlier said: "Catch hold of the other end, Makola—you beast!" and together they swung the tusk up. Kayerts trembled in every limb. He muttered, "I say! O! I say!" and putting his hand in his pocket found there a dirty bit of paper and the stump of a pencil. He turned his back on the others, as if about to do something tricky, and noted stealthily the weights which Carlier shouted out to him with unnecessary loudness. When all was over Makola whispered to himself: "The sun's very strong here for the tusks." Carlier said to Kayerts in a careless tone: "I say, chief, I might just as well give him a lift with this lot into the store."

As they were going back to the house Kayerts observed with a sigh: "It had to be done." And Carlier said: "It's deplorable, but, the men being Company's men the ivory is Company's ivory. We must look after it." "I will report to the Director, of course," said Kayerts. "Of course; let him decide," approved Carlier.

At midday they made a hearty meal. Kayerts sighed from time to time. Whenever they mentioned Makola's name they always added to it an opprobrious epithet. It eased their conscience. Makola gave himself a half-holiday, and bathed his children in the river. No one from Gobila's villages came near the station that day. No one came the next day, and the next, nor for a whole week. Gobila's people might have been dead and buried for any sign of life they gave. But they were only mourning for those they had lost by the witch-craft of white men, who had brought wicked people into their country. The wicked people were gone, but fear remained. Fear always remains. A man may destroy everything within himself, love and hate and belief, and even doubt; but as long as he clings to life he cannot destroy fear: the fear, subtle, indestructible, and terrible, that pervades his being; that tinges his thoughts; that lurks in his heart; that watches on his lips the struggle of his last breath. In his fear, the mild old Gobila offered extra human sacrifices to all the Evil Spirits that had taken possession of his white friends. His heart was heavy. Some warriors spoke about burning and killing, but the cautious old savage dissuaded them. Who could foresee the woe those mysterious creatures, if irritated, might bring? They should be left alone. Perhaps in time they would disappear into the earth as the first one had disappeared. His people must keep away from them, and hope for the best.

Kayerts and Carlier did not disappear, but remained above on this earth, that, somehow, they fancied had become bigger and very empty. It was not the absolute and dumb solitude of the post that impressed them so much as an inarticulate feeling that something from within them was gone, something that worked for their safety, and had kept the wilderness from interfering with their hearts. The images of home; the memory of people like them, of men that thought and felt as they used to think and feel, receded into dis-tances made indistinct by the glare of unclouded sunshine. And out of the great silence of the surrounding wilderness, its very hopeless-ness and savagery seemed to approach them nearer, to draw them gently, to look upon them, to envelop them with a solicitude irre-sistible, familiar, and disgusting.

Days lengthened into weeks, then into months. Gobila's people drummed and yelled to every new moon, as of yore, but kept away from the station. Makola and Carlier tried once in a canoe to open communications, but were received with a shower of arrows, and had to fly back to the station for dear life. That attempt set the country up and down the river into an uproar that could be very distinctly heard for days. The steamer was late. At first they spoke of delay jauntily, then anxiously, then gloomily. The matter was becoming serious. Stores were running short. Carlier cast his lines off the bank, but the river was low, and the fish kept out in the stream. They dared not stroll far away from the station to shoot. Moreover, there was no game in the impenetrable forest. Once Carl-ier shot a hippo in the river. They had no boat to secure it, and it sank. When it floated up it drifted away, and Gobila's people secured the carcass. It was the occasion for a national holiday, but Carlier had a fit of rage over it and talked about the necessity of exterminating all the niggers before the country could be made habitable. Kayerts mooned about silently; spent hours looking at the portrait of his Melie. It represented a little girl with long bleached tresses and a rather sour face. His legs were much swollen, and he could hardly walk. Carlier, undermined by fever, could not swagger any more, but kept tottering about, still with a devil-may-care air, as became a man who remembered his crack regiment. He had become hoarse, sarcastic, and inclined to say unpleasant things. He called it "being frank with you." They had long ago reckoned their percentages on trade, including in them that last deal of "this infamous Makola." They had also concluded not to say anything about it. Kayerts hesitated at first—was afraid of the Director.

"He has seen worse things done on the quiet," maintained Carlier, with a hoarse laugh. "Trust him! He won't thank you if you blab. He is no better than you or me. Who will talk if we hold our tongues? There is nobody here."

That was the root of the trouble! There was nobody there; and being left there alone with their weakness, they became daily more like a pair of accomplices than like a couple of devoted friends. They had heard nothing from home for eight months. Every evening they said, "Tomorrow we shall see the steamer." But one of the Company's steamers had been wrecked, and the Director was busy with the other, relieving very distant and important stations on the main river. He thought that the useless station, and the useless men, could wait. Meantime Kayerts and Carlier lived on rice boiled without salt, and cursed the Company, all Africa, and the day they were born. One must have lived on such diet to discover what ghastly trouble the necessity of swallowing one's food may become. There was literally nothing else in the station but rice and coffee; they drank the coffee without sugar. The last fifteen lumps Kayerts had solemnly locked away in his box, together with a half-bottle of cognac, "in case of sickness," he explained. Carlier approved. "When one is sick," he said, "any little extra like that is cheering."

They waited. Rank grass began to sprout over the courtyard. The bell never rang now. Days passed, silent, exasperating, and slow. When the two men spoke, they snarled; and their silences were bitter, as if tinged by the bitterness of their thoughts.

One day after a lunch of boiled rice, Carlier put down his cup untasted, and said: "Hang it all! Let's have a decent cup of coffee for once. Bring out that sugar, Kayerts!"

"For the sick," muttered Kayerts, without looking up.

"For the sick," mocked Carlier. "Bosh! . . . Well! I am sick."

"You are no more sick than I am, and I go without," said Kayerts in a peaceful tone.

"Come! Out with that sugar, you stingy old slave dealer."

Kayerts looked up quickly. Carlier was smiling with marked insolence. And suddenly it seemed to Kayerts that he had never seen that man before. Who was he? He knew nothing about him. What was he capable of? There was a surprising flash of violent emotion within him, as if in the presence of something undreamt-of, dangerous, and final. But he managed to pronounce with composure:

"That joke is in very bad taste. Don't repeat it."

"Joke!" said Carlier, hitching himself forward on his seat. "I am hungry—I am sick—I don't joke! I hate hypocrites. You are a hypocrite. You are a slave dealer. I am a slave dealer. There's nothing but slave dealers in this cursed country. I mean to have sugar in my coffee today, anyhow!"

"I forbid you to speak to me in that way," said Kayerts with a fair show of resolution.

"You!—What?" shouted Carlier, jumping up.

Kayerts stood up also. "I am your chief," he began, trying to master the shakiness of his voice.

"What?" yelled the other. "Who's chief? There's no chief here. There's nothing here: there's nothing but you and I. Fetch the sugar —you pot-bellied ass."

"Hold your tongue. Go out of this room," screamed Kayerts. "I dismiss you—you scoundrel!"

Carlier swung a stool. All at once he looked dangerously in earnest. "You flabby, good-for-nothing civilian—take that!" he howled.

Kayerts dropped under the table, and the stool struck the grass inner wall of the room. Then, as Carlier was trying to upset the table, Kayerts in desperation made a blind rush, head low, like a cornered pig would do, and overturning his friend, bolted along the veranda, and into his room. He locked the door, snatched his revolver, and stood panting. In less than a minute Carlier was kicking at the door furiously, howling, "If you don't bring out that sugar, I will shoot you at sight, like a dog. Now then—one—two— three. You won't? I will show you who's the master."

Kayerts thought the door would fall in, and scrambled through the square hole that served for a window in his room. There was then the whole breadth of the house between them. But the other was apparently not strong enough to break in the door, and Kayerts heard him running round. Then he also began to run laboriously on his swollen legs. He ran as quickly as he could, grasping the revolver, and unable yet to understand what was happening to him. He saw in succession Makola's house, the store, the river, the ravine, and the low bushes; and he saw all those things again as he ran for the second time round the house. Then again they flashed past him. That morning he could not have walked a yard without a groan.

And now he ran. He ran fast enough to keep out of sight of the other man.

Then as, weak and desperate, he thought, "Before I finish the next round I shall die," he heard the other man stumble heavily, then stop. He stopped also. He had the back and Carlier the front of the house, as before. He heard him drop into a chair cursing, and suddenly his own legs gave way, and he slid down into a sitting posture with his back to the wall. His mouth was as dry as a cinder, and his face was wet with perspiration—and tears. What was it all about? He thought it must be a horrible illusion; he thought he was dreaming; he thought he was going mad! After a while he collected his senses. What did they quarrel about? That sugar! How absurd! He would give it to him—didn't want it himself. And he began scrambling to his feet with a sudden feeling of security. But before he had fairly stood upright, a common-sense reflection occurred to him and drove him back into despair. He thought: "If I give way now to that brute of a soldier, he will begin this horror again tomorrow—and the day after—every day—raise other pretensions, trample on me, torture me, make me his slave—and I will be lost! Lost! The steamer may not come for days—may never come." He shook so that he had to sit down on the floor again. He shivered forlornly. He felt he could not, would not move any more. He was completely distracted by the sudden perception that the position was without issue—that death and life had in a moment become equally difficult and terrible.

All at once he heard the other push his chair back; and he leaped to his feet with extreme facility. He listened and got confused. Must run again! Right or left? He heard footsteps. He darted to the left, grasping his revolver, and at the very same instant, as it seemed to him, they came into violent collision. Both shouted with surprise. A loud explosion took place between them; a roar of red fire, thick smoke; and Kayerts, deafened and blinded, rushed back thinking: "I am hit—it's all over." He expected the other to come round—to gloat over his agony. He caught hold of an upright of the roof—"All over!" Then he heard a crashing fall on the other side of the house, as if somebody had tumbled headlong over a chair—then silence. Nothing more happened. He did not die. Only his shoulder felt as if it had been badly wrenched, and he had lost his revolver. He was disarmed and helpless! He waited for his fate. The other man made no sound. It was a stratagem. He was stalking him now! Along what side? Perhaps he was taking aim this very minute!

After a few moments of an agony frightful and absurd, he decided to go and meet his doom. He was prepared for every surrender. He turned the corner, steadying himself with one hand on the wall; made a few paces, and nearly swooned. He had seen on the floor, protruding past the other corner, a pair of turned-up feet. A pair of white naked feet in red slippers. He felt deadly sick, and stood for a time in profound darkness. Then Makola appeared before him, saying quietly: "Come along, Mr. Kayerts. He is dead." He burst into tears of gratitude; a loud, sobbing fit of crying. After a time he found himself sitting in a chair and looking at Carlier, who lay stretched on his back. Makola was kneeling over the body.

"Is this your revolver?" asked Makola, getting up.

"Yes," said Kayerts; then he added very quickly, "He ran after me to shoot me—you saw!"

"Yes, I saw," said Makola. "There is only one revolver; where's his?"

"Don't know," whispered Kayerts in a voice that had become suddenly very faint.

"I will go and look for it," said the other, gently. He made the round along the veranda, while Kayerts sat still and looked at the corpse. Makola came back empty-handed, stood in deep thought, then stepped quietly into the dead man's room, and came out directly with a revolver, which he held up before Kayerts. Kayerts shut his eyes. Everything was going round. He found life more terrible and difficult than death. He had shot an unarmed man.

After meditating for a while, Makola said softly, pointing at the dead man who lay there with his right eye blown out:

"He died of fever." Kayerts looked at him with a stony stare. "Yes," repeated Makola, thoughtfully, stepping over the corpse, "I think he died of fever. Bury him tomorrow."

And he went away slowly to his expectant wife, leaving the two white men alone on the veranda.

Night came, and Kayerts sat unmoving on his chair. He sat quiet as if he had taken a dose of opium. The violence of the emotions he had passed through produced a feeling of exhausted serenity. He had plumbed in one short afternoon the depths of horror and despair, and now found repose in the conviction that life had no more secrets for him: neither had death! He sat by the corpse thinking: thinking very actively, thinking very new thoughts. He seemed to have broken loose from himself altogether. His old thoughts, convictions, likes and dislikes, things he respected and things he abhorred, appeared in their true light at last! Appeared contemptible and childish, false and ridiculous. He reveled in his new wisdom while he sat by the man he had killed. He argued with himself about all things under heaven with that kind of wrong-headed lucidity which may be observed in some lunatics. Incidentally he reflected that the fellow dead there had been a noxious beast anyway; that men died every day in thousands; perhaps in hundreds of thousands —who could tell?—and that in the number, that one death could not possibly make any difference; couldn't have any importance, at least to a thinking creature. He, Kayerts, was a thinking creature. He had been all his life, till that moment, a believer in a lot of nonsense like the rest of mankind—who are fools; but now he thought! He knew! He was at peace; he was familiar with the highest wisdom! Then he tried to imagine himself dead, and Carlier sitting in his chair watching him; and his attempt met with such unexpected success, that in a very few moments he became not at all sure who was dead and who was alive. This extraordinary achievement of his fancy startled him, however, and by a clever and timely effort of mind he saved himself just in time from becoming Carlier. His heart thumped, and he felt hot all over at the thought of that danger. Carlier! What a beastly thing! To compose his now disturbed nerves—and no wonder!—he tried to whistle a little. Then, suddenly, he fell asleep, or thought he had slept; but at any rate there was a fog, and somebody had whistled in the fog.

He stood up. The day had come, and a heavy mist had descended upon the land: the mist penetrating, enveloping, and silent; the morning mist of tropical lands; the mist that clings and kills; the mist white and deadly, immaculate and poisonous. He stood up, saw the body, and threw his arms above his head with a cry like that of a man who, waking from a trance, finds himself immured forever in a tomb. "*Help! . . . My God!*"

A shriek inhuman, vibrating and sudden, pierced like a sharp dart the white shroud of that land of sorrow. Three short, impatient screeches followed, and then, for a time, the fog-wreaths rolled on, undisturbed, through a formidable silence. Then many more shrieks, rapid and piercing, like the yells of some exasperated and ruthless creature, rent the air. Progress was calling to Kayerts from the river. Progress and civilization and all the virtues. Society was calling to its accomplished child to come, to be taken care of, to be instructed, to be judged, to be condemned; it called him to return to that rubbish heap from which he had wandered away, so that justice could be done.

Kayerts heard and understood. He stumbled out of the veranda, leaving the other man quite alone for the first time since they had been thrown there together. He groped his way through the fog, calling in his ignorance upon the invisible heaven to undo its work. Makola flitted by in the mist, shouting as he ran:

"Steamer! Steamer! They can't see. They whistle for the station. I go ring the bell. Go down to the landing, sir. I ring."

He disappeared. Kayerts stood still. He looked upwards; the fog rolled low over his head. He looked round like a man who has lost his way; and he saw a dark smudge, a cross-shaped stain, upon the shifting purity of the mist. As he began to stumble towards it, the station bell rang in a tumultuous peal its answer to the impatient clamor of the steamer.

The Managing Director of the Great Civilizing Company (since we know that civilization follows trade) landed first, and incontinently lost sight of the steamer. The fog down by the river was exceedingly dense; above, at the station, the bell rang unceasing and brazen.

The Director shouted loudly to the steamer:

"There is nobody down to meet us; there may be something wrong, though they are ringing. You had better come, too!"

And he began to toil up the steep bank. The captain and the engine-driver of the boat followed behind. As they scrambled up the fog thinned, and they could see their Director a good way ahead. Suddenly they saw him start forward, calling to them over his shoulder: "Run! Run to the house! I've found one of them. Run, look for the other!"

He had found one of them! And even he, the man of varied and startling experience, was somewhat discomposed by the manner of this finding. He stood and fumbled in his pockets (for a knife) while he faced Kayerts, who was hanging by a leather strap from the cross. He had evidently climbed the grave, which was high and narrow, and after tying the end of the strap to the arm, had swung himself off. His toes were only a couple of inches above the ground; his arms hung stiffly down; he seemed to be standing rigidly at attention, but with one purple cheek playfully posed on the shoulder. And, irreverently, he was putting out a swollen tongue at his Managing Director.

The secret sharer

1

ON MY RIGHT HAND THERE WERE LINES OF FISHING STAKES RESEMBLING a mysterious system of half-submerged bamboo fences, incomprehensible in its division of the domain of tropical fishes, and crazy of aspect as if abandoned forever by some nomad tribe of fishermen now gone to the other end of the ocean; for there was no sign of human habitation as far as the eye could reach. To the left a group of barren islets, suggesting ruins of stone walls, towers, and block-houses, had its foundations set in a blue sea that itself looked solid, so still and stable did it lie below my feet; even the track of light from the westering sun shone smoothly, without that animated glitter which tells of an imperceptible ripple. And when I turned my head to take a parting glance at the tug which had just left us anchored outside the bar, I saw the straight line of the flat shore joined to the stable sea, edge to edge, and with a perfect and unmarked closeness, in one leveled floor half brown, half blue under the enormous dome of the sky. Corresponding in their insignificance to the islets of the sea, two small clumps of trees, one on each side of the only fault in the impeccable joint, marked the mouth of the river Meinam we had just left on the first preparatory stage of our homeward journey; and, far back on the inland level, a larger and loftier mass, the grove surrounding the great Paknam pagoda, was the only thing on which the eye could rest from the vain task of exploring the monotonous sweep of the horizon. Here and there gleams as of a few scattered pieces of silver marked the windings of the great river; and on the nearest of them, just within the bar, the tug steaming right into the land became lost to my sight, hull and funnel and masts, as though the impassive earth had swallowed her up without an effort, without a tremor. My eye followed the light cloud of her smoke, now here, now there, above the plain, according to the devious curves of the stream, but always fainter and farther away, till I lost it at last behind the miter-shaped hill of the great pagoda. And then I was left alone with my ship, anchored at the head of the Gulf of Siam.

She floated at the starting point of a long journey, very still in an immense stillness, the shadows of her spars flung far to the eastward by the setting sun. At that moment I was alone on her decks. There was not a sound in her—and around us nothing moved, nothing lived, not a canoe on the water, not a bird in the air, not a cloud in the sky. In this breathless pause at the threshold of a long passage we seemed to be measuring our fitness for a long and arduous enterprise, the appointed task of both our existences to be carried out, far from all human eyes, with only sky and sea for spectators and for judges.

There must have been some glare in the air to interfere with one's sight, because it was only just before the sun left us that my roaming eyes made out beyond the highest ridge of the principal islet of the group something which did away with the solemnity of perfect solitude. The tide of darkness flowed on swiftly; and with tropical suddenness a swarm of stars came out above the shadowy earth, while I lingered yet, my hand resting lightly on my ship's rail as if on the shoulder of a trusted friend. But, with all that multitude of celestial bodies staring down at one, the comfort of quiet communion with her was gone for good. And there were also disturbing sounds by this time—voices, footsteps forward; the steward flitted along the main deck, a busily ministering spirit; a hand bell tinkled urgently under the poop deck. . . .

I found my two officers waiting for me near the supper table, in the lighted cuddy. We sat down at once, and as I helped the chief mate, I said:

"Are you aware that there is a ship anchored inside the islands? I saw her mastheads above the ridge as the sun went down."

He raised sharply his simple face, overcharged by a terrible growth of whisker, and emitted his usual ejaculations: "Bless my soul, sir! You don't say so!"

My second mate was a round-cheeked, silent young man, grave beyond his years, I thought; but as our eyes happened to meet I detected a slight quiver on his lips. I looked down at once. It was not my part to encourage sneering on board my ship. It must be said, too, that I knew very little of my officers. In consequence of certain events of no particular significance, except to myself, I had been appointed to the command only a fortnight before. Neither did I know much of the hands forward. All these people had been together for eighteen months or so, and my position was that of the only stranger on board. I mention this because it has some bearing on what is to follow. But what I felt most was my being a stranger to the ship; and if all the truth must be told, I was somewhat of a stranger to myself. The youngest man on board (barring the second mate), and untried as yet by a position of the fullest responsibility, I was willing to take the adequacy of the others for granted. They had simply to be equal to their tasks; but I wondered how far I should turn out faithful to that ideal conception of one's own personality every man sets up for himself secretly.

Meantime the chief mate, with an almost visible effect of collaboration on the part of his round eyes and frightful whiskers, was trying to evolve a theory of the anchored ship. His dominant trait was to take all things into earnest consideration. He was of a painstaking turn of mind. As he used to say, he "liked to account to himself" for practically everything that came in his way, down to a miserable scorpion he had found in his cabin a week before. The why and the wherefore of that scorpion—how it got on board and came to select his room rather than the pantry (which was a dark place and more what a scorpion would be partial to), and how on earth it managed to drown itself in the inkwell of his writing desk—had exercised him infinitely. The ship within the islands was much more easily accounted for; and just as we were about to rise from the table he made his pronouncement. She was, he doubted not, a ship from home lately arrived. Probably she drew too much water to cross the bar except at the top of spring tides. Therefore she went into that natural harbor to wait for a few days in preference to remaining in an open roadstead.

"That's so," confirmed the second mate, suddenly, in his slightly hoarse voice. "She draws over twenty feet. She's the Liverpool ship *Sephora* with a cargo of coal. Hundred and twenty-three days from Cardiff."

We looked at him in surprise.

"The tugboat skipper told me when he came on board for your letters, sir," explained the young man. "He expects to take her up the river the day after tomorrow."

After thus overwhelming us with the extent of his information he slipped out of the cabin. The mate observed regretfully that he "could not account for that young fellow's whims." What prevented him telling us all about it at once, he wanted to know.

I detained him as he was making a move. For the last two days the crew had had plenty of hard work, and the night before they had very little sleep. I felt painfully that I—a stranger—was doing something unusual when I directed him to let all hands turn in without setting an anchor watch. I proposed to keep on deck myself till one o'clock or thereabouts. I would get the second mate to relieve me at that hour.

"He will turn out the cook and the steward at four," I concluded, "and then give you a call. Of course at the slightest sign of any sort of wind we'll have the hands up and make a start at once."

He concealed his astonishment. "Very well, sir." Outside the cuddy he put his head in the second mate's door to inform him of my unheard-of caprice to take a five hours' anchor watch on myself. I heard the other raise his voice incredulously: "What? The captain himself?" Then a few more murmurs, a door closed, then another. A few moments later I went on deck.

My strangeness, which had made me sleepless, had prompted that unconventional arrangement, as if I had expected in those solitary hours of the night to get on terms with the ship of which I knew nothing, manned by men of whom I knew very little more. Fast alongside a wharf, littered like any ship in port with a tangle of unrelated things, invaded by unrelated shore people, I had hardly seen her yet properly. Now, as she lay cleared for sea, the stretch of her main deck seemed to me very fine under the stars. Very fine, very roomy for her size, and very inviting. I descended the poop and paced the waist, my mind picturing to myself the coming passage through the Malay Archipelago, down the Indian Ocean, and up the Atlantic. All its phases were familiar enough to me, every characteristic, all the alternatives which were likely to face me on the high seas—everything! . . . except the novel responsibility of command. But I took heart from the reasonable thought that the ship was like other ships, the men like other men, and that the sea was not likely to keep any special surprises expressly for my discomfiture.

Arrived at that comforting conclusion, I bethought myself of a cigar and went below to get it. All was still down there. Everybody at the after end of the ship was sleeping profoundly. I came out again on the quarter-deck, agreeably at ease in my sleeping suit on that warm breathless night, barefooted, a glowing cigar in my teeth, and, going forward, I was met by the profound silence of the fore end of the ship. Only as I passed the door of the forecastle I heard a deep, quiet, trustful sigh of some sleeper inside. And suddenly I rejoiced in the great security of the sea as compared with the unrest of the land, in my choice of that untempted life presenting no disquieting problems, invested with an elementary moral beauty by the absolute straightforwardness of its appeal and by the singleness of its purpose.

The riding light in the fore-rigging burned with a clear, untroubled, as if symbolic, flame, confident and bright in the mysterious shades of the night. Passing on my way aft along the other side of the ship, I observed that the rope side ladder, put over, no doubt, for the master of the tug when he came to fetch away our letters, had not been hauled in as it should have been. I became annoyed at this, for exactitude in small matters is the very soul of discipline. Then I reflected that I had myself peremptorily dismissed my officers from duty, and by my own act had prevented the anchor watch being formally set and things properly attended to. I asked myself whether it was wise ever to interfere with the established routine of duties even from the kindest of motives. My action might have made me appear eccentric. Goodness only knew how that absurdly whiskered mate would "account" for my conduct, and what the whole ship thought of that informality of their new captain. I was vexed with myself.

Not from compunction certainly, but, as it were mechanically, I proceeded to get the ladder in myself. Now a side ladder of that sort is a light affair and comes in easily, yet my vigorous tug, which should have brought it flying on board, merely recoiled upon my body in a totally unexpected jerk. What the devil! . . . I was so astounded by the immovableness of that ladder that I remained stock-still, trying to account for it to myself like that imbecile mate of mine. In the end, of course, I put my head over the rail.

The side of the ship made an opaque belt of shadow on the darkling glassy shimmer of the sea. But I saw at once something elongated and pale floating very close to the ladder. Before I could form a guess a faint flash of phosphorescent light, which seemed to issue suddenly from the naked body of a man, flickered in the sleeping water with the elusive, silent play of summer lightning in a night sky. With a gasp I saw revealed to my stare a pair of feet, the long legs, a broad livid back immersed right up to the neck in a greenish cadaverous glow. One hand, awash, clutched the bottom rung of the ladder. He was complete but for the head. A headless corpse! The cigar dropped out of my gaping mouth with a tiny plop and a short hiss quite audible in the absolute stillness of all things under heaven. At that I suppose he raised up his face, a dimly pale oval in the shadow of the ship's side. But even then I could only barely make out down there the shape of his black-haired head. However, it was enough for the horrid, frost-bound sensation which had gripped me about the chest to pass off. The moment of vain exclamations was past, too. I only climbed on the spare spar and leaned over the rail as far as I could, to bring my eyes nearer to that mystery floating alongside.

As he hung by the ladder, like a resting swimmer, the sea lightning played about his limbs at every stir; and he appeared in it ghastly, silvery, fishlike. He remained as mute as a fish, too. He made no motion to get out of the water, either. It was inconceivable that he should not attempt to come on board, and strangely troubling to suspect that perhaps he did not want to. And my first words were prompted by just that troubled incertitude.

"What's the matter?" I asked in my ordinary tone, speaking down to the face upturned exactly under mine.

"Cramp," it answered, no louder. Then slightly anxious, "I say, no need to call anyone."

"I was not going to," I said.

"Are you alone on deck?"

"Yes."

I had somehow the impression that he was on the point of letting go the ladder to swim away beyond my ken—mysterious as he came. But, for the moment, this being appearing as if he had risen from the bottom of the sea (it was certainly the nearest land to the ship) wanted only to know the time. I told him. And he, down there, tentatively:

"I suppose your captain's turned in?"

"I'm sure he isn't," I said.

He seemed to struggle with himself, for I heard something like the low, bitter murmur of doubt. "What's the good?" His next words came out with a hesitating effort.

"Look here, my man. Could you call him out quietly?"

I thought the time had come to declare myself.

"*I* am the captain."

I heard a "By Jove!" whispered at the level of the water. The phosphorescence flashed in the swirl of the water all about his limbs, his other hand seized the ladder.

"My name's Leggatt."

The voice was calm and resolute. A good voice. The self-possession of that man had somehow induced a corresponding state in myself. It was very quietly that I remarked:

"You must be a good swimmer."

"Yes. I've been in the water practically since nine o'clock. The question for me now is whether I am to let go this ladder and go on swimming till I sink from exhaustion, or—to come on board here."

I felt this was no mere formula of desperate speech, but a real alternative in the view of a strong soul. I should have gathered from this that he was young; indeed, it is only the young who are ever confronted by such clear issues. But at the time it was pure intuition on my part. A mysterious communication was established already between us two—in the face of that silent, darkened tropical sea. I was young, too; young enough to make no comment. The man in the water began suddenly to climb up the ladder, and I hastened away from the rail to fetch some clothes.

Before entering the cabin I stood still, listening in the lobby at the foot of the stairs. A faint snore came through the closed door of the chief mate's room. The second mate's door was on the hook, but the darkness in there was absolutely soundless. He, too, was young and could sleep like a stone. Remained the steward, but he was not likely to wake up before he was called. I got a sleeping suit out of my room and, coming back on deck, saw the naked man from the sea sitting on the main hatch, glimmering white in the darkness, his elbows on his knees and his head in his hands. In a moment he had concealed his damp body in a sleeping suit of the same gray-stripe pattern as the one I was wearing and followed me like my double on the poop. Together we moved right aft, barefooted, silent.

"What is it?" I asked in a deadened voice, taking the lighted lamp out of the binnacle, and raising it to his face.

"An ugly business."

He had rather regular features; a good mouth; light eyes under somewhat heavy, dark eyebrows; a smooth, square forehead; no growth on his cheeks; a small, brown mustache, and a well-shaped, round chin. His expression was concentrated, meditative, under the inspecting light of the lamp I held up to his face; such as a man thinking hard in solitude might wear. My sleeping suit was just right for his size. A well-knit young fellow of twenty-five at most. He caught his lower lip with the edge of white, even teeth.

"Yes," I said, replacing the lamp in the binnacle. The warm, heavy tropical night closed upon his head again.

"There's a ship over there," he murmured.

"Yes, I know. The *Sephora*. Did you know of us?"

"Hadn't the slightest idea. I am the mate of her—" He paused and corrected himself. "I should say I *was*."

"Aha! Something wrong?"

"Yes. Very wrong indeed. I've killed a man."

"What do you mean? Just now?"

"No, on the passage. Weeks ago. Thirty-nine south. When I say a man—"

"Fit of temper," I suggested, confidently.

The shadowy, dark head, like mine, seemed to nod imperceptibly above the ghostly gray of my sleeping suit. It was, in the night, as though I had been faced by my own reflection in the depths of a somber and immense mirror.

"A pretty thing to have to own up to for a Conway boy," murmured my double, distinctly.

"You're a Conway boy?"

"I am," he said, as if startled. Then, slowly . . . "Perhaps you too—"

It was so; but being a couple of years older I had left before he joined. After a quick interchange of dates a silence fell; and I thought suddenly of my absurd mate with his terrific whiskers and the "Bless my soul—you don't say so" type of intellect. My double gave me an inkling of his thoughts by saying:

"My father's a parson in Norfolk. Do you see me before a judge and jury on that charge? For myself I can't see the necessity. There are fellows that an angel from heaven—— And I am not that. He was one of those creatures that are just simmering all the time with a silly sort of wickedness. Miserable devils that have no business to live at all. He wouldn't do his duty and wouldn't let anybody else do theirs. But what's the good of talking! You know well enough the sort of ill-conditioned snarling cur—"

He appealed to me as if our experiences had been as identical as our clothes. And I knew well enough the pestiferous danger of such a character where there are no means of legal repression. And I knew well enough also that my double there was no homicidal ruffian. I did not think of asking him for details, and he told me the story roughly in brusque, disconnected sentences. I needed no more. I saw it all going on as though I were myself inside that other sleeping suit.

"It happened while we were setting a reefed foresail, at dusk. Reefed foresail! You understand the sort of weather. The only sail we had left to keep the ship running; so you may guess what it had been like for days. Anxious sort of job, that. He gave me some of his cursed insolence at the sheet. I tell you I was overdone with this terrific weather that seemed to have no end to it. Terrific, I tell you—and a deep ship. I believe the fellow himself was half crazed with funk. It was no time for gentlemanly reproof, so I turned round and felled him like an ox. He up and at me. We closed just as an awful sea made for the ship. All hands saw it coming and took to the rigging, but I had him by the throat, and went on shaking him like a rat, the men above us yelling, 'Look out! look out!' Then a crash as if the sky had fallen on my head. They say that for over ten minutes hardly anything was to be seen of the ship—just the three masts and a bit of the forecastle head and of the poop all awash driving along in a smother of foam. It was a miracle that they found us, jammed together behind the forebits. It's clear that I meant business, because I was holding him by the throat still when they picked us up. He was black in the face. It was too much for them. It seems they rushed us aft together, gripped as we were, screaming 'Murder!' like a lot of lunatics, and broke into the cuddy. And the ship running for her life, touch and go all the time, any minute her last in a sea fit to turn your hair gray only a-looking at it. I understand that the skipper, too, started raving like the rest of them. The man had been deprived of sleep for more than a week, and to have this sprung on him at the height of a furious gale nearly drove him out of his mind. I wonder they didn't fling me overboard after getting the carcass of their precious shipmate out of my fingers. They had rather a job to separate us, I've been told. A sufficiently fierce story to make an old judge and a respectable jury sit up a bit. The first thing I heard when I came to myself was the maddening howling of that endless gale, and on that the voice of the old man. He was hanging on to my bunk, staring into my face out of his sou'wester.

" 'Mr. Leggatt, you have killed a man. You can act no longer as chief mate of this ship.' "

His care to subdue his voice made it sound monotonous. He rested a hand on the end of the skylight to steady himself with, and all that time did not stir a limb, so far as I could see. "Nice little tale for a quiet tea party," he concluded in the same tone.

One of my hands, too, rested on the end of the skylight; neither did I stir a limb, so far as I knew. We stood less than a foot from each other. It occurred to me that if old "Bless my soul—you don't say so" were to put his head up the companion and catch sight of us, he would think he was seeing double, or imagine himself come upon a scene of weird witchcraft; the strange captain having a quiet confabulation by the wheel with his own gray ghost. I became very much concerned to prevent anything of the sort I heard the other's soothing undertone.

"My father's a parson in Norfolk," it said. Evidently he had forgotten he had told me this important fact before. Truly a nice little tale.

"You had better slip down into my stateroom now," I said, moving off stealthily. My double followed my movements; our bare feet made no sound; I let him in, closed the door with care, and, after giving a call to the second mate, returned on deck for my relief.

"Not much sign of any wind yet," I remarked when he approached.

"No, sir. Not much," he assented, sleepily, in his hoarse voice, with just enough deference, no more, and barely suppressing a yawn.

"Well, that's all you have to look out for. You have got your orders."

"Yes, sir."

I paced a turn or two on the poop and saw him take up his position face forward with his elbow in the ratlines of the mizzen-rigging before I went below. The mate's faint snoring was still going on peacefully. The cuddy lamp was burning over the table on which stood a vase with flowers, a polite attention from the ships' provision merchant—the last flowers we should see for the next three months at the very least. Two bunches of bananas hung from the beam symmetrically, one on each side of the rudder casing. Everything was as before in the ship—except that two of her captain's sleeping suits were simultaneously in use, one motionless in the cuddy, the other keeping very still in the captain's stateroom.

It must be explained here that my cabin had the form of the capital letter L, the door being within the angle and opening into the short part of the letter. A couch was to the left, the bed-place to the right; my writing desk and the chronometers' table faced the door. But anyone opening it, unless he stepped right inside, had no view of what I call the long (or vertical) part of the letter. It contained some lockers surmounted by a bookcase; and a few clothes, a thick jacket or two, caps, oilskin coat, and such like, hung on hooks. There was at the bottom of that part a door opening into my bathroom, which could be entered also directly from the saloon. But that way was never used.

The mysterious arrival had discovered the advantage of this particular shape. Entering my room, lighted strongly by a big bulkhead lamp swung on gimbals above my writing desk, I did not see him anywhere till he stepped out quietly from behind the coats hung in the recessed part.

"I heard somebody moving about, and went in there at once," he whispered.

I, too, spoke under my breath.

"Nobody is likely to come in here without knocking and getting permission."

He nodded. His face was thin and the sunburn faded, as though he had been ill. And no wonder. He had been, I heard presently, kept under arrest in his cabin for nearly seven weeks. But there was nothing sickly in his eyes or in his expression. He was not a bit like me, really; yet, as we stood leaning over my bed-place, whispering side by side, with our dark heads together and our backs to the door, anybody bold enough to open it stealthily would have been treated to the uncanny sight of a double captain busy talking in whispers with his other self.

"But all this doesn't tell me how you came to hang on to our side ladder," I inquired, in the hardly audible murmurs we used, after he had told me something more of the proceedings on board the *Sephora* once the bad weather was over.

"When we sighted Java Head I had had time to think all those matters out several times over. I had six weeks of doing nothing else, and with only an hour or so every evening for a tramp on the quarter-deck."

He whispered, his arms folded on the side of my bed-place, staring through the open port. And I could imagine perfectly the manner of this thinking out—a stubborn if not a steadfast operation; something of which I should have been perfectly incapable.

"I reckoned it would be dark before we closed with the land," he continued, so low that I had to strain my hearing, near as we were to each other, shoulder touching shoulder almost. "So I asked to speak to the old man. He always seemed very sick when he came to see me—as if he could not look me in the face. You know, that foresail saved the ship. She was too deep to have run long under bare poles. And it was I that managed to set it for him. Anyway, he came. When I had him in my cabin—he stood by the door looking at me as if I had the halter around my neck already—I asked him right away to leave my cabin door unlocked at night while the ship was going through Sunda Straits. There would be the Java coast within two or three miles, off Angier Point. I wanted nothing more. I've had a prize for swimming my second year in the Conway."

"I can believe it," I breathed out.

"God only knows why they locked me in every night. To see some of their faces you'd have thought they were afraid I'd go about at night strangling people. Am I a murdering brute? Do I look it? By Jove! if I had been he wouldn't have trusted himself like that into my room. You'll say I might have chucked him aside and bolted out, there and then—it was dark already. Well, no. And for the same reason I wouldn't think of trying to smash the door. There would have been a rush to stop me at the noise, and I did not mean to get into a confounded scrimmage. Somebody else might have got killed—for I would not have broken out only to get chucked back, and I did not want any more of that work. He refused, looking more sick than ever. He was afraid of the men, and also of that old second mate of his who had been sailing with him for years—a gray-headed old humbug; and his steward, too, had been with him devil knows how long—seventeen years or more—a dogmatic sort of loafer who hated me like poison, just because I was the chief mate. No chief mate ever made more than one voyage in the *Sephora*, you know. Those two old chaps ran the ship. Devil only knows what the skipper wasn't afraid of (all his nerve went to pieces altogether in that hellish spell of bad weather we had)—of what the law would do to him—of his wife, perhaps. Oh, yes! she's on board. Though I don't think she would have meddled. She would have been only too glad to have me out of the ship in any way. The 'brand of Cain' business, don't you see. That's all right. I was ready enough to go off wandering on the face of the earth—and that was price enough to pay for an Abel of that sort. Anyhow, he wouldn't listen to me. 'This thing must take its course. I represent the law here.' He was shaking like a leaf. 'So you won't?' 'No!' 'Then I hope you will be able to sleep on that,' I said, and turned my back on him. 'I wonder that *you* can,' cries he, and locks the door.

"Well, after that, I couldn't. Not very well. That was three weaks ago. We have had a slow passage through the Java Sea; drifted about Carimata for ten days. When we anchored here they thought, I suppose, it was all right. The nearest land (and that's five miles) is the ship's destination; the consul would soon set about catching me; and there would have been no object in bolting to these islets there. I don't suppose there's a drop of water on them. I don't know how it was, but tonight that steward, after bringing me my supper, went out to let me eat it, and left the door unlocked. And I ate it—all there was, too. After I had finished I strolled out on the quarter-deck. I don't know that I meant to do anything. A breath of fresh air was all I wanted, I believe. Then a sudden

JOSEPH CONRAD   455

temptation came over me. I kicked off my slippers and was in the water before I had made up my mind fairly. Somebody heard the splash and they raised an awful hullabaloo. 'He's gone! Lower the boats! He's committed suicide! No, he's swimming.' Certainly I was swimming. It's not so easy for a swimmer like me to commit suicide by drowning. I landed on the nearest islet before the boat left the ship's side. I heard them pulling about in the dark, hailing, and so on, but after a bit they gave up. Everything quieted down and the anchorage became as still as death. I sat down on a stone and began to think. I felt certain they would start searching for me at daylight. There was no place to hide on those stony things—and if there had been, what would have been the good? But now I was clear of that ship, I was not going back. So after a while I took off all my clothes, tied them up in a bundle with a stone inside, and dropped them in the deep water on the outer side of that islet. That was suicide enough for me. Let them think what they liked, but I didn't mean to drown myself. I meant to swim till I sank—but that's not the same thing. I struck out for another of these little islands, and it was from that one that I first saw your riding light. Something to swim for. I went on easily, and on the way I came upon a flat rock a foot or two above water. In the daytime, I dare say, you might make it out with a glass from your poop. I scrambled up on it and rested myself for a bit. Then I made another start. That last spell must have been over a mile."

His whisper was getting fainter and fainter, and all the time he stared straight out through the porthole, in which there was not even a star to be seen. I had not interrupted him. There was something that made comment impossible in his narrative, or perhaps in himself; a sort of feeling, a quality, which I can't find a name for. And when he ceased, all I found was a futile whisper: "So you swam for our light?"

"Yes—straight for it. It was something to swim for. I couldn't see any stars low down because the coast was in the way, and I couldn't see the land, either. The water was like glass. One might have been swimming in a confounded thousand-feet deep cistern with no place for scrambling out anywhere; but what I didn't like was the notion of swimming round and round like a crazed bullock before I gave out; and as I didn't mean to go back . . . No. Do you see me being hauled back, stark naked, off one of these little islands by the scruff of the neck and fighting like a wild beast? Somebody would have got killed for certain, and I did not want any of that. So I went on. Then your ladder—"

"Why didn't you hail the ship?" I asked, a little louder.

He touched my shoulder lightly. Lazy footsteps came right over our heads and stopped. The second mate had crossed from the other side of the poop and might have been hanging over the rail, for all we knew.

"He couldn't hear us talking—could he?" My double breathed into my very ear, anxiously.

His anxiety was an answer, a sufficient answer, to the question I had put to him. An answer containing all the difficulty of that situation. I closed the porthole quietly, to make sure. A louder word might have been overheard.

"Who's that?" he whispered then.

"My second mate. But I don't know much more of the fellow than you do."

And I told him a little about myself. I had been appointed to take charge while I least expected anything of the sort, not quite a fortnight ago. I didn't know either the ship or the people. Hadn't had the time in port to look about me or size anybody up. And as to the crew, all they knew was that I was appointed to take the ship home. For the rest, I was almost as much of a stranger on board as himself, I said. And at the moment I felt it most acutely. I felt that it would take very little to make me a suspect person in the eyes of the ship's company.

He had turned about meantime; and we, the two strangers in the ship, faced each other in identical attitudes.

"Your ladder—" he murmured, after a silence. "Who'd have thought of finding a ladder hanging over at night in a ship anchored out here! I felt just then a very unpleasant faintness. After the life I've been leading for nine weeks, anybody would have got out of condition. I wasn't capable of swimming round as far as your rudder chains. And, lo and behold! there was a ladder to get hold of. After I gripped it I said to myself, 'What's the good?' When I saw a man's head looking over I thought I would swim away presently and leave him shouting—in whatever language it was. I didn't mind being looked at. I—I liked it. And then you speaking to me so quietly—as if you had expected me—made me hold on a little longer. It had been a confounded lonely time—I don't mean while swimming. I was glad to talk a little to somebody that didn't belong to the *Sephora*. As to asking for the captain, that was a mere impulse. It could have been no use, with all the ship knowing about me and the other people pretty certain to be round here in the morning. I don't know—I wanted to be seen, to talk with somebody, before I went on. I don't know what I would have said. . . . 'Fine night, isn't it?' or something of the sort."

"Do you think they will be round here presently?" I asked with some incredulity.

"Quite likely," he said, faintly.

He looked extremely haggard all of a sudden. His head rolled on his shoulders.

"H'm. We shall see then. Meantime get into that bed," I whispered. "Want help? There."

It was a rather high bed-place with a set of drawers underneath. This amazing swimmer really needed the lift I gave him by seizing his leg. He tumbled in, rolled over on his back, and flung one arm across his eyes. And then, with his face nearly hidden, he must have looked exactly as I used to look in that bed. I gazed upon my other self for a while before drawing across carefully the two green serge curtains which ran on a brass rod. I thought for a moment of pinning them together for greater safety, but I sat down on the couch, and once there I felt unwilling to rise and hunt for a pin. I would do it in a moment. I was extremely tired, in a peculiarly intimate way, by the strain of stealthiness, by the effort of whispering and the general secrecy of this excitement. It was three o'clock by now and I had been on my feet since nine, but I was not sleepy; I could not have gone to sleep. I sat there, fagged out, looking at the curtains, trying to clear my mind of the confused sensation of being in two places at once, and greatly bothered by an exasperating knocking in my head. It was a relief to discover suddenly that it was not in my head at all, but on the outside of the door. Before I could collect myself the words "Come in" were out of my mouth, and the steward entered with a tray, bringing in my morning coffee. I had slept, after all, and I was so frightened that I shouted, "This way! I am here, steward," as though he had been miles away. He put down the tray on the table next the couch and only then said, very quietly, "I can see you are here, sir." I felt him give me a keen look, but I dared not meet his eyes just then. He must have wondered why I had drawn the curtains of my bed before going to sleep on the couch. He went out, hooking the door open as usual.

I heard the crew washing decks above me. I knew I would have been told at once if there had been any wind. Calm, I thought, and I was doubly vexed. Indeed, I felt dual more than ever. The steward reappeared suddenly in the doorway. I jumped up from the couch so quickly that he gave a start.

"What do you want here?"

"Close your port, sir—they are washing decks."

"It is closed," I said, reddening.

"Very well, sir." But he did not move from the doorway and returned my stare in an extraordinary, equivocal manner for a time. Then his eyes wavered, all his expression changed, and in a voice unusually gentle, almost coaxingly:

"May I come in to take the empty cup away, sir?"

"Of course!" I turned my back on him while he popped in and out. Then I unhooked and closed the door and even pushed the bolt. This sort of thing could not go on very long. The cabin was as hot as an oven, too. I took a peep at my double, and discovered that he had not moved, his arm was still over his eyes; but his chest heaved; his hair was wet; his chin glistened with perspiration. I reached over him and opened the port.

"I must show myself on deck," I reflected.

Of course, theoretically, I could do what I liked, with no one to say nay to me within the whole circle of the horizon; but to lock my cabin door and take the key away I did not dare. Directly I put my head out of the companion I saw the group of my two officers, the second mate barefooted, the chief mate in long india-rubber boots, near the break of the poop, and the steward halfway down the poop ladder talking to them eagerly. He happened to catch sight of me and dived, the second ran down on the main deck shouting some order or other, and the chief mate came to meet me, touching his cap.

There was a sort of curiosity in his eye that I did not like. I don't know whether the steward had told them that I was "queer" only, or downright drunk, but I know the man meant to have a good look at me. I watched him coming with a smile which, as he got into point-blank range, took effect and froze his very whiskers. I did not give him time to open his lips.

"Square the yards by lifts and braces before the hands go to breakfast."

It was the first particular order I had given on board that ship; and I stayed on deck to see it executed, too. I had felt the need of asserting myself without loss of time. That sneering young cub got taken down a peg or two on that occasion, and I also seized the opportunity of having a good look at the face of every foremast man as they filed past me to go to the after braces. At breakfast time, eating nothing myself, I presided with such frigid dignity that the two mates were only too glad to escape from the cabin as soon as decency permitted; and all the time the dual working of my mind distracted me almost to the point of insanity. I was constantly watching myself, my secret self, as dependent on my actions as my own personality, sleeping in that bed, behind that door which faced me as I sat at the head of the table. It was very much like being mad, only it was worse because one was aware of it.

I had to shake him for a solid minute, but when at last he opened his eyes it was in the full possession of his senses, with an inquiring look.

"All's well so far," I whispered. "Now you must vanish into the bathroom."

He did so, as noiseless as a ghost, and I then rang for the steward, and facing him boldly, directed him to tidy up my stateroom while I was having my bath—"and be quick about it." As my tone admitted of no excuses, he said, "Yes, sir," and ran off to fetch his dustpan and brushes. I took a bath and did most of my dressing, splashing, and whistling softly for the steward's edification, while the secret sharer of my life stood drawn up bolt upright in that little space, his face looking very sunken in daylight, his eyelids lowered under the stern, dark line of his eyebrows drawn together by a slight frown.

When I left him there to go back to my room the steward was finishing dusting. I sent for the mate and engaged him in some insignificant conversation. It was, as it were, trifling with the terrific character of his whiskers; but my object was to give him an opportunity for a good look at my cabin. And then I could at last shut, with a clear conscience, the door of my stateroom and get my double back into the recessed part. There was nothing else for it. He had to sit still on a small folding stool, half smothered by the heavy coats hanging there. We listened to the steward going into the bathroom out of the saloon, filling the water bottles there, scrubbing the bath, setting things to rights, whisk, bang, clatter—out again into the saloon—turn the key—click. Such was my scheme for keeping my second self invisible. Nothing better could be contrived under the circumstances. And there we sat; I at my writing desk ready to appear busy with some papers, he behind me, out of sight of the door. It would not have been prudent to talk in daytime; and I could not have stood the excitement of that queer sense of whispering to myself. Now and then, glancing over my shoulder, I saw him far back there, sitting rigidly on the low stool, his bare feet close together, his arms folded, his head hanging on his breast—and perfectly still. Anybody would have taken him for me.

I was fascinated by it myself. Every moment I had to glance over my shoulder. I was looking at him when a voice outside the door said:

"Beg pardon, sir."

"Well!" . . . I kept my eyes on him, and so, when the voice outside the door announced, "There's a ship's boat coming our way, sir," I saw him give a start—the first movement he had made for hours. But he did not raise his bowed head.

"All right. Get the ladder over."

I hesitated. Should I whisper something to him? But what? His immobility seemed to have been never disturbed. What could I tell him he did not know already? . . . Finally I went on deck.

2

The skipper of the *Sephora* had a thin red whisker all round his face, and the sort of complexion that goes with hair of that color; also the particular, rather smeary shade of blue in the eyes. He was not exactly a showy figure; his shoulders were high, his stature but middling—one leg slightly more bandy than the other. He shook hands, looking vaguely around. A spiritless tenacity was his main characteristic, I judged. I behaved with a politeness which seemed to disconcert him. Perhaps he was shy. He mumbled to me as if he were ashamed of what he was saying; gave his name (it was something like Archbold—but at this distance of years I hardly am sure), his ship's name, and a few other particulars of that sort, in the manner of a criminal making a reluctant and doleful confession. He had had terrible weather on the passage out—terrible—terrible—wife aboard, too.

By this time we were seated in the cabin and the steward brought in a tray with a bottle and glasses. "Thanks! No." Never took liquor. Would have some water, though. He drank two tumblerfuls. Terrible thirsty work. Ever since daylight had been exploring the islands round his ship.

"What was that for—fun?" I asked, with an appearance of polite interest.

"No!" He sighed. "Painful duty."

As he persisted in his mumbling and I wanted my double to hear every word, I hit upon the notion of informing him that I regretted to say I was hard of hearing.

"Such a young man, too!" he nodded, keeping his smeary blue, unintelligent eyes fastened upon me. What was the cause of it—some disease? he inquired, without the least sympathy and as if he thought that, if so, I'd got no more than I deserved.

"Yes; disease," I admitted in a cheerful tone which seemed to shock him. But my point was gained, because he had to raise his voice to give me his tale. It is not worth while to record that version. It was just over two months since all this had happened, and he had thought so much about it that he seemed completely muddled as to its bearings, but still immensely impressed.

"What would you think of such a thing happening on board your own ship? I've had the *Sephora* for these fifteen years. I am a well-known shipmaster."

He was densely distressed—and perhaps I should have sympathized with him if I had been able to detach my mental vision from the unsuspected sharer of my cabin as though he were my second self. There he was on the other side of the bulkhead, four or five feet from us, no more, as we sat in the saloon. I looked politely at Captain Archbold (if that was his name), but it was the other I saw, in a gray sleeping suit, seated on a low stool, his bare feet close together, his arms folded, and every word said between us falling into the ears of his dark head bowed on his chest.

"I have been at sea now, man and boy, for seven-and-thirty years, and I've never heard of such a thing happening in an English ship. And that it should be my ship. Wife on board, too."

I was hardly listening to him.

"Don't you think," I said, "that the heavy sea which, you told me, came aboard just then might have killed the man? I have seen the sheer weight of a sea kill a man very neatly, by simply breaking his neck."

"Good God!" he uttered, impressively, fixing his smeary blue eyes on me. "The sea! No man killed by the sea ever looked like that." He seemed positively scandalized at my suggestion. And as I gazed at him, certainly not prepared for anything original on his part, he advanced his head close to mine and thrust his tongue out at me so suddenly that I couldn't help starting back.

After scoring over my calmness in this graphic way he nodded wisely. If I had seen the sight, he assured me, I would never forget it as long as I lived. The weather was too bad to give the corpse a proper sea burial. So next day at dawn they took it up on the poop, covering its face with a bit of bunting; he read a short prayer, and then, just as it was, in its oilskins and long boots, they launched it amongst those mountainous seas that seemed ready every moment to swallow up the ship herself and the terrified lives on board of her.

"That reefed foresail saved you," I threw in.

"Under God—it did," he exclaimed fervently. "It was by a special mercy, I firmly believe, that it stood some of those hurricane squalls."

"It was the setting of that sail which—" I began.

"God's own hand in it," he interrupted me. "Nothing less could have done it. I don't mind telling you that I hardly dared give the order. It seemed impossible that we could touch anything without losing it, and then our last hope would have been gone."

The terror of that gale was on him yet. I let him go on for a bit, then said, casually—as if returning to a minor subject:

"You were very anxious to give up your mate to the shore people, I believe?"

He was. To the law. His obscure tenacity on that point had in it something incomprehensible and a little awful; something, as it were, mystical, quite apart from his anxiety that he should not be suspected of "countenancing any doings of that sort." Seven-and-thirty virtuous years at sea, of which over twenty of immaculate command, and the last fifteen in the *Sephora*, seemed to have laid him under some pitiless obligation.

"And you know," he went on, groping shamefacedly amongst his feelings, "I did not engage that young fellow. His people had some interest with my owners. I was in a way forced to take him on. He looked very smart, very gentlemanly, and all that. But do you know—I never liked him, somehow. I am a plain man. You see, he wasn't exactly the sort for the chief mate of a ship like the *Sephora*."

I had become so connected in thoughts and impressions with the secret sharer of my cabin that I felt as if I, personally, were being given to understand that I, too, was not the sort that would have done for the chief mate of a ship like the *Sephora*. I had no doubt of it in my mind.

"Not at all the style of man. You understand," he insisted, superfluously, looking hard at me.

I smiled urbanely. He seemed at a loss for a while.

"I suppose I must report a suicide."

"Beg pardon?"

"Sui-cide! That's what I'll have to write to my owners directly I get in."

"Unless you manage to recover him before tomorrow," I assented, dispassionately. . . . "I mean, alive."

He mumbled something which I really did not catch, and I turned my ear to him in a puzzled manner. He fairly bawled:

"The land—I say, the mainland is at least seven miles off my anchorage."

"About that."

My lack of excitement, of curiosity, of surprise, of any sort of pronounced interest, began to arouse his distrust. But except for the felicitous pretense of deafness I had not tried to pretend anything.

I had felt utterly incapable of playing the part of ignorance properly, and therefore was afraid to try. It is also certain that he had brought some ready-made suspicions with him, and that he viewed my politeness as a strange and unnatural phenomenon. And yet how else could I have received him? Not heartily! That was impossible for psychological reasons, which I need not state here. My only object was to keep off his inquiries. Surlily? Yes, but surliness might have provoked a point-blank question. From its novelty to him and from its nature, punctilious courtesy was the manner best calculated to restrain the man. But there was the danger of his breaking through my defense bluntly. I could not, I think, have met him by a direct lie, also for psychological (not moral) reasons. If he had only known how afraid I was of his putting my feeling of identity with the other to the test! But, strangely enough—(I thought of it only afterward)—I believe that he was not a little disconcerted by the reverse side of that weird situation, by something in me that reminded him of the man he was seeking—suggested a mysterious similitude to the young fellow he had distrusted and disliked from the first.

However that might have been, the silence was not very prolonged. He took another oblique step.

"I reckon I had no more than a two-mile pull to your ship. Not a bit more."

"And quite enough, too, in this awful heat," I said.

Another pause full of mistrust followed. Necessity, they say, is mother of invention, but fear, too, is not barren of ingenious suggestions. And I was afraid he would ask me point-blank for news of my other self.

"Nice little saloon, isn't it?" I remarked, as if noticing for the first time the way his eyes roamed from one closed door to the other. "And very well fitted out, too. Here, for instance," I continued, reaching over the back of my seat negligently and flinging the door open, "is my bathroom."

He made an eager movement, but hardly gave it a glance. I got up, shut the door of the bathroom, and invited him to have a look around, as if I were very proud of my accommodation. He had to rise and be shown round, but he went through the business without any raptures whatever.

"And now we'll have a look at my stateroom," I declared, in a voice as loud as I dared to make it, crossing the cabin to the starboard side with purposely heavy steps.

He followed me in and gazed around. My intelligent double had vanished. I played my part.

"Very convenient—isn't it?"

"Very nice. Very comf . . ." He didn't finish, and went out brusquely as if to escape from some unrighteous wiles of mine. But it was not to be. I had been too frightened not to feel vengeful; I felt I had him on the run, and I meant to keep him on the run. My polite insistence must have had something menacing in it, because he gave in suddenly. And I did not let him off a single item; mate's room, pantry, storerooms, the very sail locker which was also under the poop—he had to look into them all. When at last I showed him out on the quarter-deck he drew a long, spiritless sigh, and mumbled dismally that he must really be going back to his ship now. I desired my mate, who had joined us, to see to the captain's boat.

The man of whiskers gave a blast on the whistle which he used to wear hanging round his neck, and yelled, "*Sephoras* away!" My double down there in my cabin must have heard, and certainly could not feel more relieved than I. Four fellows came running out from somewhere forward and went over the side, while my own men, appearing on deck too, lined the rail. I escorted my visitor to the gangway ceremoniously, and nearly overdid it. He was a tenacious beast. On the very ladder he lingered, and in that unique, guiltily conscientious manner of sticking to the point:

"I say . . . you . . . you don't think that—"

I covered his voice loudly:

"Certainly not. . . . I am delighted. Good-by."

I had an idea of what he meant to say, and just saved myself by the privilege of defective hearing. He was too shaken generally to insist, but my mate, close witness of that parting, looked mystified and his face took on a thoughtful cast. As I did not want to appear as if I wished to avoid all communication with my officers, he had the opportunity to address me.

"Seems a very nice man. His boat's crew told our chaps a very extraordinary story, if what I am told by the steward is true. I suppose you had it from the captain, sir?"

"Yes. I had a story from the captain."

"A very horrible affair—isn't it, sir?"

"It is."

"Beats all these tales we hear about murders in Yankee ships."

"I don't think it beats them. I don't think it resembles them in the least."

"Bless my soul—you don't say so! But of course I've no acquaintance whatever with American ships, not I, so I couldn't go against your knowledge. It's horrible enough for me. . . . But the queerest part is that those fellows seemed to have some idea the man was hidden aboard here. They had really. Did you ever hear of such a thing?"

"Preposterous—isn't it?"

We were walking to and fro athwart the quarter-deck. No one of the crew forward could be seen (the day was Sunday), and the mate pursued:

"There was some little dispute about it. Our chaps took offense. 'As if we would harbor a thing like that,' they said. 'Wouldn't you like to look for him in our coal hole?' Quite a tiff. But they made it up in the end. I suppose he did drown himself. Don't you, sir?"

"I don't suppose anything."

"You have no doubt in the matter, sir?"

"None whatever."

I left him suddenly. I felt I was producing a bad impression, but with my double down there it was most trying to be on deck. And it was almost as trying to be below. Altogether a nerve-trying situation. But on the whole I felt less torn in two when I was with him. There was no one in the whole ship whom I dared take into my confidence. Since the hands had got to know his story, it would have been impossible to pass him off for anyone else, and an accidental discovery was to be dreaded now more than ever. . . .

The steward being engaged in laying the table for dinner, we could talk only with our eyes when I first went down. Later in the afternoon we had a cautious try at whispering. The Sunday quietness of the ship was against us; the stillness of air and water around her was against us; the elements, the men were against us—everything was against us in our secret partnership; time itself—for this could not go on forever. The very trust in Providence was, I suppose, denied to his guilt. Shall I confess that this thought cast me down very much? And as to the chapter of accidents which counts for so much in the book of success, I could only hope that it was closed. For what favorable accident could be expected?

"Did you hear everything?" were my first words as soon as we took up our position side by side, leaning over my bed-place.

He had. And the proof of it was his earnest whisper, "The man told you he hardly dared to give the order."

I understood the reference to be to that saving foresail.

"Yes. He was afraid of it being lost in the setting."

"I assure you he never gave the order. He may think he did, but he never gave it. He stood there with me on the break of the poop after the maintopsail blew away, and whimpered about our last hope—positively whimpered about it and nothing else—and the night coming on! To hear one's skipper go on like that in such weather was enough to drive any fellow out of his mind. It worked me up into a sort of desperation. I just took it into my own hands and went away from him, boiling, and—. But what's the use telling you? *You* know! . . . Do you think that if I had not been pretty fierce with them I should have got the men to do anything? Not it! The bosun perhaps? Perhaps! It wasn't a heavy sea—it was a sea gone mad! I suppose the end of the world will be something like that; and a man may have the heart to see it coming once and be done with it—but to have to face it day after day—I don't blame anybody. I was precious little better than the rest. Only—I was an officer of that old coal-wagon, anyhow—"

"I quite understand," I conveyed that sincere assurance into his ear. He was out of breath with whispering; I could hear him pant slightly. It was all very simple. The same strung-up force which had given twenty-four men a chance, at least, for their lives, had, in a sort of recoil, crushed an unworthy mutinous existence.

But I had no leisure to weigh the merits of the matter—footsteps in the saloon, a heavy knock. "There's enough wind to get under way with, sir." Here was the call of a new claim upon my thoughts and even upon my feelings.

"Turn the hands up," I cried through the door. "I'll be on deck directly."

I was going out to make the acquaintance of my ship. Before I left the cabin our eyes met—the eyes of the only two strangers on board. I pointed to the recessed part where the little campstool awaited him and laid my finger on my lips. He made a gesture— somewhat vague—a little mysterious, accompanied by a faint smile, as if of regret.

This is not the place to enlarge upon the sensations of a man who feels for the first time a ship move under his feet to his own inde-pendent word. In my case they were not unalloyed. I was not wholly alone with my command; for there was that stranger in my cabin. Or rather, I was not completely and wholly with her. Part of me was absent. That mental feeling of being in two places at once affected me physically as if the mood of secrecy had pene-trated my very soul. Before an hour had elapsed since the ship had begun to move, having occasion to ask the mate (he stood by my side) to take a compass bearing of the Pagoda, I caught myself reaching up to his ear in whispers. I say I caught myself, but enough had escaped to startle the man. I can't describe it otherwise than by saying that he shied. A grave, preoccupied manner, as though he were in possession of some perplexing intelligence, did not leave him henceforth. A little later I moved away from the rail to look at the compass with such a stealthy gait that the helmsman noticed it—and I could not help noticing the unusual roundness of his eyes. These are trifling instances, though it's to no commander's advantage to be suspected of ludicrous eccentricities. But I was also more seriously affected. There are to a seaman certain words, gestures, that should in given conditions come as naturally, as instinctively as the winking of a menaced eye. A certain order should spring on to his lips without thinking; a certain sign should get itself made, so to speak, without reflection. But all unconscious alertness had abandoned me. I had to make an effort of will to recall myself back (from the cabin) to the conditions of the moment. I felt that I was appearing an irresolute commander to those people who were watching me more or less critically.

And, besides, there were the scares. On the second day out, for instance, coming off the deck in the afternoon (I had straw slippers on my bare feet) I stopped at the open pantry door and spoke to the steward. He was doing something there with his back to me. At the sound of my voice he nearly jumped out of his skin, as the saying is, and incidentally broke a cup.

"What on earth's the matter with you?" I asked, astonished.

He was extremely confused. "Beg your pardon, sir. I made sure you were in your cabin."

"You see I wasn't."

"No, sir. I could have sworn I had heard you moving in there not a moment ago. It's most extraordinary . . . very sorry, sir."

I passed on with an inward shudder. I was so identified with my secret double that I did not even mention the fact in those scanty, fearful whispers we exchanged. I suppose he had made some slight noise of some kind or other. It would have been miraculous if he hadn't at one time or another. And yet, haggard as he appeared, he looked always perfectly self-controlled, more than calm—almost invulnerable. On my suggestion he remained almost entirely in the bathroom, which, upon the whole, was the safest place. There could be really no shadow of an excuse for anyone ever wanting to go in there, once the steward had done with it. It was a very tiny place. Sometimes he reclined on the floor, his legs bent, his head sustained on one elbow. At others I would find him on the campstool, sitting in his gray sleeping suit and with his cropped dark hair like a patient, unmoved convict. At night I would smuggle him into my bed-place, and we would whisper together, with the regular footfalls of the officer of the watch passing and repassing over our heads. It was an infinitely miserable time. It was lucky that some tins of fine preserves were stowed in a locker in my stateroom; hard bread

I could always get hold of; and so he lived on stewed chicken, paté de foie gras, asparagus, cooked oysters, sardines—on all sorts of abominable sham delicacies out of tins. My early morning coffee he always drank; and it was all I dared do for him in that respect.

Every day there was the horrible maneuvering to go through so that my room and then the bathroom should be done in the usual way. I came to hate the sight of the steward, to abhor the voice of that harmless man. I felt that it was he who would bring on the disaster of discovery. It hung like a sword over our heads.

The fourth day out, I think (we were then working down the east side of the Gulf of Siam, tack for tack, in light winds and smooth water)—the fourth day, I say, of this miserable juggling with the unavoidable, as we sat at our evening meal, that man, whose slightest movement I dreaded, after putting down the dishes ran up on deck busily. This could not be dangerous. Presently he came down again; and then it appeared that he had remembered a coat of mine which I had thrown over a rail to dry after having been wetted in a shower which had passed over the ship in the afternoon. Sitting stolidly at the head of the table I became terrified at the sight of the garment on his arm. Of course he made for my door. There was no time to lose.

"Steward," I thundered. My nerves were so shaken that I could not govern my voice and conceal my agitation. This was the sort of thing that made my terrifically whiskered mate tap his forehead with his forefinger. I had detected him using that gesture while talking on deck with a confidential air to the carpenter. It was too far to hear a word, but I had no doubt that this pantomime could only refer to the strange new captain.

"Yes, sir," the pale-faced steward turned resignedly to me. It was this maddening course of being shouted at, checked without rhyme or reason, arbitrarily chased out of my cabin, suddenly called into it, sent flying out of his pantry on incomprehensible errands, that accounted for the growing wretchedness of his expression.

"Where are you going with that coat?"

"To your room, sir."

"Is there another shower coming?"

"I'm sure I don't know, sir. Shall I go up again and see, sir?"

"No! never mind."

My object was attained, as of course my other self in there would have heard everything that passed. During this interlude my two officers never raised their eyes off their respective plates; but the lip of that confounded cub, the second mate, quivered visibly.

I expected the steward to hook my coat on and come out at once. He was very slow about it; but I dominated my nervousness sufficiently not to shout after him. Suddenly I became aware (it could be heard plainly enough) that the fellow for some reason or other was opening the door of the bathroom. It was the end. The place was literally not big enough to swing a cat in. My voice died in my throat and I went stony all over. I expected to hear a yell of surprise and terror, and made a movement, but had not the strength to get on my legs. Everything remained still. Had my second self taken the poor wretch by the throat? I don't know what I would have done next moment if I had not seen the steward come out of my room, close the door, and then stand quietly by the sideboard.

Saved, I thought. But, no! Lost! Gone! He was gone!

I laid my knife and fork down and leaned back in my chair. My head swam. After a while, when sufficiently recovered to speak in a steady voice, I instructed my mate to put the ship round at eight o'clock himself.

"I won't come on deck," I went on. "I think I'll turn in, and unless the wind shifts I don't want to be disturbed before midnight. I feel a bit seedy."

"You did look middling bad a little while ago," the chief mate remarked without showing any great concern.

They both went out, and I stared at the steward clearing the table. There was nothing to be read on that wretched man's face. But why did he avoid my eyes I asked myself. Then I thought I should like to hear the sound of his voice.

"Steward!"

"Sir!" Startled as usual.

"Where did you hang up that coat?"

"In the bathroom, sir." The usual anxious tone. "It's not quite dry yet, sir."

For some time longer I sat in the cuddy. Had my double vanished as he had come? But of his coming there was an explanation, whereas his disappearance would be inexplicable. . . . I went slowly into my dark room, shut the door, lighted the lamp, and for a time dared not turn round. When at last I did I saw him standing bolt upright in the narrow recessed part. It would not be true to say I had a shock, but an irresistible doubt of his bodily existence flitted through my mind. Can it be, I asked myself, that he is not visible to other eyes than mine? It was like being haunted. Motionless, with a grave face, he raised his hands slightly at me in a gesture which meant clearly, "Heavens! what a narrow escape!" Narrow indeed. I think I had come creeping quietly as near insanity as any man who has not actually gone over the border. That gesture restrained me, so to speak.

The mate with the terrific whiskers was now putting the ship on the other tack. In the moment of profound silence which follows upon the hands going to their stations I heard on the poop his raised voice: "Hard alee!" and the distant shout of the order repeated on the maindeck. The sails, in that light breeze, made but a faint fluttering noise. It ceased. The ship was coming around slowly; I held my breath in the renewed stillness of expectation; one wouldn't have thought that there was a single living soul on her decks. A sudden brisk shout, "Mainsail haul!" broke the spell, and in the noisy cries and rush overhead of the men running away with the main brace we two, down in my cabin, came together in our usual position by the bed-place.

He did not wait for my question. "I heard him fumbling here and just managed to squat myself down in the bath," he whispered to me. "The fellow only opened the door and put his arm in to hang the coat up. All the same—"

"I never thought of that," I whispered back, even more appalled than before at the closeness of the shave, and marveling at that something unyielding in his character which was carrying him through so finely. There was no agitation in his whisper. Whoever was being driven distracted, it was not he. He was sane. And the proof of his sanity was continued when he took up the whispering again.

"It would never do for me to come to life again."

It was something that a ghost might have said. But what he was alluding to was his old captain's reluctant admission of the theory of suicide. It would obviously serve his turn—if I had understood at all the view which seemed to govern the unalterable purpose of his action.

"You must maroon me as soon as ever you can get amongst these islands off the Cambodje shore," he went on.

"Maroon you! We are not living in a boy's adventure tale," I protested. His scornful whispering took me up.

"We aren't indeed! There's nothing of a boy's tale in this. But there's nothing else for it. I want no more. You don't suppose I am afraid of what can be done to me? Prison or gallows or whatever they may please. But you don't see me coming back to explain such things to an old fellow in a wig and twelve respectable tradesmen, do you? What can they know whether I am guilty or not—or of *what* I am guilty, either? That's my affair. What does the Bible say? 'Driven off the face of the earth.' Very well. I am off the face of the earth now. As I came at night so I shall go."

"Impossible!" I murmured. "You can't."

"Can't? . . . Not naked like a soul on the Day of Judgment. I shall freeze on to this sleeping suit. The Last Day is not yet—and . . . you have understood thoroughly. Didn't you?"

I felt suddenly ashamed of myself. I may say truly that I understood—and my hesitation in letting that man swim away from my ship's side had been a mere sham sentiment, a sort of cowardice.

"It can't be done now till next night," I breathed out. "The ship is on the offshore tack and the wind may fail us."

"As long as I know that you understand," he whispered. "But of course you do. It's a great satisfaction to have got somebody to understand. You seem to have been there on purpose." And in the same whisper, as if we two whenever we talked had to say things to each other which were not fit for the world to hear, he added, "It's very wonderful."

We remained side by side talking in our secret way—but sometimes silent or just exchanging a whispered word or two at long intervals. And as usual he stared through the port. A breath of wind came now and again into our faces. The ship might have been moored in dock, so gently and on an even keel she slipped through the water, that did not murmur even at our passage, shadowy and silent like a phantom sea.

At midnight I went on deck, and to my mate's great surprise put the ship round on the other tack. His terrible whiskers flitted round me in silent criticism. I certainly should not have done it if it had been only a question of getting out of that sleepy gulf as quickly as possible. I believe he told the second mate, who relieved him, that it was a great want of judgment. The other only yawned. That intolerable cub shuffled about so sleepily and lolled against the rails in such a slack, improper fashion that I came down on him sharply.

"Aren't you properly awake yet?"

"Yes, sir! I am awake."

"Well, then, be good enough to hold yourself as if you were. And keep a lookout. If there's any current we'll be closing with some islands before daylight."

The east side of the gulf is fringed with islands, some solitary, others in groups. On the blue background of the high coast they seem to float on silvery patches of calm water, arid and gray, or dark green and rounded like clumps of evergreen bushes, with the larger ones, a mile or two long, showing the outlines of ridges, ribs of gray rock under the dark mantle of matted leafage. Unknown to trade, to travel, almost to geography, the manner of life they harbor is an unsolved secret. There must be villages—settlements of fishermen at least—on the largest of them, and some communication with the world is probably kept up by native craft. But all that forenoon, as we headed for them, fanned along by the faintest of breezes, I saw no sign of man or canoe in the field of the telescope I kept on pointing at the scattered group.

At noon I gave no orders for a change of course, and the mate's whiskers became much concerned and seemed to be offering themselves unduly to my notice. At last I said:

"I am going to stand right in. Quite in—as far as I can take her."

The stare of extreme surprise imparted an air of ferocity also to his eyes, and he looked truly terrific for a moment.

"We're not doing well in the middle of the gulf," I continued, casually. "I am going to look for the land breezes tonight."

"Bless my soul! Do you mean, sir, in the dark amongst the lot of all them islands and reefs and shoals?"

"Well—if there are any regular land breezes at all on this coast one must get close inshore to find them, mustn't one?"

"Bless my soul!" he exclaimed again under his breath. All that afternoon he wore a dreamy, contemplative appearance which in him was a mark of perplexity. After dinner I went into my stateroom as if I meant to take some rest. There we two bent our dark heads over a half-unrolled chart lying on my bed.

"There," I said. "It's got to be Koh-ring. I've been looking at it ever since sunrise. It has got two hills and a low point. It must be inhabited. And on the coast opposite there is what looks like the mouth of a biggish river—with some town, no doubt, not far up. It's the best chance for you that I can see."

"Anything. Koh-ring let it be."

He looked thoughtfully at the chart as if surveying chances and distances from a lofty height—and following with his eyes his own figure wandering on the blank land of Cochin-China, and then passing off that piece of paper clean out of sight into uncharted regions. And it was as if the ship had two captains to plan her course for her. I had been so worried and restless running up and down that I had not had the patience to dress that day. I had remained in my sleeping suit, with straw slippers and a soft floppy hat. The closeness of the heat in the gulf had been most oppressive, and the crew were used to see me wandering in that airy attire.

"She will clear the south point as she heads now," I whispered into his ear. "Goodness only knows when, though, but certainly after dark. I'll edge her in to half a mile, as far as I may be able to judge in the dark—"

"Be careful," he murmured, warningly—and I realized suddenly that all my future, the only future for which I was fit, would perhaps go irretrievably to pieces in any mishap to my first command.

I could not stop a moment longer in the room. I motioned him to get out of sight and made my way on the poop. That unplayful cub had the watch. I walked up and down for a while thinking things out, then beckoned him over.

"Send a couple of hands to open the two quarter-deck ports," I said, mildly.

He actually had the impudence, or else so forgot himself in his wonder at such an incomprehensible order, as to repeat:

"Open the quarter-deck ports! What for, sir?"

"The only reason you need concern yourself about is because I tell you to do so. Have them open wide and fastened properly."

He reddened and went off, but I believe made some jeering remark to the carpenter as to the sensible practice of ventilating a ship's quarter-deck. I know he popped into the mate's cabin to impart the fact to him because the whiskers came on deck, as it were by chance, and stole glances at me from below—for signs of lunacy or drunkenness, I suppose.

A little before supper, feeling more restless than ever, I rejoined, for a moment, my second self. And to find him sitting so quietly was surprising, like something against nature, inhuman.

I developed my plan in a hurried whisper.

"I shall stand in as close as I dare and then put her round. I shall presently find means to smuggle you out of here into the sail locker, which communicates with the lobby. But there is an opening, a sort of square for hauling the sails out, which gives straight on the quarter-deck and which is never closed in fine weather, so as to give air to the sails. When the ship's way is deadened in stays and all the hands are aft at the main braces you shall have a clear road to slip out and get overboard through the open quarter-deck port. I've had them both fastened up. Use a rope's end to lower yourself into the water so as to avoid a splash—you know. It could be heard and cause some beastly complication."

He kept silent for a while, then whispered, "I understand."

"I won't be there to see you go," I began with an effort. "The rest . . . I only hope I have understood, too."

"You have. From first to last," and for the first time there seemed to be a faltering, something strained in his whisper. He caught hold of my arm, but the ringing of the supper bell made me start. He didn't, though; he only released his grip.

After supper I didn't come below again till well past eight o'clock. The faint, steady breeze was loaded with dew; and the wet, darkened sails held all there was of propelling power in it. The night, clear and starry, sparkled darkly, and the opaque, lightless patches shifting slowly against the low stars were the drifting islets. On the port bow there was a big one more distant and shadowily imposing by the great space of sky it eclipsed.

On opening the door I had a back view of my very own self looking at a chart. He had come out of the recess and was standing near the table.

"Quite dark enough," I whispered.

He stepped back and leaned against my bed with a level, quiet glance. I sat on the couch. We had nothing to say to each other. Over our heads the officer of the watch moved here and there. Then I heard him move quickly. I knew what that meant. He was making for the companion; and presently his voice was outside my door.

"We are drawing in pretty fast, sir. Land looks rather close."

"Very well," I answered. "I am coming on deck directly."

I waited till he was gone out of the cuddy, then rose. My double moved too. The time had come to exchange our last whispers, for neither of us was ever to hear each other's natural voice.

"Look here!" I opened a drawer and took out three sovereigns. "Take this, anyhow. I've got six and I'd give you the lot, only I must keep a little money to buy some fruit and vegetables for the crew from native boats as we go through Sunda Straits."

He shook his head.

"Take it," I urged him, whispering desperately. "No one can tell what—"

He smiled and slapped meaningly the only pocket of the sleeping jacket. It was not safe, certainly. But I produced a large old silk handkerchief of mine, and tying the three pieces of gold in a corner, pressed it on him. He was touched, I suppose, because he took it at last and tied it quickly round his waist under the jacket, on his bare skin.

Our eyes met; several seconds elapsed, till, our glances still mingled, I extended my hand and turned the lamp out. Then I passed through the cuddy, leaving the door of my room wide open. . . . "Steward!"

He was still lingering in the pantry in the greatness of his zeal, giving a rub-up to a plated cruet stand the last thing before going to bed. Being careful not to wake up the mate, whose room was opposite, I spoke in an undertone.

He looked round anxiously. "Sir!"

"Can you get me a little hot water from the galley?"

"I am afraid, sir, the galley fire's been out for some time now."

"Go and see."

He fled up the stairs.

"Now," I whispered, loudly, into the saloon—too loudly, perhaps, but I was afraid I couldn't make a sound. He was by my side in an instant—the double captain slipped past the stairs—through the tiny dark passage . . . a sliding door. We were in the sail locker, scrambling on our knees over the sails. A sudden thought struck me. I saw myself wandering barefooted, bareheaded, the sun beating on my dark poll. I snatched off my floppy hat and tried hurriedly in the dark to ram it on my other self. He dodged and fended off silently. I wonder what he thought had come to me before he understood and suddenly desisted. Our hands met gropingly, lingered united in a steady, motionless clasp for a second. . . . No word was breathed by either of us when they separated.

I was standing quietly by the pantry door when the steward returned.

"Sorry, sir. Kettle barely warm. Shall I light the spirit lamp?"

"Never mind."

I came out on deck slowly. It was now a matter of conscience to shave the land as close as possible—for now he must go overboard whenever the ship was put in stays. Must! There could be no going back for him. After a moment I walked over to leeward and my heart flew into my mouth at the nearness of the land on the bow. Under any other circumstances I would not have held on a minute longer. The second mate had followed me anxiously.

I looked on till I felt I could command my voice.

"She will weather," I said then in a quiet tone.

"Are you going to try that, sir?" he stammered out incredulously.

I took no notice of him and raised my tone just enough to be heard by the helmsman.

"Keep her good full."

"Good full, sir."

The wind fanned my cheek, the sails slept, the world was silent. The strain of watching the dark loom of the land grow bigger and denser was too much for me. I had shut my eyes—because the ship must go closer. She must! The stillness was intolerable. Were we standing still?

When I opened my eyes the second view started my heart with

a thump. The black southern hill of Koh-ring seemed to hang right over the ship like a towering fragment of the everlasting night. On that enormous mass of blackness there was not a gleam to be seen, not a sound to be heard. It was gliding irresistibly toward us and yet seemed already within reach of the hand. I saw the vague figures of the watch grouped in the waist, gazing in awed silence.

"Are you going on, sir?" inquired an unsteady voice at my elbow.

I ignored it. I had to go on.

"Keep her full. Don't check her way. That won't do now," I said warningly.

"I can't see the sails very well," the helmsman answered me, in strange, quavering tones.

Was she close enough? Already she was, I won't say in the shadow of the land, but in the very blackness of it, already swallowed up as it were, gone too close to be recalled, gone from me altogether.

"Give the mate a call," I said to the young man who stood at my elbow as still as death. "And turn all hands up."

My tone had a borrowed loudness reverberated from the height of the land. Several voices cried out together: "We are all on deck, sir."

Then stillness again, with the great shadow gliding closer, towering higher, without a light, without a sound. Such a hush had fallen on the ship that she might have been a bark of the dead floating in slowly under the very gate of Erebus.

"My God! Where are we?"

It was the mate moaning at my elbow. He was thunderstruck, and as it were deprived of the moral support of his whiskers. He clapped his hands and absolutely cried out, "Lost!"

"Be quiet," I said sternly.

He lowered his tone, but I saw the shadowy gesture of his despair. "What are we doing here?"

"Looking for the land wind."

He made as if to tear his hair, and addressed me recklessly.

"She will never get out. You have done it, sir. I knew it'd end in something like this. She will never weather, and you are too close now to stay. She'll drift ashore before she's round. O my God!"

I caught his arm as he was raising it to batter his poor devoted head, and shook it violently.

"She's ashore already," he wailed, trying to tear himself away.

"Is she? . . . Keep good full there!"

"Good full, sir," cried the helmsman in a frightened, thin, child-like voice.

I hadn't let go the mate's arm and went on shaking it. "Ready about, do you hear? You go forward"—shake—"and stop there"—shake—"and hold your noise"—shake—"and see these head sheets properly overhauled"—shake, shake—shake.

And all the time I dared not look toward the land lest my heart should fail me. I released my grip at last and he ran forward as if fleeing for dear life.

I wondered what my double there in the sail locker thought of this commotion. He was able to hear everything—and perhaps he was able to understand why, on my conscience, it had to be thus close—no less. My first order "Hard alee!" re-echoed ominously under the towering shadow of Koh-ring as if I had shouted in a mountain gorge. And then I watched the land intently. In that smooth water and light wind it was impossible to feel the ship coming-to. No! I could not feel her. And my second self was making now ready to slip out and lower himself overboard. Perhaps he was gone already . . . ?

The great black mass brooding over our very mastheads began to pivot away from the ship's side silently. And now I forgot the secret stranger ready to depart, and remembered only that I was a total stranger to the ship. I did not know her. Would she do it? How was she to be handled?

I swung the mainyard and waited helplessly. She was perhaps stopped, and her very fate hung in the balance, with the black mass of Koh-ring like the gate of the everlasting night towering over her taffrail. What would she do now? Had she way on her yet? I stepped to the side swiftly, and on the shadowy water I could see nothing except a faint phosphorescent flash revealing the glassy smoothness of the sleeping surface. It was impossible to tell—and I had not learned yet the feel of my ship. Was she moving? What I needed was something easily seen, a piece of paper, which I could throw overboard and watch. I had nothing on me. To run down for it I didn't dare. There was no time. All at once my strained, yearning stare distinguished a white object floating within a yard of the ship's side. White on the black water. A phosphorescent flash passed under it. What was that thing? . . . I recognized my own floppy hat. It must have fallen off his head . . . and he didn't bother. Now I had what I wanted—the saving mark for my eyes. But I hardly thought of my other self, now gone from the ship, to be hidden forever from all friendly faces, to be a fugitive and a vagabond on the earth, with no brand of the curse on his sane forehead to stay a slaying hand . . . too proud to explain.

And I watched the hat—the expression of my sudden pity for his mere flesh. It had been meant to save his homeless head from the dangers of the sun. And now—behold—it was saving the ship, by serving me for a mark to help out the ignorance of my strangeness. Ha! It was drifting forward, warning me just in time that the ship had gathered sternway.

"Shift the helm," I said in a low voice to the seaman standing still like a statue.

The man's eyes glistened wildly in the binnacle light as he jumped round to the other side and spun round the wheel.

I walked to the break of the poop. On the overshadowed deck all hands stood by the forebraces waiting for my order. The stars ahead seemed to be gliding from right to left. And all was so still in the world that I heard the quiet remark "She's round," passed in a tone of intense relief between two seamen.

"Let go and haul."

The foreyards ran round with a great noise, amidst cheery cries. And now the frightful whiskers made themselves heard giving various orders. Already the ship was drawing ahead. And I was alone with her. Nothing! no one in the world should stand now between us, throwing a shadow on the way of silent knowledge and mute affection, the perfect communion of a seaman with his first command.

Walking to the taffrail, I was in time to make out, on the very edge of a darkness thrown by a towering black mass like the very gateway of Erebus—yes, I was in time to catch an evanescent glimpse of my white hat left behind to mark the spot where the secret sharer of my cabin and of my thoughts, as though he were my second self, had lowered himself into the water to take his punishment: a free man, a proud swimmer striking out for a new destiny.

Youth

THIS COULD HAVE OCCURRED NOWHERE BUT IN ENGLAND, WHERE MEN and sea interpenetrate, so to speak—the sea entering into the life of most men, and the men knowing something or everything about the sea, in the way of amusement, of travel, or of breadwinning.

We were sitting round a mahogany table that reflected the bottle, the claret glasses, and our faces as we leaned on our elbows. There was a director of companies, an accountant, a lawyer, Marlow, and myself. The director had been a *Conway* boy, the accountant had served four years at sea, the lawyer—a fine crusted Tory, High Churchman, the best of old fellows, the soul of honor—had been chief officer in the P. & O. service in the good old days when mailboats were square-rigged at least on two masts, and used to come down the China Sea before a fair monsoon with stun'sails set alow and aloft. We all began life in the merchant service. Between the five of us there was the strong bond of the sea, and also the fellowship of the craft, which no amount of enthusiasm for yachting, cruising, and so on can give, since one is only the amusement of life and the other is life itself.

Marlow (at least I think that is how he spelt his name) told the story, or rather the chronicle, of a voyage:

"Yes, I have seen a little of the Eastern seas; but what I remember best is my first voyage there. You fellows know there are those voyages that seem ordered for the illustration of life, that might stand for a symbol of existence. You fight, work, sweat, nearly kill yourself, sometimes do kill yourself, trying to accomplish something—and you can't. Not from any fault of yours. You simply can do nothing, neither great nor little—not a thing in the world—not even marry an old maid, or get a wretched 600-ton cargo of coal to its port of destination.

"It was altogether a memorable affair. It was my first voyage to the East, and my first voyage as second mate; it was also my skipper's first command. You'll admit it was time. He was sixty if a day; a little man, with a broad, not very straight back, with bowed shoulders and one leg more bandy than the other, he had that queer twisted-about appearance you see so often in men who work in the fields. He had a nutcracker face—chin and nose trying to come together over a sunken mouth—and it was framed in iron-gray fluffy hair, that looked like a chinstrap of cotton-wool sprinkled with coaldust. And he had blue eyes in that old face of his, which were amazingly like a boy's, with that candid expression some quite common men preserve to the end of their days by a rare internal gift of simplicity of heart and rectitude of soul. What induced him to accept me was a wonder. I had come out of a crack Australian clipper, where I had been third officer, and he seemed to have a prejudice against crack clippers as aristocratic and high-toned. He said to me, 'You know, in this ship you will have to work.' I said I had to work in every ship I had ever been in. 'Ah, but this is different, and you gentlemen out of them big ships; . . . but there! I dare say you will do. Join tomorrow.'

"I joined tomorrow. It was twenty-two years ago; and I was just twenty. How time passes! It was one of the happiest days of my life. Fancy! Second mate for the first time—a really responsible officer! I wouldn't have thrown up my new billet for a fortune. The mate looked me over carefully. He was also an old chap, but of another stamp. He had a Roman nose, a snow-white, long beard, and his name was Mahon, but he insisted that it should be pronounced Mann. He was well connected; yet there was something wrong with his luck, and he had never got on.

"As to the captain, he had been for years in coasters, then in the Mediterranean, and last in the West Indian trade. He had never been round the Capes. He could just write a kind of sketchy hand, and didn't care for writing at all. Both were thorough good seamen of course, and between those two old chaps I felt like a small boy between two grandfathers.

"The ship also was old. Her name was the *Judea*. Queer name, isn't it? She belonged to a man Wilmer, Wilcox—some name like that; but he has been bankrupt and dead these twenty years or more, and his name don't matter. She had been laid up in Shadwell basin for ever so long. You may imagine her state. She was all rust, dust, grime—soot aloft, dirt on deck. To me it was like coming out of a palace into a ruined cottage. She was about 400 tons, had a primitive windlass, wooden latches to the doors, not a bit of brass about her, and a big square stern. There was on it, below her name in big letters, a lot of scrollwork, with the gilt off, and some sort of coat of arms, with the motto 'Do or Die' underneath. I remember it took my fancy immensely. There was a touch of romance in it, something that made me love the old thing—something that appealed to my youth!

"We left London in ballast—sand ballast—to load a cargo of coal in a northern port for Bangkok. Bangkok! I thrilled. I had been six years at sea, but had only seen Melbourne and Sydney, very good places, charming places in their way—but Bangkok!

"We worked out of the Thames under canvas, with a North Sea pilot on board. His name was Jermyn, and he dodged all day long about the galley drying his handkerchief before the stove. Apparently he never slept. He was a dismal man, with a perpetual tear sparkling at the end of his nose, who either had been in trouble, or was in trouble, or expected to be in trouble—couldn't be happy unless something went wrong. He mistrusted my youth, my common sense, and my seamanship, and made a point of showing it in a hundred little ways. I dare say he was right. It seems to me I knew very little then, and I know not much more now; but I cherish a hate for that Jermyn to this day.

"We were a week working up as far as Yarmouth Roads, and then we got into a gale—the famous October gale of twenty-two years ago. It was wind, lightning, sleet, snow, and a terrific sea. We were flying light, and you may imagine how bad it was when I tell you we had smashed bulwarks and a flooded deck. On the second night she shifted her ballast into the lee bow, and by that time we had been blown off somewhere on the Dogger Bank. There was nothing for it but go below with shovels and try to right her, and there we were in that vast hold, gloomy like a cavern, the tallow dips stuck and flickering on the beams, the gale howling above, the ship tossing about like mad on her side; there we all were, Jermyn, the captain, everyone, hardly able to keep our feet, engaged in that gravedigger's work, and trying to toss shovelfuls of wet sand up to windward. At every tumble of the ship you could see vaguely in the dim light men falling down with a great flourish of shovels. One of the ship's boys (we had two), impressed by the weirdness of the scene, wept as if his heart would break. We could hear him blubbering somewhere in the shadows.

"On the third day the gale died out, and by and by a north-country tug picked us up. We took sixteen days in all to get from London to the Tyne! When we got into dock we had lost our turn for loading, and they hauled us off to a pier where we remained for a month. Mrs. Beard (the captain's name was Beard) came from Colchester to see the old man. She lived on board. The crew of runners had left, and there remained only the officers, one boy and the steward, a mulatto who answered to the name of Abraham. Mrs. Beard was an old woman, with a face all wrinkled and ruddy like a winter apple, and the figure of a young girl. She caught sight of me once, sewing on a button, and insisted on having my shirts to repair. This was something different from the captains' wives I had known on board crack clippers. When I brought her the shirts she said: 'And the socks? They want mending, I am sure, and John's—Captain Beard's—things are all in order now. I would be glad of something to do.' Bless the old woman. She overhauled my outfit for me, and meantime I read for the first time *Sartor Resartus* and Burnaby's *Ride to Khiva*. I didn't understand much of the first then; but I remember I preferred the soldier to the philosopher at the time; a preference which life has only confirmed. One was a man, and the other was either more— or less. However, they are both dead and Mrs. Beard is dead, and youth, strength, genius, thoughts, achievements, simple hearts—all dies. . . . No matter.

"They loaded us at last. We shipped a crew. Eight able seamen and two boys. We hauled off one evening to the buoys at the dock gates, ready to go out, and with a fair prospect of beginning the voyage next day. Mrs. Beard was to start for home by a late train. When the ship was fast we went to tea. We sat rather silent through the meal—Mahon, the old couple, and I. I finished first, and slipped away for a smoke, my cabin being in a deckhouse just against the poop. It was high water, blowing fresh with a drizzle; the double dock gates were opened, and the steam colliers were going in and out in the darkness with their lights burning bright, a great plashing of propellers, rattling of winches, and a lot of hailing on the pierheads. I watched the procession of headlights gliding high and of green lights gliding low in the night, when suddenly a red gleam flashed at me, vanished, came into view again, and remained. The fore end of a steamer loomed up close. I shouted down the cabin, 'Come up, quick!' and then heard a startled voice saying afar in the dark, 'Stop her, sir.' A bell jingled. Another voice cried warningly, 'We are going right into that bark, sir.' The answer to this was a gruff 'All right,' and the next thing was a heavy crash as the steamer struck a glancing blow with the bluff of her bow about our forerigging. There was a moment of confusion, yelling, and running about. Steam roared. Then somebody was heard saying, 'All clear, sir.' . . . 'Are you all right?' asked the gruff voice. I had jumped forward to see the damage, and hailed back, 'I think so.' 'Easy astern,' said the gruff voice. A bell jingled. 'What steamer is that?' screamed Mahon. By that time she was no more to us than a bulky shadow maneuvering a little way off. They shouted at us some name—a woman's name, Miranda or Melissa—or some such thing. 'This means another month in this beastly hole,' said Mahon to me, as we peered with lamps about the splintered bulwarks and broken braces. 'But where's the captain?'

"We had not heard or seen anything of him all that time. We went aft to look. A doleful voice arose hailing somewhere in the middle of the dock, '*Judea* ahoy!' . . . How the devil did he get there? . . . 'Hallo!' we shouted. 'I am adrift in our boat without oars,' he cried. A belated water-man offered his services, and Mahon struck a bargain with him for a half crown to tow our skipper alongside; but it was Mrs. Beard that came up the ladder first. They had been floating about the dock in that mizzly cold rain for nearly an hour. I was never so surprised in my life.

"It appears that when he heard my shout 'Come up' he understood at once what was the matter, caught up his wife, ran on deck, and across, and down into our boat, which was fast to the ladder. Not bad for a sixty-year-old. Just imagine that old fellow saving heroically in his arms that old woman—the woman of his life. He set her down on a thwart, and was ready to climb back on board when the painter came adrift somehow, and away they went together. Of course in the confusion we did not hear him shouting. He looked abashed. She said cheerfully, 'I suppose it does not matter my losing the train now?' 'No, Jenny—you go below and get warm,' he growled. Then to us: 'A sailor has no business with a wife—I say. There I was, out of the ship. Well, no harm done this time. Let's go and look at what that fool of a steamer smashed.'

"It wasn't much, but it delayed us three weeks. At the end of that time, the captain being engaged with his agents, I carried Mrs. Beard's bag to the railway station and put her all comfy into a third-class carriage. She lowered the window to say, 'You are a good young man. If you see John—Captain Beard—without his muffler at night, just remind him from me to keep his throat well wrapped up.' 'Certainly, Mrs. Beard,' I said. 'You are a good young man; I noticed how attentive you are to John—to Captain——' The train pulled out suddenly; I took my cap off to the old woman: I never saw her again. . . . Pass the bottle.

"We went to sea next day. When we made that start for Bangkok we had been already three months out of London. We had expected to be a fortnight or so—at the outside.

"It was January, and the weather was beautiful—the beautiful sunny winter weather that has more charm than in the summertime, because it is unexpected, and crisp, and you know it won't, it can't, last long. It's like a windfall, like a godsend, like an unexpected piece of luck.

"It lasted all down the North Sea, all down Channel; and it lasted till we were three hundred miles or so to the westward of the Lizards; then the wind went round to the sou'west and began to pipe up. In two days it blew a gale. The *Judea* hove to, wallowed on the Atlantic like an old candle-box. It blew day after day: it blew with spite, without interval, without mercy, without rest. The world was nothing but an immensity of great foaming waves rushing at us, under a sky low enough to touch with the hand and dirty like a smoked ceiling. In the stormy space surrounding us there was as much flying spray as air. Day after day and night after night there was nothing round the ship but the howl of the wind, the tumult of the sea, the noise of water pouring over her deck. There was no rest for her and no rest for us. She tossed, she pitched, she stood on her head, she sat on her tail, she rolled, she groaned, and we had to hold on while on deck and cling to our bunks when below, in a constant effort of body and worry of mind.

"One night Mahon spoke through the small window of my berth. It opened right into my very bed, and I was lying there sleepless, in my boots, feeling as though I had not slept for years, and could not if I tried. He said excitedly:

" 'You got the sounding rod in here, Marlow? I can't get the pumps to suck. By God! It's no child's play.'

"I gave him the sounding rod and lay down again, trying to think of various things—but I thought only of the pumps. When I came on deck they were still at it, and my watch relieved at the pumps. By the light of the lantern brought on deck to examine the sounding rod I caught a glimpse of their weary, serious faces. We pumped all the four hours. We pumped all night, all day, all the week—watch and watch. She was working herself loose, and leaked badly—not enough to drown us at once, but enough to kill us with the work at the pumps. And while we pumped the ship was going from us piecemeal: the bulwarks went, the stanchions were torn out, the ventilators smashed, the cabin door burst in. There was not a dry spot in the ship. She was being gutted bit by bit. The longboat changed, as if by magic, into matchwood where she stood in her gripes. I had lashed her myself, and was rather proud of my handiwork, which had withstood so long the malice of the sea. And we pumped. And there was no break in the weather. The sea was white like a sheet of foam, like a caldron of boiling milk; there was not a break in the clouds, no—not the size of a man's hand—no, not for so much as ten seconds. There was for us no sky, there were for us no stars, no sun, no universe—nothing but angry clouds and an infuriated sea. We pumped watch and watch, for dear life; and it seemed to last for months, for years, for all eternity, as though we had been dead and gone to a hell for sailors. We forgot the day of the week, the name of the month, what year it was, and whether we had ever been ashore. The sails blew away, she lay broadside on under a weather cloth, the ocean poured over her, and we did not care. We turned those handles, and had the eyes of idiots. As soon as we had crawled on deck I used to take a round turn with a rope about the men, the pumps, and the mainmast, and we turned, we turned incessantly, with the water to our waists, to our necks, over our heads. It was all one. We had forgotten how it felt to be dry.

"And there was somewhere in me the thought: By Jove! This is the deuce of an adventure—something you read about; and it is my first voyage as second mate—and I am only twenty—and here I am lasting it out as well as any of these men, and keeping my chaps up to the mark. I was pleased. I would not have given up the experience for worlds. I had moments of exultation. Whenever the old dismantled craft pitched heavily with her counter high in the air, she seemed to me to throw up, like an appeal, like a defiance, like a cry to the clouds without mercy, the words written on her stern: 'Judea, London. Do or Die.'

"Oh youth! The strength of it, the faith of it, the imagination of it! To me she was not an old rattletrap carting about the world a lot of coal for a freight—to me she was the endeavor, the test, the trial of life. I think of her with pleasure, with affection, with regret—as you would think of someone dead you have loved. I shall never forget her. . . . Pass the bottle.

"One night when tied to the mast, as I explained, we were pumping on, deafened with the wind, and without spirit enough in us to wish ourselves dead, a heavy sea crashed aboard and swept clean over us. As soon as I got my breath I shouted, as in duty bound, 'Keep on, boys!' when suddenly I felt something hard floating on deck strike the calf of my leg. I made a grab at it and missed. It was so dark we could not see each other's faces within a foot—you understand.

"After that thump the ship kept quiet for a while, and the thing, whatever it was, struck my leg again. This time I caught it—and it was a saucepan. At first, being stupid with fatigue and thinking of nothing but the pumps, I did not understand what I had in my hand. Suddenly it dawned upon me, and I shouted, 'Boys, the house on deck is gone. Leave this, and let's look for the cook.'

"There was a deckhouse forward, which contained the galley, the cook's berth, and the quarters of the crew. As we had expected for days to see it swept away, the hands had been ordered to sleep in the cabin—the only safe place in the ship. The steward, Abraham, however, persisted in clinging to his berth, stupidly, like a mule— from sheer fright I believe, like an animal that won't leave a stable falling in an earthquake. So we went to look for him. It was chancing death, since once out of our lashings we were as exposed as if on a raft. But we went. The house was shattered as if a shell had exploded inside. Most of it had gone overboard—stove, men's quarters, and their property, all was gone; but two posts, holding a portion of the bulkhead to which Abraham's bunk was attached, remained as if by a miracle. We groped in the ruins and came upon this, and there he was, sitting in his bunk, surrounded by foam and wreckage, jabbering cheerfully to himself. He was out of his mind; completely and forever mad, with this sudden shock coming upon the fag-end of his endurance. We snatched him up, lugged him aft, and pitched him headfirst down the cabin companion. You understand there was no time to carry him down with infinite precautions and wait to see how he got on. Those below would pick him up at the bottom of the stairs all right. We were in a hurry to go back to the pumps. That business could not wait. A bad leak is an inhuman thing.

"One would think that the sole purpose of that fiendish gale had been to make a lunatic of that poor devil of a mulatto. It eased before morning, and next day the sky cleared, and as the sea went down the leak took up. When it came to bending a fresh set of sails the crew demanded to put back—and really there was nothing else to do. Boats gone, decks swept clean, cabin gutted, men without a stitch but what they stood in, stores spoiled, ship strained. We put her head for home, and—would you believe it? The wind came east right in our teeth. It blew fresh, it blew continuously. We had to beat up every inch of the way, but she did not leak so badly, the water keeping comparatively smooth. Two hours' pumping in every four is no joke—but it kept her afloat as far as Falmouth.

"The good people there live on casualties of the sea, and no doubt were glad to see us. A hungry crowd of shipwrights sharpened their chisels at the sight of that carcass of a ship. And, by Jove! they had pretty pickings off us before they were done. I fancy the owner was already in a tight place. There were delays. Then it was decided to take part of the cargo out and calk her topsides. This was done, the repairs finished, cargo reshipped; a new crew came on board, and we went out—for Bangkok. At the end of a week we were back again. The crew said they weren't going to Bangkok—a hundred and fifty days' passage—in a something hooker that wanted pumping eight hours out of the twenty-four; and the nautical papers inserted again the little paragraph: '*Judea*. Bark. Tyne to Bangkok; coals; put back to Falmouth leaky and with crew refusing duty.'

"There were more delays—more tinkering. The owner came down for a day, and said she was as right as a little fiddle. Poor old Captain Beard looked like the ghost of a Geordie skipper—through the worry and humiliation of it. Remember he was sixty, and it was his first command. Mahon said it was a foolish business, and would end badly. I loved the ship more than ever, and wanted awfully to get to Bangkok. To Bangkok! Magic name, blessed name. Mesopotamia wasn't a patch on it. Remember I was twenty, and it was my first second-mate's billet, and the East was waiting for me.

"We went out and anchored in the outer roads with a fresh crew—the third. She leaked worse than ever. It was as if those confounded shipwrights had actually made a hole in her. This time we did not even go outside. The crew simply refused to man the windlass.

"They towed us back to the inner harbor, and we became a fixture, a feature, an institution of the place. People pointed us out to visitors as 'That 'ere bark that's going to Bangkok—has been. here six months—put back three times.' On holidays the small boys pulling about in boats would hail, '*Judea*, ahoy!' and if a head showed above the rail shouted, 'Where you bound to?—Bangkok?' and jeered. We were only three on board. The poor old skipper mooned in the cabin. Mahon undertook the cooking, and unexpectedly developed all a Frenchman's genius for preparing nice little messes. I looked languidly after the rigging. We became citizens of Falmouth. Every shopkeeper knew us. At the barber's or tobacconist's they asked familiarly, 'Do you think you will ever get to Bangkok?' Meantime the owner, the underwriters, and the charterers squabbled amongst themselves in London, and our pay went on. . . . Pass the bottle.

"It was horrid. Morally it was worse than pumping for life. It seemed as though we had been forgotten by the world, belonged to nobody, would get nowhere; it seemed that, as if bewitched, we would have to live for ever and ever in that inner harbor, a derision and a byword to generations of longshore loafers and dishonest boatmen. I obtained three months' pay and a five days' leave, and made a rush for London. It took me a day to get there and pretty well another to come back—but three months' pay went all the same. I don't know what I did with it. I went to a music hall, I believe, lunched, dined, and supped in a swell place in Regent Street, and was back on time, with nothing but a complete set of Byron's works and a new railway rug to show for three months' work. The boatman who pulled me off to the ship said: 'Hallo! I thought you had left the old thing. *She* will never get to Bangkok.' 'That's all *you* know about it,' I said, scornfully—but I didn't like that prophecy at all.

"Suddenly a man, some kind of agent to somebody, appeared with full powers. He had grog-blossoms all over his face, an indomitable energy, and was a jolly soul. We leaped into life again. A hulk came alongside, took our cargo, and then we went into dry dock to get our copper stripped. No wonder she leaked. The poor thing, strained beyond endurance by the gale, had, as if in disgust, spat out all the oakum of her lower seams. She was re-calked, new-coppered, and made as tight as a bottle. We went back to the hulk and reshipped our cargo.

"Then, on a fine moonlight night, all the rats left the ship.

"We had been infested with them. They had destroyed our sails, consumed more stores than the crew, affably shared our beds and our dangers, and now, when the ship was made seaworthy, concluded to clear out. I called Mahon to enjoy the spectacle. Rat after rat appeared on our rail, took a last look over his shoulder, and leaped with a hollow thud into the empty hulk. We tried to count them, but soon lost the tale. Mahon said: 'Well, well! don't talk to me about the intelligence of rats. They ought to have left before, when we had that narrow squeak from foundering. There you have the proof how silly is the superstition about them. They leave a good ship for an old rotten hulk, where there is nothing to eat, too, the fools! . . . I don't believe they know what is safe or what is good for them, any more than you or I.'

"And after some more talk we agreed that the wisdom of rats had been grossly overrated, being in fact no greater than that of men.

"The story of the ship was known, by this, all up the Channel from Land's End to the Forelands, and we could get no crew on the south coast. They sent us one all complete from Liverpool, and we left once more—for Bangkok.

"We had fair breezes, smooth water right into the tropics, and the old *Judea* lumbered along in the sunshine. When she went eight knots everything cracked aloft, and we tied our caps to our heads; but mostly she strolled on at the rate of three miles an hour. What could you expect? She was tired—that old ship. Her youth was where mine is—where yours is—you fellows who listen to this yarn; and what friend would throw your years and your weariness in your face? We didn't grumble at her. To us aft, at least, it seemed as though we had been born in her, reared in her, had lived in her for ages, had never known any other ship. I would just as soon have abused the old village church at home for not being a cathedral.

"And for me there was also my youth to make me patient. There was all the East before me, and all life, and the thought that I had been tried in that ship and had come out pretty well. And I thought of men of old who, centuries ago, went that road in ships that sailed no better, to the land of palms, and spices, and yellow sands, and of brown nations ruled by kings more cruel than Nero the Roman, and more splendid than Solomon the Jew. The old bark lumbered on, heavy with her age and the burden of her cargo, while I lived the life of youth in ignorance and hope. She lumbered on through an interminable procession of days; and the fresh gilding flashed back at the setting sun, seemed to cry out over the darkening sea the words painted on her stern, '*Judea*, London. Do or Die.'

"Then we entered the Indian Ocean and steered northerly for Java Head. The winds were light. Weeks slipped by. She crawled on, do or die, and people at home began to think of posting us as overdue.

"One Saturday evening, I being off duty, the men asked me to give them an extra bucket of water or so—for washing clothes. As I did not wish to screw on the fresh-water pump so late, I went forward whistling, and with a key in my hand to unlock the fore-peak scuttle, intending to serve the water out of a spare tank we kept there.

"The smell down below was as unexpected as it was frightful.

One would have thought hundreds of paraffin lamps had been flaring and smoking in that hole for days. I was glad to get out. The man with me coughed and said, 'Funny smell, sir.' I answered negligently, 'It's good for the health, they say,' and walked aft.

"The first thing I did was to put my head down the square of the midship ventilator. As I lifted the lid a visible breath, something like a thin fog, a puff of faint haze, rose from the opening. The ascending air was hot, and had a heavy, sooty, paraffiny smell. I gave one sniff, and put down the lid gently. It was no use choking myself. The cargo was on fire.

"Next day she began to smoke in earnest. You see it was to be expected, for though the coal was of a safe kind, that cargo had been so handled, so broken up with handling, that it looked more like smithy coal than anything else. Then it had been wetted—more than once. It rained all the time we were taking it back from the hulk, and now with this long passage it got heated, and there was another case of spontaneous combustion.

"The captain called us into the cabin. He had a chart spread on the table, and looked unhappy. He said, 'The coast of West Australia is near, but I mean to proceed to our destination. It is the hurricane month, too; but we will just keep her head for Bangkok, and fight the fire. No more putting back anywhere, if we all get roasted. We will try first to stifle this 'ere damned combustion by want of air.'

"We tried. We battened down everything, and still she smoked. The smoke kept coming out through imperceptible crevices; it forced itself through bulkheads and covers; it oozed here and there and everywhere in slender threads, in an invisible film, in an incomprehensible manner. It made its way into the cabin, into the forecastle; it poisoned the sheltered places on the deck; it could be sniffed as high as the mainyard. It was clear that if the smoke came out the air came in. This was disheartening. This combustion refused to be stifled.

"We resolved to try water, and took the hatches off. Enormous volumes of smoke, whitish, yellowish, thick, greasy, misty, choking, ascended as high as the trucks. All hands cleared out aft. Then the poisonous cloud blew away, and we went back to work in a smoke that was no thicker now than that of an ordinary factory chimney.

"We rigged the force pump, got the hose along, and by and by it burst. Well, it was as old as the ship—a prehistoric hose, and past repair. Then we pumped with the feeble head pump, drew water with buckets, and in this way managed in time to pour lots of Indian Ocean into the main hatch. The bright stream flashed in sunshine, fell into a layer of white crawling smoke, and vanished on the black surface of coal. Steam ascended mingling with the smoke. We poured salt water as into a barrel without a bottom. It was our fate to pump in that ship, to pump out of her, to pump into her; and after keeping water out of her to save ourselves from being drowned, we frantically poured water into her to save ourselves from being burnt.

"And she crawled on, do or die, in the serene weather. The sky was a miracle of purity, a miracle of azure. The sea was polished, was blue, was pellucid, was sparkling like a precious stone, extending on all sides, all round to the horizon—as if the whole terrestrial globe had been one jewel, one colossal sapphire, a single gem fashioned into a planet. And on the luster of the great calm waters the *Judea* glided imperceptibly, enveloped in languid and unclean vapors, in a lazy cloud that drifted to leeward, light and slow; a pestiferous cloud defiling the splendor of sea and sky.

"All this time of course we saw no fire. The cargo smoldered at the bottom somewhere. Once Mahon, as we were working side by side, said to me with a queer smile: 'Now, if she only would spring a tidy leak—like that time when we first left the Channel—it would put a stopper on this fire. Wouldn't it?' I remarked irrelevantly, 'Do you remember the rats?'

"We fought the fire and sailed the ship too as carefully as though nothing had been the matter. The steward cooked and attended on us. Of the other twelve men, eight worked while four rested. Everyone took his turn, captain included. There was equality, and if not exact fraternity, then a deal of good feeling. Sometimes a man, as he dashed a bucketful of water down the hatchway, would yell out, 'Hurrah for Bangkok;' and the rest laughed. But generally we were taciturn and serious—and thirsty. Oh! how thirsty! And we had to be careful with the water. Strict allowance. The ship smoked, the sun blazed. . . . Pass the bottle.

"We tried everything. We even made an attempt to dig down to the fire. No good, of course. No man could remain more than a minute below. Mahon, who went first, fainted there, and the man who went to fetch him out did likewise. We lugged them out on deck. Then I leaped down to show how easily it could be done. They had learned wisdom by that time, and contented themselves by fishing for me with a chainhook tied to a broom handle, I believe. I did not offer to go and fetch up my shovel, which was left down below.

"Things began to look bad. We put the longboat into the water.

The second boat was ready to swing out. We had also another, a fourteen-foot thing, on davits aft, where it was quite safe.

"Then, behold, the smoke suddenly decreased. We redoubled our efforts to flood the bottom of the ship. In two days there was no smoke at all. Everybody was on the broad grin. This was on a Friday. On Saturday no work, but sailing the ship of course, was done. The men washed their clothes and their faces for the first time in a fortnight, and had a special dinner given them. They spoke of spontaneous combustion with contempt, and implied *they* were the boys to put out combustions. Somehow we all felt as though we each had inherited a large fortune. But a beastly smell of burning hung about the ship. Captain Beard had hollow eyes and sunken cheeks. I had never noticed so much before how twisted and bowed he was. He and Mahon prowled soberly about hatches and ventilators, sniffing. It struck me suddenly poor Mahon was a very, very old chap. As to me, I was pleased and proud as though I had helped to win a great naval battle. O youth!

"That night was fine. In the morning a homeward-bound ship passed us hull down—the first we had seen for months; but we were nearing the land at last, Java Head being about 190 miles off, and nearly due north.

"Next day it was my watch on deck from eight to twelve. At breakfast the captain observed, 'It's wonderful how that smell hangs about the cabin.' About ten, the mate being on the poop, I stepped down on the main deck for a moment. The carpenter's bench stood abaft the mainmast: I leaned against it sucking at my pipe, and the carpenter, a young chap, came to talk to me. He remarked, 'I think we have done very well, haven't we?' and then I perceived with annoyance the fool was trying to tilt the bench. I said curtly, 'Don't, Chips,' and immediately became aware of a queer sensation, of an absurd delusion—I seemed somehow to be in the air. I heard all round me like a pent-up breath released—as if a thousand giants simultaneously had said Phoo!—and felt a dull concussion which made my ribs ache suddenly. No doubt about it—I was in the air, and my body was describing a short parabola. But short as it was, I had the time to think several thoughts in, as far as I can remember, the following order: 'This can't be the carpenter—What is it?—Some accident—Submarine volcano?—Coals, gas!—By Jove! We are being blown up—Everybody's dead—I am falling into the afterhatch—I see fire in it.'

"The coaldust suspended in the air of the hold had glowed dull-red at the moment of the explosion. In the twinkling of an eye, in an infinitesimal fraction of a second since the first tilt of the bench, I was sprawling full length on the cargo. I picked myself up and scrambled out. It was quick like a rebound. The deck was a wilderness of smashed timber, lying crosswise like trees in a wood after a hurricane; an immense curtain of solid rags waved gently before me—it was the mainsail blown to strips. I thought: the masts will be toppling over directly; and to get out of the way bolted on all fours towards the poop ladder. The first person I saw was Mahon, with eyes like saucers, his mouth open, and the long white hair standing straight on end round his head like a silver halo. He was just about to go down when the sight of the main deck stirring, heaving up, and changing into splinters before his eyes, petrified him on the top step. I stared at him in unbelief, and he stared at me with a queer kind of shocked curiosity. I did not know that I had no hair, no eyebrows, no eyelashes, that my young mustache was burnt off, that my face was black, one cheek laid open, my nose cut, and my chin bleeding. I had lost my cap, one of my slippers, and my shirt was torn to rags. Of all this I was not aware. I was amazed to see the ship still afloat, the poop deck whole—and, most of all, to see anybody alive. Also the peace of the sky and the serenity of the sea were distinctly surprising. I suppose I expected to see them convulsed with horror. . . . Pass the bottle.

"There was a voice hailing the ship from somewhere—in the air, in the sky—I couldn't tell. Presently I saw the captain—and he was mad. He asked me eagerly, 'Where's the cabin table?' and to hear such a question was a frightful shock. I had just been blown up, you understand, and vibrated with that experience—I wasn't quite sure whether I was alive. Mahon began to stamp with both feet and yelled at him, 'Good God! don't you see the deck's blown out of her?' I found my voice, and stammered out as if conscious of some gross neglect of duty, 'I don't know where the cabin table is.' It was like an absurd dream.

"Do you know what he wanted next? Well, he wanted to trim the yards. Very placidly, and as if lost in thought, he insisted on having the foreyard squared. 'I don't know if there's anybody alive,' said Mahon, almost tearfully. 'Surely,' he said, gently, 'there will be enough left to square the foreyard.'

"The old chap, it seems, was in his own berth winding up the chronometers, when the shock sent him spinning. Immediately it occurred to him—as he said afterwards—that the ship had struck something, and ran out into the cabin. There, he saw, the cabin table had vanished somewhere. The deck being blown up, it had fallen down into the lazarette of course. Where we had our breakfast that morning he saw only a great hole in the floor. This appeared to him so awfully mysterious, and impressed him so immensely, that what he saw and heard after he got on deck were mere trifles in comparison. And, mark, he noticed directly the wheel deserted and his bark off her course—and his only thought was to get that miserable, stripped, undecked, smoldering shell of a ship back again with her head pointing at her port of destination. Bangkok! That's what he was after. I tell you this quiet, bowed, bandy-legged, almost deformed little man was immense in the singleness of his idea and in his placid ignorance of our agitation. He motioned us forward with a commanding gesture, and went to take the wheel himself.

"Yes; that was the first thing we did—trim the yards of that wreck! No one was killed, or even disabled, but everyone was more or less hurt. You should have seen them! Some were in rags, with black faces, like coal heavers, like sweeps, and had bullet heads that seemed closely cropped, but were in fact singed to the skin. Others, of the watch below, awakened by being shot out from their collapsing bunks, shivered incessantly, and kept on groaning even as we went about our work. But they all worked. That crew of Liverpool hard cases had in them the right stuff. It's my experience they always have. It is the sea that gives it—the vastness, the loneliness surrounding their dark stolid souls. Ah! Well! We stumbled, we crept, we fell, we barked our shins on the wreckage, we hauled. The masts stood, but we did not know how much they might be charred down below. It was nearly calm, but a long swell ran from the west and made her roll. They might go at any moment. We looked at them with apprehension. One could not foresee which way they would fall.

"Then we retreated aft and looked about us. The deck was a tangle of planks on edge, of planks on end, of splinters, of ruined woodwork. The masts rose from that chaos like big trees above a matted undergrowth. The interstices of that mass of wreckage were full of something whitish, sluggish, stirring—of something that was like a greasy fog. The smoke of the invisible fire was coming up again, was trailing, like a poisonous thick mist in some valley choked with dead wood. Already lazy wisps were beginning to curl upwards amongst the mass of splinters. Here and there a piece of timber, stuck upright, resembled a post. Half of a fife rail had been shot through the foresail, and the sky made a patch of glorious blue in the ignobly soiled canvas. A portion of several boards holding together had fallen across the rail, and one end protruded overboard, like a gangway leading upon nothing, like a gangway leading over the deep sea, leading to death—as if inviting us to walk to the plank at once and be done with our ridiculous troubles. And still the air, the sky—a ghost, something invisible was hailing the ship.

"Someone had the sense to look over, and there was the helmsman, who had impulsively jumped overboard, anxious to come back. He yelled and swam lustily like a merman, keeping up with the ship. We threw him a rope, and presently he stood amongst us streaming with water and very crestfallen. The capain had surrendered the wheel, and apart, elbow on rail and chin in hand, gazed at the sea wistfully. We asked ourselves, What next? I thought, Now, this is something like. This is great. I wonder what will happen. O youth!

"Suddenly Mahon sighted a steamer far astern. Captain Beard said, 'We may do something with her yet.' We hoisted two flags, which said in the international language of the sea, 'On fire. Want immediate assistance.' The steamer grew bigger rapidly, and by and by spoke with two flags on her foremast, 'I am coming to your assistance.'

"In half an hour she was abreast, to windward, within hail, and rolling slightly, with her engines stopped. We lost our composure, and yelled all together with excitement, 'We've been blown up.' A man in a white helmet on the bridge, cried, 'Yes! All right! all right!' and he nodded his head, and smiled, and made soothing motions with his hand as though at a lot of frightened children. One of the boats dropped in the water, and walked towards us upon the sea with her long oars. Four Calashes pulled a swinging stroke. This was my first sight of Malay seamen. I've known them since, but what struck me then was their unconcern: they came alongside, and even the bowman standing up and holding to our main chains with the boathook did not deign to lift his head for a glance. I thought people who had been blown up deserved more attention.

"A little man, dry like a chip and agile like a monkey, clambered up. It was the mate of the steamer. He gave one look, and cried, 'O boys—you had better quit!'

"We were silent. He talked apart with the captain for a time—seemed to argue with him. Then they went away together to the steamer.

"When our skipper came back we learned that the steamer was the *Somerville*, Captain Nash, from West Australia to Singapore via Batavia with mails, and that the agreement was she should tow us to Anjer or Batavia, if possible, where we could extinguish the fire by scuttling, and then proceed on our voyage—to Bangkok! The old man seemed excited. 'We will do it yet,' he said to Mahon, fiercely. He shook his fist at the sky. Nobody else said a word.

"At noon the steamer began to tow. She went ahead slim and high, and what was left of the *Judea* followed at the end of seventy fathom of towrope—followed her swiftly like a cloud of smoke with mastheads protruding above. We went aloft to furl the sails. We coughed on the yards, and were careful about the bunts. Do you see the lot of us there, putting a neat furl on the sails of that ship doomed to arrive nowhere? There was not a man who didn't think that at any moment the masts would topple over. From aloft we could not see the ship for smoke, and they worked carefully, passing the gaskets with even turns. 'Harbor furl—aloft there!' cried Mahon from below.

"You understand this? I don't think one of those chaps expected to get down in the usual way. When we did I heard them saying to each other, 'Well, I thought we would come down overboard, in a lump—sticks and all—blame me if I didn't.' 'That's what I was thinking to myself,' would answer wearily another battered and bandaged scarecrow. And, mind, these were men without the drilled-in habit of obedience. To an onlooker they would be a lot of profane scallywags without a redeeming point. What made them do it—what made them obey me when I, thinking consciously how fine it was, made them drop the bunt of the foresail twice to try and do it better? What? They had no professional reputation—no examples, no praise. It wasn't a sense of duty; they all knew well enough how to shirk, and laze, and dodge—when they had a mind to it—and mostly they had. Was it the two pounds ten a month that sent them there? They didn't think their pay half good enough. No; it was something in them, something inborn and subtle and everlasting. I don't say positively that the crew of a French or German merchantman wouldn't have done it, but I doubt whether it would have been done in the same way. There was a completeness in it, something solid like a principle, and masterful like an instinct—a disclosure of something secret—of that hidden something, that gift of good or evil that makes racial difference, that shapes the fate of nations.

"It was that night at ten that, for the first time since we had been fighting it, we saw the fire. The speed of the towing had fanned the smoldering destruction. A blue gleam appeared forward, shining below the wreck of the deck. It wavered in patches, it seemed to stir and creep like the light of a glowworm. I saw it first, and told Mahon. 'Then the game's up,' he said. 'We had better stop this towing, or she will burst out suddenly fore and aft before we can clear out.' We set up a yell; rang bells to attract their attention; they towed on. At last Mahon and I had to crawl forward and cut the rope with an axe. There was no time to cast off the lashings. Red tongues could be seen licking the wilderness of splinters under our feet as we made our way back to the poop.

"Of course they very soon found out in the steamer that the rope was gone. She gave a loud blast of her whistle, her lights were seen sweeping in a wide circle, she came up ranging close alongside, and stopped. We were all in a tight group on the poop looking at her. Every man had saved a little bundle or a bag. Suddenly a conical flame with a twisted top shot up forward and threw upon the black sea a circle of light, with the two vessels side by side and heaving gently in its center. Captain Beard had been sitting on the gratings still and mute for hours, but now he rose slowly and advanced in front of us, to the mizzen-shrouds. Captain Nash hailed: 'Come along! Look sharp. I have mailbags on board. I will take you and your boats to Singapore.'

" 'Thank you! No!' said our skipper. 'We must see the last of the ship.'

" 'I can't stand by any longer,' shouted the other. 'Mails—you know.'

" 'Ay! ay! We are all right.'

" 'Very well! I'll report you in Singapore. , . . Good-by!'

"He waved his hand. Our men dropped their bundles quietly. The steamer moved ahead, and passing out of the circle of light, vanished at once from our sight, dazzled by the fire which burned fiercely. And then I knew that I would see the East first as commander of a small boat. I thought it fine; and the fidelity to the old ship was fine. We should see the last of her. Oh, the glamor of youth! Oh, the fire of it, more dazzling than the flames of the burning ship, throwing a magic light on the wide earth, leaping audaciously to the sky, presently to be quenched by time, more cruel, more pitiless, more bitter than the sea—and like the flames of the burning ship surrounded by an impenetrable night.

"The old man warned us in his gentle and inflexible way that it was part of our duty to save for the underwriters as much as we could of the ship's gear. Accordingly we went to work aft, while she blazed forward to give us plenty of light. We lugged out a lot of rubbish. What didn't we save? An old barometer fixed with an absurd quantity of screws nearly cost me my life: a sudden rush of smoke came upon me, and I just got away in time. There were various stores, bolts of canvas, coils of rope; the poop looked like a marine bazaar, and the boats were lumbered to the gunwales. One would have thought the old man wanted to take as much as he could of his first command with him. He was very, very quiet, but off his balance evidently. Would you believe it? He wanted to take a length of old stream-cable and a kedge anchor with him in the longboat. We said, 'Ay, ay, sir,' deferentially, and on the quiet let the things slip overboard. The heavy medicine chest went that way, two bags of green coffee, tins of paint—fancy, paint!—a whole lot of things. Then I was ordered with two hands into the boats to make a stowage and get them ready against the time it would be proper for us to leave the ship.

"We put everything straight, stepped the longboat's mast for our skipper, who was to take charge of her, and I was not sorry to sit down for a moment. My face felt raw, every limb ached as if broken, I was aware of all my ribs, and would have sworn to a twist in the backbone. The boats, fast astern, lay in a deep shadow, and all around I could see the circle of the sea lighted by the fire. A gigantic flame arose forward straight and clear. It flared fierce, with noises like the whirr of wings, with rumbles as of thunder. There were cracks, detonations, and from the cone of flame the sparks flew upwards, as man is born to trouble, to leaky ships, and to ships that burn.

"What bothered me was that the ship, lying broadside to the swell and to such wind as there was—a mere breath—the boats would not keep astern where they were safe, but persisted, in a pigheaded way boats have, in getting under the counter and then swinging alongside. They were knocking about dangerously and coming near the flame, while the ship rolled on them, and, of course, there was always the danger of the masts going over the side at any moment. I and my two boatkeepers kept them off as best we could, with oars and boathooks; but to be constantly at it became exasperating, since there was no reason why we should not leave at once. We could not see those on board, nor could we imagine what caused the delay. The boatkeepers were swearing feebly, and I had not only my share of the work but also had to keep at it two men who showed a constant inclination to lay themselves down and let things slide.

"At last I hailed, 'On deck there,' and someone looked over. 'We're ready here,' I said. The head disappeared, and very soon popped up again. 'The captain says, All right, sir, and to keep the boats well clear of the ship.'

"Half an hour passed. Suddenly there was a frightful racket, rattle, clanking of chain, hiss of water, and millions of sparks flew up into the shivering column of smoke that stood leaning slightly above the ship. The catheads had burned away, and the two red-hot anchors had gone to the bottom, tearing out after them two hundred fathom of red-hot chain. The ship trembled, the mass of flame swayed as if ready to collapse, and the fore-topgallant mast fell. It darted down like an arrow of fire, shot under, and instantly leaping up within an oar's length of the boats, floated quietly, very black on the luminous sea. I hailed the deck again. After some time a man in an unexpectedly cheerful but also muffled tone, as though he had been trying to speak with his mouth shut, informed me, 'Coming directly, sir,' and vanished. For a long time I heard nothing but the whirr and roar of the fire. There were also whistling sounds. The boats jumped, tugged at the painters, ran at each other playfully, knocked their sides together, or, do what we would, swung in a bunch against the ship's side. I couldn't stand it any longer, and swarming up a rope, clambered aboard over the stern.

"It was as bright as day. Coming up like this, the sheet of fire facing me was a terrifying sight, and the heat seemed hardly bearable at first. On a settee cushion dragged out of the cabin Captain Beard, his legs drawn up and one arm under his head, slept with the light playing on him. Do you know what the rest were busy about? They were sitting on deck right aft, round an open case, eating bread and cheese and drinking bottled stout.

"On the background of flames twisting in fierce tongues above their heads they seemed at home like salamanders, and looked like a band of desperate pirates. The fire sparkled in the whites of their eyes, gleamed on patches of white skin seen through the torn shirts. Each had the marks as of a battle about him—bandaged heads, tied-up arms, a strip of dirty rag round a knee—and each man had a bottle between his legs and a chunk of cheese in his hand. Mahon got up. With his handsome and disreputable head, his hooked profile, his long white beard, and with an uncorked bottle in his hand, he resembled one of those reckless sea robbers of old making merry amidst violence and disaster. 'The last meal on board,' he explained solemnly. 'We had nothing to eat all day, and it was no use leaving all this.' He flourished the bottle and indicated the sleeping skipper. 'He said he couldn't swallow anything, so I got him to lie down,' he went on; and as I stared, 'I don't know whether you are aware, young fellow, the man had no sleep to speak of for days—and there will be dam' little sleep in the boats.' 'There will be no boats by and by if you fool about much longer,' I said, indignantly. I walked up to the skipper and shook him by the shoulder. At last he opened his eyes, but did not move. 'Time to leave her, sir,' I said quietly.

"He got up painfully, looked at the flames, at the sea sparkling round the ship, and black, black as ink farther away; he looked at the stars shining dim through a thin veil of smoke in a sky black, black as Erebus.

" 'Youngest first,' he said.

"And the ordinary seaman, wiping his mouth with the back of his hand, got up, clambered over the taffrail, and vanished. Others followed. One, on the point of going over, stopped short to drain his bottle, and with a great swing of his arm flung it at the fire. 'Take this!' he cried.

"The skipper lingered disconsolately, and we left him to commune alone for a while with his first command. Then I went up again and brought him away at last. It was time. The ironwork on the poop was hot to the touch.

"Then the painter of the longboat was cut, and the three boats, tied together, drifted clear of the ship. It was just sixteen hours after the explosion when we abandoned her. Mahon had charge of the second boat, and I had the smallest—the fourteen-foot thing. The longboat would have taken the lot of us; but the skipper said we must save as much property as we could—for the underwriters —and so I got my first command. I had two men with me, a bag of biscuits, a few tins of meat, and a breaker of water. I was ordered to keep close to the longboat, that in case of bad weather we might be taken into her.

"And do you know what I thought? I thought I would part company as soon as I could. I wanted to have my first command all to myself. I wasn't going to sail in a squadron if there were a chance for independent cruising. I would make land by myself. I would beat the other boats. Youth! All youth! The silly, charming, beautiful youth.

"But we did not make a start at once. We must see the last of the ship. And so the boats drifted about that night, heaving and setting on the swell. The men dozed, waked, sighed, groaned. I looked at the burning ship.

"Between the darkness of earth and heaven she was burning fiercely upon a disc of purple sea shot by the blood-red play of gleams; upon a disc of water glittering and sinister. A high, clear flame, an immense and lonely flame, ascended from the ocean, and from its summit the black smoke poured continuously at the sky. She burned furiously; mournful and imposing like a funeral pile kindled in the night, surrounded by the sea, watched over by the stars. A magnificent death had come like a grace, like a gift, like a reward to that old ship at the end of her laborious days. The surrender of her weary ghost to the keeping of stars and sea was stirring like the sight of a glorious triumph. The masts fell just before daybreak, and for a moment there was a burst and turmoil of sparks that seemed to fill with flying fire the night patient and watchful, the vast night lying silent upon the sea. At daylight she was only a charred shell, floating still under a cloud of smoke and bearing a glowing mass of coal within.

"Then the oars were got out, and the boats forming in a line moved round her remains as if in procession—the longboat leading. As we pulled across her stern a slim dart of fire shot out viciously at us, and suddenly she went down, head first, in a great hiss of steam. The unconsumed stern was the last to sink; but the paint had gone, had cracked, had peeled off, and there were no letters, there was no word, no stubborn device that was like her soul, to flash at the rising sun her creed and her name.

"We made our way north. A breeze sprang up, and about noon all the boats came together for the last time. I had no mast or sail in mine, but I made a mast out of a spare oar and hoisted a boat-awning for a sail, with a boathook for a yard. She was certainly overmasted, but I had the satisfaction of knowing that with the wind aft I could beat the other two. I had to wait for them. Then we all had a look at the captain's chart, and, after a sociable meal of hard bread and water, got our last instructions. These were simple: steer north, and keep together as much as possible. 'Be careful with that jury-rig, Marlow,' said the captain; and Mahon, as I sailed proudly past his boat, wrinkled his curved nose and hailed, 'You will sail that ship of yours under water, if you don't look out, young fellow.' He was a malicious old man—and may the deep sea where he sleeps now rock him gently, rock him tenderly to the end of time!

"Before sunset a thick rain-squall passed over the two boats, which were far astern, and that was the last I saw of them for a time. Next day I sat steering my cockle-shell—my first command—with nothing but water and sky round me. I did sight in the afternoon the upper sails of a ship far away, but said nothing, and my men did not notice her. You see I was afraid she might be homeward bound, and I had no mind to turn back from the portals of the East. I was steering for Java—another blessed name—like Bangkok, you know. I steered many days.

"I need not tell you what it is to be knocking about in an open boat. I remember nights and days of calm, when we pulled, we pulled, and the boat seemed to stand still, as if bewitched within the circle of the sea horizon. I remember the heat, the deluge of rain-squalls that kept us baling for dear life (but filled our water cask), and I remember sixteen hours on end with a mouth dry as a cinder and a steering oar over the stern to keep my first command head on to a breaking sea. I did not know how good a man I was till then. I remember the drawn faces, the dejected figures of my two men, and I remember my youth and the feeling that will never come back any more—the feeling that I could last forever, outlast the sea, the earth, and all men; the deceitful feeling that lures us on to joys, to perils, to love, to vain effort—to death; the triumphant conviction of strength, the heat of life in the handful of dust, the glow in the heart that with every year grows dim, grows cold, grows small, and expires—and expires, too soon, too soon—before life itself.

"And this is how I see the East. I have seen its secret places and have looked into its very soul; but now I see it always from a small boat, a high outline of mountains, blue and afar in the morning; like faint mist at noon; a jagged wall of purple at sunset. I have the feel of the oar in my hand, the vision of a scorching blue sea in my eyes. And I see a bay, a wide bay, smooth as glass and polished like ice, shimmering in the dark. A red light burns far off upon the gloom of the land, and the night is soft and warm. We drag at the oars with aching arms, and suddenly a puff of wind, a puff faint and tepid and laden with strange odors of blossoms, of aromatic wood, comes out of the still night—the first sigh of the East on my face. That I can never forget. It was impalpable and enslaving, like a charm, like a whispered promise of mysterious delight.

"We had been pulling this finishing spell for eleven hours. Two pulled, and he whose turn it was to rest sat at the tiller. We had made out the red light in that bay and steered for it, guessing it must mark some small coasting port. We passed two vessels, outlandish and high-sterned, sleeping at anchor, and, approaching the light, now very dim, ran the boat's nose against the end of a jutting wharf. We were blind with fatigue. My men dropped the oars and fell off the thwarts as if dead. I made fast to a pile. A current rippled softly. The scented obscurity of the shore was grouped into vast masses, a density of colossal clumps of vegetation, probably— mute and fantastic shapes. And at their foot the semicircle of a beach gleamed faintly, like an illusion. There was not a light, not a stir, not a sound. The mysterious East faced me, perfumed like a flower, silent like death, dark like a grave.

"And I sat weary beyond expression, exulting like a conqueror, sleepless and entranced as if before a profound, a fateful enigma.

"A splashing of oars, a measured dip reverberating on the level of water, intensified by the silence of the shore into loud claps, made me jump up. A boat, a European boat, was coming in. I invoked the name of the dead; I hailed: '*Judea* ahoy!' A thin shout answered.

"It was the captain. I had beaten the flagship by three hours, and I was glad to hear the old man's voice again, tremulous and tired. 'Is it you, Marlow?' 'Mind the end of that jetty, sir,' I cried.

"He approached cautiously, and brought up with the deep-sea lead line which we had saved—for the underwriters. I eased my painter and fell alongside. He sat, a broken figure at the stern, wet with dew, his hands clasped in his lap. His men were asleep already. 'I had a terrible time of it,' he murmured. 'Mahon is behind—not very far.' We conversed in whispers, in low whispers, as if afraid to wake up the land. Guns, thunder, earthquakes would not have awakened the men just then.

"Looking round as we talked, I saw away at sea a bright light traveling in the night. 'There's a steamer passing the bay,' I said. She was not passing, she was entering, and she even came close and anchored. 'I wish,' said the old man, 'you would find out whether she is English. Perhaps they could give us a passage somewhere.' He seemed nervously anxious. So by dint of punching and kicking I started one of my men into a state of somnambulism, and giving him an oar, took another and pulled towards the lights of the steamer.

"There was a murmur of voices in her, metallic hollow clangs of the engine room, footsteps on the deck. Her ports shone, round like dilated eyes. Shapes moved about, and there was a shadowy man high up on the bridge. He heard my oars.

"And then, before I could open my lips, the East spoke to me, but it was in a Western voice. A torrent of words was poured into the enigmatical, the fateful silence; outlandish, angry words, mixed with words and even whole sentences of good English, less strange but even more surprising. The voice swore and cursed violently; it riddled the solemn peace of the bay by a volley of abuse. It began by calling me Pig, and from that went crescendo into unmentionable adjectives—in English. The man up there raged aloud in two languages, and with a sincerity in his fury that almost convinced me I had, in some way, sinned against the harmony of the universe. I could hardly see him, but began to think he would work himself into a fit.

"Suddenly he ceased, and I could hear him snorting and blowing like a porpoise. I said:

" 'What steamer is this, pray?'

" 'Eh? What's this? And who are you?'

" 'Castaway crew of an English bark burnt at sea. We came here tonight. I am the second mate. The captain is in the longboat, and wishes to know if you would give us a passage somewhere.'

" 'Oh, my goodness! I say. . . . This is the *Celestial* from Singapore on her return trip. I'll arrange with your captain in the morning, . . . and, . . . I say, . . . did you hear me just now?'

" 'I should think the whole bay heard you.'

" 'I thought you were a shoreboat. Now, look here—this infernal lazy scoundrel of a caretaker has gone to sleep again—curse him. The light is out, and I nearly ran foul of the end of this damned jetty. This is the third time he plays me this trick. Now, I ask you, can anybody stand this kind of thing? It's enough to drive a man out of his mind. I'll report him. . . . I'll get the Assistant Resident to give him the sack, by—! See—there's no light. It's out, isn't it? I take you to witness the light's out. There should be a light, you know. A red light on the—'

" 'There was a light,' I said, mildly.

" 'But it's out, man! What's the use of talking like this? You can see for yourself it's out—don't you? If you had to take a valuable steamer along this Godforsaken coast you would want a light, too. I'll kick him from end to end of his miserable wharf. You'll see if I don't. I will—'

" 'So I may tell my captain you'll take us?' I broke in.

" 'Yes, I'll take you. Good night,' he said, brusquely.

"I pulled back, made fast again to the jetty, and then went to sleep at last. I had faced the silence of the East. I had heard some of its language. But when I opened my eyes again the silence was as complete as though it had never been broken. I was lying in a flood of light, and the sky had never looked so far, so high, before. I opened my eyes and lay without moving.

"And then I saw the men of the East—they were looking at me. The whole length of the jetty was full of people. I saw brown, bronze, yellow faces, the black eyes, the glitter, the color of an Eastern crowd. And all these beings stared without a murmur, without a sigh, without a movement. They stared down at the boats, at the sleeping men who at night had come to them from the sea. Nothing moved. The fronds of palms stood still against the sky.

Not a branch stirred along the shore, and the brown roofs of hidden houses peeped through the green foliage, through the big leaves that hung shining and still like leaves forged of heavy metal. This was the East of the ancient navigators, so old, so mysterious, resplendent and somber, living and unchanged, full of danger and promise. And these were the men. I sat up suddenly. A wave of movement passed through the crowd from end to end, passed along the heads, swayed the bodies, ran along the jetty like a ripple on the water, like a breath of wind on a field—and all was still again. I see it now—the wide sweep of the bay, the glittering sands, the wealth of green infinite and varied, the sea blue like the sea of a dream, the crowd of attentive faces, the blaze of vivid color—the water reflecting it all, the curve of the shore, the jetty, the high-sterned outlandish craft floating still, and the three boats with the tired men from the West sleeping, unconscious of the land and the people and of the violence of sunshine. They slept thrown across the thwarts, curled on bottom-boards, in the careless attitudes of death. The head of the old skipper, leaning back in the stern of the longboat, had fallen on his breast, and he looked as though he would never wake. Farther out old Mahon's face was upturned to the sky, with the long white beard spread out on his breast, as though he had been shot where he sat at the tiller; and a man, all in a heap in the bows of the boat, slept with both arms embracing the stemhead and with his cheek laid on the gunwale. The East looked at them without a sound.

"I have known its fascination since; I have seen the mysterious shores, the still water, the lands of brown nations, where a stealthy Nemesis lies in wait, pursues, overtakes so many of the conquering race, who are proud of their wisdom, of their knowledge, of their strength. But for me all the East is contained in that vision of my youth. It is all in that moment when I opened my young eyes on it. I came upon it from a tussle with the sea—and I was young—and I saw it looking at me. And this is all that is left of it! Only a moment; a moment of strength, of romance, of glamor—of youth! . . . A flick of sunshine upon a strange shore, the time to remember, the time for a sigh, and—good-by!—Night—Good-by . . . !"

He drank.

"Ah! The good old time—the good old time. Youth and the sea. Glamor and the sea! The good, strong sea, the salt, bitter sea, that could whisper to you and roar at you and knock your breath out of you."

He drank again.

"By all that's wonderful it is the sea, I believe, the sea itself—or is

it youth alone? Who can tell? But you here—you all had something
out of life: money, love—whatever one gets on shore—and, tell me,
wasn't that the best time, that time when we were young at sea;
young and had nothing, on the sea that gives nothing, except hard
knocks—and sometimes a chance to feel your strength—that only—
that you all regret?"

And we all nodded at him: the man of finance, the man of accounts, the man of law, we all nodded at him over the polished
table that like a still sheet of brown water reflected our faces, lined,
wrinkled; our faces marked by toil, by deceptions, by success, by
love; our weary eyes looking still, looking always, looking anxiously
for something out of life, that while it is expected is already gone—
has passed unseen, in a sigh, in a flash—together with the youth, with
the strength, with the romance of illusions.

QUESTIONS FOR DISCUSSION

AN OUTPOST OF PROGRESS

1. What are the fundamental assumptions inherent in this story regarding the relationships among morality, humane values, and commerce?

2. What feeling about primitive society and the power of the jungle does Conrad invoke in the reader? Were Kayerts and Carlier conscious of this feeling? How did it affect them?

3. Trace the moral deterioration which is the crux of the tale.

4. An indictment is made not only of Kayerts and Carlier but of the civilized world from which they came. What is that indictment?

5. Great irony—unexpected opposites and reversals in outcome—appears in this story. In what, exactly, does this irony consist?

6. By what means does Conrad build tension and suspense?

7. The causes and circumstances of Kayerts' madness and death require explanation. What factors precipitate his madness, and what meaning does Conrad obtain by the dramatic nature of his death?

8. The mist which occurs suddenly at the end contributes atmosphere to the mysterious final scenes. What symbolical meanings do the mist and clanging bells and chaotic confusion appear to suggest?

9. What is the specific attitude of Conrad toward his theme, and how does he show it?

THE SECRET SHARER

1. ". . . I wondered how far I should turn out faithful to that ideal conception of one's own personality every man sets up for himself secretly." How does this thought establish the theme of the story?

2. The way in which Leggatt arrives and departs, the garb with which the Skipper cloaks him, the manner in which he impresses himself upon the other man, the final effect he produces—all strongly suggest he is an embodiment of the young Captain's subconscious or unconscious. Attack or defend this hypothesis.

3. "A mysterious communication was established already between us two—in the face of the silent, darkened tropical sea." Comment upon the role of the sea and its part in the ultimate unraveling of the tale.

4. "But I hardly thought of my other self, now gone from the ship, to be hidden forever from all friendly faces, to be a fugitive and vagabond on the earth, with no brand of the curse on his sane forehead to stay

a slaying hand . . . too proud to explain." With this allusion to Cain and Abel, Conrad provides probing insight into the nature of the soulful secret shared by the two "brothers." What was that deep secret, and of what has the Captain been freed by the encounter with Leggatt?

6. As a result of the encounter, the Skipper is left with a penetrating knowledge of himself that he did not have before. Explain what that knowledge is and relate it to the theme of the story.

7. Conrad suggests that the ship, finally, is virtually at the gate of hell. But she is at last saved. What compelling personal reason, beyond that of allowing Leggatt to escape, does the Captain have for taking the ship so close in to land? What relationship does there appear to be between Leggatt's departure and the ship's being saved?

A SUGGESTED INTERPRETATION

YOUTH

This tale speaks of altered spiritual states, varying approaches to life, and the search for meaningful existence. Simultaneously, it tells about the purifying power of the sea and its capacity magically to transform experience by imbuing it with passionate nobility.

Youth may be regarded as a time of spiritual innocence, a period when the power of evil has not been apprehended. Unsullied by experience and without yet having seen the wholeness of life, youth brushes aside manifestations of darkness without probing them, without understanding them, so close at hand does the ideal of perfection and fulfillment seem. Young Marlow sees the passage of the **Judea** as a journey to the Promised Land—a place toward which he looks with ecstatic yearning. Ensheathed in an armor of innocence, Marlow is able to pass through the perils of his voyage, sustained by his vision, nurtured by his faith, and protected by his singleness of purpose.

The youthful approach to life is passionate, illusory, idealistic; the mature approach to life—tempered by wisdom and experience—is rational, realistic, pragmatic. Young Marlow pledges his faith in life by giving himself to action, not hesitating for introspection and searching for significances. Bangkok represents the unattainable dream, the only kind of dream worth dreaming. The young man's life is given purpose through doing, through voyaging to never-never land. Having looked upon the East (and having the East look upon him) in such a flush of innocence and passionate dedication, never, knowing in later years what lay behind the Eastern façade, could he hope to relive his glorious earlier moment of discovery. Idealized, romanticized, the challenge to be consummated represented a perfect action, a thing of beauty. "But pleasures are like poppies spread,/ You seize the flow'r, its bloom is shed;/ Or like the snow falls in the river,/A moment white—then melts for ever. . . ." Having experienced perfection, living from that point forward could be only a series of disillusionments, a chain of disenchantments, painful awakenings. The mature Marlow, when he sighs, "O youth! The strength of it, the faith of it, the imagination of it!" is crying out against the insistence of reality, the weight of facts, the pressure of the bread-and-butter world. To have died in the passion of fulfillment and not to have survived for the inevitable letdown would have been more poetically satisfying.

And somewhere between these two Conrad-erected poles for measurement—the imaginative and the practical—life itself lies. Conrad touches upon the inscrutable power of life and the restless palpitations of the human spirit in its striving to free itself. The life of action in youth is glorified as a positive affirmation which provides proof-positive that man really **is**, that he has a consciousness of self, that he has an objective mirror by which to measure his scope.

As he creates a story that raises these elusive and mysterious and unanswerable riddles, the author tells of his mystic belief in the seas, which, with their savagery, depth, and unutterable majesty, undoubtedly contain the answers for him, or at least tease the mind to suggest they have the answers. Life is in the waters, and the waters give purpose to living, give man a mark by which to prove his mettle and establish his identity. Away from the city and its man-made institutions, way out in the ocean where "Day after day and night after night there was nothing round the ship but the heave of the wind, the tumult of the sea, the noise of water pouring over her deck," Marlow found a power he did not understand and does not even try to talk about directly in the story. With a chauvinistic flourish perhaps characteristic of one who has adopted a much-loved new homeland, Conrad suggests that England and Englishmen are nobler and stronger because their history is inextricably bound up with the sea. The sea throws a light upon one's destiny, defining it, leading one on to act out great roles, to perform great deeds of the spirit. The sea binds men in a mystic and noble brotherhood of purpose which mysteriously modifies life by giving it meaning filled with strength. "Do or die," buttressed by the presence of the sea, infuses man with an unconquerable will.

The symbolism of the ship itself punctuates the story, raising ticklish ambiguities, reverses, and paradoxes. First, as if in the world in which we live, the sands of ballast, which keep the vessel riding straight, shift, turning things all askew. The men begin shoveling to make things right. Out at sea the hold is flooded, threatening to sink them unless they pump furiously. Finally, we see the spectacle of the fire down below, with water being uselessly pumped in. And the ship explodes, goes up in flame, and sinks to death.

Throughout, difficulties appear below as the sea pounds and assaults and wrecks things above. Even the rats sense something amiss and escape beforehand. But the men tenaciously and madly fight on. Conrad appears to be talking about the accumulated weight of moral decay and racial guilt that threatens to drag life down to the bottom, the trials given to the spirit to test it, the fall from grace that is at the fundus of human consciousness. As a counterpoint to Marlow's soaring spirit, there is the malodorous rottenness below, which threatens to overcome life. But it is Marlow who triumphs—Marlow in his youthful state of belief in life and in his innocence. The old **Judea,** signaling the end of one era and the beginning of another for Marlow, burns out in the Java seas and goes down in purple flames. Yet she is the object by which Marlow comes to know himself in trial. With an expiatory explosion and flames, the ship goes down and a human spirit is released. In a surge of dynamic power and strength, with spirit and will and the blind drive to attain self-realization, man triumphs over evil.

SUBJECTS FOR WRITTEN COMPOSITION

1. The power and influence of the sea figure prominently in "Youth" and "The Secret Sharer." Prepare a paper on Conrad's view of the sea and its interrelationship with character development.

2. Unexpected outcomes and situations project figurative meanings quite different from literal facts. Explore Conrad's use of irony.

3. Through overtones of meaning and the use of ambiguities and paradoxes, Conrad talks about moral codes and the rules by which men live. Synthesize Conrad's basic moral views as reflected in these selections.

4. Present a personal interpretation of the meanings implicit in "An Outpost of Progress," "Youth," or "The Secret Sharer."

5. The theme of self-searching and the quest for self-realization are common to these tales. Through an exploration of these, explain Conrad's conception of life.

6. "An Outpost of Progress" presents views of life which we might not commonly associate with late-nineteenth-century thinking about colonialism. Discuss Conrad's approach to progress, commerce, and the impact of the European upon Africa and, more properly, the impact of Africa upon the European.

A NOTE ON TYPES

You have probably observed that the work of each author in this book is set in a different typeface. Each of these typefaces was carefully selected for its association with qualities in the author's work or with the period during which he wrote. Following is a brief description of the types used.

GREENE: Bodoni, a type cut from the early-nineteenth-century designs of Giamattista Bodoni, typefounder of Parma. Bodoni is a strong and rather heavy face, blacker in color than most text types, and is characterized by an extreme contrast of thick and thin strokes.

WARREN: Bodoni Book, an adaptation of another design by Giambattista Bodoni. The letter forms are similar to those in Bodoni, but in Bodoni Book these forms have been refined and made more delicate.

JOYCE: Fairfield, a design of Rudolph Ruzicka, first cut in 1941. Its unusually tall upstrokes and long downstrokes, combined with a pale and even color, create an effect of delicacy and elegance.

FAULKNER: Caslon, designed by William Caslon, an English typefounder of the early eighteenth century. Because of a certain unevenness of color and line weight, Caslon gives an impression both nervous and a little antique.

JAMES: Century, designed by L. B. Benton in 1890 for *Century Magazine*. This type quickly achieved great popularity because of its even, open, and legible character. Much of the writing of James's time first saw print in Century.

CONRAD: Janson, recut from designs of the late seventeenth century. This type is probably of Dutch origin, although its history is obscure. Janson has a beautiful sharpness and clarity of structure. Its letter forms are strong and without affectation or eccentricity.